Armageddon

OTHER BOOKS BY LEON URIS

MILA 18

EXODUS

THE ANGRY HILLS

BATTLE CRY

EXODUS REVISITED
  (*in collaboration with Dimitrios Harissiadis*)

SCREENPLAYS BY LEON URIS

BATTLE CRY

GUNFIGHT AT THE O.K. CORRAL

Armageddon

A NOVEL OF BERLIN BY

LEON URIS

DOUBLEDAY & COMPANY, INC.

GARDEN CITY, NEW YORK

1964

Three installments from this book appeared in
THE SATURDAY EVENING POST

This novel concerns recent history. The possibility exists that persons living today may see themselves or be mistaken by the public as characters in the novel because of a duplication of posts, commands, or political positions. There are characters in this novel who hold posts similar to those held by living people such as Generals Clay, Tunner, and Howley, the mayor of Berlin, and others. In particular, Dr. Otto Ostrowski served the people of Berlin honorably and with distinction, and should not be confused with the entirely fictitious character of Hollweg. The characters in the novel are all fictional and entirely the product of the author's imagination.

For Betty with love

A NOTE OF THANKS

It is impossible to mention everyone who helped me on this project. Some of those who helped me behind the Iron Curtain cannot be mentioned by name. However, it would be impossible not to acknowledge others.

For their logistical support, my deepest gratitude is extended to: General Lucius B. Clay; Father of the Airlift, Lieutenant General William Tunner; and to my good and true friend, Brigadier General Frank Howley, who was Commandant of Berlin in those fearsome days.

I am indebted to the United States Air Force for unstinting cooperation. To Colonels James Hunter and "Dinny" Dinsmore, who set up the complicated German and American contacts, interviews, and itineraries; to Air Force Historian Joseph Tustin; Captain Lionel Patenaude, the PIO Officer, Tempelhof and Berlin; and my pal Lieutenant Colonel William G. Thompson, who traveled with me throughout Germany and later guided me through the Airlift and flying phases of the writing.

I wish to acknowledge and thank Columbia Film Studios, which sponsored my research; the University of Southern California Library, which has never failed me; and the United States Army and United States Information Agency in Berlin.

ICH BIN EIN BERLINER

—*John F. Kennedy*

Part one

A MEETING AT THE ELBE

CHAPTER ONE—*January, 1944*

Captain Sean O'Sullivan lifted the blackout curtain. A burst of dull light grayed the room. Christ, he thought, doesn't the sun ever shine in London. He heard planes droning overhead toward the English Channel but he could not see them through the thick fog. He wondered if his brother, Tim, was flying today.

"Come to breakfast, dear," Nan called.

Sean turned into the room. It was an elegant room, the most elegant he had ever known. The photograph on the mantle of Major G. Donald Milford stared down at him particularly harshly this morning.

The dining area was an alcove of three angled windows affording a view over Bayswater Road to Kensington Gardens. It was so mucky outside, the view had vanished. Nan Milford added to the opulence of the place in a silk and lace dressing gown. She put his jacket across the back of his chair and mentioned something or other about trying to remove a spot from the sleeve.

Sean sipped the coffee, grimaced, made a mental note to bum some decent coffee from the cook. This British version of ersatz was unfit for consumption in the first place and even worse when Nan got finished overboiling it.

Nan looked pleasantly tired from love-making. She was sad because she had made love so intensely and even sadder because she had fallen in love. She watched him with obvious adoration. "How is it that a handsome Irish brute like you never married?"

"And give up all this?"

"Do be serious for once, Sean."

"The transposition of old country traditions to San Francisco, I guess."

"And how many girls have chased you as I did and how have you avoided them?"

He was about to make a crack about playing it safe with married women but thought better of it. "A bachelor develops a sixth sense that tells him when his sanctity is about to be invaded. All sorts of built-in warning systems send up flares and rockets and bells go off."

She tweaked the end of his nose. "Please," she pleaded.

"Why be serious?"

Nan stiffened. She never got overtly angry . . . only straightened her back, glared, conveyed hurt. "I am sorry I asked."

From time to time Sean was suddenly reminded that Nan could be offended easily, that he had to treat her differently than other women he had known.

"It would be hard for you to comprehend," he said apologetically.

"Am I so without understanding?"

"You've had certain advantages in your life that makes understanding impossible."

"You speak as though I'm a terrible snob."

"You are. But you are a real snob. It is nothing you deliberately cultivated. The world is loaded with people trying to be snobs who just can't make the grade. A genuine, unvarnished snob is a creature to be revered."

She liked to hear Sean talk his lovely gibberish. Of course no man had ever spoken to her that way before. Dear, sweet Donnie sat where Sean sat now. My! What a difference. Nan did not know if Donnie would be more offended by the fact that Sean was in his place or that Sean had the audacity to sit at his table with his sleeves rolled up and his collar unbuttoned.

"Are you trying to say that marriage would have held you from advancing your station?"

"Not at all, Nan. The reasons were more practical."

"Now, I'm completely intrigued."

"I haven't married for the same reason my parents didn't marry until after a ten-year courtship. He was just too damned poor to support a wife."

He gulped another swallow of the horrible coffee. Nan's soft hand on his lightened the blow. Her fingertips played over his hands. "Please don't stop, Sean. We know so terribly little about each other."

Sean's large brown eyes searched the room and then outside into the mist, looking for nothing. "When my parents emigrated to America all they had was their hands, their backs and their hearts. My father worked harder than the Lord meant any man to work. I can hardly remember when he didn't have two jobs . . . longshoreman by day, watchman by night, cable-car driver by day, janitor by night, hod carrier, ditchdigger, bouncer. And Mom spent most of her life washing dishes and scrubbing floors in places like this. It makes me want to hurt you sometimes and all the other Mrs. G. Donald Milfords whose toilets were cleaned by my mother."

She squeezed his hand tightly to let him know she understood.

"My father always said he didn't come from the old country to raise three Irish cops for the San Francisco police force. His obsession was to put his sons through college. Work now, reward in heaven."

"He must be a remarkable man."

"Yes, he is," Sean answered, "but one day his back gave out and his heart almost gave out too. It was up to mother to keep us alive. Up to me to get through college. I didn't quit. I made it through. Know how? Picking up ten and twenty bucks fighting preliminaries in little clubs around the Bay Area. One of them in San Francisco was called the Bucket of Blood. I was a good boxer, Nan. I didn't want to get hit in the face and have to explain the cuts and bruises to my mother. I fought under the name of Herskowitz, the Battling Yid. How's that? So, the Lord was good. I got through Cal and I went to my mother one day and said, Mom, you don't have to scrub Mrs. G. Donald Milford's floors any more. I'll take care of you."

"Sean . . . I'm sorry."

"Sorry for what? I'd made it and I was going to get my brothers through. We're just a black Irish family which hangs together. One day I broke my hand in the ring and got this," he said, pointing to the thin white-lined scar over his left eye, "and then my mother knew. From then on I became Schoolboy O'Sullivan the Fighting Prof. Mom nearly died every time I got into the ring." Sean slumped. "So here we are, the brothers O'Sullivan. Tim's up there flying and Liam is in a grave in North Africa. I wanted to get married, had a girl I loved, but my family came first and she wouldn't wait." He dumped an oversized spoon of mulberry marmalade over the muffin to smother the burned taste. "Nan. You're one lousy cook."

She muttered something about the impossibility of getting domestic help. The rest of the meal was in silence. Sean rolled down his sleeves, buttoned them, and fixed his tie and slipped into his jacket. The quiet became uneasy. Every time they said good-by now there was an averting of eyes. The feel of the wet cold clouds from outside had come into the room and engulfed them.

Nan knew that the God who ruled Sean O'Sullivan was pushing him to the end of their affair. "There are so many unsaid things," she whispered.

"Our whole relationship is unsaid, Nan. That photograph of your husband who cannot protest. Your children in the country who remain hidden. The words we never say when we are making love. Six beautiful months of unsaid things."

"They're going to be said now, aren't they, Sean?"

"Kind of looks like it."

A jeep horn sounded from the street below. Beep, be, beep, beep. Nan reacted. "Must he blow that horn and announce your departures to the entire West End of London?"

Sean buttoned his jacket and put on his cap. At this moment she always turned genteel, holding her cheek up for the departing buss as she did for G. Donald Milford. Instead she found herself tight against him. He let her go and she reeled back and watched him disappear down the hall.

Sean hopped into the jeep alongside Second Lieutenant Dante Arosa, who gunned the vehicle away on the fog-wettened pavement.

"Scored last night," Dante said with pride of conquest.

"Little show girl?"

"A living testimony that English women are not cold in bed. Who in the hell libeled them in the first place? Some Irishman?"

Sean was indulgent. Dante was his own age, twenty-eight, but England was his first real experience with life. He had gone from a truck farm in the Napa Valley to the University of San Francisco to an almost too brilliant law career. There was little doubt of Dante Arosa's ability as a counter-intelligence officer on duty, or his somewhat juvenile behavior off duty. Tall, thin young men shouldn't smoke cigars, Sean thought. Dante doesn't clamp the cigar in one side of his mouth solidly. It sort of hangs limply from the front of his teeth.

As they ran alongside Kensington Gardens the traffic thickened. Dante continued his testimony to British womanhood.

"By the way, don't blow the horn."

"Huh?"

"When you pick me up. One, park jeep. Two, emerge. Three, walk to door. Four, ring bell."

Dante shrugged. He didn't like Nan Milford. It was broads like her who gave the English women their bad reputations. Where does she get this Virgin Mary routine? She's just another married broad shacking up behind her husband's back no matter what kind of icing Sean puts on it.

They sank into quietness. Everything was different about London, these days. Everything but the weather. The long, harrowing nights in the bomb shelters were over. The tension had eased. The bombers were going in the other direction these days. There was an air of victory everywhere. People were looking toward the end of the war and it was evident in everyone's voice and step.

"Sean."

"Yes?"

"How far has this thing gone with you and Nan?"

"I wish I knew."

"I'll ring the bell."

Dante Arosa cut the jeep abruptly in the middle of the block. Cars before him screeched to a halt and pedestrians scattered. He beelined for a spike fence that blocked a short, dead-end street named Queen Mother's Gate. Dante hit the brakes, bringing the tormented vehicle to a halt before the terrified sentry. The sentry saluted half-heartedly and waved them through past the sign on the gatepost which read: SPECIAL MISSION, MILITARY GOVERNMENT, UNITED STATES ARMY.

The abbreviated, enclosed street held a half-dozen buildings set about a wide central courtyard. On one side were officers' quarters, enlisted barracks, administration, dispensary, mess hall. Across the courtyard stood two large three-storied block-granite buildings housing the offices and conference rooms of SPECIAL MISSION, MILITARY GOVERNMENT.

From the instant they passed through the gate toward the motor pool the problems of life and love in London were done. Dante and Sean walked crisply in step toward the first of the Mission office buildings.

The directory in the anteroom read:

Room 101: Civil Administration of German Cities

Room 102: German Legal Codes

Room 103: Public Health

Room 104:   Banking System
Room 105:   Displaced Persons/Refugees
Conference Hall A/B/C: Identification of German Cities. Aerial
                          Recon.
Room 106:   Lab.
Room 201:   Counter-Intelligence, Leading Nazis
Room 202:   Counter-Intelligence, Secondary Nazis
Rooms 203/204/205:   Eradication of Nazism
Room 206:   Military Government Orders/Rulings/Manual
Conference Halls E/F: Identification of Nazis-Nazi Organiza-
                          tions
Third Floor: Document Center

Off the anteroom they entered the officer of the day's office and signed
in, were passed through the locked portal to the inner core of quiet
bustle. A second security desk, manned by a sergeant, blocked the
hallway.

"Morning," Dante said, leaning over signing the register.

"Morning, sir."

"Morning," Sean said.

"Morning, Captain O'Sullivan. General Hansen wants you in his
office at ten hundred. And frankly, sir . . . Eric the Red has the storm
flag up."

CHAPTER TWO

Brigadier General Andrew Jackson Hansen balanced his specs on the
end of his nose. He was short, hefty, had a few sprigs of gray hair so
that the addition of a pillow under his jacket could have given him
the appearance of kindly Kris Kringle. Other men wore glasses but he
wore specs. His face was as mobile and expressive as a Punch and
Judy puppet. This bubble of gentleness was deceptive for in an instant
a stream of oaths could tell one why he was identified as Eric the Red.

He drummed his stubby fingers on the desk top and from time to
time a particularly annoying word would growl from his throat as he
read . . .

CONFIDENTIAL REPORT: Requested for the eye's only use of Brig. Gen. A. J. Hansen.

SUBJECT: Cohabitation; Nan Milford/Capt. Sean O'Sullivan.

Mrs. Nan Milford, Age 35. Wife of G. Donald Milford, Major, British Army. Major Milford was captured during the German invasion of Crete in 1941. Has been a prisoner of war three years at Officer's Lager 22; Westheim, Germany.

Before war Milford was a highly successful director of Morsby Ltd., one of Britain's leading publishing houses. Member of board of directors of a dozen lesser companies. Rated moderately wealthy. Blue blood on both sides of family. Before the war the Milfords were considered congenially married. They associated themselves with London society, art, cultural and charity affairs. Members, Church of England.

Two children: Pamela, age 10. Roland, age 12. Children are living at home of paternal grandmother in Plimlington East where they were evacuated during the heavy bombing of London.

Since husband's internment, Nan Milford has worked as a volunteer in the London Section of the International Red Cross, Prisoner of War Division.

Approximately seven months ago she met O'Sullivan who was then conducting a G-5 study on Prisoner of War Camps. In this connection he spent much time with her on official duty gathering specific Red Cross data.

O'Sullivan and Mrs. Milford have engaged in cohabitation for approx. six months. In the beginning they were extremely cautious about their rendezvous and kept away from outside social activities together. However secrecy appears diminishing. For the last two months cohabitation has occurred regularly in the fashionable Milford flat on Bayswater Road, London, W.2.

Single copy this report produced. Other records destroyed as requested.

Thos. Hanley, Major, Counter-Intelligence.

"Piss," said Hansen as he slid the report into the top drawer of his desk.

He paced the room. He did not know if he were more angry with Sean or with himself. A. J. Hansen did not like to guess wrong about people. That annoyed him. He had selected Sean for the Special Mission over several hundred experts, all older, with more experience and sounder judgment.

Why did I pick him? There was that first creeping doubt of an error in sizing the man up. Why? Because he doesn't back down from me . . .

maybe. Because any kid who loves his parents and brothers and takes
care of them at the expense of his personal happiness would love his
country that way too.

The general pouted some more back at his desk. Even when Sean
lost his brother in North Africa he pulled himself together. Women!
Goddamned women. These two have nothing in common outside the
bedroom. She's seven years older and they come from different social,
economic, and religious worlds.

Hell, nothing wrong with a stray piece. But like the report said—co-
habitate—and forget them.

Sean's got to get rid of *that* woman.

The general's orderly, a gangly acne-marked corporal from Kentucky,
announced Sean's arrival.

"Sit down, O'Sullivan."

Hansen picked up a document Sean recognized as a study he had
completed the day before. TOP SECRET. PREROGATIVES OF MILITARY
GOVERNMENT COMMANDERS IN GERMANY.

"This report was two weeks late."

"Lot more involved than I figured."

"What? The report?" Hansen thumbed through the pages, playing
for fifteen seconds of tension-building silence. "You've got a real rod
on against the Germans."

"If the General will be specific."

"The General will be specific," he aped. He adjusted his specs for
reading. "This choice morsel is on page fourteen, paragraph sixty-two.
I quote Captain Sean O'Sullivan. 'In the event the orders of the local
military commander are not carried out by the civilian population, the
commander is empowered to seize hostages from the German civilian
population and execute them at his discretion until his will is en-
forced.'" Hansen closed the report and snatched off his specs. "That's
a hell of a thing for an American boy to write."

"I didn't know our function is to spread Americanism in Germany."

"Nor is it to continue Nazism. Now by hostages, Captain O'Sullivan,
I take it you mean to define between Nazis and non-Nazis."

"If the General will tell me if the bullet that killed my brother came
from a Nazi rifle or a non-Nazi rifle."

"So in judging all Germans as being the same, you mean to take
hostages who are two, three, or four years old."

Sean balked. "Well . . . perhaps we should limit hostages to Nazis."

"There are fifteen million Nazis in Germany," Hansen pressed.

"We'll have room for them when we open their concentration camps!"

"Sit down, lad, and don't get your Irish up on me. I want the explanation of the hostage paragraph."

Sean unclenched his fists and sunk into his seat once again. Eric the Red meant business. "In my following comment I said it would never be necessary to use hostages because the Germans are orderly people and will respond to whoever represents authority. You know damned well, General, I've said over and over they won't conduct guerrilla resistance. Quote Churchill. The Germans are at your throat or your feet. They'll be at our feet when we finish with them."

"Then why did you find it necessary to put this hostage thing in."

"Because they've got their own little special missions sitting in Berlin writing their version of the same manual. You know their versions? All Germans, get under American protection at all costs where kindly GI's will supply you with cigarettes, chocolate, and short memories. We have to put that hostage rule into the record just to let them know it's there."

Hansen grunted. He opened the bottom drawer of his desk. His stubby fingers produced a bottle of rye whiskey and a pair of glasses. He poured two oversized drinks and shoved one of them to Sean. He knew again why he had picked O'Sullivan for the Special Mission.

"I lost a brother too. Mark Twain Hansen. First World War. Belleau Wood. We can't go through this with those people again. They're sick. They have to be healed. Becoming Nazis ourselves isn't the way."

"It always comes back to the same damned confusion, General. What are we going to do with them?"

"Know the facts and believe in your country. You are here on this mission because our war begins when the shooting stops. Our bullets are ideas . . . your folks are immigrants, aren't they?"

Sean nodded.

"So are mine. My father, God rest his soul, came over by steerage after the Civil War and walked from New York to Iowa in the dead of winter." The general took a swallow of whiskey and allowed himself the rare pleasure of a moment of nostalgia. "Black Hawk County, Iowa. We homesteaded a section of land. My father's name was Hans Christian Hansen, after the Danish national hero. All of us were named after American heroes . . . except my sister. She died from diphtheria in one of those damned Iowa winters. God almighty . . . I'll see my father to my dying day looking over the newly cut corn fields, standing there like a statue . . . smoke coming from his pipe. He'd look at the leaves turning and put those two big leather hands on my shoulders and wouldn't say much. At Thanksgiving he'd give a toast after he read the Bible and his eyes would fill with tears when he said . . . God bless America."

The tension between the men had passed. Sean thought of his own father and smiled. "My Dad would say, where else in the world could a shanty Irishman put three sons through the university?"

Andrew Jackson Hansen hit his hand on the desk. "That's what I mean!" his gruff voice filled with enthusiasm. "We have to love America the way our parents did . . . naïve, sentimental, unsophisticated. The good Lord has been wonderful to our republic. He has given us the wisdom to fight wars with no thought of personal gain. But this time we cannot pack up and go home. We have come of age. We have inherited both the power and the responsibility of the world without seeking or wishing it. But . . . we must face up to it. Our land has grown a magnificent liberty tree and its fruit is the richest ideal of the human soul. But, we cannot go on forever merely eating the fruit of the liberty tree or it will die. We must begin to plant some seeds."

Damn Hansen, Sean thought. He could move you from anger to tears in a moment.

"My mother was a German immigrant, Sean. She saw a son fight her native country and die in the First World War. That killed her, too. I wouldn't like the idea of my mother being shot as a hostage."

Sean nodded that he understood. The long, hard, patient way would press them for a wisdom which they did not know if they possessed. He took the report from the desk. "I'll do some rewriting."

A. J. Hansen abruptly returned to the never-ending problems needing decisions on his desk, indicating without a word that the meeting was over.

Sean made for the door.

"By the way," Hansen said, "do something about *that* woman."

CHAPTER THREE

The two huge buildings on the right side of Queen Mother's Gate were dark except for the light of two offices. A light in A. J. Hansen's office was common. This light usually burned past midnight. No one really knew the number of hours A. J. Hansen worked, but he often remarked, "It's a goddam good thing there isn't a union to demand time and a half pay for generals or we'd bust the government's ass in a year."

He pored over the usual documents, appended the usual decisions, ate the usual sandwich, drank the usual glass of milk. Tonight it was the seizure of German banks, freezing assets, issuing occupation currency. Tomorrow? Maybe German railroads, maybe German textbooks. But once during each day the immediate problem became engulfed in the greater mission. All the reports were replete with highly worded ideals, but he wondered. Have we Americans lost the stuff? Are we too self-centered, too fat to understand and face up to what has happened to us? Sure, we will fight the war to its end. But what of it when the last shot is fired?

And these sick German people. Can we treat them with kindness? Will they understand it or mistake it for weakness? Indeed, can idealism be a practical solution to a people who have only understood force?

It came to that time of night when a shot of rye and a quick snooze was needed. He stretched out on the couch and covered his burning eyes. He thought of how he mentioned his father to young O'Sullivan today. Was it strange at all? With each passing day he was reaching back to his beginnings to find answers. . . .

Andrew Jackson Hansen was second in line for the throne, the family farm, and as he put it, " didn't give a lusty crap for farming." He became the first of the Hansen family to strike out with his father's reluctant blessings. He supported himself through the University of Iowa in a classical way, waiting on tables, mopping halls. In the summer he lumberjacked some in Wisconsin and was a roustabout in the tent shows which pocked the Midwest after the turn of the century.

His first woman was a hootchy-kootchy dancer who took a fancy to him during the sophomore vacation. A. J. thought about her off and on for many years.

By World War I he had earned his degree and was teaching history, economics, and political science at River Ridge Military Academy in Michigan to upper-economic-strata boys who couldn't have been less interested in history, economics, and political science. He joined the Army.

When his father died, a revered old man in that part of Iowa, the farm went to Tom Jefferson Hansen, who had always been cut out for that life. He ran it prosperously to this day with his sons.

The end of the war found A. J. Hansen at the rank of Captain and deeply involved in a program which sent food to starving Europe and later to Russia. He remained in the Army, cursing that his administrative and organizational ability kept him from ever receiving a fighting command.

In fact his only battles were with the Congress, Army brass, and a civilian public which largely considered the military as social lepers and fascists between wars.

Within the Army, Andrew Jackson Hansen had committed the initial sin of not being a graduate of West Point and therefore not a member of the West Point Protective Association. Secondly, in the regular Army it was standard practice to stud a male heir so that he might carry on the tradition of that Long Gray Line.

A. J. married a lovely woman from the Midwest who neither lushed nor shacked during his long tours of duty away from home and presented him with three daughters, none of whom turned out to be "army brats" and all of whom happily married nonmilitary men.

Despite his blatant disregard for tradition and an inability to keep his mouth closed at the discreet moment, Hansen's genius in new programs and his unflinching acceptance of the role of whipping boy kept him at the right hand of the chiefs of staff.

In 1938 Colonel Hansen became an overnight sensation heading a committee to draw up the Army's manpower needs. His report called for the immediate integration of Negro draftees and volunteers into all combat units.

A fellow officer from Georgia on the committee loyally reported this to some fellow generals from Virginia, Georgia, and Mississippi before Hansen was to go to Congress with the report.

"Andy. We aren't going to stand by and let you push this nigger thing with the Congress," a well-known artillery officer from Alabama warned as spokesman for the purity group. "Would you want a nigger officer leading your own son into combat?"

Hansen replied that it was a problem of semantics as he had no sons and he delivered the manpower report to Congress.

This not only infuriated the southern officer corps dedicated to the preservation of a white, Aryan army, but also the southern senators and congressmen who passed upon army promotions.

When the noise had simmered down Hansen found himself exiled to one of those remote posts where the Army punishes its mavericks and gives them time to reflect sins, pay penance.

His numerous requests for transfer to command a combat regiment went unanswered. By the time Pearl Harbor was attacked the powers-to-be figured Hansen had paid for his crime . . . besides he was badly needed for a new program.

The program was G-5, Military Government.

In the beginning, G-5 trained lawyers at the University of Virginia. After the landings in North Africa it became apparent that military government law could not stop epidemics, do police work, counter-intelligence, mend broken roads and sewers.

Hansen searched both in and out of the Army for former mayors and city managers, for doctors, port and sanitation engineers, and bankers, newspapermen, linguists, and food experts and transportation and communications people, and made them officers.

At the Hore-Belisha Barracks at Shrivenham, England, he assembled two thousand experts with their British and French counterparts. Although they were older men, they worked as strenuously as paratroopers. They were assigned future German cities and towns in A, B, and C units according to size.

And in London at Queen Mother's Gate fifty hand-picked men worked and lived under rigid security. These men broke down and studied every detail of the Nazi and German structure. Decisions came after laborious, detailed appraisal and went into the manuals often only after hot arguments.

Hansen stretched his squat body, blinked his eyes open, and returned at half pace to his desk.

How damned lucky, he thought, we have been able to fight our wars, pack up and go home. This was the true heart of the matter now. The military had been given the responsibility of G-5. Yet, American

generals have never had to worry about combining a military victory
with a political victory. Their minds could only think and plan the
destruction of the enemy. Lord give me the strength to fight our own
people as well as the Germans.

CHAPTER FOUR

Sean worked far into the night, even after General Hansen had retired.
He pondered on the revisions of PREROGATIVES OF MILITARY GOVERN-
MENT COMMANDERS IN GERMANY until they were within the framework
of top policy. To hell with it, Sean thought. He'd ask Hansen to transfer him into a combat unit. But the general was even more alone than
he, and battling greater forces. There was that instinct between men
that told him Hansen needed him.

There would be little the German people would have to answer for
beyond the misery they had created for themselves. Some reparations,
some personal suffering, but nothing to compare with the tears and
the blood they had caused. Already the damned lawyers had determined there was a difference between "criminal" Nazis and "non-
criminal" Nazis.

Sean penciled through his passage on hostages and wrote instead:
"When we enter Germany the purpose of Military Government is to
expedite Allied victory. We will rule firmly but fairly, keeping in mind
American tradition of not using brutality on the enemy civilian population. Military Commanders shall use armed force only in the event of
resistance. Failure of the German population to carry out orders will
be combated by imprisonment, fines or loss of food ration in extreme
cases."

Sean jerked the paper from the typewriter. "Gott bless the gutt kind
Amerikan soldiers," he cursed, ripped the paper up and threw it into
the wastebasket. He rubbed his temples. "Oh God, Liam, what shall
I do?"

Did his brother cry out from the grave for revenge? Did Liam really
want an answer for his death? Even when Liam had been bloodied
by a bully and Sean and Tim sought to avenge him Liam said, let him

go, don't hurt him. Can't you see, he attacked me because he was scared and confused?

Fight back, Tim said. Fight back, Liam. Too many people will drink your blood if they know you won't fight back.

Liam said, revenge for the sake of revenge is immoral.

What do you remember most when it all fuses in blurs at two o'clock in the morning and when it all must be remembered in a few golden moments? Tim, Liam, Sean in the caves below Sutro Baths. The ocean pounding against the rocks. The water leaping up, trying to defy gravity. Liam O'Sullivan reading Eugene O'Neill's *Beyond the Horizon* to his two older, spellbound brothers. . . .

"Oh, Liam. Your life was too good for them to take. Twenty-two-year-old boys shouldn't die in lonely places called Kasserine Pass . . ."

The omnipresent map of Germany hung over Sean's head. He stared at it, took the torn paper from the wastebasket, and retyped it, and then he went on to the next section.

WEHRMACHT: GERMANY'S REGULAR ARMY.

Policy: The Wehrmacht has fought a conventional war against American forces. However, atrocities against civilian populations have been catalogued by counter-intelligence. Particular brutality has been evidenced against the Greeks, Slavic peoples and Jews. Military Government must determine to what extent the Nazis dominated the Wehrmacht. In those areas under Wehrmacht command where atrocities were committed we must hold the Wehrmacht commander responsible as a war criminal.

Dammit, Sean thought, I won't back down. If the army commander were allowed to blame the Nazis for atrocities in his area, we would be digging legal traps for ourselves that would leave hundreds of crimes unanswered.

Yet Sean knew in his heart that no regular German Army general would ever have to answer in a court.

Then who was guilty?

Before him were a half-dozen books, each as thick as a Manhattan phone directory. These were the "official" guilty, the Blacklist. This was the heart of the Nazi cancer. But wasn't the whole German body infected? Sean had argued endlessly that Nazism was the historical and political expression of the entire German people.

He opened the index to the Blacklist to support his report . . .

BOOK ONE: NAZI ORGANIZATION:
GROUP ONE: PARA MILITARY ORGANIZATIONS SERVING
THE NAZIS: These groupings are not the conventional armed forces
serving Germany (Army, Navy, Air Force, etc.) ALL OF THE BE-
LOW LISTED ARE TO BE DISBANDED UPON OUR ENTRY
INTO GERMANY AND THEIR RECORDS SEIZED.
SCHUTZSTAFFEL. Commonly known as SS. The SS is the prime
target of Counter-Intelligence. We shall arrest ALL MEMBERS OF
THE SS regardless of rank.
ALLGEMEINE SS. These are regional German SS charged with running SS schools, institutions and particularly "overseeing" the political
machinery of specified political districts. These people are armed only
with small arms. We shall arrest all.
WAFFEN SS. This is a fully militarized body with its own armor,
supply and administrative forces. WAFFEN SS has special duties such
as ghetto guards, concentration camp guards, slave labor camp guards,
slave labor factory guards throughout the occupied countries. In addition, WAFFEN SS units have served in combat on all battlefronts.
It is impossible to estimate the number of WAFFEN SS which will be
in Germany at the time of our entry. This is the hard core of fanatics.
We estimate they will be the center of any guerrilla resistance. Arrest
all members immediately.
NAZI PARTY STORM TROOPERS (SA). Commonly known as the
Brown Shirts. This is a para military group that was instrumental in
Hitler's rise to power and ultimate seizure of the government. The
Brown Shirts used terror tactics in crushing political opposition to Hit-
ler and brutality against minorities. The membership is 1,500,000. We
shall arrest all persons rank of Sturmbannfuehrer or above (Nazi rank:
Major). Book One lists 30,000 blacklisted for arrest.

Sean turned the page of the index. Where did it end . . . where did
it end . . .

NAZI PARTY MOTOR TRANSPORT CORPS (NSKK). A pre-mili-
tary training for Nazi Party members for future service in Waffen SS
tank or motorized units. Despite the innocent sound of name it is Nazi
drenched. Arrest all persons of rank of Staffelfuehrer or above. Book
Four lists 10,000 blacklisted for arrest.
NAZI PARTY FLYING CORPS (NSFK). This group was formed in
the early 1930's to circumvent the Versailles Treaty forbidding a German air force. They formed under the guise of a civilian flying club
but held secret military training and maneuvers, schools for glider pilots,

flyers, aircraft construction and maintenance. Arrest all of rank of Sturmbannfuehrer and above. Book Five blacklists 5,000 for arrest.

Damn, damn, damn, Sean thought. If we knew so much about what they were doing . . . why didn't we stop them?

AUXILIARY HOME AIR DEFENSE CORPS (Heimat Flak or HF). Nominally Nazi but this group is under Nazi control and direction. These are mostly factory workers, however the organization does include several thousand Hitler Youth. Abolish without arrests.

PEOPLES ARMY (VOLKSSTURM). Consists of people too old or too young for regular military service. A "Home" Army constructed for defense of German soil/German cities. Age brackets 13–16 and 40–60. Although this group is under Nazi domination the soldiers will be treated as regular army prisoners of war.

GERMAN LABOR SERVICE (RAD). A compulsory labor force for all "Aryan" males and females. These people construct military fortifications, work in land reclamation and forest conservation, road buildings and the like. We are interested only in senior RAD officers and Book Six has 250 blacklisted for arrest.

TODT LABOR (OT). A group which absorbs unemployed for "public works." This group built the Siegfried Line. Its functions overlap with above listed RAD. We have blacklisted 100 senior officers for arrest in Book Six.

HITLER YOUTH (HITLER JUNGEND OR HJ). A compulsory group for all "Aryan" males and females age 14–18. Young people are completely saturated with Nazi indoctrination. There are also nature study groups and agricultural studies, however we consider this among the most dangerous because they are young and in a formative stage. The officers and leaders are fanatical Nazis. Arrest all holding the rank of Sturmfuehrer (cadre leader). Blacklist Book Five lists 20,000 for arrest.

GROUP TWO: ORGANIZATIONS OF NAZI DOMINATED POLICE FORCES

ORDER POLICE (ORPO)

Sub 1 Schutzpolizei (Schupo). They police towns with 2,000 population or less.

Sub 2 Gendarmerie. Police open country in areas of 2,000 population or less.

Sub 3 National Fire Precaution Police.

Sub 4 Auxiliary Police. Volunteer citizens without pay used in general police work, traffic work, etc.

Sub 5 Technical Emergency Corps. Used in demolition, rescue, debris clearing. Particularly active since bombings.

Sub 6 Administrative Police. Records, payrolls, etc.

BARRACKS POLICE. DANGEROUS! A HEAVILY ARMED SHOCK TROOP KEPT AS A MOBILE RESERVE. WE CONSIDER THEM AS A POTENTIAL SOURCE OF RESISTANCE. IT SHOULD BE UNDERSTOOD THAT THE ENTIRE CIVILIAN POLICE MACHINERY IS UNDER COMPLETE CONTROL OF THE NAZIS AND IS A KNOWN LOYAL INSTRUMENT OF THE NAZIS. THEY ARE SEMI-MILITARIZED. THEIR LEADERSHIP IS NAZI. THE ENTIRE POLICE MACHINERY IS TO BE ABOLISHED AND ITS RECORDS SEIZED. THE ENTIRE GERMAN POLICE ESTABLISHMENT MUST BE REORGANIZED FROM THE GROUND UP. AFTER ALLIED VICTORY THIS IS CONSIDERED AN A1 A1 PROBLEM OF MILITARY GOVERNMENT.

GROUP THREE: NAZI POLICE MACHINERY, ITS HEAD OFFICE BEING THE REICHSICHERHEITSHAUPTAMT (RSHA), MAIN SECURITY OFFICE OF THE THIRD REICH.

SECURITY POLICE (SIPO)

Sub 1 THE SECRET STATE POLICE (GESTAPO). This is the notorious *political* police arm of the Nazi Party. It has unlimited powers of arrest. It is filled with the most fanatic of the Nazis. ALL MEMBERS ARE TO BE ARRESTED. SEIZURE OF GESTAPO RECORDS A1 A1 TARGET OF COUNTER-INTELLIGENCE. Book Six blacklists 15,000 for arrest.

Sub 2 CRIMINAL POLICE (KRIPO). An arm of the Gestapo working in the general crime field specializing in such things as black market, smuggling, etc.

Sub 3 SECURITY SERVICE OF THE SS (SD). The nerve center for spying on German citizens and using informers to collect information for the SS. NOTE: The SD has recently replaced the regular intelligence service of the regular German Army. ARREST ALL MEMBERS. Because of the ultra-secret nature of this group our lists are incomplete, but Book Six currently blacklists 15,000 for arrest.

Who were the guilty? How could this happen in but a single decade of Nazi control of the government without the unabashed support of the mass of the population? Where does it stop, Sean wondered . . .

GROUP FOUR: NAZI POLITICAL ORGANIZATIONS. THE FOLLOWING WILL BE ABOLISHED AND THEIR RECORDS

SEIZED. THOSE BLACKLISTED FOR ARREST WILL BE FOUND IN BLACKLIST BOOK FOUR.

Central Office, Nazi Party

Party Chancellory. All officers blacklisted.

Fuhrer's Chancellory. All members blacklisted.

Organization of Germans Abroad. All officers blacklisted.

Center for Volksdeutsche.

Office of the National Union for German Elements Abroad.

Office of the Reich Organization Leader (arrest top 15 officers).

Office of the Reich Party Treasurer. All officers blacklisted.

Supreme Party Court/Subordinate Nazi Courts. All justices blacklisted.

Office of the Fuhrer's Commissioner for Supervision of the Intellectual and Ideological Training and Education of the Nazi Party. All officers blacklisted.

Office of Reich Propaganda Leader. 300 blacklisted for arrest.

Office of Reich Press Leader. Top officers blacklisted.

Office of Reich Press Party Chief. Decision on arrests, pending.

Reich Office, Agrarian Population.

Head Office, Public Health.

Office for Technology.

Office for Local Government.

Office for Officials. All officers blacklisted.

Office for Commissioner for Racial Questions. All officers blacklisted.

Office for Genealogical Research. Decision on arrests, pending.

Foreign Office of the Nazi Party. All officers blacklisted.

Reichstag Party of the Nazis (Congress). Arrest all members.

Reich Woman's Leadership. Officials blacklisted.

Office for Nazi War Victims.

Regional and Local Offices of the Nazi Party Administration

Gauleitung in each Nazi Party Gau or Kreisgau (city or dist.). All Gauleiters (dist. leaders) blacklisted.

Kreisleitung of each Nazi Party Kreis (county). 700 Kreisleiters (county leaders) blacklisted.

Ortsgruppenleitung in each Nazi Party Ortsgruppe (branch, area of city). All leaders blacklisted.

Zellen and Block Officers (cells, blocks, neighborhood level). All leaders blacklisted.

The Beauftragter der NSDAP (Nazi Party Commissioners Office). Specific blacklisted persons made.

And then, the rest of it. From the police and the political machinery the tentacles spread to every vein of German life.

GROUP FOUR: NAZI PROFESSIONAL AND OTHER ORGANIZATIONS

Reich League of Doctors. Top leaders blacklisted.

Reich League of Technicians. Top leaders blacklisted.

Reich League of Teachers. Top leaders blacklisted.

Reich League for Officials.

Colonial League.

Women's Organization (working women). Top leaders blacklisted.

League of Nurses.

Women's Association (housewives).

Student Leadership Organization. Top leaders blacklisted.

Students League. Top leaders blacklisted.

Students Association.

Lecturers Association. Top leaders blacklisted.

Lawyers League in association with Notaries and Accountants. Top leaders blacklisted.

League of Former Students.

League of German Families.

German Labor Front.

Association for Physical Training.

Ex-Servicemen's League.

Chamber of Culture.

Union of Local German Government.

German Hunters Association.

Council of Population Experts and Race Politics. Leaders blacklisted.

Committee for the Protection of German Blood. Leaders blacklisted.

Relief Organization for War Victims. (Seize records as we expect wholesale larceny.)

Winter Relief. (Seize records. Grand theft suspected.)

GROUP FIVE: CIVIL AND POLITICAL OFFICES UNDER DOMINATION OF THE NAZIS.

The below listed will be suspended and all officers dismissed. Those blacklisted for arrest will be found in Book Four.

Reich Ministries (National Offices) State Secretaries, Ministry Directors. 80 blacklisted.

Land Ministers, their State Secretaries (sub-division comparable to American state). 30 blacklisted.

District Presidents. 40 blacklisted.

Department Heads of Provinces. 30 blacklisted.

Commissioner General: Medical and Health Service. (See blacklist.)

Commissioner for Shipping. Decision on arrests, pending.

Inspector-General: Water and Power. Decision pending.

Inspector-General: Transportation. Decision pending.
Inspector-General: German roads.
Reich Youth Leader. Arrests covered elsewhere.
Division Chief: Four Year Plan Office (records A1 CIC target).
Heads of Reichbank, Supreme Administrative Tribunal.
Hereditary Court.
Labor Court.
Archives.
Social Insurance.
Honor Court.
Reich Food Estate Officials.
Regierungspresidenten (governors of provinces).
Landrate (district magistrates).
Oberburgermeisters (mayors) of German cities of more than 100,000
    population. 95 blacklisted.
Officials; Reich Ministry for Public Enlightenment and Propaganda/
    their regional offices.
Reich Ministry for Armament and War Production. 70 blacklisted.
Members of German Reichstag (Congress or Parliament). All mem-
    bers blacklisted.
Members of Supreme Court.
Members of Peoples Court.
Members of Special Court.   } Arrest all.
Members of Appeals Court.
Chief Public Prosecutors.
University Rectors and Curators.
Labor Trustees. 40 blacklisted.

GROUP SIX: OCCUPIED COUNTRIES
Provisional Presidents. Reich Governors. 30 blacklisted.
Commissioner for Treatment of Enemy Property. Records are prime
    CIC target.
Head of Reichsstelle für Raumordnung (Dept. for foreign-area plan-
    ning).
Chiefs of Military and Civil administration, occupied countries. 3,000
    blacklisted for arrest.

GROUP SEVEN: MISC. CATEGORIES LISTED IN BOOK THREE
Police Presidents. 100 blacklisted.
Other key members police machinery. 320 blacklisted.
All members of the Nazi Party not accounted for otherwise holding
    rank of Beriechsleiter (group leader). 30,000 blacklisted for arrest.
Nazi Dozentenbund Officials (university lecturers).

Nazi Studentenbund (students bund).

Nazi Kraftfahrer Corps Officials (motor pools).

Businessmen and others who have accepted Nazi honors
    as Blut Orden (Blood Order)
    or Ehrendolch (Honor Dagger)
    or Ehrensold (Honor Pay).
    Lists are very incomplete.

"Sean buddy, wake up!"

Sean's head lay in the index book on his desk. Dante tugged at him. Sean's head was full of annoying half dreams and pounding with overweariness. He lifted it, blew a breath. Dante Arosa came into focus. He smelled of whiskey and cigar smoke—and perfume from the show girl. "What the hell time is it?"

"Five A.M. You weren't in the room so I figured you must have corked off."

"Yeah . . . must have dozed . . ."

Dante helped him close the volumes, lock them in the safe.

"You've got the hard job," Sean said. "All I have to do is give my opinion and watch it shoved down the drain. You've got to sit here and identify the pictures of these bastards. I was just about to explain why the Wehrmacht . . ."

"Get to bed. You're walking crooked."

"Sometimes I sit here in the middle of all this puke and wonder what in the hell we've run into. Just one big goddamned daisy chain with eighty million players."

CHAPTER FIVE

One of the things Sean found so exciting about Nan Milford was her unalterable calm. He wondered if fire or flood could unnerve her. But now Nan showed visible signs of discomfort. "From the instant we met we have been working toward this moment," she said.

"We didn't invent adultery. It doesn't bother some people. It bothers the hell out of us."

"God, I've had a splitting headache all day." She poured herself a cognac, felt it burn through her enough to soothe her leaping nerve ends.

Sean looked across the room at the omnipresent photograph of Major G. Donald Milford. "He's a nice guy, isn't he?"

"Donnie? Donnie is a lovely man. I shall tell you what kind of a man Donnie is. He would not only forgive me but he would understand."

"It would be a lot easier if you were married to a rat. I'm a nice guy, too, Nan. You've gotten to me too deeply. We're going to make a mess if we keep going."

Nan forced herself to remain calm. Sean wouldn't like a hysterical woman. What to say? How about me? I didn't bargain for this, either. Donnie was comfortable. We were the same kind . . . dull and comfortable. Can I say . . . Sean, you make an animal out of me! I crave the things you do to me and make me do. They will never happen again to me . . .

She spoke slowly and deliberately. "Donnie was gone for a year before he was taken prisoner in 1941. He was gone almost four years before I met you. That justifies nothing, of course. I would have gladly traded places with Donnie. Behind barbed wire he has no choice or conscience to fight. I think it is more difficult to be free and know you must voluntarily withdraw from the human race."

It was hard to realize that Nan Milford didn't have control of herself at every moment. Sean should have known. He should have known by the way she exploded, first in the darkness, and then here, in the dimmed lights of the living room.

"The children and I lived in the cellar every night for almost a year during the heavy bombing. I was finally forced to send them off to their grandmother. During the day I was that wonderful brave Mrs. Milford. A glorious example of stout British stuff. But when the bombs came at night I was alone . . . alone in the gray world where you are not a person but a vegetable. It becomes so when you live in that gray world; for the want of feeling another human being you are jealous of every soldier and his girl in the street, even of the damned mating birds. Sean, you didn't have a chance from the instant I met you."

"Nor did I bargain for how I'd feel."

"Nor did I. Should I be disgusted with myself because I'm not steeped in remorse or guilt? You know how you make me behave . . . in there. I've never been that way before."

Sean arose slowly and walked about the richly handsome room. Nan was neither nervous nor arrogant. She was just plain tired. "Sean, I am afraid of being alone again. You, me, Donnie . . . I don't know. I do know if you leave me I'll have to have another man and God help me because I wouldn't even care for him."

"I guess we're not supposed to be saints," Sean said. "I've got to get going now. My brother Tim is down in London for the weekend."

"Very well."

Sean put on his topcoat slowly and walked to the door.

"Sean."

"Yes?"

She was acid and angry. "You need not come back tonight. I shall be leaving in the morning to spend several days with the children."

"Okay."

"Will you be calling when I return?"

"Not if I can find the strength," he said and he left.

The hall porter ushered him out into a billow of cold wet fog. He flicked his flashlight toward the pavement to find a path through the abysmal darkness. In a second the fog had swallowed him up.

"Sean!" a frantic voice pierced the black. "Sean . . ."

He listened to directionless footsteps, leaned against a building trying to hide himself . . . trying not to answer. "Sean!" her voice cried. "Sean!"

"I'm over here."

Nan fell against him gasping for breath, wet and shivering and broken.

"You damned fool running outside without a coat . . . you damned little fool."

Nan trembled and cried. "Sean . . . I know there must be a good-by . . . but not now. I love you, Sean. I'll pay any price for having you. I swear I shan't care what shame or pain or risk will come from it. When you must go . . . we will both find the courage, somehow."

His coat was around her and he kissed her wet cheeks and pressed her into the strength of his arms. "I love you, Nan . . ."

CHAPTER SIX

Sean came in out of the fog at Henry Pringle's Blue Hawk Inn. The Blue Hawk, named after Pringle's World War I fighter squadron was the fighter pilots' hangout. Henry Pringle himself was a mechanic and had yet to make his first flight. The pub was a shrine to the heroes he never ceased to worship.

The big room was cluttered with photographs of over two hundred British, American, Canadian, French, Polish, New Zealand, and Aussie aces and as many model airplanes hung from the black beams and rafters. The walls were studded with denuded bomb casings, squadron insignia, leather helmets, framed records of kills, machine guns and pistols, bits of wings and wheels. It was a whiskey and ale aviation museum.

Nelson Goodfellow Bradbury, an American correspondent gave Pringle's Blue Hawk renewed prominence after a hibernation between wars. Bradbury reported the war from London long before Pearl Harbor. When the American volunteer Eagle Squadron flew with the RAF they discovered Pringle's place. Bradbury wrote about it, and was held in reverence by the English only slightly less than the King. He built his shrine to the fighter pilots with words. One column each week was certain to be written from "Big Nellie's" personal booth. The Blue Hawk was constantly mentioned in his deep-voiced broadcasts to America.

Despite Big Nellie's bloated wartime salary he was almost always in hock. From the time the Eagle Squadron came to England he kept a special flat as a party place for weary flyers . . . and picked up innumerable bar tabs for "his boys" . . . floated uncountable loans—some never repaid because the pilots never returned from their missions.

Sean liked the rarefied atmosphere of the Blue Hawk. The flying talk, the unshaven chins, the crushed caps, the comradery; the nervous, bragging tension of men playing with death. It was far removed from the austere gloom of Queen Mother's Gate.

Besides, Pringle had the best-looking barmaids in London, and fighter pilots were the glamour these days. Blue Hawk weddings were wild affairs—champagne corks went up like flak for three or four days.

There was too much information to be gotten around the place by a

stranger. They were not permitted. Sean was no stranger; he sat down
at Big Nellie's booth. Nelson Goodfellow hunched like a grizzly bear
over his typewriter, pecking out the end of his column over the din.

"Where's Tim?"

"Out looking for poon. He said he'd see you here soon as he makes
a connection."

"What happened to the last broad?"

"Married a Canadian sergeant."

Sean ordered a couple of drinks. "Tim owe you any dough?"

"A fin . . . a tenner . . . I don't know."

Sean paid his brother's debt. The singers around the upright piano
unloaded . . .

> Oh hallelujah, Oh hallelujah
> Throw a nickel on the grass,
> Save a fighter pilot's ass,
> Oh hallelujah, Oh hallelujah,
> Throw a nickel on the grass,
> And you'll be saved . . .

Big Nellie jerked his story from the machine. "You hear the combined
voices of the Fourth Group . . . Squadron Ten . . ."

Big Nellie began to blue pencil through his story.

> Got flak holes in my wing tips,
> And my gas tanks got no gas,
> Mayday, Mayday, Mayday,
> Got six Messerschmitt's on my ass . . .
>
> Oh hallelujah . . .

"They've got to sing loud," Nellie's gruff voice said. "They're missing
three tenors, two baritones, and a bass. Strafing a bridge yesterday,
tree-top level. The Krauts were laying up there behind a cloud. It was
a turkey shoot. How's things at Queen Mother's Gate?"

"Three casualties. One cut from a stray paper clip, another with dirty
hands from carbons, and a third got lost in the fog walking from building A to building B and hit a wall."

Nellie's laugh matched his grizzly-bear appearance. "How do you get
along with General Hansen?"

"Yesterday or today?"

"Let me tell you something about Hansen, Sean. Very few armies in

the world have a dozen generals who are too valuable to be wasted on
a fighting command. Yes . . . I said wasted. He's a Jeffersonian in uniform. I remember covering the manpower hearings before a joint committee of Congress. That little son of a bitch looked right at one of the
senators from South Carolina and said, 'We can never fight a just or
correct war so long as some of our citizens must fight it as mess-hall
boys and ditchdiggers. Our skins may be different color but the blood
the Negro offers his country is the same color as yours.'"

"I'd of pulled out of there a long time ago, Nellie, if I didn't feel
that. A lot of officers like to brag about their men following them to
hell. Hansen's the only one I'd care to make the trip with."

"I'm glad you feel that way, Sean. Hansen needs you."

"That's what I like about you, Nellie. You've always got information.
I got here early on purpose so I could talk to you alone. What is Tim
up to?"

Big Nellie's wide puss faltered.

"Come on, Nellie. We've got twenty-five counter-intelligence men at
Queen Mother's Gate. Hansen uses them to spy on me. I use them to
spy on Tim. There's been some one-man missions out of his base."

Nellie's big paw engulfed the glass of whiskey. "German rocket
bases."

"That's what I thought."

"They are well hidden, they're small, and can send up a snowstorm
of flak. We've tried several ways to get at them. Right now we're using
Invaders and Marauders. They're good birds but no hot rods. In elements of threes from medium altitude they've got a chance of getting in
and out."

"Go on."

"Our success has been limited. Tim talked his C.O. into letting him
try a one-plane, low-level sneak attack. He got back from the mission
all right. The plane looked like a sieve. But he demolished the target.
So, your brother gets to take in another plane, solo next week." He
belted down the drink, signaled for refills. "When Tim flies low they
tell me he likes to count the dandruff in the German scalps."

Oh, there ain't no fighter pilots down in hell,
Oh, the place is full of queers . . . navigators . . . bombardiers . . .
Oh, there ain't no fighter pilots down in hell.

Timothy O'Sullivan entered Pringle's Blue Hawk with a big-busted redhead on his arm. Tim had a fetish for big-busted redheads.

Nellie and Sean watched him thread his way toward their booth amid the turning of heads, the bulging of eyes.

"Where in the hell does he find them?" Nelson Goodfellow Bradbury inquired with envy. "He's only been in London for two hours."

"Hell, look at him," Sean said. Sean was prejudiced, of course. What woman wouldn't go for a strapping, handsome, twenty-four-year-old black Irishman with a fast glib tongue and wild ways. Maybe it was all brotherly pride, Sean thought . . . but then, Tim's always had to fight the women off. He and Nellie arose as Tim and the big-busted redhead reached the booth and Tim mumbled a name like Cynthia or Penelope or something like that and she was pleased to meet them, particularly Nelson Goodfellow Bradbury, whom she knew by reputation, of course . . . as who didn't. They were seated, ordered drinks. Tim and Sean traded letters from home. A wordless exchange of glances told them they were worried about their father's heart condition; he hadn't come out of it since Liam's death.

Sean said things were swell at Queen Mother's Gate; Tim said they were swell at Braintree; Henry Pringle paid his personal respects; they drank some more.

Tim was spotted and called to the piano, where the big-busted redhead delighted the flyers of Squadron Ten by standing next to him and wiggling in time to the music. Tim's entrance on the scene dictated a round of Irish ballads. A third and fourth round of drinks led directly to a seizure of nostalgia and Tim sang his father's very favorite in a handsome, rich Irish tenor . . .

> Kathleen Mavourneen! the gray dawn is breaking,
> The horn of the hunter is heard on the hill . . .

"The son of a bitch can do everything," Big Nellie said. "He'll be a cinch if he runs for Congress . . ."

> The lark from her light wing the bright dew is shaking . . .
> Kathleen Mavourneen! What, slumbering still?

After the fighter pilots of Squadron Ten had been moved to tears, the redhead excused herself to tidy up and Tim returned to the booth.

"Well done, lad. You're in fine voice tonight."

"Nellie. I'm in a bind. I need a room."

Bradbury shrugged. "There's an all-night party going on at the flat."

"So, take her to a hotel," Sean said.

"She's got a mental block about hotels."

"Here. Take the key to my place. I'll take a hotel room."

"Wouldn't think of it, Nellie."

"Sure you would," Nellie answered. "Besides I'm pushing off early. I'll be flying on a special mission tomorrow." He looked Tim squarely in the eyes as he handed him the key. "I'm going to ride an Invader. They're taking a crack at a V-1 base."

Tim took the key, avoiding both the other men's eyes. "Should be interesting," he said.

The correspondent rose to his full reaches of six feet six inches and lumbered across the room. His journey was punctuated by handshakes, back-slaps, and hi-Nellies.

The brothers were alone. "What's the matter, Sean? You look real down."

"We've got all weekend to talk about it."

"Christ, I'm sorry. I've got to get back up to Braintree first thing in the morning. Let me put whozits in a taxi and send her home. We can hole up at Nellie's and talk."

"The gesture is out of character. I'll slip into Nellie's place later and sleep on the living-room couch. We'll have a chance to talk in the morning."

Tim began to protest, but the big-busted redhead returned and her mere presence swayed the argument Sean's way. Tim and the girl left the Blue Hawk after "regretting" Sean could not join them.

CHAPTER SEVEN

"Wake up, sweetheart."

Sean blinked his eyes open. Tim, dressed and shaven, stood over him. He looked around. He was in Big Nellie's flat. He came to a sitting position cautiously. His head throbbed. His mouth held a foul taste. The smell from the kitchen of breakfast cooking added to his discomfort.

"One thing I can't stand," Tim said, "and that's a drunken Irishman."

"Where's the broad?"

"Just put her in a taxi. We never heard you come in. What time was it, anyhow?"

"Hell, I don't know. We closed the Blue Hawk and hit a private party. Pringle poured me here."

Sean wove to his feet and threaded an unsteady course to the bathroom, threw up, then dunked his head in a basin of icy water. He spread a line of toothpaste along his forefinger and pushed it over his teeth, fished through the cabinet for a brush and comb. The mirror revealed a stubble-chinned, bleary-eyed man in the throes of a monumental hangover.

He went to the kitchen, where Tim labored over the stove. Sean opened the refrigerator and mumbled about no fruit juice, but there was beer. He uncapped one. Thank God Nellie still keeps his beer cold. He flopped into a chair and asked what time it was.

"Six-thirty. I'll get the eight o'clock train from Waterloo." Tim shoved a plate of ham and eggs before Sean. He balked.

"How's the redhead?"

"Cynthia? Good lay. Besides, she is a nice kid. Lost her husband in Greece. Got a seven-year-old boy. You ought to give her a call one of these days . . . if Nan ever gives you a night off. . . . Listen, big brother," Tim pursued, "you're not the binge-throwing type. What's bothering you? Nan?"

"Partly."

"Trouble with you, Sean, you've always got to fall in love. You've got to make a big affair out of it. Christ, can't you take these women with a grain of salt?" Tim chewed a bite of ham, then waved his fork under Sean's nose. "You're going to get yourself in a real sling with this Milford broad."

"Tim . . . I love her. I love her more deeply than I loved that other girl. I've never felt like this about anyone."

Tim dropped the fork and sighed. "You poor bastard."

"I said I love her."

"Sure, I can picture it now. You, me, Nan and Dad out at Seal's Stadium drinking beer and watching the ball game on Sunday afternoon."

"Smart ass . . . smart ass."

"She's not one of ours and we're not one of hers."

"Who in the hell says we're talking marriage."

"So, what are you talking about, Sean?"

Sean shoved the plate away, snatched the beer bottle, and sulked from the table. He leaned against the wall . . . glowering, sulking, sipping. Tim's hand touched his shoulder.

"I'm on your side, Sean. A woman like Nan's got more class than you and I will see in the rest of our lives. I guess she must be pretty easy to fall in love with. But I come down from Braintree every week and see you eating your heart out. You can't get to needing a woman that much knowing you're going to have to give her up."

"You're right, of course, but it's not that easy to kiss her off. I don't know if I could stand to be in the same city with her and not call her. I keep telling myself to transfer out . . . but . . . you know how I feel about General Hansen. He's fighting the whole goddamned Army and State Department. I can't quit him, either."

"Well . . . you might as well eat your breakfast."

They both picked at their food listlessly. Sean gave up trying to eat. "Nan Milford isn't all that's bothering me. Tim O'Sullivan is bothering me too. I hear you're turning into a real hot pilot."

"Big Nellie talks too much."

"He just confirmed what I already know. You were shipped out of your fighter squadron for your own good. You were put into Invaders to slow you down because you were too reckless. Now, you've figured how to win the war single-handed."

"What the hell do you want from me!"

"Stop carrying the flag, Tim. You're always carrying the flag. When you were ten years old you wanted to join the Irish Republican Army. *Erin go bragh!* Up the Republic! At ten! And if I hadn't stopped you you'd of quit college and joined the Lincoln Brigade in Spain."

"At which time," Tim interrupted, "my brother the fighter dramatically held up his hands and said, 'I took two fights to pay your tuition and broke my hand. I'll break the other one to keep you in school.' "

"So maybe I was wrong? Maybe I did something bad?"

Tim became quiet. He shook his head. "You're never wrong, Sean. You never let me get into trouble . . . never let me get hurt."

"What is this obsession? What makes you so angry . . . hell, when we were kids and we used to climb down to the caves at Sutro . . . Liam . . . Liam would talk about the Irish poets and you would talk about the Irish terrorists."

"How in the hell can you remain so impersonal to a war that's taken our brother!"

"Don't you think I've cried for Liam?"

"You sit there day after day, week after week in those rooms at Queen

Mother's Gate. You know what the Germans have done! Don't you ever feel like you're going to break apart for the wanting to get back at them!"

Sean shook his head with a measure of guilt. "I suppose my judgment is a job qualification. I can't let personal emotions get mixed up in it."

"That's it then," Tim said, "your war is careful. Mine is another kind. And neither of us is wrong." Tim grabbed his brother's arm excitedly. "When I was a fighter pilot and we were coming over German land I almost always saw Liam's face outside the window. I would see him smiling softly the way only he could . . . I would hear him reading to us in the caves. And then . . . I would visualize Liam's grave. I want to tell you, Sean. I begged for strafing missions. I liked to watch Germans scatter and cower in ditches. I wanted to fly so low I could chop them up with my propellors." Tim's eyes became watery. His voice softened. "Private Liam O'Sullivan . . . age twenty-two. Major in literature. Liam was a poet. Poets shouldn't die. You and I would have done all right by Mom and Pop . . . but Liam . . . he could have brought us honor. Oh God! Why does the wrong brother have to die?"

Tim began to weep. He always cried when he spoke about Liam.

"Liam said revenge for revenge's sake is immoral. Call it off," Sean pleaded. "Fifty-four missions is enough. You've shot down ten enemy planes and destroyed a rocket base. Tim . . . we're winning this war, now. We'll be landing in Europe in a few months. You've got to start being careful."

Tim bolted from his chair. "Shut up. You're starting to disgust me!"

Sean grabbed his brother and shook him. "Goddamn you, Tim! Goddamn you! Don't you ever think of anyone but yourself! You want to put Momma and Poppa in the grave beside you!"

"Don't ask me to fight your war. I am what I am."

Sean's hands dropped to his sides helplessly. "I'll get myself squared away and ride down to the station with you."

CHAPTER EIGHT

A. J. Hansen saw in Sean O'Sullivan the image of himself, a defiant young officer before a superior, demanding a combat command.

"So," snorted Eric the Red, "you want a transfer. You got nut aches to be a hero. Congratulations. That's just what this Army needs, one more infantry company commander."

"I'm not cutting it here, General."

"That's damned well for the General to decide."

"You've got my report all doctored up to conform with policy and high sounding ideals, but there were just too many things I was forced to write that rubbed against my grain."

He even sounds like me, Hansen thought. How many times have I justified my existence as a desk jockey? How many nights have I gone to sleep making myself believe that I was in the most important service I could render? How many lies have I told myself after my ass has been burned?

Just today, Hansen thought . . . just today.

There had been another frustrating experience at Supreme Headquarters as Hansen pleaded with American political commanders to listen to British advice. The invasion of Europe was at hand. Hansen begged them to plan battle tactics ahead within a framework of postwar political settlement. But all those mummies could think of was how to crush the enemy, how many rolls of toilet paper to land in France, how quickly they could all get home and forget the whole ugly mess.

A. J. Hansen had kept an almost singular watch on the Russians for years. He watched the Russians snatch up eastern Europe without protest, and watched Russia spread its tentacles into American and British spheres in Greece and Italy and into the French Underground. Hansen knew his Russians from firsthand dealings. But his arguments hit a dead end.

And now, there stood before him a young man unable to reconcile himself to eating similar crow.

"It takes a rare kind of man to serve his country without the benefit of pyrotechnics or reward and a different kind of courage to keep your mouth shut and go on working and believing when you are positive those around you are wrong. We don't have enough men of this kind of dedication, Sean . . ."

"That's only part of it, sir. I've tried to stick because I know what you're up against."

"Then what is it, man?"

"Maybe I long to have a piece of this war like my brother has. I have

wished many times I could be as devout as you. But, this work here has
never given me that sort of fulfillment."

"And maybe you're looking for an easy way to end it with that woman.
Sure . . . get yourself transferred. Let the Army settle the affair for you."

"That might be part of it too."

Hansen stood and turned his back to Sean, stared through the window from his third-floor office down into the vast courtyard of Queen
Mother's Gate. "The General requests," he said, "that the Captain remain in this command."

Hansen nearly choked on his humiliation. He could go no further
now. He could not put into words the needing of Sean's keen mind, the
respect for foolhardy pride, or put into words admiration for the kind
of loyalty Sean had given him. Nor could he get into that part of it
about having three daughters and no sons. From the first bombastic
clash almost two years ago there had been that strange sort of devotion
that men find for each other in times of war.

"I'll give you your piece of this war," Hansen said. "It will mean staying here at Queen Mother's Gate, losing more arguments to stupid bastards, eating crow. It will mean that seeing or not seeing that woman
remains within your resolve."

Sean did not answer.

"This mission will set up a Pilot G-5 Team to study a German city.
This city will be learned so that every street, every citizen, every function is known. We will build a scale model in one of the conference
rooms . . . fly aerial recon flights over it, know more about it than we
have ever known about any piece of territory in Germany. This pilot
team will have to have an answer for any possible question . . . sewage
. . . Nazis . . . displaced persons . . . whorehouses. This is the textbook town from which we will gain insight to learn how to govern
Germany. When the invasion comes the pilot team will move into Germany and continue on from theory to actual practice. We will test new
laws, ideas there first . . ."

The pilot team for Germany! This was more than the piece of the
war he had reckoned on. Sean knew that on an impulse General Hansen
had taken another gamble with him. Such a command should go to
someone with solid experience in government . . . someone not so stubborn.

"I could let you down very badly, sir."

"I don't see it that way. Do you know anything about Rombaden?"

Sean's face narrowed in thought. "In Schwaben Province. Landkreis of Romstein. Sits on a big bend on the Landau midway between the Black Forest and Munich. One of the most fanatical Nazi strongholds."

"That's a good start," Hansen said. "There's a report up at Document Center by a professor in Germanic studies. He was born and raised in Rombaden, was an inmate of Schwabenwald Concentration Camp in '35 and '36. Came to America after his release. Start reading it."

Sean was too caught up in the sudden challenge to weigh the enormity of the task.

"You'll want Dante Arosa for your counter-intelligence, no doubt. The two of you go to Shrivenham and pick your team. Rombaden has an A1 rating. Take anyone you want. Any questions?"

"Why Rombaden? Why not Regensburg or Essen or Hanover?"

Hansen adjusted his specs and began to read the papers on his desk. "I have a peculiar affinity for the place. My mother came from there."

Sean got up to leave. "Funny damned war," he said.

"O'Sullivan."

"Yes, sir."

"One more thing." Hansen opened the top drawer, palmed a pair of gold oak leaves, and threw them on the desk. "I wore these very same ones, years ago. Maybe they'll bring you better luck. Stick them on your shoulder . . . we don't want any of your Englishmen to outrank you, Major."

CHAPTER NINE

CONFIDENTIAL   PRELIMINARY STUDY FOR MILITARY GOVERNMENT
CITY OF ROMBADEN/LANDKREIS OF ROMSTEIN, GERMANY

LOCATION:
Southern Germany. State of Württemberg. Province of Schwaben. Landkreis (County or District) of Romstein. The City of Rombaden is built along the north bank of the Landau River 100 miles west of Munich; 60 miles east of the Black Forest; 30 miles due north of the Swiss/German border at Lake Constance. The Landkreis (County) of

Romstein contains the City of Rombaden and continues on the south bank of the Landau into rolling foothills and farmlands. Both the city and district are surrounded by typical German forests covering 30% (about national average) of the land. Most famous is the Schwabenwald Forest.

GENERAL BACKGROUND:

First settled by Celtic Tribes two thousand years B.C. One must approach the history of this area in a context of/and as a segment of German history. For 3500 years there was no Germany, per se. There were Germanic Tribes, States, Princedoms, Kingdoms, Duchies, Landkreise all ruled by a local rank of royalty or nobility. At one time in German history there were 350 separate self-governing royal entities.

Germany, therefore, has been a collection of royal alliances heavily influenced and dominated by church alliances. Germanic tribes have sat between the Slavic world on the east and the Roman world on the west and south.

From time to time certain Germanic areas dominated the others. Prussia and Austria stand out, and personalities such as Charlemagne and Frederick the Great emerged. Nevertheless Germany did not become a united nation until Bismarck published his Elms Dispatch in 1870, a mere 70 years ago. Germany was the last land in Europe to become a nation, the last to colonize, one of the last to industrialize and the last to overcome the ravaging ruination of the Thirty Years War (1614-48).

German history has been a long bloody series of wars interlaced with power plays of royal and religious alliances inside her borders and of pressure outside her borders.

The Rombaden/Romstein District, for example, has been invaded by the Teutons, Romans, Goths, Huns, Vandals, Bavarians, Franks, Burgundians, Saxons, Bohemians, Prussians . . . among others. The Rombaden/Romstein District has sent armies into the field against the Danes, Swedes, Mongols, Magyars, Wends, Turks, French, and Italians . . . among others.

A common error is to lump all Germans together as similar persons. Germans are as different in background and behavior as is a Bostonian from a Texan—an Iowan from a New Yorker.

The Province of Schwaben, wherein Rombaden/Romstein lies, has a fiercely proud tribal-like closeness. From Schwaben emerged the branches of the Hohenzollern and Hohenstauffen families that have dominated the German royal line. The Schwaben League and Schwaben Princes have been mutinous, engineered many revolts, and have been in the balance of power plays throughout their history.

Rombaden/Romstein has always identified itself with the Catholic side of the religious struggle. The area had nearly always been in the Holy Roman Empire until it was dissolved after the Napoleonic Wars. It might be noted here that the Holy Roman Empire was neither Holy, Roman or an Empire, but a constantly shifting alliance of Germanic Kingdoms, Princedoms and Duchies with the Papal powers.

Rombaden/Romstein has been ruled or dominated by the Von Romstein Family. They are minor Schwaben nobility of the Hohenstauffen Line. The head of the family has usually held the rank of Markgraf or Graf (Count).

Rombaden City has been totally or partially destroyed at least a dozen times. War has ruined it ten of those times. Rombaden was destroyed twice during the Thirty Years War. It was so badly mutilated that the city never fully recovered from it for hundreds of years (nor did all of Germany for that matter). Rombaden was destroyed twice again during the Peasants' Uprisings, which were particularly bloody in Schwaben.

Rombaden was destroyed during the Napoleonic Wars.

Rombaden was destroyed twice during the series of wars between Prussia and Austria.

Rombaden was destroyed twice by fire.

Rombaden has been partly or almost completely depopulated by plagues a half-dozen times during the Middle Ages.

We must bear in mind that the story of Rombaden is not alien to the story of most German cities and that very few American cities like Atlanta, have ever been ravaged by war.

In addition Rombaden/Romstein has been traded, sold or bartered to consolidate royal marriages, peace treaties, etc., a dozen times.

A detailed history shows that this district has been in over 600 different alliances.

A never ending series of disasters has marked German history. Rombaden has rebuilt itself after each catastrophe with typical Germany energy.

GENERAL DATA:
ROMBADEN (Roman Baths) Population 90,000. With Romstein District, 150,000. 85% Roman Catholic. The city was named for the Roman bath antiquities found in the thermal springs in the environs. It is distinctly Schwaben in its tradition, singsong dialect, dress, etc. A great provincial pride exists. However, there are unmistakable influences of nearby Bavaria, particularly in Rombaden's architecture.

Rombaden stretches along the northern bank of the Landau. Two bridges cross into the Romstein District on the south bank. Between these two bridges is an enormous Rathaus Platz (City Hall Square) which is about a half mile in length.

The square is surrounded by dominating buildings. On the east side is Marienkirche (Mary's Church), of cathedral proportions. The single onion-dome tower is only slightly shorter than Munich's Marienkirche. The baroque interior is considered the most magnificent example of the period in all of Germany. The church was rebuilt in 1670. On the west end of the square opposite the cathedral is the Rathaus (City Hall), a square Renaissance-type structure from the seventeenth century. Under the Rathaus is the Ratskeller (City Hall Cellar or Restaurant), which is a customary meeting place in German towns. This particular Ratskeller was the scene of early-day Nazi rallies.

The half-mile long northern boundary of the square is lined with a series of buildings: the Rombaden Medical College and Research Institute and Hospital; the Roman Kunsthalle (museum); the famous puppet theater and the Opera House. The museum, incidentally, holds innumerable treasures of German masterpieces ranging from Dürer to the modernist Paul Klee.

There are three statues on the square. The statue of the Virgin Mary stands before the cathedral. Before the Opera House is the second statue—Hinterseer, the poet, and Rombaden's most famous son. It was he who wrote the *Legend of Rombaden*. The third statue stands before the City Hall, depicting two characters from the *Legend of Rombaden*, the mythical god Berwin and the goddess Helga.

This mammoth square, capable of holding most of Rombaden's population, was the scene of much Nazi pageantry.

The central business district fans out behind the northern edge of the square.

The industrial section is along the river bank. There is the big Romstein Machine Works owned by the ruling family. It is actually a complex of a half-dozen factories and is the economic backbone of the area. Since the Hitler era it has been engaged in arms manufacture and aircraft motors. Much of the factory has been moved underground since the war. It is believed to be manufacturing V-2 rocket parts. It is believed, further, that almost all of the labor consists of slaves imported from occupied lands.

There are other factories, mostly of a light-industry nature, on the river front: A brewery, a small barge-construction yard and a leather works. There are a number of the generation to generation shops in crystal cutting, the manufacture of the famous Rombaden puppets, a toy factory, etc.

Rombaden is known for its gay life. A large source of the town's income comes from the fact that it has been an overnight stopping place for Landau river-barge pilots. To facilitate their entertainment there is a three-block-long street of beer halls, bars, small hotels and brothels known as Princess Allee, which has a reputation of being a "little Hamburg Reeperbahn."

The pre-lenten ball of the Medical College Students is a riotous affair drawing artists from all over Schwaben and Bavaria for a week of unabashed revelry.

No less bombastic is the November Beer Fest in which the City Hall Square is covered by several enormous tents. A half-million liters of beer are consumed along with staggering amounts of wine, schnaps, and Schweinwürstchen.

To counterbalance these various orgies there is a splendid opera and symphony season, puppet theater, innumerable scientific seminars at the Institute and other cultural affairs.

Rombaden has its own unique pageant based on the *Legend of Rombaden,* which is a thousand years old. In medieval costume there is a re-enactment of the story of the legend. The climax is the reading, by a dozen actors, of Hinterseer's epic poem. This takes place before his statue, for upwards of a hundred thousand listeners.

ROMSTEIN DISTRICT (Roman Stone)
Upon crossing the two bridges you enter the District. It is dominated by the Von Romstein family, the Von Romstein estates and the Von Romstein castle. The area has been under such domination for eight centuries.

The family's personal estate covers nearly 100 square miles and includes its own private forest for hunting.

There are three main farming villages named after leading Von Romsteins; Ludwigsdorf, Sigmundsdorf and Ottosdorf.

The castle is an exquisite structure of seventy rooms and holds an untold wealth in art treasures. It sits back six miles from the river on the first of the rolling hills in the proximity of Ludwigsdorf.

Ludwigsdorf is also the entrance village to the Schwabenwald Forest, which has gained notoriety as the site of the Schwabenwald Concentration Camp. It was one of the first political prisons opened by the Nazis in 1934. The entire forest area is controlled by fanatical Waffen SS. (At the time the writer of this report was an inmate, 1936–37, there were some 6000 political prisoners, several priests and pastors included. The most famous inmate at the time was the old Social Democrat, Ulrich Falkenstein. It is not known if he is still alive.)

Also on the south bank of the river, somewhat removed from Rombaden, are some forty or fifty medium to large estates belonging to the wealthy and upper crust of the area. In this area are also a dozen hotels built around the natural hot springs. The Germans are ritualistic in their belief of the great curative powers of the spas. The center of this upperclass activity on the south bank is the Kurhaus, a gambling casino and rather muted version of the bawdy Princess Allee across the river.

Rombaden/Romstein has many "typical" German characteristics.

There is idol worship, tribalism, revelry and mysticism.

There is the pagan ritual of the Nazis.

As a contradiction there is strong Catholicism, a cultural and educational life and a modern industrial complex.

This tug of war, this paradox, runs deeply in the German character. It is particularly easy to see in Rombaden/Romstein. Rombaden, indeed, is representative of the eternal German, who is looking for himself and is an enigma to himself as well as to the outside world.

CURRENT POLITICAL DATA:

The Von Romstein family dynasty has been the absolute power for eight centuries. The current family head, Graf Ludwig Von Romstein, ascended to the hierarchy after a distinguished flying career in World War I. He is an intimate of Hermann Goering. The middle brother, Baron Sigmund Von Romstein, has been Oberburgermeister (Mayor) of Rombaden for nearly two decades. Count Ludwig himself is the Chancellor of the District so between the two of them they control the political apparatus. A younger brother, Kurt Von Romstein, is the Nazi Gauleiter (District Leader) but it is not certain that the older two are actual Nazis.

Graf Ludwig Von Romstein, like many Germans, was bitter and disillusioned by the Versailles Treaty. His "class" had little faith in the strength of the Weimar Republic. His district, like most of Germany, was not self-sustaining in food and had to manufacture to live. The depression, inflation, lack of food and restrictions of the Versailles Treaty wreaked havoc in the district and gave rise to a strong Communist Party.

Graf Ludwig Von Romstein gambled with the Nazis. The younger brother, Kurt, was made an active Nazi. We are certain that it was at the Count's insistence as "family" duty.

With Hitler's ascent and the rearmament, the Romstein Machine Works was one of the first to profit by huge contracts. New economic prosperity, laid directly to the Count nuzzling the Nazis, and with the Count's own brother as Nazi Gauleiter, the Rombaden/Romstein area turned into a fanatical Nazi stronghold equal in fervor to Munich, Nuremberg and the Eastern German States.

Since World War II the Machine Works as well as the smaller factories have been converted to making war material. The area has been heavily bombed in recent months.

Sean's doubts deepened as he dug more deeply into the tormented history of civil and religious wars, of blood orgies, of paganism and tribalism. Of the pride of barons and princes. Of a story of double dealings, alliances, back stabbings too complex to follow. Of the homosexuality and perversion of the Nazis. Of a deep set brutality never known by man before. Of Hinterseer, the mystic poet. Of the mystic philosophers. Of singers and musicians and writers and men of science. Intellectuals and barbarians. Brutes and scholars. Love and murder.

Sean O'Sullivan wondered, as General Hansen wondered, if any manner of man could bring sanity to a land that had never known it. What power, earthly or otherwise, could make the wonderment of an idea find its way through this lacework of muck and beauty?

CHAPTER TEN

For the next month Sean and Dante Arosa plunged into the records and backgrounds of nearly four thousand officers at the Military Government Training Center at the Hore-Belisha Barracks at Shrivenham. They weeded, weighed and then were ready to select the Pilot Team.

Dante Arosa returned to Queen Mother's Gate to assemble all the intelligence data on Rombaden while Sean stayed at Shrivenham to conduct the interviews for candidates.

Lieutenant Shenandoah Blessing entered Sean's office. He was an immense man who walked with the peculiar gracefulness that some fat people develop from constantly fighting for their balance. In the first handshake, Sean detected both the deceptive quickness and the power of the man.

"You were sheriff of Hook County, Tennessee, for nine years?"

A voice filled with folksy sweetness emerged from Blessing's moon face. He answered in the affirmative.

"And you went through a dozen special courses at F.B.I. training schools . . ."

Blessing modestly admitted to his credentials. There were a few more formal questions, but Sean had known all along that Blessing would be his man. Hook County was similar in size and population to Rombaden/ Romstein. Hook County was rough territory with difficult police problems. Despite Blessing's guise at modesty he had a known reputation for progressive law enforcement and his record was filled with innumerable examples of personal courage and ingenuity.

"The police problem in Rombaden is going to be particularly difficult because we haven't enough whitelisted Germans to direct traffic. It's Nazi top to bottom."

"How many boys am I going to be able to take in with me?"

"I think I can get you twenty."

Twenty men to handle a hundred thousand enemy civilians plus unknown numbers of soldiers, fanatics, displaced persons. They would have to be hand-picked, trained like spartans, and damned near fearless as well as cagey as hell.

"Can I pick my own people?"

"Yes."

"Well then, I reckon we'll muddle through, Major."

The oldest man Sean had tabbed was also chosen without a shade of doubt. Captain H. W. Trueblood was sixty-two years of age. His unique qualifications and determination to participate in the war had brought him to Shrivenham. Trueblood had been a curator for the National Gallery in London, specializing in the middle German periods. He spoke a fluent German and was totally immersed in German history.

Trueblood was pale as only an Englishman who never sees the sun can be pale. He spoke in hushed tones, never really addressing anyone in particular. The perfect scholar, Sean thought.

"Are you familiar with the Roman Kunsthalle in Rombaden?"

"Yes, of course." And Trueblood quickly refreshed his memory aloud. "Extraordinary representation of the second German period . . . Hans Pleydenwurff, Wolgemut. They must have several Van Soest's and I know of four Grünewalds. Then, of course, their own Schwaben masters, Konrad Witz and Lucas Moser . . ."

"Of course," Sean said, fascinated by the "foreign" language he spoke.

Trueblood suddenly reminded himself there was a layman before him and tried to correct himself. "I speak of course of the fifteenth-century Cologne and Flemish schools."

"Sure."

"There is an excellent portion given to Renaissance Germans. The Von Romstein family has supported the museum heavily, you know."

"Just how difficult is it going to be to get an accurate catalogue which will also include the cathedral and the Romstein Castle?"

"Well, one hardly knows where the paintings have been transported since the bombings, does one?" And as an afterthought mumbled, "Be a terrible pity if they lost their Moser altar . . ."

Another Englishman, Dr. Geoffrey Grimwood, had retired from the army as an Officer of the British Empire. He had served in India as a hospital director in a place where famine and epidemic were academic. After army retirement he took a high post in the public health service. Like Trueblood, he did not want the war to pass him by.

Through his sandy walrus moustache Grimwood imparted to Sean that he spoke passable German and had attended seminars on public health at the Rombaden Medical College before the war.

There was another British officer, W. W. Tidings, from the German department of Barclay's Bank, who was a wizard in that mystic realm of international currency.

There was a Canadian, Bertrand Collier, who had been a foreign correspondent in Germany, and later, news analyst for Canadian Broadcasting.

There were Americans: Dale Hickman, who was well known as an agricultural economist; Sam Alterman, a communications engineer with International Tel. and Tel.

There was Bill Bolinski, a thirty-two-year-old lawyer whose father was Polish and mother was German, and he spoke both languages well. In addition to legal officer he was made displaced persons officer.

There was Hank Greenberg, a civil engineer who was born in Germany and began his schooling at Humboldt University in Berlin and completed it at Carnegie Tech in Pittsburgh. City planning was his bailiwick. Commissioned into the Army in 1940, he had planned and constructed a half-dozen new army bases when A. J. Hansen snatched him away for Military Government.

But for the fact that he was Jewish, Greenberg had a complete Germanic appearance: thick dark brows, large brown eyes, tall limber build. He showed no reaction to Sean's hammering questions.

"You were born in Mannheim?"

"Yes. During World War I, where my father was a good German soldier. In fact he holds an Iron Cross," Greenberg answered with only the slightest trace of accent.

"Jewish, both sides?"

"Completely by birth, moderately by religion. As you can see on your record there, the Hank is really Heinrich."

"Just what kind of personal persecution did you encounter from the Nazis?"

Greenberg smiled slightly. "My father was smart enough to get out of Germany before Hitler took power. However, it was never far enough back for a Jew in Germany. Anti-Semitism is not a later-day phenomenon. It has been going on for a thousand years, Major."

"Then it must give you a vicarious thrill knowing Germany is being dismembered by the bombing raids."

"The same vicarious thrill it gives you, Major. We are both Americans."

"Do you have any pleasant recollections of Germany?"

"Of course. I spent my childhood there, became a young man there."

"What language do your parents speak at home?"

"German."

"What kind of punishment do you feel the Nazis should receive?"

"That is in your province. I am an engineer. I deal in mathematics."

Sean liked Greenberg, liked his thick skin and deliberate attitude. Yet, there was something about Greenberg he could not put his finger on. Something about him that said there was still a lot of German in the man. Was this so strange? After all, nearly one fifth of the American population is of German ancestry and emigration. And what of his own father? Still Irish to the core of his soul. Despite Greenberg's façade Sean believed there was a love-hate duel within him.

There was one key man missing from the pilot team. Someone with practical experience in government. From the records, Captain Maurice Duquesne of the Free French Forces had all the obvious qualifications. He was an elected official of an area similar in size to Rombaden/Romstein; sous-préfet of an arrondissement of the Department of Belfort, Province of Lorraine. Duquesne had lived on the German border, opposite the Black Forest, and spoke impeccable German.

But he was arrogant and from the instant of meeting let Sean know the American was a Johnny-come-lately. France knew how to handle Germany. Americans knew nothing.

The decision on Duquesne was his most difficult. Obviously the Frenchman believed he should command his own team. Yet, despite trouble signs, Sean could not let him go.

Sean remembered the first time he saw General Hansen and sized him up as a foul-mouthed, sawed-off blowhard. He learned bit by bit that Hansen was neither crass nor stupid. Hansen had the thing he lacked—experience. There was much to be learned from the man.

Duquesne had practical government experience. Through day to day intercourse he knew more about the Germans than Sean's scholastic theorizing from a distance of thousands of miles.

He gambled with Maurice Duquesne.

There were others on the pilot team—Americans and British and French. With Blessing's enlisted man's police force and the clerks and medics, he brought fifty officers and men back to Queen Mother's Gate.

General Hansen reasoned that Sean had a good team on paper, but, next to Dante Arosa, Sean was the youngest officer. Could he gain the respect of the older and wiser men? Would he be able to breathe life and fire into the plaster models of Rombaden? Could he change complacency into the spirit of a mission?

Hansen's doubts soon faded. Sean attacked Rombaden/Romstein with a zeal that turned the pilot-team studies into something of a crusade.

Even the arrogant Maurice Duquesne showed traces of respect for the energy of the man and called a truce. For now, Major O'Sullivan was a dynamo, but these maps and questions and problems in theory were far removed from the field of battle. Duquesne knew that most battle plans go awry when the first shot is fired, and he reserved his final judgment for that day. . . .

The pilot team was knitted into an exclusive, proud unit. Sean O'Sullivan had mastered a page from Andrew Jackson Hansen's textbook. He was able to muster uncommon loyalty from his men by letting a man know he was needed. At the same time he let him know he could do without him also.

CHAPTER ELEVEN

Sean entered Hansen's office. Nellie Bradbury and Henry Pringle sat chalky-faced on the big leather couch. Hansen's expressive face was wrinkled in pain.

Sean's palms became wet and his throat caked dry. Oh God! I'm dreaming! Sean tried again and again to force the question from himself. He broke into cold sweat.

"Your brother Tim is dead," General Hansen said at last.

Sean nodded his head to say that he knew, and he walked to the window and stared blankly down on the courtyard with his back to the others. Ten unbearable moments of silence passed with the only sound a deep quivering sigh from Sean now and again.

"He went after a V-1 base," Bradbury said. "This time he led some others in. They saw him get it."

Hansen took Sean's arm and lead him to a chair. "Here son, have yourself a drink."

Sean pushed his arm away. They watched him stiffen to fight off a convulsion. A numbness fell over him.

"Let yourself go," Big Nellie said.

And then, only the terrible silence again and Sean's dazed expression.

"He was one of the best, Tim O'Sullivan was," Henry Pringle said in an almost cheerful voice. "A flyer's flyer. Went out big. He won't ever be forgotten."

"Shut up, you stinking ghoul," General Hansen hissed. "It makes me sick the way you goddamned flyers worship death."

"Lay off him, General," Big Nellie said. "Pringle and I have cried for these boys till there's no tears left and no other way to send them off."

"You think we celebrate because we're happy? We're scared and sick and we all die of fright every night when the door opens and half a squadron walks in . . ."

They quieted as Sean stood and walked from the room.

The needle of his father's record player scratched out through the sound horn a distorted reproduction of John McCormack's voice:

"Kathleen Mavourneen! awake from thy slumber,
The blue mountains glow in the sun's golden light . . ."

"You listen to me, Tim. I had to take two fights to pay for your tuition. You're not running away to the Lincoln Brigade. I busted this hand getting you into college and I'll bust the other one on you keeping you there."

". . . Ah! where is the spell that once hung on my numbers?
Arise in thy beauty, thou star of my night."

A sudden shift of the wind whipped the spray into the cave and onto the three brothers. Liam shielded the book from the water. Sean and Tim watched the waves fall back, slither down the rocks and race seaward again. Liam read from the book again, in his thin voice.

> "He fell as fall the mighty ones,
> Nobly undaunted to the last,
> And death has now united him,
> With Erin's heroes of the past."

Parnell! As Liam read, Tim's eyes searched wildly for those places beyond the horizon where adventures waited, not only in daydreams. "Read from O'Casey, Liam!"

"You and your Irish patriots make me sick," Sean said.

> "Mavourneen, Mavourneen, my sad tears are falling,
> To think that from Erin and thee I must part;"

"How in the hell can you remain so impersonal to a war that's taken our brother! . . . We were coming over German land . . . I almost always saw Liam's face outside the window . . . and then . . . I would visualize Liam's grave . . . I wanted to fly so low I could chop them up with my propellors."

"Stop carrying the flag, Tim."

"Oh God! Why does the wrong brother have to die! . . . Liam could have brought us honor."

> "It may be for years, and it may be forever;
> Then why art thou silent, thou voice of my heart?"

"Your father is a very sick man, Sean. It will take months of rest and care for him to recover this attack and he will never be the same as before."

"Poppa, you're not to worry about anything. I'll take care of the family."

Private Liam O'Sullivan, a poet. A gentle boy. Dead. Age twenty-two. Kasserine Pass, North Africa. Died as quietly as he lived.

First Lieutenant Timothy O'Sullivan. Rebel. Age twenty-five. He died somewhere over Germany in a flaming pyre . . . as violently as he lived.

> "It may be for years, and it may be forever;
> Then why art thou silent, Kathleen Mavourneen?"

"Sean. It's me, Dante. You can't keep sitting like this in the darkness. Sean, for God's sake break down and cry. Curse, hit the wall, get drunk. Sean, please answer me. Sean, you can't keep sitting in the darkness . . . Sean . . . Sean . . ."

He blinked his eyes open and licked his dry lips. Father O'Brien slowly came into focus. "You've been locked in here for five days. Tim has made his way to heaven. The living must be served."

He came to a sitting position slowly, sipped some water, and lit a cigarette. He was weak and haggard and dizzy. "Father," he croaked hoarsely, "I don't want to listen to any Jesuit double-talk."

"The spiritual aspects can be explored later. I'm thinking of something more practical, like eating a decent meal. If you don't come out of here you're going to be taken to the hospital and fed intravenously."

Sean flopped back on the bed again and returned to his reverie.

"It would be a lot better for you if you sent your brother off in good Irish style. Let's go out and get drunk and split open a couple of heads."

"Father O'Brien, go to hell." Sean trembled awesomely. For the first time, a tear fell down his cheek. "Oh Timmy! Timmy! This will kill Momma and Poppa."

The priest sat beside him quickly. "You've lost your belief in God, haven't you? We've all waged that struggle, Sean. Even Jesus."

"I believe in God all right, but he is not a loving God. He's a monster. He allowed His only son to get lynched and now He keeps killing those who love Him the most. God has destroyed my family."

"This murder that was committed in God's name is not His doing. It is the folly of men who wrongly claim to do murder in His name."

"Why didn't I die instead of Liam and Tim!"

"Sean! So long as you lie flat on your back, you debase the memory of your brothers. Stand up, Sean!"

General Hansen was distressed at the weary appearance of Sean. After days of harrowing grief he looked like a combat soldier who had just waged a terrible battle.

"I'm ready to return to my command. I'm . . . sorry I put such a burden on everyone."

"There is a matter that has to be thrashed out. Are you up to it?"

"Yes, sir."

"You are the sole survivor of three brothers. Your family has given more than its share."

"I don't want to go back to the States."

"The matter is out of your hands. It is up to your parents. You realize that they have this right."

"Yes, sir."

"I contacted an old buddy of mine who is stationed at the Presidio in San Francisco. I asked him to call on your parents and explain the position."

"How are they . . ."

"As well as can be expected."

"What . . . did they decide?"

"I don't know. Your father wrote a letter. It was flown here and handed to me by personal courier." The general held the envelope. Sean read his name spelled in a tired and shaky hand. "Will you abide by your father's decision in peace?"

"Yes, sir . . . would . . . would the General please read it to me?"

"Very well." Hansen adjusted his specs, bent close to the uneven writing, and cleared his throat.

My Beloved Son:

My heart cries out for you in this time of your great need! I am so sorry I am not close by to comfort you. It is needless to say that a terrible darkness has fallen upon this house. I have always been honest with you, Sean. I will not lie now. The truth is that I do not know if either your mother or I can live long after this.

It is for you I sorrow now for you must go on living. You are the last of our seed. You are the one who will either carry our name on beyond us or forever put it to rest.

Your mother and I have no tears left. Our pain can be no deeper. I cannot in all honesty say that the death of three sons can be more terrible than the death of two. If you must join them, then you must.

I would give my life to embrace you once more, my son. I have sat for many hours to put upon paper the words that will force you to come back to us safely. Yet, I cannot do this thing. I have tried to teach you all your life that you must follow your own conscience. I cannot deny you that pursuit now. You cannot live for Tim and Liam. You must live for Sean.

You have served our name longer and more faithfully than a boy ought to. You have denied yourself for us so long . . . you have worked for us, so hard.

You are free.

I beg you, Sean, do not be consumed with hatred for it will destroy you as it did Tim. And remember, we have done all we have set out to do. I am but an immigrant laborer and I have lived to see my three sons graduate from college.

Hansen gave the letter to Sean. "What a fine man," the general said.

"Sean, I want to use you in here with me as my adjutant. I want you to give up your command."

"Give up my command?"

"You're asking too much of yourself. After what has happened I don't think you or anyone else could be placed in a position of direct contact with Germans. Your judgment would be too clouded now."

A familiar rumble outside had been building up in intensity ever since Sean entered the office. Suddenly it became overwhelming. The roar made further conversation impossible; the windows rattled and the building trembled at its moorings. Sean and General Hansen went to the window—for once the London sky was clear. Wave after wave of Liberator bombers lumbered like flying whales toward the coast. The invasion of Europe could not be far off now.

"General Hansen," Sean said. "I want my command."

CHAPTER TWELVE

Nan Milford flung the door open. Andrew Jackson Hansen stood before her. Her expression changed from anticipation to obvious disappointment.

"I am General Hansen," he said. "May I come in?"

"Of course."

All the trappings of a reunion were in evidence: a magnificent woman in an attractive hostess gown; a candlelit table in the alcove; music from the gramophone, and dim lights. He trailed her into the living room. She was, indeed, beautiful, but ice and anger too.

"Major O'Sullivan had to leave for Shrivenham unexpectedly."

"At your personal arrangement?"

"May I sit down?"

"By all means."

"Mrs. Milford. We have some unpleasant things to say to each other. I'd like a drink." Nan coldly poured him one. He did not like the situation. He would rather have taken on anyone than an angry woman.

"As long as we are going to be candid," Nan said, "I should like to know just how far your command extends into the personal lives of your men."

"Mrs. Milford . . ."

"And I should like to know why you have deliberately kept me from him at a time like this. Even my phone calls were stopped."

"Because, this is the time you should have been kept from him."

"I do not understand your ideas of compassion, General."

"That boy is so badly hurt he even denies his God."

"He's needed me, General."

"Yes, he has. Needing you is bad enough when he is sound. What if he crawls to you now and throws himself into your merciful arms?"

"Isn't love to be given when it is most needed?"

"Yes, Mrs. Milford, but you cannot give it . . . you can merely lend it."

Nan paled.

"You are offering a crutch to a wounded man. I would like to see him healed. Either prepare to go through with this all the way, divorce, re-marriage, the works . . . or let him live his own life, without you."

Nan arched her back and fought back the tears forming in her eyes. "He thinks the world of you, General Hansen. It borders on worship."

"He is worshiped, too. This boy took over the command of older, wiser men who had already cut their niches as talented specialists and he has molded them together. Since this tragedy his team has all but disintegrated. Now, all of us who love Sean O'Sullivan must give that love in the way it will help him the most. His men will give it to him through dedication. His father gave it to him through the gift of man-hood, by allowing him to pursue the dictates of his conscience. I have let him know I believe in him. I have returned him to his command . . ."

"And I . . ."

"You know what you have to do, Mrs. Milford."

"Has it been ghastly for him?"

"I have seldom seen a human being suffer so deeply."

"My poor Sean . . . my poor darling."

Nan pressed her folded hands tightly, drew a deep breath, and shook her head quickly. It was over just like that! In the end, which she had always known would come, Nan reverted to her breeding. The dreaded loneliness, the fear of time stretching endlessly before her suddenly van-ished in a well of compassion for Sean. General Hansen knew why Sean loved her so . . . why he needed her and why she could not have him now.

"I shall be leaving in the morning for Plimlington East to see my chil-

dren. I have been thinking that a holiday for just the three of us would
be a wonderful tonic. We could disappear somewhere up in Scotland.
I know of places where they don't even have a telephone."

Hansen set his glass down, walked to her, and took her hand.

"Will he forget me?"

"No, but he'll get over you."

She nodded. "That's it then, isn't it? . . ."

"You do love him very much."

"General," her voice cracked, "please go . . ."

CHAPTER THIRTEEN—*April 20, 1945*

It was evening. Major Sean O'Sullivan sped down a German country
road, second in line in the convoy of jeeps, command cars, and trucks
making up Pilot Team G-5. Sean always took the second jeep, Maurice
Duquesne the first. The Frenchman drove like a maniac; no one dared
drive with him on his tail.

The cobblestone road was rain-slick and jarring. They passed through
never ending forests, birch trees adding dark and eerie patterns to the
miserable rain-soaked road. Sean hunched closer to the windshield.

Dr. Geoffrey Grimwood grimaced alongside Sean. From time to time
low mumbles emerged through his moustache protesting the monstrous
construction of the jeep.

In the back seat, Sean's orderly, Private O'Toole, attempted to dis-
member three sticks of chewing gum. The massive Shenandoah Blessing
slept, crushing O'Toole against the side of the jeep. His moon face
rolled loosely on his neck and fell on O'Toole's shoulder. The son of a
bitch sleeps anywhere, O'Toole thought . . . through the Siegfried
Line, across the Rhine, anywhere. Look at the ugly son of a bitch sleep
with the rain leaking in and falling down his ugly neck. O'Toole shoul-
dered Blessing's head off him and tried to displace the limp body. It
all rolled back on him.

A roadblock loomed ahead. The convoy drew to a halt before a submachine-gun-toting corporal. Sean got out, drew his poncho about him,
and approached the guard.

"Password."

"Wishing well," Sean said, using the pair of "w's" designed to twist the most willing German tongue.

One of these days I'm going to say "vishing vell" and scare the hell out of one of these guards, O'Toole thought.

"Glenn Miller," said the guard.

" 'Moonlight Serenade,' " Sean answered.

"Hit me again."

" 'Tuxedo Junction,' 'Little Brown Jug,' 'Pennsylvania Six Five Thousand.' " Sean imparted distinctive Americanisms.

"Pershing Square."

"Queers."

Silly damned game, Grimwood thought. The Americans go to ridiculous extremes to identify each other.

The guard was convinced the convoy was not German infiltrators. He advised Sean they were at the end of the line and a regimental headquarters was in a farmhouse in a clearing a few hundred yards removed.

"All right. Pull the convoy over. Put on a guard. Set up a bivouac."

Sean, followed by his watchdog, O'Toole, slushed his way to the clearing and the farmhouse. Colonel Dundee welcomed them grumpily. "Dandy" Dundee, a self-made soldier, attempted to live up to his legend. His ulcer was killing him. He scratched his stubble jaw. "You guys from Military Government are always up my back."

"Matter of fact, Colonel, we've been waiting to get to Rombaden for almost a year."

"Ever drink this crap? Steinhager."

Sean accepted the bottle, took a belt, passed it to O'Toole.

Dundee brought him up to date. He had sent a patrol into Rombaden and it had gotten clobbered. He drew back, dug in, and brought up two battalions of Long Toms and a battalion of tanks. They were now getting into position in the forest. Heavy mortars were pushed up forward so they could at least reach the suburbs. Dundee meant to hit Rombaden throughout the night with everything that would reach the city. In the morning a hundred air sorties were promised. Dundee belched the belch of a man whose stomach was in constant rebellion. Then he looked at Sean devilishly, as though he were about to impart a monumental secret. "Major," he said with solemnity, "I'm going to cross the Landau tonight, two miles downstream."

"Got a bridge?"

"Hell no! The goddam engineer battalion is lost. We're going over in rubber boats."

Dundee reckoned he could shuttle a battalion of men across the river under cover of darkness. Morning would find Rombaden cut off. Furthermore, he could move part of his men to the Schwabenwald Concentration Camp to engage the expected resistance from the Waffen SS.

Sean returned to the bivouac to check his team. They had been living off the countryside since they had passed through the Siegfried Line. Blessing's men had already rounded up enough local livestock and three-in-one ration for a decent meal. Shelter halves had been set. The older men on the team—Tidings, Trueblood, Collier, Duquesne—were given the back of the trucks to sleep in. Geoffrey Grimwood qualified by age, but his long military service made him proudly refuse; he slept on the ground.

Sean went to the edge of the forest. There were only waterlogged shadows ahead. The Landau River could not be seen on the horizon, gray on gray. Rombaden was out there somewhere. The colors of the earth had been turned sallow, muck and mud alive and moving with infantrymen.

The perimeter was an open field close to the suburbs of Rombaden, interlaced with crudely dug foxholes and trenches of riflemen, mortars, and machine guns.

By nightfall the rain had stopped. In their forest bivouac the wind blew down endless sheets of water from the leaves, keeping everyone in a state of soggy discomfort.

But by now weariness had overcome the men of Pilot Team G-5. They had reached that state of delicious numbness when all pain and misery ceased, when one could hardly remember living without mud. They had devoured a pig and a half-dozen German chickens, so life was not without its redemptions; and then they slept. They slept except for the commander, for when others sleep, the commander ponders.

The Long Tom cannons and the tanks flashed up lights every few seconds as their muzzles spewed gunflame. Up forward the heavy mortars hissed and the red tracers of machine-gun bullets darted toward Rombaden.

Sean leaned against a tree at the edge of the forest. O'Toole hovered a few yards away, hands on his carbine, alert for intruders.

Well Tim, Sean thought, I have seen the Germans. I did not see them through the window of a streaking airplane, scrambling like ants from a stream of hot water. I saw them herded by the acre, dull-eyed and beaten. I saw them limp along in endless lines with their hands over their heads. I saw them slurp water from our canteens with trembling hands, and dive for our cigarette butts. I saw them too weary and disgusted to care about the disgrace of capture.

A sudden burst of fire in Rombaden revealed the outline of some buildings. Sean watched it until the flames flickered and began to fade.

It was strange seeing Germans. I didn't hate them. No desire to punch them, trample them . . . to say, "Which one of you pulled the trigger that killed Liam?" They were abstract hulks. These creatures could not have been the jack-booted, goose-stepping, hysterical *Sieg Heilers*. They were nothing . . . nothing.

Liam . . . Liam, you never got to see them at all. Maybe it is better that way. Have it quick and be done. I've got to live with them . . . and think about you and Tim.

Greenberg. What was he thinking when we entered Mannheim and he stood before a house and said that this was where he was born?

Oh God, Nan. I've been so damned lonely for you. Why were my letters returned? Why was the phone never answered? You're a cold-blooded bitch but I still love you. I love you now. That terrible moment of humiliation. At the theater on the arm of a British colonel. Nan was back to her own kind. She looked correct on his arm . . . like he was G. Donald Milford. Just a nod of the head, that's all she had for me, and the one final sentence, "It won't work, Sean. I don't want a scene, now or ever. . . ."

Well, they'll be breaking open the oflag with G. Donald Milford in it pretty soon now.

All his thoughts began to run together . . . the landing in Southern France . . . the battle up the Rhone Valley . . . the breaking of the Siegfried Line . . . the crossing of the Rhine . . . the fields of prisoners. . . .

And now . . . Rombaden lay out there.

Captain Maurice Duquesne walked from the bivouac and stood alongside Sean, looking in rapt fascination at the bombardment. He had taken bottles of wine and cognac out of France with him, and he passed one of them to Sean, who sipped and passed it back.

"What does one think of at one-thirty in the morning?"

"What have we left undone?"

When the Frenchman spoke or walked or drank wine he did it always with a certain gesture of his hands, a flair in his voice, his eyes. He was arrogant. Yet, he had been loyal to the team and, Sean thought, perhaps its most valuable officer. "Aha, our little paper battles at Queen Mother's Gate."

"You never have believed in what we were doing there."

The Frenchman shrugged. "General de Gaulle ordered me into Military Government because of my experience."

"You didn't answer my question."

"You and I have become personal friends. I do not hold you responsible because Americans are naïve."

"American naïveté is flaunted around pretty freely."

"Take the Englishman, Sean. Take Grimwood. He knows how to rule. He knows how to conquer. And we French . . . we have our little experiences also. But the Americans know neither how to conquer nor occupy. You fight your wars in behalf of neatly phrased idealism . . . and then you go back to a place that has never tasted its own ashes."

"Is it so wrong to believe in ideals?"

"Impractical. Do you really think you can learn about Germans at Queen Mother's Gate? When you Americans leave, Germany will be here and France will be here. We have lived with the German and tasted his whip and he has tasted ours. We have mingled sweat in bed with the German women and they with French women. That is the way you must get to know people."

"But your way hasn't worked, Maurice. All this sweaty mingling and all your experience has produced nothing but centuries of blood and sorrow. Perhaps you shouldn't grow deaf to the ideas of a stranger."

"Sean! You honestly think you can change the basic nature of the German."

"I have to."

"I am a cynic by experience . . . you are a fool by the lack of it."

Sean wanted to say, "I believe in my country," but he didn't. The practical politician who had conquered and been conquered would not understand anything so maudlin.

O'Toole hurried up to them excitedly. "They've crossed the Landau!"

"Well then," Duquesne said, "let us get some sleep. Rombaden faces an enlightened conqueror tomorrow."

CHAPTER FOURTEEN

Dawn came with a crispness that gave a new life to the wet misery of the soldiers; and it brought the news that during the night a battalion of infantry had crossed the Landau in rubber boats and now held the south bank.

The day was clear, and at last they saw it . . . Rombaden! The ribbon of water sweeping into the big bend, the cluster of red-tiled roofs, the lush green, and the great tower of Marienkirche. Fighter planes flying at house-top level bolted new fury into the smoking ruins.

Sean ordered the camp to be struck and the convoy to be in ready to move on the heels of a breakthrough.

At 7:22 the firing suddenly stopped. Sean rushed to regimental headquarters, where Colonel Dundee was on the phone to his forward positions. Three German officers under truce flag had come out of Rombaden and were approaching the observation post in an attempt to save the city from annihilation by a street fight.

Sean did not wait for the formal surrender ceremony. His convoy came out of the forest toward Rombaden ahead of the lumbering tanks and the infantry.

Rombaden began to take form and shape, and then an ethereal silence slowed them down as they touched the suburbs. Little fires sprouted here and there . . . there was a distant drone of aircraft looking for targets farther south . . . past the first little cottages . . . worker's quarters on the north end . . . neat little vegetable gardens . . . boxes of flowers in the windows . . . roofs with holes in them . . . chunks of plaster gouged out by bullets . . . signs in Gothic . . . "Backerei" . . . "Hofmeyer's Bierstube" . . . "Apotheke" . . . broken window fronts . . . a house blown into the street by a direct hit.

Sean turned the convoy into the main boulevard, Friedrichstrasse, that led straight through Rombaden to the City Hall Square. It was a street of the dead. Tens of thousands of white flags of surrender welcomed the victors. The flags hung limply and the three-story buildings that lined the Friedrichstrasse were in wreckage. War had come cruelly to Friedrichstrasse. There were enormous piles of waste, charred and flaming skeletons of buildings whose walls stood by some unknown determination. All of the windows were gone and most of the roofs; the street-car line was snaked out of shape and useless; power poles snapped off; trees uprooted.

The convoy slowed to a whisper of speed.

At an intersection a dead horse lay in a pool of its own blood, swarmed over by hungry flies.

How strange, Sean thought: in every town and village a dead horse has lain open-eyed and puzzled by man's folly.

The eyes of the men of the pilot team searched up at the broken windows knowing that tens of thousands of unseen eyes were on them. Only a fluttering of a curtain, a darting shadow, a muffled sound told of human life behind the ruins.

A single little boy stood in a doorway shading his eyes from the sun. He wore a pair of leather pants with such filth as only leather pants can gather. He was curious. A door opened behind him and the hand of a terrified mother jerked him from sight of the enemy.

The intersection where Friedrichstrasse met the City Hall Square was closed by a pile of brick and twisted steel ten feet high.

Sean halted the convoy. By hand signals they moved after him as he sprinted up the mound of bricks. Skittering and stumbling they came behind him to the City Hall Square on the Landau. The square was pocked by artillery-shell holes, the buildings cut up badly by the strafing. Sean looked first to the Marienkirche. The cathedral had been hit, but the tower with its magnificent onion dome stood by one of those miracles saved for the preservation of churches. The statue of Mary before the cathedral had been obliterated.

The half-mile-long row of buildings, the Medical College, the theater, the hospital, were all shakily intact. The statue of Hinterseer was headless on its pedestal.

All that broke the awesome silence was the shuffling of their trotting feet as they split up, began flinging doors open, moving in well-learned sequence toward those places they had seen on paper for so many months. Sean found himself running full head for the City Hall at the opposite end of the square, with Dante Arosa and O'Toole puffing behind him. Before the great building the statue of the gods Berwin and

Helga, of the legend, remained intact. Damned irony! Hinterseer is headless, Mary is gone, but the pagan remains!

The door had been blown off its hinges, revealing the marble foyer filled with statues of the Von Romstein family and coat-of-arms shields of each district. Sean's team moved in behind him up the spiral stairs, shoving open the office doors. Everything was in perfect order, set for a day's work.

The corner office on the second floor bore the name of the mayor, Baron Sigmund Von Romstein. Sean entered. It was a magnificent office. On one side the windows looked down on the City Hall Square, the other afforded a view of the Landau and the country beyond. He could see puffs of smoke and tracer-bullet streaks across the river in the district. Dundee's battalion had engaged the enemy, perhaps the Waffen SS from the Schwabenwald Concentration Camp. The scene on the square changed by the moment. A tank plowed through . . . now two . . . three. Soldiers began swarming in. The engineers moved to the waterfront. Both bridges were useless. A pontoon bridge was started so that tanks and artillery could cross to join the battle in Romstein District.

Then there was an ominous grinding sound. It rumbled over the square. The gears of the ancient bell clock in the cathedral tower wound up to toll the hour. It bonged nine times with earth-shaking veracity.

"Major," O'Toole said, "there's a kraut officer outside."

"Send him in."

Sean walked deliberately to the desk of the mayor and sat behind it. The German entered, stood ramrod before the desk, and bowed slightly. He was meticulously uniformed for this occasion of defeat, as though blood and mud were not a part of his trade. The German was a strange contrast to the dirty and tired O'Sullivan.

He rattled quickly that he was the senior officer and wished to know if Sean would have a surrender ceremony. Sean stood, turning his back to the German. "O'Toole, take this man to Blessing. Tell Blessing this officer is to round up his people, bring them to the square, and stack their arms."

The German began to protest that it was no way to treat an honorable enemy commander.

"That is all," Sean cut him off abruptly.

Events moved rapidly. The long training of Pilot Team G-5 was now put into play. They moved about their preordained tasks with such precision that even the cynical Maurice Duquesne was impressed.

Soon German soldiers began straggling into the square. A half-dozen tanks and a company of Dundee's infantry formed a picket around them. The Germans limped in with the same dejection that had marked other beaten men from France to Rombaden. Their plight and their humiliation was intensified by surrender inside one of their own cities. The pile of arms grew higher, until the square held several thousand soldiers.

Some of them were beardless boys in their teens. Others were old men. These were the People's Army. The last-ditch home defense.

The German officers stood in a clique away from their men as though the soldiers were contaminated.

Curious civilians began to peek about with caution. Walking close to the buildings at a creeping pace, holding a respectful distance from the prisoners.

"It is over."

"It is over."

"It is over."

They milled about and gawked in dazed confusion. Some wept with grief and some wept with relief. "It is over."

By late afternoon a dozen or more of the civic officials had been hauled in; however, neither Count Ludwig nor Baron Sigmund Von Romstein nor their younger brother Kurt had been found.

The square was now mobbed with frightened, glassy-eyed people. Sean O'Sullivan came downstairs and faced them from the steps of City Hall. He ordered the flags of the United States, Britain, France, and the Soviet Union hoisted above the building and his first order posted.

PROCLAMATION #1: APRIL 21, 1945
Attention! Citizens of Rombaden!
This city has unconditionally surrendered to Allied Forces. City Hall is hereby designated as Headquarters of Allied Forces Military Government.
No further resistance will be tolerated.
You are under the supreme command of the Allied representative.
All German courts, schools, banks, transportation and communications within city limits are hereby suspended.
All business is suspended.

The police force is hereby disbanded.

All members of the German armed forces will surrender themselves with their firearms immediately in the City Hall Square.

All firearms will be deposited at the City Hall immediately.

All motor vehicles are hereby requisitioned.

All warehouses are hereby requisitioned.

All stores and petrol are hereby confiscated.

All German penal law is hereby suspended.

Rombaden is under curfew from 1900 to 0600 daily. Violators will be shot on sight.

All theaters, cinemas, radio stations, newspapers and other publications will suspend operations immediately.

The Mayor, Sanitation Officer, District Mayors, Medical Officer, Police Chief, City Engineer and their immediate subordinates will report immediately to Allied Headquarters.

All other civilians are hereby ordered to return to their homes and stay until notified.

By order of: Sean O'Sullivan, Major, United States Army. Military Governor of Rombaden/Romstein.

CHAPTER FIFTEEN

Dear General Hansen,

As we planned, I am writing these informal impressions on the basis of the first 72 hours. Dundee's Regiment is meeting stiff opposition from the Waffen SS in Romstein District so my Team has not crossed the river, yet. We've got our hands full, here.

In Rombaden, resistance collapsed. The population is demoralized, scared stiff and getting hungry. So far we have averted panic, epidemic and serious crime, but the place is one hell of a mess.

Here's a thumbnail and unofficial survey. Hank Greenberg, my engineer, estimates 40 per cent of all housing completely destroyed, 20 per cent partly destroyed. He has a monumental demolition problem to raze the unsafe buildings. As for the rubble, he says it may be years before it is all cleared. The power plant is 60 per cent out but one of the generators is operable. No light or electricity for the civilian population is possible for months. The telegraph lines are completely down. The phone system is about 30 per cent in operation. All public transportation is *kaput*. The radio station is completely demolished and cannot transmit. Both bridges are down. The rail yard and boat yards are the damnedest messes you've ever seen. Both inoperable. The Machine Works is 85 per cent destroyed above the ground (but there is a vast underground assembly plant which used slave labor from the concentration camp) and the other factories about 80 per cent destroyed. Tell the fly boys their aim was pretty good.

Our urgent problem right now is that the sewage plant and waterworks are both out of order. Dr. Grimwood, my health officer, has declared the river contaminated. We have been using water wells and have rationed the Germans to one bucket of water per day per family.

As for sewage removal, we have set up a honey-bucket system. The buckets are collected daily and carted out of town. We have been using arrested Blacklisted Nazis on this working detail. It's good for them.

Meanwhile, the sewage plants and waterworks have our A-1 priority. Greenberg believes we can get them in at least partial working order in time to avert an epidemic.

Grimwood believes that present medical facilities can handle a small emergency (because of the Medical College) but, of course, we don't know the medical problems we face when the concentration camp is liberated.

On the plus side.

Seizure of the banks, newspapers, business firms, etc., has gone off without a hitch.

We have formed two labor battalions who, along with some 2500 POW's, have started rubble clearance, demolition, etc.

Blessing has seized the jail and has been able to keep law and order with his meager force. The people are too beaten to offer opposition. We have one of Dundee's companies doing guard duty and use them as a "back up" force. Blessing and Arosa have rounded up over a hundred Blacklist so far (our honey-bucket brigade).

The Romankunsthalle is okay. So is the cathedral. However, Trueblood will have a curator's nightmare as everything has been crated and stored in basements for safekeeping.

Speaking of irony, Dante Arosa and Duquesne found intact all the legal records, births, deaths, marriages for Rombaden/Romstein for the last three decades. Why they weren't destroyed is a mystery. It is too early to say what these records will turn up, but you can bet it will be plenty.

We weren't so lucky with the Nazi records. Kurt Von Romstein, the Nazi Gauleiter, destroyed their records, then committed suicide. So far, neither brother, Baron Sigmund or Count Ludwig, has shown up.

In all, these people have brought an unbelievable disaster upon them-

selves. I think that the quick reaction of our team held the line. I think
we can continue to hold the line and keep a semblance of human life
going except for one problem which looks insurmountable.

Dale Hickman, my food man, says there's enough stores in reserve for
about six weeks at a minimum ration of 1200 calories per day. The main
source of food is in the District but he suspects there will be a poor
harvest. Even in the best of times this area could not support itself in
food production. I have delayed issuing food-ration cards until we open
the concentration camp. I feel the inmates there rate a priority on the
food. For now, we have soup kitchens. But, the food situation must
get worse before it improves. The specter of starvation is real.

We are just too damned busy heading off disaster here to think of
either the minds of the German people or any golden futures. I hear
that things are about the same all over Germany. I have kept my promise and have not sought either personal vengeance or used brutality.
But, on the other hand, I feel neither pity, sorrow nor compassion.

Faithfully,
Sean O'Sullivan

CHAPTER SIXTEEN

Sean lifted the receiver. "Major O'Sullivan speaking."

"One minute, please, Major. We've been able to reach Colonel
Dundee."

"Good."

"Hello . . . Dundee speaking."

"Hello, Colonel. This is Major O'Sullivan. What's going on over
there?"

"We've got most of the district cleared, however these bastards are
fanatics. I wouldn't cross over yet."

"How long?"

"Well, we think we have the last of them trapped at the Schwabenwald Concentration Camp. They're using the prisoners as shields.
We've got to go slow."

"Where can I reach you?"

"Ludwigsdorf. The village is in our hands now. What's the news?"

"They say Patton has hit the Czech border and the British are about
ready to break in to Hamburg. Won't be long now."

"Son of a bitch. I wanted to hit the Austrian-Swiss border before Patton got to Czechoslovakia. How are the krauts behaving over there?"

"They're real peaceful."

"Talk to you later."

O'Toole entered as Sean hung up. "Couple krauts outside want to talk to you, Major."

"No more personal interviews today."

O'Toole handed Sean a pair of calling cards. One read: Graf Ludwig Von Romstein, Chancellor, Romstein Landkreis. The second card introduced Baron Sigmund Von Romstein, Oberburgermeister, City of Rombaden.

"Well, well. The mayor's welcoming committee. Have them wait. Round up Duquesne and Dante Arosa."

Dante Arosa and the Frenchman flanked Sean on either side of his desk. O'Toole was told to bring the Germans in. The expressions of the three men deliberately concealed their anxiety at finding the centuries-old ruling family of the area. Sean knew them instantly from their identification photos.

Count Ludwig Von Romstein was a German's German complete with dueling scar. Tall, Teutonic crew-cut blond . . . pin-striped . . . ramrod . . . a grace that belied his fifty-seven years . . . a study in German nobility . . . the head of the Von Romstein family, the chancellor.

The short, fat, nervous one walked behind him. He was Sigmund, the mayor of Rombaden. Sean now sat in his chair.

They stopped before the desk, the count remaining a step ahead of his brother. He waited for several seconds for the officers to rise and shake hands. Sean neither stood nor did he offer the Germans chairs. Count Ludwig understood that the slight was deliberate, but hid any trace of having noticed it.

"Graf Ludwig Von Romstein," he said in a clipped, immaculate English, "and my brother, Baron Sigmund Von Romstein."

"O'Sullivan, Allied Military Governor. My aides, Captain Duquesne and Lieutenant Arosa."

Count Ludwig nodded his head three times, once in the direction of each. His brother made three deep bows. The little fat one was nervous; he wrung his hands as though he were washing them.

"I should have reported here earlier," Ludwig said, obviously speaking for the two of them. "The military capitulation of Rombaden found

us across the river at Castle Romstein. It was not until a few hours ago
that I was able to get back here."

Sean said that he understood and considered the delay reasonable.

"I am at your service," Ludwig said, with a meaningless acceptance
of the status quo. His brother, the mayor, had nothing to say.

Intelligence reports were correct. Ludwig completely dominated the
family. The baron was not only washing his hands but began sweating
profusely.

"Your brother Kurt Von Romstein was Nazi Gauleiter of this district. Is that not so?" Duquesne asked.

"It is correct."

"He has committed suicide."

"I have been so informed," Ludwig said, with a passionless abruptness
that startled them. "Now that Ludwigsdorf has fallen, I should like to
have my brother's body transferred to the church there, which has been
the traditional family burial . . ."

"That can wait," Sean said.

The German nodded acceptance, showing neither anger nor emotion. Dante handed Sean a thick folder. The photos matched their subjects very well. Sean flipped page after page, scanning the known
activities that told a sordid story. He closed it abruptly, having made a
sudden decision.

He unclipped a single sheet of white paper, glanced at it, slid it to
the front of the desk. "This constitutes notification that your lands and
property are confiscated and all your known assets are frozen."

If Ludwig was annoyed he did nothing to show it. He did not so
much as look at the document. "I should like to be informed of my legal
recourses," he said.

"You have none," Sean answered. "Baron," he continued—the short
fat one stepped forward and bowed—"you are to continue as mayor of
Rombaden under my directions. Your principal function is to see to it
that the civilian population carries out our orders speedily."

"Yes . . . yes . . . I shall be honored . . ."

"As for you, Count Von Romstein. The position of chancellor is suspended. I have made no final disposition of your case. In the meanwhile
I would like your voluntary cooperation."

"I have placed myself at your service."

"Lieutenant Arosa will be conducting extensive interrogations."

"Of course. I have nothing to hide."

"You've got a lot to explain. I am putting you on your honor not to leave the environs of Rombaden. Do you have a residence in the city?"

"The house of my late brother, Kurt, will be suitable."

"Clear out of Castle Romstein immediately with your family. Take only what personal possessions you can carry in two handbags. Report your address to the clerk outside. You are dismissed."

Graf Ludwig Von Romstein smiled thinly at the three men before him, conveying the obvious message that the inferior pigs who sat in judgment constituted a temporary situation. His fat brother bowed his way out of the door backwards.

"Well," Duquesne said, "how do you like the Germans now?"

Dante Arosa blew a long breath and peeled the wrapper off a cigar he had bummed from Colonel Dundee. "You shouldn't have let them go, Sean. Both of them are right on top of the Blacklist."

"They're not going anywhere," Sean said.

"You don't sit sixty miles from the border and not have an escape route mapped out. They've probably got half their holdings in Switzerland."

"No, Dante," Duquesne said, "Sean is correct. The holdings that make them powerful are right here. The land . . . the factory. If they had meant to leave the country they would have done so before now. It is a simple matter to escape to Switzerland. He has made his decision to stay here and gamble for his estate. He was prepared for all the consequences when he walked into this office."

"Lock him up," Dante insisted.

"We've got too much use for both of them to lock them up."

Maurice, having agreed with Sean, now turned on him. "Do not think you are able to play a cat and mouse game with this Count Von Romstein. Intrigue is a way of life centuries old. With all due respects, it is foreign to American comprehension. When Dante interrogates him he will have a web of stories woven to make him look like a maiden of pure driven snow."

Sean did not argue. He wondered if by letting Count Ludwig free he had not overmatched himself.

Baron Sigmund Von Romstein, who by oversight or trickery was still the mayor of Rombaden, plopped into an overstuffed chair, devoured by perspiration, heart palpitating.

"Gone," he lamented, "everything is gone. The villages, Castle Romstein, the Machine Works. Everything is gone."

"Shut up," Count Ludwig commanded. Even at this dreadful time his sharp voice stopped his brother's babbling. "Louts," Ludwig continued.

"What are they going to do with us?" Sigmund whined.

"For the time being, nothing. They will prod us for information and use us as fronts to do their dirty laundry."

"We are clean! We have never been Nazi Party members!"

"No, poor Kurt joined the party for us."

"And now he is dead. You made him join the party. It was you, Ludwig!" he cried in a rare show of defiance.

The count slapped his brother and hovered above him in rage, his dueling scar darkening to an ugly purple. "Kurt joined the party for the Von Romstein family! Remember that! And you will control yourself, Sigmund. That is just what those people want . . . for you to lose your composure before them."

The baron gasped out that he understood.

"I have made the decision. We will remain here," Ludwig continued.

"I am afraid of that American major. He hates us."

"You need not be. He is an American obsessed by the stringent rules of fair play. What the devil do the Americans know about the game of war and conquest? What do they know about ruling a people? They are a mongrelized race protected by isolation from the realities of ashes and blood. Mark my words, when the last shot is fired the Americans will cry to go home. You can thank God the Russians didn't get here first . . . or even the French."

"I don't know. I saw something in this one's eyes. I tell you, he means to ruin us."

"Nonsense. As for the other two, it will be a pleasure for the young idiot with the Italian name to interrogate us. But . . . be careful of the Frenchman."

"Careful for what? They have already taken everything."

"We shall get it all back. The Von Romstein family has lived through this crisis a hundred times. Let them make their accusations. Let them jail us. But we have time, Sigmund. We have time and we have heirs. One year, five, ten. It will all be restored to us eventually, with proper apology. The Americans will go and the French will go . . . and there will still be Von Romstein."

CHAPTER SEVENTEEN

Sean's phone rang. "Major O'Sullivan."

"This is Captain Armour, with Colonel Dundee's outfit. We've broken into the concentration camp. Colonel Dundee says to get over here right away with your health officer."

"What's the picture, Captain?"

"It can't be described. I'll pick you up at Ludwigsdorf and lead you in."

"We'll be right over."

They crossed the pontoon bridge to the south bank of the Landau in two jeep loads. Downstream they passed the magnificent estates, the Kurhaus Casino, the spa hotels, then swung inland into the district countryside. In the excitement Sean had forgotten and let Maurice Duquesne follow him. He corrected the situation and let the Frenchman take the lead. There was Grimwood, mumbling about Sean locking up several German Blacklist doctors he needed, Blessing, and, of course, O'Toole.

In the other jeep Bolinski, the lawyer and displaced persons officer, and Dante Arosa prayed for their safety at Duquesne's wheelsmanship.

Romstein District was lush and pastoral. The unscarred villages they passed seemed to have been at peace for a thousand years. Curious farmers and villagers, knowing now they would not be harmed, studied the speeding American jeeps in half friendliness and some of the children waved.

As they approached Ludwigsdorf, which directly served the Von Romstein estates, they could see Romstein Castle on a hill in the distance. Near the highway there was a small railroad station, used to transport Romstein products; in the center of the village stood a church with a tall tower and onion-shaped dome, a replica of the cathedral in Rombaden. Within its vaults lay centuries of the Von Romstein dynasty's dead.

Captain Armour flagged them down in the square, jumped into his own jeep, and led them out. The rail line angled sharply and ran parallel with the road into the Schwabenwald Forest. They raced toward the mass of dark green with sunlight coming in flickers as the road snaked through the forest.

A large sign pocked with bullet holes blared out at them: WARNING! CONCENTRATION CAMP GROUNDS! DO NOT PROCEED BEYOND THIS POINT! VIOLATORS SUBJECT TO SEVERE PENALTY! There was a death's head insignia below the words.

A few dozen battle-weary American soldiers sat along the roadside, backs propped against trees, dull-brained from the fight, digging half-heartedly at cans of ham and nibbling at the chocolate in their rations.

A pretty wooden bridge forded a stream. Nestled about the forest were about fifty lovely cottages with little gardens planted before them. These were the homes of the married SS officers.

A few hundred yards past the cottages they broke into an immense clearing in what must have been dead center of the forest. A high, solid gate blocked them. It was flanked by two empty guard boxes, an archway over the gate. This, too, had a sign. It read: SCHWABENWALD CONCENTRATION CAMP. Below it were words of wisdom in Gothic print declaring that all who came here and performed honest labor would redeem their sins.

Once inside this outer gate they were on a street of administrative buildings and barracks of the SS Death's Head Units. Captain Armour halted before the commandant's building.

From the moment they had entered Schwabenwald Forest Sean and the others had been aware of a bad odor. They had smelled it before in places where corpses were left to rot. As they drove through the forest it persisted and strengthened. Now it was overwhelming.

From the terrible silence there was little doubt but that they had come to a place of awesome catastrophe. Colonel Dundee stood in the middle of a dozen of his officers and men. With not a single word of greeting he got into his jeep and led Sean's party down the street to a place where a ten-foot wall of barbed wire ran off in either direction for half a mile. Beyond this wall was a path six feet wide and an inner wall of barbed wire. Conductors on the poles indicated it was electrified. At precisely every thirty yards stood a wooden guard tower with searchlights and machine guns.

They drove into the heart of Schwabenwald.

When the inspection was done they sat about limp and drained and

Sean felt himself in the same nightmare as after Tim's death. How could the human race have come to this?

Colonel Dundee was a man who charted death. Dr. Grimwood had lived with the pained. Blessing had known blood. They were all stunned and silent.

Dante Arosa and Bolinski retched outside the office; young O'Toole cried.

Maurice Duquesne, who had mingled sweat with the Germans, who was arrogant about his sophistication, broke the agonizing silence. "How in the name of God could they have done this!"

"Let us just hope," Dundee said unevenly, "that this Commandant Klaus Stoll was a maniac. Let's just hope to God there are no more places like this."

"There couldn't be! God almighty, there couldn't be!"

And then the horrible silence fell on them again.

My brothers died for this! What fools ever claimed they knew the Germans! Make the sick well, General Hansen? Sure! Come have a look.

Geoffrey Grimwood rediscovered life first. "We must get on with the job," he said. "I'll need all the help I can get. Can you assign me some of your doctors and medics?"

Dundee said he could.

"I'll have to ask for supplies and advice. I don't know if anyone knows much about this. Is there any idea how many there are alive in there?"

"Maybe three or four thousand," Captain Armour said.

"We'll need a very large place to hold them."

"How about the castle?"

"No. I'd best have them moved into Rombaden. We've got to utilize the facilities of the hospital and Medical College . . ."

Sean heard the conversation only in blurs.

"We'd best sort them out and get the dead buried at once. Sean, do you have any objection to putting those captured SS brutes to work on the burial detail? I say, Sean . . . we've got to bury the dead."

"The dead will not be buried!" Sean cried.

"Come now, old man. We are all shaken up over this thing. They must be buried at once."

"No! They will not be buried. Not until every goddamned son of a bitch in Rombaden walks over every inch of this camp."

"It will take a lot of doing to force them," Dundee said.

"No one . . . *no one* will be issued a food-ration card until he goes
through this camp."

"It's six miles to Rombaden. They've got a lot of old people and kids.
You're not going to make the kids look at this," Dundee said.

"Like hell I'm not. They'll walk like they made the slaves walk every
day and every night to the factories. And if they're too old let them be
carried on the backs of their fellow Germans."

"The children?"

"Their mothers may cover their eyes, but they'll take the stench of
this place to their graves. As for the SS . . . Blessing, lock them up in
the gas chambers. Let them live in there awhile."

Sean's burst had been spent.

"I'm not going to let you do this, Major. We're buying all kinds of
trouble," Dundee said.

"I take full responsibility."

"But you're irrational."

Sean walked slowly to the colonel and stood nose to nose. "As military governor, my authority supersedes yours, Colonel. If you have a
beef, register it with headquarters. If you try and stop me, I'll have you
locked up. Blessing! Find out the colonel's pleasure!"

Colonel Dandy Dundee, a rough fighter from the ranks, was neither prepared for the ultimatum, the fury of the major, nor the consequences. Everyone about them hung frozen. Dundee broke, turned,
and walked away.

"All right, Doc. You said something about needing room?"

"Yes. Although many of them are near the end. We must prepare
for a dreadful fatality rate. It would be useless to move some of them
out."

"It is not useless. All of the living will be taken out of here. If they
are to die at least they won't die looking at this goddamned barbed wire.
They've seen enough of it." Tears of pain for those poor human animals
fell down Sean's cheeks. "Colonel Dundee. Could you please place
your motor transport at my disposal?"

"Yes, Major."

"Thank you, Colonel. Maurice. Have all German patients removed
from the hospital in Rombaden. Commandeer the cathedral. Remove all
the benches. Take beds and bedding out of as many German homes as
we will need to accommodate these people. But for God's sake, get them
out of this place! Get them out of here!"

O'Toole was ill at ease at the presence of Father Gottfried from the cathedral. The priest wore slightly different garments than American priests, his voice was deep and booming, his face dark, and his eyebrows thick. In fact, he looked very much like a German soldier to O'Toole. In one way he was the enemy, O'Toole reckoned. On the other hand he was a priest and therefore could not be the enemy. It was perplexing and made him nervous. He ushered him into Sean's office.

"I would have paid my respects earlier," Father Gottfried said, "but I can understand the urgencies you have been under."

"What's on your mind, Father?" Sean asked.

"The requisition of Marienkirche."

"What about it?"

"I understand it is going to be turned into a hospital."

"That's right."

"Of course I am in great sympathy with those poor souls, but you must try to realize, my son, that the Marienkirche is not only a house of God but a tradition unbroken for centuries that is important to us here . . ."

"Father Gottfried," Sean interrupted, "let's not horse around with each other. I don't give a damn for your unbroken traditions or what the people think. As far as you are concerned, if we examine your hands closely we will find Nazi dirt under your fingernails. I am, however, a Catholic and I cannot in the conscience of my faith jail a priest."

Father Gottfried was hardly prepared for the harsh words. Sean had cut from under him the common bond with which he hoped to appeal and he groped for words.

"Your congregation can pray with the Lutherans. The Lord will forgive them. It is about time a cathedral bearing the name of the Virgin Mother is returned to God's work."

"You are no doubt aware," the priest blurted, "that there exists a concordat signed by the Pope with the German Government over ten years ago."

"I do not believe that the Catholic Church and the Nazis are compatible. In this district I happen to be more powerful than the Pope."

"Be careful of what you say!"

"Father Gottfried. I am prepared to answer for my acts in heaven, hell, or purgatory. The Holy Father will have to answer for his."

"You are no Catholic!"

"And you, sir, are no priest of my church. The men of my church who served God properly have been locked up for five years in Compound A of the Schwabenwald Concentration Camp. You will be at the head of the line with Graf Von Romstein and lead the people of Rombaden to the camp . . . and take a good look at the fruits of your fine traditions, Father."

CHAPTER EIGHTEEN

The march macabre lasted for the entire day. The line of grumbling shufflers stretched from the pontoon bridge for six miles along the road to the forest. Graf Ludwig Von Romstein, Baron Sigmund, and Father Gottfried led them. In the opposite direction truckloads of half-dead inmates were raced out of Schwabenwald to the cathedral. The marchers turned their eyes away. At Ludwigsdorf the villagers of the district joined those from Rombaden, and together they walked, the stench growing stronger.

They saw it all. Most of them looked on in silence. Some fainted, some vomited, a few wept. The mothers, indeed, held their hands over the eyes of their children.

And when it was over they clutched their food-ration certificates in sweaty hands and stumbled back to Rombaden.

"I am old. I had nothing to do with it. Why did they make me see it?"

"Hitler brought us to this."

"It was Hitler's fault. Hitler and the crazy Nazis."

"We did not know."

"Hitler's fault."

"We did not know."

"We did not know."

"We did not know. How could we know?" asked Herr Himmelfarb, the district recorder.

Sean and Dante Arosa glared at the bureaucrat coldly.

"You must believe me," he repeated.

"Himmelfarb. How long have you been the Landkreis recorder?"

"Since 1924," he said proudly. "January 4, 1924."

Dante lifted a huge ledger and handed it to him. "What is this?"

"Death records of Schwabenwald."

"They were found in the basement."

"*Ja.* I put them there for safekeeping."

Dante took the ledger back and opened the cover. "This is your handwriting?"

"Ja."

"Your entries?"

"Ja."

"Herr Himmelfarb. We have fourteen more ledgers like this one."

"Thank goodness. I thought they might have been lost."

"Recording 116,000 death certificates issued from Schwabenwald Concentration Camp."

"Ja. That would be correct. Fifteen ledgers, 116,000 deaths recorded."

"Of these, 110,000 are listed as either heart failure or natural causes."

"Ja."

"What is meant by 'natural causes'?"

"I have no idea," Himmelfarb answered.

"Did it ever occur to you that there was something strange about being handed a thousand death certificates because of heart failure in a given week?"

"I had no thoughts about it one way or the other. My job is merely to see if the certificate is legal and then record it."

"It never entered your mind that mass murder was being committed?"

"I beg of you, Lieutenant. I am a mere civil servant. I do not have opinions. My duty is to keep records and that is all I do. Just keep records."

"Herr Himmelfarb!" Dante shouted with rising wrath, "were you a member of the Nazi Party?"

"Ja. I was a member. Please remember that my position was nonpolitical. Strictly nonpolitical."

"You wore a uniform?"

"Ja."

"With swastikas on it?"

"Ja."

"You attended Nazi Party meetings?"

"Ja, of course."

"Nazi rallies?"

"But we all had to attend meetings and rallies. Even on my day off I had to attend whether I wanted to or not."

"Did you want to?"

"Never!"

"But you did attend them."

"What choice did I have? Look, Lieutenant, I had very good Jewish friends, even."

"What happened to them?"

"I don't know. They disappeared."

"Did you ever inquire what happened to them?"

"One did not do that."

"Did you offer them help before they disappeared?"

"It was too dangerous, but I felt very badly when they were taken away."

"But you were a party member, right?"

"Don't you understand, Lieutenant. I joined the Nazi Party for only one reason . . . to keep my position."

Dante had reached the boiling point. Sean held up his hand. "Save your breath, Dante. O'Toole!"

The orderly tumbled into the office.

"Lock him up."

Dante flung up his hands in frustration. "How many have we talked to today? Twenty? Thirty? None of them say, it was my fault. None of them say . . . forgive me. 'I joined the party to save my job.' 'I had a good friend who was a Jew.' 'Strictly nonpolitical.'"

"The Jews are lucky to have so many good German friends," Sean said. "So there we have it. No one knows anything. Factory foremen who didn't know they were using slave labor . . . people working on the river front who didn't even see the slaves being marched over every day . . . doctors, nurses, professors at the college who didn't know their colleagues were at the 'research center' in the concentration camp . . . no one saw the trains coming in to Ludwigsdorf. . . . It really never happened."

"Why did they keep these records?" Dante asked.

"Because, in their warped logic, it is a basis to legalize and justify the murder in Schwabenwald. Of course we will never know how many of those poor people from outside Germany were denied even a death certificate."

"We did not know," Count Ludwig said to Sean.

"The record to date is perfect. Twenty-nine people out of twenty-nine interrogated so far did not know. Twenty-two of them had good friends who were Jewish, and twenty-four had nonpolitical Nazi affiliations to hold their jobs."

"You can not blame us for the work of a single madman. Klaus Stoll was insane, obviously."

"You might be interested in knowing that Schwabenwald was merely one of many of the same. Here's a few more names that have just come in. You read English. Read it." He handed him the paper.

Graf Ludwig read the dispatch from headquarters . . . Dachau . . . Ravensbruck . . . Buchenwald . . . reports from the Russian front indicate that in Poland . . .

"In God's name, Major. We are a civilized people."

"God's name has been used rather freely in the last few days."

"You cannot blame an entire nation for the doings of a handful of Nazis."

Sean grunted a small ironic laugh. There were stacks of files on his desk. He found the one he wanted, opened it, and walked to the count. There were photographs of the City Hall Square of Rombaden in an other day. All the buildings—City Hall, the college, hospital, museum, and even the cathedral—were covered with swastika buntings. A long row of brown-shirted SA men stood with tall, thin-tapered torches leading to a grandstand where thousands more in black shirts and death's head insignias held swastika standards. There were tens of thousands more in Hitler Youth and SS uniforms holding the Nazi salute. And there were thousands more who could not jam into the square listening over loudspeakers in joined barges on the river. It seemed as though not a person could be missing from Rombaden's population. Some women cried in ecstasy at the sight of the Fuehrer. Blown-up segments of the photographs identified the three Von Romsteins and Father Gottfried and almost all of those other "nonpolitical" Nazis.

All of this had taken place outside the window of Sean's office, where now the dead from Schwabenwald were being taken out of Marienkirche.

Masses, screaming ecstatic masses. Hear the drums! Hear his voice! Sieg Heil! Sieg Heil! Sieg Heil! The trumpets and the marching boots.

"Is that what you call a handful? Is that a handful in the square?"

"These pageants were designed to inflame the lower classes. Masses anywhere in the world are obsessed with uniforms."

Sean slammed his fist on the table. "But they don't go insane when they get in a crowd like Germans do!"

"Major, I tell you that Schwabenwald is the work of a few people. You saw for yourself how completely hidden and guarded the place was. It was a word spoken of only in whispers."

"The smell. Was it smelled in whispers? During the spring and early winter you have south winds. What happened when the smell reached Rombaden? We have twenty-six answers. Ten of them had no opinion about the smell, five thought it was a leather factory, four a fertilizer plant, one a chemical plant, and eleven didn't smell a thing. What did you think about the smell?"

Ludwig Von Romstein twitched in the first visible sign of discomfort Sean had seen.

"You are chief benefactor of the Medical College and of the Research Center. You entertained those doctors in Castle Romstein. You gambled with them at the Kurhaus. Did they discuss their experiments? Did you know your good money was going for a hundred castrations and ovarectomies a day! From Castle Romstein you can see the village of Ludwigsdorf, is that not correct?"

There was no answer.

"Is that not correct!"

"It is correct."

"Your servants and your farmers trade and live in Ludwigsdorf. You go to your church in Ludwigsdorf. It is the traditional family church. What did you think when trainloads of open gondola cars passed through Ludwigsdorf filled with corpses. Well, goddammit, what did you think?"

"All of us knew to close our eyes, our ears, and our mouths if we wanted to stay alive."

"What did you think about your factory being operated by slave labor for six years. They were marched over the bridge every day in front of the whole goddamned city! What did you think?"

"I was told what to manufacture, what my quota was. I took the labor that was assigned to me."

"You and Hermann Goering were flyers together in the First World War. Did you or did you not use your personal friendship to obtain contracts for airplane motors and V-2 rockets."

"As a businessman I am no different from any businessman anywhere in using my contacts . . ."

"And taking the Nazi Blood Order Honor."

"I was not in a position to turn down a Nazi decoration. It would have been suicide for me to refuse."

"So your brother Kurt was used as the Nazi front for the Von Romstein family and conveniently committed suicide."

"My brother made the decision on his own. I believe your concept of justice excludes guilt by association."

"Let's examine the association. Brother number one, mayor. Brother number two, chancellor. Brother number three, Nazi Gauleiter. Let me ask you, Count. In your capacity as chancellor and benefactor what did you do about the smashing of the windows of Jewish shops, the burning of their synagogues, the stealing of their fortunes, beatings in the streets, murder at Schwabenwald?"

Ludwig stiffened and fumed. The Jews! Always the Jews! What did this idiot know about Jews. Yes, as chancellor I kept them from overrunning the staff of the hospital and kept their numbers proper in the Medical College. I guarded against their filthy business ethics. Neither he nor his father nor his father's father ever had a Jew in Castle Romstein. It was a matter of family honor. There were those few distasteful civic occasions when it was unavoidable to meet a Jew . . . but, the Jews did not run the theaters and newspapers and banks as they did in Vienna and Berlin.

"I never condoned," the count said with slow deliberateness, "Hitler's program for the Jewish question. We Germans had many Jews of whom we were proud. There must have been a dozen German Jewish Nobel Prize winners. A close examination of my tenure in public life will prove I never went outside the law in the treatment of Jews."

"You didn't have to go outside the law. The Nuremberg Laws let you do anything you wished. Is there any crime on the books you can't excuse or justify, Count?"

"It is well and good for you to hammer questions at me and demand explanations," Von Romstein burst back in anger, "but I was in no more of a position to rule upon either the legality or the inhumanity of the law than you are of your laws. I am a German citizen and these were the laws and times of my country. Surely, the good Major is aware of the existence of unjust laws against the Negroes in America and surely the Major knows that Negroes are looked upon as subhumans by a large segment of the American people. We Germans did not invent race hatred."

"We Americans did not invent death factories. That is an exclusive German innovation!"

"If . . . if we could perhaps discuss this on a sane level. I can neither explain nor justify with you shouting at me and I should like you to know my position."

Sean's anger abated slowly. He told himself to gain control. "Go ahead . . ."

"May I sit down?"

Sean nodded. The count asked for permission to smoke. He drew a long puff wondering where to begin. The man opposite him was filled with righteous wrath.

"You must remember, Major O'Sullivan," Von Romstein opened, "that America has never committed acts for which she has had to answer later. Your behavior has never been judged by a conqueror. You have never had to explain. When you are not involved in the day-to-day living and temper of a times it is easy to ask questions as a casual observer."

"I'm not a casual observer. The Germans have killed two of my brothers."

"And I have lost a son. I do not wish to offend you, Major, but you must realize that the House of Von Romstein has borne the responsibility of this Landkreis since long before Columbus discovered America."

Sean was impressed by the opening gambit.

"I am not going to question your intelligence by defending feudalism," Von Romstein continued, "but it is a system that we inherited because of the limited opportunities of the land. Feudalism, the landowner and the overseer, breeds a type of tradition and family responsibility foreign to American life. As time passed we outgrew an agrarian economy and we were forced to industrialize or perish. You see, Germany was the last power in Europe to become industrial. When my grandfather made the great transition, it was a mere fifty years ago.

"Once the Machine Works was built, Rombaden tripled in size. Under an agrarian economy life was quite simple. The population was such that everyone had enough to eat. Products made in small factories where traditional arts had been practiced for generations, but . . . with heavy industry the District of Romstein, as was the case in most of Germany, was simply unable to produce enough food. This set off a cycle of dependence upon manufactured products to trade in order to import food.

"Germany is a small country with an enormous population. We do not have room to explore or expand. We do not have the natural, God-given assets of America. Germany is poor in natural wealth. Its great asset is the energy and ingenuity of the people. Things here must be orderly. Ambitions must be limited. The factory here must produce in order to maintain enough jobs. If the factory closes, Rombaden does not eat. Unlike America, we have no magic food surplus to draw upon.

"I inherited the Romstein family responsibility at the end of the First World War. I shall not debate with you the good or the evil of the Versailles Treaty. The Allies say Germany did not get enough punishment. We Germans felt it was too severe. From a practical standpoint, the Versailles Treaty closed down the Machine Works and we were not permitted to produce. The people of this Landkreis and in all of Germany were hungry and frightened and there was no work."

Graf Ludwig Von Romstein snuffed out his cigarette. He was immersed in his memories; the sea of his own words had caught him up. He drifted toward the window that looked down on the City Hall Square, that place of so much history.

"Nor will I argue either the good or the bad of the Weimar Republic. It was our first experiment with so-called democracy . . . and it failed. It was too weak to achieve the needs of the day.

"So, now that this war is ending you say to me . . . how could this have happened? I'll tell you, Major O'Sullivan. If you were a German citizen of Rombaden in 1924 you would have known. There was starvation and no work. Inflation was so bad a wagonload of marks could not buy a loaf of bread.

"And the worst of it was that we Germans had been stripped of our pride and our dignity. Pride is a German strength and a German weakness. Other people can live without it . . . the Chinese . . . the Latin Americans . . . the Slavs. But a German cannot." He pointed to his dueling scar. "This is a nonsensical pride to show my courage as a young man. Well, Hitler came and spoke to us of jobs and returning German dignity. In that square below and in other squares he staged his pageantry and a hurt lower class devoured it.

"How did the rest of us feel about this ridiculous man? We were coming to a choice in Romstein Landkreis. We either went with Hitler or to the Communists. There was no strong middle ground in the Weimar Republic. So we tried to make a temporary arrangement with Hitler in order to get people working, recover our senses, beat back the Communists, restore our dignity.

"I say in all candor to you, Major O'Sullivan, that in the days that lie ahead you Americans will discover that we were not wrong about the Communists. They may be your allies now, but you shall learn hard lessons about them.

"In the beginning, Hitler gave us more than he had promised. We had our national pride returned and we were working again. None of the people in my class believed that we could not eventually bring Hitler under control. You know the rest of the story. The tyranny imposed upon the German people was absolute. We were strangled and unable to fight back . . ."

Sean heard it all with fascination. Was the Versailles Treaty unfair? Could a Germany which plunged the world into its first bloody global war have expected less? And what about the rest of Europe, which starved and went without jobs and knew blood and sorrow because of German insanity.

And what about the Weimar Republic? Did the German people really want it to work? Did the General Staff and all the Von Romsteins give it a chance? Didn't they fight it and club it to death?

"I am sorry for what happened at Schwabenwald," Ludwig said softly. "And when the German people learn about these places they will be sorry too. We did not know."

"What about London and Rotterdam and Warsaw?" Sean asked. "Are you sorry about these places too? Are you sorry about my brothers, Timothy and Liam O'Sullivan? Did you have tears for the human race you trampled on or did you begin to become sorry when you got your brains knocked out at Stalingrad? And as for knowing. *You did not know because you did not want to know.*"

Graf Ludwig Von Romstein arose. "I assume the interview is at an end?"

"Yes."

He turned to go, then stopped and said with a pleading voice, "What you saw at Schwabenwald could have happened to any people anywhere under the same conditions."

"But it never has, Count, it never has."

CHAPTER NINETEEN

Ludwig Von Romstein betrayed his noble breeding where many Germans did, at the table. His otherwise impeccable manners eroded to gluttony satisfied with rapid shovelings of his spoon, fork, knife, and fingers (between slurps and burps) and a final sucking and picking of the teeth. The nervous rebellion made him hungrier than usual.

Sigmund had been right. The American major was obsessed with the mission of destroying him. Moreover, O'Sullivan's intelligence and his information and knowledge of Von Romstein history was startling. The interview had failed to be convincing.

From the moment he realized what was happening at Schwabenwald a year ago, he wove stories in his own mind to build arguments to prove he knew nothing about it. So did everyone else. He cursed the stupid Nazi louts. They had left everyone in a fine fix by failing to destroy the gas chambers and crematoriums. Clumsy dogs . . . leaving those fields and trainloads of corpses strewn around. Even the latest batch of castrations in the "science center" were shot in bed.

Perhaps, Ludwig thought, I should have joined the plot on Hitler's life last year. I should have covered myself with some sort of anti-Nazi gesture; smuggled a Jew to Switzerland or something. I had Jew slaves working on the farms. So, what then? I would have been strung up like everyone else involved in the bomb plot.

He convinced himself once more that he had stayed out of the intrigues against Hitler for the sake of preserving the family, but the whole Von Romstein family is tottering! Sigmund is ready to crack apart. He has been in a state of hysteria since the first air raids two years ago. What will happen when they really grill him? If only he had the good grace to put himself away as Kurt did.

Of his two sons, Johann had followed the baron's steps as a flyer. Johann was dead . . . shot down over the English Channel.

The other son, Felix, was a dull, minor bureaucrat in Berlin, without ability to carry on the Von Romstein tradition.

His thoughts turned to his daughter, Marla Frick. Marla was the only real hope the family had. But . . . hadn't she always been the only hope? Johann had been wild and irresponsible . . . fast cars, faster

airplanes. Johann would have never settled to his family duties even if
he had survived.

And the others . . . bunglers. Marla was the one real Von Romstein
of them all. A true German noblewoman. Count Ludwig had needed
someone to modernize the Machine Works. He arranged a marriage
between Marla and Wilhelm Frick to lure the brilliant industrial de-
signer away from the Krupp Industries.

The Von Romstein fortunes revolved around the Machine Works.
Wilhelm Frick could ensure its continued growth and prosperity . . .
even turn it into one of the nation's industrial giants. So what if the
marriage was not made in heaven . . . Wilhelm was ten years older
than Marla . . . he kept mistresses at the Spa on the south bank . . .
he had another in Dusseldorf, where he made trips yearly and she
accompanied him to Munich and the Riviera. But . . . what the devil,
we've all had our other women. Ludwig had not shared his wife's bed
for seven years. Even poor Sigmund kept a woman in Rombaden.

The marriage of Marla and Wilhelm had produced the necessary
heirs, fortunately two boys. These grandsons would eventually adopt
the Von Romstein name and carry the great tradition into the next
century.

But dammit, just when the big contracts were rolling in Wilhelm
Frick was drafted by Alfred Speer's ministry to organize industry in
the occupied countries. Wilhelm Frick had been captured by the Russians. God only knew when he would be seen again, if ever.

Ludwig left the table, retreated to the study of his late brother, Kurt.
The room was still plush, having been spared from the bombings. It
was in this room so many many years ago . . . how many? Twenty . . .
twenty years ago that he urged Kurt to join the Nazi Party . . . get
in on the ground floor . . . for the sake of the family. Kurt obeyed.
Everyone obeyed Ludwig. It was damned fortunate for us all, Ludwig
thought, that Kurt did not allow himself or the records to be taken. The
Nazi records showed the close intertwining of the Von Romstein control. It was in this room, too, that Kurt took his life. Poor Kurt. Ludwig
selected one of his brother's pipes, found the last of the tobacco, and
sunk into a deep chair waiting for Marla to finish putting the children
down. Damned nuisance these days without servants.

Marla was a good sport. She and Wilhelm Frick had a magnificent
smaller estate on the south bank. The Americans had commandeered it
for those louts of Polish laborers. Slaves, indeed! A decent slave can at

least put in a day's work—the Poles were less than useless. In normal times they could not have held jobs at the Machine Works . . . now these pigs live in Marla's home. God knows what they will do to Castle Romstein.

Marla Frick entered the study and said that the children had fallen asleep. She sat in a straight-backed chair near her father. She was a radical departure from the plump, large-breasted, bread-eating, beer-drinking peasant variety that abounded in Romstein Landkreis. Marla Von Romstein Frick was slim, high cheekboned, immaculately groomed. Her features were too dark and thick to give her true beauty, but her manner offset that. All heads turned at the regal bearing when she entered the casino. She was a magnificent horsewoman with a cold intriguing cruelty that could use a whip on a horse or across a servant's face. Ludwig's adoration of her was obvious, and against his better judgment he conceded that she was his favorite. He often wondered why son-in-law Wilhelm found it necessary to stray from the fold.

Marla poured her father tea and cognac. "How did the interview go with the American?"

"Not well, I'm afraid."

"What do they want from us? Haven't we suffered enough?"

"War is a foreign substance to them. They have never had to explain to an occupation force . . . what a convenient existence. We had a good chance to hold our position . . . that is, until they opened Schwabenwald. But now the world will rise in a ground swell of righteous wrath and demand retribution."

"It was disgusting . . . unbearable," Marla said, "forcing us to walk around in the middle of those corpses as though it were our doing."

Ludwig set his pipe aside. "The fact is, the family is in a grave crisis. In all likelihood your Uncle Sigmund and I will have to serve prison terms."

"But whatever on earth for, Father?"

"My pet, justice belongs to the winning side. The winners may judge the losers on any set of rules they wish. You can be assured that the Russians will never be brought to justice for their hideous crimes. Only we Germans must answer."

"Dear God, what has Hitler brought us to."

"Marla, I am completely prepared to accept a prison term. You know full well that Felix is incapable of heading the family. We do not know when your husband will be released from Russia, if ever. It is up to you, Marla."

What a delicious moment! Up to me. Up to me and my sons. *Me . . . the woman!*

"Insofar as politics is concerned," her father continued, "as a woman you are above suspect. Americans are terribly fair about that sort of thing. You know of course that sufficient funds have been transferred to Switzerland."

Marla nodded.

"Unless you are driven out you are to stay here and keep up the fight for the estate and the Machine Works."

"Yes, Father."

"Marla, the great strength of the Von Romstein family is the willingness of its members to sacrifice for our name. Your Uncle Kurt and your brother Johann have given their lives. Your Uncle Sigmund and and I are ready to go to prison. Throughout our history Von Romstein women have cemented invaluable alliances for the sake of the family."

She knew her marriage was no different. Wilhelm Frick was palatable but never desirable. From time to time she enjoyed him, but those times were seldom and only after long periods of lonely frustration.

In their public life Wilhelm Frick was always proper. The union was important to the family. It had produced the desired heirs. It protected the estates, the castle, and the Machine Works. She had known that this was to be the way of things since she was a little girl. Now was the moment of reward. Her sons *alone* would keep the name alive and *her* cunning alone would save the family.

Once she had loved someone. He was a student at the Medical College. It was the only time she remembered her father beating her. She was sixteen. Despite her rigid training, despite the fact she despised those people, she had fallen in love with a boy who was half Jew. The penance, discipline, and training that followed was cruel. There were times, of course, on a holiday away from the family when she was able to indulge in a lover. Secretly she looked for a Jew. Perhaps a Jew could help her recapture that one single moment when she was young and giving.

"Marla," her father continued, "the Americans are building a case against the family. In a way we are fortunate that legality is an obsession with them. Had the Russians come here we would no doubt all be dead. Their concept of justice is as crude as the Slavic people. With the

Americans we stand somewhat of a chance. Much of what finally comes
to court will be based on the results of the interrogation by this young
officer, Arosa."

She nodded.

"Having been interrogated by him I am convinced that his thinking
can be made flexible. I believe the case could be made much less severe."

Marla spared only a fleeting thought for her husband somewhere in
a Russian prison camp. Certainly, if and when he returned from Russia
he would want the Machine Works restored and would endorse the
urgency of the situation. Besides that, Marla had been without a man
for many months. She was hungry for sex. The young American officer
was not without appeal.

"They seem to be quite serious about this nonfraternization, Father."

Ludwig smiled. "Just so much more of their impractical unworkable
schoolboy nonsense. I am quite certain, Marla, that you could be quite
convincing to Arosa. In fact, I'd bet a fortune on it."

CHAPTER TWENTY

It was curfew. Polish slave laborers, liberated from Schwabenwald,
staggered over the pontoon bridge to the south bank, where Lieutenant
Bolinski had set up a displaced persons center in the spas, hotels, and
Kurhaus.

Shenandoah Blessing watched them from his jeep and whistled the
tune the Poles sang. The last half dozen of them over the square gathered about the jeep to bum cigarettes. One Pole, who wore a Bavarian
hunting hat and leather pants, was not content with merely shaking
Blessing's hand. He threw his arms about the fat policeman and thrice
blessed America. After that he began to weep with drunken joy and
insisted that Blessing should have his green velour hat with the big
bushy feather and the hunting pins. Blessing tolerated this all with
endless patience.

"Now come on, fellers. Let's get over to the south bank. Tomorrow
is another day."

The weeping one kissed Blessing's apple cheeks. They wove off to
the pontoon bridge with a dozen farewells.

Blessing looked around the square for any late arrivals. There were none. He tucked his belly under the steering wheel, then U-turned in the direction of the jail while pondering the immediate problems of setting out night patrols.

The whole Rombaden police force had to be disbanded. So far he could find but a half-dozen whitelisted Germans trustworthy enough to augment his meager crew. There was only one company of American infantry to guard the whole Landkreis, the POW's, and the interned SS in Schwabenwald. If there was any real trouble, he'd be in a bad fix.

He'd press Major O'Sullivan and Bolinski to let him have a few hundred Poles to put into uniform. Could he trust the Poles with weapons? In his own anger after seeing Schwabenwald, Blessing had beaten up some of the SS when they were taken out of the gas chambers. Sean let them out after three days when they began fainting from hunger, thirst, fright, and suffocation and put them under arrest.

He wheeled out of the square into a narrow street. His thoughts were halted by the sight of someone sitting atop a brick pile between two bombed-out houses. He pulled up and switched off the motor. An older man just sat and stared vacantly into space.

"Say there, old-timer," he called, "it's curfew."

The man didn't answer.

"Speaken sie English? Say there. It's *schwartz* in the *himmel*. You got to get to your *haus*."

"I speaken sie perfect English!"

"It's curfew."

"To hell with curfew, sir!"

The man did not budge. Blessing climbed up the brick pile with a deftness that belied his size. The man was not as old as he first appeared. An empty wine bottle lay at his feet. Blessing puffed to a halt before him.

"Now where in the hell do you live?"

"In Berlin, you idiot."

"Don't you go getting me riled up. Where do you live in Rombaden!"

"Nowhere!"

"You drunk?"

"Of course I'm drunk. Are you stupid?"

The policeman grabbed the man's collar with a fast reflexive move, jerked him to his feet, and had him in an arm lock. The man offered no resistance, in fact dangled loosely. In this closeness Blessing smelled the unwashed body. He knew the smell. He shoved back the sleeve on the man's left arm. The arm was engraved with the tattoo number of a prisoner of Schwabenwald. Blessing released his grip.

"Why didn't you tell me you were from the concentration camp?"

"Why didn't you ask me?" the man said, sitting down again. And then he began to babble. "I didn't drink very much. Haven't drunk in long time. It has made me drunk."

He helped the man up, but he sat down again.

"You can't sit here all night."

"I used to have friends in this place. Once this was the district head-quarters of the Social Democrats. No one is here . . . they are all gone . . . everyone is gone."

"Wait a minute. You're not a Pole."

"I sir, am German."

"Are you Ulrich Falkenstein?"

"That is correct."

The jail buzzed with excitement over the old man who lay passed out on a cot in Blessing's office. Ulrich Falkenstein! A major find. A man who had withstood Hitler persecution.

The team had all known he was a prisoner at Schwabenwald. When they broke into the camp, Bolinski and Arosa were able to determine that Falkenstein was alive up until a few days before the surrender. In the confusion, he had wandered off to find old comrades in Rombaden.

Ulrich Falkenstein and his brother were war horses of the Social Democratic Party. He had dared to stand up to Hitler even when the end had come. In the party paper and in fighting speeches he denounced the Nazis at a time when most of his comrades were either escaping Germany or frightened into silence.

In the beginning the Nazis tried to buy off the Falkenstein brothers with offers of high positions. It was rumored that Ulrich was enticed with an important post. He could neither be bought nor silenced, even though he almost signed his own death warrant by resisting.

At the epic trial in 1935, Ulrich Falkenstein made his last public statement. He predicted that this new era of tyranny would lead Germany to total destruction and universal damnation. His voice was the last of the thin cries of indignation drowned out by the thumping of jackboots and the choruses of "sieg heils." Yet, not even in 1935 did

Hitler feel strong enough to order the execution of "a foremost enemy of the Third Reich."

Falkenstein joined a legion which swelled to a half-million Germans thrown into concentration camps for real or imagined opposition to the regime. When the night of terror was done, Hitler's surviving opposition was a pitiful handful like Falkenstein and a few priests, a few writers, and a few thinkers. For practical purposes, there was no German opposition to the Nazis.

Somehow or another Ulrich Falkenstein managed to stay alive. At one time he possessed a powerful body, which resisted the beatings and kickings, the weeks and months in solitary. When it became known that no torture unto death could break his spirit he became the object of calculated degradation. The SS delighted in such humiliations before the entire prison. He bore the indignity with a dignity that increased his stature and enraged his tormentors. There could be no victory in his death unless he begged for life. And this he refused to do.

Falkenstein apologized for his drunken scene to Blessing the next morning and thanked him for his understanding.

For the first time in Rombaden, Sean O'Sullivan stood up in the presence of a German and greeted him warmly.

"I am overwhelmed," Falkenstein said, "to be remembered." He reveled in the luxury of a cigarette. The tobacco made him heady. And the coffee! A long time ago he had forgotten how to cry, but now the taste of coffee brought him nearly to tears.

As they chatted, Sean wondered what kind of man sat before him. The history of concentration camps showed it only took a year or two to completely break a normal man . . . to debase him . . . to drain his will . . . to lower him to an animal instinct for sheer survival. Those whom Hitler released from the camps never dared speak of it.

What was the thing that kept Ulrich Falkenstein defiant? What was the thing that made him refuse the exchange of freedom for the promise of silence?

Except for a tiny scar at the edge of a horseshoe of white hair on a bald head, he showed little outward signs of the punishment. He seemed a little tired. His eyes were an amazing blue, like the Danube, and he radiated a look of tenderness that sometimes one obtains only through long and difficult suffering. His eyelids gave him a drowsy look—deceptive, and concealing the thoughts that were hidden behind them.

"How does the war go?" he asked.

"The Western Front is in a state of collapse. It will only be a matter of days," Sean answered.

"And Berlin?"

"We have stopped at the Elbe River. The Russians are assaulting Berlin from the Oder-Neisse Line."

Falkenstein meditated for a long time, lit another cigarette. "I am a Berliner," he said at last. "I have a family there, a wife, two brothers, Bruno and Wolfgang, and Bruno's family of course. I suppose it is impossible to obtain information about them?"

"I'm afraid it can't be done now."

"You know, it is a pity you are letting the Russians capture Berlin."

"But the Russians are our allies. They've suffered terribly at the hands of the Germans."

"Haven't we all? It is a pity, none the less. Berliners are different. They were never truly Nazis."

Sean could not cover his shock at what seemed to be a strange pronouncement.

"You look amazed, Major."

"I am, in the light of what has happened to you, Herr Falkenstein. Not a German in Rombaden thinks of himself as anything but an innocent bystander. You left Berlin in 1935. Perhaps it was too early to realize that the Nazis truly carried out the will of the German people."

"But, Major . . . I also am a German."

"A unique German."

Falkenstein shrugged. "But, no matter how you dissect me, I am a German. Perhaps I am one of those 'good' Germans, but that does not make me English or French. Furthermore, my dear Major, I believe I know more from firsthand experience about German weakness and German sickness than you do. It still does not make me less of a German."

"It sounds incongruous coming from Ulrich Falkenstein after nine years in Schwabenwald."

"Let us say I have had ample opportunities and forceful persuasion to give up hope on the German people. What you say is true, in part. Most of the so-called 'good' Germans died in places like Schwabenwald. But now, what happens if those of us who are left turn our backs on the German people?"

The revelation of Ulrich Falkenstein's stubborn beliefs was annoying and frightening. Yet, Sean could not help but admire this man who had suffered so brutally, yet retained his identity.

"So you see, I must get back to Berlin."

Was this better or worse than those Germans who had fled the Nazis and now worked with military government? Those Germans who hated their country and their own people, who turned on all things German with savagery . . . sought revenge . . . detested their Germanness? How easy it would be now for Falkenstein to join that now fashionable anti-German clique. He was instead choosing the way of a missionary among the lepers. Sean knew the Nazis could not beat Falkenstein's love of the people from him. Yet, in Falkenstein he had an adversary, not a puppet. Still, he made their choice.

"It will be a long time before you are able to return to Berlin. Meanwhile, your services here with us are sorely needed."

"I will work with you, Major, if you will remember that I am German and my first duty is not to Allied victory but to the redemption of the people."

CHAPTER TWENTY-ONE

Sean was disturbed by the worsening scene that played below his office in the square. A dozen or more wildly drunken Poles were howling, hurling bottles against buildings, urinating in the streets, scuffling.

"We've got to put a stop to this before it gets out of hand," Sean said, turning into his office and facing Blessing, Maurice Duquesne, and Bolinski.

"Shucks now, Major," Blessing soothed, "we've got to use us a little Kentucky windage in our thinking. Some of them poor fellers have been locked up for four or five years."

"We have more complaints than we can keep track of."

"Why hell, they're just celebrating a little. Don't take very much to liquor them up. We'll sweep them off the streets at curfew."

"And what do you intend to do about the looting and the beatings?"

"Well, so they broke into some German shops and homes. They've got a lot to get out of their systems," Blessing pleaded.

"That's what I'm afraid of."

The celebration had been particularly rowdy today. A large, un-tapped wine cellar had been stumbled upon. A monumental binge fol-lowed. The streets were empty of terrified Germans.

"It's not that I have any desire to protect Germans," Sean said, "but our own authority will break down if we let the Poles go unchallenged."

"They're good people," Bolinski said. "They are what is left out of maybe a hundred thousand who passed through Schwabenwald. Less than a thousand of them left, Major. Every morning they were awak-ened at five o'clock, given a bowl of watery broth, and marched from the camp to the Machine Works. Six miles, two hundred and thirty yards, sixteen feet and nine inches. Anyone who fell down was jumped on by the dogs. The last men pulled carts to pick up the dead piled up along the roadside. They worked fourteen hours, chained to their benches in those underground hell holes, and they were marched back, six miles, two hundred and thirty yards, sixteen feet and nine inches. They were given the fine reward of fifteen hundred calories a day . . ."

"I've read all your reports," Sean interrupted.

"I say to hell with it. Let them celebrate! Let them knock in a few faces!"

Sean blew a long breath and slumped into his chair. "Bolinksi . . . you and Blessing get these Poles to work. Get them signed up for guard duty. Give them any choice jobs open. How about their leaders? Can we trust them?"

"They carry authority," Bolinski answered.

"Here's the deal. We're not going to be too technical on loot or rough-ing up a few Germans. We draw the line at rape and murder. I won't be crossed on it."

Bolinski and Blessing left to sweep up the streets.

Maurice Duquesne, who had followed the conversation with de-tached boredom, finally spoke up. "Putting them to work is an unrealis-tic solution. For these first few days they are content to drink their freedom under, but soon they will want to find out if they are still men."

"I've already thought about that. We're going to use some of Bles-sing's Kentucky windage."

A few moments later Baron Sigmund Von Romstein, still acting mayor, answered a summons to Sean's office. The sight of Duquesne made him doubly nervous. Each time he came he was certain it would be for his head to roll.

"One of the streets running off the square, Princess Allee, had a reputation for gaiety, did it not, Baron?"

"Oh yes! Many beer halls. Many night clubs. During the festivals it was one of the most raucous streets in all of Schwaben . . . and Bavaria, too, for that matter."

"I'm talking specifically about whorehouses."

The baron threw up his hands in innocence. "The Nazis closed down all the brothels. You know how Hitler was."

"According to our information Princess Allee was never entirely or really closed. Is it not a fact that you always had women working as prostitutes for the overnight stops of the river-barge pilots? Their numbers could be augmented from Munich on paydays and during festival times."

"Well, you know how these things are. Not even Hitler could stop prostitution entirely."

"What is more," Sean said, "you were mayor and your brother Nazi Gauleiter. Weren't there a number of unwritten agreements, a number of things overlooked for sake of the economy of the district?"

Sean was correct. The American was always correct. He and that abominable Dante Arosa knew everything.

"Is it not further correct," Sean pressed, "that you secretly have a registration of all the women who worked as prostitutes in Rombaden."

The baron stalled.

"Well?"

"You must understand," Sigmund whined, "there was never graft connected with this. Of course, some consideration to the police now and then. However, the registration was only to keep the situation under control. To keep out undesirable elements . . . what I mean . . . to keep the girls protected . . ."

"Strictly nonpolitical," Sean said to Duquesne, who was forced to crack a smile. "How many of them are still around?"

"Perhaps thirty or forty."

"Jolly place," Sean said. "They're going to be needed."

"For your troops?" the baron asked, hoping that the nonfraternization ruling had been rescinded.

"For the Poles."

"Oh . . ."

"Nonpolitical, Baron. I don't want to know who these women are. Furthermore, they are not to know this is coming from the Allied authority. You may be their benefactor. Beginning tomorrow the Poles will be paid in occupation currency. Any girl voluntarily going back to her chosen profession will be given triple ration."

The deflated baron mumbled that it would not be too difficult to find women, even for Poles, with triple ration.

"The alternative may be the rape of your women in the streets."

"I understand, Herr Major."

The baron was dismissed.

Maurice Duquesne laughed at the poetic justice in making Baron Von Romstein pimp for the Poles he and his brothers had used as slaves. "A clever solution, Sean, but one which will lower you in the eyes of the Germans. They will say . . . look what the American does to protect us."

"I am doing it for the sake of law and order."

"Ah, but Sean, a conqueror is not expected to be benevolent. Don't you think the women here are expecting to get raped? Don't you think the German soldiers raped the women of my province and the Polish women and the Russian women?"

"More of your centuries-old traditions, Maurice?"

"More of your American naïveté, Sean. We Europeans are not dreamers, but realists. The husbands, sons, and lovers will take their women back, tainted or not."

"I don't understand you people!" Sean snapped in anger.

"And I don't understand you. How long do you think you Americans are going to be able to keep up with this idiotic nonfraternization? How long will it be before your clean-living American boys go frantic for the touch of a woman?" And then, Duquesne laughed heartily. "By God, you are missing out on one of the true rewards for winning the war."

CHAPTER TWENTY-TWO

Rombaden gasped for life amidst its devastation. The full impact of defeat drove deeper with each passing day. No water, no food . . . ashes. Frightened movement stirred behind the charred walls as the armed Poles patrolled the streets.

The coming of Ulrich Falkenstein disturbed them deeply. The tyrannical but paternal rule of the Von Romstein dynasty was over for the first time in history. Although Count Ludwig and his brothers had governed with an iron fist, they had worked for the solid status quo of traditional life. The Von Romsteins were the father. The Von Romsteins would take care of them.

Now, Falkenstein, enemy of the Reich, scorned for two decades, sat at the right hand of the Allied governor.

Sean's first doubts about the meaning of Falkenstein's Germanness faded. Falkenstein would have no truck with the Nazis. Moreover, he could smell them. A few people from the whitelist and a few political survivors of Schwabenwald were placed in key civic positions. The Nazis were routed.

It became clear that every person in Rombaden and the Landkreis was going to have to account for his 'past activities. Rumor had it that the military government was preparing a questionnaire with hundreds of questions which every man and woman had to answer. Imprisonments grew daily.

Dante Arosa and Shenandoah Blessing played upon the shocked condition of the people to build a system of informers. The safest way for one to clear one's name was to implicate someone else. Inform. Tell on your neighbor. Informing had become a fine art during the Nazi days; no one had been safe from prying eyes. Informers had been glorified by the Nazis . . . children were rewarded for telling on their parents and parents on their children and brother on sister and cousin on cousin.

Werner Hoffman, a deputy of Falkenstein, became the unofficial liaison between the informers and the Allied authorities. Hoffman had been a minor Socialist official in pre-Nazi days and somehow survived five years at Schwabenwald. He walked bent from his back which had been broken by a guard's rifle butt. He had been made a freak whose constant pain had amused the SS, so they let him live. Hoffman was not a particularly efficient official, but he was a rare being . . . a trusted anti-Nazi.

Hoffman made the rendezvous on Princess Allee. Hoffman made the deals with the informers for extra rations and extra consideration.

This disintegration of morality added to Sean's disgust of the Germans. And it brought the usual snide and knowing observations of Maurice Duquesne. "Why are you so shocked? They are defeated and they wish to survive. You Americans have never had to live under the conditions of defeat. You have never had to account for the actions of your life. If a German army was occupying New York you would be amazed how many American tongues would waggle."

There began a wild scramble to exonerate one's guilt.

"You must make the Americans understand I joined the party because my job was at stake."

"My job was nonpolitical, strictly nonpolitical, but I was in a position to see what was going on."

"Holstein turned over four Jewish children who were being hidden."

"No matter what Herr Dunkel tells you, he was a Brown Shirt."

"When you question Bargel, remind him of how it was when he was a block warden."

"It is known that the child turned his own mother in."

"Yes, stole the entire business and house of the Jewish family when they disappeared."

The overloaded garbage can spilled and the overflow vomited and the stench mingled in Rombaden's ashes.

Ulrich Falkenstein slept in a mansion confiscated from the brewery owner. It was a twenty-two-room affair on the south bank shared with a half-dozen former Schwabenwald inmates working with the Allied Government.

At five o'clock in the morning of the beginning of the second week of occupation, his phone rang. It was Werner Hoffman.

"What in God's name do you want at this hour!" Falkenstein demanded.

Hoffman answered with a single name. "Klaus Stoll."

He spoke the name of the commandant of Schwabenwald, who had disappeared at the end of the fighting.

"Stoll!" Falkenstein repeated in a chilled whisper.

"And his dear wife, Emma. We have them both."

"Where? How?"

"The information came to us from someone who has a lot to answer for. Stoll has been hiding in the basement of a bombed-out rubble on Friedrichstrasse. He placed his trust in one of our most reliable informers."

"The Allied authorities! Do they know?"

"As a matter of fact it was Lieutenant Blessing who captured Stoll

an hour ago. He said that for the sake of certain identification it would
be a good idea if a dozen or so former inmates from Schwabenwald
interviewed Stoll right in the basement before he is taken into custody."

"God in heaven! Major O'Sullivan will be furious!"

"Major O'Sullivan knows. He said that he will be touring the Landkreis all day. And he added something quite strange. He said, 'What
I don't know won't hurt me.' What did he mean by that, Ulrich?"

Falkenstein threw his blankets off. The blood rushed through his
heart so quickly and heavily he thought his chest would break. He
fought into his clothing, called for his chauffeur, and soon crossed the
pontoon bridge into Rombaden. He was met by Hoffman in the square
in the first light of day.

They stopped before a rubble pile of what had once been Kauf-
mann's Department Store. No one seemed about. Hoffman, grimacing
from the pain of his warped body, and Falkenstein, puffing from age,
stumbled through the wreckage and down into a foul-smelling basement.

A flashlight beam hit them. "In here!" someone called.

They made their way into a cleverly concealed cell all but blocked
by twisted steel and burned-out timbers. They gasped for breath and
adjusted their eyes to the lantern light. A dozen German inmates of
Schwabenwald had been assembled.

On a bed of rags in the corner, Obersturmfuehrer Klaus Stoll and
his wife, Emma, cringed.

One of his former prisoners kicked him in the stomach. The blow
made more noise than damage. "Stand in the presence of Ulrich Falkenstein," the man demanded.

Klaus Stoll slid his back up the wall, holding his arms across his face
to ward off any blows.

Another of them grabbed Emma Stoll by her hair and jerked her
to her feet.

Ulrich pushed through the ring and stood face to face with the
Nazi. Stoll was a great brute of a man, as large in frame as Falkenstein
had once been before the flesh had been beaten from his body. He
looked from Klaus to Emma and back again. He tried to renew the
nine years in Schwabenwald in his mind. There she stood as she was.
A dull, stupid, low-class, foul-mouthed slut. Emma, who wore her
sweaters and skirts tight to taunt the inmates. Emma, who called for

naked men and women to perform for her. Emma, who collapsed in sweaty exhaustion from lashing inmates.

And Klaus Stoll, brewery-wagon driver saved from anonymity by his depraved Nazis. Klaus the braggart, who taunted Ulrich by descriptions of the gassings and how he liked to watch the castrations at the medical experiment center; how he made a half-dozen prisoners kneel head to head and bet he could put a single pistol bullet through their heads.

And Klaus Stoll's killer dog, Messer. The dog strained on the leash waiting for the command, "Kill! . . . Go for the throat, Messer!"

Klaus Stoll's dark face was stubbled, dirty, and sweat-drenched. His black Nazi uniform was torn and caked with dried blood. The swastika was gone. "I am glad you are here, Herr Falkenstein," he said in his semiliterate speech. "You are understanding. I have explained to them that I only followed orders. The Nazis would have killed me if I hadn't obeyed. They held my family as hostage to see that I carried out orders."

"Step back, Ulrich, and let us deal with them."

"Herr Falkenstein! You are a civilized man! You cannot put me at their mercy!"

"Perhaps you are right, Stoll. Perhaps we should call in the Poles."

"God no!" Emma screamed.

Stoll turned to the crippled Hoffman. "Didn't I spare you even against orders."

"Because it was amusing to see me scream in pain with my back." Hoffman snatched up a brick. "Let us see how you will bear the pain of a broken back!"

The Nazi fell to his knees and clasped his hands. "God! God be my merciful judge! I hated every minute of it! They made me do it!"

The ring closed in.

"Wait!" ordered Ulrich Falkenstein with such power and authority they halted. "Let us not be so quick. In places like Schwabenwald human beings were turned into animals so that whores and bums like Klaus and Emma Stoll would become supermen in their own eyes by comparison. Let us see if the superman is made of our stuff. Stand up Klaus Stoll," Falkenstein said in an almost paternal tone. "We shall not lay a hand on you."

Ulrich quieted the others' protests and continued. "Now, Klaus Stoll. Face your wife. Spit in her face as you made us spit on our comrades. Spit I say!"

He spat upon his wife.

"Now, Emma Stoll. Do not wipe the spit. Let it run down your face and into your mouth. Spit on your husband!"

She spat twice.

He ordered them to spit again and again and again until their mouths ran dry, and they were given water and made to spit again.

"Now, Klaus Stoll, slap your wife until her face bleeds."

"Here, Emma Stoll. Take this stick and beat the face of your husband."

And they beat on each other with sickening thuds. The prisoners of Schwabenwald shrunk back from the scene in revulsion. They beat upon each other until Emma Stoll slumped, semiconscious. The Nazi stood over her gasping and weeping and babbling to God for understanding.

"Klaus Stoll!" Falkenstein roared. "Call for your dog!"

"Mercy!"

"Call for your dog, I say!"

"Messer," the Nazi voice whimpered, "Messer."

"Tell Messer to kill! Tell him to go for the throat!"

"Kill . . ." Klaus Stoll choked.

"Aha! Messer does not answer his master's call. Get on your hands and knees and bark like Messer. Bark at your wife."

Klaus Stoll grotesquely groveled about on all fours and barked and snapped at his wife.

Ulrich Falkenstein faced the others, and they knew that he had deliberately made them disgusted with themselves.

"It is enough!" Hoffman cried, dropping his weapon. "Make him stop!"

Klaus Stoll fell exhausted and Ulrich Falkenstein stood over him. "Why didn't you have the decency to kill yourself. . . . Hoffman . . . call the Americans."

CHAPTER TWENTY-THREE

The sheets were soggy with sweat. Dante pushed off the bed on rubbery legs, groped for matches, lit the kerosene lamp, turned the wick up. It flickered shadows about the war-battered room.

The shadows played over Marla's glistening body. She lay on her side, her face buried in the pillow, her hair in disarray on the shambled bed. She was motionless except for the exhaling of deep sensuous groans.

Dante's fuzzy mind tried to work. He washed himself as best he could in the single bucket of water, and then he dressed.

The numbness caused by her bites began to wear off and hurt. Crazy! It's all plain crazy!

The rendezvous had been kept in a bombed-out apartment that her father once used for a mistress in the old days. When Dante arrived, Marla had been waiting in the darkness for well over an hour. They had both reached a kind of madness.

Marla had once been a passive lover. With Wilhelm Frick love-making was an accommodation incidentally enjoyed when times in between were long. With her lovers she asserted a sophisticated superiority which "took care of them."

When her father told her what she must do with Dante Arosa there began an excited anticipation which she had known but once, with the boy in the medical school. For that she had been beaten. And now, she avenged that beating.

The game of bringing Dante Arosa to this moment reminded her how long she had been without a man. Dante's body was hard. He was strong, terribly strong.

From the instant they felt for each other in the blackness of that shabby place Marla burst out with a sweet, brutal, surging power that wouldn't let her stop making love. It happened over and over and over again to her in a quickening succession that drove her beyond control, and it kept happening until she collapsed.

For Dante it was a wildness he had never known, draining him to exhaustion; and then Marla revived and returned to a calm and deadly sophistication. Dante had never known a woman to make love this way. Her calculated calm drew the strength of resistance from his body and his mind with each touch and stroke. These were the victorious moments for Marla, when she had a man helpless. . . . It was the kill!

Dante stood over the bed and lit a cigar. "You'll have to stay till morning. It's past curfew."

Marla rolled over on her back slowly revealing her magnificent body. "Kiss me good night, Dante."

"I'd like to break your goddamned neck," Dante said.

She rolled back again and did not move when his hand traced the line of her hips and thighs. She did not move when the door closed or at the sound of the jeep motor starting.

Dante wove through the rubble-strewn, quiet streets in a stupor. An occasional Polish or American guard stopped him, let him pass.

Oh God! What have I done! Fool! Goddamned stupid fool, Dante! Stupid son of a bitch, Dante!

All the traps she had set blurred: the sweet smell, the brushing past, the half-revealed bosom.

Keep your mind on your interrogation. Be careful of her eyes. She plays the eyes like a virtuoso. Be careful . . . careful. . . .

A long halting silence between questions; he had never met nobility before.

The third and fourth time she was called to his office . . . questions . . . more questions. The time of day stood still until she was brought in . . . .

Why don't I continue this at your home, tomorrow . . .

As you wish, Lieutenant . . .

Touching of hands . . . a kiss . . .

Marla, I've got to see you alone . . .

We could both get into serious trouble . . .

To hell with it. . . .

Dante reached the square. The light was on in Sean's office. The light always seemed to be on there. He was filled with an impulse to drive to the City Hall and tell Sean about it there and then. Sean would understand, cover for him, help him. He drove to the place where the statue of Berwin and Helga stood before the entrance and stopped the jeep. They are all killers . . . all of them . . . love and death.

Dante started the motor and sped toward the pontoon bridge and his quarters on the south bank. Go back, Dante! Damned fool, go back! Now! Now! See Sean, now!

In the three tormented days that passed Dante Arosa relived the orgy minute by minute, again and again. Neither rationalization nor self-pity nor mortification helped any longer.

On the fourth day he called in one of his MP's. "Sergeant, drive over to Marla Frick and bring her back here for questioning."

"Yes, sir."

Marla and Dante's eyes met. There was mutual hatred in both, and mutual desire. Wordlessly they both said, "Yes, tonight and every night."

CHAPTER TWENTY-FOUR

Except for a single mansion occupied by Ulrich Falkenstein and his deputies the balance of the south-bank estates had been requisitioned for American personnel. However, many members of Pilot Team G-5 rarely saw their luxurious accommodations for their working hours in those first days were as staggering as the task.

One home, formerly belonging to the owner of the river-boat and barge yard, was named the "old people's home," a dubious honor to its occupants, the senior members of the team: Tidings, the banker, True-blood, the curator, Hickman, the agricultural economist, Sam Alterman, the communications expert, Maurice Duquesne, and Dr. Geoffrey Grimwood.

No one worked, or was expected to, the hours of the commander, except for Geoffrey Grimwood, who never saw his suite or, for that matter, bothered to move into it.

Grimwood took a room in the hospital so that he might have constant command of the hourless struggle to save the lives of the Schwabenwald inmates. Most of the 3000 patients in the hospital and cathedral were on the brink of death, with few resources to combat the effects of starvation and a half dozen other death-bearing diseases.

Grimwood waged tireless battle for every life. With but marginal knowledge of starvation and its side effects he had kept the death rate under 10 per cent. There was a direct line open to a camp called Bergen-Belsen, where the British Army had run into another and larger situation much like Schwabenwald.

It was long past midnight when Sean called it quits in his office. He drove down the square to the hospital and found Grimwood bleary-eyed at his desk. They revived themselves with a transfusion of coffee.

The Englishman wiped his eyes and focused them on a pocket watch. "Oh, good Lord. I've missed the staff meeting."

"The board of directors of Rombaden Ltd. reports that the situation is still crapped up."

"How is the plumbing?"

Sean searched his weary mind. "Hank Greenberg gave me a figure in cubic meters. I can't remember it. He says he can get the distillation plant in partial operation in about a week and triple the water ration."

"Sewage?"

Sean shook his head. "The main generator was hit. We have no replacement parts. How goes the war here?"

Grimwood held up two crossed fingers. "We're giving it a go."

Sean walked to the glass separation, which looked out to a ward. "I can't believe it yet. Death factories. Murder on an assembly-line basis."

"It's the children out there who break one's heart. Poor little tykes. Most remember no life other than Schwabenwald. Just about their only contact with humanity is the fierce loyalty they have for one another . . . but love is a new experience to them. Can you imagine a child of ten who doesn't know how to smile? We may be able to mend their bodies . . . but their minds? Lord knows I've seen enough famine in India. But this! The hand of fellow man."

"Haven't you heard, Doc. There was no Schwabenwald. It never really happened."

Grimwood grunted with irony. "I should be able to deliver a memorable paper to the Royal Academy on starvation."

Sean looked slyly at the Englishman. "How about delivering a paper on hijacking medical supplies while you're at it?"

Grimwood nearly choked on his coffee. "What the devil . . ."

"If prohibition ever comes back to the States I'm nominating you to lead a gang of bootleggers."

"Damn it all, Major. We have three thousand desperately ill people. I can't wait for forms in triplicate to be acted upon."

Sean held up his hand. "Hold it. We're on the same team. I've got nothing against using Kentucky windage. Only let me know what you're doing. The surgeon general nailed me on the phone this morning."

Grimwood huffed a laugh through his moustache. "Here I thought I was being devilishly clever." He reached across his desk and touched Sean's sleeve. "Major . . . I've got grandchildren the age of some of those little tykes out there. We can't stand on formalities."

Sean nodded that he understood.

"And what the devil do I do about personnel? I can't use the Germans . . . even those you didn't imprison. Doctors, indeed! So we have six doctors for three thousand dying."

"I'm trying like hell to get you more."

"I've been thinking it over," Grimwood said coyly. "Castle Romstein is sitting empty except for that old spook Trueblood rambling about evaluating the art pieces. A hundred and twenty-two rooms. It would make a lovely rehabilitation camp."

Sean's eyes narrowed. Grimwood was a lousy poker player. He had not only been thinking it over, but had obviously devised a plan. "Go on."

Grimwood cleared his throat guiltily. "Well now, there are a half-dozen American field and base hospitals simply roving around this area. American casualties haven't been heavy enough to justify the number of medical personnel. Well now . . . one of these units would adore setting up a base in Castle Romstein."

Sean had the drift of it. "And in exchange for giving them Castle Romstein we would reach an understanding with them to press their personnel, equipment, and supplies into our situation."

"Precisely."

"The idea has merit, Doc. Let me sleep on it and give you an answer tomorrow." Sean arose and stretched heartily, shook hands, and made for the door.

"Oh, Major . . ."

"Yes."

"Bye the bye. I did just happen to run into Dr. Pobirs from the Sixty-Second Field Hospital at Stuttgart. I was up there er . . . to requisition for supplies . . . and so forth and so forth. One thing led to another and we drove down to look over Castle Romstein . . ."

"When are they moving in?"

"Tomorrow."

"Grimwood. You're a limey son of a bitch."

"Thanks, old chap. I knew you'd agree."

Sean threw up his hands in a gesture of "defeat."

"Major! With their forty doctors and nurses I'll save every man, woman, and child out there and in the cathedral."

"You don't have to explain, Doc."

CHAPTER TWENTY-FIVE

Sean kept the capture of Klaus and Emma Stoll quiet until he had received instructions from headquarters and had prepared for a flood of journalists.

Bertrand Collier, his press and information officer, had reacted quickly to the revelations of Schwabenwald. He set up tours of the concentration camp and prepared fact sheets and south-bank living quarters for the newspapermen.

The capture was announced and they poured into Rombaden. They were allowed to see Stoll and his wife from a distance in their overly guarded cells, but no one was permitted an interview.

One of the journalists to arrive in Rombaden was Cornelia Hollingshead, a phenomenon because of her sex. She was a war correspondent for Whittsett Press and its syndicate, Global Alliance. She had built a world legion of readers.

Even beneath dungarees and battle jacket, Corney was not without obvious feminine charm—long soft hair, a well-endowed bust, and sensuous lips. Femininity notwithstanding, Corney was more than a match for her male colleagues. Her ethics were under question more than once. Moreover, Whittsett Press and Global Alliance had a well-earned reputation of sensationalism over accuracy.

The Whittsett Press and their twenty-six newspapers backed Lieutenant General Arnold Cleveland for the position of Supreme Commander of Allied Forces. General Cleveland was a top man as generals went but by the time Whittsett Press and Corney Hollingshead finished glorifying him they had jacked him up to a notch over the Almighty Himself. To make matters worse, Corney was shacked up with him and trying to get him to leave his wife.

When Eisenhower was selected over Cleveland, the Whittsett Press and Corney went off like a pair of time bombs. They went so far as to call the President and General George Marshall traitors. Had the Whittsett Press published in any other country in the middle of a war, it is doubtful that they would have survived their own venom.

Corney Hollingshead romped all over England and France and Germany, a colossal pain to the authorities who were afraid to touch the sacred cow, Whittsett Press and Global Alliance.

She arrived in Rombaden determined to do a little "creative" writing to beef up the already ghastly concentration-camp stories. Bertrand Collier personally met her, gave her a beautiful suite of apartments, and a VIP tour.

She was not satisfied. She looked over officers of the Pilot Team to see who could do her the most good. Maurice Duquesne was her candidate to get her entry where other newsmen could not tread.

Duquesne accepted Corney's advances without particular personal pride. He knew what she was up to, and besides, he had not had a woman since France. Why not?

The Frenchman fenced brilliantly in her apartment without giving direct promises. The lure of sharing the bed made Duquesne intimate to her that she might have access to special information.

And so, they had an affair. The entire thing was annoying to Duquesne. He felt as though he had been raped. Corney was a very bad lover, aggressive and with about as much finesse as a bulldozer. It was sad for Maurice, for he had felt certain that a woman who depended on those particular talents as much as she would have done a better job developing them.

By morning their affair was done and through. She did not seem to mind much, she had been rebuffed before. What made her furious was that Duquesne left without a concession.

Later she drove to Schwabenwald and began to nose around the cottages of the SS officers now under Polish guard. This did not pose much of a problem. The nice lady bribed them with cigarettes with ridiculous ease and was soon inside the cottage of Klaus and Emma Stoll poking through everything—closets, drawers, desks, under beds.

In the dining room she was attracted to a rough-hewn old Bavarian china closet containing Emma Stoll's Rosenthal set and a set of silverware with intricately carved bone handles. She had found her key!

Later she went to the cathedral to interview former Schwabenwald inmates. She primed them to speak of the thousands of rumors one hears in such a place. Cornelia Hollingshead got some facts, some half truths told by sick, impassioned, hate-filled people, added rumors, and concocted a story that was the topper to the whole sordid concentration-camp chapter. Cornelia Hollingshead indeed, was not outdone by anyone! She wrote:

Frau Emma Stoll gave special orders to the SS guards in the extermination center to be on the lookout for particular types of Slavic and
Jewish skulls.

It has been substantiated by irrefutable sources that Emma Stoll personally went to the bone-crushing machines to inspect new batches of
skulls daily. She hand-picked the most suitable samples.

These skulls were used to carve the handles on her silverware . . .

Before Cornelia Hollingshead's story could be confirmed, denied, or
investigated it was accepted by a world now ready to believe anything
coming out of Germany's horror camps.

Dull, stupid Emma Stoll had gained eternal infamy as the queen of
ghouls. Emma Stoll's name would become symbolic of the universal
monster. Indeed! Human skulls for silverware handles! Belatedly, the
world cried for her head to roll!

The big American was passed by the guards to the south-bank mansion occupied by the commander of Pilot Team G-5. He used the front
door knocker. Alfred Oberdorfer opened it in behalf of his new master.

"Sir?" inquired the servant.

"*Spraechen sie* English?"

"*Nein, bitte.*"

The big American grunted and continued the conversation in a sort
of German. "Tell Major O'Sullivan that Nelson Goodfellow Bradbury
has arrived from places beyond the horizon with a duffel bag filled
with scotch, dirty laundry, and cigarettes for the black market."

Good butler Oberdorfer was puzzled. "A moment, please," he said,
bowed, and then walked to Sean's study and knocked. "There is an
American outside, sir, speaking of dirty laundry and whiskey. His name
is Goodfellow."

"Big Nellie!"

Alfred Oberdorfer watched the two men embrace and pound each
other's backs. "You ugly son of a bitch!"

Alfred was disgusted. The Americans were strange people. In the old
days such displays never took place in these halls. Things were proper
when Herr Schoof was the master. God be hopeful Herr Schoof will
return someday.

"Some layout you've got here lad."

"Joint belonged to the publisher of the newspaper. One of Von Romstein's relatives. Heidi!"

Alfred's wife answered the call in a trot, tying on her maid's apron as she ran. She bowed.

"Get these bags up to one of the guest rooms. See to it Herr Bradbury's clothes are all in order by tomorrow . . . and make us some dinner."

The husband and wife reacted to the terse commands, struggling with Big Nellie's bottle-loaded officer's bags.

During the dinner he related to Sean his adventures with Patton's Third Army when it broke into Czechoslovakia. "Patton almost broke down and cried when they ordered him back. He was dying to take Prague. When he finished crying he started cursing. He went on for an hour without repeating himself. I think we should have let him take Prague . . ."

As he spoke he saw signs of fatigue in Sean. Sean's mind seemed to react slowly, spending words as though he had to think them over three or four times before they took hold.

Something else seemed to be missing from Sean too. Tim had been the wild one, Sean was even keeled, had a quality of gentleness. He watched the near brutal harshness with which he ordered his servants about; the phone calls were taken with crackling anger; his expression of hatred of Germans was barely disguised. And, the whiskey hit Sean too fast.

"Been rough?" Big Nellie asked.

"Only on my soul," Sean answered. "I'm sorry. After sixteen hours in the boiler factory I've got to drink it under. The commander drinks alone and spills his guts to no one."

"Hi ho the dairio, the commander drinks alone."

"How in the hell could they do it!"

"Schwabenwald, Dachau, Buchenwald? I hear they've found some in Poland that make these look like resorts."

"So I get potted at night. General Hansen told me once about the beauty of military government. To most soldiers the enemy is an abstract thing, unseen, unheard. Neither Tim nor Liam ever saw him face to face or knew the hand of the man who killed them. Maybe the general was right. Maybe it is too much for me to live among my brothers' murderers. I swear I've tried to be fair!"

"Sean, I saw General Hansen before I came here. He's got it clear up to his eyeballs. Without his pilot team . . ."

"I know. Thank God I've got Ulrich Falkenstein. Trouble is, there aren't many Falkensteins in Germany."

"And your team?"

"When we were in England looking at maps, talking in abstract problems, planning like a bunch of advertising executives, Rombaden was a kind of game. In France it was a blast. We came as liberators. Maurice Duquesne spoke the language. No problems. But now . . . I'm forced to fight my own people . . . and to live alone . . . and defend Germans. And what's more I miss Nan Milford. I'm sick for missing her. I've been at the point of begging back a dozen times."

"You'll get turned down, Sean. Spare yourself that."

Sean nodded and croaked, "I know." He drank long and hard from his glass, and made another drink as his servants cleared the table. Sean looked at them with anger.

"Look at these two krauts, Nellie. Steady folks. Been here for years. *Wie lange haben sie hier gearbitet?*"

"*Zwei und zwangig jahre.*"

"Twenty-two years, Nellie. Hasn't got a mean bone in his body. These two got a dachshund. They treat that little dog like it was a baby. Alfred and Heidi wouldn't think of eating until they go through the leftovers and pick out the best for their dog. And man, you ought to see them with their grandchildren. Sentimental, loving. Germans wouldn't go hurting little kids, would they Alfred?"

The butler, not understanding, merely bowed.

"*Schwabenwald war schlecht, nicht wahr?*"

Alfred clasped his hands together and wrung them in horror in agreement that the concentration camp was a terrible place. The wife became uneasy at Sean's whiskey-inspired prodding.

Nellie watched the scene with fascination.

"Their cottage out back got a hit. Busted down the wall on one side. You should see these two on their off hours. He drags rubble from across the river to patch up the wall and momma here is getting all the window boxes painted and planted and neat. Petunias and pansies."

The table was cleared. The servants stood at attention.

"Yes sir, a kindly folk. Love their dogs, love their kids and gardens. Love their forests and poetry and music. They told me so, themselves. Lost one of their sons on the Russian front. They told me something else too. They told me people shouldn't kill each other. How about it, Alfred. People shouldn't kill people's brothers, should they?"

The bewildered man shrugged.

"Whiskey, ice, soda and *raus*," Sean snapped. "The former occupant, Herr Schoof, published the newspaper. Nazi . . . but a special sort of Nazi. The party was full of thugs and bums so they liked to get rich elite boys like Schoof. He's locked up in Schwabenwald, indignant as hell. He was truly anti-Nazi. He told me so. Nobody knows nothing. I've got two hundred SS guards from Schwabenwald who didn't even know there was an extermination center there. How about that? To-morrow," Sean continued, filling Nellie's glass, "I'll give you the com-mander's personal tour of Schwabenwald."

"Thanks anyhow. I got my baptism at a guest home for political pris-oners on the ancestral estates of the Count of Dachau. Any truth about Corney Hollingshead's story?"

"I dunno. I've sent samples to Switzerland, the States, and Sweden for analysis. I wish I could send Corney there too. She's planning to give us the pleasure of her company for fifteen more articles and she's getting nasty about an interview with Emma Stoll."

"To Corney. A credit to my noble profession. O'Sullivan, I am about to give you the antidote to Hollingshead poison. Try this on her to-morrow . . ."

Cornelia Hollingshead was outraged!

"I am not accustomed," she said in a husky voice, "to being kept wait-ing in the anteroom of junior officers. I demand to know why I was locked out of my apartment and why my press credentials were re-voked."

"Despite my lowly rank, I am at liberty to determine and act upon undesirable elements in my district."

"Dammit, I said I want to know why!"

"You filed an unauthorized and unconfirmed story having grave con-sequences."

"Don't go pulling that Little Lord Fauntleroy crap on me, buster. People want atrocity stories and that's what they're going to get."

"In this district freedom of the press is not extended to pathological liars. If you aren't out of Romstein Landkreis in two hours, you're go-ing to get jailed."

Corney leaned over his desk and began to laugh and snarl at the same time. "Major, you're begging for it. I use little boys like you to wash my panties. Maybe you don't know who I am and what I'm going to do to you. You're going to get run right out of this Army, buster."

"I'm snowed under with work, Miss Hollingshead. I would appreciate your departure without further rhetoric."

"All right, but make sure you read the Whittsett Press tomorrow. America is going to be reading about the Black Major."

"Really? What about the Black Major?"

Cornie's yellow journalistic imagination came into play.

"Did the Black Major experiment with the Schwabenwald gas chambers, using German prisoners of war as guinea pigs? How's that for a starter? Why did the Black Major desecrate the Marienkirche Cathedral and jail an anti-Nazi priest? Does the Black Major have brothels in Rombaden so his troops can bypass the nonfraternization laws? Has the Black Major opened Swiss bank accounts? Are you getting the idea, buster? Now you hear this! *You arrange that interview with Emma Stoll!*"

Sean could not believe the venom coming from this wrathful creature. "It has just occurred to me," he said, "that you are the first American I have ever met with pure Nazi mentality."

Cornelia Hollingshead's lips thinned and her teeth gnashed as she stomped for the door.

"Miss Hollingshead! Would you care to venture a guess as to what well-known lady war correspondent gave a dose of clap to what well-known major general in Paris . . ."

She stopped in her tracks and spun around. "You son of a bitch!"

"Shame on you. Gonorrhea at your age. Let's understand each other. The account of your . . . er . . . indiscretion in Paris has been written by a correspondent who has an audience as large as yours and twice as discriminating. I have it in my desk and am free to file it at will. Questions?"

The blackmailer had been blackmailed. She became amused . . . beaten badly at her own game. There was but one weapon left in her arsenal. Smiling, she walked toward him. . . .

"Have a nice trip, Corney. Besides, I hear you're a lousy lay."

CHAPTER TWENTY-SIX

TO: COMMANDING OFFICER, G-5, FRANKFURT
FROM: MILITARY COMMANDER, PILOT TEAM G-5. ROM-
BADEN/ROMSTEIN

SUBJECT: Hollingshead, Cornelia. Correspondent accredited to
Whittsett Press/Global Alliance News Syndicate.

The presence of the above named journalist is, in my opinion, detri-
mental to the best interests of the function of military government in
this district.
I have, therefore, in accordance with my authority, suspended press
credentials and ordered same from my district.

Sean O'Sullivan, Major
Commander, Pilot Team G-5

Andrew Jackson Hansen damned near had apoplexy when he read
the terse report. One did not give the shaft to Corney without dire consequences.

Headquarters in Frankfurt stood by for the cyclone to blow in from
Rombaden. To their chagrin, Corney came in meekly and filed a story
that "her" war was over in Europe and she was off to the Pacific and
battlefields yet unconquered.

Although there was a simultaneous sigh of relief, no one felt that
even the Marines deserved Corney.

A few days later, when Nelson Goodfellow Bradbury arrived, Hansen sniffed a rat and tried to pump him.

"General," Big Nellie purred, "one of these days ask General Borof
Roth why he couldn't attend the liberation ceremonies in Paris."

And that's about all he would say.

Hansen watched the reports flow in from Rombaden with obvious
pride. O'Sullivan's performance vindicated his judgment. Rombaden
was weeks, even months ahead of most cities.

May 1. Enough rubble has been cleared so we have one-way traffic, at
least, on all major thoroughfares.

May 2. 60% of all known former Nazis have been purged from civic positions and are on rubble-cleaning details.

May 3. We have restored enough power for Allied use, hospitals, and certain emergencies.

May 4. Captain Greenberg has located a generator in Munich similar to the main generator for the sewage-processing plant. He horse-traded for enough parts to improvise the rebuilding of the Rombaden generator.

May 5. All liberated Poles, Jews, and other displaced persons in the area are registered, housed, and those capable have been assigned to useful employment.

May 5. The eastern bridge over the Landau has been restored to operation.

May 6. The water-distillation plant is 20% in operation. We are therefore able to raise the water ration to six buckets per day per family.

May 7. Barge works partly reopened.

May 8. Three small factories partly reopened. All factories will use rubble as their basic raw material.
    a. Hümpelmeyer Plant formerly making steel helmets now converted to pots, pans, kitchen utensils, etc.
    b. Struger Factory formerly making hand grenades now returned to traditional toy and puppet making.
    c. Landau Works, formerly making stock handles for rifles now returned to furniture refinishing.

May 11. Leather factory reopened.

May 13. We now have seven full labor battalions on rubble clearance, demolition, and public works. Two battalions consist of ex-Nazis, two of prisoners of war; the rest, civilians.

May 14. We are happy to report that the entire population has received multiple shots for typhus and typhoid and has been vaccinated. We have completed 70% of the delousing procedures as an antityphus precaution.

May 18. Telephone and telegraph service for Allied use has been restored.

May 25. Three banks in full operation.

May 27. A makeshift public transportation system has begun using horse-drawn vehicles and carts pulled by bicycles.

June 1. The sewage plant is now in partial operation.

And so it went. Rombaden/Romstein became a pilot light. From all over the American and British sectors the urgent call was sent to Frankfurt, "What does Rombaden say about this?"

"What do the Rombaden people do in case of . . . ?"

"How are they handling this problem in Rombaden . . . ?"

"Clear it with Rombaden."

That was the new password . . . clear it with Rombaden, as men struggled to find the wisdom of Solomon and the strength of Atlas in this obliterated land. Germany's cities were as bleak as the face of the moon and there was no railroad or barges or bridges . . . no mail, no communications, no schools, no courts of law . . . no radio, no press, and damned little food.

Three million angered liberated slaves raped and looted and destroyed the western sectors; three million Allied soldiers from the West walked her land; and seven million of her men were prisoners of the West.

Ration was cut back to a thousand calories, about two thirds the minimum needed to sustain human life.

It was not only the broken body of Germany, it was the degradation they had imposed upon humanity. It was the terrible German sickness shown naked.

There was but a handful of Ulrich Falkensteins. The Nazi era had stripped the nation of government, of police, of intellectuals. Germany's jewel, her manhood, was dead, maimed, imprisoned. And a strange thing happened. For the first time, the second-class citizen, the German woman, was asked to take over the government as well as clean the mess from the streets.

June 5. I am happy to report we are beginning a master plan for the reconstruction of Rombaden.

June 7. Today, Lieutenant Shenandoah Blessing accepted and began the training of seven Germans as a nucleus for a new Rombaden police force.

June 10. Today Ulrich Falkenstein became the first German publisher of a German newspaper. In a week we are hopeful of operating a 25-watt, hand-powered radio station for the area.

June 12. Under Ulrich Falkenstein's Educational Committee, the task of rewriting the elementary textbooks has begun.

One by one General Hansen tested new laws, new ideas on Rombaden to learn if it would work out for the rest of the zone. Feeling Sean O'Sullivan had complete control of the area Hansen issued the edict there that no former Nazi could be employed at anything but common labor. This sweeping ruling was quickly followed up by the Questionnaire, the *Fragebogen,* which every adult had to fill out, accounting in full for every action during the Nazi era. In 131 soul-searching questions nothing was omitted . . . nothing left to chance. As the Fragebogen stripped every façade in Rombaden, pried behind blank eyes and sealed lips, Hansen made plans to use it in the entire American zone.

June 15. I am personally convinced that Ulrich Falkenstein has succeeded in purging the government of this district of all former Nazis. They have been replaced by people with undisputable anti-Nazi records. Unfortunately, most of them are totally inexperienced in government. However, the purging of all Nazis from official positions has brought Rombaden to an important plateau.

Henceforth, I shall turn over the responsibility and function of government to them, bit by bit, as they prove they can handle it.

In due course I will allow divergent political parties to begin to operate.

I am personally hopeful we will be able to have a free election within a year.

CHAPTER TWENTY-SEVEN

The most unobtrusive member of Pilot Team G-5 was H. W. Trueblood, an ex-curator of the British Museum. The old fellow was more than content, he was ecstatic spending his days in the cellars below the Rombaden Kuntshalle uncrating and cataloguing the museum's works. Each evening he emerged looking like a pale gopher, but thoroughly enraptured by the stimulation of being surrounded by the work of the masters.

When Sean learned that Geoffrey Grimwood had "loaned" Castle
Romstein to a field hospital, he sent Trueblood to the castle immediately
to take down, catalogue, and store the art works against theft.

Trueblood chose the immense castle library as his workroom. Room
by room, precious paintings, urns, statues and statuettes, armor and
tapestries were removed to the library until it took on the appearance
of a multimillion-dollar junk yard. A day and night guard was put on
the library as Trueblood began the painstaking work of identifying and
recording each single item.

On his third day at the castle, he phoned Sean O'Sullivan.

"I say, could you spare a bit of time, Major, and dash over here. I've
struck the pot of gold at the end of the rainbow. And bye the bye, bring
the fat policeman with you."

"Gawddamn," Blessing said when he arrived with Sean, "looks like
old Mr. Hawkins' antique store."

Trueblood led them to a corner holding a separate stack of paintings.

"I suppose you want to know why I called you over. It appears that
Count Ludwig had a passion for the French post-impressionist period.
Mind you, that is not my forte, but these works here have achieved
such a measure of renown that they are commonly known." He lifted
the first in the line. "Toulouse-Lautrec's 'Portrait of Suzanne Valadon,'
vintage 1885." Setting the painting aside he held the next two up, one
by one. "These are Gauguins . . . 'Vahine no de Taire' and, of course,
'Seashore at Martinique.' This one here we know is a Van Gogh . . .
'Field at Saint-Remy.' Quite a foursome, would you not say? I took them
out of Count Ludwig's personal quarters."

Blessing didn't understand what was so hot about the paintings but
was impressed that the Englishman called them off like names of his
children.

Sean was already ahead of it. "Where are they from?"

"The Carlsberg Glyptotek in Copenhagen."

Sean let out a long whistle.

"Let's carry on, shall we? Van de Velde, seventeenth century, 'Woman
at a Window' . . . Royal Museum of Fine Art, Antwerp. Lemmen,
'Harbor View' . . . Giroux Gallery in Brussels, and so forth and so
forth. These last three are Renoirs from private collections in France."

"You mean he stole these?" Blessing asked. "But, hell, we've got better
painters than this in the Hook County Fair."

"Certainly not. This lot represents in excess of a million dollars."

"Gawd."

"We have suspected all along that many high Nazi officials in occupied countries developed a sudden penchant for collecting art, other people's art, that is. We think Goering alone has stolen millions from France."

"Do you think there's more of them here?" Sean asked.

"I'd wager on it."

Sean thought quickly. "Come back to Rombaden with me, Trueblood. We'll try to get a line through to this museum in Copenhagen as a starter and find out under what conditions these were taken and what other pieces are missing. Blessing, round up everyone who worked in the castle or on the grounds. Grill their asses off. Promise them cigarettes, double rations, anything. We want to know every cellar, cave, secret passage . . . any possible place a cache could be hidden . . ."

"What about the count?"

"Put a twenty-four-hour tail on him."

Sean went immediately to Dante Arosa's office.

"I'm going to need everything you have on Count Ludwig right away. Matter of fact, give me the records on the entire family."

Dante was startled. "What the hell's up?"

"I'll know for sure in a few hours. Run the files into my office."

Dante laughed weakly. "Hell, there's nothing you can find out by breaking your head on the records. What is it you are after?"

In that instant, Sean sensed Dante's uneasiness. An iota of suspicion had fallen on him. "I'm not quite sure what I'm after," he said carefully.

Dante shrugged. "Well . . . they're really not up to date . . ."

Sean was disturbed. "Let's have them . . . now."

"Sure . . . sure . . ."

The voluminous files of the interrogation of Ludwig Von Romstein was studied for hours. Dates of his visits to Denmark, Belgium, Holland, and France could certainly concur with the thefts, but as Sean read on past midnight the finding of the art treasures began to take on a secondary meaning.

Dante Arosa's files began to make an ugly revelation. "Oh God, no," Sean whispered to himself. But he read on. He lifted the phone. "Operator, see if Lieutenant Arosa is in his quarters," Sean asked.

Sean dropped his head on his hands, rubbed his temples, beat his fist slowly on the desk, counting each ring of the unanswered phone.

"Sorry, sir, Lieutenant Arosa doesn't answer. Shall I try the jail. Sometimes he's there late on interrogations."

Sean looked at his watch. Almost one o'clock in the morning. "Try the jail."

"No, sir, no one has seen Lieutenant Arosa . . . shall I . . ."

"Get Lieutenant Bolinski. Tell him to report here to me at once. Then call Castle Romstein, locate Blessing . . . he's either in the castle or on the grounds. Tell him to report here."

Sean slumped back in his chair. His eyes welled with tears. Why in the name of God did Dante do it? Sean continued to read more deeply into the documents.

Bolinski was still drowsy from his rude awakening, but having worked under O'Sullivan he was used to having his sleep interrupted. Sean apologized to his legal officer for the hour; through a yawn Bolinski said it was okay.

Sean questioned him carefully. "Bo, you've been drawing up the recommendations for the indictments against the Von Romstein family. How far have you gotten on it?"

Bolinski scratched his jaw. "I've been going through the interrogations and recommendations. Matter of fact, I wanted to talk to you about it."

"How do you feel about our case?"

"Dante Arosa seems to think the count is pretty clean."

"Are we going to be able to link him with Schwabenwald?"

"Not according to Dante."

"How about crimes against humanity for use of slave labor?"

Bolinski shook his head.

"Any known collusion between Ludwig and the Nazi brother?"

"According to the interrogations the count looks as pure as driven snow. If we go on Dante's stuff we couldn't get a conviction for jay walking."

Sean nodded. "Thanks. Sorry I woke you up, Bo. Keep it quiet."

"Sure."

Sean watched from his south window, looking toward the bridge, waiting for Blessing's headlights to come into view. He watched the jeep cross the bridge, park, and the fat man make his way out.

"Lord almighty," Blessing said to Sean's back, "I got twenty men digging around in passageways inside passageways. They're turning the castle inside out." Then the weariness of the hours fell on him. "Well, one thing good about nonfraternization—been working so hard I haven't seen the end of my pecker for a month."

Sean spun about. "Where's Dante Arosa?"

"How the hell am I supposed to know?"

"If you're my police chief, you damned well better know."

"Hell's afire. You call me over here just to . . ."

"Don't get folksy with me, Blessing!"

"Can't talk to you when you're riled up like this . . ."

"You've been covering up for him, haven't you?"

Blessing turned beet red.

Sean's arm and shoulder muscles bulged with anger. "I ought to bust you in your fat stomach!"

Blessing fell into a chair. "I only knew about it for a week. I swear to you, Major, I just found out about it. I've been going through plain hell, Major . . . just plain hell. I know Dante's been doing something wrong but I swear . . . I just couldn't bring myself to telling you. I just hope to God he ain't hurt you."

Slowly Sean's anger ebbed from him. Now there were two of them in the predicament.

"In my work," Blessing said, "I have to use informers. You hate the goddamned little wart who squeals, but you've got to use him. Informers are the lowest polecats in the world. I just didn't want to become one myself. I was going to talk to Dante . . . try to set him straight . . ."

"Too late now."

"What's he gone and done?"

"Whitewashed the whole Von Romstein family. He's doctored up every report, every interrogation."

"How'd he figure he'd get away with it?"

"With so many tens of thousands of legal processes being drawn up he figured we'd be long gone from Rombaden before Von Romstein got into court. I suppose there's a woman involved?"

Blessing nodded.

"Who? Von Romstein's daughter?"

"Yeah. I followed him last week and waited until he left. I stayed until dawn and saw her come out and tailed her home."

"Where are they?"

"Bombed-out apartment down near the factory."

"Let's go."

They parked two blocks away from the apartment. They tiptoed the rest of the way through the silent streets. Blessing pointed to the second floor of a badly shattered house; then they retreated around the corner to where Dante's jeep was hidden inside an archway of a courtyard.

"We can rush it."

"No," Sean whispered, "at least let him have the dignity of being caught with his pants on. I'll stay here by his jeep. You watch the apartment and pick up the woman when she shows up later."

One o'clock.

Sean sat in Dante's jeep. Starving alley cats screamed in protest, for there was no garbage to scavenge. The rancid smell and the stillness of a death-haunted street enveloped him.

Two o'clock: Sean dozed for an instant and awoke, heart pounding with remembering where he was and what was happening. There might have been a tinge of envy, but it was drowned in anger and sorrow for Dante. What was it like to steal love in a slimy pit? . . . burning with fear . . . with guilt. What kind of love was it? Would not the urge to choke the German woman in her bed be too tempting?

Two-thirty: soft, quick footsteps. A shadow over the rubble. A trot. A long, deep and uneven sigh. Dante Arosa lit a cigar.

He felt someone alongside him. Bum joke in the darkness . . . no . . . he lit another match. Sean was there, beside him . . . no dream! Dante gripped the steering wheel and emitted only a single pathetic groan of despair.

"Drive to my office," Sean said coldly.

When they were there Sean slammed the door behind them. Dante began to cry and Sean slapped his face.

"You stupid son of a bitch!"

"Oh God! What will my mother and father say?"

"You stupid stupid son of a bitch!"

"She loves me!" Dante cried in desperation.

"She loves her father! You've been had! You're a stupid son of a bitch!"

"Oh God! I've brought shame to my family . . . oh God . . ."

"Thanks for remembering them."

Dante began to shake and sweat at the same instant. "What are you going to do to me, Sean?"

CHAPTER TWENTY-EIGHT

Count Ludwig Von Romstein could feel any shift in the wind. Already, he could detect a softening attitude on the part of the Americans. New American troops, who had not been in the battle for Germany, were coming in; they were not nearly so filled with righteous anger. Chinks were showing in the nonfraternization armor. It was a ridiculous rule, particularly for Americans. Americans wanted to be loved, even by their enemy. This was an exploitable weakness.

Weakness? The Americans were full of them. Another conqueror would have left the German people to shift for themselves in the ashes. They would have taken what they wanted as booty . . . as the Russians were doing; but the noble American seemed inflamed by the desire to restore city, state, and country to its inhabitants and return the rule to them. The Americans showed little physical brutality . . . they were childish in their de-Nazification procedures with their silly questionnaire.

There was one sure way to de-Nazify Rombaden that Ludwig knew of. That was, line them up against a wall and shoot them down. If, indeed, the first month had passed without an execution, the Nazis would worm their way back into power. To be sure they would keep in hiding until the climate was more receptive, but they would return, nonetheless. Germany boasted of sixteen million Nazis. Germany had no other trained people capable of running the country . . . the Nazis would return.

"Good morning, my dear Major O'Sullivan," Ludwig said with contempt when Blessing brought him in. "I am informed by your police that I am to be arrested."

Sean was haggard from the ordeal of the affair with Dante Arosa and grunted hoarsely at the German.

"And for what horrendous crime am I to be charged?"

"Don't glorify yourself. You're being locked up as a common thief."

Ludwig Von Romstein smarted. "I beg your . . ."

"Your passion for post-impressionist art ran away with you."

"You refer of course to the Van Goghs, Gauguins, and so forth in my apartment in Castle Romstein."

Sean nodded.

"Well, that can be easily explained. If I had any guilt, I would have hidden them. They were gifts."

"The Glyptopek in Copenhagen begs to differ."

Lout! Ludwig thought. Had he again underestimated the American? How the devil did he find out so quickly? "I . . . I am astounded to hear they belong to a museum."

"I'll bet you are."

"On my word, they were presents to me from various high officials in occupied countries. You see, I had occasion to visit Denmark, the Low Countries, and France as a member of the armaments board . . ."

"Stop the horse crap. I'm tired. We have located the entire cache in the basement of your hunting lodge and the caves near the Roman antiquities."

Good Lord! The German cleared his throat and thought with great rapidity. "Those . . . were . . . sent to me by Goering from France for safekeeping."

"Safekeeping from whom? The rightful owners?"

"I demand the right to prove my innocence. I should like to go before an American court immediately."

"First things first. You're going to be reinterrogated by the new CIC officer."

These words crashed in on him; his immaculate composure became threadbare. Von Romstein looked away from Sean's hard, disgust-filled eyes. Now he felt entirely boxed, trapped. He tried to ask about Marla . . . he couldn't.

"In case you are wondering, your daughter was put in prison this morning."

Beads of sweat popped out on the German's brow. They fell down his face, into his dueling scar. "If Marla committed any indiscretion, you certainly cannot blame me."

"Sure. You're just an innocent victim of a lot of uncouth people. Your brother the Nazi, Goering, and now your daughter. They were all out to get you, weren't they?"

"My innocence will be proved in court."

"You're not going before an American court, Von Romstein. I make that my personal mission. When we find enough anti-Nazis in Rombaden, we are going to license a German court."

"A German court!"

"Certainly you want justice from your own people."

The implications were clear. The first German courts would be on a binge of vengeance to show the world they were going to purge the Nazi era without mercy. Ludwig Von Romstein became faint with fright at the idea. All the calculations, all the carefully built plans crumbled. Why the hell hadn't he made the dash for Switzerland? Oh Lord, the German courts would be bloodthirsty for revenge. Twenty years . . . thirty . . . forty . . . Oh Lord . . . what has this mad fool Hitler brought me to?

"What are you going to do with Arosa," Maurice Duquesne demanded of Sean.

"I know what I'd like to do."

"You've got to protect that boy."

"Like hell I do."

"If he is court-martialed under this idiotic nonfraternization law . . ."

"He happens to be a counter-intelligence officer in the United States Army!"

"You know what that means, Major. Dishonorable discharge. He will be disbarred as a lawyer. What was his crime? Being human? Taking a woman to bed?"

"He picked the wrong woman."

"The army of saints!"

"Don't be so goddamned sanctimonious, Duquesne. When we entered your precious France your proud, proud citizens shaved the hair from the heads of the women who slept with Germans and sent them packing down the road, naked."

"And so? When the Americans leave and the German prisoners return, they will shave the heads of their women who slept with Americans. How fortunate! How utterly fortunate your lovely American womanhood is spared these indignities!"

"This mingling of sweat with the enemy is no justification."

"Ah, my dear Sean O'Sullivan. You have such a conveniently short memory. Have you forgotten about yourself and the English woman?"

"That's different."

"Certainly it is different. You got away with it."

Dante Arosa was gaunt and distraught when Sean went to his room. He looked up at Sean, then lowered his head. The black curly hair was in disarray . . . the swashbuckle, the vitality was flat, lifeless. Outside the long green lawn dipped into the Landau, muddy from a fresh rain.

"Say something," Dante croaked at last, "tell me what a prick I am. Tell me what I've done to my family. Tell me . . . how everyone on the team would like to spit in my face."

Sean told him nothing.

"I can't explain," Dante whispered. "It was as though . . . as though Marla was trying to kill both of us in that bed . . . like she was a messenger of death and was luring me with something wonderful . . . death and danger was in the room with us every time and it taunted me. And she pulled me closer and closer to it . . . and I couldn't break away. . . . It was hard to breathe . . . to think . . ."

Sean gripped him by the collar and jerked him to his feet. "A German woman! How could you do it with a German woman?"

And then, upset by his own violence, he opened his hands and let Dante free.

"We're just men," Sean said futilely, "just men. They made the rules too tough for some of us . . . you are confined to quarters until a new CIC man is brought in. You will acquaint him with the operations here. After that, you will be transferred to a service unit. At the soonest possible moment you will tender your resignation from the Army. I've . . . seen to it that you will receive a fully honorable discharge."

Drained of the venom of fear, Dante began to sob. "You're too decent. I don't deserve that kind of a break, Sean. I don't deserve it."

"Maybe there's some punishment in it for you, Dante. You have to go on living and knowing that if this ever leaks out, I'll have to stand the court-martial in your place."

CHAPTER TWENTY-NINE

DELIVER BY PERSONAL COURIER TO MAJOR SEAN O'SUL-LIVAN
Dear Sean,
  I am using this unusual method of communicating with you for reasons you'll quickly understand.

World opinion is creating a furor over the revelations of the extermination camps. The pressure on us for "action" is becoming unbearable.

Acting on instructions directly from Washington, Supreme Headquarters here will issue a proclamation within twenty-four hours: namely, PROCLAMATION #22. The proclamation will say, in effect, that a local military governor may request an extraordinary military tribunal for the trial of extraordinary cases. We refer, of course, to SS atrocities. The tribunal will be empowered to impose the death sentence.

Well, Sean, I'm handing the ball to you again. As my Pilot Team Commander we've tried quite a few new wrinkles out in your territory so I'm going with you again on PROCLAMATION #22. By happy coincidence you have the mother and daddy of them all in the persons of Klaus and Emma Stoll. We at Supreme Headquarters feel they're perfect for the first trial under PROCLAMATION #22.

We've got to get moving on this to let a little steam out of the vent and to show both the world and the German people we're going to be tough. We are particularly interested in hanging Emma Stoll. The fact that she is a woman will make a heavy impact.

Have your legal officer draw up indictments (recommending death sentences) and a simple paper for your signature requesting an extraordinary tribunal under #22. We'll have the court in session in Rombaden within seventy-two hours.

Destroy this document after you've studied it.

Kindest regards,
A. J. Hansen

Lieutenant Bolinski frowned and shook his head as he read Hansen's secret letter. "Well, there is obviously a lot of pressure on Washington to put up a showcase trial."

"What do you think about the legality of Proclamation 22?"

"Hell, Major, we won the war. We can do anything we want without splitting legal hairs. Now, Klaus Stoll could be hanged before any court in the world off the evidence."

"Emma?"

Bolinski frowned again, picking those little legal threads upon which a lawyer can build a mountain. "I'd say that with the interrogations and evidence I could spring her from a death sentence in any fair court."

"Go on."

"She's guilty of beating prisoners . . . none of whom suffered either death or serious injury, and she's guilty of sexual perversion. Her main crime is grand theft in the collection of Winter Relief Funds from the

German people. That's enough to stash her away for life. On the other hand, if the story of the silverware handles being carved from human skulls holds up in truth . . ."

Sean opened a file, slid a report across the desk to Bolinski. He lit a cigarette and read the letterhead. It was from a Swedish silvermaker with an attachment from a laboratory. "This came in last night," Sean said. "I sent samples of the handles to Stockholm, the States, and to Switzerland."

Bolinski drew hard on his cigarette.

IN CONCLUSION, WE HAVE ANALYZED THESE SAMPLES BY EVERY KNOWN METHOD. IN OUR OPINION THEY ARE NOTHING MORE OR LESS THAN CARVINGS ON COMMON ELEPHANT TUSKS OF AN EAST AFRICAN VARIETY.

"Christ!"

"I phoned the Swiss firm in Zurich this morning. They haven't written up their findings yet, but they told me essentially the same thing— elephant tusks."

"Thank you, Cornelia Hollingshead."

"The whole thing starts to take on the aspect of a legalized lynching."

"But what the hell are you going to do about it, Major? You can't stand up against this kind of brass."

Sean put Hansen's letter into the big crystal ashtray, lit a match to it, and watched it burst, flicker, and crumple into a hundred charred bits.

A few moments later he entered the prison cell of Emma Stoll and dismissed the guard. She knew nothing of the stories raging around the world that had made her symbolic of the evil of Nazism. He had met her before, many times. Emma, sloppy and dowdy, glowered at him with a return of some of her former arrogance.

The Americans had not killed her or Klaus and therefore they revealed their weakness. The SS had known how to rid itself of Germany's enemies. The Americans were weak . . . weak.

"You are about to be brought to trial, Emma. The only chance you have of living is by answering my questions."

"You are trying to trap me."

"I'm trying to help you."

"You lie!"

"Emma, you're not being logical. I said that you were as good as dead. What do you have to lose by telling the truth?"

It was a puzzling proposition, indeed, to the shopgirl. Lie or truth . . . what difference did it make now? They'd get her if they wanted to . . . but, "Why are you going out of your way to protect me? Why?"

"Not to protect you, Emma. To protect the name of my country."

The slow-witted girl was baffled. This Major O'Sullivan was a baffling man. Was he really as soft as she suspected? What meanings were there that she could not comprehend? "What is it you want to know?" she asked cautiously.

"I have only a few questions. None of them are tricks. Just give me straight answers. First, did you know what was going on inside Schwabenwald?"

Emma was about to make an automatic plea of innocence. She stopped herself short. She had planned to scream out her ignorance of Schwabenwald to the end . . . but . . . now . . . he did say she was good as dead. She sulked, and slumped to her cot. All the jacked-up, painted-on, manufactured attempts to be sexy had split apart in the dank cell. Her hands held a head of uncombed dirty hair. "I lived outside the actual camp," she said slowly. "You must remember that I am a German woman, a German wife. In Germany, the men run things. My husband never spoke to me about business inside the camp and I never asked him. I am a German wife."

"Did you suspect?"

"Suspect what?"

"The exterminations."

She looked up at him pitifully, wrung her hands, dropped her head again. "We all suspected."

Sean was excited by the knowledge that he had either baffled her or gained her immediate confidence or . . . that she was playing a wild gamble to hang onto life. "How much did you see of the camp?"

"Only . . . only the outer camp. My husband's office, the area around the SS barracks . . ."

"How about the medical experiment center?"

Emma sealed her lips.

"The center was in that immediate area, Emma. Did you ever go inside the experimentation center?"

"Yes," she said almost inaudibly.

"And the Gestapo Interrogation Headquarters."

"I answered these questions a hundred times for Lieutenant Arosa."

"The Gestapo Interrogation Headquarters?"

"I don't want to speak any more! Get out!"

"Last time, Emma. It's the end of the line for you. Were you ever in Gestapo Interrogation Headquarters!"

"Get out!"

"Okay, Emma. No more questions." Sean walked toward the solid iron door to thump for the jailer.

"I was in Gestapo," she said.

Sean turned back to her. "How many times?"

"I don't know."

"Forty?"

"Maybe."

"Fifty?"

"Yes . . . fifty . . ."

"And you beat prisoners and forced them to perform sex acts."

"Only Jews and Slavs!"

"And you went to the inner camp and you watched the exterminations!"

"No! No! Never! I swear! Never! I was never in there! I swear I was never in there!"

Sean knelt quickly alongside the cot, where she was weeping, mumbling prayers to God, proclaiming her innocence.

"I have one last question, Emma. Answer it carefully. Your life depends on it. Where did you get your silverware set?"

The sudden shift in questioning threw her. "My . . . my . . . what?"

"Your silverware set?"

"But I have two sets of silver."

No actress could fake it. Emma Stoll was innocent of the charge. Sean knew that now beyond question. "Well, where did you get them?"

"The good silver, I purchased in Switzerland."

"With funds stolen from German Winter Relief?"

She buried her face in her hands and wept again, sobbing now. The world would look upon her as a thief. This was more than she could bear. Sean waited until her crying spell ebbed. "And the other set. The one with the fancy carvings?"

"The old silver with the ivory handles was given to me by my father from his father. My grandfather was a soldier in German East Africa before the first war. He brought it back with him. It has become a family heirloom. It was ugly, but a German wife is taught to treasure family heirlooms . . . so I kept it."

Sean sighed deeply. His rugged, black Irish face was as perplexed as Emma Stoll's. "For reasons best known to the Lord above alone . . . I am going to try to save your life."

The next morning there was a press conference called at Supreme Headquarters in Frankfurt. Proclamation #22 was announced. The press officer intimated that a speedy trial would follow.

Those journalists who had become authorities in the American Zone quickly pieced two and two together. Within minutes of the announcement, as it was flashed around the world, there was open speculation that Klaus and Emma Stoll would be the first tried under the proclamation.

DELIVER BY PERSONAL COURIER TO BRIGADIER GEN-ERAL A. J. HANSEN, G-5, SUPREME HEADQUARTERS: I. G. FARBEN BUILDING: FRANKFURT
Dear General Hansen,

I am not certain whether your communication constituted an order or a request. At any rate, I am hereby notifying you that I reject it in either event.

In the opinion of my legal officer and in my own lay opinion, Klaus Stoll is guilty and deserving of the death penalty. However, it will take weeks to prepare proper legal documents and conclude a case . . . tried in American tradition.

Emma Stoll has done nothing to deserve a death sentence.

PROCLAMATION #22 is against my conscience, my morality, and, in my opinion, contrary to the best interests of my country.

Sincerely,
Sean O'Sullivan

CHAPTER THIRTY

Andrew Jackson Hansen's staff car and motorcycle escort wiped everything out of its path like a hurricane blowing down from Frankfurt.

Eric the Red bounced out of his car before it was brought to a full halt at the Rombaden City Hall, churned up the marble steps, down the statue-lined corridor, and burst into Sean's office, slamming the door behind him.

Sean arose. "Good afternoon, General. I was expecting you'd be down here."

"You snot-nose bastard! Are you trying to make us look like idiots!"

"No, sir. I'm trying to save you from looking like idiots."

"What the hell are you protecting that goddamned ghoul Emma Stoll for!"

"I am attempting," Sean said slowly, "to protect the good name of my country. She happens to come with the bargain. You've read the report, sir. Those bone handles are not human skulls."

Hansen leaned on his knuckles, bent forward over the desk, and aped Sean's soft, smooth speech. "But the world doesn't know. And, Major, that story will never be set straight. Corney has done her job well. And if by some miracle the story is corrected the world isn't going to give a good rat's ass. The world wants Emma Stoll's neck."

"I won't sign my name to a lynch order."

Hansen's fist crashed two, three, four times atop the desk, making it bounce under his fury. "Now you hear this, boy. Emma Stoll is going to die! The Germans will laugh in our faces if we spring her and the whole goddamned world is going to scream that we're coddling Nazis!"

"And I don't give a big rat's ass what the world screams!" Sean bellowed right back in Hansen's face. "And furthermore, I refuse to talk to the General while he is in such a rage that he has no control of his senses."

Hansen stood upright with the astonishment of a child in the middle of a tantrum who has been doused in the face with a glass of water. Sean's voice quivered for control. "What are we proving by Proclamation 22? Why bother with a sham of a kangaroo court? Let's just take them out and shoot them. Adolf Hitler proclaimed the same kind of courts to get rid of undesirable elements. They were called People's Courts. We call them Proclamation 22. Don't you think I know the German people want Emma Stoll dead even more than we do. Sure, let her die for their crimes. Let Emma Stoll die for every one of them who screamed *sieg heil*. I'm sorry I lost my temper, sir. I have strong feelings on the matter."

"Sometimes, Sean," the general said quietly, "we see our country make an obvious mistake. We go along with it without protest because

we believe in the ultimate right of what we are doing. Those times
are the most difficult when a man is asked to believe so deeply that he
will follow blindly and without question. What we have asked you to
do is not your decision . . . or mine. It is the decision of our superiors.
Nor will the ultimate responsibility rest upon you. What can I say,
Sean? This creature is not worth saving. And the world will never con-
demn you. Allow us this human mistake and go on believing."

The pressure was intensifying now. Yes, Sean thought, it would
be so damned easy to just sign the request for the tribunal. To resist
was stupid and ridiculous. And when Emma Stoll was hanged there
would be much cheering around the world and no one to grieve except
a pet dog and a grandmother. In a decade or two some obscure professor of law might point out that Emma Stoll was denied a due process
of law. But even America could make a mistake in the backwash and
confusion of the war's ending. And who would remember the name of
the major who signed the order for the tribunal?

But to refuse was to invite calamity . . . no one would understand
or want to understand his position. He could never set the truth straight
in people's minds about the ivory handles. Why in God's name stand
up in the face of world wrath to defend a slut who hardly deserved to
live.

"General Hansen, I have sat here, day in, day out, week after week
listening to one German after another repeat the same story like broken
records. They say, 'We were only following orders.' You see . . . that
is their justification for murder, castration, barbarism, degradation.
They were just following orders. And I go to my billet and I get a little
bit crocked every night and I think . . . what if a few million Germans,
or a few hundred thousand, had had the guts to stand up and refuse
to commit crimes in the name of their country. I'm sorry, General Hansen. America doesn't stand for Proclamation 22. I'm not going to commit murder in the name of my country for you or anyone else just
because orders are orders."

Hansen knew now what he had to do. "This is all beyond our hands
and our scope, Sean. That is reality. You will report to Frankfurt in
seventy-two hours with a request either for the tribunal or your resignation from the Army. I regret a willful and stubborn decision that will
bring you much unhappiness."

"I'll take full responsibility for my decision, General."

Hansen put on his cap and walked toward the door. "I'm sorry you came here, General. I'm sorry because I believed in you . . . I believed in you when you told me 'We are not Nazis. . . .'"

It rained and the Landau became muddy again and the cobblestones of the great square were slick. It rained into the leaking hovels of the bomb ruins, and the wet misery added to the gloom inside City Hall.

No one spoke of it openly but General Hansen's visit was a well-known secret. Sean gathered his people in one at a time to bring them up to date, for the obvious purpose of smoothly turning Pilot Team G-5 over to a new commander.

Pilot Team G-5 had been a grand experiment. All of them wondered if, with Sean gone, its conscience would not also leave. Maurice Duquesne would, most likely, be made commander if he would sign a request for the tribunal under Proclamation 22. The new beginning would be based upon a lie.

Maurice was perplexed by the predicament Sean had put him in. He did not wish to be confronted with such a decision. Duquesne knew that in the beginning all men are pure and driven by pure motivations. The men they believe in are also pure, in the beginning. But somewhere early in the journey all men come to that first moment of compromise. Maurice Duquesne compromised when he ran for his first office two decades before; he had gone on, hardly looking back for a moment's remorse.

He had been a good servant of his people within a framework established before him. He knew that to compromise, to overlook truth at times, to be expedient at other times, to back down instead of making a fatal stand . . . all these were practical tools of his profession. He loathed the incorruptibility in Sean that would force him into a corrupt decision; Sean's idealism was stubborn and had little to do with reality. And, in the end, he was reluctantly filled with admiration for the man he wished he might have been.

For Sean O'Sullivan the moment of sadness came with the betrayal of Andrew Jackson Hansen. At one time Sean believed that Hansen would strike back at the stars and the moon. But now he was merely a weak man bowing quietly to an unjust decision.

Could Sean believe in Hansen's reason, that ultimate American goals justified and knowingly permitted mistakes like this?

Now the doors of doubt were thrown wide open. Perhaps Hansen was merely a clever politician. Did Hansen in reality make all of his famous fights knowing and calculating in advance just how much the traffic would bear? How many other times in his career had he knuckled under like this? Had he carefully and deliberately built himself into a "colorful character," merely paying lip service to his imagined strength?

In the end Sean would be completely alone with Frau Stoll's dog and grandmother. He would be thrown into a pit of journalistic wolves to be devoured live. No, not even Emma would understand why Sean felt her life was worth fighting for. Perhaps Big Nellie would try to defend Sean or at least try to give his reasons. But to do that might mean Big Nellie would go down with him, by a world calling for blood.

In the end, there would be but a single friend, his father. Sean longed desperately to see him and he prayed that when the news reached his father, from strangers, it would not harm his heart. But no matter what . . . his father would go on believing in him . . . in the face of it all . . . his father would be there . . . and understand.

CHAPTER THIRTY-ONE

Eleven o'clock. It was time for the daily meeting with Ulrich Falkenstein and the German Council. The big conference room resembled the dining room of a medieval castle; a long wooden table; high, straightback, rough-hewn chairs partly covered with polished, worn leather; an enormous tapestry depicting a battle of the Legend of Rombaden. Those councilmen who owned pinstripes dressed in them. There were twenty Germans, with Ulrich Falkenstein at one end of the table.

As the Marienkirche bell bonged the hour, Sean entered the room and the Germans arose crisply, bowed slightly. Today Sean was without his usual contingent of American officers. "Be seated," he said. "I have excused the other officers from today's session for other business. You will examine your files and agenda to see if there is any business that cannot be held over for two or three days. I wish to consider only matters needing an immediate answer."

It was a chilling pronouncement to them. The Germans began to fish through their files nervously. They all knew what it was about, they had spoken of it in whispers. Things had gone well with O'Sullivan in Rombaden. He gave his commands with sureness and took responsibility for every decision; he was stern, but fair. They knew that other cities in the Schwaben and Württemberg and Bavaria were in chaos. With him gone . . . God knows. What if they had to deal with the Frenchman?

One by one each uttered that he had nothing urgent.

"There is one matter," Ulrich Falkenstein said. "The day after tomorrow is the twenty-second of June. For a century and a half it has traditionally been Hinterseer Day, in honor of the Rombaden poet. In the old days there was much ado and pageantry . . . in lean years the people have merely gathered in the square to hear the reading of his most famous work, the *Legend of Rombaden*. Although it must be necessarily austere this year I have been asked by all facets of the citizenry to petition you to allow the reading to take place. It would be a matter of a half dozen or so actors, a platform behind Hinterseer's statue, and some loudspeaking equipment."

On the surface of it, Sean saw no harm. So far he had forbidden large gatherings, but it could easily be controlled by the forces he had at hand. Blessing's authority was respected by them all. A reunion with traditional life would be good for morale . . . but . . . one thing annoyed Sean. The *Legend of Rombaden* was read and the pageantry had continued during the Nazi era.

"I'll read the poem tonight and give you an answer tomorrow," he said.

That was what the German Council liked—a quick final answer. "There being no further business . . ." he said, standing. They came to their feet and waited until he left the room.

Sean left his office assured that everything was as ready as possible for the new commander. A quick briefing could be made and that would be that. The command could be turned over even quicker if Duquesne were selected.

He ordered a light dinner to be brought to his study and asked that no one disturb him. He opened the book of poetry by Hinterseer and began to read with great care the German text of some forty pages. Of course, Sean knew something of the Legend of Rombaden. He had studied it as a segment of German mythology in college and in summations in military government texts.

To Sean, German poetry was truly one of the most magnificent forms of man's self-expression. Furthermore, he had flirted with German literature and poked about for the answers to the German riddle since he left high school.

The *Legend of Rombaden* was from the mythology of the Black Forest Trilogy. Sean was soon drawn in by verse of Goethe-like perfection.

Wolfram, King of the Gods, reigned over a mythical kingdom deep within the Black Forest. Although Wolfram had a powerful human body, most of his other attributes were those of animals: the rage of a boar; the speed and beauty of the buck; the strength of the bear; the whiteness of the swan; the instincts and cunning of the fox. He was all that was great and beautiful of each animal in the body of a man.

His only son, Berwin, was a warrior of incredible bravery, as befitted the Son of the King of the Gods. Wolfram ordered his son to find the purest people upon earth, with which he would populate his kingdom. Berwin wandered from land to land until he came upon the Aryans of Rombaden; and they became the chosen ones.

In Rombaden dwelled Helga, Goddess of Fertility, with whom Berwin fell in love. Before Berwin and Helga could consummate their love, the God of Snow and Mountains, Ernald, swept down from his mythical kingdom in the Alps and kidnaped Helga.

Berwin realized that the pure race would be contaminated if Helga was violated by Ernald. He gathered about him the warriors of Rombaden. In a fiery speech he exhorted them to die in battle, for only by giving their lives in the fray would they know a moment of ecstasy beyond earthly dimensions. Those who die in battle, promised Berwin, would go to Wolfram's Kingdom in the Black Forest, and live as the purest of all people.

In the final battle, Wolfram transmits to his son all of his own animal strength and cunning to help him destroy his adversary. But, in the victory, Berwin is slain.

He and all the fallen warriors of Rombaden are placed aboard flaming rafts to be drifted upstream on the Landau and into the Black Forest and the promised kingdom.

Helga, watching them float away from the shore, plunges Berwin's dagger into her breast and is then carried to Berwin's raft by a great bridge of lightning. She lies beside her dead hero on the flaming pyre and as the fire and wound end her life she extols this moment of exaltation that only death can bring. She cries out that she is being transformed into a superior form of being through death. And, in death, she consummates the relationship with Berwin, denied them in life.

And so, the daughters and sons of Rombaden who came from that union of Berwin and Helga became the purest on earth.

Sean O'Sullivan closed the book. For so many years he had probed and prodded for answers . . . and now . . . strangely . . . on the eve of his departure from Germany some of these answers were coming to him.

Was not the Legend of Rombaden in fact the story of the German people?

He began to thumb through the thin book for clues, passages to clarify a hundred hazy thoughts. And then, nagging unanswered questions began to be answered with a strange clarity.

When he had been in college and was chosen for military government, there had been endless arguments and discussions about the German mind. Scholars and practical men argued logic and theory, and then, at a certain point in every discussion, all logic about the German people dissipated into confusion. The German always ended in a cloud of mystery . . . the eternal enigma.

But here, in Hinterseer's pages, the German showed himself. Here was Siegfried! Here in the Legend of Rombaden was that longing to be the super race! Here was that strange elation at the moment of death so prevalent in the German culture! Here was the hero's reward for death in battle!

In the legend they looked upon themselves as the "chosen" people of God. But, what kind of a god? This was *not* the God of Jesus Christ! The god that they longed to identify themselves with was a pagan god! Wolfram was a god who lived in the forest and was more animal than human!

Did not the Germans, indeed, identify themselves more with the pagan than with monotheism, the Western concept of one God? Sean pondered. Once he had written what was termed a brilliant paper, on the "Origins of Anti-Semitism in the German Mind." By chance, General Hansen, in his search to find German experts, read the paper. It was this paper by an obscure political-science instructor at the University of California which brought Sean O'Sullivan into military government before the age of thirty.

Sean now tried to link his paper to the Legend of Rombaden. He had written:

No people in all of the Western world live closer to their mythology than the German people. Siegfried and other legendary figures, particularly warriors, are deep within the soul of the German people.

The German people have identified themselves indelibly with the forest, with nature, and with animals. This powerful lure of the forest has given vent to the mysticism that always follows "forest people" and a relationship to animals peculiar to them.

Take, for example, the German hunting rituals. After an animal has been slain, the German hunter cuts the throat with a special knife. The "Forest Master" dips a stick into the animal's blood and anoints the hunter's forehead. The stick is a pure phallic symbol and the purpose of the ceremony is to endow the hunter with the potency and power of the animal he has just slain . . . just as Siegfried bathed in the blood of the dragon he had killed.

The Jews gave to the Western world a formal conception of one God. The Jews handed down from Sinai the basic "laws" or rules of Western morality, the Ten Commandments.

The German hates both the one-God concept and the stringency of the "laws" in his subconscious mind. On the surface and to the world at large he is both a Christian and a product of Western culture.

However, he is a split personality. Another part of him, a vital part of his soul, remains in the forest. The German is, therefore, civilized in much the same way as a domesticated animal, for part of the German is always animal.

Despite his trappings, part of the German is pure pagan. In order for the German to become the pagan his unconscious desires he must throw off the formal concept of one God, and God's laws. Therefore, the German must destroy the Jew, who stands between him and his pagan desires.

Sean always felt that Germans hated Jews because they wanted to return to the forest. He felt the Germans loved their warrior gods; the Berwins and the Siegfrieds and identified with them more than they loved Christ and more than they identified themselves as Christians. Sean knew the old thesis that to be truly anti-Jewish, one must be anti-Christ. When you destroy the Jew, you also must destroy Christ. Therefore, the German protests Christianity by destroying the Jew.

A doctor of the mind would call the German a schizophrenic. He is, in truth, two distinct people.

One part of this two people gave man its highest and most enriching contributions to civilization through the Beethovens and Bachs and Kants and Schillers and Freuds and Mozarts and Goethes.

But the other! The hate-filled and muddled ramblings of Nietzsche and of Schopenhauer and of Hegel, of Treitschke and Fichte. And the staggering genius of Richard Wagner whose magnificent sounds extolled the glory of death, the fatherland, the chosen people . . . *chosen of pagan gods.* And who is to say that Wagner is not part and parcel of the soul of the German people?

Adolf Hitler understood this desire for paganism in the German people and exploited it. The uniforms, the blood ceremonies, the rallies were nothing more or less than pagan rituals. Hitler deliberately played to the German people's desire to identify themselves with paganism by the destruction of the Jews.

Hitler was indeed another pagan god, calling for the German people to destroy themselves in a death orgy and they answered with "sieg heil."

Sean began to recall the ramblings of the sick philosophers. Schopenhauer . . . the only honest wish man could have was that of total annihilation. Hegel, a personal beloved idol of Adolf Hitler who wrote . . . the spirit dies in order to live and that he who yields himself in death is merely yielding one's self to his other self for life is death; and Hegel wrote further that . . . every state must accept the divine right of oppression that belongs to it as a necessary state in the evolution of government; Nietzsche . . . I want to teach men the sense of their existence, which is the Superman, the lightning out of the dark cloud; Fichte, who named the Latins and French and Jews as subhumans, and Treitschke, who put the final amen on the German character . . . it does not matter what you think as long as you obey.

So, it all fit together, Sean thought. The Legend of Rombaden had produced a magic key he had sought for years that explained the anti-God, anti-Christ, anti-Jewish perversion as a drive to return to paganism.

This, then, was the answer to Count Ludwig Von Romstein and the others who argued that the Nazi era was a unique phenomenon that resulted from the First World War and a set of following crises. This was a lie, for the roots of Nazism were deep within the hearts and minds of the German people, and all of it, Aryanism, paganism, love of death, the forest, superhumanism, had been part of them for centuries and centuries!

The Nazi era then was a combined will of most of the German people over hundreds of years of cultivation and growth. The drive toward self-destruction was inevitable!

To Sean, Hinterseer and the *Legend of Rombaden* even spelled out more. The startling discovery that the *Germans worshiped death!* The German approached death in a different manner than any other Western people, who either feared it or looked upon it as an end of mortal suffering. To the German, death alone was a state of existence more wonderful than life, and the moment of death was to be worshiped as the moment of supreme exaltation!

Did this not begin to give answers, that such a people were capable of running death factories in Dachau and Schwabenwald? If death is a desirable superstate in their mystic and pagan subconscious, then it is not a mortal "Christian" sin to commit murder.

Assembly-line death could only be accomplished by an astute Western mind. It could be "justified" when the pagan overwhelms the Christian morality. The split personality in the German character made it possible.

Hinterseer and Richard Wagner told a puzzled world about the perplexing contradictions in the German. And what is more, no one is more perplexed, searches more for his own identity, is more of an enigma than the German is to himself.

CHAPTER THIRTY-TWO

Eleven o'clock. The German Council assembled. Sloe-eyed Ulrich Falkenstein appeared deceptively serene as he sat at the opposite end of the long table from the commander.

·The council sat on both sides of the table, a half dozen of them former inmates of Schwabenwald whose years in the concentration camp had earned them a badge of respectability. The others had somehow kept themselves clear of all Nazi entanglements, remnants of the old Social Democratic Party for the most part. Almost all of them were without previous government experience; five of the council were women, something new in German politics.

"I would like to poll you," Sean said, "to see if any of you have objection to the reading of the *Legend of Rombaden.*"

They looked at one another a bit puzzled, each shrugged in turn, then shook his head. No, there were no objections. Ulrich Falkenstein was not taken in; he studied Sean closely knowing the major was up to something. Sean's eyes were sharper this morning, the brow furrowed more deeply as he scanned their faces. Falkenstein knew how to read this expression.

"Frau Meissner," Sean said, "you are a native of Rombaden. Just how significant is this event to you?"

"Ach, what a question, Major. Hinterseer Day is our most important holiday. And the *Legend of Rombaden* is very close to all of us."

"You grew up with it?"

"You don't know. Among the actors at the Rombaden Theater the competition for roles in the reading was very great. It was discussed in every home, in the Ratskeller . . . even in Princess Allee. For the children, the legend was performed in the puppet theater. As a schoolgirl, the mark of my accomplishments was the memorizing of new passages."

And then, one by one, they attested to the integral part of their lives that the legend played and they praised the stature of Hinterseer and their pride in him.

Professor Hans Moltke was the intellectual of the council. He had been a teacher of German Literature until the Nazis drove him from the schools. Moltke kept himself and his family alive by losing his former identity and becoming a bank clerk during the Nazi era. "The poem," he said, "certainly must be considered among a few dozen of the world's masterpieces from the standpoint of pure literature, pure verse. Secondarily, it has attained extraordinary meaning to the people of this district. Hinterseer is Rombaden's greatest son . . . the link with immortality . . . this means provincial pride. Moreover, the reading of the legend signifies the coming of summer. The people know they will again take trips to the forest and commune with nature. The legend brings them close to nature. As you know, Major O'Sullivan, we Germans have an uncommon love of the forest."

"I am aware of that," Sean said. Then he turned to Hoffman, the deputy with the broken back who now arranged the rendezvous with the informers. "Herr Hoffman. You are not from Rombaden. What does the legend mean to you?"

"Why," he wheezed with enthusiasm at being singled out for a testimony, "every German schoolboy knows the legend. It stands with the masterpieces of Schiller, Goethe, and . . . Heine." Although a concentration-camp inmate, Hoffman stumbled on the last name . . . a Jew.

"And you, Herr Maas. Why do you suppose the Nazis allowed the legend to be read?"

"Why not, Major? It is not a political poem and it is highly Germanic in nature."

Ulrich Falkenstein listened with utter fascination as one by one they committed themselves without the slightest idea of what O'Sullivan was driving at. Sean opened his marked copy of the Legend of Rombaden.

"Frau Meissner. Would you care to venture what Hinterseer had in mind with the following passage . . . 'citizens of Rombaden, Aryans, shall we allow the sperm of Ernald to mongrelize our race?'"

Frau Meissner was puzzled.

"Well, Frau Meissner . . . do you in Rombaden feel yourself Aryans?"

"I . . . don't . . . understand . . ."

Sean thumbed through a few more pages. "Would any of you ladies or gentlemen care to make an interpretation of the following passage . . . 'You of Rombaden are the chosen children of Wolfram, King of the Gods.'"

Herr Maas began to understand. He dismissed Sean's question with a wave of his hand. "It is merely a way of saying that Rombaden is a fine city. All cities think of themselves as the best. Even in the United States there is that competition between cities."

"Fine, Herr Maas . . . then, how about this. 'I promise you a death, a moment of divine exaltation . . . this is the warrior's death . . . this is the moment of fulfillment . . . the instant your life passes from his body for the fatherland he will know ecstasy beyond ecstasy.'"

Brows wrinkled.

Sean read on. "Or this one, Herr Maas . . . 'I bathe myself in the blood of a wild pig, I castrate him, I become a superman among the peoples of the world with his strength and his virility . . . forgive me wild pig for I have a mission to rule the sub-humans which infest us.'"

Sean closed the book. He flipped it contemptuously on the table. Everyone had been frightened into silence except for Professor Moltke. He picked up their flagging banner. "But, Major, you find the same type of writing in Greek mythology . . . in Norse mythology."

"I challenge you. The Greek Gods were subtle and had delightful senses of humor and mocked their mortal failings."

"And the Norwegians and Danes. We base the Ring on their mythology."

"Yes, but neither the Norwegians nor the Danes take their gods seriously . . . you Germans do. In fact, you live out your mythology."

"I do not bend to your point, Major O'Sullivan. You can write in any meaning you wish to write in . . . any meaning you seek."

"And that is my point, Professor Moltke. The Nazis gave meaning to these legends. This poem was Nazi in conception. Adolf Hitler found it and others like it and said . . . this is what we are and the German people believed it."

"But . . ." Hoffman protested weakly. "Hinterseer has been dead for nearly two centuries."

"However, Hoffman, Nazi ideas have been alive in the German people for twenty centuries."

It was as though they had all been doused with cold water. For many moments a stunned silence prevailed until Herr Bach, the most innocuous member of the council, spoke up mousily. "I always thought there was something wrong with that poem," he said.

"Then why in the hell didn't you speak up?" Sean demanded.

"But, Major, one does not speak up against tradition."

"That is precisely the point. Your tradition demands blind obedience. So long as you are willing to be led like sheep your minds will be captured by another madman. Perhaps in a year or five or twenty some priest will deliver a sermon from the pulpit denouncing the legend or some teacher lead a group of students to protest it . . . only then will it be safe to read Hinterseer."

Falkenstein, who had remained completely out of it now spoke. "You do have tradition in America, do you not, Major?"

"If the President of the United States were to read the Declaration of Independence before the Lincoln Memorial on the Fourth of July there would be someone in America to protest and to question."

Falkenstein nodded his head, as if to say "touché." A slight smile crossed his lips as he saw the utter confusion among the council. Here they had believed themselves to be the "good" Germans. The failing then was partly theirs too; there was an iota of Nazi in them all.

"There being no further business before this council I am advising you that I will be at Supreme Headquarters in Frankfurt for the next several days. Captain Duquesne will be in command during my absence. You are dismissed," he said, eyeing Falkenstein to remain.

Sean stuffed his notes and papers into his briefcase. The two men were alone in the great hall. The legend blared down at them from the faded tapestry. Sean snapped his case shut. The coldness between him and Falkenstein was like that of the stone fireplace. "They hate me, don't they, Falkenstein?" Sean found himself saying.

"On the contrary, Major O'Sullivan. You have earned the position as their father and their leader. Those are two things a German understands. You see for yourself how well they obey you. Once the German is defeated he is quite manageable."

"But they don't even know what the hell I was talking about."

"I think you are far too impatient, Major. We may be ancient in our traditions but we are infants in the democratic experience. Our first venture with a republic, the Weimar, ended in disaster. The subtleties of democratic process are beyond their comprehension."

"But they do understand father and obedience. So we're in for another cycle of it when another father leads them to destruction."

Falkenstein straightened up a bit. "You conveniently forget the great things the German people have given the world. These are the Germans I love and believe in. This is the Germany I fight for."

Sean was tempted to argue the point. Yes, there were great contributions in literature and music and science. However, there had never been a lasting German ideal of freedom and damned few of the dignity of man. Even their greatest reformer, Martin Luther, was a dogmatic tyrant. And here, Ulrich Falkenstein, who had suffered untold brutality at the hands of this society, stubbornly refused to give up his identity or his faith. It was admirable nonsense to Sean. To believe so strongly was good; but it was beyond any man's vision to feel the German people would change. They both sensed the conversation had hit an impasse.

"We all fear," Falkenstein broke the ice, "that you have committed your last official act in Rombaden?"

"That may be so," Sean said.

"That would be a shame. You have been hard but you have never been unfair. You see, Major O'Sullivan, there are subtleties of democracy that even I cannot comprehend. For example, why does a man of your stature throw away a brilliant career in the protection of an Emma Stoll?"

"It seems to me, Herr Falkenstein, that is a strangely put question from one who was convicted by a Hitler court."

"Surely you do not intend to compare me to Emma Stoll."

"Of course not. But I do challenge a Hitler court to exist in the name of my country."

"It is a pity you won't be going to Berlin with me when I am able to. Frankly, we both have a lot to learn. On the other hand, I have a feeling that you don't really want to know that there are good Germans."

Sean shot him an angry glance, then stifled his anger. "You said yourself, I have been fair."

"Fair, yes. Like a dog trainer. But even an animal can smell when he is hated."

"Herr Falkenstein," he said, "I have written a full report for the incoming commander in case someone other than Captain Duquesne is selected. I have strongly recommended that he place full trust in you in all matters."

They shook hands with great reservation and completely without affection. Yet, an undeniable mutual admiration existed between the two men.

"Good luck, Major," Falkenstein said, and left the great hall.

And then, Sean was alone.

Sean found himself wandering through a maze of narrow streets. He had arranged that there would be no farewells, no sentimentality. In the morning he would leave, supposedly on a routine trip to Supreme Headquarters . . . no more, no less.

A battalion of laborers, prisoners of war, with Polish guards hacked into the endless rubble piles at one of the intersections. As they saw the commander the Germans stopped their work for an instant, stared, doffed their caps, and bowed as he passed. The Poles greeted him with formal salutes and smiles, but Sean was oblivious to them.

Now was the time to make one's balance sheet. There could be a balance sheet for Liam and Timothy O'Sullivan. There was one for Nan Milford . . . losses, gains, happiness, sadness. But there would be no balance for either Rombaden or Sean O'Sullivan.

A few dim, hopeful signs rose curiously in the sunlight in the sea of ruin. The people of Rombaden were working with amazing energy. They had used great ingenuity in the creation of jobs and in using rubble for raw material for a dozen enterprises.

But the digging out would continue for months, perhaps years. A single classroom had been opened without Nazi teachers or Nazi textbooks. A single four-page newspaper and a twenty-five-watt hand-generated radio station represented the press. Half the population had filled out the dreaded Fragebogen. Many of the Nazis were reduced to common labor. Now there was an application to form several trade unions and even a request to begin a political party . . . these were signs, however small.

On the other side, the scales weighed heavily. Sean knew now that de-Nazification, in reality, would never work. One does not kill two hundred thousand forming the heart of the Nazi cancer and punish sixteen million others without oneself becoming a Nazi. In the British Zone it was becoming apparent that only the top Nazis would be tried, these trials for showcasing. The French, who realistically had to continue to live next to the Germans, could only pay later for vengeance now.

Nonfraternization was starting to break down. The new troops who had not seen combat were not so hostile toward the Germans, and the good old generous Yankee hearts began to show. American soldiers could not resist giving chocolate to children. And why not, Sean wondered? Were we ever taught to let children starve? Is it our way?

Also, soldiers are men and men needed women—and they would find them, nonfraternization notwithstanding. Certainly, as commander, Sean could make it dangerous, but never dangerous enough to stop it.

Only yesterday he saw something at his own residence that set him thinking. Two of his guards were helping his old servants, Alfred and Heidi Oberdorfer, repair their shattered cottage.

"Goddamn," Sean whispered aloud, "we are lousy conquerors."

The scales had dropped even lower—another cut in food ration had been ordered. How long would the energy of the people last? And when winter comes their bodies will demand hundreds more calories for heat. Sean had a foreboding that God would make this winter a severe one.

The food crisis was hastening the black market and bringing on massive prostitution. Crime and venereal disease would follow in natural course.

Sean turned into Princess Allee. Behind the half-smashed façades there were sounds of laughing men and women. It was a strange sound in Rombaden—at least the Poles and the whores had full bellies and bootleg rotgut. The competition to become an "official" Princess Allee whore was intense.

As they saw Sean O'Sullivan walking down the middle of their street they ducked into doorways. The incongruous sound of a woman singing reached his ears; it came from a makeshift cabaret in a cellar. Sean leaned against the doorframe, looked down into the rancid-smelling den. Her husky voice sang:

> Du, Du liegst mir im Herzen,
> Du, Du liegst mir im Sinn;
> Du, Du machst mir viel Schmerzen,
> Weisst nicht, wie gut ich dir bin.

A bit of sentimental tripe from another age:

> You, you live in my heart,
> You, you live in my soul,
> You, you cause me great sorrow,
> You don't know how good I am for you.

A resounding chorus of men and women's voices picked up the song and they thumped mugs on the heavy oaken tables and sang Ja! Ja! Ja! Ja! Everything came to a terrified halt as they saw Sean. He shook his head and walked out quickly.

Sean stood musing in the great square . . . from the Romans to the jackboots. He glanced up to his office and to the statue of Berwin and Helga, and across the square to the cathedral. The statue of Mary had been repaired. Tomorrow the cathedral would be returned to the people as a place of worship as the last of the Schwabenwald inmates had been moved to the field hospital in Castle Romstein.

The bell tolled the hour. Berwin and Helga . . . Christ and Mary. Would Christ, the Son of God, ever emerge over Berwin, Son of the King of the Gods, in the souls of the people?

CHAPTER THIRTY-THREE

Andrew Jackson Hansen tossed and turned. Sean's words pounded through his drowsy brain. He snapped the night lamp on. "Goddamned stubborn Irish son of a bitch!"

He fished for his specs, focused on the clock. Three in the morning. Sean's time was up. He would be reporting in by noon. No sir, that hardheaded Irish son of a bitch wouldn't change his mind. He'd march in, walk the thirteen steps, lay his neck on the chopping block, and wham!

Hansen turned off the lamp and tried to settle down, grumbling at the overheated discomfort caused by the heavy German down comforter. He made a mental note to get a couple of army blankets issued.

"General Hansen. I have sat here, day in, day out, week after week listening to one German after another repeat the same story like broken records. They say . . . we were only following orders . . . just following orders . . . just following orders. I'm not going to commit murder in the name of my country for you or anyone else just because orders are orders . . . I'll take full responsibility for my decision . . . I'm sorry, I believed in you . . ."

The light went on again. Hansen kicked off the comforter and stared sullenly at his knobby big toes. In a moment a chaw of tobacco was tucked deeply into his jaw and he sighted in on the spittoon at bedside.

Sean was a rare officer. He had emerged from personal tragedy, assumed a vital command, performed with near brilliance. In this Army . . . no, in this whole goddam world . . . there are so few men who have the courage of their convictions . . . it's so easy to pass the buck, as he, Hansen, knew he was trying to do. That one rare man in ten thousand who says with quiet simplicity, I'll take the responsibility . . . that's it! Smack on the button. No buck passing, no wishy-washy whining.

What had happened when Sean fired Dante Arosa? General Hansen never knew. Sean merely said, once again . . . I'll take the responsibility. Those two were close friends. What made Arosa resign from the Army? It takes guts to punish a friend . . . and even more guts to defend an enemy.

What the hell . . . didn't Sean know there are times when every man must bend a little?

And what the hell was the use of trying to rationalize? Hansen knew, in his heart, that Sean O'Sullivan had made a great decision. It was that type of decision a man makes alone when all well-meaning advice is to the contrary. It is a decision in which the maker leaves himself knowingly open to scorn and danger. There were so precious few men

capable of making a great decision that it was an awesome thing to
know such a man.

"Okay, you son of a bitch," he grumbled, "we go down together."
Hansen snatched the phone. A half-dozing operator answered. "Find
Nelson Goodfellow Bradbury and have him report to my quarters im-
mediately."

With that he dressed, went to his writing desk, and began the first
of many drafts of Proclamation 26.

It was two full hours before Big Nellie could be located in Wiesbaden
at the tail end of a serious drinking bout with the Air Corps. He had to
be pried loose and sobered enough to comply with the unusual summons. When he arrived he was in a suspended state of silliness.

"Got here as soon's I could, General. What's up?"

"This," Hansen snapped, handing him a paper.

Nellie's great paws lined the paper up for reading.

PROCLAMATION #26 MILITARY GOVERNMENT HEAD-
QUARTERS, FRANKFURT A/M
Upon complete re-examination and reconsideration it is deemed that
PROCLAMATION #22 (calling for special tribunals) is inconsistent
with democratic ideals, the vision of our founding fathers, and the
meaning of the American Republic. Even suspected Nazi war criminals
are entitled to due process of law as we understand it. Therefore,
PROCLAMATION #22 is hereby null, void, and rescinded.
                          A. J. Hansen, Major Gen. United States Army

"Jesus H. Christ! When did you people decide all this?"

"We people didn't decide nothing. I decided. Frankly, I don't even
know if I have the authority. However, lad, you are going to see to it
that this is on the front page of every AP newspaper in America by their
morning editions simultaneous with its being sent through channels
here. So, if it isn't official, you make it official."

Big Nellie knew what he had to do. There was not much time. He
folded the proclamation and put it into his breast pocket. "You're an
ace, General Hansen," he said, and left.

It was about noontime of the following day, two hours after Proclamation 22 was nailed dead, that Sean maneuvered his jeep through
the streets of another German rubble pile. This one was called Frankfurt. Supreme Headquarters for Germany had been established in the

I. G. Farben building, formerly the heart of the world chemical cartel. The fact that the building stood intact while nearly everything around it had been leveled was an irony of war. The building was a gargantuan affair comparable in miles of halls and millions of square feet and numbers of elevators to the Pentagon and the Chicago Merchandise Mart.

Sean O'Sullivan, a mere major, was lost in the flood of silver oak leaves, eagles, and stars. Everyone here walked with a chipper air. None of that tired drag of the combat man. Each man felt that he carried in his briefcase the most important problem in Germany . . . if not the world.

After much ado, Sean was able to ascertain where General Hansen's office was located.

He stepped into one of those odd, open-faced, one-man elevators that move continually on a vertical conveyor belt so that stepping in and out through the open shafts on each floor called for correct timing, particularly when one was juggling one's briefcase.

"Major O'Sullivan is here, sir."

"Send him in."

Sean stepped before his desk, and accepted the extended hand. "I heard the news sir. I heard about it when I was driving through Mainz an hour ago. What will they do to you, sir?"

"What the hell do you think? They'll pin a goddam medal on me!" Hansen waved Sean into a chair. "Well, so far my ass has been chewed out by Ike and four of his deputies and three people from the State Department. At the present moment, my future is being discussed by the Pentagon and the White House. We might as well have a game of checkers while we're waiting . . . you *do* play checkers?"

"How about blackjack?"

Sean lost forty-two consecutive games of checkers while they waited. It was evening when the statement was released from the White House. A single sentence summed up the entire affair: THE RESCINDING OF PROCLAMATION #22 WAS CORRECT.

"You know," Hansen said, "we Americans have the damnedest luck. The Lord has granted us a rare thing . . . that chance to take a second look at things. And on that second time around, we usually come out all right."

Hansen looked at his watch. "Well, now that we know we are in the

Army for a while longer, I'd like you to stay over. There is something very, very important I was saving to discuss with you."

From the tone of Hansen's voice, Sean knew that another fateful decision was looming up ahead of him.

CHAPTER THIRTY-FOUR

During and after dinner the two men spoke of the matters of the day. General Hansen had completed a tour of the British, French, and American zones. The statistics on Germany's demise, now pouring into Frankfurt, staggered the imagination. Frankfurt itself had 150,000 dwellings before the war; 40,000 of these now stood. Never in the history of modern civilization had a country been so thoroughly demolished.

To add to the misery, tens of millions of displaced persons swelled the roads of Europe, and Germany was being forced to take in millions of her ethnics from Poland, Czechoslovakia, Hungary; expelled from these lands for betrayal to Hitler.

All of those things which make man civilized did not function within Germany. Now came revelations from Poland about places named Auschwitz, Majdanek, Treblinka, Chelmno that made the death factories of Dachau and Schwabenwald mild by comparison.

Hansen saw the problem in three phases: short range, intermediate, and final. The short-range problem revolved around a single word, *food*.

"We can get by on all our other problems. If the Germans get cold enough this winter they can cut down their precious forests . . . but food . . ."

In the transition period the rebuilding would begin. The Ruhr coal mines had to work again; people had to be put on jobs; and the economy had to switch from things of war to things of peace. Parts of Europe ruined by German arms deserved the first help, and to further complicate German recovery Russia had put in a multibillion-dollar-reparations claim in the form of taking out any workable machinery.

The culmination, to allow Germany to govern itself again, seemed

so far away as to be impossible. "We haven't got enough trustworthy
or trained Germans to run a good garbage dump."

Slowly General Hansen worked up a direct comment to his young
officer. "We have a fourth problem, Sean. That's really what I wanted
to talk to you about."

"Yes, sir?"

The general hedged. "How do you figure things stand in Rombaden?"

"It's going to be painful and slow just like the rest of Germany. My
outlook is parallel to yours. Of course, I do have Ulrich Falkenstein.
He's invaluable."

"And Falkenstein has O'Sullivan. Don't be modest. What about you,
yourself?"

Hansen had been working a long way around to the question; Sean
countered with a question. "What about me, sir?"

The general's poker face was gone. "Well . . . what is your own
estimation of how long you figure on staying in the Army."

"I realized when I joined military government that I would be expected to stay on for some time after the end of the war. I haven't re-
fined those thoughts down in terms of weeks or months."

"What's your personal attitude about it?"

"Shall I level?"

"Shoot."

"I'm sick of Germans. I'm sick of Germany. I promised you I'd remain
fair. I've tried like hell to keep that promise."

"Emma Stoll would testify to your fairness. How badly is it getting
you down, Sean?"

"It's bad at night. At least during the day I'm busy. I'm learning that
the lonesomeness of being commander is quite a penalty. Sure, I could
impose my comradery on my officers, but there always has to be an
aloofness . . . what the hell am I telling you about it for . . . like it's
something you don't know. So, I button up in my study and around
midnight I get to thinking about my brothers and I have to get a little
smashed to drown my hatred . . ."

"What are you going to do when all this is over?"

"Hell, that's easy. If you were a genii and could grant me three wishes
I'll tell you what they would be."

"Wish number one?"

"I want to be near my mother and father for the rest of their lives.

They deserve that much. Wish number two . . . I need a woman, General . . . I want a wife. I'm not a kid any more and I'm tired as hell. I'll probably marry the first woman who treats me with tenderness. Maybe wish number one is all mixed up with wish number two. I want my mother and father to live and see their grandchildren. I want them to know that another generation of O'Sullivans will follow." And then Sean became silent.

"You still have another wish coming."

There was an expression of nostalgia in Sean's eyes. He dared allow himself to remember now that which he had shoved into a dark corner of his mind, and he said, "A campus. A green, green campus. Big lawns, old buildings like castles, and trees. Watching the campus from my class, and those cute little things walking by swishing their cute little asses. I want that beautiful quiet before the carillons play in the tower. I want to look into the faces of students filled with hope and energy and inquisitiveness."

"And how will you get wish number three?"

"Well, I was a political science instructor, you know. I continued my own studies at night. I've got a semester for my masters and in two or three years I think I'll be ready for a doctorate."

"And in between classes you'll fight four-round preliminaries again?"

"No . . . not this time. My brothers have paid me back with their lives. Two lives . . . ten thousand dollars a life. Ironic, isn't it? Anyhow, the GI insurance will keep my parents comfortable until I finish. And then, with this new GI Bill . . ."

"Well, when you are ready for your doctorate you should be able to do a hell of a paper on military government."

Sean laughed. "Probably not enough theory . . . scholars are practical only when it doesn't disturb theory."

"Your three wishes are very simple. Have you ever thought about staying on in the Army? You've got a big rank for a young man."

"I'll stay on long enough to get my job done."

"Done? But that may take twenty years."

"I mean . . ."

"You mean, complete the first phase in Rombaden."

"Yes, sir, that's what I mean."

Hansen went through the business of finding and lighting a pipe. He longed for a chaw, but never chawed in the presence of a second party . . . except his wife. "General," Sean said, "you're a lousy poker player. What is it that you really want to ask me?"

He put out a fourth match, waved away the billow of smoke. "I'm going to Berlin. I want you to come with me."

"Berlin?"

"That's right, Berlin."

Sean collected his wits and asked shakily, "Is the General implying he wishes me to remain in the Army?"

"I am implying that his country needs him more than his mother and father or his own personal desires to find peace of mind."

The blood drained from Sean's lips. He tried to envision it. Berlin! A monstrous prison. The piles of rubble and the pall of gray devoured his beautiful green campus and the haunting lonely eyes of his father.

Sean shook his head slowly. "No, sir. I don't want to go to Berlin."

"Neither do I, Sean," Hansen said with deliberate slowness. "I've been looking for peace of mind for thirty years. I don't want to go to Berlin, either."

"But my father!"

"Ask your father!" The general got to his feet and began to pace. "Oh Christ, yes. The campus is cozy and warm. A handsome Irish buck like you will go right to the top. Pat the ass of the president's wife and smile with those big brown eyes and the world is yours by the nuts on a downhill pull. And think of the nice young stuff you can sort, stud, and train to your exact liking. Hell yes, Sean, anybody give up that green campus for a friggin' rock pile like Berlin would have to be nuts. None of the ugly things like Schwabenwald and sick Germans and rubble to contend with. Just discuss them in a scholarly manner. No decisions to make there, lad."

"Lay off, General. I don't know why the hell I've suddenly become the indispensable man in the Army."

"I'll tell you why! America is committed to the world, only America doesn't know it or believe it yet. We would all like to make a retreat to the campus, but the comforts of home and hearth are henceforth to be denied unborn generations if our country is to survive."

"You are obviously speaking about the Russians."

"You're reading me loud and clear."

"I'm not one of these automatic liberals who takes a fixed position, but let's lay it on the line, General. You're a Red baiter from the year one."

"Hear me out and see if I'm a Red baiter."

Sean had stepped into Hansen's trap! What if Hansen proved his case? The general knew all along there were senses of duty and points of logic that Sean would respond to.

"I don't want to hear it, General."

"They have men of fanatical devotion beyond our comprehension of dedication. They have them by the hundreds of thousands who perform like robots. I lay awake nights in fear of a mortal weakness in us. I fear our sons are too fat, too lazy, too complacent to sacrifice and to serve in silence. It takes no genius to figure out what is going to happen in Berlin and there are too damned few of us willing to believe it or face up to the facts. Our country is asleep. Until it wakes up I need every Sean O'Sullivan I can get in Berlin if we are to survive."

Sean was dumbstruck by the urgency of the outburst. Could he walk from this room now without even listening to the man's case?

He nodded slowly for General Hansen to begin. . . .

CHAPTER THIRTY-FIVE

General Andrew Jackson Hansen first came into contact with the Russians at the close of the First World War in the year 1920. After the Russian Revolution and counterrevolution there was an acute famine condition. As a young officer, he became part of the Hoover Commission, which fed ten million Russians a day.

Hansen contended that the Russian Revolution was not much of a revolution. The Czar's house was rotten from within from centuries of feudalism, corruption, class rule, church abuse, failure to industrialize, failure to humanize. The rotten house needed but a hearty shove to collapse. History has been conveniently rewritten by the Communists for the world to believe that the revolution was a Communist-led people's uprising. That is not true.

The Russian people, Hansen said, both by nature and by historical precedent, have proven that they are neither politically inquisitive nor revolutionary in spirit. They have tolerated a police state in one form or another from the origins of their history, for some twelve solid centuries. They have lived out their entire history in complete adjustment to police-state terror with little or no protest.

Hansen liked to point to Pavlov's experiments with dogs. The great Russian scientist experimented to show how completely an animal could be conditioned. Such an animal could be trained to perform certain feats to ward off hunger, cold, and privation. Hansen believed that in a sense, Pavlov was experimenting with the Russian people themselves. Human history has given few examples of a people who can be so thoroughly conditioned as the Russians. When the pressures reach a critical stage, another bone is thrown them and they will remain quiet. Indeed, with pitifully few exceptions the Russians are magnificently trained animals who will not permit an alien, creative, free, or contradictory idea to function within their minds. They adjust within that framework of what they are allowed to think by their peers.

In recalling the history of the ending of the first war, Russia was weary, bloody, beaten, and hungry. The moment was ripe for a gathering of divergent political parties to unite and push in the Czar's rotten house. This was the so-called revolution.

Among those divergent groups was the Communist Party. When the new government was formed the Communists were not a majority. However, they were the most tightly knit, the most ruthlessly led, the most dynamic, and the most deliberate in their ultimate goals.

In the confusion that followed the flight of the Czar, the Communists made a naked seizure of power. This was not a popular movement of the people, which they later claimed, nor was it particularly understood in most reaches of that vast land.

After a time, scattered remnants of the Czarist regime got their second wind, and along with Ukrainian and White Russian Nationalists, who hated "Mother Russia," staged the counterrevolution against the Communists.

These were the "Whites." The White Counter-Revolution was doomed from its inception. As the Whites reconquered parts of Russia, they reinstated the nobility and the corrupt system that had led to the collapse of the Czar in the first place. They tried to beat a dead horse to life.

The Reds, therefore, fell heir to the people by the default of the Whites. It was the lesser of the evils at the time. The Communists, moreover, did not sell the war-weary people on any lofty idealisms of

Marx. The Red slogan was simple and understandable . . . Bread! . . . Peace! . . . Land!

The Communists made a separate peace with Germany, withdrawing Russia from the war, and deserting their former allies. France, Britain, and the United States had both troops and equipment on Russian soil, including an Allied-trained Czechoslovakian division. Angered at Russia's separate peace and committed to guard their hordes of supplies, the Allies loosely supported the ill-fated White Counter-Revolution. For this alleged Allied treachery, the Western world earned the everlasting hatred of the Russians.

Poland, which had been partitioned into oblivion before the First World War re-emerged once more as a nation. Poland made an ill-advised move, leaping on the back of the shaky Russians in 1920, the latest in a series of wars between old enemies. However, the Red Army had gained the people's support and defeated the Poles. Poland fell into the same circle of hatred, being lumped with the West.

One of the first things Hansen learned when he came to starving Russia in 1920 was that the Russians were Asians. Western culture had been imported into only a few of the larger cities. Most of Russia and the other captive states that comprised the Soviet Union simply did not think or act like the West.

From the beginning of the Communist regime the Russians made it clear that they would take Western food, Western long-term loans, Western credits, Western trade, Western recognition. There was never so much as a small thank-you for any of it. For, the Communists made it clear from the first that they intended to remake the world in their own image.

Hansen felt that this, in essence, was more dangerous than the Nazis, who wanted to conquer only in the name of Germany. The Russian aim was more awesome. The Communist believes he has an answer for the entire world. The German arises violently and is beaten down the same way. But the Russians have oriental patience. They waited a decade for political recognition and they will wait a century to achieve the ultimate aim. A stalemate for a decade does not matter, for the machinery is always at work, always plodding on. They are convinced that their final victory is inevitable.

The Russian people knew that all invasions from Napoleon to Hitler had come from the West. Any pact they made for a temporary convenience was for their own benefit. Being allies with the West against the Nazis in no way impeded their *other* goals against the rest of mankind.

Narrowing the immediate Russian objectives was simple. The first goal was the German working class, the true birthplace of Marxism. Control of the German working class was tantamount to control of Europe . . . an old and true axiom. Hansen felt that Russia intended to capture and communize Germany as their first step against all of Europe.

But . . . in order to capture Germany . . . first, Poland, which sits between them, must go. It was in the maneuverings about Poland during the war that led Hansen to his fears.

Austria, Spain, and Czechoslovakia had been sold out to Hitler by Western ineptness. When Hitler applied the pressure to Poland, Stalin was convinced that the West would also sell out the Poles. To complicate matters, Poland refused Russian help.

So, assured of Western timidity again, knowing Polish hatred of Russia, Stalin thought it foolish to gamble further with the West.

Instead, he made a pact with Hitler. Hitler wanted the pact because Poland was next on his timetable. In the event France and Britain should honor their commitment to defend Poland Hitler did not want to risk the possibility of a two-front war. So, he set out to "neutralize" Russia. Stalin, with a clear understanding, made himself a shrewd bargain. He got half of Poland, the Baltic States, and a clear field to clean up some defensive positions in Finland, and what is more, purchased precious time to build for the attack he knew would come, sooner or later, from Germany.

In 1939 Poland was attacked. By agreement, Russia knifed Poland in the back and took the eastern half of the country. Many Poles escaped. Some got to England, where they formed the Polish Government-in-Exile. This was the universally recognized body speaking for a sovereign Poland.

A year and a half after Poland's demise, Russia was attacked by Germany and thereby became the "official" ally of England. From the outset it was a strange alliance. An alliance by default . . . a shotgun wedding . . . and a temporary arrangement of mutual convenience.

From the very start the Russians showed the coldness and aloofness they held for their allies. There was never a thank-you for the convoys of Allied material which poured into Russia through the suicide Murmansk run. The death of ships and men in the icy waters of the Barents

Sea became a legend of horror. Those who survived and landed in Murmansk and Archangel were greeted by a further coldness to match the waters.

But, the Allies kept their silence, for Russia was drawing hundreds of thousands of casualties which might have been their own.

As part of the inside diplomatic maneuverings, Russia recognized the Polish Government-in-Exile in London known as the London Poles. This took place in 1941. Russia made this recognition in order to begin pressure on the West for promises of postwar border changes in Poland.

For the sake of window dressing, the Russians went so far as to "officially" dissolve the Comintern, the instrument of international Communism. This was done to pacify the Allies. Hansen was certain, from intelligence reports, that the Comintern in reality never ceased to exist for a moment. He was positive that an intense training of foreign agents to seize a number of countries was always active and now ready to move, particularly in Germany, Poland, and the Slavic countries.

Roosevelt and Churchill retained a certain timidity about shoving Stalin because of the fact that Russia bore the brunt of the war. Stalin, however, had no such inhibitions. He continued unceasing pressure for the West to agree to postwar settlements. These he could now get "legally." The other type "settlements" would be obtained later.

The London Poles protested Stalin's proposed postwar border changes. In one of the great paradoxes of the war, the British and Americans kept the London Poles from becoming too boisterous out of fear of offending Stalin.

This "bothersome" Polish question exploded in 1943.

When Poland was attacked by Germany in 1939 many Polish officers and men chose to flee to Russia as the lesser of evils and throw themselves on the tender mercy of the Soviet Union. Many thousands of Polish officers were interned with the hopes of fighting another day.

Fifteen thousand of these Polish officers were put into camps in a place called the Katyn Forest. From the moment the Russians interned them, they were never heard from again. Hansen, who worked very closely with the British, knew the London Poles had made innumerable demands to know what became of these officers. The Russians never gave them an answer.

In 1943 the German armies advanced into Russia and came upon the Katyn Forest. They claimed to have found the bones of these 15,000 "missing" Polish officers in common graves, the victims of a massacre.

The Germans invited the International Red Cross to investigate and the London Poles joined that demand for an investigation.

The Russians became indignant and broke off recognition of the London Poles. Again, Britain and America tried to calm the pesky Poles and the charge was never allowed to be investigated.

Hansen reckoned that 15,000 human pawns were slaughtered because these Polish officers stood as a potential force against Russian aspirations in postwar Poland.

Later, when the Russians recaptured Katyn, they conducted their own closed investigation and said it was really the Germans who had murdered the Polish officers.

There were, of course, two sides and two stories in the Katyn massacres, but Hansen believed that history had proved the Russians capable of just such a slaughter. They had already made it clear they were going to have a Poland they could dominate on their border as a buffer against future invasion from the West.

There were precedents to show they would murder for political gain. Hansen reckoned the Russians had killed in excess of ten million of their own citizens in twenty-five years under Communism. Despite the frostings of peace and brotherhood coming from joint conferences he felt them neither peace-loving, kind, gentle, nor caring much for the brotherhood of man.

After the Russian Revolution the Communists first liquidated the upper class, from the Czar on down, and the nationalists of Ukrainia and White Russia, with the dispatch of the guillotine days after the French Revolution. Hansen knew of this from firsthand observation.

At the end of the 1920s Stalin initiated his collectivization of the farmlands. There were millions of prosperous or semiprosperous peasants in a class known as the Kulaks. Terror squads from Moscow swooped into the farmlands with orders to "liquidate the Kulaks as a class." History will never record the true number of Kulak families murdered on the spot or shipped to Siberia as slaves. Certainly it was no less than five million men, women, and children. Losses in crops ran in millions of bushels, millions of acres. Losses of cattle, goats, sheep, pigs ran into tens of millions. The animal losses seemed to annoy Stalin and his planners far more than the human losses.

Hansen estimated from all his sources of information that some thirteen million Russian or Soviet citizens had been forced into slave labor during the two and a half decades of Communism.

The most notable slaughter, however, was to come later during the purge trials between 1936 and 1939. A reign of terror paralleled only by the Spanish Inquisition, by the Nazis, or by the Mongol hordes was clamped on the Soviet Union. One half to three quarters of the teachers, lawyers, doctors, writers, scientists, military men, intellectuals were hauled before "People's Courts" after confessions for alleged crimes had been brutally beaten from them. They were then taken out and shot or hanged. No one was safe from the mania of Stalin. Crimes had such alluring names as "deviationism," "cosmopolitanism," "Trotskyism," "adventurism," "speculationism."

In the beginning of the war many Ukrainians, White Russians, and even Russians themselves had looked upon the German as a liberator. When the Russians reconquered these lands the carnage of vengeance was epic. Hansen believed Stalin to be the supreme monster of all ages.

The final chapter of the Polish tragedy was played out in 1944, just before the Allied landing in Normandy. Russia rolled back the German lines, moved into the Balkans, and in the north came to the Vistula River directly across from Warsaw.

As the Russians advanced on Warsaw they urged the Polish Underground Home Army to stage a rebellion. The Home Army was the official military arm of the London Poles . . . fairly large in numbers and fairly well armed with light weapons. In Warsaw, some 40,000 of the Home Army seized the strong points and controlled the city as the Russian "liberators" approached.

Then followed the epitome of treachery. The Russians halted their offensive on the Vistula, opposite Warsaw, and did nothing to help the Home Army, which they had urged to rebel. The Germans returned to Warsaw with a pair of SS Panzer Divisions and commenced to butcher the city, the Home Army, and the citizenry as the Russians watched.

London and Washington demanded that Moscow help the Poles. At first Stalin stalled by claiming the Poles had exaggerated their strength and doubted if they controlled Warsaw.

The next stall was to claim the Russian armies were exhausted from their offense and needed to regroup and resupply.

Churchill continued to press the issue. Stalin at last showed his bloody hand. In the end Stalin let it be known he had no intention of helping the embattled Poles on the grounds that the Home Army were "military adventurers." Stalin obviously wanted the Home Army de-

stroyed because it was attached to the London Poles and might stand in
the way of his postwar plans for Poland.

In final desperation Churchill asked for permission to air-drop supplies into Warsaw. Because the distances were great it would necessi-
tate Allied planes landing on Russian airfields after they made their
drops.

The Russians refused to allow either American or British aircraft
to land on their soil.

And so, Warsaw was destroyed and nearly 200,000 of her people
killed.

Hansen had continually sided with the British in their demands to
be tough with Stalin and to plan Allied campaigns with a political
objective also in mind. At the time of the finale in Warsaw, Roosevelt
was a very sick man and the State Department, held in low esteem by
Hansen, floundered aimlessly.

Earlier, the British wanted the Southern France landing canceled
and instead have a landing made in the Balkans. Hansen backed this
idea. It took no fool to realize that France, Holland, Denmark, Belgium, and Luxembourg were going to remain in the West. However,
the entire Balkans were in doubt.

Hansen contended that if the Allies had landed in the Balkans and
placed an army between Russia and Germany we would be in a position to stop future seizures like Poland. As it stood, the West might default Roumania, Hungary, Yugoslavia, Bulgaria, and perhaps even
Czechoslovakia. Moreover, eastern Germany and Austria were in danger.

Russian agents had stirred up revolutions in Greece and Italy, but
fortunately, Hansen thought, the British commanded that area of the
war and weren't going to let them get by with it.

The final card of Poland was played. After full refusal to even deal
with the London Poles, the Russians installed their own "Liberation
Committee" out of Moscow to rule the country.

Having thrown Sean into a quandary with stories he had never
known before, Hansen pressed his case home recalling an experience
with which Sean was intimate.

When the Allies landed in France, in many towns the French Underground staged an uprising to coincide with the Allied attack. As soon
as the town was liberated the Frenchmen were too busy celebrating in

accepted French fashions and too relieved with the war ending for them to keep a Gallic eye on their city hall.

In fact, some French troops advanced into towns with women in their tanks and fought the last battle with one hand around a bottle or a woman. And while the Allies and the Underground were getting buried in wine and flowers and bosoms the Communists inside the French Underground quietly seized the mayoralities and police machinery of dozens of French cities. It was Hansen who issued the order to disarm the Communists, however French they claimed to be, and eject them from office.

Hansen poo-pooed the asinine "brotherhood" proclamations that followed the "big three" conferences, particularly from Yalta. The Russians subscribed to glowing statements about democracy which they did not understand and free elections which they had never held. At the same moment they paid this lip service to freedom, their handpicked henchmen closed the book on Poland as a clear and bright signal of things to come.

Hansen decried the fact that the American General Staff had little mentality for the political situation. While the Russians and British knew enough to plan their battles in line with political advantages, the Americans walked a path of purity and innocence. This stemmed from the fact that America never was threatened by strong neighbors on her borders or even needed to keep a balance of power in her hemisphere.

Consistent with American shortsightedness, the British had to plead for permission to move across northern Germany to block it off and keep the Russians from "liberating" Denmark.

In the end American forces concentrated on an envelopment of the German Army in the Ruhr instead of choosing a rapid advance to Berlin, and Patton was called back out of Czechoslovakia. When Churchill made the last desperate plea for the Americans to dash for Berlin he was answered that Berlin had ceased to have strategic value!

When American forces pulled in back of the Elbe River, their Russian allies of the day before had begun the erection of barbed-wire barriers.

Both Russia and America had been isolationist by nature but the war changed that. Russia had become powerful. The long-smoldering giant began his move to the West. America alone could block him now.

In order to gain a right to be in Berlin, America surrendered two German provinces in another of Stalin's typical, shrewd moves.

Hansen felt that it took no genius to figure out what would happen in Berlin when the giants met head-on. Yet, an America tired of war, unready to believe their ally of yesterday was the enemy of today, unready to accept their new status of world power would call Hansen an alarmist, a man who cried "wolf."

And until their countrymen understood what was happening a few Hansens and a few O'Sullivans would have to step into the breach . . . and halt a tide in an arena named Berlin.

CHAPTER THIRTY-SIX

The moment of decision is the loneliest in human life. It must be come upon in stillness and darkness and brooding thoughts and doubts torn out from the deep reaches of the soul.

Sean O'Sullivan was a political scientist. He knew that if Hansen had spoken the truth on the Polish affair then his fears about Berlin were not only reasonable but valid. Now he labored over stacks of supporting documents, weeding truth from fiction.

We have ordered that Berlin's main radio transmitter, namely the Funkturm, be spared from bombing. Allied liaison with the Russians is so poor that we often times have to find out where the front lines are in the East from the transmission of German newscasts.

Legendary Russian secrecy and suspicion. . . . Only Churchill seemed to understand it all. In the very beginning he understood Hitler, but his warnings fell on the ears of the appeasers. And, in the end, he understood Stalin. America was suddenly without leadership. Churchill wanted us to make a physical presence in the Balkans and he wanted us to hold fast in Czechoslovakia. Churchill understood the meaning of having our forces reach Berlin first. We, in a sense, had committed the same blunder Hitler committed when he failed to recognize the importance of Moscow in the beginning of the war and turned his armies on the oil fields in southern Russia. One could now speculate seriously if Russia could have recovered from the capture of Moscow.

In our case we turned to the southern German provinces and to hacking up an already beaten German Army in the Ruhr with the fateful pronouncement that "Berlin ceases to have strategic value."

Yes, human beings make human errors. However, other human sweat and human blood must pay for those errors. As yet, no one would admit an error had been committed; and few, unlike Hansen, understood the dimensions of the error or the gravity of the situation.

In the classroom Sean would have argued that the Russian is a decent human being, peaceful by nature, gifted with scientific genius, driven by normal desires. Sean, in a classroom, might have questioned the Purge Trial statistics or whether the Kulaks were truly liquidated or deserved to be broken up. Such things as Katyn massacres, the deliberate butchery of Warsaw simply did not exist in a civilized world. Yes, a teacher would question and he would theorize.

But Sean's ability to theorize had been impaired by the months of study in Queen Mother's Gate. He learned not to hold CIC reports as fantasy. For the most part they were cold-blooded, nonpolitical in viewpoint, nontheoretical, and filled with facts which had to be accurate by the very nature and function of CIC.

Any former ideas or ideals of humanism among peoples had been destroyed the moment Sean O'Sullivan walked through the gates of the Schwabenwald Concentration Camp.

The death of Poland and the fears about Russia were truth:

Warsaw is eighty-five per cent destroyed. A quarter of a million people, mostly civilians were killed. It is positive beyond doubt that a Russian crossing of the Vistula River could have been made and prevented the entire carnage. The destruction of Warsaw and particularly the Home Army was a deliberate, calculated political move on the part of the Russians.

Was General Andrew Jackson Hansen a ranting Red baiter? For ten solid years Hansen had pleaded with the Army to form a large and effective Russian study section. He wanted to train men to speak Russian, to understand the people and the motives and the methods of dealing with them. But, like so many of Hansen's ideas, this one also hit a brass wall. The time was not fashionable. An American Army with such a department in the days before World War II would have brought the instant wrath of the liberals on their heads. Well, A. J.

Hansen would have his Russian study section now, in the flesh, in Berlin.

Sean found himself hypnotized by the summations on Russian characteristics and behavior during the war.

"In the beginning," Sean read, "the Red Army had been demoralized by the loss of more than half of their entire officer corps by the Purge Trials of 1936–38. A staggering total of 90 per cent of the colonels and generals had been liquidated by Stalin.

"In 1940, the Russian expedition against Finland bared the state of disaster facing the Red Army. The Russians fought in Finland with little heart or stamina. They were mauled and outfought by the Finns. This shocking revelation and the sudden realization by the Russian people that their "Red Army" was far from invincible brought about a frantic reorganization.

"Soviet Political Commissars are attached to each unit of size. In addition, any officer and soldier who is also a member of the Communist Party oftentimes holds the power over the actual military commander. In essence, the Red Army has a dual command; the officers on one side and the commissars and members of the party on the other. The commissars, whose existence depends upon ultimate performance, used every known fear tactic to whip the Army into a fighting mood.

"The Red Army is essentially a peasant army. The soldiers of the Red Army understand one basic plea . . . save the soil . . . and save the motherland. When Germany attacked and the Red Army reeled back the commissars were clever enough not to appeal to save Communism or the Soviet 'way of life.' As in the old days of Bread, Land, Peace . . . the commissars cried, 'Save the motherland!' Commissars, officers, and party members within the Army literally stood behind their troops with machine guns pointed at their backs to keep them from further retreat.

"The soldier from the West is fairly predictable. One can surmise what a German or a French or Italian group of men will do under certain circumstances. However, the Russian soldier is an Asian, an oriental of sorts and he is completely unpredictable by Western standards. He will fight like a wild man on a given day. On another day, under the same circumstances, he will break and run.

"In the beginning of the war, victory was within German grasp. Hitler, however, balked at ordering a frontal assault and street fight to take Leningrad, setting siege instead. The second great error was the decision not to press for the capture of Moscow but instead to drive for the oil fields in the south. Capture of Leningrad and Moscow, it is believed, would have collapsed Russian morale beyond redemption.

"Furthermore, the Ukrainians, White Russians, Georgians, and other captive states within the Soviet Union have always breathed a fire of nationalism and desire for independence of Moscow and Russia. At first, these, along with thousands of Russian intellectuals, embraced the Germans as liberators. Free from the mental prison of Communism the reception toward the Germans was a startling revelation.

"However, the honeymoon was short. The basic Nazi stock in trade was to consider the Russians and other Slavs as "subhumans." This Nazi (and German) behavior played right into the desperate Russian propaganda mills. Now, for the first time, the Russian understood fully that the Germans meant to liquidate them as a people or reduce them to serfdom. Out of sheer fear for survival the Russians rallied.

"The third German blunder therefore was the playing out of their Aryan/superman myth. A partly sympathetic White Russian, Ukrainian, and Russian public awaited them. The Germans drove them back into Stalin's arms.

"The Russian soldier may be the best in the entire world. This is because he is the most expendable. The famous steamroller tactic of World War I was renewed in World War II. This system, basically, uses humans in hordes. Chop down one line and another comes at you. Chop down a third line and face a fourth. Chop down the thirtieth and you face the thirty-first.

"Russians are like a pack of animals on the attack and otherwise. The pack strikes best in numbers. And . . . like the animal . . . he is most vicious when he is cornered.

"Like the animal, the Russian blends into the natural backgrounds of the landscape and he knows how to use terrain for protection. Like the animal, the Russian is able to endure cold and hunger . . . better than any soldier in the world. No Russian soldier would think of surrendering to the enemy merely because he is starving. He can disappear into the land like a fawn. He can survive from roots and herbs. For a Russian soldier to get frostbite is considered a crime by his superiors. And . . . like the animal . . . his instincts are sharper and his courage greater under the cover of night. He is a superb night fighter.

"Although this Russian soldier is a resourceful animal he does not exist as an individual for he is a conditioned and controlled animal. All

the thinking is done for him from above. He is never asked or expected
to make a decision on his own.

"The top commanders of the Red Army are excellent soldiers of sound
military judgment.

"However, the captains, majors, lieutenant colonels and those in the
middle 'field rank' can think only as far as the staff over them orders.
These 'field' rank commanders carry out their orders to the fraction
of a letter. They carry them out on fear of liquidation from their own
superiors or the political commissars. There have been thousands of
individual instances where a field commander has failed to exploit a
sudden breakthrough because he simply will not assume personal responsibility.

"Most Russian tactics are based on using masses of men to overwhelm
the enemy. They have good armor, equal for the most part to the German armor, but their tank tactics are crude. If the Germans knock out
a dozen Russian tanks, they face another dozen.

"Their legendary artillery is also based on using mammoth numbers
to saturate the target.

"In bedrock, the formula is waves and waves of men in a frontal assault. This is the bread and butter power play of the Red Army. Many
a time the German would stack up Russian attackers like cord wood
but they came on endlessly. The Russian Staff thinks little of expending
regiments or entire divisions to spearhead a drive or clear a field of
land mines. Human fodder, the disregard of the individual, makes the
Red Army go.

"Interviews with German prisoners state how demoralizing a Russian
assault can be. Even if the attack is beaten back, the memory of it becomes unforgettable.

"This ruthless use of the human as soldier is paralleled by the ruthless
use of the Russian civilian population. The Soviet commanders will
never hesitate to use a village, a town, or a city as a defensive position.
As they retreat they will destroy the crops, machinery, homes in order
to deny these to the Germans, but at the same time deny their own citizens the means to exist. Many's the time the Red Army has pulled back
leaving such deliberate destruction that the civilian population has no
alternative but to starve to death. Thousands of towns were destroyed
and hundreds of thousands of civilians were killed and millions more
were moved to the interior of Russia as slave labor for suspicion of collaboration with the Germans.

"Russian defensive stubbornness is legend. The Russian will not be moved from a fixed position unless overwhelmed by the enemy. However, once a position is overrun, the Russian does not retreat in an orderly manner, he plunges back. The Russian has thousands of miles of land in which to fall back.

"Leningrad, even more than Stalingrad, is the prime example of Russian defense and ruthless disregard of a civilian population. Hitler shied away from a frontal assault on Leningrad and the bloody street fighting which would have to follow. Instead, he ordered a siege with the aid of Finnish troops in order to starve the city into submission. In the first six months an estimated half-million Russians died of cold and hunger. For the balance of the thirty-month siege, another half million met death. Yet, at no time did Leningrad intend to quit, and as the siege wore on, the city actually became stronger and stronger until they broke out.

"A line of credit must go to the women fighters who appear in every phase of the service including infantry, air corps, and tank corps.

"As the war progressed, the Red Army became stronger after the initial shocks. Top Russian commanders used superlative night movements and imaginative tactics. To compensate for the lack of motor transport, infantry was often moved on the back of tanks. In the winter when the poor Russian road system broke down and literally swamped German transport, the Russians used horses and sleighs to move men and equipment.

"One of the brilliant Russian improvisations was the building of bridges across lakes a foot under the water level. All work was done by night and when a breakout or attack was ordered, the Germans were confronted with the sight of tanks and infantry moving at them, apparently riding and running on the water.

"The Russian fights best at night. The partisan units wrought havoc. Using German uniforms and the cover of the land, these units could travel for days on a few slices of bread. They had a devastating effect on the overextended German supply lines.

"This has been a ghastly war; in fact, the most brutal ever fought between two civilized nations. German rape, loot, murder of prisoners, hatred of the people was everything Stalin promised the German would be. The Russians, however, matched atrocity with atrocity.

"Damage to cities, farms, livestock, industry is of astronomical proportion. The loss of Russian life, which both sides held so cheaply, is a likewise staggering total, perhaps ten million.

"German defeat grew inevitable. In the beginning there was tactical blundering by Hitler. Then Russian space and time and weather overcame them. Russian resources grew as German resources shrunk. New Russian armies trained far back of the lines were thrown at the Germans, who didn't even know they existed.

"The new Red Army is superb. It is well-trained, -equipped, and -generaled. It continues its success on the basic tactic of the human battering ram. As German casualties mounted and equipment was permanently lost, Germany began to lose initiative. Germany had no way of shrinking the multithousand-mile front line, but instead had to thin it out.

"The winters had a crushing effect on the German. Of this, much has already been written from Napoleon's time on.

"The Red Army is a powerhouse much changed from the early days. ITS PRESENCE IN EASTERN AND CENTRAL EUROPE IN THE POST WAR PERIOD WILL HAVE A PROMINENT IF NOT DECIDING FACTOR IN CARRYING OUT MOSCOW POLICY."

"Did you get through the documents last night?" Hansen asked Sean the next morning.

"As much as I needed to see."

"And did you reach a decision?"

"Hell yes. I reached it fifty times and changed my mind fifty times. What I really want, General Hansen, is to go home. I hate Germany and Germans. The prospect of the mission in Berlin fills me with despair . . . utter despair."

"What is the greater force, Sean? Love for your country or hatred of Germany and fear of Russia?"

Sean shook his head that he did not know.

"You are asking yourself, why me? Hell, I can't explain the inequities of this. The captains and the kings depart and leave to you and me a mess to clean up. Bright young majors like you will go home and become bright young executives. We'll be out here beating our heads against a wall . . . and for it we will receive no understanding and no gratitude. But, some of us are going to have to do it anyhow. It is the miracle of the survival of our republic. Always, at the right moment, the right men seem to step forward."

"I have no aspirations to being a martyr."

"Then say no, and be on your way."

"You know goddamned well I can't say no, General. General Hansen, once in London you asked me if I would abide by my father's decision in peace. I did and neither of us is sorry. Let me ask you the same thing now. Will you abide by his decision? Yesterday you challenged me to ask my father. All right, I'll ask him."

Hansen took off his specs and cleared his throat. The man before him was not happy, did not pretend to be. He had intentionally trapped him into a situation of honor. Yet, he was asking everything of Sean . . . everything.

"As you know they are transferring dozens of squadrons to the Pacific Theater every day. I'll call the Rhein/Main base and find out if you can hitch a ride. What's the nearest Army airfield to your home?"

"Hamilton, in Marin County."

"Go and see your parents. Our first contingent will be entering Berlin on the Fourth of July. When you return to Germany it will be either to go back to Rombaden and finish your command or it will be to come to Berlin with us for as long as we need you."

"The Fourth of July? But, sir, even with good connections I won't have much more than forty-eight hours at home . . . I've been gone almost four years . . ."

"That's it, Sean. Forty-eight hours."

CHAPTER THIRTY-SEVEN

"Hey, Major O'Sullivan, take a look."

Sean responded to the prodding of the navigator of the "Vigilant Virgin," a combat-weary B-24. He unraveled himself from a makeshift bunk in the bomb bay and slipped into the flight deck between the pilots. The aircraft commander pointed out of his window.

Below, the towers of the Golden Gate Bridge poked up through a pall of grayish clouds. Beyond the bridge, the gleaming plaster and hills of San Francisco searched for the ever-elusive sun.

"The Golden Gate in '48, the broad line in '49," someone said over the intercom.

And then, there was no more talk. For this crew it was good-by Europe, hello Pacific, but the Vigilant Virgin would be gone forever. The proud possessor of seventy-five raids, including survival of the Ploesti air massacre, she would meet an untimely end and her crew would be retrained for the more powerful B-29s.

"Strap in for landing."

The "follow me" jeep led the Vigilant Virgin into a hardstand. The alert crew signaled her to cut her engines and wheel chocks were set. Her men tumbled out of the open bomb bay, and Sean and three other hitchers thanked each of the crew for the ride. The ceremony was halted by a jeep pulling under the plane's wings. A corporal from Base Operations emerged.

"Excuse me. Is Major Sean O'Sullivan here?"

"I'm O'Sullivan."

The corporal came to a sloppy salute, which an Army man tolerated from the Air Corps. "Would you come with me, sir. Sergeant Schlosberg has some poop for you at the message center."

The jeep U-turned and drove down the side of the runway as the rest of the bomber squadron was making long glides to the landing strip.

"Afternoon, sir," Sergeant Schlosberg said. "How was the flight?"

"Good as any ride in an airplane can be."

Schlosberg tolerated the nonflying mentality of a land-locked Army officer. "We've got a TWX on you about your return flight, sir. You can catch a Staff B-17 out of Mather to Washington, then ATC on the VIP flight to Orly. If you'll check Base Operations in Paris they'll get you in to Frankfurt or Wiesbaden with Theater Aircraft. Should put you back by July 3."

"Mather, that's up by Sacramento, isn't it?"

"Yes, sir. We have a staff car to take you into Frisco now. If you'll leave your address at the motor pool we'll arrange to have you picked up and transported to Mather."

"I appreciate that."

The sergeant said it was nothing at all, having been fully awed by Sean's Priority One status in his orders.

"Could I use your phone?"

"Help yourself."

Sean indicated the call was private. The sergeant excused himself. Sean lifted the receiver.

"Hamilton operator."

"This is Major O'Sullivan. I've just arrived with the 23d Bomber Squadron. I'm calling from Base Operations. Could you reach a number in San Francisco?"

"Yes, sir."

"Get me Mission 0430."

"One moment, sir."

He heard the feedback of the dialing. The phone rang. Sean's hand tightened on the receiver . . . ring . . . ring . . . ring . . . click!

"Hello."

"Hello . . . Momma . . ."

Silence on the other end of the line.

"Momma . . ."

"Oh God!"

"Momma, it's Sean."

"Oh God! Oh God! Oh God!"

"Momma . . . don't cry . . . don't cry . . ."

"It's Sean!"

"Son . . . is it you, son!"

"Hello, Poppa."

"Is it really you!"

"Yes . . . yes . . . it's me. I'm sorry I couldn't reach you sooner and let you know. I've just landed at Hamilton Field. I'll be home in about an hour."

"Are you all right, son?"

"I'm fine . . . I'll be right home."

The road through Marin ran through brown hills. At the foot of the Waldo grade stood a new city of shacks near the frantic activity of the shipyards. Then up the hill and down into the tunnel and onto the Golden Gate Bridge. Over the bay, the city showed itself flirting through wisps of clouds streaming up the gate and the wind jarred the car about.

Now, past the toll gate into the city, they turned into Van Ness, which had been a gaudy auto row in peacetime . . . on past the great brick structure of the New Saint Mary's Church.

How small, how quiet everything looked. Houses, streets, all shrunk. But is not memory always larger than life?

Sean looked down the length of Market Street to the Ferry Building. A living sea of white-capped sailors told him there was still a war being fought. The rival Market Street and Municipal Street car lines staged one of their impromptu races on the four sets of tracks.

The light changed and they crossed into Mission Street, past the armory where Sean had held his first rifle.

"Drive down to Twenty-third Street, then make a right. My house is just before Guerrero."

"Yes, sir." The driver was given with a sudden feeling of equality. The major, obviously a VIP, lived in a neighborhood that wasn't half as nice as his own in Cleveland.

Momma and Poppa stood on the rickety porch. Poppa was supported by a cane, which trembled in his palsied hand. The driver stopped, opened the door, saluted, and stood awkwardly as Sean's mother ran to meet him and the old man hobbled down the three steps one at a time to join the circle of silent embracers.

At last, when the tears were under control, Sean nodded to the driver that he was dismissed, and the three of them walked quietly toward the house.

In the grandeur of his office and quarters in Rombaden and Queen Mother's Gate he had all but forgotten how very small and very tired the old house was. Large, overstuffed, mohair-covered furniture of a bygone age, the airless, lightless living room, drooping lace curtains, cracked window blinds. The ornate light fixture with crystal tear drops hung low in the center of the room over the round oak table, and Momma's doilies covered every chair back and arm. The petit-point footstool before Poppa's rocker . . . all of it was the same, only more weary.

On the mantel, a bit removed from the cheap plaster statuette of the Virgin Mother, were photographs of the O'Sullivan brothers in uniform . . . Private Liam . . . Lieutenant Timothy . . . and himself.

He saw the decay wrought from suffering borne by his parents. The last three years had aged them twenty. That big, raw-boned, broadbacked Irishman, Pat O'Sullivan, was a withered old shell.

"You look so tired," Momma said.

"Just the plane ride, Momma. They don't build those bombers for comfort."

But it was more than that, Momma knew. All the youth had fled him.

"Now, before we get involved in Mother's nonsense about how many meals you can eat and how many socks she can mend, tell us exactly how long you are able to stay?"

Poppa had intuition . . . he knew. "I'm afraid only two days."

"So soon!"

"I'm sorry, Momma. There will be a staff car picking me up day after tomorrow at ten in the morning."

"But . . . Sean . . ."

"Now, Mother. We promised. None of that. This is an unexpected treat. We are grateful to have Sean for even this much."

Pretty soon, Eileen O'Sullivan had assumed the role of a mother whose son had returned from the wars and she was in her kitchen cooking with vengeance. Sean and Patrick sat at the kitchen table, sipping tea and trying to speak of all those things that had gone by in three years of his absence.

In his own home and with his parents Sean realized the cruelty and finality of Hansen's wish. His parents had become ancient and weak from tragedy. It would put them in their graves to tell them he was leaving for perhaps the last time. And where was the justice of it? Oh, heavenly Christ! Where is the justice? Momma kept talking about how wonderful it was going to be to have Sean home to stay. Momma talked of little else.

Yes, yes, Sean agreed. It would be wonderful.

"You said you figured about two semesters to go on your Ph.D. Are you planning to go back to Cal?"

"Yes."

And then Momma asked Sean if he had given any thought to starting a family, and Sean said yes, he had given it a lot of thought.

Patrick O'Sullivan kept his peace during dinner, for now it was Momma's moment to speak of grandchildren and ask what he ate and where he lived in Germany and how he was taking care of himself.

"Goodness no, Sean! I won't hear of you wiping dishes. It's not a fit job for a major in the United States Army. You and Pat go on into the living room. I'll be in shortly."

Pat set his rocker into motion. Much of the trembling in his hand subsided. Where to begin? What to say?

"How do you spend your days, Poppa?"

"Well, I've still the best collection of John McCormack records in the Mission. And there's the radio. Mother goes up to the church at least once a day . . ."

"Are you able to get around at all?"

"Enough. We sleep downstairs. That saves me the steps. On the sunny days I walk up to Dolores Street or to the church. And thank God, the old eyes are as sound as a dollar. I like to read. I read most of the time since the last attack. There is so much to be learned."

"Poppa, I've been thinking. It would be nice for you and Momma to have one of those pretty little houses on Lincoln Way just across from the park. They're a lot brighter and you would have the park to walk in or just sit in and read . . ."

"Come now, Sean. Mother and I wouldn't know how to live anywhere else. This tired old house may be depressing to you because you're young and have ambitions and that is how it should be. To us, it's comfortable like an old shoe. We've been here nearly thirty years. All of you boys were born here . . ."

"But . . . if I should study at Cal I'd want you nearby so we could be together . . ."

"You're worrying too much about us. That's why you've come home, because you're worried about us."

The visitors started arriving. Only a few close friends they knew Sean would want to see. And when they had gone the three of them talked far into the night. And remembering and speaking Tim and Liam's names was not so painful as he believed it would be. When you have become very, very old like Momma and Poppa, memories are a sweet drug to soothe the long hours. . . .

The next morning Eileen O'Sullivan awoke at an ungodly hour to bake more pies and cookies than any one human could possibly eat in a week. And, while his father took an early afternoon nap, Sean strolled around the neighborhood.

. . . Mission High on Dolores Street. Room 28. Mr. Whitehurst's class. That is where he had first caught the fever of political science.

. . . The Coliseum . . . the old "bucket of blood" fight club . . . "Introducing! In the red corner wearing green trunks, at one hundred seventy-five and a half, from San Francisco's rough, tough Mission . . . the dancing master . . . Schoolboy O'Sullivan!"

Stick him and run, jab and go . . . don't get hit . . . don't let Momma see you with a busted-up face . . . jab run, jab run.

. . . The boys still hung around the ice-cream parlor at Eighteenth and Dolores. Some were inside playing the pinball machine, others outside looking over the quail.

. . . Buy at Lachman's Furniture. 17 Reasons Why! The neon light blinked off and on . . . 17 Reasons Why.

. . . Bunch of kids on the corner waiting for the *Call-Bulletin* car to drop off their papers, pitching pennies against the wall.

"Hey taxi!" Sean called on an impulse.

"Where to, general?"

"Run me out to the beach . . . Cliff House."

There were no seals on Seal Rock. The gulls owned it for now. Sean walked past a monstrous structure housing the Sutro Baths, a relic from before the turn of the century. It held a half-dozen pools of varied temperatures, an ice rink, a collection of junk, curios, old autos, pre-earthquake pictures, a hundred rattly-bang music boxes, Tom Thumb's clothing, penny movies, all in this mammoth hole along with talking birds, mummies, miniature towns made out of matchsticks, bowling games, voice-recording machines, and a magic well which accepted pennies, nickels, and dimes, catering to that American mania for throwing money in pools of water.

When Sean left Sutro he was drawn magnetically to the hills behind it leading down to the ocean. Years before, stairways and caves had been carved in the jagged rock for a sea-level restaurant, but the trick tides flooded the area and caused the project to be abandoned. It had been all but forgotten, except by adventurous little boys and nostalgic soldiers on leave.

From here he was behind the Sutro Baths and could see the archway that ran through the middle of one of the Seal Rocks. Sean felt his way down one of the tunnels. Midway he could see a diffused ray of light from the ocean, and spray pounded into the hole. At the end of the tunnel he climbed out onto the rocks just above the smashing surf and looked at the ocean and its golden gateway into San Francisco.

How many hours had they sat there, the three of them, after hitching rides to the beach on the backs of streetcars. They came and watched the ships sail in and out and played games of great adventure in the rocks and caves; and Tim fought the Irish Revolution and Liam read Irish poetry.

Sean was overcome with the nearness of his brothers and he was gripped with sadness. In all those months and years away he had always looked back to this place and to his native city with affection, but now it was an infinite part of his being. His brothers, their youth . . . this city was him and he was flooded by a thousand memories of things he had believed he had forgotten.

He walked away with a leaden heart. At the end of Golden Gate Park, facing the ocean, he walked past the enshrined sloop that had belonged to the explorer Amundsen, who had sailed it into the Arctic Circle.

He walked the entire length of the park . . . past the polo fields and lakes where little boys played great seamen with toy boats; and past the buffalo pens and rowboat lakes and those hidden places where sailors and their girls made love; past the Japanese Garden, now called the Oriental Garden . . . past all the lushness . . . immersed in memory.

Suddenly he was out of the park and the great church of St. Ignatius rose up before him. Sean entered, knelt, and crossed himself. It was that time of day when a few old ladies prayed for the lives of sons they might see again and many candles burned for sons who would never return.

It had been so long . . . so very long. All those prayers Sean had set away, had doubted, had neglected, all welled up now in a single desperate cry . . . "Oh Mother of God! I don't want to go back to Germany! Help me do the right thing!"

The quiet acceptance of Sean's departure the next day made things comfortable for everyone. The matter was being treated with the idea that Sean would soon return for good. And, until he went upstairs to sleep, he could not find it within him to talk about the true purpose of his visit.

Sean tossed restlessly in his bed. His brothers were with him . . . their mementos all about him. Baseball gloves, class pictures, Liam's first notebook of poetry, Tim's medals, the crucifix on the wall, books, boxing gloves, the crystal radio. Nothing in this room had been touched. It had been kept in spotless anticipation for the homecoming of the warrior sons.

Sean heard his father struggle up the stairs and knock on the door.

"I didn't wake you?"

"No, Poppa, but you shouldn't walk the steps."

The bed creaked as Pat sat on its edge, as he had done a thousand times. He stroked his son's hair and Sean was a little boy again.

"It has been a long hard journey for you, hasn't it, son?"

"Yes, Poppa."

"Was there a woman in England?"

"Yes."

"I could sense it from the tone of your letters."

"I never could lie to you or fool you very well . . ."

"And you loved her very much?"

"Yes. She was married . . . we had to . . . break it off."

"Does that still trouble you so deeply?"

"I haven't gotten over it fully. I guess I never will."

"But there's something else?"

Sean turned his back.

"Why did you make this trip?"

It became so easy to talk with Poppa beside him this way. He always understood. He knew from the first instant that Sean was in a turmoil. "I've been asked to stay in the Army. General Hansen wants me to go to Berlin."

"Well, Mother and I won't be too disappointed. From your letters we had already anticipated there would be somewhat of a wait until your discharge."

"You don't understand, Poppa. It means . . . at least four years . . . maybe more."

"Oh . . . I see . . . well now . . . what do you think needs to be done?"

"I want to come home. I want to come home. We should be together now . . . the three of us . . . that's what is right."

"Sean, there are certain indulgences that all parents would like to have. We want the closeness of our children and the pleasure of our grandchildren, but far more rewarding to your mother and me is seeing you grow into the kind of man you have become. This great pride you have given us far outweighs our little selfish pleasures." The wise father prodded his son to turn around and face him. "What is it you aren't telling me?"

Sean pointed to the two empty beds. "I can't go on living with their murderers."

"This General Hansen. You have a great deal of admiration for him, don't you?"

"Yes, sir."

"He knows your feelings about the Germans?"

"Yes, he does."

"Knowing this and admiring you also, if he still asks you to go to Berlin it must be mighty important."

Sean swung his feet to the floor, held his face in his hands. "Yes, it's important."

"Tell me."

"General Hansen sees dangers facing us that few others will admit to. He needs to have certain people with him in Berlin who realize we have to hold a line . . . until the rest of the country wakes up to what is happening. He's afraid he might not be able to find enough people willing to . . ."

"Haven't you pretty well answered your own question?"

Sean sprung to his feet. "How about me, Poppa! Christ, I'll be in my mid-thirties before I get back. I won't be fit to compete in class with kids. I won't be able to study any more. And it may damned well be too late to start a family. And us! Oh Poppa! I may never see you again . . . I don't want to be a soldier!"

Sean O'Sullivan cried in his father's arms as he had not cried since he was a small child. "Oh God!" he cried, "I hate them . . . I want to come home. I miss Liam and Tim . . . oh God!"

"Sean O'Sullivan," his father whispered, "you must be proud to be needed this way. I am a simple man and I do not have a command of language or philosophy. There is only one question you must ask and answer. Your mother does not count. I do not count. You do not count, or your ambitions or your life. Only one question."

"What is it?"

"Is America worth it."

They were smiling when Sean left the next morning, without heroics or tears. For them, forty-eight hours was food for an eternity of reveries. An embrace, a wave . . . and he was gone.

The C-47 bounced in and out of the layers of cumulus clouds. The plane flew southeasterly over the Rhine River, past a field of shells that had once been Düsseldorf.

The copilot was crapped out on a litter in the cabin. Sean sat in his place. He put on the earphones, enjoying hearing the cryptic jargon of the flyers. The pilot flipped on the intercom switch.

"Hey, Major. Look at that friggin' wreck down there. Like, Jesus H . . . huh?"

The plane inched over Cologne. Only the twin spires of the mighty cathedral stood in the midst of a lunar landscape along the river bank.

"Pretty sharp shooting how they missed the cathedral."

"Christ takes care of his own."

"Major, those krauts aren't going to dig out of this pile of crap for a hundred years."

"Don't make book on it."

The pilot switched back to the en-route frequency and called Wiesbaden tower.

"This is Army four-seven-six-three calling Y-80, over."

"Y-80 to Army four-seven-six-three, I read you five square, over."

"This is Army four-seven-six-three. What is the present weather?"

"Visual all the way in. Winds five knots from the northwest."

As they passed over Coblenz the pilot rechecked his ETA.

"We'll be landing in twenty minutes," he said over the intercom. "Where you heading, Major?"

"Berlin," Sean O'Sullivan answered.

Part two

THE LAST DAYS OF APRIL

CHAPTER ONE—*April 12, 1945, Berlin*

The air-raid cellar beneath the Falkenstein house shifted with a sudden violent jolt. A wide split opened in one of the walls spewing a shower of granulated plaster. The precious Rosenthal china, which Frau Herta Falkenstein had meticulously wrapped and stored for safety, careened out of an overturned barrel and splintered into a million bits.

Hildegaard Falkenstein whimpered in her mother's arms.

Another blast! Another! Another! Each closer than the last. The cellar plunged into darkness. A match flame groped for the candle on the wooden table in the center of the room.

"Is everyone all right?" Bruno Falkenstein asked.

Herta and the two girls answered haltingly.

Another hit sent all four of them to the damp floor flat on their bellies. "I can't stand it any more!" Hildegaard shrieked. She beat her fists on the floor and writhed hysterically. "I can't stand it! *Kill us! Kill us!*"

"Keep her quiet!" Falkenstein commanded of his befuddled wife, but the girl continued her tantrum. Hildegaard was becoming more unraveled every day. By the second or third hour of the raids she was usually in a state. Bruno pulled his daughter to her feet, out of his wife's grasp, and slapped her hard across the cheek.

"Quiet! I demand it!"

She stifled her sobs to whimpers. "Yes . . . Father."

On the opposite side of the room Ernestine clawed through the silt which had fallen from the ceiling over her cot and nightstand. She cut her fingers digging for the little music box, clawing in desperation until she found it. A part of it showed in the debris; she worked it clear and took it up. Five of the ten figures of Prussian Hussars had been knocked off, the box was chipped and gouged. She blew off the dust and wound it ever so carefully and pulled the release plunger. The five remaining horsemen began to circle around and around on the top and the music tinkled and she hummed.

> Once there was a faithful Hussar,
> Who loved his love for a year or two,
> A year or two . . . or three or four . . .
> He swore he'd love her ever more . . .

And the crash of the bombs seemed farther away, particularly to Ernestine. They all breathed deeply during the respite. Frau Falkenstein petted Hildegaard, who had slowed to a jerky sobbing.

But the calm was short-lived. Another wave of bombers passed in on the tails of the first and another load of hell from the skies whistled down upon them and the flak crackled back and the room danced again.

Now Bruno Falkenstein's nerves were also shredded. "Pigs! Dirty American pigs! Ami beasts!"

No one seemed to hear his protest.

Ernestine had drifted into tranquility. Years and miles passed by as she watched the little music box, transfixed. "The Faithful Hussar" . . . how many thousands of years ago was it? Only six faithful years? It was 1938 then and there was peace. Peace . . . what a strange word. Could it have only been six years ago? I was only seventeen then. Oh Lord! The bombs have been falling on Berlin for a hundred years. Dietrich, my love! The bombs have been falling on us night and day for a hundred years. Oh Dietrich . . . my photo album was burned in a raid so long ago I have forgotten what you look like. Can you forgive me?

Springtime, Berlin 1939

Ernestine held the tiller steady while Dietrich Rascher took down the sail and dropped anchor. The dark-green mass of the Grunewald and the shoreline was far away. Ernestine could not conceal her joy that the two of them were able to slip away together from the rest of the Group.

How handsome Dietrich is, she thought. How deftly he moves about the boat. How beautiful his face is. Kind and thoughtful, with puppy-dog eyes.

She looked back to the shore with a twinge of guilt. The Group would be singing Nazi Youth songs. Today there was a lecturer from the party. The devil with it. It was much nicer in the middle of the lake with Dietrich Rascher.

He slipped alongside her. Dietrich could hardly control his pride. Today he had been made senior leader for the entire Dahlem District of Hitler Youth. At the age of nineteen this was quite an honor.

"Let's don't go back," Ernestine said wistfully, "ever, ever, ever. Let us set sail and blow right off the Wannsee up the canal to the North Sea, and then over the oceans to the South Seas."

"A romantic notion that conflicts with tonight's lecture."

"Don't you ever forget Hitler Youth, even for a moment?"

He shook his head. "Sometimes, Ernestine, I swear I have a feeling you don't even want to belong to the Group."

"Oh, but I do, very much. That way I can get to see you more often."

"Don't tease about such serious matters. You seemed eager enough to join in the first place."

"Well, of course, I had to. And then Father ordered Hilde, my brother Gerd, and me to be enthusiastic."

"Ach."

"I'm sorry, Dietrich. I know how much this means to you and I shouldn't tease, but I suppose I'm jealous."

He sucked in a deep breath, decided to be indulgent, then turned to her and took her hands. "I asked you to sail out here with me today because I have a secret. I am sharing it with no one in the world but you, Ernestine," he paused proudly, "I have made application for officer's training in the SS. I think I will be accepted."

A strange silence brought only the sound of lapping water. The confusion in her angered him. "I was hoping you would be proud," he snapped.

"I love you, Dietrich."

"But you don't see what an honor it is."

She only shook her head. One was not allowed to say what one truly thought in these matters. The reaction upset him. He gripped her shoulders excitedly. "The Fuehrer has done so much for us, Ernestine. Until he came we Germans had been beaten into the dirt. He said . . . lift your heads . . . be proud to be Germans. He has given us bread and jobs and land and our pride."

Ernestine squirmed uncomfortably at his tightening grip, his sudden burst of fanaticism. "We must give back to the Fuehrer what he has given us by obedience. We Germans are the only people in the world capable of giving the devotion demanded of the Aryan race."

The words had been pounded into her brain since memory. Dietrich recited them well, as any Hitler Youth Leader must. He watched her shrink away and dropped his hands from her. "What do women know of politics," he snapped. "You should be even more grateful for what Hitler has done for German womanhood."

And then, nothing.

"Well, for God's sake, say something!" he demanded.

"You were so kind and gentle when we first met. I don't want you to lose that."

He was moved by the hurt in her and he touched her hand softly, lifted it to his lips and kissed it, and she managed a weak smile. "Ernestine . . . I love you. And I trust you alone in this world. Here, in the middle of the Wannsee I can say some things that I hate myself for thinking about. There are some things about being a Nazi I have not made peace with. I do not like having to spy on my parents because of a few things in their past. They are old and harmless. Sometimes . . . I even feel sorry about a Jewish friend I had." The sound of his own confession annoyed him; he added quickly, "But we must accept the fact that there are a few unpleasant duties we must perform and we must obey without question. It is small enough a price for what Hitler is giving Germany."

"I was advised by my councilor to offer my body to you to produce an Aryan child. Do you think that it's right that we have a child now?"

"I have told you that even Hitler cannot order me to violate you."

Ernestine softened and cuddled in his waiting arms and thought . . . he will never really be an SS officer, in his heart, so long as I continue to own it.

An unwelcome breeze came up. Dietrich raised the sail, pulled up the anchor, and swung the boat away from Potsdam toward the Grunewald encampment.

"Sometimes, Ernestine, I get a strange feeling that you really don't believe in the Nazis."

"Of course I do, Dietrich. There is so much happiness in the people these days. I have seen the joy it has brought into my own home with Gerd and my mother and father. I see how much better life is . . . only . . ."

"Only what?"

"I do have an uncle in the Schwabenwald Concentration Camp."

"No one blames your family. Ulrich Falkenstein was a traitor to the German people."

"No, Dietrich," she answered softly, "he was a good man and he loved Germany very much. I am not permitted to speak his name, but I cannot be made to forget him, either, and I cannot believe he is a traitor."

"Men like Ulrich Falkenstein would have kept Germany a paupers' state. They were weak in their illusions of democracy. Germany must be strong."

"What bothers me, Dietrich, is that I have questions about Uncle Ulrich and about the Jews. I have questions about God and many other things, and I wish I knew where I could go to find another answer."

"To be a German today is to understand Germany's destiny." *You must believe without question . . . believe without question . . . believe without question. . . .*

Now only a muted breathing of numbed people could be heard in the Falkenstein cellar. For two hours the American Eighth Air Force from England dumped nearly a thousand tons of bombs on Berlin, and as the last of their flights faded from hearing, the first of the motors of the American Fifteenth Air Force from Italy began to drone above them.

Hildegaard had collapsed. Frau Falkenstein was glassy-eyed. Only Bruno Falkenstein issued small weak curses against the Americans, for Ernestine was completely immersed in memory. Remembering always helped during the long days and nights in the cellar.

A year had passed since Dietrich Rascher was accepted into SS Officers' Training at Schwabenwald Concentration Camp. He had returned to Berlin. War was with them. As a new SS Untersturmfuehrer it was a certainty he would be leaving for Poland or the occupied countries soon.

Dietrich stared sullenly from the hotel window through streaking rain down to the Kurfurstendamm. Behind him, he could hear "The Faithful Hussar" tinkle from the music box. He had brought it home to Ernestine as a gift. It was hand-carved in the Black Forest with dainty little figures of olden Prussian horsemen of Frederick the Great, and the music works were imported from Switzerland.

It should have been a moment for great happiness, but Dietrich was miserable. People below scurried along, hugging the buildings to keep dry—except for a pair of jackbooted Nazis who swaggered in the middle of the sidewalk in defiance of the rain.

Dietrich wanted to explain . . . words stuck in his throat. He wanted to tell Ernestine what the year had been like in the SS school; he wanted her to know all about the brutal training, the punishments, and the "practical work" with the prisoners inside the concentration camp. He had learned to become a bully and to terrorize. And now he had come home and had taken Ernestine with a same lack of conscience.

He wanted to tell her about the exercises in degrading the human spirit and the ease with which he beat up defenseless men; and that after his first revulsion, there was a pleasure in the power one had, in seeing men cower before you.

Dietrich turned from the window. Ernestine lay on the bed, half dressed. She looked like an innocent child, winding up the music box. As he came to her, her eyes showed him how filled with love she was.

Ernestine was reassuring herself that Dietrich had not really changed; he was compassionate, and all during that first trembling night alone he had been ever so gentle with her. Perhaps he was right about his desire to become an SS officer. It had given him manliness and respect. A man must have what he wants. Mother always told her that . . . give the man what he wants . . . the man is everything.

Dietrich sat alongside her. She tried to understand his silence, longed to make him happy, fulfill him completely. He stroked her hair. It was thick and golden and his fingers became entwined in it. Suddenly, his fingers tightened. He hurt her. He pulled his hand away and stared at it almost madly. . . .

"Kadett Rascher!"

"Jawohl!"

"I am your Hauptsturmfuehrer. Each new candidate like yourself is assigned a shepherd puppy as he enters his SS training. An SS officer must understand animals, how to train them, and how to use them. And, as our beloved Fuehrer said, how to imitate their power and virility. You shall pick a dog from this litter and after it is properly housebroken the dog will share your quarters with you."

Dietrich looked into the kennel of furry balls, lifted a puppy, and smiled as its wet nose and tongue drenched him with affection.

"Aha. The only bitch in the litter. What will you call her, Kadett Rascher?"

"I will call her Ernestine. She will be my girl until I can return to another Ernestine."

Even the cruel taskmasters were pleased at the way Kadett Rascher trained his bitch, Ernestine. There was the magnificent communication between man and beast strived for but seldom reached. No getting away from it, Rascher had a way with animals. He could get more from his bitch whispering in her ear than all the other cadets with their leashes, straps, choke collars, and throw chains. For that first year the young cadet and his dog were together day and night, the patrols of Schwabenwald, the hunts for escapees, guard duty. The hard discipline, the ugliness of the camp were all forgotten in the evening when he sat on his cot and read and reached down and was able to run his hand through the dog's fur.

A few days before the graduation ceremony, the permanent awarding of the black uniform, the death's head insignia, and the SS dagger, Kadett Dietrich Rascher and his dog were called into a blank, stone room in the kennel. His Hauptsturmfuehrer was there.

"I am pleased with your progress, Rascher," the captain said. "You have learned your lessons well. You will be a credit to the master race. Before receiving your SS dagger there is, however, a final obedience test that all SS men must take."

"Jawohl," Rascher snapped from his position to attention.

"You will, at this instant, choke your dog to death."

SS Kadett Dietrich Rascher passed his final test of obedience. With neither qualm, hesitation, nor visible show of personal emotion, he reached down, grabbed the trusting animal, put a choke hold on her, and pressured quickly to snap her neck. He then came back to attention.

"With men like you," the captain congratulated, "we are undefeatable."

A sudden wind beat a tattoo of water on the window. Dietrich continued to stare at his hand.

"What is it, darling?" she pleaded, "what is it?"

"How long can this go on?" Bruno Falkenstein moaned. "Maybe it would be better if a bomb fell on us and killed us all."

"Please don't speak like that before the girls," Herta pleaded.

"Yesterday, six hours of raids and the day before that all day. To-day, it may never end. What have we done to deserve this?"

Ernestine looked at her father quizzically. Perhaps the people of Warsaw, Rotterdam, and London wondered the same thing, she thought. Strange, father didn't seem unhappy about it then.

"Turn that damn music box off, it drives me crazy!" he commanded.

"Yes, Father."

Ernestine was shocked when she saw Dietrich on his furlough from the Eastern Front. She knew that the war would do something to him, but he was still not much more than a boy. Dietrich was twenty-two now, but all that was gentle was gone.

Furloughs were created to bring a soldier happiness and renew his vigor to fight. Ernestine had kept a belief that Dietrich Rascher would never slip beyond the power of her love. She had lost him.

Every night of his leave he was stinking from schnaps and beer. He lolled on the bed too drunk to make love . . . he babbled . . . was given to sudden wild rages and weeping incoherent confessions about unknown crimes.

Corpses . . . Jew corpses . . . tens of thousands of naked Jews . . . burning barns . . . burning villages . . . men with beards praying . . . naked mothers . . . sisters . . . grandmothers . . . pits filled with burning corpses . . . his machine gun rattled into the corpses . . . dogs ripped the Jew throats . . . the wild eyes of the cheering Ukrainians while the SS gunned the Jews into the pits . . . the nightmare, again and again . . . he drowned in blood, Jew blood . . . his hands and mouth and hair dripping and sticky with blood. . . .

"Drink! I must have a drink!"

"Dietrich! Wake up, darling! Wake up!"

"Drink! Give me a drink!"

"Oh, my darling. Please let me help you. Please don't shut me out."

"Help me tomorrow, woman. I need a drink now."

"Darling, let me love you. Please! Please! Let us marry . . . tomorrow . . . now."

"Marry you? How humorous! I am married to the SS. I have no room for another wife."

"Oh God, dear God."

"Stop your bloody weeping and get me schnaps!"

"Now you listen to me, Dietrich Rascher. This war will end one day.

I don't know what you have seen or how it has hurt you, but you will need to forget. I will be waiting here to help you. I will wait until time runs out . . . until my heart stops . . . I will never stop waiting and I will help you forget."

The all-clear sounded.

They trudged up to the demolished street. All of them stood in the dusk's fading light and stared at their broken house. Once it had stood two stories, square and solid. Most of the top floor was gone. The rest was riddled with holes, gouges, smashed and broken windows. The pretty little flower garden, so meticulously nursed by Frau Falkenstein, was destroyed. Falkenstein's auto was in flames, gutted beyond use.

The neighbors crawled from their cellars one by one and began to dig through the rubble. Reimer's house down the street, which had taken a direct hit, was flattened to the foundation. The rest of the street was a shambles. Once it was a nice street, lined with shade trees and neatly cut shrubs.

"I had better go to the store and see if there is anything left," a voice said.

"Don't bother. The store took direct hits."

"Frau Winkelmann and both her children are dead." Perhaps it was better for them, Falkenstein thought. Frau Winkelmann had been crippled in a raid a half year earlier and the children had become a burden to all the neighbors. Her husband had been killed long before in Tunis.

"Someone get over to the defense command and find out about the water main. There is no water coming into my house."

The air was grimy with unsettled dust, fires burned, and the sirens screeched all around them, hauling off the wounded, digging for the dead. There was little time for either sympathy or contemplation or to mourn dead children, broken homes, or look for bread or fill the water buckets. They knew that the American fires from the day would light a path for the British bombers by night, and when darkness came the raid would go on. Nights were somewhat better. The Americans picked an area to precision-bomb. If you were caught in the American target, like today, it could be ghastly. The Lancaster Bombers of the British tried to saturate the entire city with incendiaries so their target was spread and the chances of survival better.

The value of survival was becoming questionable, anyhow. If you lived through the British raid at night the Americans would come tomorrow and continue their checkerboard destruction . . . Dahlem . . . Wilmersdorf . . . Charlottenburg . . . Köpenick.

People were fleeing Berlin by the tens of thousands, but where to go? Perhaps, Bruno Falkenstein thought, find a nice large cathedral and stay there. The Americans were sentimental about bombing churches. Perhaps they would get a rest tomorrow. Perhaps another part of the city would get it. Lord! The Americans had come for a solid month with three hundred bombers or more and the British had come in behind them.

Their beautiful beautiful street had become a rubbish pile, like the rest of Berlin. What the hell is the use of hoping, any more.

Frau Falkenstein's mind was geared to more practical things. She sent the girls to the reservoir with buckets while she searched for something to eat. She was wily to the ways of survival, knew the short cuts around rationing, played the black market, knew how to horde and barter.

Ironically, the postman delivered Falkenstein the latest issue of the *Berliner Illustrated* during the respite. They returned to the cellar for a meal of stale bockwurst and ersatz coffee. Falkenstein read the magazine by candlelight to soothe his frayed nerves. There was not a single mention of the destruction of the German cities. It continued to picture German victories, and, like the radio, promised that secret weapons would reverse the course of the war overnight.

Falkenstein grunted. Some fools at his bureau believed fervently in the secret weapons Goebbels had promised. He had believed in them once also. His mind ran back to the speech of Goebbels in the Sportspalast . . . *"Do you want total war?"* And the masses answered with "heils." Well, we are getting it now all right. After the V rockets failed in their promise to crush Britain, Falkenstein stopped believing in secret weapons. He longed to listen to the BBC; he knew many neighbors were daring it these days. He flipped the page. It showed the new skiing costumes expected at Garmisch in the coming winter. He threw the magazine on the floor and downed the last lead-like chunk of meat.

The air-raid sirens shrieked outside. The four of them undressed in total darkness and lay in their cots, their eyes opening with each blast. It was a big raid.

"I wish it were all over . . . I wish it were all over," he moaned to himself.

Ernestine grimaced at the irony of her father's statement. Yes, everyone wished it was over. Father never wished it was over in the early days. She remembered his cries of delight, his boasts after Dunkirk and when Greece was conquered. He was proud to bursting when Gerd sent him letters from Paris.

Only since Stalingrad did they begin wishing it was over; then he began to think of Gerd's safety. Yes, since Stalingrad the war became tiresome and only then did she hear the very first words that there had been a betrayal by Hitler.

. . . Stalingrad. That was the last time she had heard from Dietrich Rascher. More than a year had passed since then. Ernestine remembered the last letter from Dietrich, carried out by a flyer friend when they attempted to air-lift supplies to Stalingrad.

My Beloved Ernestine,

More than likely this is the last you shall ever hear from me. I am relieved to be able to write you this one time speaking freely. A comrade in the Air Force has promised to deliver this to you. But even if the letter is found it shall not matter much, for by the time anyone reads it, I shall be dead.

We are beaten. I do not have the "privilege" to surrender as does the regular army. As an SS officer I must take my own life. In the long run, I may be far better off than those poor devils around me. God only knows what will happen to them when they become prisoners of the Russians.

We are freezing cold. My boots become wet, then solid. The ends of my fingers have no feeling in them and I am half blind from the glare of the snow. We are starving. I am dizzy from the lack of food. It becomes a supreme effort to move for a few meters. Our ammunition is almost gone. We are outnumbered by hordes, and now we are being outfought.

No miracle can save us here at Stalingrad. Hitler exhorts us to perform in a superhuman effort, but we cannot respond. Furthermore, we have no great desire to respond any longer. So you see, we were not supermen all along . . . only mortals.

Men here at Stalingrad speak openly about the betrayal by Hitler and the Nazis in a manner I have never heard from German lips before. In the last moments of life perhaps it is a good thing to protest. I have been a dedicated Nazi. I have loved Hitler, worshiped him. Yet, at this moment, I cannot find it in my heart to die gloriously. All I want is to sleep.

On the other hand, I cannot condone those around me now who berate Hitler. We all followed him with devotion. We all believed in the Nazis so long as Germany was winning. Only part of the fault belongs to Hitler and the Nazis. The rest of it belongs to the entire German people.

I cannot think of inspiring messages to leave you and Germany. I am just cold, hungry, and quite frightened. Now that I know that I am a mere mortal and Hitler is not my Maker, I have great fears as I go to meet my true Maker. I think He will judge me harshly for some of the things I did in the SS.

What I really wish, Ernestine, is that I was nineteen again and you and I were sailing on the Wannsee and I could have turned our boat toward a canal and sailed to the North Sea and over the oceans to the South Seas . . . forever and ever and ever.

My respects to your father and mother. My affection to Hilde, and my hopes that your brother, Gerd, returns safely from the war.

What little love I have given or received in this life has been yours. I fear it is not worth much.

Always,
Dietrich

CHAPTER TWO—*April 21, 1945*

The little stone bridge fording the Oder River was damaged by gunfire during the German retreat. It now strained under a burden for which it had never been built.

An endless parade of Stalin tanks and other treaded monsters from the bottomless Russian arsenal buckled the bridge down to its foundations. Mammoth units of self-propelled artillery, antitank pieces, the new rocket launchers, and iron-wheeled horse-drawn gondola wagons and trucks bearing the name Studebaker and Chevrolet all joined the line waiting to cross. Horses, men, iron moved toward the final day in Berlin.

Colonel Igor Karlovy, chief of engineers of the Third White Russian Front, dived below the surface of the river to study the effects on the strained underpinnings of the bridge. He surfaced and swam for shore, where a waiting party of helping hands pulled him up the bank. He was surrounded by impatient consultants as he wiped himself dry and lit a cigarette. He dressed. Igor Karlovy was a powerful, muscled man though a bit below average in height. Blond hair, a trace of high cheekbones, and ice-blue eyes gave testament to a Tartar element in his ancestry centuries before. His naked torso revealed shrapnel wounds from another battle. Once his tunic was buttoned about his neck his appearance seemed more aged than thirty-six years. It was a face that had known much, felt much, suffered much. He carried obvious authority.

"The bridge will collapse. There is no possible way to reinforce it. Erosion has set in in the foundation."

Field Marshal Popov's personal aide, a nervous major, inquired, "How long will the bridge hold up?"

"Ask the bridge," Karlovy answered.

"We have more than two thousand heavy pieces to get over in this sector. If this bridge goes it can delay the entire offensive on Berlin."

Igor merely shrugged. "Berlin is not going to run away." Popov's aide did not fathom Igor Karlovy's humor. He knew the marshal had his heart set on opening the offensive so Berlin might fall by May Day.

The entourage followed Colonel Karlovy downstream. He consulted with two other engineers and decided upon the best place to erect temporary crossings.

"The main highway will have to be diverted so there must be a rampway built to get the mobile equipment down the bank. I suggest cutting some of these lovely German trees and constructing a log road. Now, if Marshal Popov will assign a regiment of men for labor I think we can have a crossing by tomorrow morning."

"No sooner?"

"Certainly not."

The aide stomped off to get the labor. Igor drew up hasty plans for building of a crossing. Captain Ivan Orlov pushed into the circle and drew the colonel out. He pointed to his watch excitedly. "Commissar Azov is waiting for us at Eberswalde."

Captain Orlov obviously dropped Azov's name for the colonel knew V. V. Azov was more powerful than Popov himself. Ivan Orlov, the party man assigned to watch the engineers, was apt to panic at the thought of being late to see the commissar.

"Drive across the bridge before it collapses and wait until I get things set up. If the bridge goes down, I'll swim over to you as quickly as I can . . . now, please . . ."

Captain Ivan Orlov went off to the Mercedes staff car they had commandeered from a German general in Warsaw. He blew the horn with jerky violence and swung the vehicle between a pair of gargantuan SU-100 tanks rumbling over the trembling bridge.

Toward midday a human blanket of labor swarmed over the area. The masses of men and women had stripped a small forest, hand-carried in tons of fill dirt, and laid a rampway to the water's edge. Others working in the swift stream had started the temporary bridge. Satisfied that the bridge would be built in less time than he predicted, Igor turned the job over to the subordinate engineers.

Captain Ivan Orlov was near frantic by the delay. He sped the car toward Eberswalde, zigzagging between the endless lines of tanks, guns, gondola wagons, horsemen, blowing the horn incessantly, sending foot troops scurrying into the ditches. He jabbered without respite. Igor tried to ignore him. What a magnificent sight, this great great mass of men and guns. Soon the five horrible years would be over. They were at the gates of Berlin . . . Russians . . . Ukrainians . . . squat Asians from Mongol and Tartar lands . . . dark-eyed Armenians and Georgians.

Igor was disturbed by gossip in the high command that Stalin preferred a street fight for Berlin rather than allow Nazi surrender. It would be a pretext to take Berlin apart street by street, house by house. What a shame to lose many thousands of young men in this last hour of war.

Igor rolled up his overcoat, made a pillow of it, and pretended to doze in order to shut off Ivan Orlov's chatter. An intersection clogged with wagons brought them to a halt. A large-busted woman in military-police uniform answered Orlov's long, undinted horn blast.

"Out of the way, damn you, clear that road!"

"What is your great hurry, comrade?" the woman soldier demanded.

"We have a meeting with a commissar."

"Excuse me, comrade. Clear the way! Let them through!"

The People's Military and Civil Governing Group was temporarily established in the boys' gymnasium in the town of Eberswalde, some fifty kilometers north of Berlin, where they awaited the fall of the capital. White flags of surrender hanging from the town's windows clashed with the red flags atop the schoolhouse.

Captain Ivan Orlov, now an hour late, leaped from the Mercedes. He quickly identified himself to two blue-capped guards from political security and trotted down the main corridor, which still held a portrait of Adolf Hitler.

Igor was met at the door by his two junior officers, Captain Boris Chernov and young Lieutenant Feodor Guchkov. They had not seen the colonel for several days. There were embraces and backslaps.

"Have you heard, Igor? Popov's White Russian Front has approached the eastern and southern suburbs of Berlin!"

"And the Ukrainian Front is pouring in from the north!" Feodor added. "We have them in a pincers."

"It's official. We have joined hands with the Americans at the Elbe River!"

"Magnificent!" Igor Karlovy roared, "but for now I'd better get in to see Comrade Azov."

"We'll wait here," Feodor said. "Tonight the bombardment of Berlin begins in earnest. I know a place up near the front lines where we can watch it."

"Bring the vodka," Igor said, and asked for directions to V. V. Azov's office. He stopped for a moment to look into the auditorium. The Agitation and Propaganda Corps were hard at it: stacks of broadsheets holding portraits of Stalin, Lenin, Marx, Engels; stacks of leaflets; long strips of red lettering on white cloth carrying slogans would come in on the heels of the last shot.

V. V. Azov sat deadpanned behind his desk. Ivan Orlov was nervously repeating an apology of why they were late. "Marshal Popov personally asked Colonel Karlovy to look after the bridge."

Azov silenced the captain by holding up his hand without indication of belief or disbelief. He seemed remote from the elation of the great turn of events. One almost never saw a smile, a frown, or any of those indications attributed to human reactions. He greeted Igor Karlovy matter-of-factly. His thick black hair was in place and his huge moustache was combed and carefully turned. The simple tunic was opened at the throat. Behind his dull gray eyes was a brain trained to receive and disseminate information without emotion.

"I heard the news of our joining with the Americans!" Igor said. "It's marvelous!"

Azov opened his mouth slowly, began to speak with automation in expressionless tones. "We can well understand the elation of the moment. However, Comrade Colonel, we are not to lose sight of the fact that the American participation in this war has been a minor factor."

From a long-standing dealing with commissars, Igor knew how to interpret Azov's pronouncement. For several months now the Russian people had been indoctrinated to the effect that the winning of the war was a singular Russian effort. Hearing it from Azov's lips, Igor knew, was a voicing of official policy. It was for damned sure, Igor knew, that the Agitation and Propaganda people were preparing literature to downgrade the American participation.

"Of greater importance," Azov continued, "is that you and our comrades on the German People's Liberation Committee draw up the final plans for the dismemberment of Berlin's industrial complex as the first installment for war reparations."

"It shall be done, Comrade Commissar," Igor Karlovy answered.

Having run out of patience with the German People's Liberation Committee, Igor left Captain Ivan Orlov to quibble with them and sought out Boris Chernov and Feodor Guchkov. The three of them left Eberswalde in the direction of the front lines with two loaves of bread, five bottles of vodka, an accordion, a mandolin, and a balalaika. Young Feodor uncorked the first bottle and broke into song. Boris drove the battered car off to a side road filled with chuck holes. They banged their way uphill, then cut diagonally over a farmer's field to a small bluff, parked, and walked to the edge. An awesome vista unfolded below them. Thousands of individual guns of light-artillery brigades, heavy artillery, rocket-launcher regiments, and self-propelled guns were aligned wheel to wheel as far as the eye could see in either direction.

This called for a second bottle of vodka. The three men squatted on a mound of boulders eating the bread and a portion of rice from their kits, washing it down with the Polish vodka.

Igor put the field glasses to his eyes. In front of the rows of cannons, divisions of tanks were deployed and ready. What seemed to be a million infantry and horsemen swarmed through the forests, on the roads, through the fields toward the hazy outlines of the northern suburbs of Berlin.

One by one, fire control up forward called for the artillery to shoot test rounds. Forward observation posts called for necessary adjustments. With the coming of darkness the tempo increased until every firing piece in the line began to rain steel into Berlin in the most concentrated artillery saturation of a single target in the history of warfare. The guns recoiled angrily, launchers hissed their rockets away in a deadly arch, and black smoke erupted on the horizon from tortured Berlin. The guns leaped back a dozen at a time making the earth shake violently and the sky was lit with ten thousand flashes of lightning from the muzzles and the roar became horrendous. A hot wind blew up to the knoll from the unnatural agitation, bringing to their nostrils the smell of burned gunpowder.

Igor Karlovy and his two officers were becoming numbed by the fury and the vodka. Boris Chernov shook his fist toward Berlin and cursed and Feodor cheered and screamed encouragement.

"Kill the Nazi bastards!"

The barrage reached a new savagery. Igor Karlovy stood still as a statue. The light flashes reflected in his eyes and brought to him the memory of other fires. . . .

Igor Karlovy was in Leningrad in his memory and he stood on the Sovietsky Prospekt staring over the frozen Neva River. Then it was German and Finnish guns pouring it on Leningrad and the fires were all around him. He saw Children's Home #25 crumble under a direct hit! He ran toward it. The screams of agony reached his ears. The children had been caught unawares.

DEATH TO THE NAZI BABY MURDERERS! An enormous sign hung over the entrance of Factory #67. Above the sign, a portrait of a woman worker holding a mutilated infant in her arms. All over Leningrad signs and slogans snarled at the Nazi tormentors, and other signs and slogans exhorted the workers and soldiers to put up superhuman efforts.

"Look, Colonel, look!" Feodor cried, throwing his arms about Igor. His drunken tongue wagged freely. "Look at the fires in Berlin! Kill the bastards!"

How long! How very long had Igor Karlovy waited to see this glorious moment. Berlin burning! Berlin in mortal pain! How many times did he believe it would never come. All of those terrible days gone by are memory now . . . all thirty months of the siege. . . .

"Death to the Nazi bastards! Rapers of our motherland!"

When Igor Karlovy was transferred to Leningrad in 1941 it was a confused and frightened city. There was terrible shock among the people with the realization that the Red Army was vulnerable.

The first weeks of the campaign against the Finns had ended in disaster. The Finns, dressed in white, skiing as ghosts in the snow, and using their forests for cover, butchered the onrushing Reds. Here, the Russian steam-roller tactics did not work. Until the Russians learned to fight the Finnish way, they were slaughtered by an enemy a fiftieth their size.

There was Soviet indignation against the Americans, who overtly took the side of the Finns just because a few dollars had been paid yearly on an old war debt. The Americans didn't understand that Finland had military positions on the Karelian Isthmus at Leningrad's throat, and that the Finnish dictator, Mannerheim, had been sleeping with the German staff. For the Soviet Union not to challenge these Finnish positions would have been to court suicide.

Just as the Finnish campaign ended, Igor Karlovy went to Leningrad. The city had a meaning, like Moscow itself. Not only was it a great Soviet cultural center and seaport, but the cradle of the October Revolution. With the Soviet Armed Forces reorganizing, it was a time and a place for a young officer to make his name.

The sneak attack by Germany against the Soviet Union came in June of 1941. By September, thirty German divisions and the revenge-seeking Finnish Army were pressing on Leningrad.

The masses of the city were confused and angry! Never before had the leaders heard so much open bitterness against the regime. The masses cried "betrayal." They had been duped into thinking the Red Army was invincible and further betrayed because Leningrad was literally defenseless and without stores.

Then passivity overcame them. It was not that they welcomed the Germans, for they knew they would be dealt with harshly, but that, with great relief, they knew the Communists would soon flee.

The panicked Communist leaders were packed and ready to go when ordered by Stalin to stay, and Leningrad was commanded to hold no matter what the cost.

A million workers from factories and schools and the Army went out to build a great belt of defenses against the approaching Nazi armies.

Yes, it was a time a young Red Air Force engineer could make a name. Although primarily concerned with runways, air traffic, and air installations, the needs of the day took him into other fields of engineering. Igor Karlovy demonstrated a type of initiative and inventiveness desperately needed in the construction of defenses. It was he who conceived a plan to dismantle the unfinished stadium and use the thousands of concrete slabs on the perimeters.

By the time the Red Army had fallen back into Leningrad, the Russian people had come to learn that the German was no liberator. Driven by sheer fear, tens of thousands of men and women formed into defense battalions and manned the parapets.

Within sight, feel, and smell of Leningrad, Hitler went against the advice of his generals and ruled against a street fight. With the Finns as an ally, Germany set siege to the city. Hitler was certain the siege would break the Russians just as demoralization, bombardment, and starvation had worked in Warsaw and other unfortunate cities of Europe. Hitler felt the Russians were subhumans so the will to resist would quickly be crushed from them. One of the monumental sieges of all time had begun.

The Red Army artillery continued the bashing of Berlin in unabated fury into the night. Young Feodor was passed out drunk. Boris Chernov slept in the back seat of the car. Igor Karlovy alone retained the watch, for he was sober and the pain of memory now stuck sharply.

He recalled the unmerciful agony of the winter of 1941. Leningrad was cut off from Russia except for a single passage over Lake Ladoga at their backs. There were not enough ships on the lake to either evacuate the old and young or to bring in sufficient fuel, food, and ammunition, and they were forced to cross under the guns of the enemy.

The Communist leaders, harangued from Moscow, in turn harangued the masses.

In those days, a Red Air Force engineer slept little. Igor was involved in the building of a half-dozen small airstrips to attempt an airlift of supplies. The plan fell woefully short.

When Lake Ladoga froze he and the other engineers performed the perilous feat of cutting roads over the top of the ice to keep the meager convoys of trucks and sleds moving.

There was that grim day when all the wooden homes in Leningrad were ordered dismantled for firewood and the peat bogs around the islands had to be worked by battalions of women under German artillery fire.

Yet, somehow, the people bore it. The Russians demonstrated their limitless capacity to endure suffering. In Leningrad, as in all of Russia, practically no civilian goods were produced. The workers were compelled to labor unbelievable numbers of hours for the meagerest existence. In the hinterland twenty million men and women were armed and trained in the nation's singular dedication to survival.

In Leningrad ration cards became the key to life and the means of controlling the masses and inducing more labor from them. Inside every factory, labor battalion, and army unit was the political commissar, the party member, political intelligence, and the informer to apply unrelenting pressure and fear tactics. There was a shortage of almost everything except slogans and portraits of Stalin. The news of German atrocities was pounded into the brains of the masses day and night. There was no respite even in this hell.

As coal reserves diminished, power failures stopped industry, transport, light, and heat.

The dagger of death in 1941 was an icicle and the dagger struck 400,000 civilians dead. The sight of frozen corpses in Leningrad's gutters became as common as the sight of the slogans. Starved, bombarded from within and without, frozen, half crazed with fear, the people of Leningrad clung to the thread of life and were driven to exert yet one more ounce of energy.

As the siege guns pounded, the unyielding stone of Leningrad began to crumble away, bit by bit. The casualties in hospitals, schools, and factories were appalling. Stukas and Messerschmitts screamed down from the skies . . . days . . . weeks . . . months . . . years. . . .

In the spring of 1942 a recovering Red Army broke through from the south to open an eight-mile corridor in the siege ring called the Schlusselberg Gap. Karlovy's engineers and hordes of women laborers built a rail line through the Gap and constructed bull-dog defenses on either side of it. The Germans were never able to close this thin bottleneck. Hitler continued in the belief that he could starve the Russian into submission, but from the first trainload of supplies through the Schlusselberg Gap to Leningrad, the city was destined to hold.

Despite this life line opened to the rest of Russia, the saga of the siege was still being written. The hunger, disease, artillery, air raids, and cold of two more Russian winters would claim yet another half-million lives.

DEATH TO THE NAZI BABY MURDERERS!

Yes, a million dead. That was the price for Leningrad.

Igor was standing on the Sovietsky Prospekt when Children's Home #25 crumpled under a shell hit. He ran toward it with the screams of the children drumming in his ears. "God! My baby is in there! My baby! Yuri! Yuri!" Yuri Karlovy was born, lived and died during the siege.

At dawn the Russian guns were white-hot and warped from firing. Boris and Feodor still slept. The thrice-decorated hero of the Soviet Union, holder of the Lenin Order for Courage, gathered his boys up and drove back to Eberswalde as the mighty Red Army stormed the gates of Berlin.

CHAPTER THREE

The stage was set for the grizzly playing out of the German death wish. From the chancellory bunker, Adolf Hitler brought on ultimate self-destruction by a deliberate decision to fight to the last. Indeed, it was all in the tradition of the fiery deaths of the idols of Teutonic legends; this was, however, no myth.

Like Berwin of Rombaden, he exhorted his warriors to perform superhuman feats. However, unlike the Aryans of the legend, Hitler's "Aryans" existed in name only, and they could not respond. He commanded nonexistent paper armies to come to the rescue and counter-attack. He went through an odious ritual of a marriage ceremony with Eva Braun, a woman as stupid and dull as Emma Stoll. And, in the last moments, he ranted that all of Germany had betrayed him and was unworthy of his genius.

The Russians, whom he had declared subhumans, followed their monstrous barrages by frontal assaults into the bowels of his kingdom. As the tortured city gurgled in its death throes, he waited until the enemy was within touching distance, and then he ordered the torch set to his body.

Children and old men of the People's Army, disorganized military units, and frantic Nazis bloodied the Russian intruder mightily. The final bath of blood was a fitting sacrifice to the end of the pagan gods.

The German fought from the bunkers and the rooftops and the street corners and the windows. Berlin was a city of mighty stone and steel, as was Leningrad, but unlike the Germans, the Red Army did not shy away from a street fight.

In the last days of April Russian victories were counted in inches, casualties in tens of thousands. No siege, this; batter it out foot by foot, room by room; isolate it house by house, street by street, section by section; reduce it to shambles. Artillery and tanks fired down great streets at point-blank and walls grotesquely buckled and crashed. Human fodder, bearing bayonets and flamethrowers, gutted and gored its way forward. Rivers of blood spilled into the gutters. The back of the Nazi was being broken by unstoppable sledge-hammer blows. The German committed suicide, fought, bled, escaped, surrendered. The civilians cowered and starved and became dehydrated from anguished thirst.

The magnificent Unter Den Linden and Siegesallee with their immense boulevards and great massive structures were reduced to hideous shells. Sizzling bridges collapsed into the Spree and the Brandenburger Gate was riddled to a sieve; the castles and Reichstag smoldered and the factories that somehow lived through the months of bombing crumpled under short flat hits of cannon and the incessant tattoo of machine guns, grenades, and mortars. This violent racket went on without respite until exhaustion beyond exhaustion overcame the defenders. And then they were systematically cut off and their ammunition fell to the zero point.

By the first day of May white flags sprouted by the tens of thousands and the upraised hands of surrender followed. The sound and the fury diminished as lone fanatical suicide units made the final futile gesture.

On the second of May Red Army vehicles rolled freely through those places not blocked by wreckage. They controlled a city that had undergone more damage at the hands of man than any single place on earth. Berlin was obliterated from one end to the other and a hundred thousand dead civilians lay beneath the mountains of brick.

Months before, as the Red Army began the final offensive, Russian journalists, with official blessings, promised the soldiers that Berlin and all in it would be spoils of the victors.

As the combat troops gained complete control they were suddenly and strangely withdrawn from Berlin, battalion by battalion, and replaced by garrison forces of inferior quality. The replacement troops contained a great number of Asians from distant Soviet Republics. They began the final chapter of horror on the beaten enemy.

During the last days of April the Falkenstein family and all their neighbors locked up in their cellars as SS officers from a nearby camp made a last-ditch stand in the Dahlem District. The whine of bullets, the crash of mortars, and the burst of shells made them flinch and cower through the pitched battle.

Fear made them forget hunger. In the Falkenstein cellar there was a new sound, unheard for years—the voice of Bruno Falkenstein praying.

Their minds had grown hazy. Radio gone, toilet unworkable, a single candle left, no water, no food.

There was a short and violent exchange of gunfire early in the third morning of the battle, and then great, unearthly silence. The quiet lasted for what seemed hours; no one could remember such silence for years.

The longer the stillness held, the more terrifying it became. The four of them, grimy, stinking, starved, sat in their stupor for over an hour without uttering a word. At last Frau Falkenstein creaked her large body from the cot and labored up on a stool to look through a window on the level of the street. She drew the boarding and blanket aside and squinted into an eternal grayness that revealed nothing.

"What shall we do, Bruno?"

"I don't know," he rasped.

"We must find food and water or we'll all be dead."

"I'll go up and see if anyone is there," Ernestine said. Her father protested, but she insisted she was better able to move around than the others. "Don't come up looking for me and don't leave here until I get back."

"For God's sake be careful, Ernestine."

She climbed the steep stairs, shoved the trap door open, and glanced about the shambles in the hallway. Her body was slight and deft. She hoisted herself out carefully, dropped the trap door down, and as an afterthought dragged a carpet from the anteroom and covered the door.

The living room, shattered long before, was boarded up from the rest of the house. She pushed open a temporary door and peered outside. Not a sign of life in the streets. The scars of battle were much in evidence, the street smoldering from one end to the other.

She decided to try a dash straight across the way to their neighbors the Kaisers. She ran, moved even more swiftly by the sound of her own steps.

In the middle of the street her heel fell into a small mortar hole and she crashed to the pavement, twisting her ankle. She emitted a cry of disgust and pain, rolled over onto her hands and knees, and tried to lift herself. The foot gave way. She gritted her teeth and tried to drag herself, when she saw, out of the corner of her eye, someone moving.

Ernestine peered up slowly. A few yards away, at the intersection, two men with tommy guns over their backs stopped and watched her. They wore crossed bandoliers, bloomered brown trousers, short boots, and red stars on their caps. Russians! They moved at her cautiously, smiling.

Her ankle throbbed; she stifled the impulse to attempt to run. One of them now had his weapon pointed at her. Both of them seemed to be boys in their late teens; one was a blond and rather husky, the other dark with a shaggy growth of hair.

"*Kumm frau,*" the blond said, sneaking up to her. "Kumm frau."

"Tick, tick, tick, tick," the shaggy one said, pointing to her wrist. He leaned over, grabbed her arm, tore the wrist watch off, and put it to his ear and laughed. "Tick, tick, tick, tick." His comrade listened, also amused.

She tried to crawl away while they played with the watch, but they walked behind her taunting, "Kumm frau!"

Ernestine sprang to her feet, tried to run, staggered blindly, limping on the pained ankle. The blond one snatched her long hair and flung her ruthlessly to the pavement again. "Kumm frau!" he repeated, looking about for some place to take her. As he reached down she saw the eyes of a wild man and heard the breathing of a dog in heat. She lashed at his face and tore it open with her fingernails. He wrestled her to her feet, banded his arms around her, and dragged her toward the garden plot in the Kaiser yard. She dared not scream for that would have brought others up into danger, but she kicked and squirmed in fury and her teeth found their way into the Russian's hand. He bellowed in pain, and released her. The shaggy-haired one smashed his fist into her mouth.

Ernestine spun under the impact of the blow, landing hard in the dirt. It went into her mouth and nose and eyes. The world whirled crazily. She clawed at the wet ground to stop the spinning . . . saw her own blood dripping, herself sinking into it . . . and slowly pushed herself up to a sitting position, holding her head, groaning. Another punch from the shaggy one knocked her flat on her back. He grabbed her arms and pinned her down to the earth digging his knees into her wrist. The blond one knelt over her grunting, his trousers down.

An hour later Ernestine knocked almost soundlessly on the trap door. It creaked open. She dragged her body over the edge, spilled down the steps, and lay crumpled on the floor. Her dress was in shreds, both breasts bared, both eyes swollen shut. Blood gushed from her mouth. She gurgled a single long groan, and then blessed darkness rendered her unconscious.

Bruno Falkenstein reached under his pillow, snatched his luger pistol and lunged for the steps. His wife threw her arms around his legs. "No! Don't go outside armed!"

"I'll kill those bastards!"

"Bruno! Give me the gun and find Dr. Hahn! For God's sake listen to me! She may be dying!"

The locating of Dr. Hahn became a monumental task. Falkenstein lost his watch to the first Russian, a second roughed him up for not having a watch, and a third beat him for the sport of it. Several times he was ordered to go back, forcing him to use round-about methods. When at last the doctor was found, he was treating a nine-year-old girl who had been raped by six Russians. The child was mutilated and in shock. He promised Falkenstein to come as soon as he could.

It was yet another long hour before Dr. Hahn was able to get to the Falkenstein cellar.

"The little girl?"

"Dead. They're going crazy up there. There's no end to it."

The physician who had brought both Ernestine and Hilde into the world as well as their brother, Gerd, knelt alongside Ernestine's cot. He rolled her over gently, forced her swollen eyelids apart, and flashed a light into her pupils. The blood from her mouth had caked dry; heart and pulse were weak but steady; there were massive cuts and bruises. He ministered to the wounds from his diminished supply of drugs, cleaned them with a solution, and then waved an ammonia stick under her nose. She groaned to a sort of consciousness.

"Ernestine. It is Dr. Hahn."

She shook her head that she understood.

"I want to probe for breaks. You will tell me how badly it hurts."

He probed about her body, then remained in utter frustration for a long moment. "She is not in shock and that is good. The ankle is not broken, only sprained, but I suspect a couple of ribs fractured and perhaps a concussion. Needless to say she is badly off from the beating and violations. I don't know what we can do about either food or medicine . . ."

Everyone froze simultaneously at the sound of feet shuffling overhead.

"Lord! We forgot to close the trap door," Bruno whispered.

"Quiet!"

The sounds above became more pronounced . . . laughter . . . talk in a strange language . . . something was kicked over and crashed. Frau Falkenstein grabbed Ernestine beneath the armpits and rolled her under one of the cots as the candle was doused.

Falkenstein wanted to go for his pistol, but the footsteps were just above them now! The ray of a flashlight probed through the trap-door opening, along the walls, and stopped as it found Hildegaard's face. She shrieked!

A soldier dropped to the floor, whirled his submachine gun at them, called up to the others. Three more followed. They were Mongols, short and squat with yellow skin and long, drooping moustaches. They were ragged and foul-smelling from drink. The last of them carried a square canvas filled with loot: clocks, silverware, porcelain pieces, candlesticks.

The leader, swaggering and nearly senseless from alcohol, stepped up to them. "Tick, tick, tick, tick," he said.

"They want your watches," Dr. Hahn said. "Give them up."

Hildegaard and Herta Falkenstein nervously took them off and put them on the center table. The leader snatched them, listened to the movements, and attached them to his left arm, where he already wore a dozen watches.

He jabbered an order to the one with the submachine gun, who smiled through brown and yellow decaying teeth as he separated Dr. Hahn and Falkenstein from the women, leveling a gun barrel at their chests and motioning them to turn their faces to the wall.

"Kumm frau," the leader said, advancing toward Hildegaard Falkenstein.

"Listen," Dr. Hahn said rapidly, "it is useless to struggle. They might kill you. Do as they say . . . don't resist."

"Mother!" Hildegaard shrieked, and clung inside Herta's inept protective grasp. "Mother! Tell them I'm sick! Tell them not to make me do it!"

Herta Falkenstein held her daughter tightly for an instant, and then they pried her loose and flung her onto the cot under which Ernestine was hidden.

"Animals! Bastards!" Bruno screamed as he turned and lunged. He caught the barrel of the guard's gun over the bridge of his nose, sending his glasses to the floor, smashed. Another crack on his jaw with the gun butt sent him sliding in slow motion to the ground, now on his hands and knees, pawing around senselessly. One last blow flattened him and a pool of blood began to form under his face.

The leader tore the clothes from Hildegaard's body. This sent the other three soldiers into spasms of laughter as the girl screamed, tried to shield herself, prayed, and cried. He knocked her flat, and mounted her. Another of the soldiers shoved Herta Falkenstein onto another cot. Her fat, flabby body and immense hanging breasts delighted the Mongols. They chortled and whooped as they forced themselves on her.

The two women lay rigid and unprotesting. When the first two assailants were done, they traded women. The other two became angry and pushed their comrades off and took their own turns. All of this went on as the leader began vomiting from liquor and the others urinated and moved their bowels on the floor. Each new disgusting act was considered terribly humorous, causing them to scream with laughter.

Two hours after they arrived, they shot up the shelves in the cellar in a last burst of vandalism and left.

As Dr. Hahn went to the women, Bruno Falkenstein crawled toward his cot, took his pistol from under the mattress, and stuck the barrel in his mouth. The doctor leaped on him and kicked the pistol from his hands. He writhed on the floor weeping.

"You idiot! Help me with your women!"

"Why did you stop me? What is there to live for? We are all ruined!"

Old Dr. Hahn stood in this chamber of horrors with the fetid smell reaching deeply into his nostrils. He saw the agonized man beating the floor with his fists, and he saw the shambles and heard the three women groan.

Frau Herta Falkenstein crawled from her cot and knelt beside her prostrate husband and touched his head. He pulled away from her.

"Bruno," she moaned, "go to Hilde. Tell her you love her. Please go to
Hilde and tell her you love her."

"Ruined," he wept. "We are ruined."

CHAPTER FOUR

Heinrich Hirsch walked alone and unarmed in the middle of a street
still smoldering from battle in the Neukölln District of Berlin. He
stopped before a three-story building on Geyer Strasse 2. A bullet-
pocked sign, "Backerei," groaned back and forth. The window was
smashed and boarded. He looked up to the second floor. A window
box held petunias that drooped wearily.

The young man was tall and slender. He had thin Semitic features
revealing he was half Jewish, from his mother's side of the family. He
wore shiny new boots, semimilitary garb, and a red star on his arm band.

He walked the creaking steps to apartment four at the front of the
building, second floor, and knocked. The door was opened slowly by a
frightened old woman. Upon seeing his Russian attire, she paled.

Heinrich shoved the door wide and entered the room. The old woman
flattened herself against a wall and watched his movements as he came
to the center of the room and let his eyes play everywhere. "Don't
worry, old woman," he said. "I lived here once. I only want to look
around."

Was it only ten years ago? . . . ten years, nearly to the day. He remembered walking into the room and seeing the grim faces of the comrades. He was ordered into his room to go to sleep.

Heinrich walked to a small hallway and shoved open a door to a tiny
bedroom. He lay there that night ten years ago listening to the arguments of the comrades. He had lain awake many nights in those days
listening. The comrades were confused about the Nazi stampede. What
to do? Where to hit back? How to fight?

One by one important party members disappeared. Names of the concentration camps, the Oranienburgs and Dachaus, began to be heard.

And then . . . it came his father's time. They had talked that night
until late. When they left, his mother and father went to sleep in the
next room in their big soft bed with its great down comforter.

He remembered wakening to the sound of whistles in the street . . . then footsteps racing up the steps and angry thumps on the apartment door . . . and last . . . his mother's scream!

Much of what followed was in blurs. For several days he and his mother hid in the home of comrades in Spandau in a basement. The news came back that his father, Werner Hirsch, a Communist official, had been spiraled into martyrdom, beaten to death in Gestapo headquarters.

Heinrich remembered a wild drive in the middle of the night to Rostock on the Baltic Sea and hiding in the hold of a stinking old fishing boat that stole over the straits to the sanctuary of Sweden, where other comrades kept them hidden.

After three weeks his mother told him, "The comrades have decided that we should go on to the Soviet Union. We will be safe at last."

The Soviet Union! From earliest memory his mother and father had labored, lived, struggled for the dream of a socialist state in Germany. The Soviet Union was the womb, the mother. It would be almost like coming home for the very first time.

Heinrich remembered the swell of tension in the gray Finnish morning as they boarded the train for the ride to Leningrad. Tears fell from his mother's eyes as she first saw the great stone buildings of this mighty fortress of socialism. . . . They would soon be in Moscow.

In 1935 Communist refugees from Germany were treated as heroes, for they were the living symbols of the struggle against Hitler. The son of Werner Hirsch was to be a student at School #78 in Moscow, which had been established exclusively for the children from Germany, Austria, and German-speaking countries. School #78 was given great attention. It was a modern four-story building; the children lived in and were given special diets of German food, the best uniforms, tours about the country; were given special seats in cultural events and the most superb health supervision. Outside school a League of German Communists coordinated their activities.

For fifteen-year-old Heinrich Hirsch it was the most wonderful life he had ever known. The dank meeting halls in Berlin, the shabby life, the terror were all behind him.

School #78 was spared that drab, lusterless place called Moscow. The children were only allowed to see a few gems in its sea of dejection.

Heinrich's mother worked as a translator of German documents in one of the political bureaus. He was allowed to visit her one day a week.

The two had been exceedingly close, and their weekly meeting brought
on an uncomfortable situation. There was scarcely a place where they
could be alone to talk; surely not in the German Culture Center, for
they would not have a moment's peace; even in the parks there was a
constant blare of loudspeakers eulogizing Soviet life, playing nationalistic music, or reporting the news.

They spent their time in her room. It was a single small room in the
apartment of a comrade from Berlin in an abominable old wooden house.
The foundation had sunk and the outer walls were propped with timbers to keep them from collapsing. Some twenty persons from five families shared a single bathroom and kitchen.

But this was the best that could be arranged. Heinrich had been
thoroughly indoctrinated that these housing conditions were a result of
the first war, the counterrevolution, the devotion to industrialization,
and the pressure of the imperialist countries. His mother seemed quite
content with her lot, particularly the good fortune of her son.

Several months after their arrival, Heinrich Hirsch stood on the stage
of the auditorium of School #78. Above the stage hung a great portrait
of Stalin, and in blood-red lettering his words, THERE IS NO FOR-
TRESS THE BOLSHEVIKS CANNOT STORM!

He received a red scarf in a ceremony making him a member of the
Pioneers and repeated the oath: "I solemnly promise in the presence of
my comrades and parents that as a Pioneer of the Soviet Union I will
fight bravely for the interests of the working class and to safeguard the
sacred legacy of Lenin."

Then a buckle, engraved with five logs representing the five conti-
nents and the three flames of the fire of International Communism, was
slipped on the scarf.

This was the formal opening of his religious studies. Denied the God
of his mother, he adopted Communism as his religion. Karl Marx was
god, Lenin the son of god, and Stalin the great disciple.

Their writings were studied as meticulously as a Jesuit studies Christianity, and under greater discipline. Like all religions, this one, too,
promised a heaven that seemed beyond the reach of the living.

The first time Heinrich Hirsch knew mortal fear it came in the form
of Nazis and Brownshirts marching in jackboots.

This time it came on a knock on the door in the middle of the night.
The purges!

There were new banner headlines and inflamed speeches and the loudspeakers harangued: SPIES! TRAITORS! FASCIST HIRELINGS! AGENTS! SPECULATORS! SWINDLERS! DEVIATIONISTS! PROVOCATEURS! TROTSKYITES! MUTINEERS!

There was advice to FIND THEM! SHOOT THEM! DESTROY THEM!

And each new blast ended with a solemn prayer: LONG LIVE COMRADE STALIN AND OUR GLORIOUS COMMUNIST PARTY!

Things began to change at School #78. Almost overnight the food became gruel, like that of the rest of the Russians, and the pampering stopped. One by one teachers disappeared; the parties, the weekend dances, the fun and laughter stopped.

On a Saturday, eighteen months after his arrival in Moscow, Heinrich Hirsch went one day to the room of his mother. The door was sealed and padlocked. Frantically, the boy tried to open it, then ran through the house pleading with everyone, one by one, to try to find out what had happened. No one heard anything, saw anything, knew anything.

Three weeks later he received a postcard. The message was printed. The signature might have been his mother's. It read: "I have been guilty of provocations and confessed to treason against the Soviet Union and have voluntarily accepted deportation to Siberia. Forget about me."

Mother a traitor of the Soviet Union! Impossible! Impossible!

Then, other children of School #78 went out on weekends and found sealed doors and received postcards from parents confessing to treason.

The teachers were too frightened to speak about it, but after a time the students talked among themselves. Each one knew that his own parent was not guilty, but the intense indoctrination paid off. They each came to justify the fact there would be a few mistakes of justice under the urgencies of the times.

Despite this black mark against him, Heinrich Hirsch had shown such great skill in political studies that he came to the second stage in his career as a Communist. He was called for an interview with the possibility of joining Komsomol, the Young Communist League.

He recited his new duties flawlessly:

"To study the works of Marx, Engels, Lenin, and our beloved Stalin; to encourage the masses toward our ideals; to carry out all resolutions, proclamations, and edicts of the Supreme Soviet and the Communist Party without question; to protect our great socialist heritage with sacrifice; to acquire knowledge, culture, and develop physically and never cease working for the Motherland against its enemies and to never cease the struggle until all peoples are freed of fascist and imperialist bondage through International Communism."

"What is the principle upon which Komsomol is founded?"

"The principle of democratic centralism."

He was admitted to higher institutions for languages, then Marxism, and then International Communism. Heinrich Hirsch closed his mind to the things happening around him. Names of men who were heroes of the Revolution yesterday became the names of traitors today. Marshals of the Red Army, members of Lenin's Politburo, members of the Central Committee all fell under the ax of the purge. Suicides of great names often took the place of official confessions. One had no choice but to study and keep his nose clean.

At Institute #16 for advanced studies of foreign Communism Heinrich again saw Rudi Wöhlman, titular head of the German Communists in the Soviet Union. Wöhlman had come to Institute #16 for a series of lectures on German Communism.

He remembered Heinrich as a little boy of five in Berlin and, of course, remembered his martyred father, Werner Hirsch, very well. Often times Heinrich heard his father speak of Rudi Wöhlman as the great hope of the German Communists.

Wöhlman had left Berlin for special schooling in Moscow in the mid-1920s, but never returned. It was a great disappointment for the German Communists. After his training in Moscow, Wöhlman was assigned as a commissar of the Soviet Union's German-speaking Volga Republic.

No wonder Heinrich looked forward to his lectures with great anticipation. Here at last was the link between Moscow and Berlin. What followed was a terrible disappointment. Rudi Wöhlman's speeches were a recitation of the current political line; he delivered them with parrot-like perfection, the words a rehash of a hundred speeches Heinrich had listened to before.

Rudi Wöhlman showed himself to be a shrewd politician rather than a man of thought. He had a sheen of glibness which hid the lack of depth or intelligence. He used the same verbal acrobatics all the teachers used. Wöhlman kept it safe, worked around the core of delicate

problems, kept clear of personal opinions, and sidestepped pointed questions by having the students argue them, then placing himself as a final
judge. A man of slight build with an immaculately trimmed goatee and
darting eyes, each thought and word was calculated to keep him out of
trouble.

By the end of the third lecture, Heinrich came to the conclusion
that Rudi Wöhlman was a German in name only. He had not suffered
during the Nazi era, nor did he show any allegiance to the German
working class. Wöhlman was another of those "foreign" comrades whom
Moscow kept because they had meaningful names in their former native
lands. In fact, they had no grasp of the struggle in the countries they
pretended to represent, but merely carried out Moscow edicts.

Heinrich's own father, although a devout Communist, was nonetheless a devout German. He had impressed in the boy that Marx and
Engels and the Communist idea were all German. The Soviet Union
had merely borrowed them. Wöhlman's lectures left no doubt that Moscow now was the mecca of Communism.

The first disasters of the campaign against Finland and the vulnerability of the Red Army threw him into a quandary.

The great shock came with the Soviet-German Non-Aggression Pact.
Barrages of written and verbal explanations came from the propaganda
organs to "prove" that the pact was a scientific treaty consistent with
socialist aims. But, explain as they might with all of their persuasive
forces, the complete reversal overnight of Soviet foreign policy and
avowed Communist goals had a lasting effect upon him and thousands
of others. Heinrich Hirsch could not remember when he was not fighting Nazis. These Nazis, now in pact with Russia, were the very same
who had murdered his father.

The recourse? There was no way to either question or protest—only
justify. He reasoned that if there were flaws it was not in the system,
which was scientifically perfect, but with the mortals who ran it and
the pressures of the outside. After all, if the Western imperialists had
not placed the Soviet Union in such circumstances, he reasoned, we
would never have made an agreement with the Nazis.

The German panzers spilled into the Russian motherland in June
of 1941, canceling the Pact. The words "fascist," "Hitlerite," and "Nazi,"
which had not been heard in Moscow for the nearly two years of the
treaty's life, now poured out again in damnation of the aggressors. And

all newscasts, speeches, writing ended with the cry, "Death to the Nazi enemy."

On a night in September of 1941, three months after the German invasion, Heinrich Hirsch was awakened by a knocking on his door. Four NKVD men gave him ten minutes to gather a few personal items in a single bag. At secret-police headquarters his papers and Komsomol card were revoked. He was issued a new identification paper stamped with the words GERMAN and JEW, placed into a waiting truck filled with others who had been processed, and driven in the predawn hours to a barbed-wire enclosure on a rail siding on the outskirts of Moscow. A train of eighty-odd cars, some of them freight and cattle cars, stood by.

Every few moments another truckload of deportees arrived. By morning they had been crammed into the train cars. The windows were barred. Obviously these very cars had made other excursions with "suspect elements." The shades were drawn, the doors locked and guarded. The train left Moscow in a southeasterly direction toward an unknown destination.

There were seventy persons packed into Heinrich's car. He found himself to be one of the few true Germans in the lot. For the most part they were made up of persons of German ancestry from the Volga Republic. Rumor spread, even through locked cars, that the entire Volga Republic was being deported en masse; some had a German mother or father . . . some had Germanic names . . . some had no idea why they were there.

It was a torturous trip of stop and go. The car stank from the lack of air. Rations and water were thrown in once daily as one feeds a pack of animals in a cage. The only way one could relieve himself was through a twelve-inch hole cut in the floor in the center of the car.

Ten days and a thousand miles later they were allowed to lift the blinds for the first time and leave the train for a stretch. There were dead to be removed from the car, and seriously ill to be left to die. The station was a mob scene of refugees. Tens of thousands of homeless persons who had fled in the face of the German assault were wandering aimlessly, unfed, desperate.

From the signs and the appearance of new guards and rail workers with dark eyes and yellow-brown skins and stubby legs, Heinrich reasoned they had passed beyond the Volga River into the foothills of the Urals in the faraway Soviet Republic of Kazakh.

They continued their journey south, far far past the Urals to Lake Balkesh, at that place where the borders of Siberia, Mongolia, and China meet, and then swung north to the remote city of Karaganda and even beyond that for several hundred miles.

On the twenty-sixth day of this nightmare, the train came to a halt at a wooden shed at a siding of a village bearing the name: Settlement #128. The passengers debarked. Dozens of horse-drawn carts awaited them. The roll was called:

"Bloss. Settlement #89."

"Hauser. Settlement #44."

"Bauer. Settlement #123."

Heinrich Hirsch watched them trudge off to the carts with only a small bundle of their belongings. So this was it, the land of the exiles! Villages without names a thousand miles from nowhere. Here were the survivors of the Kulaks, the independent farmers whom Stalin exiled in his drive to collectivize agriculture at the end of the twenties. Here were the political survivors of the purges. Here were German prisoners from the first war who had never been returned. No doubt his mother was in one of those nameless villages. He dared not inquire.

The odyssey of Heinrich Hirsch could have ended with him going off in the back of a cart down a dirt road into oblivion except that the regime had other uses for him. He was returned to Karaganda.

Heinrich had heard about the city. Karaganda, built under the first five-year plan, was praised in meeting after meeting.

Karaganda could disillusion the most stalwart servant of the party. This planned city of a quarter of a million, the epitome of the Soviet pioneering spirit, turned out to be a dirty, dilapidated hole beyond description, with an evil film of coal dust infecting it.

On the outskirts Heinrich Hirsch saw thousands of large holes in the ground. These were covered with rags, wood, and tin. These oversized graves served as homes for the less fortunate Kulaks who had not been resettled in the nameless villages. A great number of them were aged, crippled, and helpless. In this place they lived on scraps and awaited merciful death from the final horror of "People's Socialism."

There were a few modern buildings in Karaganda. They belonged to the NKVD, the Town Soviet, District Committee of the Communist Party, and the Educational and Cultural Institute. In this forsaken hole, Heinrich Hirsch assumed new duties as a reinstated Komsomol member of the Agitation and Propaganda Corps.

There were two objectives. First, the entire German Volga Republic had been deported, many into this district. He had to continue to enlighten the exiles, and keep up their agricultural and manufacturing quotas.

The second objective became more apparent as the war wore on. Trainloads of German prisoners arrived and were encamped. Heinrich Hirsch was on one of the teams to re-educate them. He found German defectors, obtained signatures for petitions against Nazi Germany and used them for broadcasts and newspaper articles.

He retrained them as Communists. Repentant German prisoners could become members of the "anti-Fascists" who were slated to become important in Russia's postwar occupation plans for Germany.

Hirsch did his job well. In 1943 Rudi Wöhlman traveled to Karaganda and assigned many Germans to new duties. Among the appointees was Heinrich Hirsch, who had undergone his third redemption.

Once again he crossed the great Kuzkah desert. This time he traveled on an unguarded train and with new papers without the damnations GERMAN and JEW stamped on them. His destination was the city of Ufa in the Autonomous Republic of Bashkir, some eight hundred miles east of Moscow.

As the Russians evacuated citizens and machinery into their vast lands certain cities received certain types of evacuees with similar characteristics; Alma Ata and Tashkent became wartime centers of artists and scientists; others drew manufacturing complexes and became transport or training points.

Ufa became the center of International Communism. Under agreement with the Western Allies, the International Comintern had been officially dissolved. But in remote Ufa, it continued to operate under a different set of titles.

Heinrich Hirsch was attached as a member of the International Society for the Aid of Class War Prisoners. In Ufa he joined the cream of foreign Communist trainees.

Like most Soviet cities in the hinterlands, Ufa was jammed with starving refugees and the horrible privations of wartime. However, this did not affect the comintern trainees who continued to live splendidly.

His particular school was known as Technical School #77 for Industrial Economy. In this institute Germans, Czechs, Austrians, Spaniards, Bulgars, Poles, Italians, French, South Americans, and Africans all trained for the singular purposes of infiltrating, subverting, and destroying their former homelands.

In this inner sanctum of hard-core trainees the tactics of keeping the imperialists on the defensive were emphasized by use of constant, prodding harassment and pressure. Lenin remained the infallible source of inspiration. "Push out a bayonet. If it strikes fat, push deeper. If it strikes iron, pull back for another day."

In order to learn how to counter imperialist propaganda the students were exposed to Western books, newspapers, speeches, broadcasts. For in Ufa, the enemy, the true enemy, was everyone who was not a Communist. This meant the temporary American and British allies just as it had meant the Nazis during the Non-Aggression Pact days.

During the meticulous courses in counterpropaganda Heinrich Hirsch, for the first time, was exposed to Jefferson, Lincoln, and Paine and Western thought. All of the Anglo/American ideologies were thoroughly dissected and destroyed in the classrooms, but at the same time, a new flood of thought opened.

For the first time in his life he was able to read that all of the world's ideas were not discovered by Marx, Lenin, or Stalin. Added to his earlier confusions and disillusions, Hirsch knew that he could become an agent of the revolution only through the fear of power and the silencing forever of his own voices of inquisitiveness.

Something else happened to him in Ufa. Heinrich had reached his twenty-third year without ever having sex with a woman. He had always been too tired from his studies and too dedicated to indulge in such nonsense.

In Ufa he met Maria Majoros, the young daughter of a Spanish Communist who, like his own father, was a martyr of the Communist world.

At what moment does one try to describe the first awakening? What happens when the long suppressed emotion bursts alive like springtime? How does one tell of the sensation of first love? First a meeting of the eyes . . . then, perhaps, stolen glances . . . going out of the way to be at a place where you know she is passing . . . a first rendezvous filled with trembling and fumbling, and then . . . a knowing of love.

It was discovery that there were other things on this earth that belonged to most men that had been denied him.

Wild great cries of love to each other in stolen places . . .

BULLETIN!
HEINRICH HIRSCH AND MARIA MAJOROS WILL APPEAR
BEFORE THE KOMSOMOL COMMITTEE FOR THE PURPOSE
OF SELF-CRITICISM.

Who told on them? Did it really matter? Was there ever life away
from prying eyes?

They took their medicine. They stood side by side daring not to look
at each other. The portrait of Stalin glared down at them; it always
did. The angry eyes of the Komsomol Committee executives scorned
them, and they confessed their shame.

"I beg for the understanding of my comrades for this *petit bourgeois*
indulgent act I have committed," Heinrich Hirsch said of the love of
the only woman he had known. "I am humiliated for allowing myself
to forget my Communist upbringing and behavior unworthy of a member of Komsomol."

For an hour Heinrich Hirsch was berated; and then, Maria Majoros,
a woman of proud Spanish blood, blurted her "confession":

"The manifestations and provocations of my act with Heinrich Hirsch
are contrary to the duty of a socialist woman. I beg mercy from my
comrades to prove myself again worthy of making my contribution to
world revolution."

When the further debasement of Maria Majoros was over the girl
was sent away from Ufa, never to be heard from again.

Heinrich Hirsch, the twenty-five-year-old deputy to Rudi Wöhlman
on the German People's Liberation Committee, had now finished his
journey into the past at the flat on Geyer Strasse 2.

The old woman in the room was still filled with a fear of the strange
young man.

"Don't be frightened, *Mutter*," he said softly, "I just wanted to see
what it looked like."

He walked outside into the shambles of Berlin. The homecoming
was done.

CHAPTER FIVE

Igor Karlovy requisitioned a mansion in Karlshorst for his billet. It was relatively undamaged, and the twelve rooms were the most luxurious he had ever been in. The headquarters office was established in the main drawing room; he did his own work in his enormous, lush bedroom. Reports poured in from all over the city with data for the dismantling of the Berlin industrial complex. In a few days he was due to hand in his own findings to Commissar Azov and the German People's Liberation Committee.

A sound of singing reached his ears, the voices of his men. Igor took off his glasses, put them down for a moment, and listened from his desk. The song, known to him from childhood, was called "Volga, Volga," a song of the cossacks and their lure. It was Russian, melodic, and mournful. Young Feodor's voice sang with nostalgia.

A fine boy, young Feodor, Igor thought . . . my most promising officer. They had been through it all together, Feodor and the colonel. They were more like brothers than senior and junior officers.

The voice of Ivan Orlov joined in the chorus. Ivan sings well, Igor thought, but that is about all. He hangs too closely on the words of the commissars and the edicts. He spies on us.

Igor stretched, yawned, patted his flat hard stomach, and slipped into his tunic without buttoning it and went into the living room. The singers were warmly comfortable after the first flushes of victory and the afterglow of vodka. They sat about in the deep comfort of the great house with their boots off and their tunics open.

"Sit still, sit still," Igor said as he entered.

Feodor tossed a mandolin to the colonel; he perched his foot on a stool, lit a cigarette, and caught up in the chorus:

> Volga, Volga you're my mother,
> Volga, you're a Russian stream . . .

Captain Boris Chernov came in from the outside just as the song came to its sorrowful end telling of a young princess being thrown into the waters as a sacrifice.

"You're late," Igor admonished. "I've been holding up the entire report on your account."

"Forgive me, Comrade Colonel," Boris said, slyly holding up a woman's delicate watch. "I got delayed by a little German dumpling."

Ivan Orlov laughed. Igor set his instrument down, snatched the papers out of Boris' case, and returned to his bedroom slamming the door behind him.

"What bothers the colonel?" Boris asked.

"He thinks our officers shouldn't screw the German women," Feodor snapped, coming to the colonel's defense.

"Nonsense," Ivan Orlov said.

"Let me tell you that many officers are condemning the whole thing and want to put a stop to it."

"I was at headquarters"—Boris laughed—"an old woman was complaining she was raped eighty-four times. The doctor insisted she was enjoying it or she wouldn't have bothered to count."

Ivan laughed; Feodor got more angry.

"Come now, Feodor," Boris said. "Do you think the Germans deserve better?"

"The hell with both of you," Feodor answered. "Besides, I don't think much of your taste. As for me, I wouldn't stick mine between a German woman's legs."

Igor Karlovy was standing in the doorway, his fists clenched. "Carry on your goddamned discussion elsewhere. I'm trying to finish my work."

Forty-eight hours after his report was filed, Commissar Azov summoned Igor to meet with the head of the German People's Liberation Committee.

V. V. Azov, who made a fine art of keeping himself inconspicuous, mysterious, and anonymous, had a mansion in Potsdam on the Wannsee. His house was in a forest, shades eternally drawn, grounds heavily guarded.

The usual portrait of Stalin hung over the conference table in the dark-paneled room replacing an oil of Prussian nobility. Even in the worst days of Leningrad, Igor thought, there was never a shortage of Stalin's portraits. V. V. Azov looked expressionless and bored as he took his place at the table.

Two members of the German People's Liberation Committee sat opposite him. Igor personally disliked most of the Germans on the committee. It was true that all of them were tested Communists who had fled Hitler, yet he felt there was too much German left in their souls.

Rudi Wöhlman's face reminded Igor of the little field rats that used to attack the grain stores on the family farm . . . thin face, thin beard, glinting front teeth. He had brought with him his young aide, Heinrich Hirsch.

"To get directly to the point," Azov said, "I find your report unsatisfactory."

Igor had dealt with party people successfully all during the siege and the great offenses out of Russia, across Poland, East Prussia, and Germany. He wished they would let him stick to Air Force problems, but his own talent trapped him; he knew the language. "If the Comrade Commissar would get to specifics I am certain I can offer explanations."

"Many of our recommendations have been rejected," Heinrich Hirsch said sharply.

"Let us take the transfer of railroad cars as an example. You deleted it," Azov said.

"I am certain," Igor answered, "the Commissar is aware there is a different gauge in the German and Soviet rail systems that make their rolling stock useless to us. With our transport and distribution problems the rail cars have better use in Germany."

Azov nodded that the point was well taken. "However," he said drolly, "the German and Polish rail systems are compatible. Our Polish comrades have suffered untold brutality at the hands of the Nazi beasts. The Lublin People's Committee for a Free and Democratic Poland have asked us to help them in rebuilding their shattered homeland. Delivery of the rail stock in the Brandenburg Province will be among the first Polish reparations."

Igor pretended to study his folio in order to give himself time to decipher the true meaning of Azov's rhetoric. Dozens of such conferences had taught him not to be taken by a surprise announcement of policy. What he unscrambled was that the Lublin Poles had been installed to run the country.

"It poses a technical problem," Igor said carefully.

"Which is?"

"The Brandenburg Province, and Berlin in particular, has never been self-sustaining in food even in the best of days. Furthermore, food surplus must come from eastern German provinces. This means we

need rail stock. Also, I have studied the draft of our agreement with
the Americans and British. As I interpret it, the immediate areas around
Berlin are responsible for feeding the city. This will all be impossible
without freight cars."

Azov tapped his fingers on the tabletop, digesting Igor Karlovy's line
of logic. Wöhlman looked from one to another, not daring to venture
an opinion at this point.

"Your interpretation of the treaty with the Western Allies is incorrect," Azov said. "The Americans and British must feed their own sectors of Berlin from their own sources. Therefore, we will be responsible
for feeding less than a third of the city."

Again, Igor tried to separate political implications from realities.
Azov's words, which were official policy, said that Russia would find a
way to break the treaty. America and Britian would be compelled to
bring in food from a distance of at least two hundred kilometers, if not
from overseas. Furthermore, Berlin depended upon coal for industrial
power from the Ruhr. The loss of freight cars was obviously intended
to place such a burden on the Western Allies that it might be impossible
for them to stay in Berlin. Igor nodded that he understood. "Certainly
our Polish comrades should have the rolling stock," he said. "I will re-
evaluate the situation at once."

Next Azov listed several classifications of machinery which had been
omitted from the report.

"The machinery you speak of," he answered, "cannot be integrated
into the Soviet system. It is useless to us. Furthermore, it will take tens
of thousands of man hours to dismantle it and move it by rail and unload it for the sole purpose of letting it rust in depots. It is an expensive
waste of both rail space and man power."

"However, Comrade Colonel," Azov came back with "policy," "even
if the machinery is valueless to us it has great value to the Germans,
particularly if they entertain the notion of a war of revenge against the
Soviet Union."

Wöhlman now felt safe in handing Azov a list. He cleared his throat.
"I call your attention to the recommendations of the German People's
Liberation Committee in paragraph twenty-two, which we presented
to you as far back as Warsaw. You have not included them, Comrade
Colonel."

This coming from Rudi Wöhlman was too much. For an instant Igor
almost lost his composure. He felt like shouting, "What the hell side are

you on, Wöhlman? Are you a German or not?" Of course, he said nothing, stifling his anger with a slight smile.

Colonel Karlovy knew the notorious paragraph twenty-two from
memory. It listed the removal of Berlin's toilets, sinks, doorknobs, window sashes, wiring, light bulbs, chairs and desks, typewriters, window
shades, bidets, and many dozen other such items as part of Berlin's
"industrial complex." How eager to please Rudi Wöhlman was! He'd
even take the toilets out of Berlin!

"I fail to understand," Igor said, now calming himself, "how German
toilets will either add to the wealth of the Soviet Union or to future
German war making potential. If Comrade Wöhlman would be so good
as to explain?"

Comrade Wöhlman was flustered long enough for Azov to step in
and save him. "Before the re-education of the German working class
they must be made to realize what happens to those who dare attack
the Soviet Union. Only after the Germans atone for attacking our
motherland will the Liberation Committee be in a position to build
socialism." With that pronouncement Igor knew the conversation was
at an end. "I take it then," Azov continued, "you are aware of the de-
ficiencies in your report."

The moment had come. Igor Karlovy nodded his head and mumbled
an apology for his mistakes.

"Whatever you do, give priority attention to those sections of West
Berlin scheduled for American and British occupation. We want everything cleared out before they come."

The meeting was abruptly ended upon Igor's promise to have an
amended report ready in seventy-two hours.

"If you will drive me in to our headquarters," Heinrich Hirsch said,
"I will get ready the lists of our original recommendations."

"By all means, Comrade Hirsch."

They passed through the gates of Azov's mansion onto Königs Road
and the devastation of Berlin. Heinrich Hirsch was the least offensive
of the Germans to Igor. He was the youngest member of the committee
and obviously Wöhlman's right hand. Small wonder. In the meetings
they had had, he found Hirsch's tongue like a razor, an astute brain
reacting quickly with a depth of knowledge of the dialectics. Most of
the party people pondered on each word, weighed their answers meticulously; not so Hirsch. Igor knew he was the son of a martyred German
Communist. Beside that, only a few hazy half facts. One never asked

about another's background or experiences. One had to treat another with basic distrust, for he never knew if he was talking to a spy or just how words would be used against him someday. The fact that Hirsch had emerged as a member of the committee at such an early age testified to his stature. For a long while they were wordless. They passed near the lake with the pale green birch trees forming a mantle on both sides of the road.

"I agree with your position," Hirsch said at last.

"What position?"

"Your attempt to save Berlin from being stripped down to the last nail and screw."

"It was not a position, Comrade Hirsch. I am merely an engineer. Positions, as you call them, come from Commissar Azov."

"Nevertheless," Hirsch countered quickly, "you chose to ignore Rudi Wöhlman's recommendations and drew up different plans."

"On what I believed to be a purely scientific basis. I was only thinking in the mathematical terms of work hours and transportation. Now that I have been made aware of the political considerations my position, as you call it, has been clarified."

It was the kind of wording both of them knew well. "Hell, let's face it," Heinrich persisted, to Igor's discomfort, "it's damned bad business. Not only the stripping of the city but abuses by the soldiers."

Igor stared directly ahead, pretending to be bored. His brain worked feverishly to avoid being drawn into such a discussion. Igor took the road that cut diagonally across the Grunewald. There was not too much damage in this area. "The present behavior of the Red Army is destroying a great image."

"Just a minute, Comrade Hirsch. The Soviet Union did not invite the Nazis to invade, destroy our cities, burn our fields, kill our children, and rape our women," Igor recited from the standard line. "Our men have fought hard and have been bloodied for thousands of miles. After what has been done to us, the German people would be fools to expect less. Besides," he added as an afterthought, "soldiers are soldiers."

Hirsch struck back immediately. "In all candor Comrade Colonel, this continued rape can only diminish the stature of the Red Army regardless of the provocations. Both Marx and Lenin have pointed out that in order for us to successfully carry out world revolution we must first have the support of a socialist German working class."

"The German working class will be rebuilt after every vestige of the Nazi is purged from him."

"But, Comrade Colonel, I raise the question of whether our soldiers are discriminating between Nazis and non-Nazis in their . . . er . . . sport. Certainly the rape of a ten-year-old girl will do nothing to induce the Germans to accept the Soviet way of life."

"There are bound to be a few mistakes," Igor answered weakly.

"A few hundred thousand is more like it. Colonel Karlovy, I dare this conversation with you out of mutual love of the Soviet Union. I have begged Comrade Wöhlman to speak to Azov. The fact of the matter is that Wöhlman at times appears to be more intent on pleasing the commissars and keeping in their good graces than he is of representing the new Germany. If these abuses are allowed to continue it must end in earning the everlasting hatred of the German people and it must sow the seeds of a war of revenge. You are a hero of the Soviet Union in a position to exert pressure. Many Red Army officers are disgusted with the events in Berlin."

Igor was now terribly uncomfortable. They had emerged from the forest and were moving toward the wreckage of central Berlin. Igor knew nothing could stop the rape and looting except orders from Azov. Acts of "individualism" was just the type of thing that killed half the officer corps off during the purges. "Comrade Hirsch, many things you have said to me could bring you grave consequences. For this time alone, I will forget you ever opened your mouth."

Heinrich Hirsch stared at Igor. There was no more to be said. They reached the Brandenburg Gate, where the red flag hung limply atop the monument to former German victories, and crossed beneath to the Unter Den Linden. The avenue of former grandeur was perhaps the most horrible in all of Berlin with its massive gutted shells. Hirsch asked to be let out.

"I'm sorry I spoke to you, Colonel Karlovy," he said. "I was gravely mistaken. I thought you were different."

Igor, smarting from the last remark, watched Hirsch go off. He gripped the wheel of the car tightly . . . damned bastard!

He was wearing thin with the whole mess in Berlin. And now, this business of stripping toilets. What the hell, political decisions were not handed down for discussion. As one who was trained in the days of the purges, Igor knew how to go into mental vacuums. The officers' training created situations to compel the men to inform on each other.

Spying was an accepted way of life. One had to be careful not to form lasting friendships for he could never tell when the most innocent complaint would be twisted against him. Spying kept minds alert and prevented cliques of military deviationists from forming.

Despite this conditioning Igor Karlovy was reachable. There were memories to haunt him. Always at a time like this the ghost and the voice of Peter Egorov was heard. He drove back to his house, forgetting his work, locking his door behind him, drinking quickly to drown out the memory of Peter.

He lay on his bed and the sweat began to form in cold beads. Damn you Peter Egorov! Damn you! Why did you do it? Will you leave me in peace! You know you were a fool . . . you know that.

More vodka . . . yes, more vodka to burn away the memory.

Lieutenant Peter Egorov and Feodor Guchkov were the favorites of Colonel Karlovy. All of the young engineers looked to Igor as their idol during the siege of Leningrad. His ingenuity, bravery, and bravado had become legend. What was more, Colonel Karlovy was not a party member. Things in his command were relaxed. Members of his immediate staff were like family. What a hell of a time they had, the three of them. Loving, fighting, and drinking. Igor, Feodor, and Peter Egorov.

What a brilliant young officer Peter was! A superb engineer with endless talents for improvising, particularly in keeping up factory production. So bright was Peter that those factories in his immediate command even increased production in the middle of the siege.

Peter had a Cossack's lust for life. Perhaps that is why Igor, a Cossack himself, was drawn to the younger man. He had all the attributes . . . he sang like a nightingale or fought like a tiger as the occasion demanded. He loved women and women loved him.

When the siege was broken and the lines rolled westward, Igor was borrowed from the Red Air Force and promoted as chief engineer of the entire front. Peter and Feodor came along on his staff. Throughout the offenses of 1944 and 1945 the engineers moved with the armies through the Baltics, White Russia, and into Poland, erecting bridges, blowing up other bridges, repairing ports, laying airstrips, demolishing unsafe buildings, cutting roads, repairing rails.

The White Russian Front rolled up to the gates of Warsaw and halted on the east bank of the Vistula River in the industrial suburb of

Praga. After Praga was cleared a queer edict came down from the top not to pursue the Germans across the river into Warsaw.

At first the field commanders were told that the entire front had to regroup and resupply. Later the word was passed down that there was an uprising inside Warsaw by "military adventurers" representing the imperialist London Polish Group. Although these explanations were hazy, officers of the Red Army were conditioned too well to inquire further. They could, nevertheless, see the destruction of Warsaw just across the river with their naked eyes.

Days wore on that brought counterrumors that Nazi panzer divisions were being allowed to reduce Warsaw to the ground and that civilians were being massacred.

In the meanwhile a Moscow-trained People's Committee for Free and Democratic Poland had been installed in Lublin, to the south. The Red Army could feel the anger and resentment of the Polish population. Igor smelled the rage of the Poles; he knew such things from his own childhood. The Lublin committee was apparently having a difficult time convincing the Poles that the Soviet Union had truly liberated them.

One night during the second week of the fighting in Warsaw Peter Egorov came to Igor's quarters.

"Many of us are fed up with the butchering of the people in Warsaw," he said. "We know we have the strength to cross the river and help them."

"Calm down, Peter. It is unfortunate that a few civilians are caught in the middle. You know that this Polish Home Army is nothing more than a fascist tool."

"For God's sake, Colonel! They are Poles fighting for Poland against Nazis!"

"Be careful how you talk, Peter."

"I've been careful how I've talked all my life. For once I want to shout out what is in my heart. Colonel . . . listen to me . . . there are other officers who feel as I do. Among us we can organize several hundred troops. We plan to lay down a bridge upstream and bring over weapons to the defenders and stay on and fight. With you, Igor Karlovy, leading us, five thousand troops will cross behind you. Believe me, Colonel . . . this is the way to go out."

For an instant Igor's heart was seized with the fire!

"Imagine. If the Red Army came to the rescue of Warsaw then the

Poles would know we are their liberators instead of their captors," Peter cried.

Peter was a Ukrainian and a Pole. Igor had long ago sensed the dangerous trait of "nationalism" in him; it had lain dormant, but began seething beneath the surface. Now, as they stood opposite Warsaw, it exploded.

"I will forget you spoke to me, Peter, and I suggest you forget your madness."

Peter did not forget. He and six other junior officers and fifty soldiers of the rank were betrayed on the night before they were to attempt their crossing.

Commissar V. V. Azov ordered a special three-man military court to try them. One of the judges was Igor Karlovy. He was deliberately selected because Peter Egorov was a member of his engineering staff. Who had betrayed them? It did not much matter. Perhaps it was Ivan Orlov. Everyone knew he was the party man. Perhaps it was someone else. It would never be known.

Before the court convened, confessions were obtained by the secret and political police. The young rebels were questioned around the clock in the Praga prison. Old hands at obtaining confessions, the secret police broke the rebels down one by one, mainly by a promise of sleep. Fifty-six sworn statements all confessed to "an anti-Soviet plot for the purpose of committing sabotage, treason, and collaboration with the enemy." The "enemy," in this case, was the Polish Underground.

A secret trial followed. The court convened in the warden's office beneath a portrait of Stalin and a slogan speaking well of Soviet justice.

Justice was delivered quickly. There was a reading of the charges, a reading of the confessions, brief deliberations by the judges, and the pronouncement of the death sentence, to be carried out immediately.

V. V. Azov did not take part in the proceedings but stayed on merely as a "spectator" in the interest of the state. The three judges signed the execution order. Azov gave Igor Karlovy a demonstration of the finality of his power.

"Comrade Colonel," Azov said, "you will personally supervise the executions."

How strange . . . how terribly strange. As Peter Egorov was led into the courtyard and placed against the firing wall he wore a smile on his face. It was a look of fulfillment, of satisfaction, of knowing a great secret. Until the last instant of his life, Peter Egorov smiled mockingly into the eyes of Igor Karlovy . . . until he slumped over dead.

CHAPTER SIX

The colonel remained in a black mood the next day. He was testy while the stream of appointments worked through his office and several times during conferences on redisposal of labor forces he snapped at subordinates in a manner unlike him.

Ivan Orlov attributed the colonel's behavior to the fact that he had been dressed down by Azov. The other dozen officers and men stationed in the mansion kept silent. Only Feodor really knew that the ghost of Peter Egorov had returned. He had seen the colonel like this before. If enough vodka was in him he'd sometimes babble to Feodor that he had done the right thing at the trial and that Peter had brought on his own death.

Heinrich Hirsch had touched it off. Why must one always come back to that situation of being forced into a decision against the regime? Igor told himself that he was an engineer. All he wished was a chance to build again—that and a little peace of mind. Why did this damned situation recur and recur?

By evening Igor retreated to his office in his bedroom. A tray was brought to him and he locked himself in. After a long while, immersed in figures, he calmed down. The mocking eyes of Peter, the blood-drenched paving stones of the prison yard, the challenge of Heinrich Hirsch all melted into the rows of numbers.

The night was warmish. He took off his tunic and placed it on the back of his chair, shoved his papers to one side, walked to his balcony, and leaned against the doorframe. A restless breeze rustled the leaves of the trees. Hirsch was right, of course. It was shameful, all of it . . . raping of thousands of little girls and old women. The women of Berlin were creeping around with mud on their faces to make themselves appear repulsive. Others pretended to be feeble-minded so the soldiers would leave them alone. It would take years, if not forever, to make the German people believe in the Soviet way after this. But, what the hell!

Hirsch was as foolish as Peter Egorov had been. Only orders from Azov could stop it.

He looked over his shoulder back into the room to the waiting work but was in no mood to concentrate. The balminess of the night soon consumed him with sentimentality. He hummed, and then sang softly to himself . . . "Daleko" . . . "Daleko" . . .

> Far, far away,
> Where the fog swells,
> Where gentle breezes,
> Sway o'er the wheat,
> In your own land,
> By a hill in the Steppe,
> You live as you did,
> Think often of me,
> Day . . . night . . . all the time,
> From me far away,
> Await my love . . .

A strange sound stopped his song; he cocked his head to listen. Something was rustling about in the bushes of the garden. Perhaps a stray cat. No, wait! He went to the rail . . . a heavy thrashing . . . angry grunts of a man's voice, then! a short sharp cry of a woman!

Igor hand-sprang the rail and dropped gingerly to the ground. A fierce struggle was going on.

"Kumm frau!"

Igor sprinted to the place and pushed the bushes aside. In the semi-darkness he could make out a man in Russian uniform atop the writhing figure of a woman pinned to the earth. Igor swung his boot up, kicking the soldier on the side of the head, knocking him off the woman. The soldier crawled to his hands and knees, dragged himself up to receive a thunderous fist in his mouth. The soldier went down again flat on his back. Igor glowered over him.

"Animal!"

He reached down, gripped the dazed man, jerked him upright, and dragged him into the light. Feodor! "Oh Mother of God! Not you, too, Feodor! You who were too good to touch a German woman! Not you, too, Feodor!"

Feodor wiped the blood from his mouth with the back of his hand. Igor flung him to the ground, enraged, kicked his ribs, and jammed the heel of his boot into the pit of his back. "Get out of my sight!"

THE LAST DAYS OF APRIL

Feodor crawled off as Igor tried to hold back tears of rage and disgust. The woman thrashed and groaned. He went to her and knelt beside her.

"Are you all right?" he said abruptly in German.

She answered with a whimper. He helped her to her feet and braced her as they walked into the light. She stood swaying . . . trying to hold together her ripped clothing. Igor took her face firmly in his hand, turned it to the best light, and examined the cuts and bruises. She was very young, and although quite dirty and bloody he could see that she was extremely pretty.

"You are just a child," he said. "All right, stop your babbling. I am not going to hurt you."

The girl began to regain her self-control, gulping great gobs of air and shuddering. "What the devil were you doing inside these gates?"

"I could smell the bread baking."

"You are so hungry?"

"I haven't eaten in three days."

"That is quite unlikely. You could go to the soup lines."

"I did. Two soldiers pulled me out of line and took me into the rubble. I did not go back."

Igor reacted with a grunt of revulsion. "Very well, I'll give you something to eat and have a car take you home."

"I have no home. Your soldiers took it."

"Parents?"

"They were both killed in an air raid by the Amis three months ago."

"Friends? Relatives?"

"My relatives all live in Dresden. Friends are all scattered. It is not easy to get around these days. We stay off the streets. I don't know where most of them are."

Suddenly she toppled in a dead faint. Igor caught her, swooped her into his arms, and walked toward the house. The questioning eyes of Ivan Orlov met him at the front door. "Are you going to bring her in here?"

"What do you propose, Orlov?" He shoved past the captain harshly, then turned. "You have time enough to run to Azov and report this. As for now, have my orderly prepare something warm to eat and see if there is woman's clothing in any of the closets."

Feodor was waiting before the colonel's door. "I am so ashamed," he whispered.

Igor spat at the young officer's feet, entered his bedroom, and laid the girl down. He wiped the back of her neck with a damp cloth, applied smelling salts, and as she came to, made her sit on the edge of the bed and put her head between her legs.

"Come along, child. You are all right."

The girl's hand trembled so badly Igor had to feed her at first. He made her sip slowly from the hot cabbage borsch filled with chunks of meat. Her shrunken stomach rebelled at the sudden onslaught of food.

"Don't eat so quickly or you'll throw it all up."

She nodded, then ate until she thought she would burst. She pushed the dark rich bread around in the bottom of the bowl.

"What is your name, girl?"

"Lotte. Lotte Böhm."

"How old are you?"

"Nineteen."

"Well . . . how do you feel now?"

"Better."

Igor had his orderly clear the room. The soldier said he had found some woman's clothing. Igor told him to unlock the adjoining bedroom and not disturb him further.

When the soldier left he considered the situation. The girl seemed to have recovered her senses and appeared none the worse for wear . . . a few minor bruises. However, she might be too weak to go on out alone. Out to what, of course, was conjecture. All that appeared to wait for her, if her story could be believed, was another rapist. Naturally, he felt no obligation to protect her; nevertheless, one would have afforded the same courtesy to a beaten dog.

"Your story had better be completely true," he said. "I intend to check it."

"I wish it were not true. I wish I had a home and parents."

He came to a sudden decision. "I shall allow you to sleep in the next bedroom tonight. You will not be disturbed. Help yourself to whatever clothing is in there. Tomorrow I will see what can be done about arranging a safe place for you."

"You are very kind," she said and began to cry.

Igor wanted to say that not all Russians were like those in the streets now . . . even after a war that had taken his only child and his beloved Natasha. Yes, even after Natasha, mortal enemies must have some humanity left. He opened the door to the next bedroom.

Lotte Böhm wiped her tears. "Do you have water?" she blurted.

"Water?"

"To wash."

"Yes, of course."

"I have not washed decently in a month."

"Well, help yourself."

"Could . . . could I . . . bathe?"

She knocked timidly at the half-opened door. Igor turned from his desk. "Well now, let's take a look at you. You look quite decent with your face scrubbed."

Her youth had made possible a revival of body and spirit. She breathed deeply and happily and bounced about her bedroom pinning up her hair in long graceful rolls. She wore an oversized night coat, making her appear very tiny. "I was thinking about how nice you are all the time I was bathing. You must be someone very important."

"Just a soldier." He pointed to the bed. She slipped between the covers, stretched and purred with joy and felt the pillows and the satin spread as though she were in a wonderland. "I'll die if I wake up and find this is a dream. I'll die if I wake up in the cellar."

Igor sat on the edge of the bed and smiled indulgently. She was so small and helpless. So like . . . Natasha. Unconsciously, his hand reached out and touched her cheek, startling her. He drew his hand away quickly.

"I did not mean to frighten you."

"You do not frighten me." She rolled away so that her back was to him. "I have been living in a cellar alone for six months. I have been half starved all the time. The Amis came with their bombers every day and the British every night. And since the Russians . . ."

"I know."

"I am more grateful to you than I can say."

"We are just people . . ."

"I must show you how grateful I am. I want to please you."

"It is not a condition for being human to one another."

"But I want to thank you. I have no other way. The others took what they wanted from me. Once I was left for dead in the gutters when three of them had finished with me. At least let me give it once, willingly."

"Go to sleep and shut up."

"When I was out there, struggling on the ground, I . . . I heard a voice singing . . ."

He leaned over, bussed her cheek, touched her hair. "Good night, Natasha."

"It was your voice, wasn't it?"

He flicked off the light and walked to the door.

"Please don't make the room dark," she called out.

"I will be working at my desk in the next room. I will leave the door open."

Igor usually liked the hours of night to work. In the complete quiet of night one's thoughts could be immaculately clear, but ghosts of the day followed him into this night. Things ran together. Drab statistics and engineering problems were invaded by the haunting smile of Peter Egorov and the sharp voice of Hirsch—and now Natasha was with him!

From time to time he heard the girl thrash restlessly and heard moans of what seemed to be a continuous nightmare. He found himself standing in the doorway looking at her as though drawn by an uncontrollable force. The light from his room fell across her body. What a magnificent little creature! She is young . . . I was young once. Where did it all go?

And, as though Lotte had been awaiting him, she awakened from her sleep and saw him. They looked at each other for a long time without movement or speech. She did not blink and barely breathed as she drew him toward the bed, slowly. He sat down on the edge.

Her little hand reached out, took his powerful hand, and led it beneath the comforter and placed it on her throbbing breast, and then she drew the covers aside for him.

Her body was deliciously young and firm and warm.

Softly, he kept repeating to himself, softly. Be very gentle with her. Handle her with delicacy and make up to her for all of those miserable brutes. Be tender and make her want me as Natasha wanted me.

He worked her up slowly until the nerve ends leaped from her skin. They taunted and teased each other, but the girl was being driven mad. She groaned with the joy and tried to draw him in and devour him. And then came a time when control and judgment fled and they burst into convulsions . . . and now, at last, Lotte slept a deep, quiet, peaceful sleep.

Igor Karlovy remained awake. He lay on his back, the girl's body curled up against him. His eyes were wide open. . . . Now I am no better than the rest of them . . . but then, have I ever been? Have I ever really been?

CHAPTER SEVEN

The village of Glinka on the Kuban River in southern Russia in the year 1921:

Igor finished his chores in the barn. He crossed through the chicken yard to the pump, took off his square, beaded cap and embroidered peasant's shirt, drew a pail of water, and splashed it over his face and the back of his neck and hands.

He glanced pensively toward the cottage. Muffled, angry voices filtered out of it into the evening air. His father and his brother, Alexander, would be at it again. It was like this every night now, one heated argument after another. Last week his father had struck Alexander in a rage.

It was the same all over the village. Everyone walked about with long faces, curses on their lips, and suspicion in their eyes. Many of the younger villagers like Alexander had joined the Reds and fought with them. But there were others, mostly from the elders, who had been with the Whites.

Igor felt the presence of someone and turned to see Natasha inching toward him shyly. She smiled with obvious adoration of first love, for she was ten and he was twelve. She reached down and handed him his shirt.

Igor tolerated her as one tolerates a small sister. He had known Natasha from earliest memory. She lived three cottages down the road. Well, perhaps it was more than a toleration; she was a faithful friend. They even shared a secret hiding place near a bend in the river. Oftentimes they would meet there and discuss their most intimate thoughts.

"Please don't be so sad, Igor," she said.

"I don't like to go into the house any more."

"It is no better in my house."

"Yes, I know. Alexander says the fighting is over. We all have to accept the new order. Only Poppa . . ."

"Igor, come down to the river tomorrow and meet me?"

"I don't know. We will be sacking grain most of the day. Besides, I have to study. You know how Alexander insists I learn how to read and write."

"Please."

"Very well. But only for a few minutes when the others are taking their midday rest."

She ran off, climbed the rail fence, then ran down the road toward her cottage after a last look and a wave.

"Igor! Come in!" Momma's voice called.

The crude room was held by an awesome silence. Igor's father, Gregory Karlovy, a leathery, bearded giant sat at the rough-hewn table with his great hands folded, glowering at the floor. Opposite him, twenty-year-old Alexander sat with his face muscles twitching with tension. Igor slipped alongside his father as quietly as he could.

A great pot of chicken broth and dumplings was put on the center of the table. As Alexander reached for a chunk of bread his father raised his head and glared at him. Alexander retreated by dropping the bread, folding his hands, and mumbling a short prayer and crossing himself.

It was another of those silent meals, frequent of late, the only noise an occasional slurp. With each spoonful Igor saw the wrath building up in his father. Finally the old man brought a hamlike fist down on the table making the entire room rumble. "My own flesh and blood leaving the house and the land of his fathers!"

Alexander nearly choked trying to swallow past the lump in his throat. His father roared again. He dropped his spoon. "I'm telling you for the fiftieth time. I am going to Rostov at the invitation of the District Planning Committee. It is the greatest opportunity in my life. We will be reorganizing clear down to the Georgian border. Can't you understand how important this is to me?"

"Nothing is more important than your own farm."

"You're wrong, Poppa. The revolution is more important."

"It seems to me," the father answered with a trembling voice, "that we have lived through enough years of bloodshed and sorrow. First the war took half our sons, then the revolution, and then the counter-revolution. Is there to be no peace? What kind of a revolution is it that turns a son against his own father and his own land."

"The old ways are gone."

"Gone, hell! Generations of Karlovys have been born, lived, and died on this land! Don't you tell me they're gone!"

"Poppa, for God's name. The counterrevolution has failed. We've been bled dry for centuries. The people want a new life."

"I will thank you not to repeat Red slogans under this roof."

"This is not a slogan, Poppa. Glinka has stood here for three hundred years without a school or a hospital. Don't you want to see Igor read and write. Don't you want to see women like your own wife give birth without losing three or four children."

The old man shook his head sadly. "Freedom is life, my son. We have heard all of the talk of reform before. Here . . . this land . . . this is freedom. You are a Kuban Cossack and that is freedom. If there is anything we have learned it is to smell out those who would take freedom from us."

The young man pushed away from the table. "What the hell's the use of talking."

An impasse had been reached. A final impasse. The flame of revolution was destined to burn in the young man's heart, alone. The father was lost to the son just as the old ways were gone. Alexander turned, shoved open the curtain across his alcove, and grabbed his carpetbag. His mother and his brother began weeping.

He went to her and kissed her and he tousled his brother's hair. "Study Igor, study. The future will belong to those who study."

The father and the son stood face to face. "Shall we shake hands, Father? Will you wish me a good journey?"

Gregory Karlovy arose, but his hands remained at his sides. He turned his back. "May God protect you," he whispered after the door slammed shut.

Igor whistled their secret code, three times like a marsh swallow, then skittered down the bank through the tall grass to the clearing where Natasha waited for him. They were on the slightest of knolls on a point in the bend of the river; nearby stood a huge and ancient willow tree whose limbs draped to the water's edge.

It was midday. The air hung still, the land aflame with oranges

and reds and golds. A raftsman swirled past them, poking his long pole
into the opposite bank to push him back midstream. Voices of song
drifted to their hearing from over the fields.

Natasha's great brown eyes were filled with fear and she was trembling. "I'm so glad you're here, Igor . . ."

"It wasn't easy to come," he said, mindful only of his own problems.
"Alexander left home for good last night. He has gone to Rostov to
join the Reds. I lay awake all night trying to think of what life will be
like without Alexander. I could hear Momma crying and Poppa moaning in his sleep."

"I'm so sorry."

"Never mind. Well, what is so important?"

Natasha drew a deep breath and tried to speak, not knowing if she
could; and then he saw her anxiety.

"The Reds," she quivered at last. "They have talked to my brother,
Sergei."

"Where? When?"

"When we were at market three days ago in Armavir. Poppa went
to the Jew's quarters to trade with them and left Sergei to watch our
stall. When I came he was gone. He didn't tell me until this morning
where he had been. The Reds had taken him away."

"What did they want?"

"What they always want. They wanted to know where the village
was hiding the grain."

"He didn't tell, of course."

"Not at first. Then they told him we were all saboteurs and provocateurs . . . whatever that means . . . and that the people in the city
were starving."

"Damn them! You know what the Reds give us for our grain! A piece
of paper no one can read."

"They . . . they promised to make Sergei a hero of the Soviet Union
if he told."

"A hero for telling on his own parents?"

"Sergei told."

Igor bolted to his feet. "You should have told me immediately."

"I . . . I only found out about it . . . and I was afraid . . ."

"I've got to warn the village!"

Igor raced across the fields yelling at the top of his voice. He ran all
the way back to the village center, a muddy street, gasped dizzily,

grabbed the rope of the alarm bell, and pulled for all his worth, bringing villagers on the run from fields in all directions.

Igor blurted out the story, and Sergei, his own age of twelve, was brought into the square and questioned until he broke down and confessed. His father dragged him off to their barn and thrashed him to within an inch of his life as Natasha screamed. The Cossacks frantically scrambled to remove their hidden grain to another place. In the middle of all this the Reds swooped in and caught them. Natasha's home was burned to the ground and her father hung by the neck in the square.

When he was cut down and buried and the grieving was done and the shock settled, Natasha and her mother went off to live with relatives in the next village.

Sergei was carried off by the Reds to Armavir to a children's home, which was soon renamed in his honor. He was extolled by the Reds as the first of the youth heroes of the Kuban Cossacks. Over a period of time sixteen villages, twenty factories, ten collective farms, eight tractor stations, and dozens of Children's Homes and Pioneer Camps were named in his honor.

During the years that followed in the 1920s, Alexander Karlovy became an official of considerable influence in Rostov. The fact that he was a Cossack from the land and at the same time a dedicated Communist proved of great value. He was among the key planners to get greater production from the farmlands of southern Russia.

Fantastic changes were taking place all over the Soviet Union. This awakening giant trembled into a new century, having to pay in toil for past failures to educate her people and industrialize. Now the sweat of the workers and the farmers driven before the unrelenting Communist whip shoved them into this new world.

The Kuban Cossacks of Glinka clung to their land. These new ways remained strange to them; many of their sons were gone and the village wore unhealed wounds. The agitators sent in to enlighten them were treated with suspicion. Their beliefs were as simple and primitive as their lives. The Cossacks had been sent as border guards centuries before by the czars to outposts on the Don and Kuban in Siberia and on other borders. In times of emergency they had raised armies. In exchange, they were granted a status as free men. This, and nothing more, nothing less, was what they desired from the Reds.

Igor Karlovy reached young manhood with a basic faith in the old ways. He suppressed his personal desires to examine this great new world, for it would have created an untold hardship to follow Alexander from the family farm. Gregory Karlovy had grown very old. Despite his furious pride he could not deliver a full day's work and so Igor subordinated his curiosity to family duty.

A fire for knowledge remained alive though, and each night he read and studied on his own until his eyes burned. When the school came to Glinka he begged for books and periodicals to feed the growing hunger to learn.

Although more and more writing became available, the books began to fall into a dull pattern. Everything had been rewritten so that it was ultimately a glorification of the Bolsheviks.

Igor taught himself both German and English in order to find new avenues of thought away from the repetition of the Communist books. He discovered that he could read great Russian writers of the past in foreign languages as many were no longer published in Russian. It was the same with Russian history, which seemed to begin, so far as the Bolsheviks were concerned, with the birth of Karl Marx.

In other ways, Igor was the son of his father. In true Cossack tradition he became a magnificent horseman, sang with the sweetness of the marsh swallow, and developed into a drinking man of no small accomplishment. His heart, frivolous at times, never truly strayed or really ever belonged to anyone but Natasha.

Days and sometimes weeks seemed endless until that glorious moment when she rode in from her village and they could go off together to a place known to them alone, away from all the world. But they had come to that time in the springtime of life when meetings brought frustration and partings became a thing of pain.

Natasha understood his yearning to seek the world, his predicament and imprisonment. She did not press him to the promise of marriage, for to have done so would have sealed him to Glinka forever.

And so, on a summer's day when Igor was eighteen and she sixteen, they came to know each other's bodies; it happened in their secret place by the Kuban River.

At the end of the 1920s a vast change swept the land. The order came from Moscow to collectivize the farmlands. The planners made an edict that farm production had to catch the march of industrialization. It was not an edict understood by the Kulaks, who were free farmers, or the Cossacks, who were free men.

The Kuban Cossacks armed and rode their horses out to defend their land and charged wildly into fusillades of Red Army guns which cut them down like stacks of wheat.

At last it became Glinka's turn to collectivize. Alexander Karlovy returned to the place of his birth out of sentiment. A meeting was called. Alexander pleaded with the villagers to accept it peacefully for the good of Russia, and warned that only by quiet acquiescence could Glinka be spared the fate of hundreds of blood-soaked villages. It was beyond his power to do more.

The villagers of Glinka, led by old Gregory Karlovy, gave their answer. They burned their crops and slaughtered their livestock.

And so, it came to pass that the centuries-old tradition of free men ended. The people of Glinka were rounded up and deported for slave labor to Siberia, never to be heard from again. Only a single villager was spared. By trickery, Alexander had his young brother Igor come to Rostov to visit him at the exact moment of the deportation.

Igor, of course, sensed that something terrible had taken place, but travel permits were almost impossible in those days. Furthermore, Russian life had conditioned him not to inquire. In due time Alexander told him of what had happened and that their father and mother had chosen not to escape to Rostov.

The farm was gone forever, yet there were a number of compensations in living in Rostov with Alexander and his family. Mainly, new doors opened to learning in the great drive to educate the masses. As a Communist official Alexander had his own two-room cottage. He was able to fix up a shed outside so that Igor had his own six- by ten-foot room; this was a luxury for a single man.

Igor threw himself into that vast, faceless legion of toilers going to work in one of the new tractor factories and continued his studies by night.

It was impossible to bring Natasha to Rostov because of the travel papers. Even if he had been able, there was no way to support her or ask her to share the shed. She learned to read and write so there were letters to sustain them. Then, once each year, he was able to go off with her for a week to the Black Sea.

During the early 1930s he formulated his ideas about his future life.

He hated the factory; away from the freedom of the land he thought of himself branded, like a cow, and expected to produce so many buckets of milk. He hated the four walls filled with slogans and portraits; he hated the charts and the pitting of his team against the other teams in a never-ending search to push production.

During the lunch breaks and two or three days a week after work they were compelled to attend lectures by the agitators and the Komsomol extolling their "way of life." It was explained that life was temporarily difficult because of the backwardness of the country inherited from the Czar, the bloodshed, and mostly, the outside pressures of the imperialists to crush them.

The Action Squads made up of party and Komsomol members Igor detested the most. The Action Squads saw to it that the workers showed up 100 per cent for all lectures and activities. The Action Squads led them on "spontaneous demonstrations" for visiting dignitaries and holiday parades. The Action Squads saw to it 100 per cent of the vote was cast for the party in the "elections." It was the Action Squads who visited lagging teams to induce them to "donate" free days of labor to increase quotas.

The pressure became so unbearable that workers desperately met in secret for the intention of organizing a strike. The Action Squads along with the secret police rounded up the leaders and shipped them east. Then the Agitators came in and explained that strikes in the Soviet Union were illegal because there was no need to strike. The workers owned the factories and therefore they would be striking against themselves.

The only way to gain recognition as a worker appeared to be to work one's self to an early grave through donation of almost every free hour. For this, the worker's reward was a medal, the Labor Order of the Red Banner, to wear on his shabby suit.

The farm had been primitive, but the words of Igor's father were never forgotten . . . *"freedom is life."* He realized that the Communists were trying valiantly to make the Soviet Union a modern country and that harsh methods were called for. He also came to understand that the West was the true enemy of the masses. Nevertheless, he had to escape the factory.

His brother Alexander's revolutionary fires had been dimmed. Alexander was now in a jungle for survival. The only way to prosper was to follow classical party lines. The early idealism was replaced by the never-ending terror. Alexander attempted time and again to have Igor join Komsomol. As a Komsomol member new opportunities would open. Igor was determined to escape the fanatical discipline and the distasteful duty as an agitator or member of an Action Squad.

He found his way through the study of science and set in a number of improvisations in the factory that won him the attention of the planners and finally a medal as a Hero of Soviet Labor. As an engineer Igor knew he had a chance for a better life because engineers were desperately needed.

He pressured Alexander to arrange for him to take entrance examinations for the great University of Moscow. It was a far-reaching dream. The university belonged to the Komsomol faithful and the sons and daughters of the new ruling class. A Cossack boy from Rostov simply did not have a chance. But Igor persisted, and won the dream.

Natasha wept on his last visit before his departure. Moscow was 1000 kilometers away. Igor would be gone for four years with little or no chance of seeing her and just as small a chance of getting papers for her to come to Moscow. Afterward he had to give two years of free service to the government to repay his education and would most likely be sent to Siberia to the virgin lands.

Igor tried to comfort her by promising that the years would fly by and they would still be young enough to make a life. His last words were a vow to return to her.

Igor Karlovy never went into Siberian service. Upon graduation from the University of Moscow he was commissioned into the Red Air Force and sent to Leningrad. The Army and Air Force were frantically reorganizing trying to recover from the purges and the fiasco of the Finnish campaign.

The eve of the Great Patriotic War found him designing and constructing bulwarks on the Karelian Isthmus for the defense of Leningrad. Natasha moved to Armavir to a war factory, but after a short while communication was cut off between them.

June, 1942
My Beloved Brother, Igor,

The war has kept contact from us for a full year. I have not heard from you in all this time, but I know from friends you are stationed in the same place as where you were assigned after you left the university.

The bearer of this letter, a colleague in the Party, is being transferred to your district and has agreed to try to get this message to you.

My family and I have been evacuated into the interior. We are settled, and now to the task of organizing food production. We are faring quite well.

I have terribly bad news. Natasha is dead. She was among the defenders of Armavir. Many survivors are now in my area so the accounts of her death are authentic. I fear to say the entire business is most distressing. She was wounded and captured by the Nazis, abused, and done away with in a most brutal manner.

My deepest pity is for you at this moment of grief. I beg you to be of stout heart and take vengeance on the Nazi monsters for what they have done to Natasha and our glorious Motherland.

Long live the Communist Party! Long live Stalin! Death to the enemy!

Your loving brother,
Alexander

The Russian lands are cold and morbid, and a long shadow of death and tragedy hovers over her people. The woeful cries of toil and grief and poverty fill her music and her poems; life is suffering, suffering is life. The winters are as brutal as life is brutal.

All that is tragic in Russian heritage struck down on Igor Karlovy where he lived among the freezing and the starving in the Siege of Leningrad. The letter was the most painful chapter in a pain-filled journey through life. The death of his beloved Natasha all but sucked the will to survive.

When is it that a man like Igor Karlovy seeks out a woman such as Olga Shiminov? Is it when his soul wallows in a bottomless pit of grief? Is it when he clings stubbornly to a thinning thread between hope and complete depression?

Or perhaps it was the warmth that first brought him back to life, the warmth of Olga Shiminov's apartment. Outside the dead were stacked like frozen logs in the gutters; the starving walked about in trances; Finnish and German cannon beat upon them without respite. Was it something so simple as the cold and the rumble of hunger in his belly that drew him to Olga Shiminov?

She was one of the most important Komsomol leaders in Leningrad. As a deputy in charge of women's labor battalions she came into frequent dealings with Igor in the numerous engineering problems in building fortifications, roads over the ice, demolishing dangerous buildings, clearing rubble.

It was on a night in December during one of their many conferences that they became unbearably cold in his heatless office and Olga suggested they finish their work in her flat, where it was warm. Warmth . . . that is what one needed in the Leningrad winter. For the masses there was no fuel. Every wooden structure had been demolished and long consumed as firewood. Everyone was cold and hungry . . . except important officials like Olga Shiminov.

She had her own room with a private bath and kitchen. It was a luxurious palace in that frozen tomb of a city. And her cupboards held tea and vodka and potatoes and bread and beef.

Did he sell himself for warmth or was it just a weariness of life that afforded him no resistance? In truth, Igor never looked at her as a man looks at a woman in all those months they had worked together. Olga kept herself drab and severe as befitting an official of the party.

She was entirely without Natasha's female wiles, sensuous looks, soft touches, desirable body. Olga was a daughter of the revolution, the ultimate product of this new way of life. She carried her breasts with a sort of defiance, as though they constituted a challenge to her equality. Olga was a slogan, a dedicated heartless mold which functioned with the machinelike efficiency of the new breed of Russian. Nonetheless there was still something of her that was "woman" . . . there was female flesh. No matter how well it was Sovietized, it still existed.

Igor was an attractive man. Despite her objections that he had no background as a Communist, there was a special wartime dispensation for heroes of the Red Air Force. He was of the new legend. Wounded by gunfire, a man of great ingenuity and great courage, a hard-drinking Cossack surrounded by loyal officers. Perhaps it was Igor's total indifference to Olga that awakened a challenge in her. He took her because he had reached the depths . . . and her apartment was warm.

The marriage was not made in heaven. It was a convenient bargain on both parts to make the best of a miserable life.

Neither Igor's patience or tenderness was able to penetrate Olga's obsessed dedication. Sex life, such as it was, was dispatched with mechanical efficiency. It was always arranged so as not to interfere with a committee meeting or a lecture to factory workers.

Igor Karlovy, now a decorated major in the Red Air Force, strayed from his warm nest when springtime came and the thaw set in. He sought out his old comrades to drink with and soft and tender women to love.

Olga Shiminov was not without recourse. Igor was hauled before the Central Committee of the Communist Party of Leningrad. He was roundly admonished for his wild Cossack ways and warned that the husband of a leading functionary could not treat her as if she were a peasant woman. If rank and career meant anything to him, he had better stay home evenings. Finally, he was informed there were climates he could be sent to even colder than Leningrad.

Olga became pregnant between speeches. From her immensely practical point of view it was no time to have a child. Aside from room and food, a child would be a damned nuisance and interfere with her work. She made out a standard application for an abortion, against Igor's wishes.

On this occasion the Central Committee took Igor's point of view. The comrades "suggested" to Olga that it would be good for the morale of the masses if one of their leaders gave symbolic birth in the middle of the siege. Never a deviationist, Olga adhered to their "suggestion." She presented her husband and the people of Leningrad a boy. Igor wished to name his son for his father, but the comrades "suggested" that the child be named Yuri after a young boy who had a martyred death at the hands of the SS early in the invasion.

The birth of his son gave Igor a reason to renew his desire to live. Slowly, he began to emerge from the great darkness . . . until one day the shell of a siege gun hit Children's Home #25.

When Igor awoke, the German girl, Lotte Böhm, was staring at him. He had seen such an expression of fulfillment in a woman's eyes a long time ago when Natasha used to look at him that way.

"Why do you look at me so?" he asked.

"I did not know it could be like this."

He closed his eyes and pressed her young body against him. Tears filled his eyes and ran down his cheeks. Oh Virgin Mother, he whispered, let me have a few moments of her again.

He washed and dressed silently and returned to his work in the next room. Lotte watched him from the doorway, her eyes riveted on him. At last he snapped his pencil in half, walked to the French windows and flung them open as if choking, and breathed in deeply.

"I wish to make an arrangement with you," he said. "I shall see to your protection and that you are properly housed and fed."

"You will not be sorry. I will make you very happy."

CHAPTER EIGHT

Commissar Vasali Vladimarovitch Azov drank a glass of white chalky medicine to soothe his burning ulcers, wiped droplets from his thick black moustache, belched, and munched the second half of his meal, crackers. A portrait of Lenin "Speaking to the Workers" hung behind his desk; and a portrait of Stalin was over the fireplace opposite him. He held the new directive from Moscow in thick peasant hands and studied.

END VICTORY CELEBRATIONS IN BERLIN AND STABILIZE SITUATION

Azov was glad the directive finally came. As a man who lived largely by a sixth sense he felt the rising anger among the officer corps over the rape in Berlin's streets.

The last time the fires erupted in his stomach was during the offensive in East Prussia. Tens of thousands of German troops had been enveloped and trapped in a pocket and attempted to surrender. Azov was ordered to "liquidate the pocket" on the grounds that the Germans were all suspected of being SS troops. For this task Azov brought in Siberian Cossacks, Mongols, and Tartars. The Germans were first disarmed, then slaughtered. During the ten days it took to complete the unpleasant mop-up Azov's ulcers burned like the fires of hell.

He made a mock salute to the portrait of Stalin with a second glass of medicine and thought that he should switch portraits with Lenin's so that he would not have to look at Stalin all day. However, in the Soviet life the ritual of taking down pictures had all sorts of connotations. Portraits that suddenly disappeared signified a person had fallen into disfavor; thus, the portrait switching could be reported by some member of political intelligence and used against him.

Azov had not made up his mind whether he liked or disliked his present exalted position. It was the most important of his illustrious but anonymous career. He would remain a mystery man, an enigma to most everyone in Germany; but as Chief Political Commissar and Advisor to German Affairs his "suggestions" to the Army and the Germans would be carried out to the letter. Indeed, this subdued mansion would be the true capital of the eastern parts of Germany.

Azov was painfully aware that the chance for a grave mistake, a miscalculation or error in judgment was much greater in his present post. He did not fathom the exposed position, had deftly avoided it all his life. His mind was like a delicate sail boat, able to react instantly to the slightest shift in the wind.

In the beginning, three decades ago, Azov had caught the eye of Lenin. In those days the Communists supported their illegal activities largely through hold-ups of banks and other robberies. Azov proved a perfect henchman in these operations; he was drab, but entirely dependable; he executed orders without deviation or regard for others.

After the new regime he worked with both the secret and political police as a liaison to Lenin, remaining on the fringe of the inner circle.

After Lenin's death he stayed clear of involvement on either side of the power struggle that followed. Sensing ill winds, he shifted his sails toward Stalin without ever really expressing an opinion.

Azov was next sent to re-educate a large section of the Ukraine to the new way of life. There was great hope in the Five Year Plan to modernize industry and later collectivize agriculture of that backward land.

Kulaks, the independent farmers, abounded in his territory. This led to his first ulcer. The Ukrainians were always fired with a nationalistic spirit. The Kulaks wished to be Ukrainians first, had no desire to give up their land, and did not understand socialism. There was massive resistance by the burning of crops and destroying of livestock. Azov commanding Action Squads, Agitators, and the Red Army from Russia stamped down the resistance without mercy. The blood bath and deportations brought the economy to the brink of ruin.

He proved to be utterly merciless. Still a man without an opinion, he carried out the edicts to Sovietize the Ukraine with brutal efficiency. His personal hand sealed the fate of a quarter million people.

Once the resistance was crushed he set about building the secret police, military and Propaganda and political units so that they were controlled by Russians, not Ukrainians.

Azov did his job so well that he was recalled to Moscow as a top deputy of the NKVD. His speciality was obtaining confessions and his pride was that no one ever went to trial without first confessing.

This position brought him the usual rewards; he had his own three-room flat, a phone, a car at his disposal, a daughter in Komsomol, and a son in the University of Moscow.

In the beginning of the purges, Azov became one of the most dreaded of the inquisitors. Tens, hundreds, thousands broke before him; he found the weakness of each person. On some there was use of brutality, on others, starvation. Some broke from the lack of sleep, others quickly succumbed to terror. Eventually he got them all.

But as the purges wore on they began to turn on the hunters. More and more members of the NKVD and OGPU received their own fatal midnight summons. Each day brought another former colleague to Azov to confess.

During these years of the terror he slept with one eye open awaiting the knock for him. The knock often came between midnight and one in the morning. He would lurch up in panic, his heart thumping, and dress in a state of drowsy fear. He would try to recall what he had said wrong or to whom he had spoken. Perhaps it was his own son! They had argued!

By some miracle the summons for Azov always came from Stalin. He would be whisked through the empty Moscow streets in the middle of the night at terrifying speeds to the villa in the suburbs hidden in a pine forest. Here Stalin held his nightly court. Those people summoned arrived one by one in black cars. Each time the cast changed; only Molotov and a personal secretary were there every time.

Stalin, in plain proletarian tunic, looking much like the millions of his portraits, greeted them and led them into a banquet room. The table buckled beneath the weight of roast pig, steaks, caviar, champagne, vodka, borsch, and rare lamb dishes of his native Georgia.

During these nightly orgies of food and drink the business of the Soviet Union was conducted by despots. Molotov and the aides made quick notes of Stalin's edicts and random ramblings. Sometimes a word or a nod meant moving a half-million persons, putting a thousand to death.

The nights Azov attended it was generally for the purpose of getting the list of new persons to liquidate in the purge for the charges of being a Trotskyite, Bukharanite, deviationist, saboteur, speculator, traitor, opportunist or anti-party. He was stunned to receive names of marshals of the Red Army, members of the Politburo, heroes of the revolution, and great Leninists.

At four or five each morning Stalin would become quite drunk and took pleasure in berating everyone in the room, making them the butt of crude jokes. He shredded their dignity with drunken boisterousness.

But Comrade Stalin never got so drunk as to lose his astuteness or deadliness.

"Comrade Azov! I have proposed a toast in honor of our Chief Prosecutor for People's Justice, Comrade Vishinsky. Why do you refuse to drink? Fill his glass!"

Stalin knew very well of Azov's ulcers, but Azov drank and his insides turned to flame and his eyeballs rolled back in his head and he burst into an icy sweat. Once during each summons Stalin made him drink a whole glass of vodka. Azov dared not pass out until the meeting broke up at dawn and he was in the car on the way to his office to carry out the new liquidations.

The years of the nightmare waned slowly with the police arms devouring each other and their own members. It was, indeed, a delicate time for Azov.

The climactic Purge Trial ended with a bit of poetic justice when Yagoda, the head of NKVD, was brought to people's justice. V. V. Azov's supreme achievement was in obtaining Yagoda's confession.

Because of his past experience in Sovietizing the reluctant Ukraine, Azov was assigned during the Great Patriotic War to form a German People's Liberation Committee.

And now, here in Berlin, it was Azov's turn to do the midnight summoning. His table was not so lavish as Stalin's, but his rule in Germany was as absolute, and what was more, no one could force him to drink vodka at this table.

Azov peeked through the drapes. In the driveway below the cars began to arrive: Wöhlman, Hirsch, the rest of the Liberation Committee, Red Army commanders, and military government officials.

Tonight would be special indeed. Tonight he would introduce a secret plan detailing *The Harassment of the Western Allies in Berlin.*

Part three

THE LINDEN TREES WILL NEVER BLOOM AGAIN

CHAPTER ONE—*July 1, 1945*

Daybreak came at 0548. Sean O'Sullivan's convoy assembled in the parade grounds of the former Wehrmacht barracks in the town of Halle where they had been gathered, and waited with growing restlessness to move up to Berlin among the first American echelons.

A curious mixture of vehicles took to the road, conventional military trucks and jeeps interspersed with a variety of confiscated German automobiles. Four armored troop carriers hauled a platoon of infantry to guard against attack by German Werewolves and straggler bands.

Sean rode in a Horsche sedan which had been unsuccessfully hidden by its former Nazi owner. Shenandoah Blessing and Bolinski, who spoke some Russian, shared the huge touring car. Nelson Goodfellow Bradbury and a photographer drove in a jeep directly behind Sean.

The convoy progressed north to Dessau, and crossed the Elbe River on a pontoon bridge built by American engineers, who left it to the Russians after they withdrew.

The first curious contact with their Russian allies was made when a Russian military policewoman of elephantine proportions signaled them to halt with a pair of traffic flags, then leaped ungracefully on the running board of Sean's Horsche and pointed down the road. They slowed their speed as they passed beneath a flower-bedecked, newly erected archway which held portraits readily identified as comrades Lenin, Stalin, and Marx. A blaring red and white sign leaped out at them: WELCOME TO DEMOCRATIC GERMANY!

Just beyond the "welcome" arch they came to a vicious-looking barrier on the road flanked by barbed wire and concrete emplacements.

"This looks meaner than trying to run moonshine into Kentucky," Blessing said.

"The dawn came up like thunder," emoted Big Nellie.

The woman MP shouted at a pair of drowsy Russian soldiers who raised the barrier. Sean swung his car to the head of the convoy and drove through. The next point of contact was a farmhouse near the roadside. A half-dozen Russians kept reserved and suspicious distance from the arrivals as a slovenly dressed officer emerged from the house, leaned into the sedan, and snarled, "You are now under the protection of the Union of Soviet Socialist Republics. I demand that your soldiers put their weapons away."

Bolinski translated to Sean, then answered, "The weapons are for the purpose of protecting the convoy from German stragglers."

"Not allowed," the Russian answered. "Soviet territory."

Sean recalled the specifics of his orders: *Get the convoy to Berlin without incident.* "Tell the admiral here," he said to Bolinski, "that I will order my men to keep all weapons out of sight."

The Russian figured that was compliance enough to suit him. He got into his own vehicle, a badly abused German auto, ordered the convoy to follow him, and turned off the four-lane *autobahn*.

"This isn't the way to Berlin," Big Nellie said to his photographer.

In a half hour they came to the town of Wittenberg and halted at the Rathaus, which now served as Russian Headquarters for the district. The Russian quickly disappeared into the confines leaving Sean's convoy waiting. They were being observed by Russian soldiers from a cautious distance. It was a far cry from the pictures of the brotherhood of Russians and Americans embracing on meeting at the Elbe only two months earlier.

Sean appraised the Russians. These troops were neatly uniformed, well-armed, appeared to be under good discipline. He guessed they were NKVD, political troops.

Twenty minutes went by before a new officer, a Russian lieutenant, came from the building and introduced himself in broken English. "I demand," he said, "that you and your men come inside for an official welcome."

Sean's troops followed him into the typical bulky German city-hall affair, down an oil-painting-lined corridor of heroes, to a foyer which would serve as a reception room, smack into a platoon of Cossacks, who were, to a man, tall, blond, spit and polish, and obviously show troops.

The Russian lieutenant whirled around, was handed a document by a subordinate, stood ramrod before Sean, and read:

"I am pleased to welcome this, the first convoy of Americans on this route. You are privileged to join us in Berlin after the Soviet Union's glorious victory over the Nazi aggressor. Soviet victory was inevitable, but came sooner because of your aid. You are welcome to Democratic Germany as our guests."

Sean faced his own astonished men and with an expression warned them to keep their mouths shut.

"I should like to see the commanding general of this district," he said to the Russian.

"He is not available."

"I should like his name and information on where, when, and how he can be reached."

"That information is not available."

"When you find out who and where he is, give him this medal from my government for being the first to reach the Elbe and join forces in this area."

The Russian looked in his hand, puzzled. He studied the medal, confused, ordered the Cossacks to sing, and left the reception room quickly without excusing himself.

Two dozen bellowing Cossacks prevented too close a discussion of the situation.

"What are you going to do, Major?"

"Damned if I know."

He drifted over to Bradbury. "Don't take any notes and better tell Mac to keep his camera out of sight. It's a cinch they'll take the film."

Nellie nodded.

A new song began with a bellowing opening verse, and stopped instantly as a heavily decorated Russian colonel entered the foyer.

"I am Antonov, the colonel general's aide. I thank you for the decoration."

"Now that we have warmly welcomed each other, Colonel, I should like to proceed to Berlin."

"But!" Antonov said with an expression of shock, "we have many more songs prepared and we must have some toasts."

Sean looked at his watch. "I'm sorry, Colonel."

"A moment," he said huffily, "and we will get your orders cleared."

The moment stretched to ten and then twenty. Accordions and balalaikas continued a history of Russian folk song. The Americans stood around stiffly, embarrassed. Forty minutes later Antonov returned and took Sean into a side office.

"I am most regretful," he said, "that you cannot proceed to Berlin with your present complement. It is in direct violation of the Brandenburg Agreement."

"Colonel, I am impressed by the warmth of your welcome and I am moved by the magnificence of your artists. However, as one soldier to another, my orders are to bring my convoy to Berlin with all possible speed. I am unaware of the existence of the Brandenburg Agreement."

"So? Well, I see. The agreement drawn up by your government and mine puts numerical limitations on all convoys moving through Democratic Germany. You are not permitted with a convoy of more than twenty vehicles, twenty officers, and forty enlisted men. The agreement specifically states that the men may not be combat troops, but I will overlook this technicality."

"Just when was this Brandenburg Agreement drawn up?"

"Weeks ago. I cannot assume responsibility that your government has not informed you properly."

"Colonel Antonov," Sean pressed unruffled, "I want to see your copy of the agreement. I am certain your government informed you well enough to send you a copy."

Antonov looked angrily at the American whom he now recognized as an opponent who would not be bullied. He smiled, threw his hands open. "Unfortunately, Major, no copy in English."

"Russian will be fine," Sean said.

"I see." Antonov excused himself.

His absence stretched. Sean knew no course under the restrictions of his order but to ride it out and keep firm. The harassment was obviously deliberate and well-planned. He had left Halle in the morning certain there would be no trouble on something so routine as a convoy of G-5 personnel.

He had discussed with his people the possibility of some red tape and the natural curiosity of two distant allies seeing each other for the first time. What was happening now was the creation of an incident out of thin air.

In the foyer he could hear the singing continue. He peeked out.

Vodka and some food had been brought in. The Russians were toasting to peace and friendship.

Another half hour passed before a beefy, swarthy brigadier general returned in place of Colonel Antonov.

He looked at the American major with disdain. "You are a guest of the Soviet Union," he said abruptly. "You are under our protection. You have offended us by bringing armed troops into this zone in direct defiance of the Brandenburg Agreement."

Sean watched the game played out. The weight of rank was designed to wear him down. The whole damned thing was childish. He contained his anger. "I question the existence of a Brandenburg Agreement," he said.

"That is a grave provocation," the general answered sharply.

"Nonsense. Let me refresh the General's memory on an agreement that does exist. The United States has ceded the provinces of Thuringia and Saxony in exchange for a sector of Berlin."

"The provinces of Thuringia and Saxony have been given us out of historic justice. The Soviet Union alone is responsible for the death of Nazism."

Sean smiled in a way that the Russian did not like. "I understand, General, that the Russians only cover their dead with six inches of dirt and leave them unmarked."

"I do not understand . . ."

"We Americans keep an accurate count of our dead. If you will look very hard over my shoulder you will see American crosses all the way back to North Africa."

"The capitalistic press is known for its blatant lies."

"Take it easy, General. Two of those crosses belong to my brothers."

The Russian paled. "The Brandenburg Agreement limits convoys on this road to . . ."

"Twenty trucks, twenty officers, forty enlisted men. Okay, your round. I will return half my complement to Halle. Believe me, tomorrow will be another day."

"What did you say your name was, Major?" the Russian asked threateningly.

"Gable. Clark Gable."

Sean walked quickly into the foyer where the Cossacks were now leaping over tables and chairs. He bellowed, ordering his men outside.

As a precaution, Sean had Big Nellie send the photographer back
with the group going to Halle. A Russian major sat between Sean and
Bradbury to "direct" the convoy to Berlin. Bo and Blessing sat in the
back seat bitching about the Russians' behavior.

As they now suspected, they were led away from the autobahn,
plunging deeper into secondary roads in the countryside. Sean alerted
his people to keep their eyes sharp. At least there might be some intelligence to be gained out of the zigzag detour.

To the men in the ranks, this first meeting with the Russians ended
in a semishock. Their Russian counterparts had refused to do what any
man does when meeting on a distant field. They did not show pictures
of wives, sweethearts, children. They did not tell where they were
from, what work they did. They kept asking why the Americans were
trying to commit aggression.

"This is a lousy day, Sean," Big Nellie said. "I wanted to believe this
sort of thing couldn't be true."

"It's only the beginning."

The convoy passed through dead villages and untended fields. There
seemed to be no sign of German life; it was eerie.

Russian road blocks continued to bisect the most remote country-
side lanes. Unlike the disciplined NKVD troops at Wittenberg, the
Russian soldiers in the countryside were a scrubby, filthy, ragged lot.
As often as not they showed up drunk, bogged down under sacks of loot.
A dozen times the convoy was stopped. The halting was followed by
demands for American cigarettes and chocolate.

They plunged deeper into detours on tortuous dirt roads on the thin
excuse that the main highways were closed due to "technical difficulties."

At evening their winding course brought them to the southern approach to Berlin, where they were once again halted in the town of
Werder before the rail crossing. The accompanying Russian major exchanged words with his people, then ordered Sean to have his convoy
remain in their vehicles.

Big Nellie nudged Sean, pointing to the woods that ran alongside
the rails. On close look one could see that the ground in the woods was
pocked with thousands of holes dug out by human hand and covered
with tree branches, corrugated metal, cardboard, and lumber scraps.

These holes were home for tens of thousands of liberated slave laborers and concentration-camp victims from eastern Europe. They had worked their way to Werder in an attempt to get back to Poland and Russia.

The trained eyes in the convoy sized it up quickly. There was no facility for registration, food, or medical help.

A train of some eighty open freight and cattle cars jiggled back and forth blocking the road crossing, and puffed to a stop. It was followed by an awesome sight of thousands of refugees suddenly pouring from their holes in the forest. Some held a single pack or suitcase. Some had nothing. A line of bayonet-bearing Russian soldiers held at bay this growing horde of the backwash of war.

A Russian officer blew a whistle; the guards opened their line. An insane scramble ensued as the mass of human misery swept up to the train. They shoved and kicked and clawed and screamed their way aboard. Old, young, and weak were hurled mercilessly down the rail bed. In but a moment the cars were crammed beyond capacity.

Another whistle and the line of soldiers re-formed and clubbed back with rifle butts those who did not make it. Pleas fell on deaf ears. The train chugged into motion with its bulge of misery.

The Russian in Sean's car giggled. "See how anxious they are to get home."

Sean and the others looked at him with revulsion. It was, in a moment, a ten-year indoctrination course.

Sean snapped on the ignition, fought to keep from shouting at the outrage. The convoy cleared the crossing, watching the unsuccessful refugees trudge back to their holes to wait for another train on another day.

Just beyond Werder they saw a now familiar sight. The bridge ahead was blocked by a pair of submachine-gun-toting Mongols who waved the convoy to halt.

Sean was blind with anger. He pressed his foot on the accelerator and beaded in on the bridge.

"That a boy, Major," Blessing said, "frig 'em!"

The Russian began to yell, "Nyet! nyet!" He tried to shove his foot on the brakes. Sean jammed an elbow into his ribs and at the same moment Blessing and Big Nellie clamped him frozen.

The convoy closed up behind Sean and bore down on the bridge at seventy miles an hour!

The Mongols waved their guns threateningly! At the last split second they leaped over the bridge rail into the river and the convoy passed over.

At seven o'clock, thirteen hours after their departure, Sean's convoy had traversed the German landscape endlessly for a mere forward gain of a hundred miles.

At last they pulled into the former SS *Kaserne* in Babelsberg, a suburb of Potsdam, across the Havel River from Berlin. Before coming to a proper halt, Sean was pounced on by A. J. Hansen's gangly orderly who saluted, then grabbed his arm. "General says get up to his quarters before the Russkies get ahold of you." The two trotted over the parade grounds as a half-dozen Russians descended on the convoy to liberate their man and to find a Major Clark Gable.

No smile greeted Sean from Andrew Jackson Hansen, First Deputy Military Governor of Germany. "Come in, Major Gable," he scowled. "Goddammit, O'Sullivan, I friggin' well told you to keep your ass out of trouble."

"Sir, I have been the epitome of restraint . . . only . . ."

"Only what!"

Big Nellie came in. "Only we saw something at Werder."

"The Russian refugee transfer point?"

"Yes, sir," said Sean.

"That still didn't give you license to run those bridge guards into the river. The next convoy will face concrete road blocks. Sean, you've got to learn to hold your water. This isn't Rombaden and this isn't your show."

"Yes, sir."

Big Nellie watched Sean try to digest the end of one war, the beginning of another. Again he would be the soldier without the gun . . . patience, restraint, wisdom.

The journalist looked out of the window, down into the courtyard of the Kaserne. "Looks like a prison."

"The Russians insist our presence is hypothetical until the Potsdam Conference signs a treaty," Hansen said.

"Will I be able to get into Berlin and look around?" Big Nellie asked.

"Maybe. It would make our position more difficult if you were to write a column on what you saw today."

Hansen could have invoked censorship, but preferred to put the matter to a reliable old friend in another way. Big Nellie nodded that he understood.

"Check in with the intelligence office and tell them what you saw today."

Big Nellie said he would and left. Hansen took Sean to the next room, where Major General Hiram Stonebraker and Colonel Neal Hazzard waited.

Stonebraker was known in Air Corps circles as a salty, hard-shelled genius with the speciality of air transportation. He was considered the true creator of the Hump Airlift, which flew supplies from India to China. Transferred into Europe as the war ended, he was detached for advisory duty to the President for the forthcoming conference at Potsdam. This was to be his last mission for he was slated for retirement.

Colonel Neal Hazzard, commandant-elect for the American Sector of Berlin, had been an outspoken fighting soldier most of his career. A wound gave him the choice of discharge or military government. He was brash, direct, honest.

"Tune out Moscow," Hansen said. Hazzard went to a half-dozen places in the room where the Russians had planted microphones. To counter it, a member of the staff had rigged up a two-cell battery connected to a buzzer, which set off a steady hum when connected. This noise, directed into the microphones, screened out the other voices from the Russian listening post in the basement.

"Okay, Sean," Hansen said, "what happened today?"

He related the bizarre incidents. It tallied with reports of a half-dozen other American convoys which had come to Berlin on other routes. It added up to a plan of deliberate harassment. The "welcoming" officer was always below the rank of the American convoy leader. This was a deliberate belittlement. The negotiating officers were always above the rank of the American—Russian logic set to establish their people as superiors.

Sean looked squarely at the three men as he finished his story. "Had I been given freedom of action in my orders, I could have gotten the convoy through to Berlin on the autobahn."

"That's a rash statement," Hansen said. "We are in no position to afford the luxury of an incident."

"There would have been no incident," Sean said firmly. "They were bluffing."

"What makes you think so?" Stonebraker asked.

"Ask a pair of wet Russian soldiers."

"That will be all," Hansen cut in. "My orderly will show you to your quarters. There will be a guard on your door. Other than intelligence interrogation, talk to no one."

"Yes, sir."

When he left all that could be heard for a time was the steady buzz into the wire taps.

"We're getting our pockets picked," Neal Hazzard growled. "We should have captured Berlin. Now, we compound the original stupidity by giving the Russians two lush German provinces for a foothold in this rock pile."

Hansen answered, "The Russians have been isolated from the West for three decades. Since the end of the war they've broken out of their cocoon. They are awed by their sudden new position of being a world power. But, they are suspicious. It's going to take time for the strangeness to wear off, but we are going to have to learn to live with them."

"That crap may go in a classroom, Chip," Stonebraker said to Hansen, addressing him by a nickname used between generals. "Your young major is right. We're playing their game and they're going to con us out of our jock straps."

"For Christ's sake, sir," Hazzard added, "do you really believe they're not going to try to elbow us out of Berlin."

"That's academic," Hansen answered. "The facts are that we have to do business with them."

"How do we do business, Chip? I'm for the young major's way."

"This is 1945. The American people wouldn't give a lusty crap if we handed over all of Germany or even all of Europe to the Russians. They want to finish the war against Japan and forget the whole goddamned thing. We will receive no public support for a strong stand against the Russians."

These were, indeed, the ugly facts of life.

"Fine," Stonebraker said, "we're in Berlin. Maybe someday we'll know why. We've seen what happens to our convoys. You'd better prepare for an alternate route."

"Where?"

"In the air. Define air corridors from our zone to Berlin, put it on paper, make it part of the Potsdam Agreement."

"How can we justify it without getting them heated up?"

Crusty Stonebraker gave a craggy smile. "Tell the Russians it's for their own good. We all need an air-safety setup because of the volume of traffic. They'll buy it now. They won't in a year."

Hansen didn't like it. Air lanes were foolish. It was a part of Crusty Stonebraker's vanity.

A knock on the door brought Hansen's orderly. A sealed envelope was delivered from Russian Marshal Alexei Popov. As Hansen read, the others detected the urgency. He looked from Hazzard to Stonebraker, read aloud. "This is to advise you that the Americans will not be permitted to take possession of the six boroughs of Berlin tomorrow, as previously discussed. It is felt by the Soviet High Command that there must be a formal written agreement and the establishment of a four-power council first. Signed, Marshal Alexei Popov."

"All right, Crusty. Draw up a plan for air lanes. Neal, bring O'Sullivan up here. He's going to get an opportunity to find out if the comrades are bluffing or not."

CHAPTER TWO

Andrew Jackson Hansen, Hiram Stonebraker, and Neal Hazzard all looked down to the Kaserne courtyard. They saw Sean O'Sullivan and Blessing get into the touring car with two enlisted men.

Hansen looked at his watch. It was seven in the morning. This hour was picked because he knew the Russian command didn't come to life and function until around noon.

The motor chugged, fought the brisk cold, roared into life. The car was stopped at the gate by a drowsy Russian guard. Sean showed him an order signed by Hansen directing Sean to Tempelhof Airdrome to pick up an incoming VIP. The Russian was impressed by the big car and passed it through.

In a few moments three jeeploads of men passed through the gate, ostensibly on routine missions to Berlin.

During the two weeks of his semiconfinement in the Babelsberg Kaserne, Colonel Hazzard kept as many vehicles as possible moving in and out of Berlin for as many reasons as he could invent without rousing Russian suspicion. The vehicles were dispatched along a variety of

routes and, whenever possible, photographed the streets until Hazzard's
master map became studded with information. Ordinary Russian troops
seldom challenged them for they seemed to hold an equal fear of cam-
eras and maps.

Sean sped along the southern rim of the Wannsee Lake into the
Grunewald, whose enormous acreage comprised a great part of the land
in the western districts of Berlin.

The forest had not suffered too much war damage and in the morning mist the greenery shielded the sight of the horror of Berlin. He ran
parallel to the smaller chain of lakes that bordered the forest and at the
crossing waited. In a few moments the other three jeeps arrived from
different directions at the rendezvous.

They bisected the forest on Onkel Tom Strasse, turned into Argen-
tine Allee, coming out directly before a magnificent complex of administrative buildings. It had been part of the Hitler Barracks and served
as Luftwaffe Headquarters for the Central Germany Command. The
Luft Gau buildings and barracks fringed the woods, showed little damage for it had been selected as the future American Headquarters.

Blessing pointed to a central building in the complex with a convenient flag pole on the lawn before it. The area was void of life. Sean
waved the convoy in, raised the American flag to the top of the mast,
and posted a large hand-painted sign on the front door in English, German, and Russian.

ATTENTION: THIS IS THE PROPERTY OF THE UNITED STATES OF AMERICA
AND HEREBY DESIGNATED AS HEADQUARTERS FOR THE AMERICAN SECTOR
OF BERLIN COMPRISING THE BOROUGHS OF STEGLITZ, ZEHLENDORF,
SCHÖNEBERG, NEUKÖLLN, TEMPELHOF, AND KREUZBERG.
SIGNED:
Colonel Neal Hazzard, Commandant American Sector by authority
of Major General Andrew Jackson Hansen, First Deputy Military
Governor.

Marshal Alexei Popov was awakened from a deep, vodka-induced
slumber by a phone call at his Potsdam mansion at the unlikely hour of
eight o'clock.

"What do you mean, American troops are at the Hitler Barracks?" he
yawned.

"They have proclaimed it as American Headquarters, Comrade
Marshal."

How could they invade, he thought, they don't have enough troops?
"How many?"

"Fifteen."

"Fifteen! Fifteen Americans declaring a headquarters! Fifteen!"

"Yes, Comrade Marshal. Fifteen. What shall we do?"

Popov stretched, scratched his head, and squinted at the clock. What
an uncouth hour to start trouble. "Send up a battalion of tanks and
stand opposite them. Have a battalion of infantry see that there is no
further movement in or out of the area."

Popov slammed the receiver down, wrestled out of his pajamas,
wended his way to the bathroom. His soldierly figure belied sixty years
of age. He shaved, doused his face, combed his great full head of soft
silver hair, of which he was quite proud, dressed, and called for breakfast in his room, calculating the true meaning of the problem.

The simplest thing to do would be to lift the phone and ask Commissar V. V. Azov for instructions. That would, however, be a sign of
weakness. Popov had worked his way through every rank in the Red
Army, was among its founders, had survived the purges. He had not
come this far just to prove to a political commissar that he was unable
to deal with fifteen Americans. Obviously, the Americans had something up their sleeves. What was it?

An aide came in with word that Russian troops had the Americans
completely cut off and a field phone was in operation. He put in a call
to his commander at Hitler Barracks.

"Marshal Popov speaks here."

"Good morning, Comrade Marshal, Colonel Vanyev here."

"What is your situation?"

"I have ten tanks and a hundred men deployed opposite the Americans. The streets are blocked off. They merely stand before the door
of the building."

"Send someone across the street and rip down their proclamation."

"And what if they open fire?" Vanyev asked.

"Call back for instructions."

He finished his coffee, stood before the mirror, struck a small pose.
The Americans called him the Silver Fox. Not bad at all, he admitted
to himself. The phone rang, Vanyev reporting.

"Did you rip their proclamation down?"

"It was attempted. One American opened fire, wounding our soldier.

Fortunately, we have a good photograph of him. Do you have further instructions, Comrade Marshal?"

"Stand by!" he said as he set down the phone, now frowning with worry. "Call my car! Reach the Americans and tell them I am on my way to speak to General Hansen," he snapped at his aide.

He was driven under siren-shrieking escort into the Babelsberg Kaserne, marched with a trail of aides up to Hansen's suite, ordered them to wait in the hall, and entered. Neal Hazzard was in the outer office.

"Good morning, Marshal Popov," he said. "What brings you out so early?"

"My business is not your business. I demand to see General Hansen."

"Sorry, sir. General Hansen is not available."

Popov blanched. "It is advisable that he becomes available."

"Yes, sir. If you will have a seat I will attempt to get the message to him."

Hazzard left the room. For the next thirty minutes the Russian cooled his heels. The instant he saw General Stonebraker return in Hazzard's place he realized he was being fleeced at his own game of musical chairs. Popov's voice lowered ominously. "I demand to see General Hansen without further delay."

"He is not available."

"General Stonebraker. Please believe me that my patience is at an end. If I do not see General Hansen in exactly two minutes I will order my troops to open fire."

Hiram Stonebraker sat behind a desk, opened a file of papers, began to read through them as though he were alone in the room.

"The minute I leave this office you will have condemned your soldiers to oblivion!"

Crusty Stonebraker looked up slowly. "Marshal," he said, "we are going to have to live with each other for a long time. You've got to start learning to say please."

Popov's anger grew, but he knew to conceal it. "For the sake of the lives of your innocent soldiers, I request an interview with General Hansen."

"In that case, sir, come right in."

"Morning, Marshal Popov," Hansen said. "What brings you out so early?"

He looked from Stonebraker to Hansen, regained his threadbare temper, and tried to understand the situation. His confidence had wavered. The Americans were bluffing, he knew . . . yet, they were not the kind to risk lives on such a gambit. What was behind it?

"Why do you push me to force my hand," he said.

"We are only asserting our rights in Berlin," Hansen answered.

"There is no formal agreement!"

"How about the Brandenburg Agreement?"

"The what?"

"The same crap you have been using to harass our convoys and to keep us locked up here," Hansen said. "The game works two ways, Marshal Popov."

"I assure you I am not bluffing."

Hansen looked at his watch deliberately. "In a half hour, American troops are scheduled to begin evacuation of Saxony and Thuringia. If you are advising me we are not entitled to take physical control of our six boroughs of Berlin, I am advising you that American forces will remain in those provinces."

Popov's physical and strategic advantage was leveled. His decision held implications too vast. He was faced with a *fait accompli*. He smiled warmly, and became amazingly friendly as he picked up the phone and ordered his troops out of western Berlin.

When Popov had left and confirmation of the Russian withdrawal phoned in and the guards in the Kaserne lifted, Hansen allowed the luxury of a sigh of relief.

"O'Sullivan is a smart young man," Stonebraker said.

"I guess we all learned something today, Crusty."

The phone rang and Hansen answered. It was Lieutenant General Hartly Fitz-Roy, the British Military Governor of Germany who called from the other wing of the Kaserne.

"I say, Hansen. What the devil are you chaps up to. You can't take unilateral action like that, you know. Here, we have already set up negotiation meetings with the Russians."

"Negotiations are finished. You can occupy your boroughs at once."

"Can't do that. We need all our troops to welcome the Prime Minister for the conference." He continued to protest American rashness.

Hansen shook his head when the conversation ended. "Sometimes I think I understand the Russians, but I'll be goddamned if I'll ever understand the British."

CHAPTER THREE

Ernestine answered the knock. She pushed against the makeshift board that served as a door until it gave enough to see an older-appearing man. He was large, a bit stooped, and seemed tired. She studied him curiously. "Yes? What is it you wish?"

"Falkenstein?"

"Yes."

"May I come in?"

The voice drew on her memory. She pushed the board open wider. "Are you . . . my uncle? Are you Ulrich?"

"I am."

"I am Ernestine."

"You? Little Ernestine?"

"I am very happy to know you are alive. Please come in."

Bruno's eyes widened at the sight of his brother, he arose slowly, backed up. "You!" he whispered harshly. "You! Ulrich! Alive!"

"Quite."

"But . . . but . . . but . . ."

"You need not fear, brother. I am thoroughly decontaminated."

Bruno was distraught with confusion. "You! In Berlin!"

Herta Falkenstein kept her wits. She knew that he must be among the clean Germans and must have come in with the Amis. "You have never been out of our thoughts," she said quickly. "Please forgive us, but you come as quite a shock."

"Humpf." He looked past the candlelight to where Hildegaard sat near her cot, puzzled. "You must be Hilde."

Hilde did not know how to greet the man whose name had been spoken in curses from childhood memory. After long spells of silence her father raged that both of his brothers were traitors and their record limited his advancement in his bureau. She was only ten years old when Uncle Ulrich was sent away. She hardly remembered him.

"Stand up, Hilde!" Frau Falkenstein commanded. "Let your Uncle Ulrich see how you have grown." She stood awkwardly, bowed stiffly.

"Gerd?"

"He is in a prison camp in America."

Bruno began to recover his composure, and caught his wife's eyes to leave them alone. "I am sorry there is nothing to offer you to eat," she said.

"I am not hungry."

"This is a great occasion. We all wish to be with you but I know you and Bruno want to speak." She herded the girls from the room.

The brothers Falkenstein were alone. Ulrich looked at the shambles, the gaunt, stubble-bearded man. "There is so much to say, one does not know where to begin," Bruno said.

"With general rejoicing to a glorious homecoming," he answered bitterly. "What have you heard of my wife, Hannelore?"

"You did not know of the divorce?"

"Rumors reached me."

"She divorced you when the war began, moved to Vienna. It was difficult for her because of your . . . opposition. She passed away last year."

Hannelore, dead without the steel to see it through. It must have been dreadful for her.

"Where is Wolfgang? I have searched high and low."

Bruno shook his head, his voice broke. "Our brother is dead."

Ulrich let out one long deep pitiful groan of resignation. "Everything is dead."

"You must have heard of the July plot to kill Hitler. Wolfgang was involved. There was a terrible revenge."

"How did he die?"

"He was hanged."

Ulrich dragged himself to his feet wearily, flopped his arms to his sides. "I shall not wear out my welcome."

"Ulrich! We are still brothers. Nothing can change that."

"No, nothing can change it."

"You don't know what it has been like," Bruno sobbed. "You can't imagine how we have suffered."

Ulrich's deceptively drowsy eyes did not conceal his disdain.

"Of course you have suffered too," Bruno bumbled on. "We all have. I've seen my wife and daughter raped before my eyes. Look at me. We are half starved. I am ruined . . . I have nothing left."

"We must get together sometimes and trade horror stories."

"For God's sake, all I want to do is forget it happened."

"You mean the same way you forgot that Wolfgang and I existed?"

"So, we were taken in by Hitler. Just because I held a minor post
with the Nazis, am I to go to jail and leave Herta and those poor girls
alone? I tell you, we have paid."

"Not enough, Bruno, not enough."

How bitter came the destruction of the long dream. Ulrich Falkenstein had come from the blackness of Schwabenwald to an even greater
blackness of Berlin.

Wolfgang and Hannelore were dead and the old friends gone.

Berlin was worse than dead. A great, beautiful goddess hacked up,
prostrate, gasping for breath . . . the last of life's blood oozing from her
body.

The old man was stooped with sorrow as he trudged down the Unter
Den Linden, that mammoth boulevard that rumbled under the wheels
of Prussian cannons, clicked under the heels of genteel ladies, heard the
shouts of protesting workers, the gunfire of insurrection, the boots of
pagan rallies, the circumstance of glory.

At Friedrichstrasse he stood and looked down the flattened street.

> So long as the old trees bloom Unter Den Linden,
> Nothing can befall us,
> Berlin remains Berlin . . .

The voices that once came from the cabarets of Friedrichstrasse were
stilled forever. Sentimental voices, bawdy voices, angry voices . . . still
. . . so still. Now a man hacks away at the carcass of a dead horse.

> You are my old love,
> Berlin remains Berlin . . .

Ghastly, ragged men stagger and fall into the streets from hunger.
Urchins beg, women barter . . .

> So long as the old trees bloom Unter Den Linden,
> Nothing can befall us,
> Berlin remains Berlin.

He stood now near the Brandenburg Gate at the Pariser-Platz at
what was the heartstone of his beloved city. The reigning royalty of the
thriving culture lived here on the square and watched from their windows as the pageantry of history flowed beneath the Brandenburg Gate.

The Berlin theater songs, the bitter satire of the political cabarets, the exciting theater, the grandness of the opera . . . all the voices were still.

Atop the Brandenburg Gate the Quadriga of Victory once had her chariot drawn by four lusty steeds. The chariot had no wheels, the horses no legs; they lay in a heap and a limp red flag hung over the prostrate shambles. The gate itself remained up only from memory. Great chunks of the massive columns had been bashed away.

He looked back down the Unter Den Linden to the gutted shells of the massive buildings of the opera and the university, the museums and the cathedral, and he walked through and toward other gutted shells of the Reichstag.

The magnificent floral wonders of the Tiergarten were ravaged. The Column to Victory of other wars dismantled, and Victory Allee a lane of strewn rocks.

For three days he picked his way across that expanse of three hundred and fifty square miles that once constituted Berlin. Only an ugly scar on the landscape was left in this place of beauty and pomp, ideas and energy. The great forests were in ruin; the hunting lodges of the electors of Brandenburg and the castles were battered beyond comprehension; the workers' houses were in ashes, and the lakes and rivers putrid.

> You are my old love,
> Berlin remains Berlin . . .

After a number of days, Ulrich was able to locate the first of his old comrades, Berthold Hollweg, who existed in a clapboard hovel on the Teltow Canal below Tempelhof Airdrome. It was a single room, earthen floor, windowless, toiletless. There was a futile attempt to grow a few scrubby vegetables among the rocks and weeds.

In the old days, Hollweg had held a number of high posts in the Democratic Party. He had been chairman of Brandenburg Province and held a seat in the Reichstag until the last free election.

Time and tide had reduced him to the meagerest level of existence. He had aged as Ulrich had aged. The first moments of seeing each other were filled with disbelief, and then Hollweg recounted the past.

"When your trial was over and you were sent away, that signaled our end. Some fled, some disappeared, others blended into the scenery to make themselves anonymous."

"What about our Jews? Ginsberg, Jacobs, Adler, Davids? They were among the heart and brains of the labor movement."

Hollweg shook his head. "They are all dead. For a time we made an attempt to hide Adler and his children, but they had to leave."

"You turned them out?"

"It was next to impossible to hide a Jew in Berlin. Adler understood . . ."

Frau Louise Hollweg began to weep at her husband's recollections.

"Tell me about Wolfgang," Ulrich whispered harshly.

Hollweg lowered his eyes, spoke blankly. "From the moment you were sent away the Gestapo watched him day and night. We knew he was being used as bait. We had to split up. It was impossible to hold a meeting. Spies were everywhere. Things got so bad we couldn't even recognize each other when we passed on the street. Wolfgang was a contact. Finally . . . we had to tell him to stop trying to see us. It was the only way to survive. Ulrich . . . spare yourself the rest of this . . ."

"Go on."

"When the plot was made against Hitler, Wolfgang became involved and he got many of the old comrades involved. His job was to print the proclamations that Hitler was dead and to get them posted around Berlin with the announcement of the new government. The plot failed. Hitler went insane with vengeance. Wolfgang was among the first dragged into a People's Court. You know the procedure."

"Was there no one who spoke for him? Not a single German voice!"

"In many ways, Ulrich, it was better you were in Schwabenwald. You will never know how totally crushed we were."

There was no use to berate Hollweg, only pity him. "And what of you, Berthold?"

"We lost our son on the Russian front. Me? I went from one job to another, each time hounded by spies and the Gestapo. I was forced to reduce my existence. In the end I was a doorman at the Adlon Hotel, but even there the Gestapo thought I saw too many important people come and go. I found my true niche in life as guardian of the men's toilet at the Am Zoo Hotel."

Ulrich wondered if there was anyone left who could say he was a German who fought Hitler. There were too few to really be counted in the first place. "Maybe it would have been better if I died in Schwabenwald than return to this."

"No, Ulrich, one by one the Berliners will begin to climb out of the ashes. They will need you if we are to put the pieces together again."

Ulrich grunted.

"We did the best we could, Ulrich . . . the best we could . . ."

At last, Ulrich Falkenstein made the last stop of his bitter homecoming. As the light of day faded, he had found his way to the Plötzensee Prison, which bordered on another ravaged woods and stood opposite the destroyed inland harbor. He got out of the military jeep which had brought him and walked alongside the high brick wall. The main gate was guarded by a post of British soldiers. He showed them his papers.

"Do you speak English, sir?" an officer asked.

He nodded.

"We have received a call from the Americans that you were coming. If you will follow me, sir."

The gate clanged open. The officer's hard boots cracked on the stones. They crossed out of the main compound into a dirt courtyard just beyond the main wall and came to a small brick building of twenty by twenty feet.

The officer pushed the door open. Ulrich entered. The room was concrete and bare. A single iron beam bridged the room. From the beam dangled a half-dozen meat hooks. Six thousand men and women were hung by Hitler in revenge for the bomb plot. They had dangled from piano wires in slow strangulation. His brother, Wolfgang Falkenstein, was among their number.

Ulrich stared out of the narrow, barred window. The red wall of the prison and a high chimney hovered over them. That was the last thing that Wolfgang saw.

He walked from the place. The door slammed behind him.

CHAPTER FOUR

"Just before the battle mother!" sang Shenandoah Blessing,
    "I am thinking most of you!
While upon the field we're watching,
    With the enemee in view!"

"Slob! Quiet!" Sean demanded. "You're gonna wake up Bo."

"Filled with thoughts of home and Gawd!
  For well they know that on the morrow . . .
Some will sleep beneath the sod!"

"Friggin' blubber!" Sean puffed as he lugged the massive, enormously drunk policeman up the steps. They stopped on a landing, Sean propped the big man against the rail and caught his breath. Blessing threw his arms apart and bellowed . . .

"Farewell mother you may ne-ver,
  Prrrrrreessss me to your heart agin!
But oh, you'll not forget me mo-ther,
  If I'm numbered with the slain!"

"You'll be numbered with the slain all right if you don't shut up!" Sean draped Blessing's limp arm over his shoulder and continued the tortured climb. "Bo!"

Bolinski's door opened.

"Help me with this fat son of a bitch!"

"You woke up Bo." Blessing emoted, switching suddenly from latent musical aspirations to a crying jag. "Goddam, Major, they don't write songs like that no more . . .

Hark! I hear a bugle sounding,
  Tis the signal for the fight,
Now may Gawd protect us, moooother . . ."

"This bastard must weigh a ton," Bo said.

"How about it, Major, baby? Did yore little ole' fat boy here clean the Russkies? Did we win a pile or did we win a pile? Huh, Major, baby?"

"You're a sweet old fat bastard," Sean admitted.

The strangeness between the Russians and their former allies ended explosively. Throughout the ruins of Berlin parties at all levels of command erupted. There were enlisted men's brawls in makeshift cellar night clubs, and plush vodka and caviar affairs of the top echelon . . . brotherhood flowed freely.

General Hartly Fitz-Roy, the British governor, gave a boar hunt from a lodge, still intact, once belonging to an elector of Brandenburg. The Englishman was aghast when Marshal Popov showed up with a sub-machine gun. It was damned unsporting, but as host he could say nothing except for a mumble under his breath.

The French arrived in Berlin and threw a great feast in their own honor. General Yves de Lys grimaced in horror at the way the Russians belted down their superb wine.

Russians wept out songs of the motherland, Cossacks made great leaps, Mickey Mouse watches became a gift of the proof of lasting friendship.

Sean and Blessing had helped launch a new Russian junior officers' club. Halfway through uncountable litres of vodka and gallons of beer, past innumerable songs and toasts, the light heavyweight champion of a Russian division issued a challenge to any man in the room regardless of weight or nationality. The offer proved irresistible to Sean.

A British lieutenant gave them both lengthy discourses on fair play, and in a makeshift ring Sean dazzled everyone with his dancing-master tactics—until his vodka-rubbered legs left him open for a wild hook that knocked him flat on his back.

Sean decided upon arising, no more fancy work. He cold-cocked the Russian in forty-six seconds, collecting for his backers numerous watches and great denominations of occupation currency.

Shortly thereafter it came to light that Shenandoah Blessing had once been a wrestler, working his way through college under the nom de plume of the "Mad Russian."

The frivolity continued as he threw six Russians, an Englishman, two Americans, and a Frenchman in succession. Finally motorcycle escorts brought in a 300-pound Siberian with a handlebar moustache. Blessing was rather tired and he was dethroned. But, by this time, the Russian officers were cleaned of a month's pay and their new club a shambles.

The party broke up at six in the morning with the Russians serenading their guests farewell and declaring them the salt of the earth.

Sean and Bolinski unloaded their burden on a bed never meant to absorb the shock of so large a falling body. Bed and occupant crashed to the floor and there they let him lie.

"Come on into my room," Bo said. "I've got some coffee warmed up."

Sean flopped into a big chair and began laughing. "Haven't done that since I was a kid at a couple of Irish wakes." He pulled out large wads of occupation currency from every pocket. "Got to send some of this crap back to the Russkies tomorrow to help pay to repair their club."

Bo Bolinski watched the major with a bit of fascination. Sean was always proper, at times somewhat pompous. Bo counted a black eye,

ten scraped knuckles, buttons off his shirt, saw a mellow drunk with a
cigar stub entrenched in his jaw.

"What the hell you doing up this time of the morning?" Sean asked
as he sipped the coffee.

"Colonel Hazzard asked me to study these regulations for the four-
power occupation. He wants an opinion on them today."

"They stink," Sean said.

"Looks like you've made a private peace tonight with the Russians,
anyhow," Bo said.

"We're under orders to play up this brotherhood crap and con each
other for information. Once the Russkies loosen up, they're not too hard
to take. Anyhow, they're not Germans."

Sean stood up, dispensed with the cigar, walked into Bo's bathroom,
and rinsed his mouth out. There was coldness between the men. In all
the time they worked together Sean knew little of Bo except the statistics; lawyer, Notre Dame, married and two children, Chicago. Not
that Bo hadn't been loyal and efficient.

"Bo, you pissed at me because I pulled you out of Rombaden and
brought you to Berlin?"

"No one forced me into G-5, Major."

"What's wrong?" Sean said abruptly.

"I can't hate Germans like you do, Major. I get sick when I see kids
digging through our garbage cans. I get sick everytime I drive into
Berlin."

Sean did not answer.

"Morning, O'Sullivan," Hansen smirked at his hungover officer. "I
understand you and your fat friend tried to annihilate the Russian officer corps last night."

"All in the spirit of brotherhood, sir."

"Were you able to get any information on this V. V. Azov?"

"They clam up the minute his name is mentioned. It's my guess that
he's the signal caller."

"It's starting to add up that way."

"Sir, I want to bring up these rules governing the Berlin occupation."
"Shoot."

"We're in trouble if we accept them."

"Neal Hazzard put you up to this?"

"We've discussed it."

"For a so-called fighting soldier, Hazzard does a monumental amount of bellyaching."

"He's got a right to if he's expected to be commandant by these rules. However, we reached the same opinion independently. So did Lieutenant Bolinski. The whole document is written by Russians, in Russian, and for Russians."

"No matter what the rules are," Hansen answered, "the success of the four-power occupation depends solely upon the desire of the Russians to cooperate."

"Why do we have to bend over backward to let them know we're not going to hurt their feelings? They're not bashful. Pretty damned soon they're going to have us believing that they won the war single-handed."

"It's about all we can do to prevent them from giving the Yugoslavs a sector of Berlin. The Russians say they're entitled to it more than the French. How do you answer that?"

"Colonel Hazzard has his work cut out for him."

"We all have."

"All four licensed political parties, headquarters, Russian Sector. Police Headquarters, Russian Sector. Radio Station, Russian Sector. City Hall Assembly and Magistrat, Russian Sector. University, Russian Sector."

"Sit down, Sean. I hate to make that headache of yours worse this morning, but you'd better read this."

TOP SECRET. RECOMMENDATIONS, POTSDAM CONFERENCE

Sean had worked on some parts of this himself.

RECOMMENDATION:
We must make the Russians spell out their reparations demands or they can stretch them for infinity. The Russians must be made to account for what they have already taken out of their zone of Germany and apply it against the total bill.

We must establish four-power control to govern the flow of reparations to the Soviet Union. Inasmuch as Russians demand great deliveries from the Western Zones of Germany we should not agree to make such deliveries until they agree to an accounting and controls.

REJECTED:
The spirit of mutual trust which we hope to establish will be damaged if we offend the Soviet Union in this manner.

Sean flipped the page.

RECOMMENDATION:

We must force the Soviet Union to adhere to the principle of running Germany as a single economic unit. This is being made impossible because the Soviet Union has already physically cut off their zone of occupation from the rest of Germany. We must insist on open borders, open commerce, and free interzone travel.

REJECTED:

This would make the Soviet Union feel that we are against their moving the Polish borders west to the Oder/Neisse line. Although we have not agreed to these border changes, the Soviet argument of setting up a buffer has merit.

"They didn't ask us about any goddamned border changes," Sean said. "They just did it."

"Read on, Major."

RECOMMENDATION:

There is grave concern over allowing the Soviet Union to use our currency engravings and plates to print occupation currency with no method of accounting. The Soviet Union could flood our zones with paper money, buy out Western Zone resources and create inflation.

REJECTED:

Fiscal and monetary experts agree these arguments are possible. However, the Soviet Union would greet the demand to return engravings as a direct question of their honesty.

RECOMMENDATION:

The declaration of the Potsdam Conference guaranteeing freedoms to the German (and Slavic) people and further guaranteeing free elections is a farce.

The Soviet Union cannot guarantee something for other people they dare not give their own people. The Russian people have lived under a police state in one form or another for the entire 1200 years of their recorded history.

We must insist on a definition of freedom, free elections, and democratic institutions.

REJECTED:

A proclamation at the end of the conference is necessary. It would take two decades to negotiate the exact meanings.

There was more, much more. Sean handed the file back to General Hansen quietly. "It was all I could do to push through things like the air corridors. So, we've got to sit still and wait for them to push us too far."

"Will we know it when they do?"

"Not today," Hansen said. "The war against Japan ended a week ago. Today we see American boys in the uniform of their country parading through the streets of enemy capitals demanding to be sent home. It is going to take time for our countrymen to realize that Americans can never go home again."

CHAPTER FIVE

Ernestine awakened sharply from her nightly funk, sweaty, terrified. For hours she fought off sleep, for the darkness brought horror. Then a complete exhaustion drugged her into a semiconscious state far into the night, and she wandered into that torment of blood and ghosts and hollow voices.

She dressed in a half daze, walked pasty-faced into the kitchen, where the family was taking breakfast of a sort of gruel.

None of them had gotten over the shock of the Amis requisitioning their house, forcing them into a bomb-battered set of rooms in Friedenaü of the Steglitz Borough. Bruno and his wife slept in the kitchen, the girls in an oversized alcove with half a wall shorn away.

Bruno bemoaned the latest cruelty of fate, the loss of his house; he, a government official of status; he, who had a chauffeur-driven automobile until late in the war. Now he was reduced to waiting on tables in a French soldiers' beer hall.

Thanks to Ulrich they were not all in labor gangs and had a few extra grams of ration. However, hatred between the brothers did not waver. Bruno felt his brother could do more. The family was barely staying alive. Hilde could not hold a job. She had always been pampered and her head was filled with illusions of becoming an actress.

Bruno's pride was damaged at the idea that his wife had to work as a chambermaid in an American officers' billet. She had never held a job in her life and one could hardly consider her a common *hausfrau*.

Ulrich got her the job. The Americans were generous with the bones they tossed out for her doing their laundry.

In the beer hall Bruno decided the indignities of rowdy Frenchmen had to be borne in order to survive. Soldiers left half-smoked cigarettes, wanted girls, and had access to food; neighbors needed to barter, so he served as an intermediary in small dealings. In spite of the degradation Bruno and his family subsisted better than the starving neighbors around them.

Ernestine sat at the table. Her mother looked from her to Hilde. By contrast, Hilde seemed to show no effects of the times. "You look bad this morning," Herta said.

"Who looks well in Berlin these days," Bruno mumbled. "Everyone is a walking ghost."

"I am just a little tired," Ernestine answered.

"Your Uncle Ulrich offered you a job at Democratic Party Headquarters. I want an explanation of why you refused," her father said.

"I would rather not talk about it," she answered.

"It will be talked about. I cannot bear more drunken Frenchmen— and I don't like the idea of your mother cleaning floors for Amis."

"I won't work for Uncle Ulrich," Ernestine protested.

"I demand to know why. You are trained as a legal secretary. You worked for one of the finest law firms in Berlin."

"There is no German law, any more."

"But you know that your training makes it possible to do a number of things. So long as Ulrich is throwing us a few bones you could think of your family."

"I have decided against it, Father," she said shakily.

"Ernestine," her mother said, "what is disturbing you about Ulrich?" She tried to eat. It was impossible.

"Can't you talk at all?" her father demanded.

"It's those places," she blurted impulsively.

"Places? What places?"

"The things they are saying about us at Nuremberg."

A terrible silence followed. At last, Herta took her daughter's hand. "It is all over. We must forget."

"But, if what they say is true . . ."

"Truth?" Bruno said. "What is truth? Do you believe you can get truth from a Russian radio? You are a German, girl. Do you think your people could have done these things?"

"The pictures . . ."

"Ernestine," her father said testily, "you should be able to recognize propaganda. Our faces are being rubbed in the mud. We have no way to answer back. Even if there was a shred of truth, how can you feel that you and I are to blame?"

"Your father is right, Ernestine. Close your ears, forget the lies. They are trying to turn the world against us."

Yes, Ernestine thought, Father is always right . . . always. Father is never wrong. "Did you know about slaves in your Labor Bureau?"

He smashed his fist on the table. "How dare you!"

"Apologize to your father," Herta demanded.

"I am sorry, Father. Forgive me."

Her sister, Hilde, pushed away from the table and walked away. Arguments! Always damned arguments!

"Where are you going?"

"Out."

"Where?"

"Just out of here."

"When will you be back?"

Hilde shrugged and left.

"All day she is gone," Bruno said. "Where does she spend her time? Where does she get that stuff to paint her face?"

"Uncle Ulrich gave it to her," Ernestine said quickly. "I must go to work."

"Think about Ulrich's offer. Think about us," her father said as she left.

When in the devil will she learn to leave the past alone, Bruno thought when she left. Life is hard enough. The future looks hollow. Fate has been cruel.

Herta packed a small sack containing a tin with five ounces of tobacco strained out of cigarette butts that Bruno had gathered at the beer garden and she put in a number of bars of soap made from laundry scrapings that she had remelted. Herta was clever in the ways of the open barter market in the Tiergarten, where trading was permitted.

She learned to stay clear of the Russian soldiers who had been paid in occupation currency which was near worthless in Berlin and which they could not send home. They were forced to work the barter market themselves, and bullied merciless bargains.

"Try to get a camera," Bruno said. "I have a line with some Ami soldiers. I will be able to get up to a dozen cartons of Ami cigarettes for a decent one."

A dozen cartons of Ami cigarettes! A dozen bags of gold!

The underground took Ernestine out of Steglitz to the center of the city. She had to take a round-about way to get to the hospital where she worked in Neukölln as a nurse's aide. In the last-ditch fighting many parts of the subway system had been flooded, forcing innumerable detours.

The car was filled with sallow, ragged people. She was a bit light-headed, now remorseful about the question she had asked her father. Of course he would not know about slave labor. It was the times. One had to remember father was a respected official and had given them all a good life. It was a pity to see so proud a man reduced to poverty.

How could she really tell him why she worked for Dr. Hahn and could not take Uncle Ulrich's offer?

Hospital? It was a sorry excuse for a hospital. Half bombed out, boarded windows, stripped down to the bedding by the Russians. It was filled with patients, even in the corridors, and there was a shortage of everything. So many old people died these days in a state of confusion, and the newborn screamed into a world of hunger and fear.

Only yesterday the gas was turned on in a section of Neukölln and the hospital received nearly a hundred suicides and attempted suicides. Ten yesterday had died of dysentery, typhus, and diphtheria. Half were little children.

Ernestine followed the lethargic line of trudgers to Potsdamer Platz, close to what was once the heart of Berlin. It was too horrible to walk in Berlin any more. The city was a grotesque, surrealist graveyard palled in a gray mist. The half lifeless who staggered about were damned and tormented.

Dietrich Rascher was dead. When she grew fuzzy-minded she thought of him. At first she would not accept that he would never return, even after the last letter from Stalingrad. But there would be no miracle.

In the last years, through the agony of Berlin, it was Ernestine who was the one of calm strength in the Falkenstein family. They all looked to her, even her father. She held them together during the bombings, the news of Gerd's capture, the rape by the Russians. But now, Ernestine was unable to keep from plunging into deep smoky pits and mazes.

She came to the Tiergarten; barter market and black market were in full swing.

She stared at ravaged trees and gardens and for a moment in her haze she was once again strolling with father and Dietrich down flower-lined paths and the band was playing Strauss waltzes and the people drank strawberry beer . . . Berlin! Paris on the Spree, the Athens of the East!

She was carried with the moving river of human misery into the subway again. The melancholy that had been running days and nights together closed in on her. She put her face in her hands. The train wheels sang out . . . Dachau . . . Dachau . . . Dachau. . . .

The visions came to her as they came in her terrible dreams: a clear recollection of sullen silences in her law office before the war; there were questions that were not asked; a clear recollection of those long moments of searching her father's eyes when he did not want to look at her; a faint recollection of the names of Jewish playmates; a blurred remembrance of Uncle Ulrich's strange disappearance and of the whispers after the hanging of Uncle Wolfgang.

More than any of it, Ernestine vividly relived those moments when Dietrich Rascher was on leave from the Eastern Front and of his drunken babblings. She remembered the little music box he had given her and a rain-streaked hotel window where they loved . . . she remembered him blurting out the name of Blobel . . . Colonel Blobel . . . Kiev . . . Commandos 4A Special Action Group C!

"Auschwitz station!"

She looked up horrified.

"Grenzalle station," the trainman repeated.

It was a mile to the hospital. The surface transportation was either by ricksha bicycle or horse-drawn street car. The street car was filled beyond capacity, no rickshas around. She walked on foot down Rudower Allee. It was dangerous because it was close to the Russian Sector and oftentimes they crossed over and accosted Germans on the streets, and other Germans were powerless to stop them.

"Hey, fraulein," an American soldier said, blocking her way.

She looked at him. He was young, like Gerd, and he was nervous about trying to pick her up. "Ich have cigaretten . . . and . . . uh . . . chockolade . . ."

"Bitte," she pleaded, and brushed past him quickly.

She was alone on the dead street. Walls of shorn buildings like large fingers hovered above her. With each step, Dietrich Rascher's mumblings beat into her brain.

Then, yesterday she heard it! "This is the People's Radio. We announce a massacre outside Kiev at the pits of Babi Yar. It is now confirmed that 33,000 Jews were gunned down in open pits. It was the work of Colonel Blobel, Special Action Group C!"

Dietrich Rascher! Ernestine struggled up the last three steps to the hospital door. Her eyes rolled back in her head and she toppled to the ground.

No one got excited. This sort of thing happened every few seconds in Berlin these days.

CHAPTER SIX

Even at this moment of self-criticism there was an undeniable air of satisfaction as Heinrich Hirsch reviewed the accomplishments of the German People's Liberation Committee.

Rudi Wöhlman closed his eyes, pressed his fingertips together, and nodded in rhythm to Hirsch's monologue as though he were beating time to music.

The other two Germans present formed the inner circle. There was Adolph Schatz, appointed president of police, and Heinz Eck, appointed deputy mayor of the city.

V. V. Azov sat dull-eyed at the end of the table, in his usual posture of no commitment of pleasure or displeasure.

Heinrich flipped a page. The final tally was that 85 per cent of the Western Sectors were stripped of "war-making" potential before arrival of the British and Americans.

Before the arrival of the West:

A banking monopoly had been established in the Soviet Sector, controlling the finances of the city;

A food ration system was established in five categories. The highest ration was twenty-five hundred calories a day and the lowest twelve hundred. Control of the ration system was in Soviet hands. Use of the ration system was proving an effective way to gain converts. Top rations went to those who cooperated best with the Soviet Union.

Hirsch reviewed the positions of each of the two dozen members of the German People's Liberation Committee, how they moved into pre-selected positions, each holding a key to life.

Hirsch reported that hundreds of other Germans who had been Russian prisoners of war and converted into an "anti-Fascist league" were placed in the school system, the union, the police force.

Adolph Schatz, nominally a German like Rudi Wöhlman, had been with Azov as an officer in the NKVD; now he was president of police with headquarters in the Soviet Sector.

Rudi Wöhlman led the Communist Party, licensed under a thin guise as the People's Proletariat Party. He moved into the city's civic machinery, grabbed the abandoned judiciary, filled the courts with judges from the party. The Berlin Magistrat, the city's executive branch, had some two-dozen departments covering education, welfare, transportation, public works, police. Wöhlman loaded them with Communists. The personnel director of the Magistrat was a member of the German People's Liberation Committee and personnel directors of eighteen of Berlin's twenty boroughs were either Communists or in tune with Wöhlman's directives.

Hirsch reported that a single labor union had been licensed and was under absolute control of the Communists. The union formed "Action Squads" for use in demonstrations and to persuade other workers to stay in line.

Wöhlman's most clever move, however, came in the digging up of the old Democrat, Berthold Hollweg. He was found in a shack on the Teltow Canal, adjudged harmless, and appointed as Oberburgermeister. Hollweg suited an excellent purpose. He still had a name from the old days and could be used as window dressing and "prove" how demo-cratic the Communists were in appointing a non-Communist as lord mayor. Hollweg made a fine figurehead to be controlled by Deputy Mayor Heinz Eck of the German People's Liberation Committee.

Young Hirsch took the post on the Magistrat as secretary of edu-cation and a second post as secretary of culture and information. From here he could control the texts and the teachers. At the university he formed and controlled a student organization on the lines of an Action Squad.

The single radio transmitter in the city was under Hirsch's super-vision.

While the Communists set their roots deeply, entwined their tentacles tightly, the other political parties were in no position to protest. Even after the arrival of the West, they were not permitted a rebuttal in their newspapers for the source of all newsprint was controlled by the Communists.

The German People's Liberation Committee moved in from Moscow with an awesome speed and efficiency. Before the West could get bearings they were faced with the accomplished feat of the police, Magistrat, courts, union, banking, ration, education, information, mayor's office, all under Russian control.

Heinrich Hirsch concluded his report. The West would not be able to get out of the hole. The rules governing the four-power occupation *Kommandatura* saw to that.

When the report was concluded, each of the four discussed the next moves.

They had begun the classic maneuver of infiltrating the other three political parties using both police pressure and the Action Squads.

V. V. Azov was rather pleased. All the planning during the war had paid off. The West had done no planning. The instruments to shove the West out of Berlin were established.

Heinrich Hirsch was told to remain after the others left.

"You sent a note that there was a matter you wished to discuss with me privately, Comrade Hirsch?" Azov asked.

"Comrade," he began with caution, "I must express concern regarding the use of former Nazis, particularly in educational and police posts."

"You are, perhaps, speaking for a group?"

"Only for myself. And only because I feel this is harmful to our aims. Even if we are able to hide the facts from the West, the German people will recognize it. They may tend to doubt our sincerity."

Azov had to be careful not to be drawn into an argument with Hirsch, for he was certainly the most articulate of the Germans. "Tell me," he said, resorting to standard trickery, which Hirsch recognized from years of schooling, "do you know why we are in Berlin?"

"Of course," Hirsch said. "To Sovietize the German people in accordance with Lenin's words that he who controls the German working class controls Europe."

"Now, Comrade Hirsch, why are the Americans and British here?"

"As a symbolic token."

"Ask ten Americans what they are doing in Berlin and you will get ten different answers. Most don't know. However, we do know."

Hirsch became irritated as the dialogue of justification continued.

"If Berlin is not evacuated by the West it will turn into an outpost of spying against us," Azov said. "And the longer they remain the greater the risk of building Germany for a war of revenge."

"How do we serve our purpose by stocking our own bins with Nazis?"

Azov smiled, and kept walking around a trap. "This question has been pondered by the Politburo of the Communist Party, by Comrade Stalin, by our great dialecticians. We realize that the Nazis are so deep in every phase of German life that we cannot carry on normal functions without using them. At the moment, the West is our greatest enemy. You yourself worked at persuading German prisoners over to the anti-Fascist bloc."

"Using common soldiers and officers is one thing. Using SS men and hiding wanted Nazi war criminals is another."

Hirsch was neither to be convinced nor bullied. He was adamant.

"Many Nazis," Azov said, "are truly repentant about their past. They have seen the light through Communism."

They have saved their asses through Communism! Anger began to gnaw at Hirsch. He knew now he had to keep his tongue from wagging further. The whole sordid business was becoming a windfall for hundreds of Nazis all over the Soviet Zone. If the Nazi could be of use, there was a simple formality to purge him of his past. The Russians knew they would be willing workers for the Communists for their past records were held over their heads as blackmail.

Azov saw the young man was backing off, and applied the final wisdoms. "We who believe in world Communism must overlook a few injustices in the light of the over-all aspirations."

Heinrich's eyes flashed black. Those were Hitler's words and the Nazis' excuse to justify criminal behavior and genocide. But what was so different? Hadn't the Soviet Union always found an excuse for purges, deportations, privations? Hadn't the excuse always been that it was justified for the great goal? Hirsch packed his notes quickly and left.

The exchange continued to annoy the commissar. He knew that Heinrich Hirsch was disciplined to realize the consequences of challenging a Moscow decision. But Hirsch had done the same thing earlier in protesting the removal of war reparations and he knew Hirsch had gone to Marshal Popov regarding the behavior of the Red Army upon entering Berlin.

Azov wondered what this strange blind spot was in the man that gave him the effrontery to break party discipline.

For a long time he had sensed this flaw in Hirsch's character, felt he gave too much loyalty to being a German. He smelled that Hirsch was groping for independent German thought and action. This touched upon the two cardinal sins of nationalism and deviationism.

Yet, Azov was reluctant to take measures against him. He was the most brilliant member of the German Liberation Committee—Adolph Schatz was a clod and a bully, Heinz Eck a pawn. Rudi Wöhlman was clever and a good organizer but never added new ideas for he was determined only to please and to stay out of controversy.

But Hirsch had ingenuity, was sharp in analyzing the West, was brilliant. Yet, the damned blind spot was there, a flaw in his strain. He is half Jew, Azov thought, all Jew by character. Stalin had an uncommon suspicion of Jews. Azov recalled many a night he was summoned to Stalin's villa and handed a list of Jews to purge. Stalin had an intuition about Jews. But, for the time, Hirsch was needed.

Heinrich Hirsch ordered his chauffeur to drive him to People's Proletariat Party Headquarters.

He damned himself for not holding his mouth. The entire discussion was an invitation to receive a knock on the door in the middle of the night. Yet, he was unable to contain himself, even with party discipline drilled into him for a decade. . . . They were pardoning the men who had murdered his beloved father.

CHAPTER SEVEN

Ernestine blinked open her eyes. A wind blew at the canvas patch over the broken wall. Hilde sat on a wooden crate before a small mirror. Ernestine watched her sister pull on a silk stocking, holding out her slender leg to admire its shapeliness.

Hilde spotted Ernestine watching her through the mirror, turned, and said, "Good morning. How do you feel? Any better?"

"I'm fine," Ernestine said.

"You don't look so fine. You screamed again in the middle of the night."

"I am sorry I disturbed you."

"I'm getting used to it," Hilde snapped. "Why don't you put on a little makeup. The circles under your eyes would not show so much."

"It does not matter."

Hilde sighed, tossed down her lipstick, regretted her sharpness. She sat alongside the bed she shared now with Ernestine, ran her fingers through her sister's hair. "It's this living on top of each other. Erna, you're your own worst enemy. Dr. Hahn has said so. You take life too grimly."

"There is nothing to be joyful about in Berlin."

"Fine, so make the best of it." Hilde returned to the mirror.

"Hilde," Ernestine said. "I want to talk to you about the things in your trunk."

The younger girl was startled.

"It was by accident," Ernestine said. "I was looking for your red sweater to borrow. The lock was open. Besides, where does one hide a trunk, or anything, in this place? Where did you get cigarettes, chocolates . . . those stockings?"

"I made contact with some old friends."

"I am your sister, Hilde. I will not be set aside."

"All right."

"We have been taught right from wrong."

Hilde laughed bitterly. "There is no right and wrong in this place. There is only survival."

"No matter what has happened, we still have our decency."

"Decent? Are we decent? Have we ever been?"

"Hilde, you are getting yourself into serious trouble. There is no justice today, not even from the Amis."

Hilde shrugged, and flipped the powder box shut. "Your baby sister gets around. You could also make life easier for yourself."

"Easy? It only looks easy."

"Have it your way, Ernestine. I'll leave something to eat for you on the table. Dr. Hahn should be here soon."

"Hilde! You are only twenty years old. It is too soon to give up on life."

"It seems that you are the one who has given up. I'm just trying to get along with a bad situation. Erna, you will promise me you won't say anything to father about the trunk."

"I promise," her sister whispered in defeat.

"You're a dear." Hilde leaned over, kissed Ernestine's cheek, and went out of the alcove.

In a few moments old Dr. Hahn arrived. "Well, how is the patient today?"

"I am afraid I am causing everyone a lot of trouble."

He creaked to her bedside, pinched her drawn cheek. "If I could only put a little color back into that pretty face. Are the sleeping powders helping you?"

"For part of the night."

The drugs had been obtained on the black market at great cost. He would find more, somehow. "I don't want to keep you using it. It is bad to start at your age."

Ernestine looked up to the same old grizzly face she remembered from earliest childhood. It seemed to her that Dr. Hahn was born old. She knew the touch of his hand as he examined her and she knew the familiar grunts of his meditation. He pulled the covers back over her shoulders, slipped the stethoscope from his ears.

"I am not going to lecture you, young lady. But you cannot get better until you help yourself."

He packed his instruments into a battered bag, rummaged through for his almost diminished supply of drugs, and refilled a bottle at her bedside.

"Ernestine, someone came with me today. I want you to see him."

"Who?"

"Your Uncle Ulrich."

She rolled away, turning her back. "No," she said shakily.

He went out into the hallway where Ulrich Falkenstein had waited. The two men had known each other for nearly three decades. Hahn shook his head. "Physically, she is in weak condition. Not enough to eat, overwork. It is the same as everyone in Berlin. Yet, I do not believe she is ill enough to be in bed."

"I am told by her mother that she lies there day after day and that she screams in her sleep."

"My dear Herr Falkenstein. Yesterday, the Amis released the information that they, along with the British, dropped seventy-five thousand tons of bombs on Berlin in forty days of continuous air raids at

the end. She has been brutally raped by Russian soldiers. Her fiancé is
dead and her brother is in a prison camp. Anything she has ever known
of a normal life is gone. The illness that afflicts her is mental exhaustion."

"Is that a reason for her to refuse to see me?"

"Have you not noticed, Ulrich, when someone speaks to you they do
as I. They look into the shadows on your right or left, but never into
your eyes. To some of us you are the mirror of German conscience, the
living reminder of what we have done."

"I have had a long time to wonder, Dr. Hahn, who are the guilty? I
cannot blame her for the Nazis."

"Nor can you keep her from blaming herself. The true guilty draw
a curtain on the past. The most innocent assume the guilt. Unfortunately there are too few Germans like that girl."

"I must go to her," Ulrich said.

"Be careful."

Ernestine heard him come in and cringed into the folds of the bedding.

"Ernestine," he said.

"Please go, Uncle."

"Ernestine." He reached out and touched the girl and she began to
sob softly. "You must turn around and look at me now." His hands
were firm. He dried her tears. There were large black circles beneath
her eyes.

"Is it true?" she asked.

"It is true."

She slumped back. "I am so ashamed," she whispered. "Dietrich . . .
shot them down in cold blood. I loved him. He shot them down in cold
blood."

"You did not know, child."

"Because I did not want to know. No one could have lived in Berlin
in these years and not know." It was not so hard as she believed to look
at her uncle. At the moment it seemed a burden was lifting.

"Every German must face the past before he can face the future.
Otherwise, there can be no redemption. You have taken the first cruel
step, my child, and tomorrow you must start all over again."

She reached for his hand and pressed it to her cheek.

"You can sleep now," he said.

CHAPTER EIGHT

Neal Hazzard, American commandant, was the most gregarious of the brass and the best-known occupation officer in the city. The Berliners loved his gruff bravado, his showing up at rubble-clearing sites, in beer halls, schools, union meetings, churches. Mostly he traveled alone and unarmed, a distinction in Berlin.

From the start the rules of the four-power Berlin Kommandatura were stacked against the West by the presence of a veto. He was compelled to accept all the Russian entrenchments before American arrival.

Even though Hazzard operated in a deep hole, he took a personal liking to the Russian Sector commandant, Colonel Nikolai Trepovitch, who, like himself, was from the ranks and had held fighting commands. Trepovitch was the most outgoing of the Russians, having a sparkling pixyish sense of humor.

However, the meetings of the Kommandatura often as not turned into a nightmare, with translations and conversations going in senseless circles for hours. What would, on the surface, appear to be a routine matter could suddenly turn a session into hairsplitting, bickering, and endless dialogue. Trepovitch and his deputies could haggle for hours and neither Hazzard nor the other Western commandants knew from one time to the next what the Russians had in store.

Hazzard realized that Trepovitch was allowed little room for flexible thinking, having to carry out his directions to the letter. He never pressed the Russian when he knew he could not give; Trepovitch appreciated it.

Hazzard was unable to achieve this silent rapport with the British colleague, Colonel T. E. Blatty, who would argue for hours for no other purpose than to keep the game by the rules. The Englishman, a classical officer, would never anger, never raise his voice, never become vexed. His endurance was the antidote to Trepovitch's ponderous attacks.

The fourth member of the Kommandatura was Colonel Jacques Belfort. Trepovitch made the Frenchman aware that his country's presence in Berlin was more of a gesture than a reality. The friction between these two was the most obvious. Belfort made up in sheer pride what he lacked in actual power, and it was his intent to make himself conspicuous for the sake of French prestige.

On certain issues the Russian would not budge. Attempts to regulate the currency with closer four-power control, attempts to liberalize the courts, quit the use of rations for political control, all met with filibuster and evasion.

On other matters the four worked together rather well. Housing was the worst of any civilized city in modern history, and worsened by the occupation powers requisitioning the best of what remained.

There was universal cooperation in the field of public health where mass inoculations tried to stem a rampage of typhus, typhoid, and diphtheria. The mushrooming incidence of tuberculosis, the terrible dysentery, and venereal disease taxed the medical facilities of all four powers.

The number of hospital beds was a third of prewar level and much equipment had been carted off by the Russians as reparations. The four powers set up joint garbage removal, sewage treatment, and other crash programs to head off epidemic.

Transportation was crippled in the broken city. There were no private German automobiles, buses, or taxis. Many chunks of the elevated were down and sections of the underground flooded in the last days of the fighting. Hundreds of rail cars had been shipped off to the Soviet Union. Traffic was perilous because of collapsing walls and half the streets were blocked by debris. Ricksha bikes and a few trams drawn by horses were a poor supplement in the gigantic area of nearly four hundred square miles. Berlin had an extensive canal system and an inland harbor and more bridges than Venice. Half of them were twisted into the Spree and Havel rivers, blocking the barges. The West Harbor was a shambles.

The phone system and the telegraph system collapsed. The Russians had carted off what was left of the switchboards, telephone instruments, generators. They had to be built from the ground up.

Before the war the power plant near the West Harbor was used only to augment during peak hours. The plant had been stripped of generators by the Russians and only part of the shell of the building remained. Neal Hazzard was faced with another accomplished fact . . . the power for the city was entirely supplied by the Soviet Union. Ironically, much of the power came through lines from Saxony and Thuringia, the provinces surrendered by the Americans.

A subcommittee of the Kommandatura began the arduous task of de-Nazifying 30,000 postal employees to restore some kind of mail service.

Most of the other utilities were gone. Some gas was being restored.

The city was patrolled by squad cars usually holding one soldier from each of the occupation countries. It was an outward show of unity for the Berliners.

Dozens upon dozens of orders were signed by the Kommandatura and passed along to the Berlin Magistrat for action.

While cooperation existed on many matters, Neal Hazzard slowly, with great determination, chipped away at the Russian entrenchment in other directions. Colonel Trepovitch, alone among the Russians, realized how enormously persistent the American was.

Hazzard put top priority on the selection of a deputy police president who would be more cooperative to the West; Adolph Schatz was owned by the Russians. Nothing could change this since all appointments before Western arrival had to be accepted.

Hazzard was not without recourse. New appointments had to be approved by all four powers. He was in a position to hold up Trepovitch's appointments until they gave him his deputy police president.

The finding of the German to fill the job went to Sean O'Sullivan's trouble-shooting unit, a little group of a dozen men without portfolio or official designation. They filtered intelligence reports, watched straws in the wind, prepared data for Hansen on the Supreme German Council and for Hazzard in the Kommandatura, made predictions, acted as liaison between Berlin and the rest of Germany, and performed innumerable special details. Sean and his unit were in and out of Berlin daily, apt to show up anywhere on unique missions.

Neal Hazzard read the report pulled by the unit recommending Hans Kronbach for the position as deputy police president. His record seemed immaculate. Kronbach had been chief of detectives for the city of Berlin. He resigned in protest after Hitler came into power and went into private business, buying out a small-parts factory. He had no known involvement with the Nazis. At the end of the war three former slave laborers in his plant came forward to volunteer testimony to the treatment they received. Further, Kronbach had saved a number of lives and hidden a number of Jews. The war bombed his factory out in the last days.

Currently he worked as a plainclothesman on a black-market squad in Prenzlauer Berg Borough.

Hazzard set the report down, looked at Sean and Blessing. "What kind of a cop did you make him out to be in your interview, Bless?"

"Nothing he doesn't know about police work. Knows how to supervise men, do administrative work, the whole business. I'd take him on my force in Hook County in two minutes."

"How did he impress you, Sean?"

"He's pro-West, no doubt about that. A Democrat by affiliation. I don't think we can own him. He's got a mind of his own. German first."

"A good one," Blessing said.

"We're not looking for a stooge like Schatz," Hazzard said. "One thing bothers me about Kronbach. Until the last two months, he hasn't done any police work for a decade. The Russkies will lean on him, hard."

Blessing smiled. "Took a hell of a lot more guts to stay out of the Nazi police than it did to collaborate."

"Good enough," Hazzard said. "I'll get ahold of Blatty to put his nomination on the agenda tomorrow. Bless, find him, tell him what we're up to."

"Yes, sir. You going to be able to push his nomination through?"

"May take ten hours. I'll just have to wear Trepovitch down."

"Damned if I see how you can stand them meetings, Colonel."

"I can't," Hazzard answered.

CHAPTER NINE

Blessing left the meeting with full instructions to find Hans Kronbach and get him moved into the American Sector that night.

He called for his patrol jeep, stood on the steps of the Headquarters building, and paused for a moment as the sun set. The flag hung limply; greenery had been renewed about the building; it was a nice time of day.

Across the boulevard two young German girls walked in slow, dull unison, their heels sounding on the pavement. He took off his hat, wiped the inside of the band, and squinted at them.

Eveningtime brought the girls out on the streets. They prowled the American Headquarters, the woods behind and the barrack area was a good place for a quick trick. Blessing thought most of them had little choice but to hustle. They had real hunger in their stomachs and many had kids and old people to keep alive. Bad business to whore to stay alive.

Nonfraternization was still on paper, but it had never really worked. It was dragged out once in a while to pacify a visiting congressman or clergyman. Sometimes, women's clubs in the States put up a stink. Colonel Hazzard was ordered to make an "example" awhile back. The first two he got his hands on were a pair of respected judges working in his legal section. Hazzard made them go off hard liquor for a month as punishment. They got so stoned on bad wine he relented at the end of the week.

Bless remembered how he handled it in Hook County. He warned the roadhouses to keep their noses clean and police themselves. Whoring was all right as long as the girls didn't cadge drinks, clip, and kept being examined for VD. Hell, a miner on payday has to have a woman . . . so does a soldier. So does a cop, for that matter, he thought. Bless had been without a woman for a long time. No one thought a fat jolly cop needed a woman like everyone else.

Police work had taught him to mask fear, act impassive to tragedy. The dark side of the world, its hardness, and its misery was just part of a day's work.

Bless knew there was a souring point that came to a lot of cops. When a man gets too callous he can turn into a cynic or a brute.

The two German girls reached the corner, turned, and retraced their steps.

Damn, I'd like to see Lil! He smiled at the thought of his wife. She is a good ole' gal. And she still cuts a fine picture of a woman.

Lil had come out of the hill country, knew nothing but hard times all her life. When she was sixteen she married a bastard just to escape. Used to beat hell out of her. Lil ran away.

Bless knew a woman like her, with all she'd been through, wasn't going to go playing around, because she had a good man who treated her square. He and Lil had something wonderful going for them and two of their own . . . cutest kids in Hook County.

Such a long time. He wondered how many times Lil needed to have a man in the past two and a half years. She was human and a lot of woman. Bless knew she would go about it in the right way. She'd go off to Memphis for a week, where nobody knew her, and she'd be damned careful. He would never ask her about it because it wouldn't mean a damned thing.

A radio jeep with constabulary markings was driven up by one of Blessing's squad, Corporal Danny Sterling. The kid was going to make a good cop, Bless thought, switching his mind back to duty and piling into the jeep.

"Where to, Lieutenant?"

Blessing pondered. Contacting Hans Kronbach was not a simple matter. He was in the Russian Sector so Bless would have to dig up a German informer and send him out as a liaison to set up a secret rendezvous.

"Let's go over to the provost marshal at Tempelhof and find us a kraut fink."

Danny gunned the jeep away. The two German girls watched cautiously as the police jeep passed them. Blessing whistled softly "Just Before the Battle, Mother."

The pressure of Berlin was reaching him. He wanted out of the rat hole before he went sour. There was suspicion in the Germans . . . there was hatred, fear, and tension. He knew by long experience the face and the actions of desperation, for he had read it in the sallow, pinched faces of the farmers when their crops were wiped out and their kids went hungry. He had seen it at the mines in the mass hysteria of the strikers as they cursed the scabs, and he had seen it at the mines in the eyes of the women waiting for the news of a cave-in.

He had seen it in the eyes of lynch mobs; he knew it in the faces of the Negroes of Hook County. All of this was the face of Berlin.

Bless picked up the microphone, switched on the transmitter. "Rebel two-eight reporting, over."

"This is Baltimore calling Rebel two-eight. Who's that man making big gains for Green Bay?"

"Don Hutson," Blessing answered, assuring the authenticity of his call. "We are leaving Baltimore en route to Atlanta Provo, over."

"Roger, and out."

As they passed out of slightly damaged Dahlem, heavy with American Headquarters and barracks, the horror of Berlin was worsened by block after block, mile after mile of gutted shells. They were slowed to a halt by demolition work near the canal.

As they cleared they saw a German policeman running down the middle of the street waving and calling frantically. They halted. He stopped beside them, gasping, jabbering too quickly for them to understand.

"Was gibt's?"

The German pointed, tried to make himself understood, then remembered the cards he carried in his pockets. He brought out a stack, each holding a single word: RAPE, ASSAULT, ACCIDENT. He stopped at the card reading ARMED ROBBERY, and kept pointing to it.

"Russkies?"

"Ya, ya, Russkies."

"Now what the hell they doing all the way over here," Bless grunted, shoving the German into the jeep and picking up the mike. "This is Rebel two-eight calling, over."

"This is Baltimore. Go ahead Rebel two-eight."

"We are proceeding to investigate a sixty-four now taking place vicinity Südende. We think there are Ivans involved. Will report exact location when I have it, over."

"Roger, we'll move in your direction."

Baltimore sent out a call for a half-dozen other cars to converge on the general area.

The German policeman stopped them before the Südende S-Bahn elevated station. He pointed up to the platform. Blessing told the German to stay put. It was a situation with occupation troops and he was not permitted to interfere. Moreover, he was unarmed. "Danny, call in our exact location, then back me up."

Blessing took the steps two at a time, stopped at the far end of the platform. Twenty-five yards away, three Russian soldiers had herded a dozen Germans against the cashier's window and were stripping wallets, taking wrist watches, rummaging through handbags.

He understood the situation instantly—two did the looting, the third held the Germans at bay with a submachine gun. He heard Danny run up the steps behind him, turned, and motioned him to freeze.

Bless walked toward the Russian with the submachine gun. "Tovarich!" The Russians saw him for the first time, like startled deer. "Nyet, nyet, American Sector."

The Russian with the submachine gun recovered his senses, waved Blessing back. The big cop kept moving forward, pointed his thumb east. "Russian Sector . . . go."

A spray of bullets erupted at his feet!

Blessing smiled, held his arms apart in friendly greeting, and as though he were a defenseless cub, walked toward the amazed Russian. The soldier shoved the barrel into Blessing's stomach. In a lightning move he disarmed the Russian, knocking him flat on his back.

The other two reached for their pistols.

"Nyet!" Bless cried.

They continued to draw. Two shots barked from Blessing's .45. Two Russians toppled over. The third had jumped up and fled down the railroad track as Danny tore up the stairs firing.

The Germans screamed and scuttled away from the pools of blood forming on the deck.

Bless heaved a great sigh, wiped the sweat from his face, and replaced his pistol. "Let him go," he said to Danny. "All right, calm down, calm down, it's all over. Any of you people speak English?"

"Ya, I do."

"There is a German officer at the foot of the steps. Get him up here. I want him to record everyone's name and address and the story of what happened. Tell these people they will be informed where they can claim their possessions."

"Thank you, sir."

"Calm down now. It's all over."

Bless knelt and turned one of the Russians over. The shot had been true, through the heart. The other one was a grotesque sight, a bullet through his face.

They could hear the sirens of support cars.

"Ambulance?" Danny said, fighting off sickness.

"They're both dead," Blessing answered. "And the damned fool thing about it is I know they were bluffing. They got to learn if they go for their guns to use them."

Bless leaned against the building, and bit his lip hard. "You okay, Lieutenant?"

"Yeah . . . . I'm okay."

CHAPTER TEN

Neal Hazzard arrived at the two-story Kommandatura building in Dahlem fifteen minutes before the general session was due to begin for a special meeting with T. E. Blatty, the chairman for the month.

T. E. Blatty, always the perfect gentleman, tall, sandy, well-groomed, arrived a moment later, and as he passed into the confines the Union Jack was raised on the second of four masts, and a British sentry took a post next to the American already posted there.

The two commandants met in Blatty's office.

"I want to take the nomination of Hans Kronbach off today's agenda," Hazzard said.

"You seemed quite keen on the chap when you telephoned me and I think he would be good for us."

"It has nothing to do with Kronbach. Two Russian soldiers were killed by us last evening. They were caught in the middle of an armed robbery."

"I heard rumors of it."

"It's a lead-pipe cinch Trepovitch is going to blow his top. Today is not the day to push for the nomination of a deputy police president."

"Speaking quite frankly," the Englishman answered, "you're making it a bit awkward, are you not? We can never expect to establish order if we jigger the agenda around every ten minutes."

Neal Hazzard stifled an impulse to wring Blatty's neck. "Hans Kronbach is too important for us to lose. Just don't make a federal case out of this and let things cool down before I put his name up."

"See here, Hazzard, I'm only trying to run the show properly. Once we impress the Russians that we play the game by the rules through thick and thin they're not so apt to bugger us around."

"For Christ's sake. We're not on the goddam sporting fields of Eton."

"Well!"

"I mean, close your eyes this once."

"If you insist, Colonel Hazzard, but I act under duress."

Hazzard sighed with relief. "I'll return the favor."

The tricolor of France was raised on the third flag pole as Colonel Jacques Belfort arrived. They all met on the first floor in the main conference room around a square table, with seats behind theirs for advisors and translators.

At precisely nine o'clock Colonel Nikolai Trepovitch arrived with a bevy of staff following him. Hazzard watched the Russian carefully. His face was frozen in a cold glare, he was sullen, and there was an absence of greeting. Hazzard knew it was going to be a long, hard day.

Trepovitch nodded curtly to the chairman, Blatty, sat, adjusted his glasses, unloaded his briefcase, and picked up the agenda.

"This session is called to order," the Englishman said. "We have a request to remove from the agenda the nomination of a deputy police president." He looked at Hazzard. "This is a unilateral action of the Americans. Do I hear an objection?"

Trepovitch's interpreter buzzed into his ear and pointed to the agenda. To Hazzard this was another bad sign, for Trepovitch's English was better than passable when he so desired. He had a knack of forgetting English in order to force slow, tortuous translations.

Blatty continued. "The first order of business will be to continue discussion on a subcommittee report regarding the removal of Berlin's dairy herd by the Soviet Union before our arrival in the city. The vote stands three to one that we should not be compelled to replace the herd, that being the duty of the Soviet Union. Whereas," Blatty droned on, "we have agreed to feed our sectors, an original source of food has been deliberately removed in the Soviet act of spiriting 7000 cows away. Speaking for His Majesty's Government as well as the American and French governments, it is our position that the Soviet Union owes us 5000 cows . . ."

"Last night," Nikolai Trepovitch began as though he had not heard a word the Englishman said, "two soldiers of the Soviet Union were murdered."

"I say, Colonel Trepovitch, you are most out of order."

"They were shot down in cold blood by American aggressors."

"We are discussing the dairy herd, sir."

"The guilty murderers are to be found, full restitution made to their grieving families, and a public apology is to be rendered to the Soviet Union."

"There is a proper place allotted on the agenda for the discussion of emergency contingencies. In due course we shall examine your charges."

"This was an arrogant murder of two soldiers of the Soviet Union who fought the Nazis with valor only to be slaughtered in the streets by American police brutality."

Thus far, Neal Hazzard had kept a slight smile on his lips, and had otherwise remained expressionless.

"See here, now," Blatty answered, "you simply cannot twist the agenda about because you are in a fit of pique. It is not done."

The Russian brought his fist on the table. "There is no other order of business until this is settled!"

"Sir, is it the position of the Soviet Union that you refuse to allow the business of this body to proceed?"

The fist fell again.

"As chairman of the Kommandatura, I shall not submit to threats or highhanded methods. Now then, if you are finished pounding on the table, we will continue to examine the question of the dairy herd."

"Is it your position then to protect paid murderers?" Trepovitch broke into an impassioned speech filled with such names as warmongers, fascist bullies, gangsters, lynchers. Within moments the translators were unable to keep up and the translation broke down. Trepovitch didn't mind. He ranted on, alone.

Blatty waited until he had spent his passion. "Inasmuch as Colonel Trepovitch refuses to recognize the orderly procedures and is attempting to submit us to anarchy, I adjourn this council."

The Russian jumped to his feet, pointed a finger at Blatty, and further accused him of covering the American crime. He snapped out orders to subordinates, and began to stuff his briefcase. The obvious threat of a walkout existed.

"Gentlemen," Neal Hazzard said, uttering his first words, "I am completely willing to waive the other order of business to take up the Soviet Union's charges."

"That is commendable," the French commandant said quickly, "and in keeping with the spirit of working together."

"Sporting gesture," Blatty said, "but if we permit this we would be endorsing chaos."

Son of a bitch, Hazzard thought. Between the two of them, you could go nuts. Blatty was so adamant he would even allow a disastrous Soviet walkout.

"I'd like a vote," Hazzard said.

"I will veto if I am outvoted," Blatty warned.

Hazzard had guessed that part of Trepovitch's tirade was pure play acting, but the Englishman was genuine in his stodginess.

"Yes or no?" Trepovitch demanded.

"Sir! Does His Majesty's Government take that to be an ultimatum!" The Russian continued with the business of preparing to walk out.

"I propose a ten-minute recess," Jacques Belfort said.

It was stiffly agreed to by all parties.

When the session reconvened, T. E. Blatty made a final stubborn retreat. "Inasmuch as I am rotating the chairmanship to my French colleague tomorrow and inasmuch as Colonel Hazzard voices no objections, I will recognize a change in the agenda provided that Colonel Trepovitch places his proposition in the form of a request rather than a demand."

Face had been saved.

"It is a request," Trepovitch agreed. He replaced his glasses, sat, unloaded his briefcase.

"You heard the charges, Colonel Hazzard. Are you prepared to answer?"

Hazzard nodded, looked over his shoulder to Lieutenant Bolinski, who had the crash job of investigating the case and preparing the report overnight. Bo sat beside Hazzard and read slowly.

"Three soldiers of the Soviet occupation forces were intercepted in the act of committing armed robbery against a dozen German civilians at the Südende elevated station at approximately 1630 yesterday evening. An American peace officer arrived on the scene and attempted to dissuade the Soviet soldiers and to have them return to their sector. One of the Soviet soldiers fired several shots at the feet of the American peace officer from a submachine gun, and further menaced him to a point where the American peace officer had no choice but to disarm him and otherwise defend himself. The other two Soviet soldiers reached for their side arms against the advice of the American peace officer, and when they refused to comply were shot dead."

"A fabric of lies!"

Bolinski placed a sheaf of papers on the desk. "These are the supporting statements of the twelve German civilians and a German police officer."

"The Soviet Union will never accept the testimony of fascist liars. I demand to interrogate the aggressor you are hiding."

"Colonel Trepovitch," Hazzard said, "one of your people escaped. He should be easy enough to find. He's most likely in the same unit as the two men who were killed. If you will produce him, we will produce our peace officer."

Trepovitch changed the subject. "Do we kill your soldiers? Are they not all welcome in the Soviet Sector? What about your black marketeers with their cigarettes? Do we send them back in coffins?"

Hazzard knew now that Trepovitch really did not want an investigation but satisfaction. He answered deliberately. "According to rules adopted by this body we categorized major and minor crimes of our occupation forces. Petty black-marketeering and the breaking of non-fraternization are in a misdemeanor category. However, rape, murder, armed robbery, and assault are considered by this Kommandatura as major crimes." He nodded to Bolinski, who was now proving to be a walking fact sheet.

"In the last sixty days," Bolinski said, "we have arrested or apprehended six hundred Soviet soldiers in the American Sector. Over five hundred of these arrests resulted with us taking back your soldiers to your sector for drunk or disorderly conduct. However, we have made a hundred arrests in the major crime category and have, in addition, another hundred German complaints of unsolved cases. To date no American soldier has been arrested in the Russian Sector for rape, armed robbery, or murder."

Trepovitch turned hot under the collar. "We've been damned patient," Neal Hazzard said. "It is a miracle that more of your people haven't been killed. This homicide was in self-defense and entirely justified. Your people are going to have to learn that six boroughs of Berlin are under protection of the American flag."

The Frenchman sensed that Trepovitch had been paid back double. "I suggest that a neutral committee of ourselves and the British investigate the charges."

"Neutral! You are both hirelings of the Americans!"

This brought the expected outburst from both Blatty and the Frenchman.

Hazzard knew the Russian was being pressed too far. The points had been won and a face-saving settlement was all that was needed. "Gentlemen," he shouted over the oratory, "inasmuch as this matter concerns ourselves and the Soviet Union, I suggest that we be allowed to work it out ourselves."

These were the right words at the right moment.

The Kommandatura returned to the business of Berlin's missing dairy herd, and, after four hours of argument, ended in a deadlock.

Later that evening they all met with their staffs at the French Head-quarters, the Napoleon Quarters, for the banquet traditionally given by the outgoing chairman. This month, however, the French were to take their first turn as chairman and Colonel Belfort was allowed the honors.

The Americans gave the most austere of the receptions, the Russians the most lavish. British liquor was excellent although the food poorly prepared.

Now, Jacques Belfort was determined to give Trepovitch a run for his money. The spread was lavish and flanked with the finest French wines and champagnes. All was harmony again. There were toasts to Allied unity and brotherhood.

Colonel Trepovitch, whose English had deserted him earlier, found it again. He cornered Neal Hazzard as the entertainment got under way.

"Confidentially," the Russian said, "we are not so concerned with the shootings. There are some ruffled feathers in our command."

Hazzard nodded. It was an opening gambit for some down to earth horse trading. A platter of *pâté de fois gras*, France's answer to Trepovitch's pounds of caviar, passed between them.

The Russian continued. "A note from the Americans would smooth a lot of things out, particularly to the Germans."

"A note might be possible."

"In exchange for approval of the nomination of Hans Kronbach?" Trepovitch said.

"Quite likely."

What Hazzard did not know was that a quick line was drawn on Kronbach by the Russians. Hirsch, Wöhlman, Eck, and Schatz all struck an attitude that anyone who was as anti-Nazi as Kronbach was automatically sympathetic to the Soviet Union. In their basic philosophy, the West and the Nazis were similar inasmuch as both were enemies of the Soviet Union. Kronbach was anti-Nazi and, therefore, pro-Soviet.

Trepovitch passed on Hans Kronbach's appointment to deputy police president. Neal Hazzard read a note regretting the death of the Russian soldiers.

A new attitude of respect was visible by the behavior of Russian soldiers visiting the American Sector. Russian crime halted.

The surprise at the next meeting of the Kommandatura was not the quick agreement, but that Nikolai Trepovitch returned promoted to the rank of brigadier general, a notch higher than his Western counterparts. The meaning was obvious.

CHAPTER ELEVEN

On the highways, the rail lines, the canal ways into Berlin the warning was posted: KEEP OUT OF BERLIN! BERLIN IS FORBIDDEN!

The hundreds of thousands of refugees pouring east to west and west to east in search of homes and loved ones were steered wide of the prostrate city. It was said that a crow flying over Berlin would have to carry his own provisions.

Winter chilled the air. The cold brought new terrors as the great forests of the city dropped their leaves and the waters of her seventeen lakes danced under wind-whipped whitecaps. It was that time of year when heavy gray clouds looked eternal and sleet and snow poured from their misery.

Schools and factories closed, transportation froze to an agonized trickle. The old died in bed of freezing and the young lay under piles of rags and papers in numbed confusion.

Berlin was a spawning ground for those who lived best in slime and who moved best in shadows. . . . Hildegaard Falkenstein was drawn to them.

It began, innocently enough, with an accidental meeting of an old schoolmate, Elke Handfest, who had also been in her troop of Hitler Youth.

Before the war Elke was remembered by Hildegaard as plump, acned, and homely. Elke covered her physical misfortunes with a riotous sense of humor with which she played out the part of a buffoon. Her humor was a defense created out of sorrow, but proved of great value later.

Elke's search for love taught her that, as a woman, there were things men wanted from her and many would overlook her appearance if she supplied the commodity liberally.

In the wild years of the war, Elke Handfest plunged from one affair to another. Although she looked quite presentable now, her humor had deepened to a morbid and scathing kind of self-damnation. She had been forced into sex for recognition; she had never received happiness from it. The more she tried to find its pleasure, the more it eluded her, the more it all became distasteful. And she drifted powerfully toward her own sex and began to find it fulfilling.

When the Amis dispossessed the Falkenstein family from their Dahlem home, chance placed them near where Elke lived with her aged and helpless parents.

At first meeting Elke was excited by Hilde's beauty and encouraged a renewal of their friendship. Little by little, Elke revealed tangible evidences of good fortune.

"Elke! Where did you get this Ami cigarette?"

"Just enjoy it."

"I insist on knowing."

"Where does anyone get anything these days?"

"The black market?"

"No. More of an exchange market."

"Elke, stop teasing me. I've smelled your perfume and I've drunk real coffee and tasted real butter."

"I have good friends. Perhaps some day I will introduce you to them."

"Today."

"You were always jealous of anyone having anyone or anything you didn't."

"It's been so long, Elke."

Maybe long enough, Elke thought. Maybe she is hungry enough to want these things. "I must think about it, Hilde. Why don't we visit in a few days and I'll let you know."

Hildegaard thought of it too; she thought of little else . . . cigarettes, coffee, silk underwear. Elke's luxuries gnawed at her innards.

Elke, too, thought of little else. She appraised her own situation with murderous objectivity. She was neither as beautiful as Hilde nor even very pretty. The competition among women in Berlin was growing unbelievable. The first harbingers of winter pushed more and more out on the streets. Elke wondered how long she could last under the competition.

The physical beauty of Hilde thrilled her, but she knew she had to approach that with care. First, she had to let Hilde's greed trap her.

Then she would train Hilde carefully. With a partner like Hildegaard Falkenstein and her own connections she could make her life last much longer. Her fulfillment with Hilde would come later.

"So, you are still interested in knowing my friends?"

"Yes."

"It is a matter of taking dates with occupation soldiers."

"You mean, sleep with them."

Elke shrugged. "It is better than working on a rubble pile. Besides, I have my parents to keep alive."

"Do you . . . walk the streets?"

"Of course not. That is for the old hens. I have one of the best connections in Berlin to arrange my dates."

Hildegaard pondered it for days. Elke Handfest lived well under the circumstances, better than her own struggling family, even with Uncle Ulrich's help. A few times Hilde tried to work but found it dreary and impossible.

Elke's proposition presented moral aspects against her teaching, but morality in such times was a flexible item. Almost everyone was doing something to live that they would not do in normal times. Hilde rationalized that having dates arranged with occupation soldiers was not the same as being a common whore. It even had a ring of respectability. And, if Elke did well, she could do better.

Hilde remembered her own experiences before the Mongol soldiers raped her. The first time she had sex, she was just fifteen. It was encouraged in Hitler Youth as not only honorable but a highly patriotic duty to bear a baby. Illegitimacy did not exist in the Third Reich. In this intense nationalistic atmosphere she and a boy, whose name and face she could hardly recall, decided to try it out with each other.

There was a week-long encampment of Hitler Youth in the Berlin State Forest on the Müggel Lake. They arranged a rendezvous in the woods in much the same way as dozens of other couples.

The boy was awkward and fumbling and caused her pain. He cried afterward because he had done so badly. All she got from it was disgust and anger. He was a stupid clod, like most men.

There was a second experience during the war when Hildegaard realized true womanhood. Berlin, before the big bombings, was a place of gaiety and excitement and a bit of madness. A young submarine officer on leave, named Sigi, pursued her with wild, heady abandon and made her forget the other unpleasant experience.

Hilde cared for him . . . well, for a while, anyhow. When his leave was over and he returned to his submarine she forgot him almost completely . . . at once. His whining letters annoyed her. Although she had enjoyed Sigi, the affair revealed to her many things. What Hilde craved from him most in those fifteen crazy days were those moments he was unable to restrain himself at the sight of her loveliness, when he lost control simply by touching her. The supreme thrill came when he was in a state of utter exhaustion and unable to function.

When Sigi left, Hilde decided that falling in love so intensely again was a bother and took too much out of her. She saw the example of her sister immersed in misery and pity with Dietrich Rascher, saw her tear herself to bits. No man was worth what Ernestine went through.

Hilde decided that the next affair would be approached with cold calculation with someone who could help her with her ambition to gain lazy comfort. Hilde was self-centered enough to deny herself the giving of love. She pampered her beauty for the right moment, and as a woman of twenty she was an enormously handsome woman in a classical German sense.

The horrors of Berlin told her that the old life was gone. The chances to fill her ambitions also gone. In this tomb she could not understand how they could not be gone forever. Yet, her craving for things that Elke Handfest had attained began to overpower her.

When she saw Elke again, she said, straight-out, "I would like to try a date with you."

Elke was pleased that Hildegaard had taken the first step. "I will see what can be arranged."

"Of course, I would prefer an Ami officer."

Elke laughed. "You will have to take what is arranged."

"Do you mean . . . I might have to accept a Russian?"

"Some of them are quite nice, Hilde. Being a beautiful creature does not mean everything. You must please the men you are with. If you don't, you'll wash out quickly."

Elke tutored her on the rest of it. Never tell a soldier your troubles. He doesn't give a damn about your crippled mother or the hole you live in. Too many girls spend their evenings boring a man. A man wants a stupid, happy girl who can make love like an animal, laugh at his jokes, allow herself to be possessed. Don't drink, Elke warned. A girl needs her wits; stupid girls drink. Forget modesty.

"And don't fall in love, Hilde. But of course, you will never fall in love. You love yourself too much for that."

"You need not worry about me, Elke," she answered, both terrified and excited by it all.

The Paris Cabaret now stood in a cellar near Alexander Platz in Mitte Borough, Russian Sector, in the bashed-down heart of Berlin. Fritz Stumpf remained proprietor on a Russian license. Stumpf was wounded badly in the first days of the war. A crippled left arm returned him to Berlin for the duration.

In the good old days before and after the First World War, the Paris Cabaret belonged to his late, lamented father. It stood on the Friedrichstrasse in the middle of pulsating night life and was a meeting place for theater people and writers.

Berlin was a wonderful, wicked, wild city in those days. A bawdy bohemia of artists, free love, and sex. It was a pompous and proper place with the highest order of opera and concerts.

From here sprang the weird charm of a Mac the Knife and the husky voice of Marlene Dietrich told the world for the first time that she was, from head to toe, consumed with love. It was a Berlin of the immortal Elisabeth Bergner and Tilla Durieux. Negro bands and shimmy dancers and ponderous Wagnerian sopranos all made the magic blends of Berlin.

It was Käthe Gold and the miracle plays of Reinhardt. Fritz Stumpf remembered his father lamenting the departure of the Jews from the Berlin scene. All those magnificent impresarios and virtuosos and fiery journalists had gone. His father said the Jews gave Berlin much of its charm just as they had given Vienna its charm.

Nonetheless, one had to live with the times. By the time Fritz took over from his father the Paris Cabaret had changed to a rendezvous for Nazis who tried to elbow in on the old culture hoping some of it would rub off on them. They came from the ministries that lined the nearby Wilhelmstrasse . . . and the old days died.

When he returned early in the war with his wound, Berlin, for the moment, caught the restless sensation-seeking beat of the twenties. Then the Paris Cabaret was bombed out as indeed all of Mitte Borough was, and Stumpf moved into the safer cellar location. The end of the war left the Paris Cabaret in a shambles, but Fritz Stumpf was a clever man and quickly adapted once more to the new masters.

He quickly contacted high-ranking Russian officers, obtained a license, and set his house in order. Three Russians of the rank of colonel were cut in in exchange for protection, an arrangement that worked well for everyone. In the Nazi era, he took care of the needs of Nazi officers. In these days, he took care of his Russian friends.

Fritz Stumpf's girls were young and pleasing, for the competition to work in the Paris Cabaret was keen. It was cold outside and the Paris Cabaret was as warm as the beds and mansions of the occupation officers.

Elke Handfest retained a popularity for the fun she was, the experience she had, and the fact that she would go along with any party. When she approached Stumpf on the matter of Hildegaard, insisting she was extraordinary, he agreed to look her over.

The front door of the Paris Cabaret was flanked by a pair of American military police. A sign read: OFF LIMITS FOR AMERICAN MILITARY PERSONNEL. This was all part of a show for visiting dignitaries. In a day or so they would be gone, the sign would come down, and the MPs would go away. Colonel Hazzard would, once again, drop by for a late beer on the way home from the Russian parties.

Hildegaard walked down the ten steps into the depths of the cafe and was watched from all over the room as the new girl. The place was smoky and noisy and put together out of odd chairs and tables. The bar girls were tightly corseted to enhance their bosoms and the girls lined up on the other side of the bar jealously watched and feared this unpainted, angelic-looking competitor in their midst.

A musically uncoordinated band played a theater song of the twenties, adding to the discordance by the presence of a badly out-of-tune piano, and girls danced together waiting for dates.

Fritz Stumpf kept a private booth on a balcony a few steps over the main floor. They were ushered to the booth by Hippold, Stumpf's bodyguard and an ex-middleweight champion of Germany.

Stumpf arose, took Hildegaard's hand, kissed it, and asked her to be seated. She saw in traditional pinstripe a maitre d' of the old school. He was monocled and wore a pearl stickpin. His withered left arm was permanently held against his body, the hand covered by a black leather glove and on its second finger an outlandish diamond ring, a mark of either great vanity or great hurt.

He spoke softly, questioned her carefully, and Hilde answered well. She was obviously from a good family, was well groomed, well mannered, well schooled. Her body appeared to be as lovely as her face. The only question was her ability to handle men. Elke assured him that, if they worked as a team, she would train Hilde.

As they spoke, Hippold, the bodyguard, palmed Stumpf several notes. There were already a half-dozen requests around the room to meet Hilde.

A drum rolled, an excited master of ceremonies introduced Renate, an immaculately groomed chanteuse who looked with moony eyes over the tarnished place and sobbed:

> "Berlin, Berlin, I hardly recognize you,
>   Where is your reckless light heart?
> Where are the good old songs
>   You seem sad and lost . . ."

Elke nodded to Hilde and they excused themselves and retreated to the temporary sanctity of the women's room, sat side by side and repaired their makeup.

Hilde was baffled. She fully expected Stumpf, as "master," to try out the new girl first.

"He is a fascinating man," Hilde said cautiously.

"The old-school charm."

"Is he involved with a woman?"

"He has many."

"I have a feeling he does not like me."

"Part of his arm was not all that was shot away during the war."

Hilde changed the subject. "I take it we have dates."

"Yes."

"What about our pay?"

"Don't get greedy, Hilde. You have been accepted on Herr Stumpf's payroll as a hostess. He takes care of his girls. Remember, he does not deal with money and it is just as well we don't get involved in the transactions. Besides, if you are a good girl, the soldiers will be generous with their tips."

The thought disgusted Hilde. She was thankful Elke was with her to ease things. Elke bussed her, with a bit too much affection. "Come on."

They were led to a table toward two British officers.

"Berlin, Berlin I could cry for you,
The most beautiful city in the world you once were."

The sentiment struck deep. Renate continued with another verse on the demise of the beloved city.

The two British officers stood. Elke was impressed by Hilde's quick adaptation. The British major made a sweeping gesture in offering Hilde a seat. She smiled as though she were a very little girl and someone had given her a big, beautiful doll.

"How nice to ask us over," she said in English. "My name is Hilde . . . Hilde Diehl."

Fritz Stumpf watched the scene with a never-ending fascination. It was the endless game he and his father had watched played a thousand times. A new queen bee was in the hive to start a short and fruitless reign. In a small time she will be in such demand she will be heady with success. She will be a favorite of colonels and generals. But, in these days, there were no mistresses in the grand style, only prostitutes. She will become greedy and start making arrangements for herself. They always try.

Stumpf desired her for himself, but in a new girl there is always a certain amount of pride and temper. She could not be degraded immediately. That was a way to ruin a good race horse. Sooner or later she would degenerate by herself. He would be patient until the facts of life softened her up.

Such were things! In the old days, girls like her loved for love and adventure. The Paris Cabaret rocked with laughter and not this dirgelike sentimentality. Beautiful women could not swim the treacherous channel today . . . they had to crash into the rocks.

But . . . without me, he rationalized, they would be prowling the streets and making love in rubble piles for worthless occupation currency.

A note was handed him. It was a lucky night. A case of excellent champagne was being offered for five women to come to the French officers' billet.

After the first week Hildegaard seemed most annoyed by her lack of guilt. Moreover, she had an insatiable desire to return. She enjoyed the game, enjoyed withholding, hated the lust of the men.

They all fell into one of several categories, which Elke had defined, but there was a basic reaction by all of them. Appeal to his vanity, feign interest in his babbling, let him act possessive, laugh at his idiotic jokes, touch him, watch the evening grow, watch his anticipation rise. The drive through darkened streets to billets they had requisitioned. In the final act, Hilde played out a role of demure innocence that brought them to a passionate pitch.

She had never loved a man in her life and what she was forced to do came out in a hatred in the dark. She was drawn to make them plead for her body, and when she submitted she went berserk until the man collapsed. As he lay moaning, she was always awake with the twinge of victory. She was the ultimate whore that every man craves in woman, one who could run the gamut from innocence to savage lover.

At the Paris Cabaret they said here was one girl who made love and loved it. Fritz Stumpf alone seemed to realize that she was, in truth, committing murder through the sex act. He saw that she stuck close to Elke, enjoyed Elke's morbid humor, which condemned their lives.

Stumpf became suspicious when Hilde curtly told him one day she would accept only two dates a week. This could only mean one of two things. Either she had a steady lover or was making her own arrangements. He had Hippold watch her and was puzzled to learn that she rarely left her room on the days she did not come to the Paris Cabaret.

Hilde's motives were simple. On those nights she worked, she wore herself into exhaustion. She cared too much for her beauty to use it up. In addition, she was earning more in two nights than most of the others in an entire week.

She was determined to come out of the experience whole. Yet, exposure brought risks. She realized that Elke was a Lesbian with designs on her; the cool patience and mystery of Fritz Stumpf frightened her . . . she could run into roughness and ugliness. One had to fight against slipping and staying out of serious trouble.

One night, as it comes to all in that ancient trade, Hilde found herself in a desperate situation. Her date, an Ami officer, grew quite drunk. As he did, his remarks about Germans became more vicious. He was a Jewish boy, and in bed his hatred of himself and of her erupted and he beat her up.

Her father and mother apparently accepted the story that she was accosted by Russian soldiers on the street, but Ernestine knew otherwise.

She tended Hilde day and night and watched her sister sink into a deep wordless depression on the realization that there was no coming out whole.

Ernestine was awakened by Hilde's sobbing.

"The scar on my breast won't ever go away."

Ernestine was glad to hear Hilde's first words since the incident. "Those are not the only scars. You cannot see the others, Hilde, but they are there and they may not go away either."

"Don't!"

"We must talk, Hilde. We used to talk to each other. We were so close."

"My breast used to be perfect . . . those Russian beasts!"

"I know all about Hilde Diehl and the Paris Cabaret," Ernestine said abruptly.

Hilde buried her face in the pillow. "You spied on me!"

"I am your sister."

She forced Hilde to turn over and dried her tears and stroked her hair. "Oh, Erna! I am so terribly confused. What has happened to us?"

"It is hard to realize but there will be a tomorrow someday without this nightmare."

"There is no tomorrow here in Berlin," Hilde said.

"We have to live to believe there is. But every time you enter that place you destroy your tomorrow. I have sat here night after night waiting for you to come home and I say to myself . . . how have I failed Hilde? How can I make her understand?"

"You have always been too good, Erna. You have always suffered for others. When we were little . . . you would take the blame when Gerd and I were naughty. I used to think . . . I can be a bad girl, Ernestine will pay for me being bad."

"Shhh."

"You are too good for all of us. But all your goodness cannot help here. Look at this place. I walk there at night and I see that street . . . and I know . . . the linden trees will never bloom again."

"Oh no. In a little time Gerd and our boys will come home. You must not be tainted then, Hilde."

Hildegaard laughed bitterly. "A German boy? Exist in this rat hole? I will find an Ami officer who will marry me and take me to America."

"Hilde, Hilde, when will you stop dreaming?"

"It is you who is the dreamer, Erna. What else is there in this rotten world our dear father made for us?"

"Don't speak against father."

"No . . . don't speak against father," Hilde mumbled. "But who made them hate us? Don't you know their hatred of our German souls? Don't you know I feel that hatred from all of them? Our beloved father and our beloved fatherland brought us to this."

CHAPTER TWELVE

A subcommittee of the Kommandatura worked with the Germans to update the 1920 Constitution of the city. The Berlin Assembly, the lawmakers, would consist of 130 members voted from the twenty boroughs.

The Assembly, in turn, would select an Oberburgermeister and two deputy mayors to be approved by the Kommandatura.

The Magistrat, the executive branch, held eighteen civic departments running the functions of police, transportation, welfare, education, and the like.

As the Constitution neared completion it would signal a city-wide election for a new Assembly.

This election was pondered broadly by the commissars, for the Communist Party in Austria had been soundly beaten in an open election and they were not looking forward to a repetition in Berlin.

Rudi Wöhlman felt that, with his control of the labor union and the propaganda apparatus, and with Communists already imbedded in the government, a victory was sure. Furthermore, the People's Proletariat Party were the true anti-Fascists and would be accepted as the way to redemption by choice of the German people.

Heinrich Hirsch was not so certain. The opposition Democrats had come out of the war the strongest and by sheer weight of numbers had the most people working in the Magistrat and could control the new Assembly. Some of the Democrats could be frightened, bought, bent, terrorized . . . but not Ulrich Falkenstein. How deeply did Falkenstein's influence run with the people?

As both Constitution and election grew imminent, V. V. Azov received instructions from the planners in Moscow: UNIFY ALL POLITI-

CAL PARTIES IN BERLIN INTO A SINGLE ANTI-FASCIST FRONT WITHOUT DELAY.

They were calling for a textbook maneuver to swallow the other parties.

There were three free parties in Berlin. The Christian Party was a religious front, Catholic-dominated. Its main strength was in western Germany along the Rhine, and in Bavaria.

The smallest of the parties was the Conservatives, who represented right-of-center businessmen's ideology.

Ulrich Falkenstein's Democrats were the plum and the target. Berlin was traditionally a labor city and the Democrats their political arm; Berlin, furthermore, was the Democratic stronghold of Germany.

Wöhlman decided to lop off the Democrats first, leaving the other opposition stripped. A meeting between the two executive committees was arranged in the office of Berthold Hollweg, the appointed Democratic Oberburgermeister who was also on the Democrat's Executive. Hollweg was weak, but still carried a good name and the Democratic tag. It was widely known that the Communists who flanked him—Heinz Eck, first deputy, and Adolph Schatz, president of police—held the true power of his office.

The third member of the Democratic Executive was Hanna Kirchner, a grandmother and the leading woman politician in all of Germany. She had fled to Sweden early in the Nazi era, kept a liaison with the first cousins of the German Democrats, the British Labor Party, and the Social Democrats around Europe. During the war she worked for the International Red Cross.

The Communist/People's Proletariat Executive consisted of Rudi Wöhlman, Heinrich Hirsch, Deputy Mayor Heinz Eck. The fourth man was there for no other purpose than a naked display of police terror. He was Adolph Schatz.

"Comrades," Rudi Wöhlman said, smiling his toothy smile to all sides of the conference table, "we have requested this meeting to put forth a proposal which we know will benefit Berlin and help clarify the political confusion. We are now pulling in separate directions. Soon, a new Constitution will be granted. It is time for us Berliners to work together to put this city on its feet."

Berliners, indeed, Falkenstein thought. None of the four Communists remembered Berlin, they had been in Russia so long.

"It is our proposal that we form a single political group . . . one great anti-Fascist front. With such solidarity and strength, the Nazi elements will never again be able to rise and destroy the German people."

So that was it! It was so transparent, Ulrich had all he could do to keep a straight face as Hirsch and Eck added their voices. When they were done, Ulrich quickly averted an open discussion. "We will talk about it and reach you," he said.

The three remained after the Communists left.

"It is an outrageous attempt to swallow us up," Hanna Kirchner said, "under a guise of unity. Oh, certainly, they'll put us in a few posts as window dressing."

"Why must we suspect the worst," Hollweg said.

"Because this is the worst," Ulrich answered.

"But what can we do to stop it?" Hollweg retorted. "You know the pressure we are going to come under. We are not strong enough to stand against the Russians and the Americans are not going to lift a finger in our behalf."

Berthold Hollweg had come out of a shack on the Teltow Canal to assume an important role in the rebirth of the Democratic Party. Much of his old iron had been taken by the humiliations of the Nazi years, but still Ulrich knew that he spoke truth.

When Ulrich and Hanna left, Heinz Eck, the deputy mayor, came to his office.

"It was a good meeting," Eck said. "I have a feeling you see the merit of the plan."

The gambit had begun. Hollweg knew they were to be singled out now and brought under pressure. Heinz Eck was an automatic functionary, a robot—a man with neither mind nor soul.

"It would be comforting for us to know you intend to support the anti-Fascist front," he pressed.

"I must think it over carefully."

"By all means, examine all aspects. Only then can you realize it is the only way for Berlin. How else are we to build? How else can we stop the rebirth of Nazism which the West fosters in our midst. May I say more? We in the People's Proletariat Party have long recognized you as the true strength of the Democrats."

A detestable lie, Hollweg thought. I am a relic of the past, living on past glory.

"Speaking with frankness, Comrade Hollweg, we would support your candidacy as Oberburgermeister again in the election."

No doubt with you as my first deputy, Hollweg thought. "A fair price for services," he mumbled.

"Can we say that we can depend on you?"

"I said, I would think it over."

Immediately following the meeting the Action Squads, supported by the political section of Schatz's police, began to single out Democrats to "convince" them of the merit of the unity plan. Those who were "convinced" set up a demand for an open meeting of delegates to vote in the form of a referendum.

Ulrich and Hanna knew that such an open meeting staged in the Russian Sector of the city would put a rubber stamp on the anti-Fascist front and be the death warrant of the Democrats.

Neither the Christian nor Conservative parties were in a position to do anything but follow the Democrats. They were too weak by themselves and Wöhlman had maneuvered to lop them off one at a time.

When Berthold Hollweg announced he supported the open meeting, Ulrich knew he was being brought under heavy, heavy pressure. He also knew he was out of maneuvering room.

Sean greeted Falkenstein at American Headquarters. Each made half-hearted apologies for not seeing more of the other since they had been in Berlin.

"We have followed your work with great interest. You've done a hell of a job of putting the Democratic Party together."

"Which may all prove in vain," Ulrich answered. "We always spoke to each other straight-out in Rombaden, Major O'Sullivan."

"Shoot."

"The Communists are trying to force us into a political union. It is an old trick."

"We know all about it," Sean said.

"Good. Now, what do you intend to do?"

"Nothing."

"I have always known the Americans are naïve." He held up his hand to stop a retort. "How long do you expect the free parties to survive?"

"Officially, we have to consider this a German family affair."

"Nonsense. The Communists are no more German than you are.

They are men with German names being backed up by Russian guns. How do you conclude it is a German affair?"

"Herr Falkenstein, freedom is not something that can be presented to you, compliments of America, in a neatly wrapped package."

"Your country has never been exposed to the ugly facts of life we face."

"I challenge that, Herr Falkenstein. We won our spurs in a bloody Civil War and we have fought the German people twice in a lifetime because of ideas."

"Do you really think then that you can stay here and keep from getting your hands dirty? I am telling you how this works. I have seen the terror before and it is all coming back. The Action Squads used to be called Brownshirts and there is no difference, sir, between the NKVD and the Gestapo. They will single out weak men, break their spirit, convert them. The slogans and speeches are all the same. You Americans have to know there are Germans here who speak for the West and you cannot conveniently turn your backs on us."

Sean knew what was taking place. But how many were there like Falkenstein, ready to stand up and be counted?

"The fact of life is this, Herr Falkenstein. I could not convince a single man in authority to trust a German politician no matter what label. We do not believe in your people."

A dull throb pained Falkenstein's chest. His voice grew harsh. "You are making a grave, grave mistake."

"Are we? If you truly believed in the courage of your people, you would not come running for help at the first threat. You know they are weak, but your freedom is not something to be handed you at the end of an American bayonet. If we are ever to be convinced, it will be because you earn it with the blood of men willing to die."

Falkenstein was sallow. "Seeing all this happen again is like being an observer at your own funeral. I plead with you, make a gesture so I can rally my party."

"You told me the first day we met in Rombaden that Berliners are different."

"They are! This is the birthplace of free thought!"

"It is also the birthplace of Prussian militarism. Sure, Berliners are different. They just happen to like a parade."

Ulrich Falkenstein pulled himself to his feet heavily. Tears welled in his eyes. "You will see!"

CHAPTER THIRTEEN

A meeting of the Democratic Party was licensed by the Soviet Union to be held deep inside the Russian Sector for the purpose of voting on the anti-Fascist front referendum.

The site selected was the Lichtenberg Workman's Hall, suitable because of only minor bomb damage.

Sean O'Sullivan arrived as a curious observer along with Nelson Goodfellow Bradbury, the sole Americans. They drove with a German named Lenz who worked in American Headquarters. As they neared the Workman's Hall they were all quick to spot police from the SND, designation for Special Nazi Detachment. The SND was, in fact, Adolph Schatz's hand-picked political police, the new Gestapo. The SND was augmented by Russian NKVD observing every route to the Workman's Hall.

Sean was there early as the first of over a thousand delegates filtered in from all parts of Berlin. Ulrich Falkenstein was engulfed by old friends, most of whom he had not seen in a decade. His drowsy eyes found Sean and he nodded coolly; Sean returned the nod.

Lenz pointed out that among the early arrivals were members of Communist Action Squads who scattered through the hall in pre-arranged locations.

The hall buzzed with excitement as reunion after reunion took place. More "observers" from People's Proletariat Party drifted in. The stage was being set for a stampede. Sean felt sorry for Falkenstein.

"They're not leaving anything to chance," Big Nellie said, pointing to the different colored "yes" and "no" ballots to be cast in case of a voice deadlock.

A murmur arose as the *grande dame* of the Democrats, Hanna Kirchner, made her entrance down the center aisle. She was swamped with well-wishers.

In the meanwhile, Berthold Hollweg had arrived almost unnoticed by a side entrance and slipped quietly onto the stage.

For two weeks smaller meetings all over Berlin argued the referendum. They met in bomb shelters, hovels, and factories to select delegates, give instructions. Whenever a meeting was known either the SND or Action Squad people hovered nearby.

At last the hall was filled and Hanna Kirchner and Ulrich Falkenstein took their places on the stage behind a long table covered with a green cloth.

The Burgermeister of Lichtenberg Borough, himself a Democrat, gave a formal welcome to this, the first free assembly of a decade. A few more speeches followed and the chair revolved to the district chairman.

"We are to accept or reject a proposition to join the anti-Fascist front . . ."

Both catcalls and applause greeted him. He demanded order and continued. "Inasmuch as our Executive Committee is not unanimous we cannot provide you with a recommendation. Before floor discussion and a vote we will call on individual members of the Executive to give their personal views."

The full-blown Executive Committee of seven argued the issue back and forth. Ulrich realized that some good people had been cowed by Schatz. He also knew that it boiled down to the last three speakers—himself, Hanna Kirchner, and Berthold Hollweg. Throughout the speeches he searched Hollweg for a sign. The old pro played out a bored detachment.

"Frau Hanna Kirchner!"

Half the room rose in respect. She stood to her full height of five feet and four inches. A funny hat was precariously perched on a knotting of silver gray hair. As she approached the rostrum a bevy of catcalls erupted from the Action Squad members who attempted to push her supporters down and drown them out. Schatz's SND was busy writing down the names of her friends. Fist fights broke out and the chairman threatened, then begged for order.

Hanna rode the storm with calm. She was a wily politician whom Hitler could never cow.

"Those of you gentlemen sent here by Comrade Wöhlman will kindly finish your performance."

Quiet soon followed.

"Now," she said, "that is better. I will get in my two words if it takes all day so kindly refrain from further spontaneous celebrations until I am finished."

A ripple of laughter. Even the American major smiled.

"What a broad," Big Nellie said.

"Where does this great anti-Fascist idea originate? From no less a beloved Berliner than Rudi Wöhlman."

Laughter.

"His belated interest in his native city is very touching."

More laughter of the kind that destroys opposition.

"We see the faces of old friends in this hall today, but we also see the faces of new friends, our guests. We did not invite them, but they came to see that we carried out an orderly, democratic meeting and then voted with different-colored ballots."

The crowd was warming.

"Who are these beloved Berliners? Adolph Schatz, whose Gestapo is so very busy writing down our names for future social calls . . . at night, of course. The kindly Russian NKVD, who have us surrounded so that peace will prevail. Deputy Mayor Heinz Eck, who was thrown out of college as a panderer at the age of eighteen and fled to the Soviet Union and has now returned to give us the benefits of his good advice. And we cannot help but feel the presence of Rudi Wöhlman, whose unseen hand guides us on the path of right. Berlin is fortunate to have so many who love her.

"Comrade Wöhlman wants clean and pretty store windows, but inside he is peddling the same old rotten tomatoes."

When Hanna Kirchner finished her slashing attack there was sustained cheering. When order was restored, the chairman called upon Oberburgermeister Berthold Hollweg. He was yet one of the grand old men of the party. Time and terror might have taken something from him, but his power was still there.

His eyes were red from sleeplessness and his voice so soft it forced an ethereal silence on the assemblage.

"I stand," he said slowly, "in favor of the anti-Fascist front. We in the Magistrat have worked well together, all four parties. In these days cooperation among us is urgent and this can be attained only by pulling together. And . . . we must be strong enough through such unity that never again will a Nazi madness take us over."

The rest of what Berthold Hollweg said was hardly important. When a figure so great made an acceptance so spiritless, it brought them all back to reality.

Hollweg continued, in effect, to say: Where are the Americans with their great democracy? Why do they leave us naked? Where are the British? Where are the French? Why fool ourselves into believing we can do something about all this. Why invite the terror again. We are alone, abandoned, and weak, and the alternative is the midnight summons, the beatings, the kidnapings.

Tears welled in many eyes. Truth was bitter, but truth was truth.

When Hollweg returned to his seat the Action Squad people stomped and whistled, but the rest of the hall was stunned.

"I call upon Ulrich Falkenstein."

He walked alongside the long, green-covered table, stopped for a second behind Hanna Kirchner, his hand squeezing her shoulder, and she could feel the tremor boiling within him. He stood at the rostrum for several moments, looking down on them like an angry Moses whose children had betrayed God. The face of Ulrich Falkenstein, a mirror of German conscience, penetrated every soul in the room and they became transfixed.

In that instant Sean O'Sullivan realized a giant was among them, and Nelson Goodfellow Bradbury knew a moment of magic was happening.

"Berliners!" Ulrich Falkenstein said in a way that hypnotized them.

"Berliners! Are we to hand over our freedom twice in our lifetime without raising a finger!"

"No!" someone shouted from the rear.

"No!" another voice cried.

"Does any man or woman in this room doubt what this referendum means?"

"No!"

"No!"

"Berliners, if we do not stand, we deserve another Hitler!"

Men began standing around the room.

"We will not bend! We will not kneel! We will meet this test and the next and the next and the next! We will be free!"

The hall was on its feet. The roar became deafening!

"Freedom!" he cried from the depths of his being.

"Freedom!" responded the delegates.

"Those of you who stand for freedom will cast your vote now by following me from this hall!"

Hanna Kirchner was at his side. The two of them walked from the stage into a sea of aroused humanity. The SND and the Action Squads were dumbstruck at the sudden massive uprising.

A chant began as row after row emptied behind Ulrich and Hanna. "Freedom! Freedom! Freedom!"

And in a moment there was a handful of them left in the hall and the two colored sets of ballots remained on the stage. Berthold Hollweg sat ashen faced.

Sean O'Sullivan shook his head. He looked out into the streets where the chant rose to a new height.

"Freiheit! Freiheit! Freiheit!"

CHAPTER FOURTEEN

YOUR BELOVED FATHER PASSED AWAY QUIETLY IN HIS SLEEP LAST NIGHT. YOUR MOTHER IS HOLDING UP WELL UNDER THE CIRCUMSTANCES.

The emergency telegram, sent through the Red Cross, was signed by Fr. Dominick Fragozze, a priest Sean had known all his life.

It was not the same as losing Tim and Liam. This was a decision he and his father had made together and knew would happen. He was now given to wondering if he should have stayed home and done more. It was the hour of guilt every man knows after losing a parent.

His friends came by to express their sorrow, and realized he wished to grieve quietly, to remember his father and relive words and scenes of earliest childhood.

And General Hansen came by and asked him how he was holding up. "Here are all your emergency leave papers. Transportation is working out the best route home. We have you on an ATC flight out of Tempelhof in three hours."

"Thank you very much, sir."

"Sean, I wish I knew how to help you. Words can really never ease your pain and particularly with a man as fine as your father."

"I appreciate the General's concern," Sean answered.

Andrew Jackson Hansen's face drew tight with memory of his own. "I remember my father in his last days. He told me something very wonderful when he realized he was going. He said, 'You have done us proud, Andrew. Your family and your country. You have brought food to starving people and more . . . you have given them hope. What a good thing it is to be an American . . . God bless America.'"

Sean lifted his eyes.

"My father told me something else. He said, 'Andrew, the way you have lived your life has made it possible for me to sleep in peace.' Your father would have said the same words to you, Sean. The way you have lived your life has given him the gift of being able to sleep in peace."

"Thank you very much, sir."

When the burden of the funeral was done, Sean closed the old house forever. His mother and a widowed sister would share their days in a small cottage in the sun.

CHAPTER FIFTEEN

Igor was never entirely certain about his arrangement with Lotte Böhm. Circumstance brought them together for mutual convenience. From any point of view, the girl had a good thing in a Russian colonel, yet an attachment of great warmth developed.

Lotte seemed to adore him, stopped at nothing to please him, catered to his whims, moods, instinctively knew how to comfort him. Igor was pleased, but determined not to be deceived. He knew the girl had an overpowering fear of the realities of life in Berlin without his protection. As in all women, except his unlamented wife, Lotte was part actress. There was an outside chance she loved him, but he would not be fooled.

Families of high-ranking Russian officers began to arrive in Berlin. Igor held his breath until he received a letter from Olga that the importance of her work would keep them parted. He silently thanked the party.

For months he traveled through the Russian Zone of Germany stripping one factory after another as part of the reparations program. As that program was ending he was assigned to study reparations claims in the Western Zones.

Millions of German ethnics had been expelled from Poland, Czechoslovakia, and other countries. They moved west in search of new homes. It was a simple matter to plant hundreds, then thousands of Soviet agents in their number to infiltrate everywhere.

Prime assignment of these agents was to gain information to be used to mount Soviet reparations claims. They photographed every factory, piece of machinery, rail yard, harbor, airport, and canal in the West. They drew mountains of data on mineral deposits.

Igor sifted this intelligence so that the Soviet Union could hand-pick the things it wanted. He noted at his weekly meeting with V. V. Azov that the arrival of Madam Azov did nothing to mellow the commissar.

"Comrade Colonel. The British are now ten thousand tons of coal behind schedule in deliveries to us. What have you to report on your negotiations?"

"I can report that the British are stubborn," Igor answered.

"They owe us the coal. It must be demanded."

"It is not quite so simple. The Ruhr mines are capable of only one third of their prewar capacity."

Azov assumed it was for a lack of miners and offered to send "volunteers" from the Silesian districts of Poland.

"It is not a question of either miners or techniques. The English know the mining business. The machinery is obsolete. The miners do not receive sufficient ration for such difficult work. Transportation is broken down. These are technical problems that would only bore the commissar. Our own mines in the Soviet Union are suffering from the same problems."

Azov hated engineers. They hid behind a foreign language. He insisted the pressure must be increased.

Igor insisted you cannot pressure an Englishman. "Besides, the British argue they don't owe us the coal."

"What kind of nonsense is that?"

"For one thing, we have not returned fifteen thousand freight cars in which previous shipments were made."

"A legitimate reparation."

"Yes, of course. However, the British also claim we are behind in our shipments of brown coal to Berlin by some thirty thousand tons."

Azov mulled it over. There was an agreement to exchange the industrial coal of the Ruhr for the brown coal from Silesia to heat the city. This was part of the general plan to exchange the natural assets of the four zones to keep Germany operating as a single economic unit. This was what the Potsdam Agreement said. The Soviets took the hard industrial coal for their own use in Russia and never delivered the soft

coal from Silesia. Fortunately for Berliners the winter of 1945 was
mild.

"The Silesian mines," Azov said, "are no longer a part of Germany
and therefore do not come under the economic exchange regulations.
They are the property of the People's Democratic Republic of Poland.
We cannot force the Poles to send coal to Germany."

Igor digested the commissar's words. He had offered quickly enough
to send in Polish miners, then in the same conversation defended the
"autonomy" of Poland against delivering Silesian coal. Igor was on
tricky ground.

"The British do not recognize the border changes ceding Silesia to
Poland until a peace treaty is signed."

Azov changed the subject.

"The West has agreed to an on-site inspection of the industrial complex preparatory to a reparations conference. You are assigned as a
member of the inspection group."

Igor nodded.

"You will begin next week in the American Zone. After inspections
of the zones you will be assigned as a technical advisor to our delegation at the conference. The conference will be held in Copenhagen."

Igor realized that Azov was watching carefully for a reaction to the
name of a Western city.

Once, during the war, as the Soviet Union swept west along the
Baltic he had seen plans to send three Soviet divisions into Denmark
and occupy it. Unfortunately, the British got there first. He had not
believed he would see a Western city outside of Germany in his life.

"Traveling in the West is a great responsibility. There will be a
session tomorrow to discuss your behavior. Captain Ivan Orlov will ac-
company you as an assistant."

Igor was not annoyed. He had lived with commissars and NKVD
too long.

"One last thing. Your friend, Lotte Böhm."

Igor started.

"She has relatives in Dresden," Azov continued. "We have issued
travel papers for her to visit them and remain there until you return."

Lotte would be a hostage. They had decided that he was deeply attached to the girl.

"Fraulein Böhm will be delighted to learn of her trip," Igor said
sadly.

CHAPTER SIXTEEN

When Sean returned from his emergency leave he was assigned to escort the Russian inspection group. Later, in Copenhagen, General Hansen would lead the American delegation in the reparations claims conference.

The Russians sent twenty-two officers and civilian experts. American intelligence revealed that the group leader, General Lipski, and half the delegation were from political security and the balance technical experts.

Most of the Russians had been exposed to the Americans in Berlin but nevertheless arrived at Tempelhof Airdrome to board General Hansen's personal plane filled with suspicion.

The first stop was American Headquarters, I. G. Farben Building, Frankfurt, where they were given a two-day briefing on what to look for in the way of reparations and what to expect in the way of bomb damage.

The Russians, to a man, were impressed, for the Americans briefed them with a depth of technical knowledge and in an open manner of discussion that was unknown to them. Each member of the Russian group was quietly aware of the vast amounts of American motorized and mechanical equipment, the efficiency, the facilities for common soldiers which would be luxurious even for Russian officers and were caught in an over-all spell of the wealth of the great power.

When the briefings were done, General Lipski reckoned Russian suspicions were based on good reason. The Americans told them, in effect, that Western Germany's industrial complex was all but destroyed. Their own agents did not report such ruination. Obviously the Americans were trying to cheat them out of usable machinery.

They conferred in General Lipski's quarters after the NKVD members turned the place inside out looking for hidden microphones and were exceedingly nervous when they were unable to locate any.

"The Americans are trying to trick us," Lipski said. That was the end of his knowledge. He was in NKVD and had no understanding of technical affairs. There was general agreement that the Americans were up to something, but the question was how to prove it.

Igor Karlovy confined himself to studying the documents listing the factories, rail centers, refineries. He took no part in the accusations, but suggested that the American liaison, Major O'Sullivan, be contacted and more facts provided.

Sean came later that night to Igor Karlovy's quarters in the Officers' Club at the I. G. Farben Building.

"Major O'Sullivan," Igor said bluntly. "We demand to see a more comprehensive report to back your claims."

Sean understood it as Russian mistrust. He said he would begin to gather data immediately.

Igor reported this to General Lipski. Knowing his own operation, Lipski said they were in for days of American evasions. He began to draft a sharply worded protest and planned to dispatch it to Marshal Popov the next day.

The protest was never sent. Within twenty-four hours Colonel Karlovy was handed the organizational charts and missions of the Eighth and Fifteenth American Air Forces listing every plane, every installation, every mission, every bomb load, and supporting reports on the results. He promised the same data from the Royal Air Force within forty-eight hours.

Igor Karlovy was chagrined.

"General Hansen believes that if we are to work together in the next weeks, it might be well if you understood America's global war effort. This document will acquaint you with the nature of our forces and our conflict in every corner of the world."

Igor eyed the thick record out of the corner of his eye. The cover read: UNITED STATES OF AMERICA ARMED FORCES AND SUPPORT IN WORLD WAR II. PRELIMINARY SURVEY. He was most eager to read it but thought better of it. "It has nothing to do with the work of this inspection mission."

"We believe it has, Colonel Karlovy. Your propaganda that you won the war single-handed is incorrect. Once familiar with the extent of our effort you are apt to approach the work here with a little less suspicion and hostility. I'd like to call your particular attention to pages eighty-four through ninety-nine listing war materiel shipped from the United States to the Soviet Union."

He handed the document back to Sean. "It has nothing to do with this mission," he repeated.

"Nothing you care or dare to see?"

"Major O'Sullivan, I think we had better rule politics out of our discussions," Igor said. "You deal in theory. We deal in reality. Invasion of your borders, destruction of your homeland changes one's point of view. We have lived with war inside our country for centuries."

Igor Karlovy, the most knowledgeable of the group in air matters, studied the reports on the Eighth and Fifteenth Air Forces with a rising disbelief! If the Americans had what they claimed, then the Red Air Force was a pigmy alongside it.

Igor had seen with his own eyes the bomb damage in Berlin, but that had been attributed mostly to Soviet Artillery. He had seen damage in the Russian Zone of Germany and believed that the West concentrated their air power against East Germany while they preserved the industry and cartels in the Western Zones for a war of revenge.

In the ensuing days they inspected Frankfurt, Munich, and Stuttgart with American Air Force experts and engineers. The precision destruction of transportation centers and manufacturing capability tallied in close detail with the American claims.

A confusion grew within the Soviet group.

And then they came to Rombaden, where the plum was to be the Romstein Machine Works.

They arrived in a convoy of cars late in the afternoon and before receiving billets went to the Rathaus to the offices of the military governor and the Oberburgermeister for the official welcome. At first a few curious people gathered at sight of the Russians. Then the word spread that Major O'Sullivan had returned.

Within minutes hundreds of people had poured from the buildings on the square and the city band was hastily assembled. When they all left the mayor's office they were greeted by a rendition of "God Bless America"—in waltz time.

Igor and his Russian companions were stunned by what was happening. They knew by now that O'Sullivan disliked Germans intensely and had been a stern master. What a strange welcome for a conqueror!

The spontaneous outpouring continued. School children paraded before him on the Rathaus steps, bowed, and curtsied, and the portico became filled with bouquets of flowers. Everyone wanted to shake Major O'Sullivan's hand.

Then beer barrels rolled in on horse-drawn brew wagons and an impromptu festival took place right on the spot.

General Lipski allowed his group to mellow a bit. As Igor watched the folk dancing he remembered his dozens of trips to East German cities, where all that ever greeted him was fear. And as the Germans nodded and bowed and smiled to O'Sullivan he remembered the look of hatred in the eyes of the Polish people in Warsaw.

O'Sullivan was intimate with the destruction of the Machine Works. Russian agents had sent back false reports.

The tour went on. Knowing now that the original briefings in Frankfurt would be borne out, the Russians began to relax.

Darmstadt: September 11, 1944. RAF raid. 300 planes dropped multithousand incendiaries in 45 minutes gutting 72 % of the city and turning it into an inferno. It took a week for the place to cool off.

Mainz: Rail center and arteries destroyed. Center of city a mass of brooding stone.

Offenbach: 60 % destroyed. 93 % of war-effort factories destroyed.

Kassel: Wartime armaments factories made it a priority for Allied bombers. Not even Berlin took such a pounding for its size. Inner city entirely leveled.

And so it went in one city after another. The political section of the group spoke among themselves about the efficiency of American Military Government, the de-Nazifying procedures, the new legal codes and the speed of open elections.

Wiesbaden. The inspection of the American Zone was coming to an end. Now they saw an undamaged German city. And this, too, made a mark on Igor Karlovy. It was a great, plush old spa of sumptuous beauty, the likes of which he had never seen, something he had believed existed only for czars. The Taunus Mountains looked down on lush forests and the people had bathed in spas from the times of the Romans. Seeing this unspoiled place enabled Igor to put together bits of the ancient German culture that he had seen in the jigsaw of rubble.

At the Schierstein Harbor they boarded the yacht *City of Cologne,* which once belonged to Adolf Hitler, and sailed down the Rhine to the little sporting town of Rüdesheim and docked. Here the full splendor of that fabled river revealed itself. The Watch on the Rhine, the statue of Germania, stood high above the magnificent terraced vineyards.

German school children gathered to sing a welcome in their high-pitched voices. They sang the traditional "Lorelei" and the village dancers and band and singers added their odes to the ethereal beauty of the Rhine.

This was a side of Germany Igor Karlovy had never known. In the warmth and sentimentality of their songs, so like his own, he realized there was something in the German character other than brutality and militarism. How puzzling! But after all, did he not love a German woman? Had he not seen these things in her?

After an elegant banquet at the centuries-old mansion of Krone they tasted the wines at Castle Crass. As ancient wine-tasting ceremonies ensued, the party loosened up, and then . . . brotherhood came about. Even NKVD General Lipski enjoyed himself and those limber ones among the Russians were soon showing off a few dance steps of their own to the delight of the American hosts and the German entertainers.

They boarded the *City of Cologne* at dawn with bombing hangovers. As the boat pulled away the children were there again, singing the "Lorelei."

The boat moved down the river. Major O'Sullivan walked among the group shaking hands with each of them. In two short weeks he had gained their respect after the passing of the initial hostility. He seemed to be an unusually open and honest man as well as extremely pleasant.

Sean sat at the rail, caught up for a moment with the overwhelming beauty of the river. Igor Karlovy sat alongside him.

"Well, Major O'Sullivan, what will we do without you?"

"The British will take good care of you."

"Will we be seeing you in Copenhagen?"

"Probably."

There was general excitement as the yacht came around a treacherous bend and they could see the great basalt rock that rises out of the river and hovers in a large cliff over the water. The voices of the children singing the haunting "Lorelei" still reached their ears.

"So that is the 'Lorelei,'" Igor said.

"Don't listen too closely to the voices of the sirens, Colonel, or you may crash on the rocks."

Igor smiled. "You would make an excellent dialectician."

They rounded the bend passing those long low river barges and the outlines of the Mäuseturm showed itself against a gray sky over the terracing.

"I was told only last night that you returned from America from an unhappy event. Your father, I believe."

"Yes."

"I am so sorry."

"Thank you, Colonel. He was quite old and quite tired."

"And you have family left?"

"There is only my mother and myself. I lost two brothers in the war." This shattered Igor into a long silence.

"And you, Colonel?"

"I lost . . . a childhood sweetheart . . . and my son."

"Then we really should be friends, shouldn't we," Sean said.

"I guess so. What part of America do you come from?"

"San Francisco."

"Oh yes. California was once settled by Russians."

"We stole California from the Spanish in a war of aggression . . . however, we did purchase Alaska from the Russians, legally."

Igor laughed. "From the Czars. We would not have made such a bad bargain." Igor lit a cigarette. "Tell me, what did your family do?"

"We had all more or less just graduated from the university. I was teaching. My younger brother aspired to be a writer. He was a student of literature. The middle brother . . . a follower of causes."

"Three sons in the university. Your family must have had great wealth."

"My father was an immigrant from Ireland. He was never more than a laborer."

"Very interesting."

Ivan Orlov, as always, hovered nearby. The NKVD had made a small error in assigning him to watch Colonel Karlovy . . . he spoke no English. He made his presence so annoying that Sean asked to excuse himself. When he left, Ivan Orlov said, "Beware of Major O'Sullivan. He is a spy for American political security."

At Cologne the American escort was joined by the British escorts. It was the same story. Cologne, Hanover, and the ports of Hamburg and the American enclave of Bremerhaven utterly mangled.

But the very worst they saw in all of Germany was the devastation of the Ruhr industrial complex. Düsseldorf, Essen, and Dortmund were all but wiped out.

The Soviet inspection group proceeded to the Copenhagen conference sobered. Neither the British nor Americans had hidden a thing.

Igor Karlovy had to admit to himself that Germany was more thoroughly destroyed than the Soviet Union.

What was horribly clear now was that the Soviet Government had deliberately lied to keep the Russian people from knowing the strength and participation of the West. Indeed, Western Germany had not been spared for a war of revenge.

CHAPTER SEVENTEEN

The clock in the tower of the Copenhagen City Hall tolled the hour of seven. Igor Karlovy paced his room. Most of the staff would be asleep for another two or three hours. He opened the curtain, stepped out onto the balcony of his room at the Palace Hotel.

In the center of the street arose a column, and on it a pair of vikings blowing long trumpets. The Danes joked that the trumpets would sound when a virgin passed.

Raadhus Plaza stretched below. Copenhagen was starting a new day with wonderful briskness. Tens of thousands of Danes pedaled their bicycles, weaving around automobiles, and the square was alive with the sounds of cooing pigeons, sharp heels on stone, voices of the rapid, indistinguishable language.

How different from the movement of the troubled grim masses in Moscow, Igor thought.

Colonel Igor Karlovy was a man deeply disturbed. The five-week inspection tour of the Western Zones and the conference in Copenhagen were drawing to a close. He had felt uneasy about the safety of Lotte Böhm. No communication between them had been possible. The separation had made him realize that he loved her . . . and he had committed a cardinal sin in losing his hatred for Americans. . . . Questions gnawed at him. They could never be asked.

One could watch Copenhageners for hours, Igor thought. The Soviet delegation was housed in a wing of the Palace Hotel in the heart of the city. The Americans were a mile and a half away at the D'Angleterre. Between them ran Frederiksborg Way, a narrow street lined with exclusive shops and department stores.

The Russians always tried to hold meetings and luncheons at the American hotel so they could walk Frederiksborg Way. The shops were filled with goods they had never seen . . . watches, silver, porcelain, furs. The people were handsome, they smiled, and they were well dressed; and all this was in an austere period at the end of a war. Was this capitalistic decadence?

If Major O'Sullivan and the other Americans and British he had dealt intimately with were proof of Western imperialism, then the proof was wrong. Most of them came from humble backgrounds with at least one parent from another land. They were hard-working, intelligent, and friendly.

Why did Azov send me on this mission?

Igor remembered his complaint to a British major about the fact that the coal miners in the Ruhr were striking and holding up Russian reparations shipments.

"But these chaps have every right to strike, you know," the Englishman answered.

"They have no rights. They are Germans and you are an occupying power," Igor had insisted.

"Poor devils have been fainting from hunger. A miner can't do a decent day's work on two thousand calories. Damned healthy sign when they got enough dander up and had the cheek to strike."

In the Saar, German students were protesting French occupation regulations. A French captain shrugged. "Students always demonstrate. It is a student's prerogative to demonstrate. Works off energy."

Damned if students demonstrated in Moscow! How could it be a healthy sign to disobey authority! In all his life Igor had accepted orders without question.

How could the Americans, British, and French permit freedoms to the Germans which he, as a Russian, did not have?

The Americans and British were at ease. They were so sure of themselves. Perhaps they were so sure of their way of life! Or perhaps the Russians were unsure of theirs. Was that it? The Russians feared themselves, feared each other?

Igor hungered to know truth and he walked on dangerous ground.

Major O'Sullivan had become his friend. If there was only a way to speak to him. . . .

That evening Captain Ivan Orlov, NKVD, sat at his desk at the Pal ace Hotel finishing a report to his superiors giving his findings on those members of the Soviet delegation he was assigned to watch.

Colonel Karlovy would come in for bad days, at last. All through the end of the war, Karlovy had belittled him, ignored him; till now there was nothing to accuse him of.

Now there were solid suspicions that Colonel Karlovy was getting a soft attitude toward the West and had even engaged in a friendship with Major O'Sullivan, an American spy!

Ivan Orlov was fulfilled! After all, one is assigned to watch someone and there can be no accomplishment unless you catch him at something. Ivan dreamed of a promotion when the report was rendered.

A knock on the door. A short square man in black chauffeur's uniform introduced himself as the driver for the Soviet Ambassador to Denmark.

"The ambassador demands your presence," the chauffeur said.

Ivan was elated! The ambassador himself! Perhaps General Lipski discussed his work and the ambassador wanted him to remain in Copenhagen. What an idea!

A somber Mercedes with a pair of Red flags attached to each fender waited. In a few moments the car was moving north out of Copenhagen speeding toward the Danish Riviera in the direction of Elsinore.

"The Comrade Ambassador wanted to hold the meeting with you in private," the chauffeur said. "There are too many Western spies in Copenhagen. We are driving to his summer residence."

Ivan nodded that he understood. The chauffeur was undoubtedly NKVD also. He was too well disciplined in the secret ways of political security to question an ambassador.

An hour later the last of the farewell parties unfolded at the great velvet and mirrored Wivex restaurant, the largest in Europe, which was on the edge of the Tivoli. Although it was too early for the Tivoli's season, the million lights were turned on in honor of the occasion to set up a fairyland of color and magic.

Participants of the conference arrived: ambassadors bedecked in sashed elegance; generals and admirals bogged under decorations; ele-

gant ladies. The room was filled with tables, each holding small flags
of the various nations, and a formally dressed Danish orchestra played
Russian laments, French love songs, American jazz, and British airs.

Long tables of smörgasbord, aquavit, Carlsberg beer, open-faced
sandwiches of tiny shrimps, ham, and cheese, buckets of iced champagne—all attributed to the fact that this was a banquet of the victors.

Colonel Igor Karlovy, one of the most popular of the Soviet delegation worked his way around the room, shaking hands, saying good-bys
to Belgians and Poles, Dutch and Danes. Igor felt something was wrong.
He had been in the place for nearly a half hour without seeing Ivan
Orlov . . . he began to feel naked.

Igor's face lit up as he spotted Major O'Sullivan on the balcony facing
the Tivoli and speaking to a Danish girl he had seen several times during the conference. Igor cleared his throat.

O'Sullivan introduced him to Miss Rasmussen, a Danish translator.
She excused herself, knowing there was to be some men's talk.

"We have arranged a private party as soon as we can gracefully get
out of here. Would you come, Colonel Karlovy?"

"Who will be present?"

"Some of the boys from the Marine Embassy Guard have a house
just a little out of town."

"I am afraid that would be impossible."

"I seemed to have overheard that Captain Orlov took ill or something," Sean said. He looked directly into Igor's eyes. "Orlov won't be
around tonight."

On an impulse Igor said, "Hell, why not?"

Master Gunnery Sergeant Michael J. Flynn, USMC, of the American Embassy Guard was assigned as an assistant to Major O'Sullivan
for the conference. They discovered they had much in common beside
Irish parents. Both were Mission District San Franciscans out of the
same high school. Flynn took to the major right off the bat, remembering having seen him fight at the old Bucket of Blood arena. The sergeant and four other staff NCO's pooled resources and were able to
rent a lovely place on the sea in Taarnby, a suburb of Copenhagen.

Igor's apprehension about accepting the invitation faded. The Americans were almost like children in their desire to be friendly. They
showered little gifts on him and were consumed with curiosity about
his war record.

The Marines all had lovely Danish girls as dates. Sean was with Miss Rasmussen; Igor insisted he did not want a girl.

It was a nice gathering. They could look over the water to Sweden from the porch; the sky held a billion stars, and there was a gentle pounding of the surf.

They all had their tunics off and drank as comrades without rank. The Marines made a number of jokes about the inferiority of the American Army at Major O'Sullivan's expense, but he had the right answers. Igor had once been warned by Russian intelligence that the American Marines were an elite corps like the Nazi SS. It did not seem possible, meeting them like this. They were plain boys from many places and three of the four had wounds from the war in the Pacific.

The living room was dark except for the light from the fireplace. The Marines and their girls sat about on the floor and sang. One, from Wyoming, had a guitar and they sang British songs about the jolly sixpence and "Bless Them All" and they sang about the Heart of Texas.

The pace of the evening slowed and the Wyoming Marine sang a spiritual of the American Negro—that he was a wayfaring stranger alone in a far land. Igor thought it was beautiful.

He took the guitar from the Wyoming Marine and sang to them about Russia and they thought . . . what a hell of a nice guy.

The hour became late and they drifted away, two by two.

Only Sean and Miss Rasmussen were left as the fire dimmed to its coals. Igor saw that Miss Rasmussen was looking at Sean with loving eyes and that his farewell should be made.

"I must go back to Copenhagen but first you must tell me what happened to Captain Orlov?"

"One of the boys in the Marine detachment has Russian-born parents. They spoke it at his home all the time. We got him a chauffeur's uniform, borrowed a car from the embassy motor pool, and stuck a pair of Red flags on the fenders. Captain Orlov was driven to Elsinore to see the Soviet ambassador."

"But . . . but . . . the ambassador was at the Wivex tonight."

"You don't say."

"But . . . but . . ."

"He was driven to Hamlet's castle and told to knock on the gate. The car drove off. Well, Orlov speaks only Russian and we figured he'd have

a hell of a time finding a Russian-speaking Dane. He should get back
to Copenhagen tomorrow sometime . . . if he's lucky."

Igor Karlovy laughed until his stomach ached and tears rolled down
his cheeks. "That stupid bastard!" Orlov was probably making out a
report on him. Now, he could never turn it in because he would have
to admit being tricked by the Americans. When he gained control of
himself he thought the time for a farewell had come.

"It was a nice journey, Major O'Sullivan."

"See you around, Colonel."

Sean thundered out of a deep sleep, fished around for the nightstand lamp, and switched it on.

Igor Karlovy hovered over him, roaring drunk. Miss Rasmussen
screamed and threw the blankets over her head.

"You son of a bitch! It's four o'clock in the morning!"

"I intend to go," Igor said, "but first I demand to know why you want
to destroy us!"

"Because, you simple bastard, we crave the latest Moscow fashions!"

CHAPTER EIGHTEEN

The American Army band marched beneath the reviewing stand striking up "The Stars and Stripes Forever." The honor guard, a crack
drill team of Negroes, followed the band in double cadence, executing
an intricate close-order drill.

Marshal Alexei Popov waved his hand in appreciation. The Russian
was in a jovial mood. Great medals adorned his tunic from armpit to
armpit, chest to navel. Elements of the mighty Second American Armored Divisions followed with their tank treads setting up a rumbling
din.

Standing next to Popov was Lieutenant General Andrew Jackson
Hansen, First Deputy Military Governor. Hansen remembered a year
back. The President was in Berlin for the Potsdam Conference and
drove between two solid lines of tanks of an entire division. American
might was then on display. Soon parts of the division would be pulling
out of Berlin, once again reducing the garrison.

A year ago, at the end of the war, there were three million American troops in Europe; now less than a third of the number and shrinking fast. The stampede was on to bring the boys home and to hell with European involvements. Hansen had pleaded in council after council that twenty divisions had to be left in Europe. The Congress led the parade of deaf ears.

That was why Marshal Popov was in a genial mood. All along, Soviet experts had predicted the American withdrawal. Soon the Americans would be too weak to withstand concerted pressure.

The parade honoring the first anniversary of the occupation of Berlin made a public show of unity. In the beginning the Berliners looked upon the Americans as liberators and were shocked. During the first year in the Berlin Kommandatura and the Supreme German Council the Americans seemed to be doing everything possible to please the Russians.

Colonel Neal Hazzard stood in the row behind Hansen, beside his adversary, Brigadier Trepovitch. The latest tirade from the Russians was over the American formation of a sports program for German children with GI's acting as instructors and coaches.

Trepovitch harangued that it was an attempt to encourage the rebirth of German militarism. When the Russian saw how the children flocked to the American soldiers, he attempted to institute a duplicate program in the Russian Sector.

Neal Hazzard said he knew why the Russians used the knight as their favorite chess piece. "It's like a Russian. It can move in eight different ways . . . all of them crooked."

As Scotch pipers of a tradition-rich regiment set up a wail in the streets, Neal Hazzard wondered how far the Russians were going to push before we began to push back.

"Neal," General Hansen said, "we are pleased with the way free elections have gone in Hesse, Bavaria, and Württemberg-Baden. I'd like to press for them in Berlin."

"There's a difference, sir. We don't have Russians to contend with in the zone."

"The Constitution is ready to be handed down. Take a crack at it in the Kommandatura."

"Yes, sir."

Hazzard brought the matter up, expecting a stalling act from Trepovitch.

The Russian returned at the next meeting with instructions, and,
to everyone's surprise, suggested elections at an early date in October.

Neal Hazzard was baffled. He went to O'Sullivan for advice.

"Sure the Russians want elections," Sean said. "We both do for different reasons. We want them to dispose of our responsibility. They want
them to entrench themselves."

"How do they figure they can win?"

"They're dealing to us with a stacked deck."

"They can't win after what they've done to this city," Hazzard insisted.

"They've made a calculation, Colonel, that we won't lift a finger to
help the free parties. They'll have them demoralized to a pulp."

Sean's estimation was based on the way the Communists had
squeezed the life out of the political opposition in the Russian Zone
of Germany. In city after city the Democratic Party leadership along
with the other free parties were coerced into the anti-Fascist front.
The pattern was the same. For window dressing a Democrat or member of the Christian Party sometimes held the post of mayor. But always he was flanked with deputies like Heinz Eck and the police,
education, propaganda, and food control was in Communist hands.

After smarting from Ulrich Falkenstein's rebellion, the Communists
went to work on the Democrats in the Russian Sector of Berlin where
the West could not operate. Systematic terror lopped off Democratic
and Christian leadership.

Despite Falkenstein's earlier pleas, his party was being splintered
away.

Feeling no Western opposition, Trepovitch then presented the petition to license the anti-Fascist front as an operating group in Berlin
"because it was in existence in the Soviet Zone."

In England, the Labor Party, first cousins of the German Democrats,
brought pressure on their occupation officials to stiffen British opposition. It was Colonel T. E. Blatty who answered in the negative to the
anti-Fascist front.

Then a strong French stand by Jacques Belfort said that France
would recognize the anti-Fascist front, but only as a continuation of
the Communist Party. This was the first feeble beginning of resistance.

At American Headquarters individual officers such as Sean O'Sullivan acted on their own initiative to help the free parties in dozens of "unofficial" ways.

For the most part, the West remained ineffective as Rudi Wöhlman and Heinrich Hirsch engineered an election campaign to put the most uncouth ward heeler to shame, by comparison.

Russia, controlling Berlin's only radio, refused to give the free parties a single minute of air time.

Mitte Borough, the center of the city, began to look like Moscow on May Day. Banners in defiant red and white hung from nearly every wall.

THE SOVIET UNION IS THE FRIEND OF THE GERMAN WORKING PEOPLE!

FREEDOM AND DEMOCRACY THROUGH THE PEOPLE'S PROLETARIAT PARTY!

TURN BACK THE WARMONGERS!

NEW GERMANY MARCHES TO PEACE WITH OUR SOVIET BROTHERS!

REBUILD GERMANY THROUGH THE PROGRESS OF THE PEOPLE'S PROLE-TARIAT PARTY!

WE STAND WITH THE WORKERS!

Sound trucks flooded the Russian boroughs and their newspapers and broadsheets inundated the city.

Sixty days before the election People's Radio announced that all fruit and vegetables for Berlin would be supplied by the benevolent Soviet Union.

Under the auspices of the People's Proletariat Party there was a display of free food such as had not been seen in years.

Free People's Proletariat cigarettes were distributed at the factories.

The school system under the management of Heinrich Hirsch passed out free pencils stamped with the initials of the party and free notebooks carrying pictures of Marx, Lenin, and Stalin, with suitable quotations. The children were lectured on how to instruct their parents to vote.

"Spontaneous" parades and demonstrations were apt to erupt by the well-groomed Action Squads.

The specter grew ugly. Schatz's SND brazenly kidnaped and beat free party candidates. The Action Squads grew bolder stampeding free party rallies right inside the Western Sectors.

Democratic, Christian, and Conservatives who wished to speak in the Russian Sector were forced to submit their speeches in advance and put their lives in jeopardy when they crossed over. As often as not free party rallies in the Russian Sector were canceled at the last moment for an imaginary infraction.

Hansen watched it grow to a point where the Americans were looking like damned fools. He did not trust either Falkenstein or the Democrats, but he could not justify American continuation in the city if they allowed a Communist take-over. His own staff quarreled over the intention of the mission. One group, largely from his State Department advisors, felt they had to get along with the Russians at any price. Neal Hazzard led the opposition, demanding American involvement in behalf of the free parties.

Hansen went to both the Pentagon and the State Department for policy instructions. *There was no clear policy on the Berlin election!*

Five weeks before the election a candidate of the Democratic Party from the Soviet Sector in Köpenick Borough disappeared. His body washed up on the Müggel Lake, days later.

On the fifth day of September, a month before the elections, a new sound was heard by three million Berliners.

"This is RIAS calling. This is Radio in the American Sector. This is the voice of freedom."

The microphone was turned over to Ulrich Falkenstein, who began with his rally cry, "Berliners!"

Operation Back Talk had begun.

CHAPTER NINETEEN

Berlin was full of homecoming soldiers and others in transit from the Soviet Union. They were emaciated and scraggly, mostly shoeless, with large rags wrapped around their feet. Once proud uniforms were tattered and stinking. Hollow eyes and bony faces told stories of horror.

Most of the Berliners ignored them. Once they had marched away as a symbol of German superiority. They crawled back now. The Prussian military tradition gave no glory to the bearers of defeat.

Other prisoners of war came from the West. These were more fortunate. Among their number was Gerd Falkenstein.

"Gerd! Gerd is home!"

Ernestine fell into his arms; Herta wrung her hands and wept, and Bruno pulled a hand free and pumped it.

"Oh God, oh God!"

"Son! How did you find us?"

"The Ami Red Cross. They are very efficient. Look at you Hilde! You are a woman!"

"Come in! Come in. Don't stand in the hall."

Gerd put down his worldly possessions, a single knapsack. They pulled him into the room and stood around him. He looked rather well: he was lean and a bit tan; his uniform was shabby but neat and he wore new shoes.

"You look wonderful," his mother wept.

Gerd smiled. "If you must be a prisoner, by all means be a prisoner of the Amis. What has happened to our home? Was it bombed?"

"The Amis took it, but let's not talk of that now."

The meal was edible, enough to fill Gerd's stomach. They listened to his adventures.

He admitted he was lucky. His antiaircraft bunker on the coast of Normandy received a near hit by the British naval bombardment.

"I was unconscious for three days. When I woke up I was on an American hospital ship in the prisoners' ward."

The rest of the story was internment in a camp in Maryland, the most decent food he had eaten since he left home, work on a road gang, schooling, and good entertainment.

"It is a small miracle, but here we are all together again."

Well, not quite all. Gerd inquired after old friends. They were dead, badly butchered, or missing in Russia. "I am sorry to hear about Dietrich Rascher. He was a fine fellow."

Ernestine paled. Gerd was pleased that she still mourned Dietrich. That was good after all the things he heard about German girls these days.

"You might as well know," his father said, "your Uncle Wolfgang was involved in the plot against Hitler and hanged."

Gerd took the news with no show of emotion. "Sooner or later he had to go that way."

And then they settled and Gerd recounted it all from the beginning. He told of the battles in North Africa when they were winning and the collapse of the Low Countries and France before that. His hands drew images of the brilliant strategy, the hordes of panzers, the fury of the Luftwaffe. Ernestine watched her father's eyes light as he talked of the parade through the Arch of Triumph in Paris. It was a way he had not looked since before Stalingrad.

She felt herself sinking. After the first warmth of greeting, Gerd seemed distant, and his voice was filled with cynicism and arrogance.

"Your Uncle Ulrich is here in Berlin."

"So, he is still alive. I hardly remember him."

"He has been very good to us," Ernestine said quickly.

"And why not? He made us live with his shame for years."

"Things are different now. Uncle Ulrich is an important man."

"Strange," Gerd said, "we decent Germans end up living like this, or worse, like those poor devils down on the street. And the traitors are given our country."

Bruno listened to his son with a warm glow. It was music he had not heard for so long.

The next day was Sunday, but father and mother had to work. Hilde excused herself on the pretense that she had an unbreakable date with a girl friend.

Ernestine and Gerd walked. The air was nippy. There was a terrifying feeling that the winter might be severe. Autumn's eternal gray brought the sky down to the tops of the dilapidated buildings. They walked until they found their old street in Dahlem and stood before their former home.

"Who lives there?"

"Four American officers."

"Well, it is better than Russians. We will get it back sooner than you think."

"Don't torture yourself, Gerd. Let's get out of here."

They were swallowed by the Grunewald, where the paths were filled with bright, shedding leaves. For a moment the misery of Berlin was hidden.

They turned toward the Kummer See, one of the smaller lakes. Gerd whistled, "Raise the Banner," the SA marching song, known as "Horst Wessel."

"You must not whistle that song," Ernestine said shakily. "It is forbidden."

"Forbidden? Your own music, forbidden?"

"Please, Gerd, they are very strict."

They came to the edge of the lake and sat on a boulder. "Remember the encampments, Erna? Hitler Youth. The air was filled with such music then."

"All during the bombings I came here and sat by the lake," she said. "Dietrich and I sailed here. Gerd . . . those days are gone."

"Hail the conquering hero," he said with acid in his voice. "What a damned mess this place is. But don't fret, Erna. We will have those days again and the next time we won't make the same errors."

"There won't be any next time, Gerd."

"Of course there will."

"Do you know what happened to us at Stalingrad?"

"A strategic blunder."

"Do you know what happened to Berlin in the last hundred days?"

"It won't happen again."

"Gerd! Hilde and mother and I were violated by Russian soldiers. We have all had enough."

Gerd's lips narrowed. "That is why there will be a next time. Only we will choose better allies than those sniveling Italian bastards. The Amis will be on our side. They are strong but they are also naïve. We will control the alliance."

"Gerd! Germans have to change their ways!"

"How, Erna? Do you believe a doddering old fool like Uncle Ulrich can lead the German people? Do you believe the German people will be kept down? We have energy and brains. We are not nigger slaves or wailing Jews." He laughed with irony. "Even this destruction will have its compensations. Homes and factories have to be built and we need machinery and guns. This will bring Germany jobs and prosperity. Total destruction means total reconstruction."

"For God's sake! Don't you know about Auschwitz?"

"Of course. In the prison camp the Amis held classes called reorientation to democracy. We were told at great length about our wicked ways. It was a joke among the prisoners."

"You feel no shame?"

"Why should I? What did I do? Besides, let us not pretend we suddenly love the Jews because we lost the war. I think it's a pity we didn't kill all of them."

Ernestine jumped off the boulder. Gerd reached for her. She stiffened at his touch. "Dietrich Rascher always told me you took things too seriously."

Hilde was getting more nervous around Elke Handfest. Elke's hand was constantly touching her, squeezing her leg, brushing her bosom.

One night she asked Fritz Stumpf not to give her any more dates with Elke.

But she was no longer in a position to make demands. Her day as queen bee was over. Berlin swarmed with beehives and queen bees. Women came in too many varieties and men were too fickle. It was an echo of the orgy running wild all over Germany.

Hilde began to suspect that Fritz Stumpf was deliberately withholding dates from her. Evening after evening now she sat alone in a booth at the Paris Cabaret. She looked bitterly at the new girls, listened to the same tired songs, heard the same complaints. Her dates were with lower-ranking officers and enlisted men, fewer Amis, more Russians. She became fearful that she was losing her beauty. She needed a drink to keep her composure.

When a good date came it always was double with Elke. That made her nervous and she needed a few drinks before leaving the Cabaret.

Hilde toyed with the idea of leaving the Paris. But she knew that all similar places with good connections cooperated with each other. And what if she went out on her own and contacted gonorrhea again. Only someone like Stumpf would be able to supply penicillin.

Trying to leave could bring the risk of blackmail against Uncle Ulrich, or worse, physical harm to herself. Fritz Stumpf had a few more around like the ex-pug, Hippold. There was talk that Hippold had a speciality of using a knife to scar a girl's face and body. The thought of mutilation of her beautiful body began to bring her to nightmares like Ernestine used to have. In these dreams glass cut her and animals' teeth ripped her.

She knew now about the velvet room in Stumpf's apartment. The war wound had left him impotent. His pleasure was watching women with each other in the velvet room while a trio played Bach and an ancient actor read the poetry of Schiller and Heine. She cringed with fear now, as Stumpf would often summon a half-dozen girls without dates to come to his apartment.

Gerd's homecoming set off problems. She remembered Ernestine's warnings that she was killing a chance for a normal life with a German boy. Chances were slipping that an Ami would have her.

In the days after Gerd's arrival Hilde began drinking heavily. Sometimes her date found her angry and other times found her remorseful and complaining about her terrible situation. She had started along the path that Elke had warned her against in the very beginning.

"Herr Stumpf wants to see you," Hippold said.

Fritz Stumpf was no longer gentle or elegant to her. "Hilde," he said, "your bar bill is growing too large. Last week you drank more than you earned."

The girl was still beautiful, but the childish charm had hardened and she no longer played at innocence.

"You do not get enough dates for me."

"There are over a quarter of a million lovely girls in Berlin. Thousands of them would change places with you in a moment. Do you need a drink now, Hilde?"

"Yes."

She used both hands to steady her glass.

The chanteuse sang the old Kurt Weill Berlin theater song:

"Oh, the shark's teeth,
How they bite. . . ."

"We are having a little party at my apartment later," Fritz Stumpf said. "Some of your friends will be there. Elke asked me particularly to invite you. You might be surprised. Things could become better for you again. Shall you be there, Hilde?"

She closed her eyes and nodded . . . yes.

CHAPTER TWENTY

A week before the elections the weather began to be cold.

In the Potsdam palace of Commissar V. V. Azov, Rudi Wöhlman and Heinrich Hirsch went over final campaign plans.

"It is time for the American radio," Azov said. He turned the power on and dialed RIAS, paced in a slow gait, hands clasped behind him, eyes on the floor.

"This is the Voice of Freedom."

Rudi Wöhlman laughed. A slight twitch developed on the right side of the commissar's face. Heinrich Hirsch prepared to scribble notes.

"This is RIAS, Radio in the American Sector. The next voice you hear will be Colonel Neal Hazzard, commandant of the American Sector."

Azov stopped his pacing and hovered over the radio.

"My friends. In keeping with American policy of bringing the truth to the people of Berlin, I will debunk the latest lie written in the Soviet newspaper, *Täglische Rundschau,* yesterday. The article by Heinrich Hirsch gave false figures on the contributions of the four occupation powers in the feeding of Berlin. Soviet contributions have amounted to 10 per cent of the total although a third of the population is in the Soviet Sector. Furthermore, this food has been taken entirely from the economy of the Russian Zone of Germany. The United States has spent sixty million dollars of the American people's money to bring food to this city in the first year of occupation . . ."

Azov snapped the radio off, returned to his desk, drummed his fingers. The portrait of Comrade Stalin seemed to glower at him.

Wöhlman wiped his glasses, replaced them. "RIAS has some nuisance value. It will have no effect on the election."

Wöhlman had reasons to be cocksure. He had engineered a classical campaign mixing inducements with threats. Feed them with the right hand, hold a club with the left.

"Let us continue," Azov said testily.

Heinrich Hirsch had plotted a whirlwind campaign finish. The usual demonstrations, speeches, and inundation of literature. "In addition, we have the special events. Four days before elections a fifteen-car trainload of wheat and potatoes will arrive and be distributed with extraordinary news coverage."

There was more. Ten thousand tons of Polish Silesian coal would arrive for the winter.

The final coup would take place two days before the election. Five Democratic candidates for assemblyman had been "persuaded" by Schatz's SND to join the anti-Fascist front, legal only in the Russian Sector. They would make their announcements at almost poll time.

It all looked well on paper. Yet Azov was not entirely certain. Brigadier Trepovitch had reported a stiffening Western attitude at the Kommandatura. Moreover, the Western military government personnel had too much experience in open elections to fall for trickery. The Russian attempt to have different-colored ballots for each party failed.

The West insisted Trepovitch submit the list of eligible voters and that he use the stamping of ration books to assure a single ballot to a single voter.

British, French, and American officials would be on hand at every

polling station in the Russian Sector. . . . It would be damned hard
to rig.

"These bourgeois gestures do not disturb me," Wöhlman said.

While Wöhlman exuded confidence, Heinrich Hirsch wondered. He
had known Wöhlmans, Azovs, Schatzes, Ecks all his life. At a certain
point their ability to have individual thought processes stopped, and
their minds were completely dominated by party thinking. They functioned without a shred of anger, curiosity, or protest in their being.
They were unable to have concepts of right or wrong.

Men who had no anger, curiosity, or protest in themselves could not
understand how it could exist in other people.

Hirsch had never entirely lost these traits despite his training. He
feared that their efforts had been a deception so transparent that the
people of Berlin were going to rally behind Falkenstein in a display of
defiance.

Azov was looking at Hirsch. The younger man had been under suspicion, but he possessed a mind far keener than Wöhlman's.

"What is your opinion, Comrade Hirsch?"

"I cannot completely share Comrade Wöhlman's confidence. We
should win in a stampede. Yet, some final dramatic gesture is called for
on the eve of the election."

"But we have spent millions of rubles to bring in food and coal."

That was what annoyed Hirsch. In the coal negotiations with the
British they were forced to stick to the line that the Soviet Union could
not force the Poles to give up Silesian coal. When Azov wanted coal
as a campaign gesture, Polish sovereignty did not exist.

Wasn't this last-minute flood of food rather obvious when it was
known the Americans had maintained the ration for over a year? And
now they had RIAS to give their story. Had they all underestimated
RIAS?

"Comrades," Hirsch said, "I believe I have the type of message the
Berliners will understand."

Two days before the election, Heinrich Hirsch's plan unfolded. The
Soviet Union controlled the flow of electricity to the Western Sectors.

At darkness, the people of the Steglitz Borough discovered they had
no electricity.

Twenty minutes later the lights went out in the French boroughs of
Wedding and Reinickendorf.

An hour later the central British boroughs of Tiergarten and Charlottenburg were plunged into darkness.

Alternating borough by borough, the lights went out in a wordless bit of last-minute electioneering. Without Russian electricity there would be no industry, transportation, sewage disposal, communication, schools, or hospitals.

The day of October 20 in the year of 1946 was a misery of cold and drizzle. For the first time in a decade Berliners went to the polls. The outpour of people brought mile-long lines of ragged humanity huddling for warmth against the first real bites of winter. Ballot boxes were crammed to elect the new Assembly of 130 members.

At dawn of the next day, Berlin was awakened by a now familiar voice:

"This is RIAS calling. The results of yesterday's election is as follows. The Democratic Party, 1,015,000 ballots giving them sixty-three Assembly seats with 49 per cent of the vote.

"The Christian Party was second with over 460,000 ballots, winning twenty-nine Assembly seats and receiving 22 per cent of the vote.

"Third, the Communists under the name of People's Proletariat received 400,000 ballots, twenty-six Assembly seats and 19 per cent of the vote.

"The Conservative Party won the balance of twelve seats with 195,-000 ballots constituting 9 per cent of the vote.

"The free parties have swept the election with a staggering combination of 81 per cent."

CHAPTER TWENTY-ONE

The stinging defeat at the polls presented a new tactical problem to V. V. Azov. He realized the new Berlin Assembly would never elect a Communist Oberburgermeister and so he threw their strength to retaining the old Democrat Berthold Hollweg, whom they could control.

The Communist Heinz Eck was unable to attain to higher than second deputy mayor.

In the Kommandatura a new wrinkle was added as Nikolai Trepovitch ordered investigations into the backgrounds of a great number of free party assemblymen for "suspected Nazi pasts." He was thus able to keep them from taking their office.

Although the West grew passive again after the election, the first open break between America and the Soviet Union had taken place that wild autumn of 1946.

The Berliners were certain that the few gestures of the West were in the nature of face-saving. They remained cool to each other.

Repercussions of the election continued to be felt throughout all facets of the society. At the university a rumble grew and grew.

Heidi Fritag and Matthias Schindler shared the common heritage of having parents murdered by the Nazis.

Heidi was half Jewish, her father once a professor at the university. Except for the "taint" in her ancestry, the intense girl was a physical personification of Hitler's Aryan dream; tall, full-busted, blond. When her father was taken away, Heidi and her mother lived in seclusion in that low caste of being daughter and wife of a Jew.

Matthias Schindler's story was one of pure horror. His father had been a Democratic Party leader in Brandenburg. He was sent to Dachau early in the regime as a political undesirable; his mother died shortly thereafter. Matthias was placed in a series of work camps for children of political prisoners and Jews. The end of the war found him having survived a dozen camps and working as a slave laborer of the Krupp Industries and the death of his father confirmed.

The university had a tradition sweeping back a century and a half with such honored names as Humboldt and Niebuhr and the Brothers Grimm. War had ravaged many of the main buildings on the Unter Den Linden.

Heinrich Hirsch re-established the university in the Russian Sector, appointed a Communist rector, filled the faculty with hand-picked teachers, texts, and curriculum to convert it into a school of Marxism.

All the new students were carefully screened. Both Heidi Fritag and Matthias Schindler were clean of Nazi taint and thought to be pro-Russian.

The returning professors and many of the students did not fit neatly into Hirsch's vision of the institution. They began to complain to the Americans for a liberalization of studies.

In the autumn of 1945 American policy had been to cooperate with the Russians at any price. Neal Hazzard brought up the question of the university at the Kommandatura, taking the view that it should be under four-power control.

Trepovitch made one of his unmovable stands. Hazzard let the matter die. The Russian position was that the university was physically in the Russian Sector and of no interest to the West.

During 1946 Hirsch consolidated his grip. Every political, historical, and philosophical study was derived from a base of Lenin and Marx. All student clubs were under domination of young Communists on the campus. Likewise, the faculty organization was run by Communist professors.

Both the students and faculty came under heavy pressure to join Communist activities. Often students were threatened with being expelled if they did not attend special lectures, join demonstrations, donate time to the Action Squads.

After the Berlin Assembly election of the fall of 1946, a number of Communists were taken out of the educational system in the Magistrat. A ground swell started among the students and non-Communist teachers for reforms.

Heinrich Hirsch used the textbook tactics dictated by Lenin. In the light of the elections and the temper of the moment he made a temporary retreat by granting a number of small but unimportant concessions.

The stirrings grew. Heidi Fritag and Matthias Schindler emerged as the opposition leaders on a crest of unrest. The two personally petitioned Colonel Hazzard for an American license to form a Democratic Students' Club on the campus and publish a weekly newspaper. Even though the school was in the Russian Sector, it would be keeping within the contention that the university was rightly under four-power control.

Hazzard warned the youngsters that they would be in danger and out of reach of American help, but they were adamant.

RIAS and the American newspaper announced the granting of the club license followed by an appeal from Heidi Fritag urging the students to join. What happened caught Heinrich Hirsch flat-footed. Over half the students flocked to the Democratic Club.

In the Kommandatura Nikolai Trepovitch raged at the "illegal" organization and promised to break it up. Neal Hazzard did not budge.

In a few days the first issue of the Democratic Students' Club newspaper, *Justice*, was printed and distributed. The two-page tabloid carried a front-page editorial by Matthias Schindler.

WE DEMAND!
Academic Freedom!
An end to Marxist indoctrination!
Democratic student power!
Texts of Western philosophy!
Courses in religion!

Heinrich Hirsch stood with eyes cast down, figuring out the pattern on the Persian rug. V. V. Azov flung a copy of *Justice* at his feet.

"The blood of the Soviet Union drenches every millimeter of German soil! Do you think we have spilled it to stand by idly and allow the rebirth of Nazism!"

Hirsch's voice trembled. "It would be difficult to consider Matthias Schindler or Heidi Fritag as Fascists."

"All Germans are Nazis at heart!"

My father was not a Fascist, Heinrich said to himself.

"You will learn once and for all, Comrade Hirsch, that no German nationalism is tolerated and the German people will learn that their only salvation is through the Soviet Union!"

The abduction of Heidi Fritag and Matthias Schindler by unmarked cars of the SND was swift and efficient. Schatz's political police bound and gagged them and whisked them out of Berlin. The kidnap was followed by an Action Squad from the university breaking into the print shop of *Justice* and destroying it.

The kidnap cars sped south and were swallowed up in the darkness of the Russian Zone of Germany. They halted at a castle on a former Prussian Junker estate near Jüterbog. The captives were hustled into dungeon cells where V. V. Azov, himself, had come to supervise the confessions. They had to be carefully staged, recorded, and photographed.

In the old days Azov was able to estimate within minutes how long a person could hold out. Most of those who had been brought to him during the purges had already appraised their predicament and confessed without resistance, but during the purges they only wanted to keep alive and continue as partners in the crime.

Matthias Schindler and Heidi Fritag held on to something a purged Russian never knew; the usual promise of sleep, food, water, cigarettes did not work.

The commissar could not understand their stubbornness. Five nights and days of round-the-clock questioning failed to break them. Matthias Schindler, with the glistening marks of other beatings from the Nazis, smiled and spit at them.

Heidi Fritag, the damned Jewess, merely sat erect, tight-lipped, defiant.

Azov sweated. He ordered the use of drugs, for he was getting the worst of the questionings. His stomach had turned to fire. The drugs produced blurted ramblings unsuitable as evidence to the world. As a last ditch, he decided upon torture. It had to be done with care so that no visible mutilations would show.

Schindler got it first. He broke and signed a confession.

Heidi Fritag continued to hold out.

She was stripped naked and lashed to a table. Mirrors were rigged up before her eyes so she was able to see the entire length of her body. Candles were placed on both breasts and lit. As they burned lower and lower the hot wax dripped on her. Lower . . . lower . . . she convulsed with pain. One of Azov's commissars sat close by, drumming questions into her ear, promising relief.

On the eleventh day after the kidnap a "trial" was held. Heinrich Hirsch was forced to observe everything.

Present in the castle were members of Adolph Schatz's Special Nazi Detachment, NKVD, and two carefully selected journalists. V. V. Azov sat at the end of the room as an "interested" observer.

Matthias Schindler had been cleaned up so that he might be photographed, and was dragged into the room under heavy sedation.

A prosecutor read his confession. "I admit to undercover activities dedicated to the rebirth of fascism at the university . . ."

A sentence of twenty-five years was passed.

Schindler was dragged away and Heidi Fritag was called.

A member of the SND came into the room and whispered into Azov's ear, "The girl died a few moments ago." Azov stood and asked to address the court.

"Heidi Fritag has attempted suicide out of guilt. She cannot appear in court. However, we have her signed confession."

The journalists wrote "interviews" with the defendants in which they expressed extreme remorse for their "crimes." Tapes were edited and photographs retouched. . . . People's justice had been done.

Sean O'Sullivan was brought out of his sleep by a sharp knock on the door. He turned on the lamp. It was three in the morning. Blessing stood at the door.

"Get dressed," Bless said. "Pack a bag, quick. We're taking a trip."

Sean did as he was told without question.

A staff car waited at curbside. Bless got in the front seat next to the driver and Sean in the back. Neal Hazzard was waiting. They sped along the Unter Den Eichen.

"We have General Hansen's plane standing by at Tempelhof. We're carrying out a single VIP to London. Keep him company. Write down what he says. See that he doesn't try to knock himself off."

"Defector?"

"A big one. Heinrich Hirsch."

CHAPTER TWENTY-TWO

V. V. Azov had forced Hirsch to attend session after session of the questioning and torture of Heidi Fritag and Matthias Schindler to break this strange streak of resistance in him.

Hirsch watched the whole event like a witness at his father's death. The circle was complete. He, a victim of tyranny, had now seen the same merciless destruction imposed on an enemy. He, the Communist, had killed in the same manner as his father had died at the hands of the Nazis.

Azov's attempt to debase his spirit was the final disillusion of what was once a golden idea. He still believed in Communism, but had come to detest the men who had perverted it beyond recognition.

Yet, the last thread of defiance did not break. He would not submit to this final humiliation . . . to become a Communist robot without a soul.

Months earlier he had gotten wind of certain happenings in the American Sector that planted a seed of escape in his mind.

Jews, freed from death camps in Poland, trekked west to attempt to get to Palestine, the only door open to them. They were carefully shepherded by young Palestinians who slipped them to French and Italian ports. Immigration to Palestine was deemed illegal by the ruling British mandate.

Although it meant going against his British colleague, Neal Hazzard quietly established a refugee camp for the Jews in the American Sector and saw to it they got what they needed in the way of displaced persons documents.

General Hansen unofficially encouraged his officers all over Germany to help the transit of the Jews to embarkation ports for Palestine.

The Russians learned of this and watched the American-protected camps with suspicion.

Heinrich Hirsch alone stumbled onto the information that one of the leaders in the Jewish underground in Berlin was the American chaplain. On closer scrutiny Hirsch discovered that many Russian Jewish soldiers visited the chaplain's house to attend services forbidden in the Russian Army. The rabbi's place was a social center for Jewish soldiers of all four occupation powers. Here they met Jewish girls from the camp, or others who had been hidden and were trying to get to Palestine.

The NKVD was baffled by the disappearance of some forty Russian Jewish soldiers. Hirsch figured that they would rendezvous with the chaplain in civilian dress, he would issue them displaced persons papers, and they would disappear into the American camp.

He never reported his findings to his own authorities. After the fate of Matthias Schindler and Heidi Fritag was sealed, Hirsch made his own rendezvous with the chaplain.

His confession and the revelation of Heidi Fritag's brutal death hit Berlin as hard as the first rages of winter. The classes at the university emptied and refused to reconvene despite the threats of Communist students' Action Squads.

Hostile bands of students circled aimlessly looking for a voice as the pitch boiled to a fever; and then a half-dozen new leaders stepped forward from both the student body and the faculty.

They announced defiantly that a memorial service would be held for Heidi Fritag on the steps of the main building.

The People's Radio reacted quickly to denounce Heinrich Hirsch as a traitor and his confession as a lie. The threat was made that a demonstration would be broken up by force and all participants expelled.

Neal Hazzard had taken Heidi Fritag's death very hard. As a combat commander he had sent men into battle with a reasonable chance of defending themselves. Heidi Fritag died helpless . . . as helpless as the students would be if they tried a demonstration.

The British and French commandants entered the Kommandatura conference room without greeting Nikolai Trepovitch. The Russian, stripped of flamboyance, stared emptily at the papers before him.

Colonel Neal Hazzard arrived last. He looked at the Russian for the first time with absolute hatred.

Nikolai Trepovitch had just finished a merciless session with Marshal Popov. As chairman, he called the meeting to order.

"I have requested this emergency meeting to discuss illegal activities planned at the university. Heinrich Hirsch is a traitor, a liar, and a provocateur. We have signed confessions of the accused. Unless this demonstration is called off we will resort to necessary measures."

"I take it then," T. E. Blatty said, "you propose to massacre students in the streets."

"I propose to stop a demonstration of Fascist militarism."

"But sir, you established the university, you screened these students, you chose their studies and their teachers."

Trepovitch fell back to the second line of defense. The plan was to hold out bait of a promise of four-power control of the university in exchange for stopping the demonstration. Once the West agreed, Trepovitch could haggle over the control mechanism until the incident died down.

"We are a peace-loving people," Trepovitch said. "The Soviet Union wishes to avoid bloodshed. For the sake of Allied unity we would consider the possibility of four-power control."

"No," Neal Hazzard said. "No four-power control, no one-power control. The school belongs to the people of Berlin. They have shown now they are ready to run it."

The Russian could not buy it. It would mean the end of their domination completely. "You want this school to foster German militarism and rebuild the Nazis! We will not tolerate it!"

Neal Hazzard appealed to the cooler heads among the new leaders of the university and convinced them to hold their demonstration in the American Sector.

Twenty-five hundred students walked the Stresemann Strasse spanning from curb to curb, and behind them walked 25,000 Berliners. At a place where Goebbels' Propaganda Ministry once stood they came to a halt, looking across the street into the Soviet Sector, a leveled field that once held Hitler's Reich Chancellory. It was filled with Soviet tanks and guns.

The students wore black arm bands, carried black-bordered photographs of the first martyr of a new age, Heidi Fritag. Other placards demanded the freedom of Matthias Schindler.

At the head of their number walked Colonel Neal Hazzard.

CHAPTER TWENTY-THREE—*Winter, 1946–47*

It was the coldest in the history of Europe.

In Berlin blustery north winds and snow dropped the temperature to twenty and thirty below zero. People froze to death by the dozens, helplessly covered with rags. The infant mortality rate skyrocketed; the water supply froze; filth bred epidemic; rampages of pneumonia and TB swept the city along with a diphtheria epidemic. Gonorrhea and syphilis had long ago found a home in the orgy-filled town.

Berlin was an icebox with bare shelves. Emergency soup kitchens attempted to stave off starvation. People were driven from the heatless shells of buildings down into the underground railroad and to bomb shelters.

In one of the desperation measures, the Kommandatura gave permission for Berliners to cut down their forests for use as firewood. This became the most terrible symbol of the defeat. They trudged in the face of a frigid death from their hovels to gather armloads of kindling.

In the Western Sectors the Grunewald and Tegel forest heard the ring of the ax as did the woods bordering the medieval section of the city at Spandau. In the Russian Sector the great State Forest on the Müggel toppled to the same fate.

When the Falkensteins were not at work they huddled around a single unit of warmth, a wood-kindled kitchen stove from turn of the century vintage, or they lay bundled beneath stacks of covering.

Ernestine was able to use her former legal training in obtaining a position in the Magistrat in the reorganization of the laws and courts. She worked for American jurists in the military government, which also kept her out of the physical cold a part of the day.

At home she tried in vain to bring her family back together. Hildegaard preyed on her mind always. She remained a regular at the Paris Cabaret, taking that sordid life as against the risks of the bitter weather and life outside. Hilde had a third case of gonorrhea and an abortion. Ernestine saw the arrogance fade from her sister. Hilde was the chattel of Stumpf, the mistress of Elke Handfest. Yet, despite it, the girl went into her twenty-first birthday with much of her early beauty.

Ernestine was unable to bear it any longer. Talks with Hilde had no effect. She went to her mother.

"I have suspected Hilde's activities for a long time," Herta said.

"Why in the name of God haven't you done something?" Ernestine demanded.

"I tried to speak to her, but she will admit to nothing. She passes me off. Besides, in these times who is to say she is wrong? It will all pass in a few years."

"Mother, we must do something for Hilde now. We can't wait. She must be sent out of Berlin."

"That is not possible without your father knowing why."

"Of course, he will be told."

Herta stood fast. "Your father must not know. He has enough troubles."

Gerd Falkenstein proved to be energetic, industrious, and ingenious. These were the traits, he boasted, that had made the German people superior and God's chosen.

With an old comrade and money from his father's savings, Gerd was able to buy up several thousand surplus gas masks and convert the metal casings into pans and ladles. As his parents worked to support his enterprise, he received a license to reclaim rubble and with his partner rigged a device to resurface bricks and stone into standard sizes. Their operation was carried on in a patched-up shell of a small, bombed-out factory in Schöneberg Borough in the Ami Sector. He boasted openly that the family would stop working one day and return to the old standard of living.

While his ambition was commendable, Ernestine feared his other attitudes. One of his workers was found to be an ex-Nazi in the Waffen SS and she knew that Gerd had helped him escape to the British Zone of Germany, which was the most lax on de-Nazification.

There was more that worried Ernestine. Gerd tried to obtain a license to form a veterans' organization, and when this was unsuccessful he continued to have weekly gatherings at his factory, where the old songs were sometimes sung and the exploits of the war recounted.

"There's nothing wrong with getting together with a few old friends," he told his sister. "Don't take it so seriously."

Lieutenant Oakley Oakes of Frog Creek, Missouri, was one of the most anonymous and at the same time obnoxious officers in military government. He had not come out correctly. Oakley stood an insignificant five feet, five inches tall, had wiry hair, and a pocked face. His personality was equally homely. His singular achievement was matriculation at a university where he joined the ROTC and this eventually brought him a commission in the Army.

He worked in the ration-control section of the Steglitz Borough and, as such, gained a running knowledge of many German families.

As a social failure back home, he luxuriated in his new status in Berlin, bragging constantly about his "exploits," to the boredom of fellow officers.

One day, in the winter of 1946, a new officer named Tom Jones was assigned to his section. Tom Jones, a few months out of college, was awed by the sophistication of the "old-timer" and his apparently limitless connections with German girls. He accepted Oakley Oakes' offer to "show him Berlin."

They started in Zehlendorf, near Headquarters, drinking at their own club, then working up toward Wedding Borough in the French Sector where Oakes assured Tom Jones he knew a Frenchy joint with the best poon in Berlin.

Oakley Oakes and companion burst into the French garrison's Bier Garten, a big noisy room that smelled of malt and hops and sauerkraut and pungent sausages. He waved and loudly greeted real and imaginary acquaintances as though he were part owner and certainly the most popular man in the city.

They plopped into heavily hewn chairs. Oakes smacked a pack of American cigarettes on the table and pointed to the bar lined with waiting girls. "There's the poon."

Tom Jones had been impassioned by the long evening of drinking and urged Lieutenant Oakes to make a connection quickly.

"Man, you acting like a boar hog in stud. Take it easy, man. Berlin's just one big poon town."

Oakley drank two large mugs of dark beer while playing out the role of complete nonchalance. He began to remember why he really wanted to come to the Wedding Bier Garten and remembering through the alcoholic haze turned him into a mean mood.

"How about the redhead?" Tom Jones panted.

"Nothing . . . she ain't nothing."

"That's nothing!"

"Stick with me, kid. I'm gonna get you laid good."

A third mug of beer made him fuzzy and thick-tongued and his posture decomposed. He turned bleary-eyed, opened his blouse and tie to get air. Cigar ashes dripped down his shirt. He remembered the Paris Cabaret and the humiliation of a week before. He was very drunk then, too, and tried to get a date with one of the girls; they hustled him out into the street and told him not to return, and the MPs drove him back to the American Sector.

"Son of a bitch," he mumbled.

"What you talking about, Mr. Oakes?"

"Can't fool this old boy. No, sir, not Oakley Oakes. Man, I know every goddam ration book in Steglitz Borough. I know that broad. I seen her up there for her book. She's the one that turned me down at the Paris . . ."

He put two fingers in his mouth and blasted out a whistle. "Hey, you, boy!" He snapped his fingers at Bruno Falkenstein. "That's how you gotta treat these kraut bastards."

Bruno stood before his table and bowed.

"I'm interested in some tail."

Bruno reddened and squelched his anger. This little sandy-haired wart had always been a troublemaker.

"Elsa will be in soon."

"She's a pig."

Tom Jones was getting sick.

"I will do what I can, Herr Lieutenant," Bruno said, hoping the damned Ami would pass out. He bowed again and tried to take leave but Oakes grabbed his sleeve.

"I want me Hilde Diehl."

"Diehl? But sir, I know of no Hilde Diehl."

Oakes' face wrinkled and he snarled. "Hilde from the Paris Cabaret."

"I am sorry, Herr Lieutenant. I do not know anyone from the Paris Cabaret."

"Bullshit."

"Hey, leave him alone, Mr. Oakes," Tom Jones pleaded.

"Don't you lie to me, boy. I said I want me Hilde Diehl."

"Herr Lieutenant, I swear to you, I know no one by that name."

"You know her you kraut pimp. She's your daughter."

Hilde's screams brought Ernestine running up the stairs past the open doors of the neighbors. She broke into the room. Her mother was at the table, head buried and weeping, and Gerd stood immobile in a corner.

Hildegaard cringed on the floor. Bruno stood above her, flailing both fists on her back as though he was wielding a sledge hammer.

"Pig! Slut!"

The veins of his neck and face throbbed with rushing blood. His color was as purple as his rage and the sweat poured from the exertion. He kicked his daughter in the ribs. "Pig! Pig! Pig!"

Hildegaard shrieked. As Ernestine tried to get to her, Gerd blocked her way and grabbed her arms. "Leave him alone."

She tore out of her brother's grip and flung herself on the floor as a shield to receive the last blows of his strength. Bruno gasped, reeled around the room, fell onto his cot, and groaned between curses.

"Shhh . . . shhh . . . shhh . . . he won't touch you any more . . . Ernestine is here . . . Ernestine is here . . ."

She struggled to her feet and got Hilde upright somehow. Gerd walked toward them, menacingly. Ernestine backed Hilde into a corner and stood between them.

Gerd stopped and smiled cruelly.

"Oh God in heaven!" Ernestine cried in anguish. "Look at what has become of us! This is our victory!" She turned to her beaten sister, took off her own coat and put it over Hilde's shoulders, and wiped at the blood spurting from the girl's nose and mouth. She held her tightly in her own thin arms and braced her to walk slowly over the room.

Her mother looked up. "Where are you taking her?"

"Away from here! Away from you!"

"I forbid it!" Bruno rasped. "I forbid it!"

They continued toward the door. Herta climbed clumsily to her feet, knuckles on the table. "Obey your father!" the mother commanded.

"I forbid! I . . . forbid!"

"Go to hell, Father," Ernestine said.

"I won't stand for you to talk to Father like that!" Gerd roared.

"My father," Ernestine whispered. She spat on the floor and led her sister.

"Stop them! I demand it! Stop them!"

Gerd blocked the doorway. He saw in Ernestine's eyes something more intense than the frenzy of a Nazi mob, more bitter than enemy soldier to enemy soldier. He stepped aside. "Let the little whore go."

Ulrich Falkenstein set his book down, shuffling to the door in response to the urgent knocking.

"My God!" he cried at the sight of Hildegaard.

Ernestine held her hands open desperately. "We have been walking for hours all over Berlin. It is cold. We have no place to go. She is sick. Please help us . . ."

Ulrich stood at the door of the bedroom watching Ernestine at her sister's bedside. She was like an angel, speaking softly, giving warmth.

Hilde's cheekbone had been fractured and several ribs broken. Her face was puffed and discolored, but the pain was now blocked by a wall of drugs.

"Ernestine. You are so good! I love you. Oh, Ernestine . . . you are all that is left of us that is decent . . ."

"Please rest . . ."

"You tried to tell me what a fool I am . . ."

"Don't go back there . . . ever!"

"Russian officers are in back of Stumpf . . . Hippold . . . they may kill me."

"I'll get you out of Berlin. I swear it!"

"Oh, God, Erna . . . I'd give anything . . . anything . . ."

Hilde's eyelids became heavy and she passed into sleep begging her sister not to leave her. Ernestine held her hand for an hour, and at last Ulrich took her back to his study.

She painfully told her uncle the story of Hilde's downfall and of Gerd and her parents.

"I am the worst of them all," she said. "I did not help her. But I wonder, Uncle . . . do we deserve better?" And then Ernestine began to cry softly. "I have turned on my own father."

She felt Ulrich's hand on her shoulder. "It is high time some German sons and daughters do that."

"There is good in Hilde. I swear I'll do anything if she is given another chance."

"First, she must mend. And then she will leave Berlin. There are friends in the Western Zones who will take her."

It had been a long, long time since Ernestine felt the warmth of another human being. She knelt before her uncle's chair and laid her head on his lap and let herself be comforted. "You are so kind," she said.

"And you, my child, what of you? You cannot go back there."

"I don't know."

"This is a lonesome place for an old man," he said.

She looked up at the scholarly, slovenly room filled with books he had not been able to read and music he had not heard.

"Would you share this place with me, Ernestine?"

Perhaps, she thought, I can help him too. We do need each other. I will take care of him.

"You will stay?"

"I love you, Uncle Ulrich . . . and I have been so cold for so long . . ."

CHAPTER TWENTY-FOUR

Blessing covered the door opening with his hulk, leaned against the frame, and chewed on a strip of beef jerky, which Lil always sent in the packages. Bo Bolinski finished packing, wordlessly.

Bo lay the last three khaki shirts in a battered canvas officer's bag, buckled it shut, set it alongside his foot locker, and looked about the room.

"I guess that's everything," he said, looking at his watch. Two hours to traintime. Bo sat on the locker and lit a cigarette. His unhappiness was apparent. "We've been together a long time, Bless. The major and you and me. London, France, Rombaden."

"We're all that's left of the team," Bless said.

"The captains and the kings depart."

Bo had received an excellent opportunity from a large and important law firm in Chicago. Its attorneys and most of its clients were Polish-Americans. At the end of the war the firm became flooded by those trying to re-establish contact with lost relatives or claim lost fortunes.

It was a natural situation for Bolinski. He was a good lawyer, experienced in displaced persons work, spoke fluent Polish and English, was an expert on indemnification and restitutions, and had built up contacts. It was the time and place for a young man to go far.

Bo sent Major O'Sullivan his request to resign from the Army. In a few months he would have been eligible for discharge, anyway, and Sean pushed it through.

Somehow the return to the States did not bring him the expected exaltation . . . not leaving Berlin or even the anticipation of the reunion with his wife and children. He had convinced himself he had done enough and was entitled to leave. Yet . . .

"It's going to be a funny feeling to see a city not wrecked by bombs . . . and look at people who aren't hungry."

"I reckon so."

"What about you, Bless?"

"My discharge should be coming up in three or four months."

"I'll be glad when you get out of here. This city is like standing over a trap door waiting for the Russians to pull the lever."

"We all want to go home," Bless said. "That's our national anthem."

"We can't all be made like the major."

"Reckon not. The Lord put his finger on certain people to do the dirty work for the rest of us."

"Don't be so sure it's out of love. He hates the Germans enough to stay here for a century so long as they're suffering."

"I wouldn't say that, Bo."

"Anyhow, it's time to go in and say good-by to him."

Shenandoah Blessing watched Bo's train disappear from sight and hearing. He wheeled his jeep from trackside and drove back toward Headquarters. Bo felt guilty, but no one could blame him for wanting home, Blessing thought. Hell, everyone who could was pulling out these days.

They had offered him captain's bars to remain in Berlin two more years. Small compensation for the losing battle being fought. Lil and his kids hungered for him and he for them.

Bless knew he was pushing forty-five. The law of the land said that Hook County had to reinstate him as sheriff. His first deputy, Charlie Durkin, had held the office for five years now. Charlie knew his way around and was a good officer. No doubt he had built his own political connections and had become entrenched. Blessing would have to face him in an election.

Had he returned at the end of the war, he would have won any election, hands down. But the days of returning heroes were gone. The war was over for nearly two years and wanted only to be forgotten by Americans. There would be resentment against him now. Soldiers in uniform were big people when there was a fight to be won, but these were the days when soldiers in outposts were forgotten.

A month after Bolinski left for the States, Captain Shenandoah Blessing stood at dockside at the American enclave of Bremerhaven in the British Zone as the first shipload of American wives and children arrived through a North Sea's mist.

There was much weeping and embracing on the dock. Lil and the two kids dragged down the gangplank as did most of them, weary from the voyage. They stood and looked at each other.

"Hi, Bless," she said.

"Hi, Lil."

He scooped up his sons and they hugged him and said hello daddy and he said, my God, they've grown and the four of them walked slowly and tightly together for the shed.

Later a heavily armed train chugged through the unfriendly German countryside toward Berlin. After a barrage of questions the boys fell off to sleep and Lil curled up in his arms, poked his belly, and said she was glad he hadn't gotten skinny.

"Honey," he said, "I was never able to put into words why I thought I should stay here and I swear, I don't think I ever can."

"Bless, you don't have to. We'll make out. We always have. I know you're doing the right thing."

CHAPTER TWENTY-FIVE

At the end of 1946 the lead story around the world for the day told that Andrew Jackson Hansen had been named a full general and assumed the position of military governor of Germany.

Shrewd observers like Nelson Goodfellow Bradbury felt it came just in time, for the situation was degenerating badly.

In a quiet and efficient way Hansen had built a dazzling record. As first deputy he had sat as a member of the Supreme German Council for several months. At the end of the war he moved in on cartels, froze German assets, and broke the backs of a number of those evil industrial combines. He spearheaded the de-Nazification of two million Germans in the American Zone through the questions of the Fragebogen. A hundred thousand criminal Nazis were in American stockades, and an additional 300,000 were allowed to work only at common labor.

Hansen was tough, yet guided by an overriding principle that the American Zone had to establish its own democracy rather than exist under a military tribunal.

As quickly as clean Germans could be found, the courts and de-Nazification procedures were put into their hands.

Free elections were held in three "lands" in the American Zone with new constitutions governing them and schools reopened with new texts. A free press and radio returned to Germany after a long absence.

Hansen was instrumental in the spurring of youth groups formed on new principles and he encouraged the church to purge any Nazi taint.

Andrew Jackson Hansen was more responsible than any other man for bringing into military government leading American educators, jurists, clergymen, labor leaders, mayors and civic officials, doctors, engineers, and police who lent their skills in fashioning a new path for the German people. He arranged for Germans to travel in America to study American methods and establishments.

He spurred the revival of the opera, the symphony, the theater, and the arts.

On Hansen's orders three battalions of Negro troops were converted from service units to infantry. A new pride changed them from outfits with severe discipline problems to first-rate troops. His own honor guard in Berlin was a Negro unit. Hansen alone predicted the next step had to be full integration. He felt that the example of a moving, living democracy would have the greatest possible effect on the German people.

A corner of America was established in Germany. The arrival of large numbers of wives and children in the early parts of 1947 did much to put a skid to the occupation orgy.

Schools were built and women's clubs, PTA's, and a social life put a large dent into the beer-hall and prostitution business. The reinstatement of family and communal life came as a saving grace in many cases.

The occupation forces published their own newspapers, had a radio network, built movies, servicemen's clubs, bowling alleys, and libraries. Inexpensive vacations in Bavarian resorts were arranged and schooling through college made available to every soldier.

Law and order were maintained by a magnificent American constabulary of 30,000 mobile police. These white-helmeted, yellow-scarfed troops constituted a crack force that commanded the respect of the Germans.

The most spectacular victory was won by the friendliness of the Americans. The Germans realized that they had come not to bleed the economy or debase the vanquished, but to protect, cleanse, teach, and rebuild.

While General Hansen and his country established a record of progress, the other side of the coin was a dark picture. He took command on the heels of a cruel winter that had paralyzed all of Europe.

In Germany canals froze, putting more burden on the wrecked rail system, now short thousands of cars and running on obsolete engines and punctured lines. There were no spare parts either in the transportation or the manufacturing complex.

As the coal mines functioned at but a fraction of capacity, and the means to transport it collapsed, manufacturing all but stopped.

The land failed to respond because of a lack of fertilizer and there were few seeds.

Housing remained the worst of any civilized nation and the cold brought all normal functions to a standstill.

The terror was compounded when seven million Germans were expelled from Hungary, Poland, East Prussia, and Czechoslovakia and poured into the American and British zones.

Hansen had observed the dwindling of the American Army. He inherited a force so thin it would not be able to meet a direct military challenge.

There was confusion among the Americans on what to do with Germany.

A harsh line wanted to reduce Germany to an agrarian economy. Hansen knew this plan would never work. Germany had a land area of less than the state of California and ten times the population with almost no natural wealth. In her best days, Germany had never been self-sustaining in the raising of food. Germany had to manufacture and trade to survive. This was an absolute economic law. The plan to reduce her to a vast farm would have invited mass starvation and sown the seeds of another war.

A second plan was to chop Germany into small territories and have each neighbor annex a piece. However, none of these units by themselves were sustaining and would create a burden on the annexing country which would be also compelled to take a hostile German minority. This plan could only foster a German "unification" dream.

Hansen had to take the unpopular view that Germany had to manufacture and trade. Moreover, the occupation zones had to be reunified, for the country could respond only as a single economic unit. The American Zone had pretty Bavarian scenery, but no ports or great industry; neither could the British or Russian zones survive by themselves.

Yet, Hansen inherited a situation where each of the four occupation zones was cut off from the other with little exchange of product, ideas, or population.

On the Supreme German Council, the French position broke Western unity. General Yves de Lys argued out of fear of Germany; the French wanted economic domination of the Saar and Internationalization of the Ruhr.

The Ruhr represented Germany's chief asset. Without it Germany could never establish a trade balance. Such a French plan would have continued the British and American zones as liabilities, costing billions to sustain.

The French wanted a permanent four-power army on the Rhine, but Hansen would have no part of Soviet troops beyond the Elbe.

General de Lys continued to operate on the contention that business could be done with the Soviet Union and the French did not want to offend them.

Marshal Alexei Popov bogged down the Supreme German Council on the basic issue of operating Germany as a single economic unit with free trade between zones governed by a common policy. He deceitfully paid lip service to unity, but in fact sealed the Russian Zone from any contact with the West.

Every attempt to establish four-power administrations over trade and industry was blocked by Popov as the Russians continued to strip their zone and reshape it in the image of a Soviet puppet.

Reports filtered back to Hansen that thousands of German prisoners with technical skills had been detained in the Soviet Union. Russia's grand plan for her zone was much the same as what Hitler intended to do with Poland, reduce it to serfdom and set it up as a buffer.

Popov aided the elaborate Communist scheme by holding Germany down, draining off reparations from current production, and keeping her from re-establishing a trade balance.

All this brought joblessness, hunger, and all the other breeding grounds of Communism.

The key issue at the Supreme German Council was a four-power agreement on German steel production. Popov wanted a figure large enough to deliver reparations, but small enough to prevent a German recovery. Even though all of Europe was coal-starved, the Ruhr mines were permitted to operate at a fraction of capacity, for the collapsed economies of France and Italy also played into the path of Soviet aims.

One of Hansen's first moves was to travel to Washington and urge the Secretary of State to come to Germany and deliver a statement of policy to the people.

They were shaken from the winter, frightened of what lay ahead, and a lethargy had engulfed them.

The Secretary of State spoke at Heidelberg reaffirming America's aim to unify the zones and return its institutions to the people. It had a galvanizing effect on the demolished nation.

Immediately thereafter, Hansen began negotiations with the British for the purpose of making the American and British zones a single economic and political unit. This forced the Soviet Union to step up their own timetable, for they knew that the French would have to follow suit. The unity of the Western Zones could build up a powerful German threat and end their own plans of domination.

All four powers jockeyed for position for a Conference of Foreign Ministers. In preparation, Hansen flew to Washington to brief the American delegation. His opening remark threw off the last pretenses:

"Gentlemen, the Soviet Union will cooperate with the West only as long as they receive reparations from our zones. The instant this stops they will proceed with plans to stop unification of the Western Zones. They will endeavor to remove us first from Berlin, then from Germany, then from Europe."

CHAPTER TWENTY-SIX

The tragic strains from Beethoven's "Pathétique Sonata" reached Sean's ears as he approached the door to Ulrich Falkenstein's flat in Kreuzberg. He stopped for a moment, listened, then rang the bell. The music inside stopped.

"Lieutenant Colonel O'Sullivan?" Ernestine asked.

"Yes."

"Please come in. I am Ernestine, Herr Falkenstein's niece. My uncle telephoned to say he would be a few minutes late, that he was distressed by the delay and hoped you would not mind."

"Certainly not."

She led him into the only patched-up room that had been made cozy, which served as both living room and his study.

"Could I prepare you some tea?"

"No thank you."

The bookshelves sagged under hundreds of volumes. Sean walked along and browsed at the titles in German, French, English, consisting of both profound comments and the popular fiction of the mid-thirties. He found himself at a row containing Jefferson, Paine, and Thoreau.

"Quite an assortment."

"He reads incessantly and usually far into the night. He is trying to make up for those years he lost in Schwabenwald."

Her words struck Sean as rather strange. He thought about it for a moment, and then discovered that in all the time he had been in Germany he had never heard a German before mention the name of a concentration camp in casual conversation.

He stopped at the piano. There was a photograph of Ulrich's brother Wolfgang, who had been hung by Hitler. And another photograph, perhaps Falkenstein's wife, whom he never mentioned, but likewise never forgot. Sean hit a few notes in a vain effort to read the music.

"You must play very well," he said.

"Gallant but not true, Colonel. I play poorly. Nonetheless it is the first time in years I have had either an opportunity or the atmosphere. As you see, the rooms are not damaged and it is quite peaceful. One of the first things lost in the bombing was my piano. My sister joked that the American flyers must have heard me and aimed at our house."

Sean turned to look at her. He had noticed her graceful movement from the moment she answered the door. The fingers that played the piano were long and artful, but had also known hard work. Her face was particularly elegant, with flawless skin set off by deep, sorrowful, expressive eyes. Her hair, immaculately groomed and businesslike, was however, entirely feminine. Her voice was unusually soft and without Germanic abruptness. Ernestine began to fidget.

Sean ended the tour.

"Are you sure?" she asked, pointing to an array of richly colored liqueurs in cut-crystal bottles on the coffee table. He sat on the opposite end of the couch and said she could buy him an apricot brandy.

Ernestine opened a tin. "This is Leubeck flat cake. The wife of an old comrade of my uncle sends us one each month. You will find it quite different."

He took a bite and agreed.

Ernestine looked at him from the corners of her eyes, and was unable to constrain a small giggle. "So you are Major . . . I'm sorry, Colonel O'Sullivan."

"That's me."

"Of course, my uncle Ulrich has spoken of you innumerable times. I was expecting someone quite different."

"How's that?"

"Well, I saw you as much older . . . and . . . "

"And?"

"You won't be offended?"

"Promise."

"Rather stern . . . you know, like a Prussian."

She did not know what compelled her to be so familiar except that Uncle Ulrich's description drew a picture of a man of iron discipline and surly nature. He seemed terribly young to have been governor of Rombaden.

"I'm glad you don't find me . . . like a Prussian."

Ernestine jumped to her feet at the sound of the door opening. Ulrich Falkenstein puffed into the room with apologies. She took his coat, wiped the perspiration from his brow, chastised him for walking so hard, and inquired if he had taken his pills. He had forgotten, as usual. She settled him into a chair, and when certain he was comfortable and calm, she took her leave.

Sean watched all this with curiosity, wondering if she was pampering him because of the comforts he could offer or if their relationship was true.

Ulrich sipped his tea. "She babies me, that girl. It is such a comfort having her. Congratulations on your promotion."

"Thank you."

"What extraordinary calamity brings you into a German home?"

Sean smiled. Falkenstein was the one German whose needle did not annoy him.

"Right to the point?"

"I never expect less of you."

"All right," Sean said. "It's not pleasant news. We have conclusive evidence that your distinguished Oberburgermeister, Berthold Hollweg, is in complete collaboration with the Russians."

Falkenstein set his tea down, digested Sean's words. "All of us in the Democratic Party know he is not the same man he once was. We also know of the pressure he has been under. Hollweg has been my comrade for decades, since we were boys. Weak, yes. Movable, yes. But collaboration . . . never . . . never . . ."

"It's in his own handwriting, Herr Falkenstein."

Falkenstein's face showed astonishment. He did not believe it.

"Not only does he obey Rudi Wöhlman's orders," Sean continued, "but there are also some interesting numbered bank accounts in Switzerland."

"No!"

"I'm sorry, sir. It is absolutely conclusive."

Falkenstein shook his head, pulled himself out of the deep chair, paced disquietly before the books. "What do you want of me?"

"When the exact moment is ripe, your own people have got to confront him with the charges."

"You do it! You do it in the Kommandatura."

"No. You have to do it as an internal affair."

"And while you Americans keep your sanctimonious, official, and holier-than-thou status, duly elected members of the Berlin Assembly and duly selected officials of the Magistrat have been kept out of their offices by so-called investigations of the Russians. The Soviet Union doesn't know we won a free election, but they do know the Americans will continue to sit on their hands. God knows what Hollweg has undergone. Members of my party are harassed day and night . . ."

"Herr Falkenstein . . . I came out of personal respect for you," Sean interrupted. "Permanent reforms can come only from the will of the German people . . . if they desire it. You know damned well that you and not I must read Hollweg out of the party."

"You lost your calling, Colonel. You should have been a minister. How convenient for you to continue to say you do not trust Germans. Well, sir, we do not trust Americans. Of course, we are beholden for the fact that you have not mutilated or starved a defeated enemy. But here in Berlin, where there is someone to test your iron, all you do is hurl phrases at us. Ask my niece what goes on in the judicial system. The presiding judge is straight from Moscow and hasn't enough legal background to be a blacksmith. Four judges were kidnaped last month because they made decisions on behalf of the West. Believe me, the Russians take care of their people."

"That's just the point," Sean said. "You're not our people. Will you familiarize yourself with the evidence against Hollweg or not?"

"Very well," he said in defeat. "When is the lynching to take place?"

"When the moment is correct for a coup, not before, not after."

Their heated words had gotten beyond the room. Ernestine stared angrily at Sean. He looked from one to the other and said a terse good night.

CHAPTER TWENTY-SEVEN

In the Kommandatura the chess game went on. Neal Hazzard became quite a player. . . . He made a move to break the Communist control of the Labor Front.

At first, Falkenstein and the Democrats supported the idea of a single organization, feeling that the lack of labor unity in Berlin weakened their position in fighting Hitlerism. They were soon to learn that the Labor Front was designed and staffed with Moscow-trained Germans who dominated the locals as well as the executive offices.

Hazzard dropped his bomb when RIAS announced that a new union had been authorized in the American Sector.

"Illegal!" Trepovitch bellowed. "The rules clearly state that the Labor Front is the only legal organization to be recognized! You have imported American labor thugs, hirelings, and goon squads to terrorize the workers into reactionary lines and rob them of their freedom."

"Would you care to comment?" T. E. Blatty said when Trepovitch finished. "I do believe you have something to explain, Colonel Hazzard."

"The Constitution governing the Labor Front as passed by this Kommandatura calls for elections of the executive every year," Hazzard answered. "As of now elections are eight months, two weeks, four days, and six hours overdue because of General Trepovitch's delaying tactics. Now, either we're going to have an election or the new union which I have authorized will begin functioning. It's up to you, General."

Faced with the reality of losing their grip over labor, Trepovitch returned to the Kommandatura with an elaborate scheme. He would agree to an election of the executive if the West agreed to retain the present executive and merely expand it by the election. A quick check of mathematics told Neal Hazzard that if non-Communist candidates won every post in such a plot, the Communists would still have a numerical superiority.

The plan was bluntly rejected. It was so transparent that T. E. Blatty and Jacques Belfort announced that they, too, would recognize the new union in the American Sector. Trepovitch had to agree to an election.

It was the city elections of 1946 all over again, beginning with a Communist fanfare . . . that all workers in the Russian Sector would henceforth receive a free, hot meal at midday.

On the day of the elections, Western officials were bluntly barred from the polling stations in the Russian Sector, which issued two colored ballots. The result, nevertheless, was another monumental defeat for the Communists.

Following the same pattern they used after the other elections, the Russians delayed the seating of the new executive. All non-Communists were bullied from taking office because of "investigations" of their suspected Nazi backgrounds.

There was more than one way to win an election. The West stood by as the abuses against the winning candidates became an open scandal.

At last Neal Hazzard announced that the new union was authorized to begin operation. As the workers in the Western Sector flocked to it, the Communist stranglehold was broken.

The American action was not long in being countered. The Russians did so with a display of raw terror never seen before in the occupation.

On a single night the SND along with the NKVD rounded up four hundred German technicians living in the Russian Sector, herded them aboard a train, locked them in, and shipped them to the Soviet Union.

When T. E. Blatty hurled the charge at Trepovitch, the Russian commandant smiled like a fat Cheshire cat.

He puckered his lips, opened his briefcase. "I have here," he began, "signed contracts for the four hundred German volunteer technicans. It is conclusive proof there was no kidnaping. These lies spread by the Western press are sinister provocations for which we demand an apology."

"Just keep you goddamned forgeries in your briefcase," Hazzard snapped in the first open rage he had ever shown.

Trepovitch remained calm, too calm, Hazzard thought. The Russian whispered to one of his aides, and a moment later a German civilian was marched into the room and asked to be seated at the conference table.

"What is your name?" Trepovitch asked.

"Joachim Mangold."

"And why did you ask for permission to appear before this body?"

"I am the spokesman for the Committee of Four Hundred Free German Technicians."

"You are authorized to speak for all of them?"

"Yes. I was selected in a free and democratic election."

"You are aware of American and British charges that you and your colleagues were abducted."

"That is a lie. We volunteered."

"Not forced?"

"No force was used."

"Why do you wish to work in the Soviet Union and why did you seek us out and ask us for contracts?"

Mangold cleared his throat and recited carefully, "Because in the Soviet Union my comrades and I will have the opportunity to work and research for the benefit of mankind. Here, we fear we will be used for warmongering imperialist purposes of the reactionary West."

"Jesus H. Christ," Hazzard blurted aloud.

The outrage set off a chain of demonstrations. With mixed desperation, anger, and fear the free parties sent out a call for unity.

In a showdown the Soviet Union had displayed naked power and there would be further atrocities, for the West did not answer the kidnapings . . . and the Berliners were trapped.

CHAPTER TWENTY-EIGHT

V. V. Azov's ulcers flared when Captain Brusilov arrived from Moscow. Despite his inconspicuous rank, he was a personal courier of Stalin. Azov was aware that Captain Brusilov was never dispatched for the purpose of passing out medals.

His entry into Berlin just before the Foreign Ministers' Conference was no accident.

In his career, Azov had known some of Stalin's other couriers. When he was Sovietizing the Ukraine a word from one of them could set off a hundred thousand deportations. During the purges, a message often sealed the doom of a marshal of the Red Army or a ranking member of the Politburo. During the war a courier gave him orders to slaughter the Germans who had surrendered in an East Prussian pocket.

Captain Brusilov traveled in a private plane in the company of fifteen NKVD and spoke to no one outside his immediate circle.

Of the five couriers Azov had known prior to Brusilov, each had disappeared as Stalin's abnormal suspicions doomed them for possessing too many secrets.

The night before he was to confer with Brusilov, V. V. Azov displayed open fear that only Madam Azov was aware of. He told his wife that he was growing old and had served faithfully for nearly four decades.

Had he not made a Soviet State out of the Russian Zone of Germany? Certainly Stalin could not complain about that. Yet, he knew Comrade Stalin could find fault without apparent reason. Had he fallen from favor? What was his crime? He had never been able to explain the defection of Heinrich Hirsch to the West. This stayed on his record as a blunder. He cursed General Hansen and those British and American officers for making his troubles. Yet, he had pushed them as far as Moscow had permitted.

For a long time, Azov dreamed of retirement to a small *dacha*, a modest pension, and complete anonymity.

The memory of the past terrorized him. In his time he had obtained "confessions" from hundreds of political commissars. After they had achieved the rank he now held, few of them died in bed of old age.

NKVD spies were all around him, watched his every move, monitored his words, speculated on his thoughts. Had they detected his secret yearning for peace? Had they reported to Stalin? He moaned as the fires in him flamed.

The next morning Azov fell back on years of experience to cover his fears.

Captain Brusilov admonished him for allowing the Soviet Union to get tricked into the labor election. "It is obvious," Brusilov said, "the German people don't know what is good for them so their votes are meaningless. Otherwise, they would have never allowed Hitler."

Azov was further berated for failure to drive the West out of Berlin, but as he spoke he revealed that there was further use for the commissar. Azov breathed easier, knowing he would live a while longer.

"Our sacred mission is to collapse morale of the West before the Foreign Ministers' Conference next month. The Western ministers must arrive in Berlin realizing that it is a Soviet city."

Any last pretenses for the benefit of the German people that four-power unity remained was destroyed by a massive assault on the West with the Americans coming in for the heaviest battering. The People's Radio and the Russian newspapers spearheaded the drive with the planting of rumors and the hurling of falsehoods.

THE NEW ARCHITECTS OF FASCISM, THE ILLEGAL COLONEL HAZZARD AND THE CORRUPT GENERAL HANSEN!

Stories were printed about their "sordid" past and their current secret work on behalf of the rebirth of Nazism. Ugly cartoons depicting them as savages and animals found a daily place on the editorial pages.

SS WAR CRIMINALS FIND SAFETY AND REWARDS IN THE WESTERN ZONE!

NAZI BEASTS FILL WESTERN GOVERNMENTS!

MURDERERS RUN GERMAN POLICE IN AMERICAN ZONE!

IMPERIALISTS USE NAZI OFFICERS TO REBUILD SS FOR A WAR OF REVENGE!

After each session of the Kommandatura, Nikolai Trepovitch printed his version of the proceedings in a column which carried such headlines:

WEST BLOCKS HOT MEALS FOR GERMAN WORKERS!

HAZZARD DELAYS HOUSING PROGRAM!

WEST ADMITS IT IS AGAINST UNIFICATION!

In the Soviet Sector of Berlin, thousands upon thousands of signs covered the walls. Bombed-out buildings wore red banners reading:

THIS BUILDING WAS DESTROYED BY AMERICAN BOMBS. IT MUST NEVER HAPPEN AGAIN.

The Soviet Union advanced the theory that their Zone of Germany had selected communism and their Germans were therefore redeemed and had purged themselves of guilt in the Nazi era. On the other hand, the West which now fostered Nazism stood guilty for all of Hitler's doings.

The newspapers carried front-page stories and photographs of lynchings in the South, child labor in factories, Chicago gangster murders, race riots, skid row bums, labor strife, Hollywood orgies, poverty-stricken Oklahoma farmers, American backing of South American dictatorships, and oriental war lords. The Western decadence of Henry Miller and boogie-woogie, prostitution in New York, and the striptease joints of New Orleans all came in for special beratings.

This attack was paralleled by stories depicting happy Soviet workers on their collective farms building the socialist future. Social realism in art and literature was displayed alongside the corruptions of Picasso and Hemingway.

The stage was elaborately set in Berlin for a move on the West before the Foreign Ministers' Conference.

CHAPTER TWENTY-NINE

A new playground had been bulldozed from a rubble-strewn square in Zehlendorf. A baseball team of German boys, trained by GI's under the youth program, played a team of Americans from the garrison families. Neal Hazzard umpired.

The ball ground was surrounded by curious Germans. In the second inning Hazzard called a particularly bad and obvious decision against the Americans to keep the score within bounds.

The American boys ganged around him screaming in protest. Both German team and spectators were astonished at this defiance of authority . . . against Colonel Hazzard, no less. Fortunately, Colonel Hazzard won the argument and the game resumed.

Between innings Lieutenant Colonel O'Sullivan drove up in a staff car. "The Russians have seized the Railroad Administration Building."

Hazzard looked baffled. It was deep inside the American Sector. "Hansen know about this?"

"He's on the way to Headquarters now."

Hazzard appointed an umpire to replace him, announced his regrets, and went off with Sean, speeding directly to Hansen's office.

When they entered, General Hansen had just concluded unsuccessful attempts to reach Marshal Popov and General Trepovitch. The Russians were "not available." Colonel Mark Parrott, commander of the American garrison, was present. He told them a company of Russian infantry crossed into the American Sector a half hour earlier, evicted all the German workers from the Railroad Administration Building, ran up a Red flag and stood guard.

The three officers looked to the general; there was no time to procrastinate. Either they had to respond immediately or accept it as an accomplished feat.

"Move in your troops, Mark, cut the area off. Don't shoot first, but if they try to send in relief, open fire."

Neal Hazzard beamed.

The staff car bearing him and Sean O'Sullivan barreled through the streets, sirens screaming. It slowed at Friedenau Platz, where a crowd had gathered. Sean ordered everyone off the streets, then walked toward the building with Hazzard. They were blocked by a submachine-gun-toting Red Army soldier at the door.

"I want to see the officer in charge," Hazzard said.

The soldier shrugged and pointed the gun at them. They turned and recrossed the street. In a matter of moments Mark Parrott pulled up with several truckloads of soldiers and quickly dispersed them so that the building was cut off.

Inside, Colonel Igor Karlovy watched the American movement on the street. He picked up a telephone to call Russian Headquarters. The line seemed dead. In another instant an aide confirmed that the Americans had cut the telephone wires.

"Colonel Hazzard is approaching the building again. This time he has a dozen soldiers around him."

"I will see him, myself," Igor said. He went downstairs and stood at the entrance. Neal Hazzard told his escort to stand fast and walked with Sean to the Russian.

"I know him. Let me talk to him, Neal."

"Go ahead."

"Afternoon, Colonel Karlovy," Sean said. "What are you people up to?"

"This is the property of the Soviet Union!"

"It's two miles inside the American Sector. How do you figure?"

"The location is only a technicality."

"Go on."

"The Kommandatura agreement states that all railroad operations in Brandenburg Province are to be run by the Soviet Union."

"That is correct."

"This building is the administration headquarters of the railroad system and therefore legally within Soviet jurisdiction."

"In a pig's ass," Neal Hazzard cut in. "Here's your situation. No one is going to enter this area. You are, however, permitted to leave and return to the Russian Sector. If you want to stay here, you can starve to death. That's your business. If there is any attempt to bring troops in, you're going to get blasted. My people have orders to open fire at the sight of Russian troops." Hazzard left.

Igor smiled at Sean. "So, we meet again. I see you have come up in the world. Well . . . one day you seize American Headquarters, one day we seize the railroad building. It balances out."

"There's a difference," Sean said.

"What is that, my friend?"

"We're not bluffing."

The reopening of the State Opera was a great event in Berlin. The partly reconstructed Opera House was located on the Unter Den Linden in the Russian Sector. The Soviet high command hosted the evening.

General and Agnes Hansen sat as guests of Marshal Popov in a box shared with British General Fitz-Roy and French General de Lys and their wives. In the opposite box Neal and Claire Hazzard and the other commandants were guests of General and Mrs. Trepovitch.

Representatives of the State Department and of the foreign ministries were there. The diplomatic corps of seventeen Allies were there. Leading German Communists were there. . . . It was a glittering affair.

The opera chosen for the event was Verdi's *Nabucco*, appropriate for this night because it had been banned during the Hitler years because of its Jewish theme.

A splendid party followed the opera, during which not a single word was exchanged regarding what was taking place at the Railroad Administration Building. During the night, Igor Karlovy and his company looked into floodlights from American batteries and began to wonder if there had not been a gross miscalculation.

At seven o'clock the next morning, Neal Hazzard's orderly woke him to inform him that General Trepovitch was on the phone.

Hazzard smiled when he saw the time. It was an ungodly hour for the Russians. He knew they had been sitting up all night pondering.

"Morning, General Trepovitch. Beautiful event last night."

"Yes . . . indeed . . . beautiful. Candidly, Colonel Hazzard, I wish to discuss the situation at the Railroad Administration Building."

"Shoot."

"If you will agree to withdraw your forces I will agree to an emergency session of the Kommandatura today to discuss the matter."

"If you're looking for bargains, try Sears, Roebuck."

"What?"

"Nyet."

Trepovitch's voice lowered to that familiar pitch that was about to unleash a threat. "If you do not remove your forces, we will take appropriate measures."

"We'll be there."

Trepovitch set the phone down. Marshal Popov, V. V. Azov, and Captain Brusilov from Moscow were in the room. They waited until the translations were made and read them. Captain Brusilov had been sent to create an incident before the Foreign Ministers' Conference to establish *de facto* Russian control of the city. He crumpled the translation in his fist. Azov felt a slight comfort for the moment. What would the great courier do now? Call Moscow for instructions?

"Withdraw our forces from the building," he said.

CHAPTER THIRTY

"Lieutenant Colonel O'Sullivan speaking."

"This is the sergeant at the main gate, sir. There's a Fräulein Ernestine Falkenstein to see you."

"She has an appointment. Have her checked through and brought up to my office."

"Yes, sir."

Ernestine stepped into the security shack, signed in, and deposited her identification papers and ration book at the desk. A spit and polish corporal from the Constabulary led her briskly into the compound.

Ernestine shrank back. She had been here before when it was the Luft Gau Headquarters for Central Germany. Her law office had sent her to witness a court-martial as a "friend of the family." In those days a swastika flew from the mast and the entrance had a large, stone German eagle. There were black uniforms and jackboots.

The corporal led her down the long, somber corridor and she shuddered a little. At last they stopped before Lieutenant Colonel O'Sullivan's office. The corporal knocked, opened the door, saluted, and gawked at the woman as she went in.

"I'll call you if I need your help, Corporal."

The soldier was embarrassed and beat a hasty retreat.

"Won't you have a seat?"

"Thank you. And thank you for seeing me."

"What can I do for you?"

"As you might have suspected, it regards my Uncle Ulrich. This information on Berthold Hollweg has come to him as a great shock."

"It would be strange if it didn't upset him."

"They have been comrades for decades. The thought of having to bring him up on charges and thrown out of the Democratic Party is more than he can bear."

"Your uncle has a great capacity for absorbing punishment. He understands his duty as clear-cut."

Ernestine fumbled with her handbag. "Can't someone else bring the charges? They are the same no matter who makes them."

"We've been through all that, fraulein."

"There is something else. I know you're going to want him to become Oberburgermeister of Berlin."

"That's right. He should have been elected instead of Hollweg in the first place. We were trying to accommodate the Russians. We're not so anxious to do that, any more."

"Perhaps I am not making myself clear, Colonel. He is not a young man nor is he in good health. I fear that this burden might be too much for him."

The girl was clever and well trained and more, she had perception.

"We are being drawn into a situation where we must become more and more involved with your politicians. It is a condition your uncle has argued for from the beginning. If we are to start giving up on backing then we cannot settle for less than the best man. No one has the stature of Ulrich Falkenstein."

"But, Colonel," Ernestine persisted, "he may not have it left in him to give. He has done enough and deserves a few years of peace."

"Some men are never born for peace."

"My uncle is very, very tired. I hear him thrash during the night and cry out reliving the horror of Schwabenwald. I see the exhaustion and the deterioration that others don't want to see. This will kill him." At the moment, Sean felt a touch of compassion for the girl.

"Let him continue as the spiritual head of the party but find a younger and more vigorous man and begin to groom him," she pleaded.

Sean shook his head. "History chooses people. It is never the other way around, fraulein. He is the man who can rally Berlin. Each day here the battle becomes broader and clearer. Your uncle is a general who must assume his command. Like all soldiers, we are expendable if God wills it."

"I'll fight you," she said.

Sean's eyes narrowed. He was damned angry. He leaned forward almost hissing his words at her. "Did you fight to keep your brother out of uniform? Did you fight to keep your Nazi boy friend from butchering innocent, defenseless people? Not one of you fine German women seemed to fight too much to keep your men from marching off to die for the fatherland. Now you listen to me. There are things in this world more worthy of dying for than Deutschland Uber Alles."

Ernestine came to her feet, watery-eyed. "I am sorry that your beautiful democracy has no mercy for its weary fighters."

"Not if we are going to win."

"I have seen men like you before, Colonel O'Sullivan. I have seen them in this very building, in these very offices. Blind obedience to duty. They were in Nazi uniform."

CHAPTER THIRTY-ONE

Sean wrestled on the floor with Shenandoah Blessing's two roly-poly boys, held them fast, tickled them, then allowed himself to be pinned and mauled. Lil Blessing finally pulled the boys off Uncle Sean and hustled them to bed.

After dinner, Shenandoah buckled on his duty belt, kissed Lil, told Sean he'd see him later and went off.

Sean settled with a cognac while Lil checked the boys and warned them of dire consequences if they weren't asleep immediately. The German maid was dismissed. Lil picked up her knitting.

"That was a hell of a dinner," Sean said. "I haven't had hush puppies since I was a kid. I had an aunt and uncle in North Carolina. My brothers and I visited them one whole summer. Hush puppies, grits, hawgs' knuckles. No wonder your old man is so fat."

"I like him fat. Gives me something to bounce around on."

"How's garrison life?"

"Can't complain. It's good for the boys seeing another part of the world. Kind of feel bad about how hard things are for those folks in Berlin."

"They can't expect any better."

"I'm having tea with some of the ladies from the British garrison tomorrow. We're going to have us a forum on the problems of raising kids in the occupation. How about that?"

In the few months that Lil and the kids had been in Berlin they had become like old friends. Sean gave up his cottage to them, a neat little wooded place in a development once belonging to SS people. He took a flat in Dahlem large enough to suit him.

"Sean. You're sure not yourself, tonight."

"It's all this damned preparation for the Foreign Ministers' Conference."

"That's not all that's bothering you."

Sean rolled his cognac glass in the palm of his hand.

"You're sure wonderful around the kids," Lil went on. "Any man who gives up all his off-duty time to coach them ought to have a couple of his own."

"Hell, you women are all alike. None of you can stand a happy bachelor."

"You're talking to Lil, honey. You're not happy."

"I didn't know I set off a signal."

"Any man who works as hard as you do for the privilege of coming home to an empty room can't be happy. Things aren't made that way."

"About once every three months I get to wondering about the bargain I made to come to Berlin, but it always passes."

"Time is passing, too, buster."

"Lil. I never got this blue until the American families came." Then, on an impulse he said, "Are you my very good friend?"

"You bet I am."

"Seems like I've got a penchant for going for the wrong woman. I think I've got it down to a science."

"Getting mixed up with a German girl?"

"Not exactly. I know I want to see her again and I know I shouldn't feel that way."

"She encouraging you?"

"All I've gotten from her was a rap in the mouth."

"The way you think about Germans you probably had it coming."

"Maybe. Lil, am I a blind, arrogant Prussian?"

"My, my. Sounds like that girl said a mouthful."

"She did. I guess there was enough truth in it to bother me."

"Tell her what a nice girl she is. It's not going to kill you."

"I can't. Not to a German girl. Besides, I guess I owe her an apology."

"Sean . . . there's something human in the worst German who ever lived." Lil picked up the knitting-instruction book, pulled out a number of stitches, counted carefully. "Did Bless ever tell you about us?"

"No."

"I spent my first fourteen years on a dirt farm, the kind you read about in *Tobacco Road*. Ran away from home at the age of fifteen, pregnant. I lost that baby. Ended up in Harper, Tennessee, the county seat of Hook County."

Lil set her knitting down, lit a cigarette, and poured herself a drink from the bourbon bottle. "I wasn't much good for anything but hanging around roadhouses, but at least I was able to learn to read and write, have a dress on my back, have a room of my own with a light, a radio, plumbing.

"When I first met Bless he had been voted sheriff of Hook. Bless didn't bother the girls so long as they didn't steal. Matter of fact, he helped a lot of them out of trouble. Bless was always sweet on me, but he was too busy or too shy to do much about it.

"One night he pulled a raid on a place running a big game. I was caught in the roundup. I was pretty drunk, noisy, and seeing me hurt him, inside. He roughed me up so bad I ended up in the hospital. Hell of a romance, huh, Sean?

"There was never a minute in my life like the next morning when that fat, wonderful man bumbled into my hospital room and asked to be forgiven. A man can look big in his own eyes and in the eyes of other men when he shoves people around. A man really looks big in a woman's eyes when he is humble enough to say he is sorry."

"Mind if I come in?"

Ernestine looked up from her desk as Sean closed the door behind him. She was too surprised to speak, but showed that she was unforgiving.

"I had some documents to deliver to Judge Cohen," he said, referring to one of the American jurists in military government. "I thought I might drop in. So, this is where you work."

The office was a clutter of law texts. Ernestine was working on translations of British and American volumes dealing with lower-court appeals.

"As a matter of fact," Sean continued, "I am glad this opportunity came up, because I've been wanting to speak to you about our last meeting. Fraulein, my choice of words showed a lot of bad manners and bad taste."

Ernestine watched his discomfort, but even his attempt to apologize was being carefully phrased. The colonel did not say he was sorry, had spoken untruthfully, or that he had changed his mind.

"What I should have said was that your uncle came back to Berlin out of choice and knowing how great his chore would be. But a long time before that he had made up his mind that the things he believed in were far more important than his own being. I believe that if you attempted to dissuade him from what he knows he must do, he would reject your plea."

"You are right, Colonel O'Sullivan. He has rejected my plea."

"I am sorry for your sake because I understand how much you love him."

"It is kind of you to make this gesture."

"As for my other remarks . . ."

"You need not try to apologize. It is quite true that my fiancé was involved in the Babi-Yar Massacre and God knows what else. I am aware of what we Germans have done to the human race. I am not in the position to atone my shame and guilt, nor are you in a position to grant me forgiveness. Now please leave my office . . . and please leave me alone."

CHAPTER THIRTY-TWO

A few days before the Foreign Ministers' Conference in Berlin the Truman Doctrine was declared stating that any further attempt to expand communism would be met with force.

From the end of the war there had been innumerable meetings of heads of state and their deputies in Washington and London, Moscow and Paris.

Conferences were directed now to easing the growing antagonism between the Soviet Union and her former allies. Now it came Berlin's time as the site to attempt to determine a settlement for Germany.

"Mrs. Hansen is on the phone, General," Sean said.

"Hello, Mother."

"Andrew. I just received another of those calls. Some terrible things were said about you."

Agnes sounded shaky. He was tied up with preconference work until very late. Tomorrow dignitaries would start arriving. All the members of his staff and their wives were receiving anonymous telephone calls at all hours promising death if the Americans did not get out of Berlin.

General Hansen and Colonel Hazzard were both sleeping with pistols at their bedstands after refusing to put guards on their homes.

"Mother," Hansen said, "I'll send a car for you. See if Claire Hazzard will go to the movies with you. Go to the Staff Club afterward and I'll fetch you on the way home."

"I'll do that, dear. I am sorry to have bothered you."

Sean dispatched a car for Mrs. Hansen. "Those calls are damned hard on some of the women," he said. "Don't you think you'd better put a guard on your house for Mrs. Hansen's sake?"

"Hell no. When you think about it, Sean, it must be terrible for defenseless people behind the Iron Curtain to be subjected to such naked terror with no way for them to fight back. I guess the Russians must be real successful there."

The day the delegates arrived in Berlin the Soviet Union announced they were holding war games and the sky became black with fighter planes. They buzzed the incoming transports menacingly.

Hansen called Lieutenant General Barney Root, the USAFE Commander in Wiesbaden. The American Secretary of State landed at Tempelhof under an escort of the new jet fighters, followed by other squadrons flying in formation spelling out the letters U.S.A. The Soviet planes cleared the corridors.

It was on this note of hostility and tension that the Berlin Conference of Foreign Ministers convened.

The main arena was in the Sanssouci Castle in Potsdam, but throughout Berlin subcommittees argued the points of difference.

At the Napoleon Quarters, French Headquarters, the most important

Committee on Reparations met with General Hansen heading the American delegation. His old adversary from the Supreme German Council, Marshal Alexei Popov, sat on the far side of the U-shaped table.

The first session was not more than a half hour old when Marshal Popov set down the Russian reparations demand of ten billion dollars from the Western Zones from current production.

Popov, the gray fox, finished, leaving the place almost stunned. There was some parliamentary small talk, but everyone was waiting until the floor rotated to the Americans.

Andrew Jackson Hansen took off his specs, folded his hands, and looked straight at Popov. "My government is going to reject your demands," he began bluntly. There was a buzz around the room.

"Let me explain our position, Marshal Popov. The United States is not going to make any further reparations until you agree on German iron production. The ten billion dollars you are now asking for could well be the entire output of German industry. America is in Germany for the purpose of allowing the Germans to establish a trade balance so they can take care of themselves."

"To build for another war!"

"Now, you just wait a minute. I'm not finished. My country is pouring hundreds of millions into Germany. Your country is taking hundreds of millions out. What are you after? A direct payment from Washington to Moscow?"

Popov's face reddened.

Hansen continued firmly. "We want the zone borders opened and Germany run as a single economic unit. You've avoided this issue for two years. Furthermore, we want an accounting on how much the Soviet Union has already taken out of Germany."

Popov tried to interrupt.

"I haven't finished yet. The Soviet Union on its own has seized German lands with a tax valuation of twelve billion dollars. It has taken land from Poland with a tax valuation of two billion dollars. The question is . . . how many times and in how many different ways are you going to try to collect the same ten billion dollars?"

Popov could hold still no longer. "The Soviet Union will continue to be guided by policies that prevent the enslavement of the German working class. We know all about the concentration camps in the British Zone of Germany. We know about the Hitler-like campaign preventing the Communist Party from delivering the workers in the American Zone. It is you who are intolerant of democracy."

"I appreciate your rhetoric," Hansen answered, "but you haven't answered my questions."

"It is the Soviet Union who suffered at the hands of the Hitler aggressors and the Soviet Union leading the German people to peace!"

"Will you or will you not give us an accounting of what you have taken out of Germany?"

"I see no sense in continuing this meeting." Without further ado, Marshal Popov and his staff walked out.

Marshal Popov's performance was duplicated on the other side of the city by Soviet Foreign Minister Molotov, who insisted American money was pouring into Germany for the war of revenge and enslavement of the German working class.

After Molotov's walkout, even the conciliatory French had had enough.

The Berlin Conference ended with the United States, Britain, France, Holland, Luxembourg, and Belgium jointly declaring that the three Western Zones of Germany should coordinate economic policies, and further, that steps be taken to draft a constitution for a German Republic.

Europe was weary. The horrible winter of 1946–47 had brought a final collapse of industry and agriculture. People were undernourished and machines were destroyed or obsolete. The skilled labor force had been depleted. The farms lay in ruins; the mines did not run; the will of the people to survive was failing.

Although the Truman Doctrine did much to stop the impetus of armed Communist take-overs, something more was needed. For in this filth, fear, and hunger, the cancer of communism grew fat in Italy and France.

A monumental program of aid to Europe was envisioned by a wise old soldier who had ascended to Secretary of State and knew that guns were not enough.

The question now was to get the European Recovery Act/The Marshall Plan through the Congress before it was too late.

America was coming of age. The price to rebuild Europe meant acceptance of American leadership. And for America, the age of her seclusion was done.

The tired nations of Europe were asked to convene in Paris and make their needs known as the machinery of Congress worked toward enactment of the law.

CHAPTER THIRTY-THREE

The notice read:

The new library in Amerika Haus will be formally dedicated this Thursday. Special Services has arranged a concert by the eminent pianist, Sergeant William James.

This library, which will eventually hold 50,000 volumes, is a gift of the American people through donations to the German-American Friendship League. It would be appropriate on this occasion that personnel who wish to attend invite German guests.

A formal invitation read:

Colonel and Mrs. Neal Hazzard request the pleasure of your company at a cocktail party at the Dahlem Press Club directly after the concert of Sergeant James.

Sean had the invitation on his desk for a week. A number of times he had stared at it, pondered it, reread it, doodled on a scratch pad next to it . . . two days till the concert.

He picked up the phone and asked the board for an outside number.
"Hello."
"Fraulein Falkenstein?"
"Speaking."
"This is Lieutenant Colonel O'Sullivan."
"Oh yes, Colonel."
"There is to be a dedication of a library at the Amerika Haus. I wonder if you and your uncle would consent to be my guests?"

Ernestine took the invitation impersonally, in the nature of a semi-official request, as her uncle would ordinarily attend such a function.
"What day, please?"
"Day after tomorrow."
"Oh? Let me check his calendar . . . Hello . . . he has a district

meeting in Spandau on Thursday and I believe he has said it was quite important."

"How about you going with me?"

"Me?"

"We have a fine young pianist who will play a concert. I understand he is going to do a Beethoven sonata."

"I don't know," she whispered.

"Please, fraulein. This is not an order."

"Well . . . very well, I'll go."

"Good. I'll come by for you about six-thirty. My regards to your uncle."

Sergeant William James lived up to his advance notices as a forthcoming giant among the virtuosos.

Sean and Ernestine met with what seemed to be dedicated determination to be polite to each other. The first moments were stilted and awkward. They hardly spoke all the way to Amerika Haus.

Then by some mystic communication, Sergeant James played the "Pathétique" and Sean and Ernestine were given an awareness of each other that said that a long dormant awakening was taking place.

On the way to the Press Club they had something to talk about and it helped them relax.

At the door, he offered her his arm and they walked down the reception line. Eyebrows were raised; they felt it.

Neal Hazzard studied Ernestine from head to toe in a second or so. He caught Sean with a glance that read: "Jesus, what a dish."

"Fraulein Falkenstein, I'd like you to meet Colonel Hazzard, Mrs. Hazzard."

"Lovely affair."

"Any relation to Ulrich Falkenstein?"

"My uncle."

They tried to avoid the voices trailing after them.

"Say, is that O'Sullivan with a German girl?"

"For her, he *should* make an exception."

"That's Falkenstein's niece. She works in Judge Cohen's section."

"I'll bet General Hansen told him to bring her. Show of friendship and all that."

While the gossips had their say, Sean found the friendly, homely face of Nelson Goodfellow Bradbury deep in a mug of beer at the bar.

He introduced Ernestine and they retreated to a quiet table in the
garden and Sean excused himself to report his whereabouts to Headquarters.

In all the time they had been in Berlin, Sean had never been seen
socially in the company of a German. His dates were either American
girls or those working in the foreign missions.

Big Nellie sat with the girl and remembered a lot of things from way
back. He was the one who had told Sean his brother was dead. And in
Rombaden, Sean confided his unadulterated hatred of Germans.

Was it this particular girl because of her obvious intelligence and
beauty who broke the barrier, or was it because she was the niece of
Falkenstein? Was this the beginning of a softening process?

"I have enjoyed your column over the last year and a half," Ernestine
said.

"I didn't realize I was read here in Berlin."

"My uncle has an arrangement to receive a number of American
and British papers. You have been a friend of the Berliners."

"Because the Berliners have been our friends."

"I understand you and the colonel are old comrades?"

"We go back a ways."

There was an awkward second. Perhaps a question she wanted to
ask; perhaps one he wanted to ask.

Sean returned and after a moment Big Nellie ambled away.

They talked for a long time about things that both of them liked:
the kind of music they heard tonight; the kind of books she had read
since living with her uncle. There was much in common.

When it was time for them to leave, Sean drove her home and both
of them said it was a nice evening and perhaps . . . sometime again.
. . . And the moment he drove away he was annoyed with himself for
enjoying it and wanting to see more of her.

Ernestine slipped quietly into the apartment. The light was on in the
living room.

"How was the evening?" Ulrich asked.

"The concert was lovely. It was a pity you couldn't attend."

"And the colonel?"

"Quite civilized. In fact, he can be quite charming. As you know he
can discuss many things on a wide range of subjects."

"All O'Sullivan and I ever talked about was good Germans and bad Germans."

"We avoided that."

Ernestine brewed some tea and felt uncomfortable with her uncle's obvious cynicism.

"Ernestine, darling," he said, "Colonel O'Sullivan has had to set aside some deep feelings to be seen with you."

"Under it all, he is just a human being. He was bound to become lonely. We all become lonely, Uncle."

"And you? I have never seen you look as radiant as when you came in just now."

"I am sure the invitation was mainly for you to make a public show of friendship."

"And you will see him again?"

"Perhaps."

"You are a young woman in the bloom of life. How long has it been since you had a date? Isn't it strange that the first time you have gone out in months, it should be with an American?"

For a time, Ernestine made dates with German boys she had known and colleagues at work. She saw in them something of Dietrich Rascher, her father, her brother. She was frightened of all of them.

"Certainly O'Sullivan is civilized to stifle certain emotions, but eventually his hatred will burst through."

Ernestine wanted to defend Sean. Her uncle had worked with him in Rombaden under severe circumstances. Uncle never got to know him as a warm and gentle person. That image of the iron-willed dedicated Prussian faded when he spoke. Why was she defending him in her own mind? She knew she wanted to see him again.

"It is strange how enemies are irresistibly drawn to each other. But love between enemies is not love. It is a desire to destroy each other," Ulrich said.

"You are making a lot over nothing."

"If it is nothing, then promise you won't see him again."

"I did enjoy the evening so much, Uncle."

"I don't want you hurt, Ernestine . . . I don't want you hurt."

CHAPTER THIRTY-FOUR

Igor shaved. In the mirror he could see the image of Lotte in the doorway behind him putting on her negligee. She was pouting.

"Are you going out?"

"Yes."

"This makes four nights in a row. What is so important?"

"I am a colonel. Nikolai Trepovitch is a general. He ordered me to a meeting. I go."

"Why must you always hold your meetings in the middle of the night?"

"So we can sleep late in the morning."

"But I can't sleep when you are gone."

"You are a delightful fraud. When I return I always find you dead to the world."

"That is because I take pills."

He doused his face, rinsed his razor, and put on a lotion that he had obtained from an American at the Air Safety Center.

Lotte had her arms around him, squeezed him. He lifted her up and carried her into the bedroom, deposited her, and tugged on his boots.

"When will you give me a baby?" she asked.

What a liar! Oh, maybe she did want a child in the same way a little girl wants to play with a doll. She was clever enough to please him with the thought. They had been discreet, never showing up together at public functions. That was tolerable to the command. But anything like having a German mistress bear his child would mean immediate banishment.

A month earlier, Igor had gone through particular hell. The party, for some reason, decided it would be of propaganda value to dispatch his wife, Olga, to a convention of the League of German Women Communists and an inspection of Russian Berlin. Igor was compelled to stand like an adoring clod at the airport with a bouquet of flowers and embrace her with emotion at the ramp for the photographers. She was as drab as he remembered her.

For a week Igor escorted her on a well-documented tour of the Soviet

Sector with the story sent out to the Communist world of this son and daughter separated by their dedication to the greater cause.

Olga visited a site in Treptower Park which would become a great memorial cemetery to the Russians who died storming Berlin. She visited an orphanage and had words for the future comrades. She attended a church service as visible proof of the Soviet Union's democratic attitude toward religion.

Olga addressed the convention of German Women Communists with venom against the imperialists trying to enslave them and pleading for German motherhood to protect the peace by giving their sons and daughters to the forward march of world communism.

There was a final banquet at which Olga surprised her husband by presenting him with the Order of Lenin at the command of Comrade Stalin.

The agony ended with him rushing back to Lotte to calm the distraught girl an hour after his wife flew back to Leningrad.

"I do want your baby," Lotte said again. "One day you must leave. All soldiers leave."

Igor knew she was right. The shuffling of officers and party officials was a constant game aimed to prevent the formation of power cliques. In fact, it simply added to a ponderous and wasteful administration. Igor had remained clear of the recalls because he was an engineer with particular skills outside the political and military ring. Yet one day he, too, would leave.

He tucked Lotte in, patted her cheek, and told her to try to sleep. He had never lost that same feeling for this wonderful little imp as the first night he saw her.

As he was driven to Trepovitch's house, Igor thought about the money he was putting away, a tidy sum he would leave for Lotte. Igor was in a position to do many favors in Berlin and, like most of the Russian staff, took advantage of it, always making certain not to go too far.

He hated himself for the notion, but he knew the money would be safer in a bank in the Western Sector. Daring to put the money in a Western bank was "speculation," a crime that brought twenty-five years imprisonment, and sometimes death.

After he had returned from the Copenhagen Conference he had impressed Marshal Popov that the Americans and British had a number of engineering capabilities worth studying.

As long as there were areas of cooperation, Igor felt it was common sense to establish Russian missions any place they might benefit. He put people in with the Americans and British in heavy construction, road building, sanitation engineering, and the like. This brought him into contact with Western officers; he became known as the most agreeable of the Russians.

He looked for the proper American or Englishman through whom he could transfer his funds for Lotte, but each time he nearly made the decision he faltered.

The one officer he did trust was Sean O'Sullivan, but friendship with an American was a crime as serious as money speculation and Igor meticulously avoided Sean after his return to Berlin. Any meetings were by chance and the only amenities were exchanges of polite nods. Sean fully understood.

As an Air Force officer, Igor's own particular pet project was the four-power Air Safety Center. The West was at least a decade ahead of the Soviet Union in matters of traffic control and safety. He was able to have the Americans establish a school to train Russian personnel, and he attended. He was considered the top man in his own command in this field.

Nikolai Trepovitch paddled around in bedroom slippers and a shaggy old robe after a warm greeting to Igor. Igor was concerned for his comrade. In the old days Trepovitch had been a fun-loving, robust fellow. He was now on a strict diet that permitted only mild drinking and no smoking.

"I don't see how you can stand to sit there for hour after hour in those meetings at the Kommandatura," Igor said.

"It's terrible. If only I could return to a combat command. Life was good then. Between Colonel Hazzard and that Englishman, they've killed the inside of my stomach, but that's no reason you shouldn't have a drink."

Igor poured a stiff one.

"Tovarich, there is a highly delicate matter you have to attend to in the next forty-eight hours."

"Yes?"

"Some of the geniuses from Moscow are flying in. You must be prepared to give an opinion on whether or not the Americans and British can supply Berlin by air."

"It would strain them, but they should be able to get in enough for their own garrisons."

"No, no, Igor. I mean, supply their sectors of Berlin."

"Berlin? All the Western Sectors? Food, coal, medicine . . ."

Trepovitch nodded.

Igor set his drink down, stunned.

"It is a hard game we must play. They cannot be permitted to remain."

Igor recovered his bearings. "I must have a great deal of intelligence information."

Mid-February, 1948

Colonel Igor Karlovy went into Potsdam to a mansion hidden in the woods. The assembled were V. V. Azov, Russian Commandant Nikolai Trepovitch, Marshal Alexei Popov, an Air Force Intelligence colonel from Moscow, a colonel general attached to Stalin, a party member of the Politburo, and a top official of the NKVD. Last, the mysterious emissary, Captain Brusilov.

Igor had committed nothing to paper as he addressed this powerful group.

"Attempts at major air transport of supplies have usually fallen short." He outlined the attempt to supply Leningrad by air, a situation he knew intimately. It was a primitive operation and a failure.

"In the spring of 1944, Imphal in the state of Manipur in the India-Burma area was supplied from the air by the American Troop Carrier Command to the extent of twenty thousand tons. It is estimated that a combined force of fifty thousand British and Indian troops were sustained for three months. Also, the Luftwaffe backed up the parachute landings on Crete with an air-supply operation. However, these two cases are of a military tactical nature for an immediate objective.

"In the large picture, the German attempt to air-supply Stalingrad ended in fiasco. All they needed, logistically speaking, was three hundred tons of material a day.

"History shows one great air-supply operation which succeeded was by the Americans, again in the India-China Theater. From the Assam Valley, the Bengal Valley, and the Calcutta area their transports flew over the Himalayan Mountains landing in some nine airfields in China in the Chengtu and Kunming areas. They called it jumping the Hump, or some such. This operation, which lasted from the end of 1942 to the end of 1945, achieved notable results with a major cargo of oil and petroleum."

Igor went into great detail showing that the Hump deposited as much as sixty-five thousand tons of material a month in China which called for brilliant operational and logistical support, skillful and courageous flying.

"However," he concluded, "this operation does not parallel the problems of supplying a city the size of Western Berlin and its two million civilians."

The main cargo, Igor rationalized, would have to be coal and no one knows how to fly coal. In the Hump they had nine fields to land on and innumerable choices of routes. Flying the corridor would call for a precision never achieved in aviation history and there was only Tempelhof in Berlin to land on.

A member of the Moscow group spoke. "Comrade Colonel. Is it your opinion it cannot be done?"

"On a purely mathematical basis one would have to say the Americans and British have sufficient equipment, crews, economic reserve, and skills. In theory, mathematical theory, it is possible."

"Then, Comrade Colonel, it is your opinion they can succeed?"

"Only in theory. There are too many imponderables. I can present you with the mathematical figures and then those things which detract from the figures."

"Such as?"

"A calculation must be made of American public reaction and determination to go through with such an operation."

"Determinations of this sort will be made by our political experts," V. V. Azov said testily, trying to return Igor to the statistical end of the business.

Igor would not be stampeded by the commissar. "You must calculate if the Americans are willing to commit their global air transport power, MATS, into a single operation."

Marshal Popov, from earlier meetings, knew this was a key question. Would the Americans dare make themselves vulnerable elsewhere?

"The entire strength of the United States," Igor continued, "must be put behind this effort. As for the British, they may be able to deliver a quarter of the tonnage. They are short of crews, craft, and in a weak economic position. France? They will give speeches about French national honor, but can make no contribution."

Trepovitch laughed. He had received his fill of lectures on the glory of France from Colonel Jacques Belfort.

Igor got down to bare facts. The minimum requirements for food, coal for industry, and power sustaining the barest level of existence would make this an undertaking unknown in history. It was not merely a question of the number of craft committed, but the number of engines in reserve, the number of trucks on the ground, and the number of crews. He estimated the supply of aviation fuel alone would demand a fleet of oil tankers.

In theory a craft carrying ten tons must land, unload at Tempelhof, and be on the way back to the Western Zones every eleven minutes, twenty-four hours a day, day and night.

"In the winter months the weather should defeat this operation. Beginning with autumn fogs, the weather can be below flying minimums sixty to eighty per cent of the time."

This calculation warmed their hearts. Igor threw the statistical bomb at them. "If we were to chart the cities in America with the worst weather record, Pittsburgh would be at the top of the list. If we were to list Pittsburgh with all airports in Germany, Pittsburgh would be the best. In other words the best German weather is worse than the worst American weather in the winter months. You can depend on Berlin to be shut down fifty per cent of the time."

From his own studies at Air Safety with the Americans, Igor knew their rigid standards. In bad weather the stacks of planes would pile up over Berlin, unable to land. It would have to result in chaos.

"And I must say, comrades, no matter how good the attempt or how lucky, it can only succeed with the support of the Berliners. It is impossible for me to believe that the people would not look to the Soviet Union for protection. And lastly, the cost would be staggering, even for the Americans. It would run millions every day."

The meeting went on for hours. Every eventuality was discussed.

That night the Moscow group and Captain Brusilov departed with the opinion: *It is impossible for the West to supply Berlin by air.*

On March 20, 1948, Marshal Popov staged a final walkout of the Supreme German Council.

CHAPTER THIRTY-FIVE

A ROLL CALL OF THE DEAD by Nelson Goodfellow Bradbury. For three years, since the end of World War II, reports have flowed in from American Embassies, military attachés, Counter-Intelligence, and journalists on what is happening in Eastern Europe. Americans did not seem to care. Now that the Truman Doctrine has been declared and a Soviet walkout has ended the function of the Supreme German Council it is well to review the past so that we understand the future.

Here is the roll call of the dead:

In the beginning Estonia, Latvia, and Lithuania were gobbled up and annexed into the Soviet Union as "People's Republics."

Poland fell through a textbook take-over by the Moscow-trained Lublin Committee. Except for a faint gasp by the Church and some traditional alliances with the West, Poland has become another odious "People's Republic."

Albania: The most brutally administrated and backward country in the Western world was in Communist hands at the war's end. Hoxha is an absolute dictator ruling this domain which has little political or economic value. Yet, it is geographically located for guerrilla action against Greece and as a base for a possible move against Italy. There has been the pretense of an election; the usual single slate of candidates. The constitution is modeled on that of the Soviet Union.

Bulgaria: At the war's end there were almost no Communists, but they quickly infiltrated under the protection of the occupying Red Army and forced the other political parties to form a "Fatherland Front" which they could dominate through naked terror. The "Fatherland Front" won the election, to be sure. In 1946 bloody purges wiped out an estimated 20,000 major and minor figures of the prewar government. After the purges, a "People's Republic" was declared.

New general elections supervised by the Red Army announced a majority to the Communists. Who knows?

Georgi Dimitrov, exiled before the war to Moscow, was dusted off and returned to be named Premier.

Petkov, leader of the harassed opposition Agrarian Party was arrested and put to death, his party outlawed. Opposition to the Communists is thoroughly crushed.

Hungary: The first free election in late 1945 was swept by the anti-Communist Smallholder's Party under the leadership of Zoltan Tildy.

Using the Red Army to support them, the Communists then forced the Smallholder's Party to form a "unity" front. Bela Kovaks, Smallholder's Secretary, was arrested for "crimes against the occupation" and a purge of the Smallholder's followed. The Communists forced the Democrats to merge into the "unity" front, followed by a purge of the Democrats.

Deputy Premier Makoki, the Communist, became the true ruler of Hungary.

Cardinal Mindszenty, the last voice of opposition, was arrested before a new election presenting a single slate of candidates. A constitution along Soviet lines has been adopted, a five-year plan along Soviet lines adopted, and a final ousting of all non-Communists has taken place in the government.

Rumania: Under Red Army occupation the Communists forced the other political parties to form a "National Front." Because of King Michael's presence, the Americans and British were able to exert some pressure to keep a balance in the first government, but a massive terror campaign preceded the election of November 1945. Under Red Army supervision, the Communists were declared the victors.

Julius Maniu, leader of the opposition Peasant Party, was arrested along with thousands of members. Treason and espionage trials broke the back of the Peasant Party.

Ana Pauker was named the Communist Premier, forcing King Michael to abdicate.

A new "People's Front" was formed. The new election gives the

Communists 90 per cent of the vote followed by adoption of a Soviet-type constitution.

Purge trials wiped out all existing political opposition, all Roman Catholic bishops were arrested and their congregations dissolved, agriculture was collectivized and industry nationalized.

The game today is called "Slavic Unity," a name reeking of the memory of other unities now deceased.

This is the most repetitious column I have ever written, but the pattern is bare for us all to see. Only in Yugoslavia has Moscow made a gross miscalculation. One might refer to them as the Martin Luthers of communism. Yugoslavia in World War II has the distinction of being the only occupied country to liberate itself. Stalin has made what might prove to be a classical blunder in believing that because Yugoslavia is Communist it will subject itself to the dictates of Moscow. Yugoslavia alone in the Red Bloc has a good army and Stalin does not doubt that it will be used if pushed. Moscow has backed away. This is the first dim clue that there is vulnerability within the Communist world and someday great new rifts may develop.

This great red mass has poured West like a river of molten lava devouring everything in its path. Defeat is recognized as temporary, victory inevitable.

Here in Germany we have seen the Soviet Union slicing off the Eastern Zone and rebuilding it along the recognizable lines. I believe, however, that the event that finally touched Americans was the second fall of Czechoslovakia. Two times in a single decade this innocent people fell victim to a sellout. Once at Munich, now again by an apathetic American public, which did not lift a finger as the Red Army and the Communists chewed up the Czechs. The murder/suicide (?) of the hero, Jan Masaryk, stilled the last voice of freedom, but as it died in agony, perhaps it was the sound to awaken the sleeping America.

Will other nations join the Roll Call of the Dead? Finland was "invited" by Moscow to join a mutual defense pact. Turkey has been coveted as an entrance to the Mediterranean by Russia for centuries. Italy and France are staggering close to communism through collapse of their economies.

In Greece, the Truman Doctrine is meeting its first great test. Left in a shambles by one of the most terrible of the Nazi occupations, Greece saw nearly a third of her population starved, murdered, frozen, or diseased. These valiant people, often divided against themselves, were asked to fight a most horrible civil war.

Greek Communists using bases in Yugoslavia to hit and hide have kidnaped tens of thousands of Greek children, divorced them from their lives and parents, and are training them as future agents of this barbaric order.

As the Greek tragedy wore on, a tired Britain became unable to guarantee the freedom of the Mediterranean. As massive American aid pours in, the Communists are being driven deeper and deeper into the hills.

The Achilles heel of communism, Yugoslavia, first to stand up against Moscow, is closing its borders to the guerrilla bands and it appears that an end may be in sight.

The only ray of light in this bleak picture is the accommodation worked out to neutralize Austria.

In a few years the Soviet Union has swallowed up Eastern Europe and now stands on the brink of creating an empire from the Baltic to the Mediterranean to the English Channel. It is so vast that not even a Hitler dreamed of it. The Soviet Union has patented a method of results without the death of a single Red Army soldier. In Berlin we have been subjected to every harassment short of open warfare. We take our cue from the Greeks that when free men hang tough, they will prevail. If Berlin falls, then the take-over of Western Germany and Western Europe becomes academic.

All that stands between the Soviet Union and the English Channel is a thin line of American and British soldiers and the resolution of free men.

CHAPTER THIRTY-SIX

The tension in Berlin was like that brief lull between the time the air-raid siren stopped and the first bomb fell.

The rumor was planted and spread that the Americans were about to pull out, that food reserves were nearly gone in the Western Sectors, and that there was no room "for the adherents of partition."

With the Supreme German Council no longer functioning, the only official contact was through the Berlin Kommandatura where the moves and countermoves increased the tempo toward the showdown.

On April 11, 1948, the Berlin Assembly continued to defy the Soviet Union by once more voting down the anti-Fascist front.

Two days later General Trepovitch attempted to seize the police force by declaring it wholly under Soviet command. The Western commandants were able to block the take-over because Neal Hazzard had been farsighted enough to have Hans Kronbach appointed as deputy president months before. Kronbach had quietly built a strong pro-Western force which could splinter away from the main body.

On April 16 all Western papers in the Russian Sector were seized, all printing plants confiscated.

Along with this there began a harassment of German civilians traveling in and out of Berlin. The rail lines and highways were entirely within Russian-held territory. After getting away with the pressure on the Germans, Trepovitch ordered harassment on the daily American trains which ran personnel, mail, and supplies to and from the zone.

Each train leaving Berlin was now forced to submit to tedious inspections on the Russian contention that the Americans were supporting black-marketeering and smuggling.

On the autobahn, trucks were compelled to submit manifests and their cargo was inspected carefully. Soviet checkpoints made these inspections last for hours, lining up hundreds of vehicles waiting for clearance.

Then the canals were hit and barges waylaid. . . . The Soviet Union had succeeded in snarling traffic hopelessly.

At last Neal Hazzard warned that no Russian troops would be allowed to board any American train or convoy.

Trepovitch quickly adjusted to the tactic. Without prior warning the rail lines and highways would be shut for hours for "repairs" or due to "technical difficulties."

Berliners watched it all happen with growing apprehension.

By mid-April the American garrison began to feel the pinch. General Hansen phoned the USAFE commander, Barney Root, at Air Force Headquarters in Wiesbaden.

"We're going to need supplies flown in to take care of the garrison."

"How much do you figure, Chip?"

"Eighty tons a day."

"Eighty tons! Hell, Chip, all we've got around here are a couple dozen old Gooney Birds. They can handle only about two tons a flight. Let me get together with my people and see what we can scratch up. Send us a list of requirements and we'll get it to you somehow."

Barney Root was able to locate a few Douglas Skymasters in Italy and the Middle East. These four-engine craft had a ten-ton capacity. Crews were called in from bases in England and two days after Hansen's call the first of them touched down on the runway at Tempelhof to begin the "milk run" to Berlin.

Meanwhile, General Hartly Fitz-Roy worked out some sort of relief for the British garrison and both supplied the French.

At the Air Safety Center, still under four-power operation, and through spies around Tempelhof, Igor Karlovy was able to study the proceedings. In bad weather the planes stacked up overhead resulting in minor chaos. It all confirmed Igor's findings. The West was having trouble getting in a few hundred tons of supplies a day for their garrisons. The greater task of supplying two million people needing thousands of tons daily was beyond comprehension.

To make matters more tense, Russian fighter planes ran through the corridors on the contention that the corridors were illegal, did not exist, and the skies were Russian-owned.

Into this city came Senator Adam Blanchard.

It had long been fashionable for members of the Congress to tour Berlin, get themselves photographed, make a statement or two for posterity, and generally lend themselves to the "glamorous" situation.

Hansen and Hazzard and other top staff officers were compelled to spend hundreds of hours at Tempelhof welcoming the junketing legislators. Some were hard-working and sincere men desiring to help the situation, others were utter bores and nuisances. . . . Hansen deliberately lived in a small house without guest facilities.

Adam Blanchard was not a common-garden-variety senator. From the minority party, he held seats on both the powerful Senate Foreign Relations Committee and the Armed Forces Committee. Although no one could figure what good he could do in Berlin, everyone knew he could do a great deal of harm. The silk-glove treatment was ordered.

Blanchard, as suspected, had come to Berlin with a purpose in mind. He was to run for re-election with a swell of discontent in the party hierarchy of his state. Key industrialists, traditional conservatives, and crusty old isolationists controlled the party machinery. They were sick as hell of being taxed to death to feed undeserving and ungrateful Europeans and keeping a costly American occupation army "over there."

Blanchard had gone along with the Truman Doctrine earlier, bringing further growls that he was getting a little "pinko" around the edges. The senator was now on tenterhooks on how he would vote for the Marshall Plan. He evaded that issue.

His advisors conjured up the idea of a "fact finding" trip to Germany, and Berlin in particular, after which he would make a declaration to soothe the troubled waters back home.

At the end of four days of briefing and tours in Berlin, Adam Blanchard's people called a press conference which was arranged for the entire corps, Communist as well as Western journalists in attendance.

"We want to get out of Germany as soon as possible," Blanchard said. "The first step will be to hand over the authority to the State Department and pare down this costly occupation force."

"That son of a bitch!" Neal Hazzard said.

"Calm down, Neal," Sean warned.

"Calm down, my ass."

On General Hansen's desk lay a copy of *Tägliche Rundschau*, the official Russian newspaper in the German language. The headline blared: KEY AMERICAN OFFICIAL CONFIRMS WITHDRAWAL OF AMERICAN FORCES FROM BERLIN.

A sampling of newspapers around the world played the same theme:

YANKS PULLING OUT OF GERMANY

U.S. WEARY OF OCCUPATION COSTS

AMERICAN ABANDONMENT OF EUROPE BEGINS

"This could not have come at a worse time," Hansen said.

"That bastard just played the Russian trump card. It's just something like this that will stampede the people."

"Neal. Get Falkenstein and the other leaders together and get them calmed down."

"They don't believe us any more, sir. We're sitting on our prats letting them shove our traffic all over Germany. General Hansen, we've got to face up to the fact that their next move is going to be a complete blockade."

"I haven't come to that opinion yet. The Russians are going to be careful about turning world opinion against them."

"The Russians don't give a Chinese fart what the world thinks of them as long as they get away with what they're trying. We're the ones who are always afraid of how we look."

"That will be all, Neal."

"Yes, sir."

He left. Hansen pushed away from his desk and looked at Sean.

"Colonel Hazzard is right, sir. They're going to blockade."

"I know it, Sean, but I can't let either Neal or the Germans know that I believe it, yet."

The general left to pick up Senator Blanchard for a luncheon at British Headquarters. The senator's people were so proud of the headlines they urged him to remain in Germany another week or two. Hansen dreaded the consequences. He considered the matter in the back seat of the longest, blackest, shiniest Cadillac in the American garrison as it sped toward the VIP guest house surrounded by a covey of motorcycles.

The house was a magnificent affair once belonging to Himmler. It sat on the Wannsee Lake. The living room had a great plate-glass wall that could be raised and lowered, a velvetlike lawn that swept to the water's edge, and a private dock.

Senator Blanchard got into the car beside Hansen, the sirens screamed and the flags on the fenders fluttered as they moved north, skirting the Grunewald and the chain of little lakes as they moved toward Charlottenburg Borough.

Adam Blanchard was a handsome, lean man in his early sixties. He spoke with the smooth assurance of one who had survived many political dogfights over three decades.

He was aware of the coldness of the Berlin garrison after his press conference. In a very nice way he let Hansen know he was annoyed.

"As a matter of fact, Senator, this gives you and me a chance to talk. We are having a very bad time straightening out some misunderstandings as a result of your statements."

Blanchard knew he was sitting beside one of the few military men he could not bully. He decided upon the blunt route himself. "Your record of antagonism toward the Congress is well known."

"The basis of my antagonism has always been that the military has been more farsighted than the Congress. The fact that our country was forced to enter World War II unprepared because of a lack of appropriations or appreciation of the danger vindicates my position. You know, Senator Blanchard, if the United States had been strong, there might never have been a Second World War. And only strength will stop a third World War."

The slap was unmistakable. Before the war Blanchard was among those die-hard isolationists; his new position on the Foreign Relations Committee had not changed the spots on the leopard.

"General Hansen, I admire your candor. Let me speak with equal candor. I have found waste and inefficiency in this military government operation appalling. Incompetence in the military is a subject with which I am familiar."

"Senator, have you ever been aboard an aircraft carrier?"

"Certainly."

"That piece of machinery is worth over a hundred million dollars. It takes three thousand men to operate her. She is the most advanced product of the nation's talents, carrying the most sophisticated electronic devices known to man. Yes, sir, an aircraft carrier is something."

"What is your point, sir?"

"The officer who commands such a ship makes nine to eleven thousand dollars a year. What do you suppose such a man would get from private industry running a hundred-million-dollar corporation with three thousand employees?"

"Now just a minute . . ."

"I haven't finished yet. It has become fashionable again to portray the military as stupid, shiftless clods. I'll tell you something about what we've got here in Berlin. We have a cross section of the most brilliant brains our nation can produce. Our sector of Berlin is administrated by judges, police, labor leaders, engineers who could run any city in the United States with greater efficiency than it is now."

Blanchard flustered. He had never received such a tongue-lashing by an Army man. "You, General, intend to foster world tension to justify huge military expenditures. I know all about this goddamned country club you're running."

"I'm a man in my sixties," Hansen said softly. "I have $1800 in the bank. In thirty years in the service my wife has had twenty-one places she has called home . . . but we know why we are in Berlin. And I also know why you are in Berlin.

"You don't want to leave here knowing why America must stay because that might make you unpopular in your state. I'm dealing with the same deaf man I dealt with before the war. But don't think we can leave Berlin, free. We will pay for it with ten thousand per cent interest.

"You're in a fight, Blanchard, because I've got a press corps here who knows what we are trying to do and you start on us and you'll get it right between the eyes."

The car passed on the southern circumference of the park holding the Olympic stadium and sports complex, where Hitler once attempted to prove Aryan superiority on the playing fields.

The two men had no more to say.

At the north end of the Olympic Park, the sports administration building now was the location of British Headquarters. A glum Adam Blanchard lit up as the British honor guard came to attention and the band played a "fanfare for a dignified occasion."

He emerged from the car, walked toward ramrod stiff, swagger stick-bearing Hartly Fitz-Roy and pumped his hand, slapped his back, and waved at the guard as though he were soliciting their votes.

CHAPTER THIRTY-SEVEN

Neal Hazzard paced the living room of Sean's apartment angrily. "What the hell is the matter with General Hansen? Is he blind or something?"

"He is being hampered by a little system known as democracy," Sean answered.

"What about the threat of blockade? Why doesn't he know?"

"He knows. But he can't do anything until it is imposed. You know how it is, pal. The military cry 'wolf' and no one believes them. The only way it will be believed is when Berlin gets its Pearl Harbor."

Hazzard shook his head. "We have to stand here flat-footed waiting for the Russians to belt us."

"That's because we represent a society dictated by public opinion."

Hazzard had chewed his cigar beyond mercy, flung it into the fireplace. "Sean. I think I know the people of Berlin as well as anyone."

"I'll buy that."

"They've got strong nerves. If we could only give them our guarantee that we are going to stay."

"We can't do that, Neal."

"I know the Russians too. I know them from two hundred and fifty-eight meetings of the Kommandatura with Nikolai Trepovitch. They'll quit short of a fight."

"That's no secret."

"Goddammit, I'm going on RIAS and tell the people of Berlin this garrison is staying."

"Neal, for Christ's sake. If you do guess wrong you can commit us to a bad situation."

"I'm an old infantryman, Sean. I know that when the battle gets so screwed up the generals behind the lines can't control it, a few men in the thick of it have to improvise."

Sean had once stood in Neal Hazzard's shoes in Rombaden ready to face the wrath of the world for something he believed. He was a soul mate. If there was one single thing that being an American meant to Sean it was the ability to think for one's self. Not in times of comfort, but under nerve-wracking stress. Hazzard knew he was right. Sean believed it too.

"You've got a partner," Sean said. "How do we do this?"

"I'm going to go over to RIAS and make the announcement right away."

"With the right moves," Sean thought aloud, "we can dump Hollweg as Oberburgermeister and stop the Russians for long enough to clean the Adam Blanchard stink."

"Like my old pal T. E. Blatty says . . . let's get cracking."

At the invisible boundary between the American and British sectors on Kufsteiner Strasse 69 on Innsbrucker Platz stood a five-story, semi-circular, gray-stone building which had become one of the most powerful locales in the world.

RIAS was the only radio planted deep inside the Russian Empire. A brilliant staff, which refused to be cowed, succeeded in obliterating the Russian propaganda assaults. RIAS was one of the few positions anywhere where the West took the offensive. Each day the reportage of Soviet atrocity was heard by millions of the enslaved. RIAS was a voice in the dark forest of Eastern Europe. To the Russians, the American Radio had become the most hated symbol of the West, and behind every move to get the West from Berlin was the plan to still its voice.

This station was so feared that six hundred Russian jamming stations tried to blot out its signal. To counter this, RIAS staggered its programs to the Russian colonies. Then once a day the entire power output was combined and over a million watts thrown into a single program, which nothing could jam. It is said that when RIAS went on full output it could be received in the silver fillings of your teeth two hundred miles away.

Colonel Hazzard was an old friend at RIAS. He went to the director's office. All transmissions were ordered to halt to put the full power at the American Commandant's disposal.

"This is Colonel Hazzard, commandant of the American Sector of Berlin. My friends. I have a most important message from my government. For the past several weeks the Soviet Union and their flunkies, led by Rudi Wöhlman, have deliberately spread a rumor that the American garrison is going to withdraw from Berlin. I am here to nail this new lie dead. An opinion expressed recently by an American senator was entirely his own and has been completely discredited in Washington."

Hazzard closed his eyes, crossed his fingers.

"An official spokesman of my government has sent me this message and I quote. 'The United States is in Berlin by irrevocable legal agreements which make Berlin separate and independent of the occupation zones of Germany. This is a four-power city and will remain so. The United States garrison will not withdraw now or in the future until an accord is reached and ratified by the people of Berlin. We will continue to fulfill our obligations.' End of quote."

"Colonel Hazzard," the guard said at the main gate, "General Hansen wants you in his office, immediately."

Hazzard came to a stop before the general's desk, eyed an ashen-faced Sean standing nearby.

"You're fired," Hansen said.

"Yes, sir."

"You will proceed with Mrs. Hazzard and your family to Frankfurt and report to the Provost Marshal. You will remain there until I can act on your formal resignation from the Army."

"Yes, sir. I'm homesick for Kansas City anyhow."

When Neal Hazzard had gone Hansen sat speechless for ever so long. "I should have done this a long time ago," he mumbled to his deputy. "He's a hothead."

Sean did not answer.

"All right, get it off your chest," the general demanded.

"You've made a mistake, sir."

"Hazzard takes too damned much on his own. He's gotten us into hot water before."

"Rugged individualism. Yes, sir. That's a bad thing."

"I said get it off your chest!"

"Yes, sir. This is an army. It is not intended to run on democratic principles. Generals should not go chewing the asses off senators."

"Goddammit, Sean . . ."

"I haven't gotten it all off my chest, sir. What we need is more blind obedience. You can be friggin' sure that no Russian colonel would take that responsibility on himself. You can be sure of that."

Berthold Hollweg was thunderstruck by Neal Hazzard's broadcast. When Ulrich Falkenstein went home he pretended to be delighted by the American attitude, but in his heart he feared more pressure from Wöhlman, Schatz, and the Russians.

Since Sean had confronted Falkenstein with the sellout, his relations with Hollweg had gone cold. Hollweg's desire to appease the Russians was so apparent it was becoming an open scandal in the Democratic Party.

"There is so little left of forty years of friendship," Ulrich said sadly, "we can at least spare each other the sham of wearing two faces now."

"What are you trying to say, Ulrich?"

"The time has come for you to resign as mayor of Berlin."

Hollweg paled, grew faint. He recovered enough to become indignant.

Ulrich stopped him by throwing before him a copy of the reports that damned him as a Russian collaborator. Berthold Hollweg lifted the first page and began to read, then turned his back and wrung his hands.

"The truth!" Falkenstein demanded.

"They made me sit for hours in an empty office in police headquarters," he mumbled. "Schatz came . . . three, four nights a week . . . I was followed everywhere . . . they threatened to kill my little grandson . . . you can't imagine what it has been like!"

"Yes, I do know what it is like."

"Great God! All men cannot be like you!"

Ulrich Falkenstein's final disdain ruled out pity. "Was there nothing left for the things we lived for? Was there nothing left of the memory of our comrades that Hitler destroyed? Was there nothing left to cry out in anger at Rudi Wöhlman? Was there nothing left?"

Hollweg wept.

"Fool!" Falkenstein cried.

"You are the fool!" his friend screamed back. "How long will the Americans stay before they are sick of the German business? How much blood will they spill for us? Do you really believe the Russians can be stopped? You are the fool, Ulrich! I cannot live through it, again."

Ulrich flopped his arms helplessly. Beneath him writhed a person whose innards were eroded by the political terror of two decades.

Falkenstein unfolded a sheet of paper, placed it before Hollweg, and handed him a pen. "You will sign this. It is your resignation from the Democratic Party and as Oberburgermeister of Berlin."

CHAPTER THIRTY-EIGHT

It happened with lightning speed!

The session of the Berlin Assembly came to order in the red-brick, churchlike structure on Rathaus Strasse. The banner of the city with its symbolic Berlin Bear looked down on the great room from behind the rostrum.

During the early morning hours, Ulrich Falkenstein had quietly marshaled his forces and held secret meetings with the leaders of the Conservatives and Christians. The air was still supercharged by Colonel Hazzard's broadcast. A new ounce of courage was in them all.

The chief clerk of the Assembly stood, and read the resignation of Berthold Hollweg as Oberburgermeister.

Rudi Wöhlman never knew what hit him! Before he could gain his wits, the free parties had elected Ulrich Falkenstein to the office.

Collaborating with the American guarantee, Sean had used this precious timing to inflict a catastrophic setback on the Russians. It was the first real display of offensive action as against defensive reaction.

General Hansen was too wise not to understand the temper of the moment. He displayed another quality of his many-sided character by the admission that he had made a mistake and he set out to rectify it.

Hansen now took responsibility for Hazzard's broadcast and argued with the State Department that it was entirely within his discretion and general American policy. Washington now was faced with rebuking their military governor publicly. They backed down with an announcement of their own: THE AMERICAN GARRISON IS REMAINING IN BERLIN.

"General, we have contacted Colonel Hazzard in Frankfurt. He is on the line."

"Neal?"

"Speaking."

"Hansen, here."

"Yes, sir?"

"Neal, on second thought, Berlin needs you more than Kansas City."

"To hell with Berlin, General."

"I'm trying to say, I'm sorry."

"You don't have to, General. I knew what I was doing. I'm the one who is sorry I had to put you in hot water."

"Will you come back?"

"No, sir. I'm tired of sleeping with a pistol under my pillow. I'm tired of my wife being threatened. I've got children sixteen and seventeen years old. I want to get a quiet job and have enough money to put them through college. General, I've got a wife in the next room crying her heart out. She really hasn't enjoyed the country club we're supposed to be running in Berlin. I've never seen Claire cry before . . . not in twenty-two years of this. We've just had a belly full."

Sean lifted the extension. The general nodded that it was okay to speak. "This is Sean. We need you here."

"Find another pigeon."

"Listen, dammit. Hollweg resigned as mayor and Falkenstein was named in his place. The Russians never knew what hit them."

"You're kidding . . ."

"We've got to make this stick. Your pal Trepovitch is screaming for an emergency meeting of the Kommandatura. You've got to go in for us."

"Hold on."

Both of them could hear him talking to Claire Hazzard. We've got to go back, he was saying. No I can't guarantee it won't happen again.

"General, if we get a plane this evening we should be in Berlin by midnight."

"I'll dispatch mine right away," Hansen said.

When the call was over Hansen said to Sean, "I wonder if Senator Blanchard thinks a shiftless clod like Neal Hazzard really earns his eight thousand bucks a year?"

"Veto! Veto!" Nikolai Trepovitch said darkly. "We veto the resignation of Berthold Hollweg. He must continue to serve in office. Therefore, the election of Ulrich Falkenstein is illegal . . . and we veto that too."

Hazzard, the chairman of the month, recognized T. E. Blatty.

"I say, General Trepovitch, you can't veto Hollweg's resignation. It is clearly permitted under a constitution which you personally agreed upon and gave to the city of Berlin. Nor do I see how you can veto Herr Falkenstein as it specifically states in Article Twenty-three of the same constitution that the Oberburgermeister shall legally be voted into office by the Berlin Assembly. You just can't go around vetoing, my dear fellow."

"We have substantial suspicion that Ulrich Falkenstein is engaged in black-marketeering. We demand an investigation."

"No dice," Neal Hazzard said. "Either present charges or forget it."

Trepovitch began banging on the table. "It is a Western plot! We will never allow Falkenstein in office!"

An advisor whispered into the Russian commandant's ear. He was warned to beware of an American trap. Remembering how Hazzard allowed the new labor union to form in the American Sector there was a danger he might try the same trick with the city government. Under no circumstances could the Soviet Union risk removal of the Assembly and Magistrat from the Soviet Sector.

"For the sake of Allied unity," the Russian began hollowly, "I shall propose a compromise. We will accept Hollweg's resignation on the condition that Falkenstein's illegal election is set aside. We will agree to Hanna Kirchner as acting mayor until the problem is fully worked out."

Hazzard smelled victory, but Blatty was at it. "Don't you know," the Englishman said, "that we can't do all this mucking around without consent of the Berlin Assembly."

As chairman, Neal Hazzard called a recess before Blatty went off on a full-scale parliamentary tangent.

In his office he reached Ulrich Falkenstein and advised him of the Soviet proposal.

Falkenstein was delighted. "Hanna will make an excellent Oberburgermeister. The Russians believe that because she is a German woman they have found another weak spot like Hollweg. They have picked on a tough hen."

"How about the Assembly?" Hazzard asked.

"I am certain I can get them to agree."

For the following half hour the three Western commandants locked themselves up in Blatty's office, the other two convincing the Englishman to accept the compromise. If the Kommandatura were to "suggest" this to the Berlin Assembly, perhaps the Assembly would make the accommodation.

At last Blatty gave in.

Hanna Kirchner was "suggested" and the Berlin Assembly approved her as acting Oberburgermeister. She had achieved the highest political position of any woman in Berlin's history.

On People's Radio from the Russian Sector, the "voice of the masses" brought Berthold Hollweg to the microphone.

"My fellow Berliners," his weary voice said, "I have resigned as Oberburgermeister of Berlin because I found it impossible to conduct the office under the constant threats of Colonel Hazzard and his imperialist henchmen Blatty and Belfort. They imposed upon me a reign of Fascist terror and attempted to have me work against the working class of Berlin. My conscience could no longer bear it. I have asked Comrade Rudi Wöhlman to allow me to serve the interests of freedom through the Democratic Party in the Soviet Sector in the anti-Fascist front."

CHAPTER THIRTY-NINE

Ernestine opened the door quickly, put her finger to her lips and stepped into the hall.

"Shh," she whispered, "Uncle Ulrich has dozed at his desk. I don't want to awaken him."

Sean helped her into her coat, took her arm, and led her to the Horsche sedan.

"What time does the concert start, Colonel?"

"I have a confession, Fraulein Falkenstein. I lured you out tonight under false pretenses."

"So?"

"We have met four times. One piano recital, one dramatic reading of Goethe no less, one museum exhibition, and one opening of a play. The way I look at it is this . . . there is only so much culture a man can absorb."

"And what do you have in mind, sir?"

"A table at a nice French restaurant on the Tegeler Lake. Are you angry?"

"As a matter of fact, there is only so much culture a woman can absorb."

He clicked on Armed Forces Network, where there was apt to be music no more serious than Glenn Miller, and swung to the northern end of the city past the medieval borough of Spandau.

In the middle of the French Sector, the Jungfernheide and the Tegel forests surround the Tegeler Lake. At the lake's edge the French Officers' Club operated a lovely restaurant for occupation forces.

It was that kind of warm and balmy night that, with the freshness of the woods, made Berliners boast about their rare brand of air. Their table was ready on the outside terrace.

"What a lovely idea," she said.

Sean excused himself as he always did when they arrived at a destination. She watched him leave to phone in to Headquarters and give his whereabouts.

After their first date they did not see each other for ten days, until Ernestine phoned him to ask him to the opening of a play. She was glad he had decided to drop the "cultural" pretext as a reason for seeing her. They were quite at ease with each other now, in a formal sort of way. What was it besides his rugged good looks that made him so attractive? The inevitable comparisons with Dietrich Rascher and the other men she had known came to mind. She realized that Sean and her uncle were the most interesting people she had ever known. His range of knowledge and his ability to express it seemed limitless, like the teacher he was.

There was a certain peace within Sean that was apparent. He did not need to prove the masculinity that obsessed most German men. He was certain of himself about so many things.

The opening of a warm and sentimental side began when Sean tried to apologize to her. No German boy would so humble himself; it was a new experience for her.

But there were other moments when she felt she could read his thoughts and those thoughts were ugly. He constantly seemed to be reminding himself he was sitting with a German woman, asking himself why. "German woman . . . leper."

Ernestine was curious to know if she could loosen him from an obsessive hatred of Germans. Or was their friendship nothing more than two lonely people who needed to talk to each other? Would Sean's hatred always lurk and suddenly be triggered?

He returned to the table.

The menu was a bit on the thin side, but the French could do wonderful things with sauces, even over Rhine River eel. Fortunately, there was no shortage of champagne.

He raised his glass. "To our first noncultural affair."

Their other encounters had given way to a rising number of long silent spells, lingering glances, and greater occasion of the need to touch each other. In this setting both of them knew that these feelings had to find their way through. It became a moment of both anticipation and fear.

She reached over and took his plate. "Here, let me cut that for you. Only an old eel *fresser* can do it properly."

Sean watched her movements as she made thin, true slices down the middle of the fish and removed the backbone. He thought she did everything delicately.

They were conscious of their own silence. They drank and watched the lake, and were annoyed by the intrusions of the waiter. Sean tipped the last of the bottle into her glass.

"*Prosit!*" she said without thinking, but Sean did not react to the German toast.

He ordered another bottle of champagne.

Ernestine giggled. "I should have warned you. It does not take much to make me tipsy."

Her eyes shone and she was radiant. The barriers were tumbling.

Behind them, the musicians switched from French to a German medley. Ernestine hummed, then sang, and her voice was sweet too. She remembered that she had not sung for years and years. "You are a pretty man . . . yes, you are a pretty man . . . that is better, Colonel . . . you do have such a nice smile when you use it."

> *Du kannst nicht treu sein—*
> *Nein, nein, das kannst du nicht,*
> *Wenn auch dein Mund mir*
> *Wahre Liebe verspricht.*
> *In deinem Herzen*
> *Hast du fuer viele Platz,*
> *Darum bist du auch nicht*
> *Fuer mich der richt'ge Schatz.*

Ernestine thought she saw his face grow tense at the German lyrics and stopped singing.

"Please go on," he said.

There, the damned hypersensitivity again. "It is nonsense. A silly, sentimental song."

Sean took her hand. "I am very glad we decided to become friends."

"May I have some more champagne?"

"I don't want to give you a hangover on our first noncultural meeting."

"I wish to get utterly drunk. I have been prim and proper for lo, six hundred years. I am going to kick off my shoes, forthwith, and wade into the lake and make you carry me to the car . . ."

Sean poured her another glass.

She sipped long and sighed deeply. "Oh Lord, it is lovely here. It hasn't been so lovely for so long."

"To a lovely friendship," he said.

She tweaked his nose. "We have a nice German custom when people decide to become friends . . . oh, excuse me, Colonel . . . you don't like German customs."

"If it's a nice one."

"Extremely nice. First, you hold your glass and I hold mine. Now, we reach over . . . so . . . and intertwine arms. There. Now, we drink."

"This is a nice custom."

"The best is yet to come."

They sipped from each other's glass, their locked arms brought their cheeks close.

"After a kiss we can call each other by the familiar form of . . . Du."

He felt the velvet of her cheek. "I like Du," he said.

"And I like Du."

"Du smell good."

"I wore it for Du."

Their lips touched.

"Hello, Sean."

"Hi."

Even on the veranda lit with little more than moonlight it was difficult to miss the hulking form of Shenandoah Blessing as he spoke to the headwaiter, who, in turn, pointed to their table.

"Sorry to disturb you," he said.

Sean tumbled back to life, excused himself.

"Take the young lady home. I'll meet you at Security soon as you can get there. I have your fatigues and side arms in my jeep."

"Was gibt's?"

"Don't know, but it sure smells big."

CHAPTER FORTY

When Sean reached a secret room in the basement of Headquarters, Blessing was there with a dozen hand-picked enlisted men from the Constabulary. Likewise, a British Major Whitehead and a squad of their military police were present. General Hansen, General Fitz-Roy, and the Commandants Hazzard and Blatty were there. General Fitz-Roy addressed them:

"You gentlemen have been selected and assembled for a secret, urgent, and delicate mission. Within forty-eight hours our headquarters will issue a joint communiqué announcing a currency reform in the American and British zones of Germany.

"Further, it is now anticipated that the American Congress will enact the Marshall Plan into law momentarily. These two events will no doubt bring a violent reaction from the Soviet Union.

"We anticipate the Russians will attempt to issue their own currency and make it universal in Berlin. We are here to prepare for that eventuality.

"Your mission tonight is to fly to Munich and proceed to a destination known as Hüttendorf, where you will bring back a special currency for Berlin. We will hold it ready if the Soviets try to eliminate four-power currency.

"Captain Horniman of British Intelligence will brief you in detail."

Horniman spoke for an hour outlining the mission. It had been meticulously plotted.

With a final warning that no one was to make contact with persons on the outside, the briefing ended.

According to the plan they were to proceed in twos, threes, and fours to Tempelhof over a staggered time so their arrival would not create suspicion. A four-engined Skymaster was in ready named "Cherry Picker." The flight plan called for Hamburg with the passengers listed as troops going on furlough or routine military business. After a roll call, Tempelhof tower cleared the Cherry Picker slightly after midnight and she swept over sleeping Berlin into the northern air corridor toward Hamburg.

Sean had worked secretly on certain details and aspects of the currency reform. Now that there was no doubt that cooperation with the Russians was impossible new currency would be needed for the planned merging of the Western Zones. It was an integral part of the raising of German production levels, halting inflation, opening up consumer goods, rebuilding and establishing a trade balance.

Yet, the currency reform was a daring tactic in that it issued the Russians a direct challenge. By legal agreement, Berlin was a four-power city not belonging to any Zone. Therefore, the currency to be used in Berlin would be marked with a "B."

The Cherry Picker passed out of the Soviet Zone at the Dannenberg beacon beyond Soviet surveillance and instead of continuing for Hamburg she swung south.

At the Munich airport a convoy of closed armored trucks stood by at their parking space. As the Cherry Picker cut engines, a company of infantry surrounded her restricting the pilot and crew aboard. It was daybreak.

Members of the mission boarded the waiting vehicles according to preassignment; they drove south from the city into the rolling foothills of the mountains in the direction of the Austrian frontier. This was Bavaria in its unspoiled form.

Off the main road they passed through villages filled with decorative wooden houses with brightly colored murals on their outside walls, churches with tall towers and onion-shaped domes, and cobblestone streets and still lakes. It was one of the few corners of Germany untouched by the war.

Once past Tegernsee the hills grew more severe and the forests thickened. The convoy swung onto a dirt road blocked by a guard station.

HÜTTENDORF 3 KMS. PASSAGE ON THIS ROAD IS FORBIDDEN!

They plunged into the forest and threw up a swirl of dust; the land was void of human life. The rising sun flickered through the trees as they passed another series of roadblocks and were checked through carefully.

So far as the Germans in the area knew, Hüttendorf, a tiny village of ten families, had been confiscated in total as a stockade for upper-echelon Nazi war criminals. Trained never to ask questions during the Hitler era, they said nothing and knew nothing about this "forbidden" place. The village was surrounded by a wall of barbed wire.

Colonel Hill, the C.O., met Sean and Major Whitehead at the main gate and led them to an inner compound completely walled off from the outer village and watched by an intricate guard system.

Inside the compound Germans and Americans had volunteered to live for four months with no contact with the outside for the purpose of establishing an engraving and printing plant for the manufacture of the new currency. The security was in the hands of select personnel who also volunteered to be isolated.

Inside the inner wall stood a half-dozen buildings; two barracks, the former community barn, and three other wooden constructions holding the plants and warehouse.

The convoy was lined up alongside the barn. Colonel Hill unlocked the door. The barn was filled with neatly crated boxes containing billions of marks in the new money. The special Berlin B marks were triple-checked and loaded. Signatures were traded, another roll call made. This was the sixteenth roll call.

The convoy rolled back to Munich, where the Cherry Picker was loaded. To further avoid suspicion, half the mission was left in Munich confined to tightly guarded quarters.

The Cherry Picker took off to retrace the earlier flight, reversing the procedure and pretending to be coming from Hamburg.

Late that evening six tons of wooden crates were unloaded at Tempel-hof marked BOURBON, GIN, SCOTCH WHISKEY, and VODKA.

Russian agents reported to Soviet Headquarters that a large shipment of liquor had arrived. This led to a great deal of mirth in the Russian Command. Obviously the West was feeling the pinch of the traffic harassment. If there was going to be a blockade, the West did not intend to run out of liquor. What made it doubly funny to Nikolai Trepovitch was that the British and Americans had forsaken the French by failing to bring in wine.

Sean O'Sullivan, Blessing, and the rest of the men in the mission were confined to McNair Barracks until public announcement of the currency reform was made.

CHAPTER FORTY-ONE

June 17, 1948, is a day that will live in humanity's memory. The Congress of the United States enacted into law the European Recovery Act. The weary, the hungry, the frightened were told that the Marshall Plan would bring them tractors and butter and hope. The Marshall Plan was the light to rekindle the flame of freedom.

On June 18 the British and American headquarters jointly announced the currency reform for Germany, except Berlin. And with this, the Soviet Union's march to the English Channel came to a halt.

It was widely announced that Marshal Alexei Popov had an extraordinary proclamation. Every radio set in Berlin was tuned to People's Radio as the Russian took to the air.

"The conditions under which the West was invited to Berlin no longer exist. Because of broken Western treaties their presence in Berlin has become illegal.

"Berlin is geographically, economically, and historically part of the Soviet Zone of occupation. Four-power occupation is hereby ruled null and void.

"As of tomorrow, the former currency is no longer of value in Berlin. The Soviet Union will issue new currency which will be the only legal money in the city."

Sean went to the general's office where Neal Hazzard had set up a billow of cigar smoke.

"Sean," General Hansen said, "you know Ulrich Falkenstein better than any of us. Shoving our currency in against the Russians isn't going to be enough. There is no doubt that the Berliners will give an expression of where they stand. The danger is not from the Berliners; it's from the Communists. We need the B marks approved by the Assembly. Can Falkenstein do it?"

If not Falkenstein, then no one, Sean thought, but it would be difficult. The City Hall sat inside the Russian Sector. The free assemblymen would be in danger.

"It will be tough," Sean said.

"I say Falkenstein is strong enough to pull them through," Hazzard said.

"He's the leader," Sean agreed. "That's the one thing a German understands . . . follow the leader."

"And that's the one reason I'll never buy these people. They won't stand up for an idea because it's a good idea," Hansen said.

"It's a hell of a lot better to follow Falkenstein than Hitler," Hazzard answered.

"What a hell of a funny place," Sean said. "Our ally is now our enemy and our enemy is now our ally. Well, sir, we all agree that Falkenstein is the best of the lot."

"And I don't trust him," Hansen said.

"General, I don't think you trust any politician."

There was a relief of laughter.

"At least he's as good as Senator Blanchard," Hazzard added.

"All right, all right, send for him," Hansen said.

"I don't think we'd better do that, sir," Sean said.

"Why not. You two are selling me this guy."

"What we are now asking is that the people of Berlin become our partners."

"What the hell are you driving at, Sean?"

"We need Ulrich Falkenstein and the Berliners as much as they need us. No more, no less. We can't go into this partnership acting as conquerors. Falkenstein won his right to be our equal in a concentration camp. I think this occasion calls for us to get in a car and visit him at his home."

"I second the motion," Neal Hazzard said.

Andrew Jackson Hansen was appalled at the notion, but the point had been made. Things were changing. He grumbled to Sean to order a staff car.

Falkenstein's maid nearly passed out when she opened the door.

"You want to kick it off, Sean?" the general asked.

"Herr Falkenstein. We have flown in five hundred million marks of the new currency. It is exactly the same as that in the zone except it is stamped with a B. We are prepared to disburse it to the banks in our sectors within an hour."

Well, well, well, Falkenstein thought to himself. They were answering the challenge with the strongest indication yet of a determination to remain in Berlin. "I am certain you have examined the consequences."

"Any consequence is better than handing them the city."

"After we make our announcement, we want the Berlin Assembly to pass a resolution favoring our B marks," General Hansen said.

"That is a tall order."

"We think you are a tall man," Hazzard said.

Falkenstein's mind ran in practical channels. Would he be able to hold his people together and push a vote through in the Russian Sector? Yet, the Americans and British were committing themselves to risk, too, for the first time.

The alternative? Give the city to Rudi Wöhlman. How long would it last? As long as Prague . . . as long as Warsaw.

Falkenstein did not like the alliance with the Americans. They were hedgy. They came to him only out of self-interest. Yet, there was no one else, there was no place to go.

"When do you plan to announce the B marks?"

"Over RIAS in the morning so that it will be covered in the afternoon papers."

Falkenstein nodded. "I have a busy day's work then."

"There is a question I am forced to ask," General Hansen said. "Knowing what might happen, are the people of this city going to hold?"

"And you, gentlemen. Will you hold?"

"I don't know," Hansen answered. "If we do leave we will pay for it with the blood of unborn generations. But the question is here and now. At this moment we have a way out and you don't. How are the people of Berlin going to choose to go this time?"

With his hot and cold love of the city, Ulrich Falkenstein had made himself believe that Berliners were different . . . but they had endured the Nazis, the bombs, the rape of their city. Was there enough left in them to resist? Would fear of the Russians band them together to accept this half-hearted alliance with the Americans; or would the history of the past tell them that resistance is useless and would they then stampede to the Russians as the best way to survive?

He looked directly at the American military governor. "You have my word, sir, that so long as the American garrison remains in Berlin, the people will stand with you."

They shook hands. Hansen and Falkenstein looked at each other with a mutual lack of warmth.

CHAPTER FORTY-TWO

The day after the announcement of the B marks, the Soviet Union suspended canal and rail traffic for "technical" reasons and the movement on the autobahn slowed to a trickle.

Hovering on the brink of a complete blockade, Ulrich Falkenstein presented a bill to the Berlin Assembly to accept the Western currency.

Rudi Wöhlman used the full bag of parliamentary tricks to stall and the SND of Adolph Schatz worked overtime to apply terror on the assemblymen.

On the day of June 23, 1948, the vote could no longer be delayed. As he had done many times before, General Hansen sent Sean O'Sullivan into the eye of the hurricane. He was dispatched to the office which the Americans kept at the Berlin City Hall.

Berlin's Rathaus sat well inside the Soviet Sector a short distance from the rubble-strewn Unter Den Linden and two full miles away from the junction where the British, American, and Russian sectors came together.

The former Lust Garten at the end of the Unter Den Linden had been cleared and made into a huge plaza, renamed Marx-Engels Platz, and served as a massing place for shows of Soviet solidarity.

On this day Action Squads from the factories, the university, the political clubs, and the youth groups assembled in the plaza and placards were passed among them.

DOWN WITH THE IMPERIALIST WARMONGERS!
AMERICANS, GO HOME!
PEACE AND PROSPERITY THROUGH OUR SOVIET COMRADES!
HITLER! HANSEN! HAZZARD!

On cue they filed out of the Marx-Engels Platz, crossed the bridge over the Spree River, and took up their posts at the Rathaus and at the Magistrat a block away. The police were nowhere to be seen.

The arrival of the first Democrats from the Western Sectors started catcalls and shoving. As more came some rocks were hurled and the last through were mauled and the clothing torn from them.

In his office Ulrich Falkenstein received word from one of his floor deputies that the Communists were creating pandemonium, refusing to come to order. He walked to the balcony overlooking the Assembly and watched the Communists throwing ink bottles, shouting, and stomping.

"Call Lieutenant Colonel O'Sullivan."

Sean watched for some ten minutes. Every attempt to bring order was drowned out.

"All right," Sean said at last, "you've got my clearance."

Falkenstein walked down to the floor and over to Rudi Wöhlman, who stood on a desk top exhorting his people. He tugged at Wöhlman's trouser leg and motioned for him to come down.

"Comrade Wöhlman," Ulrich said, "if you do not establish order in your ranks in one minute we are authorized to leave and conduct the business of this Assembly in the American Sector."

Wöhlman had been warned by V. V. Azov not to let such a thing happen. He got his people quiet, held a quick caucus, and announced a boycott of the "illegal" bill before the Assembly.

With the Communists refusing to vote, the Berlin Assembly voted in behalf of the Western B marks, rejecting the Russian currency unanimously.

When the session ended, the physical violence outside reached a new peak with Hanna Kirchner being severely beaten at the Magistrat and hospitalized along with two-dozen assemblymen from the free parties. . . . But the vote stood.

Any comradery that once existed between Neal Hazzard and Nikolai Trepovitch was gone. Hazzard looked angrily at the Russian at what was obviously going to be one of the last meetings of the dying Kommandatura.

"You have used the Red Army as thugs, bullies, and hoodlums to terrorize defenseless people in country after country. Is this your glorious way of life? Threatening to starve two million people. You were not wanted in Poland. You were not wanted in Czechoslovakia and you're not wanted here in Berlin. I only regret that my country was not in Prague and Warsaw to prevent their rape."

Trepovitch was pale. He was ill from the strain of the past days. "The Soviet Union vetoes the illegal action of the Berlin Assembly," he recited.

As the Russian spoke, an aide whispered to Neal Hazzard that General Hansen was on the phone. Neal was excused and left the conference room for his office.

The instant he was gone, Trepovitch sprung to his feet. "The Americans have walked out of the Kommandatura!"

"Nonsense," T. E. Blatty answered, "he slipped me a note requesting to be excused to take a phone call."

"A lie! This was a direct provocation! The Americans have deliberately walked out in the middle of my arguments! The Soviet Union will no longer tolerate such indignities!"

And with that, the Russian led his staff from the Kommandatura, duplicating Marshal Popov's abandonment of the Supreme German Council. The flag of the Soviet Union was lowered from the staff before the building, never to be raised again.

The free parties of Berlin called for a unity rally in the still battered great Olympic Stadium. It was jammed to overflowing with 125,000 aroused Berliners. Yet, it was an orderly demonstration as only German demonstrations can be. The passion in them was under control.

As their leaders arrived and mounted the rostrum a swell of cheers arose, but the great ovation was reserved for Colonel Neal Hazzard, who clasped both hands over his head like a victorious fighter.

Those on the rostrum who led the Democrats and Christians and Conservatives realized that the people cheered the man rather than his nation, for the alliance was shaky.

Hanna Kirchner came from her hospital bed and the thunder swelled. One by one they stood before their people and begged them to be firm and begged the world to look upon them. And then, Ulrich Falkenstein:

"Berliners! We have been asked if we have the courage to stand! Give me your answer!"

A long and loud plea for freedom swelled the air!

"Hear us in Moscow! Hear us in Washington! Hear us in London! The spirit of Berlin was never Nazi and will never be Communist! From the depths of our souls, our will to be free will build a mighty dam that will beat back the raging Red Seas which try to drown us. Berlin will be free!"

The next day the Soviet Union announced that the bridge on the Elbe River was closed for "repairs."

Berlin was blockaded by land and by sea.

Part four

THE LAST OF THE GOONEY
BIRDS

CHAPTER ONE

Another morning.

Another gathering of Germans over the boulevard from American Headquarters. They stared through a Berlin mist as the color guard marched to the flag pole and continued to watch silently as the Stars and Stripes went up the staff, unfurled, fluttered. Certain now that the Americans were in Berlin for another day, the clump of Germans broke, carrying lunch buckets, shopping bags, briefcases, and trudged toward the U Bahn.

Outside city limits three divisions of Soviet troops with heavy armor continued nerve-wracking maneuvers, ostensibly poised to strike into the Western Sectors.

People's Radio increased the tension. They began with a water-shortage scare, then a rumor that the West had annexed the Ruhr. "Food riots sweep West Berlin as thousands are thrown out of work. Babies are dying from the lack of milk! This cruel imperialist policy is bringing new untold suffering to the workers!"

On the third floor of American Headquarters, General Andrew Jackson Hansen wrestled with the most pressing of his problems. Barney Root, the USAFE commander, had been able to fly in between eighty and a hundred tons daily of supplies and the British were flying in enough to handle their own immediate needs. But now, food for the entire population of Western Berlin was in a growing crisis.

With the food shortage was a power shortage. Before the war there had only been a single power plant in the Western part of the city. It stood on the Hauswehr Canal opposite the West Harbor, the inland barge port.

This plant was the most modern in Berlin, but used mainly as an auxiliary during peak hours. The Russians had stripped it and only a few of the generators had been replaced. Most of the power for the Western Sector came from Saxony through Russian-controlled lines.

The Russians cut the electricity, causing an industry shutdown and a sweep of unemployment.

Sean O'Sullivan worked with the Magistrat experts to determine the immediate situation. He brought the grim tidings to Hansen.

"We have a thirty-six day supply of coal for the power plant. We can generate enough power to run our own installations, move minimal transportation, prevent a communications collapse, and keep certain emergency facilities going. No coal for German civilians, and almost none can be spared for industrial purposes."

Hansen lifted the receiver of his red, emergency phone and told the switchboard to put him through to Army Headquarters in Heidelberg. Commander of combat forces, Lieutenant General William Warren Crossfield answered on his red phone.

"Scramble the conversation."

Each pressed a scramble button, a device to jumble their voices against a phone tap.

Crossfield spoke excitedly. "We just heard news of the food riots. Do you need help?"

"There aren't any food riots. That's Radio Moscow crap. There was a little excitement over a water-shortage scare, but we've settled them down. Billy, I want you to assemble an armed convoy and have it stand by."

"Are we going to try to break through the autobahn?"

"If Washington lets me."

"Chip, I'll personally lead that convoy but we'd better not have our bluff called."

"The Russians are the ones bluffing."

William Warren Crossfield had commanded an Army Group north from Southern France and over the Rhine. He was not given to being a flashy leader, but he was a shrewd, steady tactician who had an immaculate grasp of logistics, supplies, support, and all the other nuances of battle . . . and he was a cold-blooded realist.

"We're playing with fire," he said, "and we don't have a damned thing to put it out with."

"It's not that kind of a fight. This is a battle of will power," Hansen answered.

"Maybe you're right, Chip, but I know that Marshal Popov knows that the whole United States can't call up two reserve divisions of infantry."

A few hours later General Hansen arrived at USAFE Headquarters in Wiesbaden for a conference with General Barney Root.

"You've got to think of flying in five, six, seven hundred tons of supplies a day. We need coal as badly as food, and somehow we've got to get some more generators in."

Barney Root stared at Chip Hansen as though he were crazy. "Would you repeat that?"

"If I can't sell Washington on an armed convoy, I'm going to sell them on supplying Berlin by air."

Barney relit his cigar butt. "Three years ago we had twelve thousand aircraft in England and on the European continent. Right now our air transport consists of eighty-two worn out Gooney Birds. My crews are punchy. They're flying almost triple the number of hours we consider safe. We didn't even ask them to fly this way in the war. Chip, I haven't got enough spare parts in Europe to rebuild the ass end of a Piper Cub."

"Barney, I intend convincing Washington to send over Skymasters to replace the Gooney Birds and I'm going to ask the President to recall Hiram Stonebraker."

"Look, I'm with you all the way. I'll keep scratching around for aircraft and crews. I've already assigned Shorty MacDonald on the Berlin supply run exclusively. He's the best transport man we've got." Barney Root squashed out the dead cigar.

"You don't believe in this, do you?" Hansen asked.

"I'm a bomber man. I don't know enough about transports."

"You don't believe in it?" Hansen repeated.

"You're going to need a hell of a lot more than Stonebraker and Skymasters."

Back in Berlin the sound of Russian gunfire could be heard in the suburbs.

Communist agitation cars roamed the streets broadcasting food

scares, blaming the situation on Western greed, justifying the blockade by swearing the bridge over the Elbe had collapsed.

Lil Blessing had been looking for Calvin for an hour. She sent the
other children in the neighborhood to scour around for him. This was
unlike little Cal.

Trying to avoid panic, Lil sat by the phone on the brink of calling
Bless when she heard muffled sobs coming from the hall closet. She
threw open the door. Cal was huddled in a corner, ran into his mother's
skirts, and buried his face.

She lifted him, torn between kisses and a scolding, carried him to a
rocking chair, and tried to calm him. After a while his sobs softened
to spasmodic jerkings.

"What's all this about, Calvin Blessing?"

"Everybody in school said it."

"They said what?"

"The Mongols are coming back and chop our heads off. The German
kids have seen them before."

Lil pressed the boy closer to her.

Yes, People's Radio had announced that Mongolian regiments had
joined the maneuvers outside the city to rekindle the memory of Berlin's
capture and Cal's fears were echoed by everyone.

"You think your daddy is going to let anyone hurt you?"

"I want to go home."

"This is our home, Cal."

✦

"Teleconference with Washington is ready, General."

In the vaulted room beneath Headquarters in Berlin, Hansen was
joined by Generals Crossfield and Root. Sean O'Sullivan wrote out
the first message, handed it to the teletype operator. In a moment the
message was coded, radioed to Washington, decoded, and flashed on a
screen in the Pentagon.

THE FOLLOWING ARE BERLIN PARTICIPANTS: GENERAL HANSEN, MILI-
TARY GOVERNOR; OSCAR PENNEY, POLITICAL ADVISOR, STATE DEPART-
MENT; LT. GENERAL CROSSFIELD, COMMANDER GROUND FORCES; LT.
GENERAL ROOT, COMMANDER USAFE; BRIG. GENERAL HAZZARD, COM-
MANDANT, BERLIN; LT. COL. O'SULLIVAN SPECIAL ASSISTANT TO HANSEN.

Washington returned their complement:

FOLLOWING PARTICIPANTS: GENERAL COLLOWAY, CHIEF OF STAFF, U.S. ARMY; HARRY KING, SPECIAL ADVISOR TO PRESIDENT; LT. GENERAL BRONSON, DEPUTY CHIEF OF STAFF, OPERATIONS, U.S. AIR FORCE; JOSEPH PECK, STATE DEPARTMENT, CHIEF OF GERMAN DESK.

Hansen jotted out the first message. Barney Root nodded approval and Billy Crossfield gave a reluctant okay. It was handed to the teletype operator.

TOP SECRET: BLOCKADE EFFECTIVE. SITUATION DESPERATE IN TWO WEEKS. REQUEST PERMISSION SEND AN ARMED CONVOY UP AUTOBAHN AFTER ANNOUNCING OUR INTENTION TO RUSSIANS. CROSSFIELD, ROOT IN AGREEMENT. GO AHEAD.

In several moments a message started appearing on the screen.

TOP SECRET: PECK, GERMAN DESK. STATE DEPARTMENT IDEA IS TO MAKE OFFER TO WITHDRAW B MARKS FROM BERLIN IN EXCHANGE FOR GUARANTEED ACCESS RIGHTS TO CITY.

"In a pig's ass," Neal Hazzard grumbled.
"Take it easy, Neal."
"Yes, sir."
They huddled, discussed it quickly. All agreed that the proposal spelled disaster.

TOP SECRET: PENNEY, POLITICAL ADVISOR STATE DEPARTMENT. ADVISES WITHDRAWAL B MARKS FATAL OUR POSITION AND COLLAPSE CONFIDENCE GERMAN AND ALLIES.

A general uneasiness fell on them as they waited for an answer from Washington. The next transmission came from the Chief of Staff of the Army.

TOP SECRET: NOTHING IN CONTINGENCY PLANS TO COVER ARMED CONVOY.

Peck of the German desk continued the message:

ATTEMPTING RENEWAL DIPLOMATIC DISCUSSIONS RUSSIANS. SAME TIME PUT BERLIN QUESTION ON UNITED NATIONS AGENDA. RASH ACTION NOW MAY ENDANGER TALKS.

Eric the Red's blood pressure began rising. It was beyond his comprehension that the State Department could be so naïve as not to know that the Russians would stall talks until the city was on the brink of starvation.

TOP SECRET: REPEAT. IT IS OUR CONSIDERED OPINION WE CAN BREAK BLOCKADE BY IMMEDIATE SHOW OF STRENGTH. REPEAT REQUEST PERMISSION TO SEND ARMED CONVOY ON AUTOBAHN.

As the chips were down, the tension could be read on their faces.

TOP SECRET: REQUEST DENIED.

They were deflated, and talked among themselves quickly, trading ideas.

TOP SECRET: REQUEST YOU CONSIDER MOVING B-29'S WITH ATOMIC WARHEADS TO BRITISH BASES AS PSYCHOLOGICAL DETERRENT.

From Washington, a thread of hope.

IDEA ALREADY UNDER CONSIDERATION. FOR YOUR INFORMATION CODE NAME TOP HAT.

"Well, they're not completely dead," Hazzard said.
"We can't leave it hanging this way," Hansen said.

TOP SECRET: HANSEN SENDS. REQUEST URGENT MEETING JOINT CHIEFS AND NATIONAL SECURITY COUNCIL IMMEDIATELY. ADVISE.
TOP SECRET: KING SENDS. WHEN CAN YOU BE IN WASHINGTON?
TOP SECRET: WILL ADVISE MY ETA. ANYTHING FURTHER?
WASHINGTON: NOTHING FURTHER.
BERLIN: OUT.

Hansen's rubbery face was knotted as though he were in pain. If Washington decided to move the B-29's it might throw the Russians off long enough for him to make a last appeal.

Back in his office, his aide called Tempelhof to have the general's aircraft commander prepare for the trip.

Hansen phoned his wife, instructed her to pack, as she had done for him a thousand times, and bring his bags to Tempelhof. As he swept out of the main gate, an ever-present knot of Germans waved to him. On the way to the airport he droned instructions to his people.

His plane was in ready upon his arrival, warming up under the canopy. His Air Force captain and his aide hastily cleared a flight plan with Operations.

Hansen shook hands with Barney Root and Billy Crossfield, Sean, and Neal Hazzard.

"We'll be here when you get back, General," Sean said.

In a few moments Agnes Hansen arrived.

"Mother," he said, "you don't know how hard it is for me to leave you here alone but you do know why you must stay."

She smiled. "If you have time, call the children from Washington."

"Damn," he said, "you're a good trooper."

They watched as the General's Skymaster lifted him from the runway and banked out of sight.

CHAPTER TWO

Sean groaned like a happy puppy as the sun poured down on his back. It was the first real hot spell of the summer, driving off the fogs and mists and the first time he had had enough free hours to relax by the lake.

At that place where the Little Wannsee and the Greater Wannsee merged with the Havel River there was a strip of luxury mansions. The waters were still, with no breeze to billow disappointed sails. An occasional barge glided into the canals toward the Russian Sector.

Overhead there was a constant drone of American Gooney Birds pulling up from Tempelhof, and just over the lakes their British counterparts, the Dakotas, were landing on the Gatow airstrip.

There was a thin strand of imported-sand beach behind which rolled a long, lush lawn and this was filled with patio chairs and umbrellas, and there was a pool. The great house had been converted into an American Officers' Club. Like most of the other mansions on this strip, it once belonged to a top Nazi who had stolen it from a Jew who could not return from the grave to reclaim it.

Ernestine sat alongside Sean, her head on her knees, arms about her legs. She knew the eyes of every American officer looked her over. She had not been looked over this way for a long time and she liked it.

The American women were looking her over also, in grudging admiration. Sean was breaking that unwritten law against bringing a German girl into their midst, socially. Well, she could hear most of them say, she is not as bad as most German girls . . . after all she is the niece of Falkenstein . . . and a pretty thing . . . if you like the type.

The gossips did not matter much to Ernestine. The day mattered. Sean mattered. . . . Long ago she was in a tiny boat on the Wannsee and she told Dietrich Rascher she wanted to sail up to the canals, and then into the sea and away . . . forever and ever.

Ernestine did not believe she could ever come to this place again and be happy. The other love had ended in blackness. There was a tiny promise that this might be the first real happiness of her life.

She took a handful of sand and let it trickle through her fingers on Sean's back. From his drowsing, he reached behind him to brush away an imaginary fly. She persisted.

"Let me sleep, woman."

"A handsome young colonel asked me to come to the beach with him. Tell me, old man, do you know where he went?"

Sean rolled over on his back and stretched as the sun greeted his face. "Jesus, what a day."

Ernestine knelt above him so that her warm flesh touched him.

"You are like the other woman who sits on that rock on the Rhine whistling to poor souls and making them crash on the rocks seeking her mystic charms."

"Sean, it is getting too painful to be funny."

He sat up so they were side by side looking into the other's eyes.

"You and I would be like a couple of freight trains hitting each other head on."

"Does it have to be that way?"

"Yes."

"Damn you. You sound like Uncle Ulrich."

"He's a wise man," Sean said, and lay back on the sand and stared at the sky. She lay beside him. Their eyes followed a Dakota circling, then falling toward the treetops and out of sight.

CHAPTER THREE

Shenandoah Blessing sat at Cal's bedside until the boy fell asleep. He padded into the living room and turned on the radio to American Forces Network for a delayed broadcast of a baseball game between the Cards and the Brooklyn Dodgers. Lil handed him a bottle of beer and a hank of yarn. He put his big paws through the wool, sneaking a sip now and then as she wound it into a ball.

There was too much truth in the little boy's fears and no one knew the urgency better than he. For several weeks Bless headed a special detail to train people recruited from the free political parties, the free union, and the Western Sector students in the tricks of in-fighting, riot control, and all of the brawling tactics known to the Communist Action Squads—plus a few of Bless's own innovations.

These Order Companies were quick to spot Communist agitation cars and troublemakers. It was becoming unprofitable for the Communists to cross into the Western Sectors as the Order Companies toughened.

Blessing had also worked in the build-up of a system of spies and informants, for the facts of life demanded quick, accurate intelligence. Dozens of volunteers had buried themselves in the ranks of the Communist Party and even became Action Squad members for the purpose of keeping American Headquarters informed of moves.

That is how he knew that the talk of Mongol troops was true and their presence outside Berlin deliberate.

Blessing was among those Western officers singled out for abuse over People's Radio, which described him as a strikebreaker, lyncher, and fascist bully in the tradition of the Storm Troopers. He came in for cartoon treatment in their papers, which depicted him as obese, stubble-bearded, fanged, clawed, drooling, hairy.

His answer to the last attack was to take Lil and the two boys to the Russian Sector and have a Sunday picnic on the Müggel Lake.

He lowered the volume on the radio as Gil Hodges took a called third strike. "What are the girls gossiping about these days?"

"Usual PX talk. Who's sleeping with who. Who's drinking too much."

"What do they say about the situation here?"

Lil shrugged, feigned innocence. "Not too much. Bless, that sure is a nice girl Sean has. We got to have them come to dinner again soon."

"Come on, Lil. What's the talk?"

She dropped the ball of wool, lit a cigarette, and glared at him with that expression that said he was acting like a cop. "They're all scared to death."

"You?"

"I know we can't leave. I'm trying as best I can not to show it to the kids."

"And the rest of the girls. They want to leave?"

"Stop grilling me."

"We got to know."

"Well, a dozen I know of, maybe more, have asked to be evacuated."

"If they start to move out, every dependent in the garrison will want out, except Agnes Hansen and Claire Hazzard."

The phone interrupted them.

"Blessing," he said.

"Hardy," a Constabulary officer said, "better get over here right away."

"What's up?"

"Tide's coming in tomorrow. We're going to have to send out the fishing boats."

Bless turned his back to Lil to get a grip on himself before he set the phone down, but she saw the receiver wet with perspiration.

"Honey, rig me up a thermos of coffee and a couple sandwiches. I got a little extra duty."

He left the room quickly to dress.

She had seen him react this way too many times not to know there was danger. In a few moments he returned, strapping on his duty belt and checking his pistol. He slipped his MP arm band on, she handed him the white Constabulary helmet and a lunch bucket.

"Keep the boys home from school tomorrow and stay in the house."

"Tell me."

"You can't communicate this to anyone, Lil. The Commies are going to try a *Putsch* in the morning."

"How serious is it?"

"There is a pistol in my closet in the inside pocket of my winter coat. I don't want you and the kids to be taken alive."

CHAPTER FOUR

For several days informers working inside the Russian and Communist groups had alerted the Americans that they were brewing a "workers' Putsch."

The logical time to try it would be early in the morning during rush hour when the trains exchanged populations from sector to sector. The Communists first would infiltrate organizers who would move to key points in the Western boroughs.

The leaders would be followed by Action Squads, armed with concealed clubs, knives, stones, bottle bombs, and small arms, who would be loaded on the underground and elevated trains from various points, cross into the Western boroughs where their leaders would be waiting at the town halls, the power plant, radio transmitter, RIAS, and key factories. When they reassembled they would begin riots and seize their locations.

The plan was to create chaos in several dozen places and force the West to commit its garrisons to restore order. Then a second wave of Communists would cross over in trucks and grab dozens of new targets. This follow-up group would include Soviet soldiers and Schatz's SND police dressed as civilians. By now, the West would be spread too thin to cope with the new mayhem.

At this point, General Trepovitch would offer to send in his troops from the outskirts of the city provided the Western troops agreed to return to their barracks. Tempelhof and Gatow airdromes were the prime targets and would be closed due to "technical difficulties."

With the West in their barracks, the Russians would "in fact" control the entire city in a bloodless coup.

The propaganda organs would then leap into action and explain that the workers, tired of Western imperialism and unemployment, had rebelled. Only the benevolence of the Soviet Union prevented a blood bath.

0515. Putsch day.

Blessing's breath darted out, evaporated in the morning chill as his driver, Danny Sterling, pulled up to the Kreuzberg Town Hall where a temporary command post had been established in the foyer.

The Borough of Kreuzberg lay directly across from Mitte Borough in the Russian Sector where a series of rail lines would exchange the heaviest traffic.

Blessing had checked his subway and elevated stations, which were due to take the first shock of the Putsch. It was deceptively calm.

Deputy Police President Hans Kronbach, who had quietly built a force loyal to the Magistrat, made his decision earlier to commit them. They were staked out along with the newly trained Order Companies to spot Communist leaders.

The Constabulary under Blessing would act as a mobile force. In the Russian Sector, dozens of American informers were in Mitte, Pankow, Friedrichshain, Treptow, for the purpose of watching for Communist movement.

The final back-up force was the regular garrison under Colonel Mark Parrott with headquarters at Tempelhof and all troops poised to move to trouble spots.

Blessing stepped outside the Kreuzberg Town Hall, uncapped the thermos jug, sipped some coffee, and offered some to his driver. The street was gray and quiet with only the first small sounds of the day, wheels on the pavement, a pair of angry hungry cats.

He walked over to Victoria Park, where a group of police were hidden, and spoke a few words to the German officer. The quiet made him restless. He got into the jeep and told Danny to drive him toward the major subway and elevated transfer point on the Yorck Strasse. It was 0545. If their information was correct, the Communists would be coming soon. Bless tuned in on the British and French frequencies and heard them checking in. They stopped at Yorck Strasse and waited. 0600.

The sound of wheels on steel rails humming in the distance from the direction of the Russian Sector grew louder and louder. The train leaped into view with a smell of brakes as it screeched to a halt. The doors opened and the first rush of morning passengers exploded onto the platform.

Four known Communists were buried in their number to take up a position at the Kreuzberg Town Hall. At the foot of the steps they were spotted by a member of an Order Company.

Four American Constabulary walked quietly alongside each, snapped on handcuffs, and walked them away quickly and efficiently toward a holding station. One of the Communists began to protest. The soldier locked his arm with a billy club and pressured so that it would break. The Communist became quiet.

Blessing picked up the microphone in the jeep. "This is Sportsfisher One calling all piers. The tide is coming in. How is fishing in your area?"

"Hello Sportsfisher One, this is Redondo," the squad at Moritz Platz subway radioed back. "One small sand shark."

"Sportsfisher One, this is Venice Pier," Koch Strasse detachment called, "the tide is coming in fast but no fish yet."

"This is Long Beach Pier calling Sportsfisher One," called the key complex of Anhalter Banhof, with its numerous exchange points and masses of movement in proximity to the Russian Sector. "We picked up two sand sharks, three blues of about sixty pounds, and a man-eater."

"This is Sportsfisher One calling Long Beach. Are they hitting hard?"

"This is Long Beach. No, they're kind of sluggish. We reeled them in easy."

The pattern was beginning to open. Blessing listened to the British and French frequencies again. All along the line Communist leaders were getting picked up as they departed the trains.

"This is Santa Monica Pier," called Grozgorschen Strasse elevated. "Couple of big blues hanging around right here. I think they're waiting for the school of mackerel."

Bless returned to his command post at Kreuzberg and phoned over a direct line to Colonel Parrott at Tempelhof. In the first fifty minutes they had snagged some seventy Communist agitators.

At Potsdamer Platz, the key exchange point, the first school of mackerel, an Action Squad, was bagged.

A Joint Command in the British Sector assessed the information. By 0620 three hundred known agitators and Action Squad members with no explainable business in the Western Sectors had been spotted and swept up in quick, sure movement.

At 0702, two railcars containing the largest load yet, three hundred Action Squad people, moved for the destination of Beussels Strasse elevated, where they were to disperse for the joint targets of the power plant, the Plötzensee Prison, and the West Harbor. A tip-off came ahead of them and they walked off the train into a mixed company of French and British soldiers with fixed bayonets.

By this time the Russian monitors smelled a Western trap and this

was confirmed by the fact that none of their leaders had reported back
to Putsch headquarters. And then a frantic call came to Schatz by one
Communist who had slipped the Western net after seeing his comrades rounded up.

"They were waiting for us!"

A nausea-wracked, trembling Adolph Schatz phoned Soviet Headquarters and cried, "We have been betrayed!"

Trepovitch tried to head off the disaster of sending more people in.
At this rate the West could deplete their loyal core of Communist
strength in an hour and it would take weeks, if not months, to build
up for another try. He branded Schatz as an incompetent German
lout, called off the attempt, and shouted that he was surrounded by
spies.

Brigadier General Neal Hazzard entered the mess hall of the Staff
NCO Club and the 250 officers and men came to attention. He asked
them to be seated and told the guard to shut the door.

"I'll get right to the point," Hazzard said. "Fifty of you people have
requested to evacuate your families. I have asked the rest of you here
so as not to identify and embarrass the others. Here's the score. When
General Hansen left for Washington we told him we'd be here when
he got back.

"By that I mean the United States would be in Berlin. In this
garrison, the United States of America particularly means our wives
and children. For the next two weeks no request for transportation
out of Berlin will be acted upon . . . as my old friend Trepovitch would
say . . . for technical reasons."

A murmur of puzzlement greeted his terse announcement.

"To walk out of here with our tails between our legs would be giving
aid and comfort to the enemy and would make a spectacle of our
country. This garrison stays . . . men . . . women . . . children."

CHAPTER FIVE

The meeting of the National Security Council was going badly against
General Hansen. The President, for the most part, listened to the

divergent arguments, interrupting only now and then for a sharp question.

The room housed a glitter of silver stars and braid of admirals and their banks of ribbons to attest to bravery. These were the Joint Chiefs of Staff. The Secretary of Defense was there; the Secretary of State was there; the Secretary of the Treasury was there with the Vice President and the ambassador to the Kremlin. Behind them sat their experts and planners.

The forces seeking accommodation, settlement, compromise, appeasement had built an insurmountable case. The State Department had treated the Berlin blockade as an accomplished Soviet victory and sought ways to get off the hook with the least loss of face.

"The B marks have to be withdrawn from Berlin."

"Throw the matter open to the United Nations while attempting to make a direct political settlement with the Russians."

Practical men from the Pentagon with slide rules and charts had their turn.

"Berlin is dead weight. The city not only has to import food, but it has to import raw material to keep its industrial complex functioning. As a former national capital the city has tens of thousands of former government employees with no new means of support. Berlin has 300,000 pensioners."

"Berlin is still in ruin."

"Berlin cannot be saved."

"Mr. President. I do not believe anyone can make a determination of how long we would have to be committed. General Hansen speaks in terms of forty-five to sixty days, but suppose it has to go longer. It could well run into months."

"We have been unable to draw up a cost estimate, but it will run millions a day. The Soviet Union might deliberately keep the blockade going in an effort to bankrupt our economy."

"Berlin cannot be defended. It is entirely indefensible."

The generals gave their opinions on the condition of the defense establishment. The country could not call up enough reserve to deter the Kremlin's planning. Hansen's own commander, Billy Crossfield, had told him the same thing.

"Sure, we could send an armored convoy up the autobahn, but it is a calculated risk that could mean total war. Suppose the Russians did make a challenge or suppose the closeness of the situation made them fire by accident. Our forces would be swamped."

"Mr. President. It is suicide to put all of our air transport capability into supplying Berlin. It simply makes us too vulnerable to pressure everywhere else in the world."

"Mr. President. I do not believe it is possible to supply Berlin from the air, not even for the forty-five days General Hansen desires."

The ambassador to the Kremlin reported complete frustration in attempts to see Stalin or Molotov, much less pin them down to a meeting.

General Hansen was not without his champions. Hard-line men demanded action, but they spoke more out of pride and anger, for on this day practical men brought home the unpleasant facts of life.

"General Hansen," the President said, "I think we should wrap up this meeting. Is there any more you believe we ought to know?"

Andrew Jackson Hansen studied the room. They were all there. Friends and a few adversaries of three decades. They were hard-nosed, brilliant, dedicated men and he was beaten, for this was not a situation that could be solved with logic. How could one convince wise men to go against the grain of their knowledge?

Yet, there had to be a flicker of hope, for in the final analysis it was not a joint decision, but that of the lone man at the end of the table, the President. He would have to weigh and decide on the words of the day after his captains departed. He was an earthy man, the President, and he was strong on the issue of stopping communism. He was ahead of his countrymen, his diplomats, his Congress, and even some of his military.

There was little room spared in the pages of glory for a general whose fate or talent kept him from the romance of a combat command, the utterance of a salty slogan under enemy fire, or the drawing of a gory wound; but Andrew Jackson Hansen believed, and he placed those beliefs on the line now. The general was pale and watery-eyed from a persistent cold. His chest was heavy from four days of argument at conference tables.

"Mr. President," he began hoarsely, "gentlemen. A few years ago we concluded a war with the naïve hope that an accommodation could be achieved with the Soviet Union to bring us a lasting peace. I shall not insult the intelligence of this distinguished body by a recounting of tragic errors made . . . not by you and me alone . . . but by the temper of the American people. We know that all that has prevented total collapse has been that thin, thin line of British and American troops on the European continent."

An uncomfortable fidgeting began around the table from those who had followed the line of try to reason with the Soviet Union.

"If there is one lesson we should have learned it is that the Soviet Union looks upon diplomacy as merely another means of waging war. They do not come to the conference table to seek peace or solutions . . . they come to seek victories.

"The blockade of Berlin is designed to force this country to negotiate under pressure."

He left his chair, walked down the length of the table so that he stood at the opposite end of the table from the President and the eyes of every man could be seen by him. His voice grew more harsh and slower and the room was awesomely silent.

"What are the objectives of the Soviet Union? Above all to prevent us from the formation of a democratic Germany, but if they accept that as an accomplished fact, they fall back to the second goal of ejecting us from Berlin.

"Germany's only chance of being rebuilt along democratic lines and our only chance of converting her into an ally is possible only as long as the United States stands behind her. And who, who will trust the United States after we leave Berlin? Who in Europe and Asia will believe that the United States will not abandon them too? And, gentlemen, I ask you . . . will we believe ourselves?

"Lenin said, give me the currency and I will control the nation. Take the B marks out of Berlin and we have lost Berlin! But is the currency or even the formation of a democratic Germany the true issue? It is not." His voice quivered.

"The Soviet Union will engage us in a war for one reason and one reason alone . . . because they think they can win. Do you think they need a currency issue? They'll invent any damned issue that will please them when they feel the time is ripe.

"Gentlemen. Mr. President. We have fought two wars against the German people in our lifetime. I know some of you here who have lost sons. And God knows there is no love of Germany from me. Yet, we find ourselves in this alliance and the man and the woman in Berlin shows us he is made of remarkable stuff."

Hansen's fist pounded the polished oak.

"Contrary to every evaluation made here today I flatly state that the people of Berlin will not crack." And his voice fell to a whisper.

"We have been told that this city cannot be supplied or saved or defended. I say that it is not expendable. Have we lost the imagination, the skill, the guts that has made our nation perform two centuries of miracles? Are we too content to defend ourselves? Have we lost faith in ourselves?

"You speak of costs, gentlemen. Has anyone calculated the cost to our coming generations if Europe is lost?

"If we leave Berlin, the Soviet Union is then free to consolidate its empire behind a closed border. As long as we retain our outpost in Berlin, communism can never consolidate.

"We cannot abandon the one place on this planet where we hold an offensive position.

"This is no ordinary city. Berlin . . . is our Armageddon."

Hansen leaned forward, his knuckles pressed against the table and turned white. He looked now at the President alone. "In the name of God, Mr. President, the future of freedom on this earth requires our presence."

The full misery of Hansen's cold crashed down on him with the feeling that his mission had failed. He returned to his hotel, the Hay-Adams, and received a score of old comrades rather listlessly.

Those who had attended the meeting tried to buck him up, but he hadn't the spirit for it. The repeated specter of the national apathy that preceded the war had come back to haunt the military. The country was a fat cow riding a postwar boom and things over there just did not matter.

By evening his aide insisted that he accept no more visitors and take no more calls, but get into bed and send for a doctor. Hansen growled against medical attendance, ate a bowl of hot chowder, had tea spiked with brandy, then sat in the greatest dejection of his life staring at the White House just over the way. He sat alone recounting the past four days.

What had gone wrong? He blamed himself for failure to bring home the truth. There was small solace that the man in the White House now wrestled with this problem.

Beyond the White House jutted the illuminated obelisk pointed skyward in memory of George Washington, and past that the circle of lights and airplanes taking off and landing in quick succession at the Washington National Airport on the river. He did not believe he could ever see an airplane again without thinking of Tempelhof.

Weariness overtook him. He dozed in his chair.

He did not know how long he slept, but when he was awakened by the phone it was dark outside. He squinted at his watch. It was three in the morning. He was certain his phones had been shut off by his aide.

"Hello," he rasped.

"General Hansen?"

"Speaking."

"Sorry to disturb you at this hour, but the President would like to talk to you."

Hansen looked out of the window again and drew an image of the Chief.

"General, how's that cold of yours?"

"I'll live, sir."

"I've sent a couple bottles of Jack Daniels over to your hotel. Best thing in the world. Take a couple of stiff belts before you go back to sleep. I'll send a doctor over to see you in the morning."

He was about to spout that he didn't want a doctor, but thought better of it.

"General, I'm going to send you those Skymasters you want. You get back to Berlin and tell those people we intend to stick by our word."

A long grateful silence followed.

"It is going to take a little time to convince everybody here, but you just leave that to me. You can depend on the first squadrons arriving within the week. Now, what else do you need?"

"I'd like General Stonebraker recalled."

"It has my approval."

"Good. I'll leave for California in the morning to see him."

"Give him my best and get over that cold."

By the next morning Hansen had made a remarkable recovery. His aide had his plane stand by at the MATS terminal and as he flew out for Los Angeles to see Hiram Stonebraker, the Defense Department announced that Skymasters would be on the way to Germany shortly. More B-29's marked for less peaceful missions touched down on

British airfields loaded with A-bombs as Operation Top Hat was put into effect.

And then the British Parliament was stunned by a couple of fiery speeches by the Prime Minister and the Foreign Secretary. In cold anger seldom heard in the ancient Commons, the British lion, minus a few of the old teeth but none the less still potent, said bluntly that tampering with British rights in Berlin meant war.

This powerful reaction from the West gave the Kremlin reason to re-evaluate. The Russian troops in Berlin suddenly melted away and with open-armed benevolence for the "sake of world peace," they invited Western missions to come to Moscow and talk over a Berlin settlement.

CHAPTER SIX

A staff car drove Hansen between a pair of whitewashed brick pillars, down a gravel-top road that was flanked by young hedge and bisected an orange grove, and continued to a bluff that hovered above the Pacific Ocean. Along the bluff rambled a California Spanish-style house.

When Hiram and Martha Jane Stonebraker greeted him, he thought how wonderful they both looked. Deep healthy tans had erased the signs of fatigue that came with the constant pressure of duty.

They showed him around the layout with obvious pride. The Stonebrakers had four acres which ran from the highway to the bluff and included a beach below. The land held an orchard, a small corral with horses for the general and visiting children and grandchildren, and an extensive garden for Martha Jane. It was located near the Ventura County line at the end of Malibu strip. The Malibu movie colony was fifteen miles away with only a few ranches between them and the nearest settlement.

Hansen saw it all with a twinge of envy. He and Agnes had never known this kind of peace and he wondered if such a place was ever in the cards for them. He had misgivings for his mission of taking Crusty away from it.

Hours were needed to fill each other in on old comrades and the situation in Germany. They sat the afternoon out on a patio which stood at the far edge of the bluff where it sloped gently to the shore and was covered with a wild array of multicolored pelargoniums. The tide was out and they could see the rock-filled surf surging ever so gently.

As the sun moved behind them, M.J. brought cocktails and sweaters so they could enjoy the last sharp contrast of sea and sky.

"How do the days go here?"

"I take a horseback ride on the beach every morning, summer and winter, check out the orchard and stable. And . . . I've got a bit of correspondence and a lot of reading."

"Ever get a yearning to be back in harness?"

"Hell no. Chip, I made more money last year as an advisor to private industry than I ever made in uniform in a year. Seems I know a thing or two after all. I have been invited to sit on the board of two airlines to develop their freight services . . . if I wanted to work that hard."

"It's good to see you like this."

"It took a long long time to get here and it's only for a short stay."

The light failed and the breeze became stiffer. They walked toward the house. "I've got a boat at the cove about five miles down the highway. Let's go fishing tomorrow."

During dinner, Hansen continued to avoid the purpose of the visit. M.J. was suspicious and sent out a number of indirect questions.

After dinner, the two men settled in Crusty's study. The room was filled with mementoes of the Hump and photographs and gifts of presidents and kings and grandchildren.

"Okay, Chip, let's have it."

"I brought some papers with me that I want you to study and give an opinion on."

"About this Berlin situation?"

He nodded. "We are committing ourselves to supply Berlin by air."

"For how long?"

"Long enough to take the pressure off negotiations. Forty-five days . . . sixty. Talks are starting in Moscow next week and it could end sooner than that."

"And if negotiations collapse?"

"We will have to supply the Western Sectors indefinitely."

Crusty Stonebraker, who once insisted on air corridors to Berlin, showed no sign of emotion. The reports would reveal the situation accurately. "I'd better get started reading."

Hansen could see from his bedroom across the patio to Crusty Stonebraker's study. The light burned until very late and on several occasions Crusty paced the patio bundled up in an old flying jacket looking out to the sea as if hoping to find mystical answers coming in with the tide.

Breakfast the next morning was in silence. Crusty grunted through the meal and said, "Let's go fishing."

They drove in a jeep down the highway and turned off onto a eucalyptus-lined road that ran down to the ocean. The sun was trying to force its way through the morning fog as they parked at the foot of a long wooden pier.

The *Betty-Lee*, a rock-cod sportsfishing boat, was just pulling away filled with half-asleep anglers.

Crusty grabbed the tackle box and poles and they walked down the pier to the bait shop.

"Morning, General."

"Morning, Bob. Where are they hitting?"

"You can jig or troll for bonita."

"Got a freezerful waiting to be smoked."

"Yesterday the half-day boat came in with a dozen good size halibut at Trancas and the bass were going crazy right in front of your place. I'll run you out to your boat."

They took the stairs that ran down the pilings to a floating platform dock and got into the skiff and putted out to where the *M.J.*, a practical and stout twenty-six-foot cabin cruiser, was moored.

The dock hand helped pull the canvas cover back, held the skiff fast while the two men transferred, and pulled away calling, "I'll wait for you at the bait receiver, General."

Crusty went about the business of blowing out the bilge, checking the hose fittings and levels, starting, warming up, connecting the live-bait tank. The *M.J.* showed that its owner was obviously a man of great knowledge in the science of the proper use of space.

Hansen cast off the painter and Stonebraker pulled alongside the bait receiver, handling the boat with the sure touch of an old barnstorming pilot. They took on a scoop of anchovies and headed out of Paradise Cove.

Chip Hansen fixed the poles with halibut leaders as they turned

Point Dume, ran up the coast awhile, and began a drift on the edge of the kelp beds.

They sat with their lines in the water for several moments. Crusty pulled in a calico bass, put it into the gunny sack, and studied the horizon. The water was warming up. Soon the albacore and yellow tail would be running near Catalina.

His wife had become quite a fisherwoman in the past three years. They had been looking forward all winter and spring to trips to Catalina and the Channel Islands.

"Well," Chip broke the silence, "you read it?"

"I read it."

"It can be done, then. We can supply Berlin by air."

Crusty Stonebraker did not answer.

"Well, what do you think?" Hansen asked.

Crusty stared at his old friend. "I think you're out of your friggin' mind."

Hansen handed Stonebraker his orders from the President recalling him to active duty. He said he knew Crusty all along would do it and told him a plane and crew were at his disposal.

"I'm going to have to have my own people and I don't want any interference."

"You've worked with Barney Root. He's a good troop and all for you. The President has given this mission top priority and I'll damned well back you up."

"Chip, I'll do my best to hold things together, but you've got to make a political settlement or we're going to fall flat on our ass."

"Have you told M.J.?"

"She smelled a rat the minute you phoned from Washington. I'll follow you to Germany in a couple of days. I've already prepared a list of people I want transferred to Wiesbaden. I want to stop off in New York and see if I can get a particular man for production control . . . and I've got to call my daughter-in-law and see if she can come out and keep this place running."

That same day Crusty gave instructions to his lawyer and went over everything with the maintenance couple. He was in his study going through the last of his papers.

Chip Hansen sat in the kitchen with M.J. grabbing a sandwich,

and avoiding her eyes, for she was frightened and on tenterhooks.
"Isn't there someone else?" she blurted.

Chip saw her on the brink of tears.

"No one in the world knows more about air transport than Crusty.
We have our backs to the wall."

She sat opposite him, gripped his wrist. "He has a heart condition,
Chip."

"I know. I hope you can get to Germany as soon as possible and take
care of him."

She got up and tried to work at the sink. He gave up on eating his
sandwich. They could hear the car coming down the road.

"Chip, I don't blame you. Don't make this your responsibility. You've
got enough to think about. Anyone in your place would have come for
his help and he would have agreed."

"Thanks, M.J."

"All right," Crusty Stonebraker bellowed, "let's get the goddamned
show on the road."

The driver loaded their bags.

Hiram Stonebraker pushed out his leathery face, looked around the
corral and the orchard, and for a long time at the sea. "Don't worry,
M.J.," he said, "we'll clean up this mess in two months and we'll be
back here when the yellow tail begin to hit."

CHAPTER SEVEN

Clinton Loveless's swivel-hipped secretary entered his office. "General
Stonebraker has arrived," she said.

Clint sprung from behind his desk, walked the long deep-carpeted
corridor hastily, and pushed through the double mahogany doors that
led into the plush reception room.

"General Stonebraker! What a wonderful surprise to have you in
New York, sir."

"Hello, Clint."

He grabbed the general's arm, led him down the sumptuous corridor
to his office. "By golly, I can't get over how fit you look. How's Miss
Martha Jane?"

"M.J. is fine. She sends you her warmest regards."

He led Hiram Stonebraker into an office that reeked of prosperity. The general studied its oversimplified elegance that looked down on Madison Avenue from a height of thirty stories.

"You're looking pretty prosperous yourself, Clint."

"Not much like the old field shacks on the forward bases of the CBI?"

J. Kenneth Whitcomb III had been alerted to the arrival of General Stonebraker and burst into Clint's office at that instant. Pudge Whitcomb was an incurable celebrity collector and the acidy old general would be a great name to drop at his club or a cocktail party.

(My good friend, General Hiram Stonebraker, you know . . . the boy who engineered the Hump . . . well, anyhow, he was just saying to me the other day . . . Pudge, I like your new product.)

"General, meet Pudge Whitcomb, president of our firm and my new boss. Pudge, my old boss, General Stonebraker."

"A pleasure and an honor to meet you, General. Clint told me you were dropping by. Anything we can do for you while you're in New York? Theater tickets . . . limo . . ."

"I'm just fine, Mr. Whitcomb. I'll be leaving for Washington directly after lunch with Clint."

"Oh, that's too bad. I was hoping you'd drop by my office and we could exchange views."

"About what?"

Pudge smiled that smile of his with his face going lopsided as though someone had hacked his mouth on a diagonal angle with a meat cleaver. He excused himself asking Clint to step into the hall.

"Lovable old codger," Pudge wheezed.

"Like hell he is. He's one of the meanest sons of bitches who ever crapped between a pair of GI shoes."

"Well . . . time slows them all up, I guess. He's earned his right to be grumpy."

"He was born that way. And he also happens to be one of the most brilliant men in our country."

Pudge did a repeat of his slash-mouth smile, chortled an asthmatic laugh, and slapped Clint on the back. "See you in the A.M. Big, big think session on the Robson account."

"Check."

Clint returned to his office, pushed down the intercom button. "Miss Paisley, make luncheon reservations. '21' okay, General?"

"Ate there once. Too goddamned noisy and they ought to be shot for their prices. While you're at it I don't want to sit in one of those restaurants where they line you up against the wall like sides of beef in a butcher window."

"Check. Miss Paisley, try Charles à la Pomme Soufflée. Tell Maurice I want a table so the general and I can sit opposite each other. Yes . . . opposite . . . not side by side."

"Well, Clint, what the hell does a production-control man like you do up to your ass in all this carpet and mahogany?"

Clint chuckled. "I head a specialty group. A team of experts in merchandising."

"Sounds interesting."

"Whitcomb Associates is the only complete service of its kind in the country. We take a product, build it, beef it, sell it; test market, direct mail campaigns, complete ad agency. The whole works."

"I guess I follow you."

They jammed into an elevator which plunged them down to the lobby at a terrifying speed and they became an infinitesimal part of that faceless mass of scurrying ants yelling, "Taxi, taxi."

En route Clint continued his dissertation.

"In this country we build obsolescence into our products. Our national economy is based on waste. People buy because things look good and are packaged attractively. Take toilet paper, for example. We are starting to manufacture it in color. Our test market hops prove conclusively that pale green sells best in St. Louis while pink is big in Boston."

A look of utter vexation exploded on Hiram Stonebraker's face.

"We have editors to snag the public by verbal gymnastics; brown isn't brown, it's tawny brown. We subtly key in sexually stimulating music to back up radio commercials. We know that men like blue-colored after-shave lotion. Sanitary napkins will soon be packaged in boxes of various shapes with striped and polka-dot wrappings. So who cares how the motor runs as long as the upholstery has eye appeal and the exterior is junked up with enough chrome?"

"What project demands your talents these days, Clint?"

"Television. Big coming field. My team works on visual appeal. Our beer account will have the best-looking foam in the industry."

They arrived and were seated. General Stonebraker could not believe that the man who sat opposite him was once considered a young genius at locating and solving industrial riddles.

"Clint," he said sadly, "right after the war you went into a partnership with a real bright guy from Wichita. You formed an efficiency team to fix up sick companies. Clint, I seem to recall that you put a small steel mill back on its feet. What happened?"

Clinton Loveless looked as though he had been struck.

General Stonebraker was telling him now what he had told himself once or twice a month since he came to New York.

The general was intimating that if Whitcomb Associates were blown from the face of the earth, no one would really ever know they were gone.

"The efficiency team was a long time ago, sir. I guess we weren't doing too badly, but you know how those things are. It would have taken a long time to really get into the black. Anyhow, Pudge Whitcomb tracked me down and made a pretty attractive offer. I guess Judy and I have always wanted New York."

"Then you're happy?"

"What makes you think otherwise?"

"Well . . . it's just that I've been wiping my ass on plain white toilet paper for almost sixty years and I can't figure out any difference and I wonder if you really can."

"It's all in a day's work, General. I didn't invent the American way of doing things. I'm just a member of the crowd. Let's order lunch."

Everything was served in sauce far too rich for Hiram Stonebraker's catholic taste, but he decided not to mention his further discomforts. He set his knife and fork down carefully, wiped his lips with his napkin.

"Clint. I'm entangled with a logistical problem of feeding and supplying raw material and fuel to sustain a population of over two million persons by air."

"It's that Berlin business," Clint said. "I've been following it. I heard on the news last night that you were going to Germany."

"I've been able to get all the CBI boys together. They're en route to Wiesbaden right now."

"General, somebody's crazy. There's no way to do it." Clint took out a pencil and began to scribble on the tablecloth, a crude but acceptable New York custom. Hiram Stonebraker watched his pencil work with stunning rapidity and knew the spark was still in the man.

"You people," Clint said, "have to be talking in terms of five million gallons of aviation fuel a month."

"That's right. We have had to stop four oil tankers at sea and rush them to Germany to finish out this month."

"The Gooney Birds are only flying by instinct. They're shot."

"We're going to bring over C-54's."

Clint was ahead of the general. "C-54's were designed to carry troops over long distances. You say you will make them carry freight on short hauls. How are those engines going to stand up under so many take-offs and landings with heavy loads?"

"We don't know yet, for sure."

"What kind of facilities do you have to overhaul them?"

"I don't know that, either."

"Where in the hell you going to find spare parts and trained people?"

"I can't answer that either, Clint."

"And what about landings. The C-54 has a fragile nose wheel. How the hell is it going to hold up under the poundings of heavy loads? You'll burn up tires and brakes faster than they do at Indianapolis."

The general saw Clint Loveless get caught up in his own enthusiasm for a moment.

"Spark plugs are going to cost you between fifty-five and sixty-one cents a copy. We've got to be talking about forty thousand a month. And what is this crap about flying coal? How do you fly coal?"

"That's what I mean, Clint. These problems worthy of you. I'll make you my vice chief of staff or something. Mainly I have to have a production-control man who knows what the hell he's doing."

Clint buried his head in his hands and said, "No, no, no, no. I just got carried away for a minute. It's out of the question."

"We need you, Clint."

"My two wives would never sit still for this . . . Judy and Whitcomb Associates."

"They can spare you for a few months."

"General, Judy has been sparing me most of our married life. She worked as a hashslinger, salesgirl, and maid to put me through college. I graduated just in time to trot off to war. In ten years of married life we've had a fat fourteen months in which we weren't worried about the next meal. Pudge Whitcomb has limited loyalties. They're limited to Whitcomb Associates. I'm thirty-seven and I've found a happy home.

I make seventeen thousand dollars a year and I have a two-thousand-dollar expense account."

"That's a lot of money, Clint. I've never had that much."

"And I'm not going any place but up."

"That all depends, Clint, on what you consider to be up."

CHAPTER EIGHT

The Fourth of July was celebrated in the American Sector and elsewhere in Western Berlin with exchanges of oratory and promises of mutual loyalty. There were modest picnics, small parades, and sports contests.

In Steglitz Borough, Oberburgermeister Hanna Kirchner was due to make an appearance with Brigadier Neal Hazzard on the Insulaner, a great hill built from rubble and converted by thrifty, tidy Berliners into a park. It was one of a half-dozen man-made rubble mountains and now the highest point in the city.

When Hanna did not arrive, Ulrich Falkenstein was conveniently present for the speech, but when neither appearance nor word came from Hanna by the end of the ceremonies, there was cause for concern.

It was not until late that night that she arrived at Ulrich Falkenstein's apartment and he immediately called Neal Hazzard, Sean, and the British and French commandants.

The woman was obviously shaken as she told her story. She lived in Prenzlauer Berg Borough in the Soviet Sector. The Russians knew she planned to participate in the American Independence Day Celebrations.

"Schatz and four of his SND came to my door and ordered me into a car. I was driven to the Magistrat Building and kept in a file room with guards both inside and out. An hour ago, General Trepovitch came and handed me these documents."

There was a Russian order to Oberburgermeister Kirchner advising the Magistrat to stop paying occupation costs to the Western Allies.

A second order for the Postal Department of the Magistrat to stop all mail delivery to the Western Sector.

A third order stated that all municipal salaries would be paid in Soviet currency.

These papers were signed by Trepovitch in a new role, as "Military Governor of All Berlin."

The next morning Sean and twelve of his people went into the Soviet Sector to their liaison offices in the City Hall and the Magistrat. Sean called together the Magistrat department heads.

"The Soviet Union yesterday attempted to claim sole authority in Berlin. We are increasing our liaison in all offices in the Russian Sector. If you are accosted in your office by Soviet officers you are within your province to demand the presence of an American, British, or French officer."

The move did much to stop the harassment of the German officials during working hours, but a steady campaign of sheer terror was mounting against those who lived in the Russian Sector. Yet, the Germans were showing increased resistance as the West became more and more committed.

Having failed in the "workers' Putsch" and now meeting stiffening resistance from German officials, the Russians turned their efforts to an attack of the hated B marks.

All along the sector borders search stations were set up. People were pulled off trains, off the streets, out of restaurants, and dragged into shacks and searched for B marks. The round-ups were particularly evident on payday in West Sector factories. Some fifty Berliners were given severe prison sentences for carrying "illegal" Western money.

Despite growing unemployment in the Western Sectors, the further reduction of power to a quarter of normal; despite the diminishing coal and food stores, the B marks were clobbering the Russian currency until it took ten to buy a B mark. The Russian money became known as "wallpaper marks."

The Soviet Union had a vast coal store on the West Harbor and other depots and dumps along the canals, mainly in the British Sector. One day, shortly after the Fourth of July, the Russian guard was ejected and a British guard placed on all Soviet dumps.

With no formal contact between them, General Trepovitch, who advertised himself as sole ruler, tore over to British Headquarters to speak to T. E. Blatty.

The Englishman handed the Russian a receipt for the precise inventory of the dumps they had seized.

"We aren't taking them, General Trepovitch. We are merely borrowing them until you lift the blockade."

Anger over the blockade grew. Every night in the Western Sectors there were a half-dozen meetings of the three political parties. These gatherings drew thousands of people . . . solemn, orderly, and now able to protect themselves from agitators. Along with Falkenstein and the indomitable Hanna Kirchner a whole new crop of stubborn leaders emerged.

A counteroffensive was launched. The Berlin Assembly, on a bill by Falkenstein, voted to return the university to the Magistrat. Trepovitch ignored the mandate but both he and Rudi Wöhlman were puzzled by the growing anger and wondered where the next strike would come. . . . It did not take long to find out.

Hanna Kirchner summoned Adolph Schatz into her office in the Magistrat.

In the presence of the department heads of the Magistrat and the leaders of the Assembly she addressed the tormentor of Berlin.

"I accuse you of collaboration with the Soviet Union against the people of Berlin by police brutality, by the hiring of ex-Nazis, by the use of political terror through your so-called SND and for participation in the 'workers' Putsch.'

"Yesterday, you attempted to fire five hundred policemen because they are members of free parties. You will either answer these charges here and now satisfactorily or you are discharged as president of police."

Adolph Schatz, a bully all of his life, blinked with disbelief at the little woman behind the big desk. He growled that all of them would regret it and stormed from the place beelining for Soviet Headquarters.

Trepovitch naturally denounced the Magistrat action as "illegal."

At the same time People's Radio ridiculed the move, Hans Kronbach entered RIAS. Adolph Schatz's forte was political terror. He was neither a good organizer nor an efficient administrator. While his strong-armed squads ran rampant for three years, Hans Kronbach had constructed an excellent police force predominently loyal to the Magistrat.

Hans Kronbach as the new police president issued an order for all police to report to the Western Sector. The next morning 90 per cent of the Berlin force crossed over to where Hans Kronbach established a new office.

Adolph Schatz had outlived his usefulness, but for the sake of saving Russian face he continued to run a police force in the Russian Sector. Berlin now had two police forces.

This was the first break within the city government but there were more to come as department after department underwent merciless harassment. The Germans, now finding safe haven, fled to the West.

The British returned to the people of Berlin their Victory Column commemorating the Bismarck Wars.

The United States redesigned the eagle at Tempelhof as an American eagle and set it atop the building.

Trepovitch said that this was all a return to militarism and in the same breath announced there would be no more midday meals for workers from the West in the Russian Sector.

At the Tempelhof elevated station, throngs gathered each day to watch the Gooney Birds take off and land.

Dozens of men were gathering in Wiesbaden from all over the world wearing the China/Burma/India Theater of War arm patches and waiting for the arrival of the boss, Major General Hiram Stonebraker.

Although the first load of coal had been dramatically flown into Berlin, the situation was desperate. The Gooney Birds were weary beyond weariness and so were the crews. Rain leaked into their cabins and there wasn't so much as a spare windshield wiper left in Europe.

CHAPTER NINE

Clint lay on the bed with his back propped up sipping a martini and watching Judy dress. It was a repeat performance of a ten-year ritual that neither of them seemed to tire of. Judy had a rounded voluptuous body, soft without being fat. She always sat before the mirror putting on her face without a bra because she knew Clint liked to look at her. When she finally did slip into the bra, it was the signal for him to begin

shaving and showering as the timing would work out for both of them
to be dressed at the same time.

Clint reached to the nightstand, grasped the martini pitcher, swirled
it, drained out another half glass.

"Who are we?" he intoned abstractedly.

"Sweet people on the high road to becoming sweet rich people."

"We are perverters of the American dream. We prostitute for the
worthless products of a flabby society."

"That nasty old man must have upset you, lover. You haven't been
yourself all week."

"That nasty old man is Hiram Stonebraker, humanitarian. He handed
me a mirror and said, look at you, Clinton Loveless. Will the American
people pull through with white toilet paper? Will womanhood survive
with the old, gray telltale boxes?"

Judy slipped into her bra delicately and glanced into the mirror.
Clint wasn't even looking.

"It's that thing in Germany with all the airplanes."

"Yes . . . that . . . thing."

"I don't know that I'm in favor of spending tens of millions feeding
Nazis. What for? Another war?" She opened her closet. "Clint, start
shaving. We'll be late for dinner."

"Who are we?"

Judy went to him, rumpled his hair, lifted his legs, and put them
on the floor. "We'll ditch Milt and Laura early and get back and make
love like animals."

Clint stretched and walked into the bathroom.

"I'll put the children down," she said putting on a robe.

Clinton and Judy Loveless met Laura and Milton Schuster in the
lobby of the restaurant. Clint and Milt shook hands; Judy and Laura
bussed cheeks and each said, "Darling how lovely you look," or words
to that effect and Milt said, "Let's have a drink." He had come straight
from the office and was in need.

The restaurant was noisy. The meal was smothered in sauce. The
four of them sat side by side along the wall with other fashionable
New Yorkers . . . like sides of beef in a butcher shop window.

Milt Schuster was a pale, articulate lawyer in one of the big ad
agencies and as a matter of company and personal policy gave his dissertation on "that idiot in the White House."

Clint didn't know about that. He thought Harry Truman was doing a hell of a job both feeding the world and keeping it from moral collapse. American prestige had never been so high. However, he did not wish to intrude on Milt Schuster's soliloquy because it wouldn't change Milt's mind anyhow.

Laura began chattering about an Italian film by a newly acclaimed genius, Dino Massavelli. "The picture has such honesty, such realism . . . so earthy. Why can't Hollywood make such films?"

"Because it would bore the crap out of people," Clint said. "Laura, you liked that picture because it showed a couple of Dagos pissing in an alley and the leading lady refused to shave her armpits. Otherwise no one, including Dino Massavelli, had the slightest idea what the picture was about."

Milt Schuster said that business was on the skids because of the bureaucracy in Washington. Laura said they simply must see the Cuban-African Dance Group at Town Hall. Clint knew she got kicks from it because of a half-dozen six-foot Negroes built like there was no tomorrow, muscles glistening in their own sweat. Looking at Milt, who could blame her? They had to gobble down the last course because it was getting close to curtain time.

The check came to $61.00, which never failed to hit Clint like a kidney punch. He greased his way out of the place passing the bulwark of captain, maitre d', check-room attendant, wash-room attendant, and a frantic doorman who blew his whistle desperately for a taxi that never came.

It was only six blocks to the theater . . . let's walk it. They galloped off at a half trot. Fortunately the curtain was fashionably late. They were forced to split up because seats were hard to get, even at fifteen bucks apiece. As was the custom, Clint drew Laura Schuster.

The theater was another of those New York atrocities, an ancient firetrap that seemed to have been constructed for the discomfort of the audience.

The play was a ridiculous bore from six minutes after the first curtain. A grand old team, who were once fine performers, went through the motions and would continue to do so as long as smart New Yorkers plunked down fifteen bucks a ticket.

By the second act Clint had hypnotized himself into complete detachment. His mind was on airplanes flying and landing in rhythm, unloading, pouring life blood into a city of two million human beings.

Clint had thought of little else since General Stonebraker had come and gone.

He thought of writing to the general to give him some ideas on the removal of long-range navigation equipment which wouldn't be needed on the short hauls and the removal of other compartments which, with proper loading, could increase each pay load by a ton in a Skymaster.

What the hell, Clint thought, Stonebraker's staff will think of these things. Goddam, they'd all be there . . . Perry Sindlinger, Matt Beck, Sid Swing, Pancho, Lou Edmonds . . . what a wild-assed bunch of reprobates. . . . The bubble burst with a merciful final curtain.

The narrow, dirty street was swarmed with a sudden outpour of humanity from other drafty, uncomfortable theaters. They wrestled with the usual indecision of how to round out the evening. Judy suggested a chanteuse and combo at one of those East Side cabarets, also constructed for human torture with postage-stamp-sized tables.

Laura Schuster thought maybe that clever, clever little review at the Side Alley. She knew Milt would like it because it ripped the hell out of the Truman family. Laura also suggested a screamingly funny singer down in the village who was on the brink of being closed because of obscene lyrics. "He's so witty," Laura explained.

Milt Schuster suggested they go to Sardi's because Milt didn't have much imagination and Sardi's was the traditional place to go.

Clint envisioned further discomfort and mob scenes and preposterous tabs.

They joined the new flock of sheep converging on Sardi's, waited for forty minutes, and after proper apologies from a profusely perspiring headwaiter they were seated against the wall.

"The play was utterly divine," Laura Schuster said.

Milt thought it had its moments.

Judy said there was still a lot of magic in the team of Hunt and Martin.

"The play was unadulterated crap," Clint said. They tittered because Clint was in one of his cleverly candid moods. "This evening cost us a bill . . . one hundred dollars to eat garbage and sit on planks to hear a crusty old fart mumble lines completely without conviction. Clara Martin has a grandson in Princeton. I resent a talentless playwright telling me she is a desirable mistress. And I am about ready to throw up listening to you three literate people justifying this crap."

They grinned at him sickly.

"Tomorrow night we may debase ourselves by going to a comfortable neighborhood theater and for two bucks watch a great movie, but God almighty, we have to rip it apart because it was made in Hollywood. You know what we are. We're not only phonies . . . we're suckers."

Judy quickly patted Laura Schuster's hand. "Clint will call you sweet people tomorrow and tell you how sorry he is. Good night, darlings."

On the way home the cab driver said, "Why in hell should I be loyal to the goddam Dodgers, I ask you? In 1928 I had a good business, I had a house paid for, I had dough in the bank. Comes the crash, I'm wiped out. Lemme ask you somethin' pal, did the Dodgers care about me? Hell no. So, why should I care about the Dodgers?"

Clint gave an exorbitant tip for his friendly philosophy; then resented the doorman because he always felt capable of opening his own door.

Judy knew there was a choice of two ways to handle him, either have a counterexplosion of her own, or give him overwhelming sex for a week to smother his discontent.

He loaded a glass with scotch and stared morosely out at the perpendicular cement prisons of Manhattan, again not watching Judy undress and this worried her. She scented herself, slipped beside him.

"Lover . . . momma wants."

"Who are we? My kids don't even know what sunshine looks like. It's rationed out here in cheap, grotesque snatches when their Nana parades them over to that hood-filled excuse for a park."

"Clint, honey, I told you Pudge Whitcomb talked vice presidency at the last cocktail party. He means it, and when it comes through we can move to a wonderful penthouse with our own roof garden . . ."

"Filled with false hedges because no self-respecting plant would grow here. Do you suppose we'll ever see the moonlight again? Does it ever shine over this place or are we too damned busy elbowing our way into Sutton Place to look for it."

She pressed her bosom close to him. Clint got up and left the chair. "We're antiseptic. We don't even get dirty on vacations any more. The white linens of Nassau for Mr. and Mrs. Clinton Germless. We don't even draw ants on a picnic!"

"Clint, that's enough."

"You know what I once did, Judy? I helped that nasty old man lift a half-million tons of oil and rice and fly it over the highest mountains in the world. We did it through monsoons and low freezing levels and on muddy airstrips. We put more material into China by airplane than trucks did on the Burma Road . . . more than the ships brought into their ports. We did it with airplanes. By God, I was somebody in those days."

"You can't live that for the rest of your life. You're a big boy now. We've worked too damned hard to get what we have."

"Have? We deserve this. This is why Judy Loveless was a hashslinger to put her husband through college. All for this . . . phony, overpriced suckersville down there." He belted the drink down and refilled his glass. "You're right, Judy, that nasty old man shouldn't have come. He shouldn't have said . . . Clint . . . we need you . . . he shouldn't have said that."

CHAPTER TEN

The next day Clinton Loveless sported a fearsome purple hangover. His swivel-hipped secretary patched him up as best she could with a limited supply of drugs and coffee and followed him, pad in hand, to the sacred inner sanctum where J. Kenneth Whitcomb III was about to conduct a top-level think session.

As the brain trust gathered, the level of tension mounted. Pudge's father inherited railroads, lumber acreage, and oil holdings from his own tycoon father, a robber baron at the end of the last century.

During the 1920s Pudge's father was dissatisfied with the way many of his products were being sold and so created Whitcomb Associates as his own ad agency to sell a better corporate image. The advertising agency was never designed to be other than a minor holding. Pudge was the family black sheep; at will-reading time it was the perfect inheritance for a son held in low esteem.

Pudge proceeded to fool all of his contemptuous brothers and sisters by becoming a business phenomenon and the first of the clan to make the covers of both *Time* and *Fortune*. Whitcomb Associates took on new accounts that made his father scream from the grave and turned losers into winners. He was an American success story.

The seat of Pudge Whitcomb's genius lay in his ability to exploit other people's brains. The inner sanctum proved this point. Counterclockwise there was Dick Buckley, a lawyer who could be described only as brilliant and who, in his youth, dazzled as a court-room performer. His days were now spent weaving a maze of verbal gymnastics designed to keep Whitcomb Associates and some of their borderline accounts within the hair-split of the law. He was immersed in keeping the Pure Drug and Food people off their backs "because it was run by those Pinks in Washington."

Next to Dick sat Jerry Church, who, in younger days, won fellowships for biochemical research. He was over his eyeballs in a home in West Hampton and all of his talents became vented in one direction, self-survival. The colors mixed for pre- and after-shave lotions dominated his research.

Charlie Levine was next in line. Charlie once had a love affair with the English language and believed in finding talent to perpetuate its beauty. As an editor he had to prepare twenty-five to thirty books a year by established authors, mostly bad. There was the business of making contracts with literary agents, fighting the blood-curdling inner-office political wars, giving razz-matazz speeches at sales meetings, belting down two and three martinis at luncheons with visiting royalty among the authors.

Once in a while Charlie ran across a promising manuscript, one that would need a few months of dedicated work. Charlie was too damned tired and overworked to give it the devotion it needed.

Charlie took a dislike to himself upon realization that most books were mediocre and a publisher would push a bad one because of its exploitation value. Not that this in itself was evil. It was the pretending of standing on a pedestal that was evil, when one was really just another Madison Avenue whore.

Charlie decided to become a good whore as long as he was one. Pudge Whitcomb ran a good whorehouse. He now used the words he loved to insult the intelligence of the reader and listener, but if pounded into the brain often enough became part of the bastardization of the language he loved.

On the other side of the table was Gustav Von Gottard, a slick Viennese psychiatrist who was retained at an exorbitant salary to associate products with basic human desires for them.

And there was Clinton Loveless, a production genius.

J. Kenneth Whitcomb III made his entrance. . . . It was alleged he played some thirty minutes or so on Yale's varsity before he was booted out of the school. It was known that he saw Pat O'Brien portray a famous coach and never got over it.

"This is the big game," he began, "and that is why you, you, you, and you are here. You are my first-string team."

Look at the stupid sons of bitches taking notes, Clint thought.

"We're picking up the ball on our own ten-yard line and we're going to hit hard, we're going to hit fast. We're going to drive, drive, drive, and we won't stop . . . we won't stop till we score."

Pudge's male secretary dutifully, reverently, placed ten bottles of aspirin tablets in a row on the table.

Pudge lifted the product of Robson Drugs and pushed it forward. "Here's the ball. Duo-Aspro."

Robson Drugs had been hauled before the courts four times in six years for unpure products and cited for false advertising . . . by those Pinks in Washington.

"Professor?"

Gustav Von Gottard stroked his beard, looked off into space dreamily, swung on the swivel chair. "Ve know zat ze deep colors, ze reds und purples iss making people sink of hangovers."

Clint winced.

"Zerefore ve muss sink softly . . . a soft blue of ze sky . . . ze pink of a voman's flesh . . . ze color must be subtle . . . soft . . ."

"Got that Jerry?" Pudge asked his chemist.

"Check."

"Go on, professor."

"I am sinking zat ven man iss in pain he needs varmth . . . he looks for ze vomb . . . for ze bosom for comfort."

"Tit-shaped aspirin . . . subtly, of course. Charlie, your play."

Charlie Levine, former editor, chewed on the end of his pencil sincerely, scanning his notes. "How do we hit this? Do we go with a cold-turkey sell or do the science bit? Do we figure on added new ingredients and make it something unpronounceable but highly medical or do we swing with the doctor in the white coat. This is off the top of my head, but why not stick with the pounding hammers, the bubbles being released in the stomach, and call it pain-go or sooth-o."

Dick Buckley interjected, "We've got to go easy on the man in the white coat. The Pinks have been persecuting Robson Drugs . . . because old man Robson gave a big donation to the Republican Party."

"Dick's our defense," Pudge said.

"Check," Charlie Levine said. "I'll lay out the blurb with drums pounding and *segue* to soft music after Duo-Aspro gets in the blood stream."

"Chopin music," Gustav Von Gottard said.

"Check."

"Jerry, got everything so far?"

"You want pink, tit-shaped aspirins with baking soda added."

"Clint, baby, you're being awful quiet this morning."

Clinton Loveless got to his feet and looked grimly from one to the other. "Gentlemen," he said, "I have an important announcement."

They leaned forward, with bated breath.

"Gentlemen," Clint said, "the Confederates have fired on Fort Sumter."

And with that, he departed Whitcomb Associates.

"I'm not going to let you do this," Judy cried.

"You're not big enough to stop me. Let's don't end ten years of marriage with me knocking you flat on your back."

"What in the name of God has come over you? What will you do when you come back from Germany?"

"For the next several months Hiram Stonebraker is giving me the opportunity to practice and relearn my chosen profession. Once I saved a little steel mill from going under. I might just do the same thing again."

"And we ate canned beans for a year while you were doing it."

"And two hundred people went back to work when I finished the job. Cut it. It's all talked out."

"All of it, Clint . . . all of it? How about you and me?"

"That's up to you."

"I know you love me, Clint."

"Almost enough to give up my self-respect."

A half hour later, Clint's bags were at the front door when the Loveless apartment was graced by the presence of Pudge Whitcomb himself. The slash-mouth smile was more diagonal than usual. Judy said, "Thank God you're here . . . talk some sense into him."

"Clint, baby, you've been playing the game too hard. You're a little down."

"Nonsense. I haven't been working hard enough."

"You're our star halfback. Forget the Robson account. One more citation from the Pinks and we're going to drop them anyhow. In the meantime, here's a pair of ducats for Nassau for you and Judy and a bonus to cover expenses."

"I don't like Nassau. I might want to go someplace crummy, like Atlantic City."

"Name it."

"Germany."

"Clint . . . a little over a year ago when I asked you to join the team . . ."

"Can it."

Pudge began to perspire. "Big deal feeding Germans! Don't you think your own American people come first! This country needs you! The team needs you!"

The doorman phoned up that a taxi was waiting. Clint picked up his bags.

Pudge stood in the doorway. "I'm tearing up the old contract and writing a new one."

"Spell it out."

"All right, it goes like this. Vice presidency, stock options, member of the board, twenty-five grand a year, and a five-thousand expense account."

Judy's eyes pleaded.

"Ass was always overpriced in New York," Clint said. He brushed Pudge Whitcomb aside and left.

CHAPTER ELEVEN

The sign on the desk read: THE BUCK ENDS HERE. Hiram Stonebraker had once seen it on the President's desk, admired its philosophy, and the President sent him a copy.

The men in his office had been assembled from all over the globe. They had created the first miracle of air transport, the Hump.

"You people," Stonebraker crackled, "were brought here because you once had a reputation as can-do people."

Perry Sindlinger, now a full colonel, would serve as chief of staff;

Colonel Matt Beck, a flyer's flyer, would run Operations and as such be chief pilot; Lieutenant Colonel Sid Swing was back at logistics; Lieutenant Colonel Jose Mendoza, considered the most ingenious maintenance man in the old Army Air Corps, was there, as was Deputy Chief of Staff Lieutenant Colonel Buck Rogers, who had been spirited away from the Army to supervise cargoes and ground transportation and act as staff liaison with the Army; Lieutenant Colonel Ben Scudder, who set up communications on the Hump, would do it again with the new sophisticated electronic aids.

There was Major Lou Edmonds, a forlorn weatherman; and last, old Colonel Swede Swenson, who had put down a string of airfields in the Assam Valley and Bengal Valley and Kunming and would again supervise air installations.

"In the few days since I have arrived to assume this command you people have treated me to a monumental amount of bitching about living quarters and being torn away from families. This goddamned mission is not part of the occupation country club. You are here to work, and what I mean is, if you don't have a coronary in two months I'll know you're not putting out."

Hiram Ball Breaker was back in the saddle. He hadn't changed a bit, they thought.

"This mission is to be considered as war. You might encounter a little less flak, but if the Russians don't fire it, depend on me. Now, as for getting yourselves out of this mess, consider twenty years . . . if you're lucky."

Jesus Christ, Swede thought, I'll bet the old bastard couldn't wait to get back into uniform so he could start chewing asses.

"I expect a full survey of the situation and your reports within twenty-four hours. Remember, an aircraft grounded is of no value. Until spare parts get here we have to cannibalize. Now get in gear and come back with answers."

The first blow to Stonebraker was the recall of Barney Root to Washington, with General Buff Morgan named the new USAFE chief.

Hiram, like Chip Hansen, was not a member of the WPPA (West Point Protective Association) and had had innumerable run-ins in the past with Morgan.

"Buff, this is Crusty. What kind of crap are you giving my people on housing."

"Just hold your water."

"Hell. My people have been pulled away from their families on twenty-four hours' notice. I hate to disturb this magnificent occupation plant, but I suggest you move your country club to the suburbs and give us the housing so we can get at our work."

"Now, you just wait a minute there, Crusty."

"Got no time to wait. I have a thousand technicians coming in in the next couple of days and I'm not going to hold up this mission because the grand occupation country club won't get moving. I have to have six hundred billets immediately."

Buff Morgan grumbled that he would get on it. An old scenery chewer himself, he held the lifeless phone in his hand cursing at it for two minutes after Stonebraker hung up.

Stonebraker had come in like a hurricane. Buff Morgan was upset . . . everyone in USAFE was upset.

Stonebraker noticed a young officer pace about in his outer office, had spotted him before the Staff meeting.

"You!"

"Me, sir?"

"You. Get your ass in here."

"Yes, sir."

"What the hell are you doing here?"

"That's what I'd like to know, General. All I know is day before yesterday orders came for me to report here directly to you."

"Where were you stationed?"

"Andrews Air Force Base."

"What's your name?"

"Beaver, sir. Woodrow Beaver."

"Beaver! Goddammit, you're not Beaver!"

"Begging the General's pardon, I regret that I am Woodrow Beaver. At least, I'm quite certain I am."

"Hell, they sent me the wrong Woody Beaver!"

"It looks that way, General. I suggest, therefore, I return my ass to Andrews immediately."

"Not so fast, Beaver. What do you do?"

"I'm a PIO officer."

Stonebraker chuckled. "Two Woody Beavers and both PIO people."

He squinted closely at the young officer. "You don't look too bright to
me."

"I am extremely bright."

"I didn't say you weren't. I said you didn't look like it."

He had learned his first lesson in living with Hiram Stonebraker
. . . never back down.

"Beaver. I'm going to give you forty-eight hours to learn to be PIO
for this mission. Take the office next to mine and come back tomorrow
with extremely good suggestions."

"Yes, sir."

Perry Sindlinger returned from message center and handed a teletype to the general.

CLINTON LOVELESS AO 359195 HAS REPORTED TO MATS, WESTOVER,
REQUESTING SPACE TO WIESBADEN. SAYS HE IS A MEMBER STAFF,
MAJOR GENERAL STONEBRAKER. HE HAS NO ORDERS. ADVISE AND FOR-
WARD ORDERS.

"I've already answered," Perry Sindlinger said. "It will be good to
have Clint here."

Clinton Loveless arrived at Wiesbaden in the middle of the night
dazed by the sequence of events following his departure from New
York. Judy's tears, Pudge Whitcomb's asthmatic laugh, the children's
bewilderment all fogged together and an utter weariness was sealed
by a bouncy bucket-seat flight across the Atlantic.

Perry Sindlinger was at the ramp to meet him. They drove back to
the general's headquarters in the center of Wiesbaden, where, in the
middle of the night, carpenters were knocking walls out of adjoining
buildings to expand the work area.

"Hello, General," Clint rasped.

"It's about time you got over here. I've got a plane standing by at
Rhein/Main to run you to Berlin tonight."

Clint bucketed down a quart of coffee while Perry and the general
brought him up to date.

"Hansen's trouble shooter, a Colonel O'Sullivan, will meet you at
Tempelhof. You get together with the Germans in the Magistrat and
find out just what it is going to take to feed these people. Cut everything to the bone. Swede and Buck Rogers are in Berlin looking over

the air installations and ground facilities. See them. Come back with a rounded, thumbnail picture."

"Yes, sir. What are we landing in Berlin now?"

"The day I took over the command, a week ago, we put down a thousand tons with the British."

"How far can we push this?"

"With the present setup, not another ounce."

Clint understood, and got up to leave. The general gave ever so slight a nod that said he was glad Clint had come.

"By the way, sir. What am I?"

Stonebraker scratched his head. "Lieutenant Colonel, I think, vice chief of staff, or something."

"Air Force or Army?"

"Air Force. We're all Air Force. Even Buff Morgan and his country-club set."

The situation was worse than Chip Hansen or the President realized. Stonebraker's chief of staff told him bluntly that if C-54's didn't arrive, the whole mission would turn into a fiasco.

They were short on every kind of personnel: weathermen, crews, mechanics, engineers, radiomen, radarmen, office personnel, cooks, doctors, carpenters, drivers.

Housing, food, medical facilities were substandard. Rhein/Main, the key base outside Frankfurt, was at 150 per cent of capacity with more people pouring in each day. There were no beds and a food shortage loomed. Rhein/Main had the worst living and working conditions of any American air base in the world. It was called, without affection, Rhein/Mud.

With lives left dangling all over the world in a peacetime mission, morale was bound to collapse.

Air Installation reported that the two American bases of Rhein/Main and Y 80/Wiesbaden were inadequate in length of runways, taxiways, hardstands, fueling facilities, loading and unloading facilities, hangar space, dump space, administration buildings, and all lighting; floodlights, approach lights, hangar lights were below standard.

Communications told General Stonebraker that most existing equipment was obsolete. Beacons and ranges to and from Berlin could not control precision flying in the narrow corridors. There was no ground-controlled approach systems to "talk down" pilots in bad weather.

Ground transportation had to have more and larger trucks and trailers, spare parts, garages, mechanics, drivers. Better roads and storage dumps were an urgent necessity. Rail lines and spur lines had to be built to bring in aviation fuel from the port enclave of Bremerhaven; rail lines were needed to bring in the Ruhr coal; loading and unloading of aircraft was erratic and awkward and cargoes were bulky, improperly packaged, improperly weighed, improperly tied down.

Colonel Matt Beck told Stonebraker in his report that crews were flying too many hours. Coal was a dangerous cargo, with explosion potential. The weather was the worst in Europe and the approaches to Berlin were treacherous, running over Russian airstrips, demanding steep angles of glide into the midst of a jammed city.

The two Berlin airports of Tempelhof and Gatow were only ninety seconds apart by air. More radar was urgently needed to keep control of everyone's position. Unless ground-controlled approach was installed to maintain positive air discipline, mid-air collisions were possible.

The staff meteorologist, Lou Edmonds wrote: "If we were to list all airfields in the United States in descending order, the worst would be Pittsburgh. If we were to list Pittsburgh among the Central European cities, it would be the best." He promised late-summer fogs, violent turbulence from thunderstorms, and in the winter, low icing levels and crosswinds.

The logistics and maintenance men added the final amens. The Gooney Birds were covered with dangerous grime from coal and flour cargoes that was wrecking delicate instruments and setting in corrosive action on cable systems. The numerous take-offs and landings with heavy loads placed unmerciful stress on engines, brakes, tires. There were no facilities for proper maintenance; the spare part situation was beyond mere desperation. . . . This was Hiram Stonebraker's inheritance.

Clint returned from Berlin and gave the general further bad news.

"Both the Tempelhof and Gatow strips are breaking down. Just stand there a half hour and watch the Gooney Birds land and see the blue flames shoot off their tires. With C-54's hitting the runway with triple the present loads, Swede figures the runways will be knocked out in a matter of a few weeks."

Clint had drawn a list of urgent needs. A new runway at both Tempelhof and Gatow, and then the repair of existing ones. New aprons were needed for loading and unloading, new lighting. Finally, they had to find the site for a third airfield.

"We can fly in pierced steel planking and asphalt," Clint said, "and we are certain we can use the rubble in Berlin for a base. Labor is no problem. The ball breaker . . . pardon me, General . . . the clinker is how to fly in bulldozers, steam rollers, graders, rock crushers. There aren't any in Berlin."

The question of flying in heavy machinery was a new monster. There had to be a certain amount of food brought in daily before they could move in the asphalt and planking.

"You worked with the Magistrat, what's the food picture?"

"Stores are running very low, General. Less than a month's supply of staples."

"How much, Clint?"

"We're going to have to fly in fifteen hundred tons of food a day."

"What the hell are those people doing, glutting themselves in an orgy? Christ almighty, we've only reached a thousand tons a day of everything with the British. That has to be re-evaluated and cut in half."

Clint shook his head, no. "It would be lighter to fly in flour and have them do the baking in Berlin. Allowing for a one per cent loss we can squeeze by with six hundred and fifty tons a day."

"What the hell else are those people gorging themselves on?"

"By dehydrating potatoes and vegetables and powdering milk we can swing it with a minimum of eighty tons of potatoes, forty-four tons of vegetables, and twenty-one tons of milk. Sixty tons of fat, a hundred tons of meat and fish, all boned."

Stonebraker grunted.

"Thirty-eight tons of salt and ten tons of cheese."

"What the hell do they need ten tons of cheese for?"

Clint continued to drone out the meticulously planned list of the most valuable foods supplanted with vitamins. There would also be need for whole milk, special foods for hospital patients, food for the zoo, and for seeing-eye dogs. When he was done, Stonebraker knew Clint had figured it down to the ounce. In truth, they were asking two and a quarter million people to cling to bare threads and forget every comfort and most necessities known to a civilized community.

"Hello, M.J.," Hiram said, bussing his wife's cheek. "How was the flight?"

"Just fine, dear," she answered, searching for signs of fatigue on him.

"How are things at home?"

"Dorothy and the children are all settled in and will stay for the duration."

"Good, it was wonderful of Jack to let her come."

The town was mostly dark when they arrived except for the lights burning at his Headquarters complex. M.J. commented that it appeared to be a pretty city. Hiram said he didn't know as he hadn't seen much of it.

"It was spared," he said, "because some people had designs on it as an occupation country club."

As she suspected, he lived in a hotel within walking distance of his office. A pinstriped, cutaway-dressed German manager of the requisitioned Schwarzer Bock Hotel welcomed M.J. profusely. It was a magnificent hostelry in the grand old style with great high ceilings, marble fireplaces, enormous baths, glass-fronted wardrobes, glittering chandeliers, antique clocks, seventeenth-century writing desks, and an abundance of marble. Their suite looked down on a small square, the Kranz Platz, which was the site of the original Roman spring.

When the attendants were finally shooed out, M.J. loosened the general's shoe laces, and went about doing those things to force him to relax, then she unpacked.

"How is the mission going, dear?"

"Just fine. We have a few minor problems, but those will be ironed out."

From the hall came the sound of an alley-cat chorus of nonharmonizing voices.

> We are poor little lambs,
> Who have gone astray,
> Baa, baa, baa.
> We are little black sheep
> Who have lost our way . . .

M.J. opened the door and Perry Sindlinger handed her a great bouquet of roses and Clint Loveless held two magnums of champagne. They piled in . . . Pancho, Ben Scudder, Swede, Sid, and Lou Edmonds.

Crusty mumbled that unfortunately he would have to bounce for drinks. After a good and true welcome they crawled off wearily, well past midnight.

At last the general and his wife settled into bed. Just as M.J. rolled over to get comfortable, Hiram sat up, turned on the lamp, and grabbed the bedside phone.

"Get me Colonel Loveless at the Rose Hotel. Hello . . . Clint. Get back up here, right away."

Hiram was out of bed, wrestled into a bathrobe, and paced the living room until his vice chief of staff arrived from the hotel down the block.

"November, 1943," Stonebraker said. "I sent you to the Assam Valley to get some tractors flown into Chengtu."

"By God!"

"Think, Clint!"

"By God!" Clint's voice trembled. "By God. We had a little sergeant in maintenance. I remember now. He was a regular impresario with a cutting torch."

"Remember how we got those tractors over the Hump, Clint!"

"Yes, sir. This little guy cut them each up into fifty parts, numbered each part, flew with them to Chengtu and welded them back together."

"Why in the hell didn't you think of this earlier?"

"Because . . . sir . . . I've been too busy keeping the goddamned food down to fifteen hundred tons."

"All right . . . what was his name?"

"Christ . . . let me think . . . a real gook name . . . Homer . . . Halbert . . . Remus . . . something like that. Freshwater."

"Goldwater?"

"No . . . let me think . . . we sent him a citation. Drinkwater! Clarence Drinkwater!"

"Get back to Headquarters, find out where he is, and get him over here."

Clarence Drinkwater, auto wrecker and junk dealer from Atlanta, Georgia, was approached the next afternoon in his yard by a man from Air Force Intelligence.

He was very happy because he spent his days cutting up junk with a torch and was pleased to know that his rare talent was needed. He packed an extra case of chewing tobacco for he always needed a chaw to help him concentrate.

Twenty-four hours later he arrived in Germany at the Hanau
Engineer Base into the waiting arms of Clint Loveless, who nearly
broke into tears watching Clarence begin cutting up rock crushers,
graders, bulldozers, and all the heavy machinery needed to make new
runways in Berlin.

Big Nellie sat in Hiram Stonebraker's suite listening to the general
explain the mountain of new projects that had been initiated to support
the mission. Work had begun on rail lines, highways, airstrips, dumps.

A spare-parts base had been established outside Munich at Erding;
MATS announced the first Skymasters would be on the way from
Hawaii and Alaska and Tokyo and the Caribbean, and the President
had authorized the call-up of ten thousand reserves.

"I'm hoping to be able to give the order to stop the cannibalization
of the Gooney Birds. It is still a great old craft and I hate to see them
lose their integrity. If we intend to airlift Berlin . . ."

"Excuse me, General. What did you just say?"

"I said, if we intend to airlift Berlin . . ."

"Airlift . . . my God . . ."

"Never thought much about it."

In his column, Nelson Goodfellow Bradbury told America that a
new word had been given to the English language by the rightful
father, Hiram Stonebraker. It would capture the imagination of the
world. . . . The word was *Airlift*.

CHAPTER TWELVE

Honolulu

Master Sergeant Nick Papas, a sizable and burly man, made into
Tiger Quong's Gentleman Bar in Pearl City. Tiger was weary, making
motions of mopping the bar, waiting to close. He poured Nick a beer.
Nick chug-a-lugged it.

"Where's the sleeping beauty?"

Tiger pointed to a tiny office off the hallway. Nick entered. Captain
Scott Davidson was passed out cold, sprawled on a cot. Nick had been

looking for him all over Honolulu when the Tiger chased him down by phone.

He stared down at the captain. "Christ, what a sorry-assed sight," then brought Scott Davidson up to a sitting position. He was like a limp rag doll. Nick slung an arm over his shoulder and dragged him into the men's room, where Tiger was waiting with a bucket of ice water. The frigid dousing stunned him from his reverie.

"You son of a bitch," Scott moaned, "you son of a bitch. I'm sick . . . I may die . . ."

"Go in the can, stick your finger down your throat, and vomit."

"Goddamn you, Nick. You've got no respect for rank."

"Puke already. Tiger's tired. He wants to go home. I want to go home."

After Scott did as he was told, he recovered enough of his senses to study his sorrowful appearance in the mirror.

"You better get some sleep. You're due at the CO's office at 0730. There's flak up we may be flying out to Germany."

"I can't go back to the base looking like this."

"I'll take you to Cindy. She's been looking for you."

"Did she find me?"

"No."

"Then let me sleep at your place."

"I said, she's waiting for you."

"With a pickax. I can't take any of her static tonight. She started me on this bender in the first place."

"Sure, she's got a hell of a nerve getting teed off just because you tried to pick up another broad right in front of her . . . a married one at that."

"Nick, you going to let me sleep at your place or not?"

"Come on . . . Captain . . ."

Nick shoved a fin into Tiger Quong's protesting palm. The two of them assisted the wobbly flyer into Nick's car and he drove toward Honolulu, then up to the Pali Hills, where Nick maintained a flat that belied his rank.

Nick Papas had been a flight engineer for fifteen years and remained in the Air Force because it supplied a source of new blood for his card-playing proficiencies. Nick backed a number of enterprises in Chicago's Greek section staffed by relatives; a bar, a garage, a piece of a laundry, and a small hotel.

Despite his harsh appearance he was a pushover, with deep loyalties to persons other than Greek relatives. He supported the Church heavily and a string of charities from an orphanage to an animal shelter.

Scott Davidson was about his closest buddy. He had flown with the captain for nearly two years, and during the war Nick was there when Scott's plane cracked up on a jungle runway.

With rough gentleness, Nick helped the captain undress and spilled him into bed. Scott clung to it, groaning, as the room started to whirl.

He folded Scott's rumpled uniform, pinned a note on it for the house-boy to press it first thing in the morning, then set the alarm and lay in bed mulling over whether or not to call Cindy.

He wondered why bastards like Scott Davidson always tied up with nice girls like Cindy. Nevertheless it was something to watch him wheel and deal. Scott was a sort of alter ego.

"Hello, Cindy . . . this is Nick. Sorry to call you so late."

"Did you find him?"

"He's at my place. I thought it would be better. I got to hustle him down to Hickam first thing in the morning."

"Is he all right?"

"He'll live."

"Thanks, Nick."

"Good night, Cindy."

The next morning, with the help of thiamine chloride and charcoal pills, tomato juice and coffee, and in a rejuvenated uniform, Captain Scott Davidson was able to make a creditable appearance in the office of Colonel Garrett, commander of the 19th Troop Carrier at Hickam Field.

In thirty-six hours Scott would lead a group of eleven Skymasters as chief pilot on orders reading "extended training mission." The flight plan was Hamilton Field in California to Westover, Massachusetts, to the Azores, and end at Rhein/Main in Frankfurt, Germany. Everything in the squadron would go; spare parts, office equipment, all crews, all personnel. Colonel Garrett said everyone should carry enough gear for two months "temporary duty" in Germany. He confided to Scott that twelve Skymasters of the 20th Troop Carrier Squadron at the Panama Canal and nine Skymasters from the 54th in Alaska were getting ready for the trip to Germany. A big show seemed to be shaping up.

Scott had to get off his binge quickly. As chief pilot there were stacks of paperwork, briefings, meetings, inspections. Late in the afternoon all personnel were called and Colonel Garrett dropped the bomb with less than twenty-four hours to go. The meeting broke up with a stunned scrambling. Half the men were married, and others deeply committed to the area with apartments, cars, and furnishings. Once the shock set in, a breakneck scurrying ensued to salvage, say farewell, get the squadron ready.

Scott took a last look around the pleasant little studio apartment that stood along the Ala Wai Canal. There wasn't much for him to take, a few shirts, a change of uniform, some toilet gear. Most of what was there, Cindy had brought and put the touches and frills that made it warm. Scott began to scribble a note saying good-by and asking her to sell his car, his only visible asset. He heard a key in the lock and his heart sank. He was hoping to get away before she came.

Cindy was still wearing the white uniform of a dental assistant. "I was passing by on the way home," she said. "I saw your car parked out front." She went to the phone, called her home, and told the house-keeper to go ahead with dinner for the children, she would be in late. And then she saw Scott's handbag and uniform.

"You don't have to leave," she said. "I'll settle for half a loaf."

"I'm flying out tomorrow."

She looked at him curiously.

"I was ordered out. We're going to Germany on that supply run to Berlin."

"How long do you expect to be gone?"

Scott shrugged.

"And it all happened so fast you weren't even given time to say good-by," she said acidly.

"I'm chief pilot. The whole squadron goes. I've been over my eyeballs in work."

"Too busy to phone."

"I was just writing a note."

"So long, Cindy. See you around, sometime," she said with sarcasm. Those were the exact words he had planned.

"I want you to sell the car," he said, "keep half . . ."

"For practical considerations?"

Oh Christ, he thought, she's simmering to a boil and getting good and bitchy. He was hoping to avoid a scene, but that seemed impossible.

He sighed, now resigned to an unpleasant raking over. For some reason they all went in for the dramatic exit.

"I was hoping," she said with her wound showing in every inflection, "that there was some feeling between us."

"There was a lot."

"I even thought, for a while, we had grown to mean something to each other. You were so good with the kids . . ."

"Cindy, there were never any promises. You went into this like a big girl."

"You have a lovely way of making a girl feel like a cheap whore."

Here comes the self-condemnation bit, he thought. In the beginning a game was played. She wanted a husband, most of them did. He maneuvered to have her without commitment. Cindy knew what the score was. She had been divorced for five years. She'd been in other beds before, and she would again after he left.

Even though she accepts the rules in the beginning she has to begin to justify the affair by making herself believe it is more than an affair. She wants to feel needed. That is the face-saving stage. And then the initial excitement fades and she gets possessive and jealous. About that time another woman begins to look exciting.

"Don't pretend you haven't enjoyed it," he said. "Why can't we call it a day like nice people. We buried it last week, anyhow."

She turned away from him to fight off tears. She'd be damned if she would cry in his presence.

The bastard had it all down to a science, even the farewell scene. She gained control of herself and looked at him. Lean, blue-eyed, curly hair. She had committed the cardinal sin of falling in love, and when she saw him slip away she compounded the sin by becoming desperate.

"So long, punk," Cindy said.

"Cindy . . ."

"Get out."

The Skymaster lifted majestically over Mamala Bay, banked, gained altitude, and made a great horseshoe turn over Waikiki. Scott had a single fleeting thought for Cindy as he looked out of the window. By the time they passed over Diamond Head, he blew a long breath of relief. The orders had come just in time. Soon there was nothing below but blue water.

Scott's copilot and friend of years, Stan Kitchek, had been glaring at him all morning. They barely exchanged a word beyond the official language of the checks. Stan switched off the radio to the intercom.

"You're a no good son of a bitch," he said to Scott.

Scott didn't answer.

"I went over to say good-by last night. You couldn't even spend the last night with her? You couldn't even make a little game like you were sorry to go? She was crying her heart out. You're a no good son of a bitch."

"Fly the goddamned plane," he snapped, "I'm going to sack out."

He wrestled out of the seat and started for the makeshift bunk at the back of the cabin. Nick Papas' big square frame blocked his way.

"All right, Nick, I didn't beat her."

"You should of, it would have been better."

"Don't kid yourself. There'll be somebody else in the sack with her in a week."

"You're a prick . . . Captain . . . sir . . ."

Scott took the cigar out of Nick's teeth and stamped on it. "No goddamned cigar smoking in the cabin."

Scott shoved past him angrily, curtained himself in the bunk. Soon, he thought, the sweet music of the engines would sing him to sleep and he could forget. Everybody's pissed at me . . . Cindy . . . Stan . . . Nick . . . half the squadron. Nobody can stand to see a happy bachelor escape.

The music of the engines did not work. Scott squirmed, bunched his jacket beneath his head. Once he had gotten hooked and it ended in disaster. What do women want, disaster? I'm doing them a favor by kissing them off.

Scott Welton Davidson, a son of Norfolk, Virginia. From the beginning, Scott had it his way. A comfortable home and too much doting. He was a three-letter athlete at Matthew Fontaine Maury High School and touted as one of the best in the state.

It was easy to smile his way through. He carried it out of Norfolk to William and Mary College where coeds adored him. The studies were easy, the girls were easy, the games on the field were easy.

Scott was among the first to enlist when the war started and one of the first in all of Virginia to come home on leave with flyer's wings on his chest and new officer's bars on his shoulders. Merely another chapter in the success story.

In that strange crush of war, furloughs, sentiment, Barbara Lundy somehow managed to win out over the competition. The Queen of the Chesapeake Festival, the senior class president, was in many ways Scott's female counterpart.

Scott and Barbara. New flyer's wings, big war, and lots of patriotic fever . . . new wife.

It was a picture-book marriage of the All American Boy to the All American Girl. Norfolk was the proudest city in the country. It was a scene to sell War Bonds.

No one in Norfolk was really surprised when Scott Davidson became the first Virginia ace of World War II. In a dogfight over Bougaineville he shot down three Jap Zeros in a single day to bring his tally to seven.

And one day, Barbara received the dreaded telegram:

YOUR HUSBAND HAS BEEN WOUNDED IN ACTION.

Scott's squadron had been rammed in one of those crazy last-ditch suicide orgies. Both he and his craft were badly torn up, but he managed to nurse it to a belly landing on a New Guinea airstrip. Nick Papas was one of those who pulled him out of the ship before it exploded.

A Red Cross girl in Australia wrote for him, "Don't worry honey, it was only a scratch."

At the age of twenty-three Scott Davidson refused to believe the big lark of life was over. In a hospital in Australia, identified to Barbara only by a mysterious APO number, he fought to a remarkable recovery.

It was disappointing not to be able to get back into fighters, but the big, slow transports of the ATC had their compensations. He could move around to a number of civilized places where he was able to break marriage vows he never intended to keep in the first place.

As a flyer he became enthralled with the precision-flying of four engines and learned to love his new home in the clouds. He was tried time and again as a squadron commander but Scott had no mind for turning in reports on time or taking the responsibility for other men. He just wanted to fly. . . . And then, one day, the war was over.

Scott returned to Norfolk, bemedaled, to accept the latest chapter of glory, the worship of the returning war hero.

He weighed a number of offers. In those days it was good to have Scott's name in your business.

He made a vague pass at reorientation to civilian life. Soon he left his young wife confused and weeping by his strange, morose behavior. Scott was still out there, maybe flying over a nameless island, shooting, drinking, gambling, singing . . . loving. After her naïve desperation passed, she saw a stranger who looked not at her, but through her. The humiliations piled until she had no choice.

"You're a spoiled little boy. You've had it all your own way all your life. You can't love anyone because you love yourself too much."

Scott took it like a gentleman and with a sense of relief that he would soon be free of this trap. And all the while Barbara was cutting their ties, she loved him.

"You haven't got the courage to live in this world and take your share of its responsibilities and its bitterness. You think you can go on living in the clouds, but you're fooling yourself. One day life is going to catch up with you and you'll crash harder than you did on that jungle airstrip and when you do there will be a lot of people whose hearts you have broken standing on the side lines and cheering."

Scott justified the final phase with Barbara by saying he was a lousy husband and she deserved better.

Scott flew off with his infectious smile and easy way, seeking the thrill of new conquests, and he left a trail of damned fool women like Cindy who thought for a moment the wings of the eagle could be clipped.

CHAPTER THIRTEEN

Scott cut engines at the hardstand at Rhein/Main and growled for Nick and Stan to secure the craft. He was weary. He stretched, looked forward to a hot soaking tub, securing a three-day pass, and shaking down Frankfurt for quail.

As the last craft of the squadron cut engines, a burst of activity erupted. The planes were engulfed by ten-wheel army trailers whose crews began pulling out the cargo; first sergeants assembled the squadron personnel on the apron, and maintenance men queried each captain on the condition of his ship.

Colonel Matt Beck, head of Operations and chief pilot on Stone-braker's staff, met Scott at the bottom of the ladder.

"Would you come over to Operations with me, Captain," he said. "We want to run down the personnel and condition of the craft."

"Excuse me, Colonel . . . what's the fire?"

"These ships will be worked on tonight and stripped of certain components. They'll be flying cargo to Berlin tomorrow."

"We're beat, sir . . ."

"You'll bed down on the field tonight and be ready to fly tomorrow."

Scott's bath and the great treat that lay in store for German woman-hood went up in smoke. He got into Colonel Beck's jeep, drove down the row of Skymasters.

The first thing Scott saw of Rhein/Main was a coal dump fifteen feet high covering an acre of land, and a field of antennas that covered another acre. He had never seen anything like it. Bustle was every-where. Huts were being hammered together for enlisted personnel like a Gold Rush boom town. Maintenance docks, hangars, warehouses, fire stations were being erected; roads were being built on a base of mud. They passed an immense park of the transportation corps jammed with newly arrived trucks and trailers. The sign read: 24TH TRANS-PORTATION TRUCK BATTALION, UNITED STATES ARMY. Negro soldiers were shaking them down.

Across the road, Colonel Beck pointed to a small city of displaced persons who were the laborers. The movement, the gray dinginess, the mud that encased the entire field, the temporary structures all re-minded Scott of wartime. Rhein/Main was a far cry from the neat lawns and hedges of Hickam Field.

Matt Beck stopped before another temporary building marked 7497TH AIRLIFT WING. He was asked to wait in the colonel's office. The place meant business, he thought. He stretched and tried to doze.

Hiram Stonebraker, who had been inspecting the new building projects entered the office wearing a pair of grimy fatigues. "You the chief pilot of the 19th out of Hickam?"

Scott blinked his eyes open.

"What's the status of your craft?"

He didn't answer.

"What the hell's the matter with you. You tongue-tied?"

"So far as I know, you're a kindly middle-aged gentleman in dirty dungarees. I never give them classified information."

Stonebraker looked at his coveralls, stifled a smile. He walked out of the office right into Matt Beck, who had heard the end of the conversation in horror. "I'll tell him who you are, sir."

"Never mind. Get his record over to Wiesbaden, then shoot his ass over there."

The thing that ultimately made Hiram Stonebraker a major general while other men remained majors was his gift of selecting and using men.

He read the book on Scott Davidson, found two men in his Headquarters who knew of the captain personally.

Scott was a hot pilot, guts and ice water. He had knocked down eleven Jap Zeros with a P-38, and later, flew a Thunderbolt. He had more strafing and ground-support missions on Marine and Army invasions than could properly be recorded.

He had survived a miraculous landing in a badly damaged craft, suffered wounds that might have finished a lesser man. He made an even more miraculous recovery, as the medical record showed, to fly again for ATC and MATS, where he was considered a superb pilot.

Hiram Stonebraker liked what he read . . . except for certain things on the fitness report: THIS OFFICER IS A POTENTIAL LEADER BUT IS LACKADAISICAL, IS ALWAYS LATE WITH REPORTS, AND AVOIDS RESPONSIBILITY.

"We met earlier today, Captain," Hiram Stonebraker said.

The two silver stars adorning each shoulder were much in evidence now. "I had a sort of feeling I may have made an error in judgment . . ."

"You were within your rights. I'd have chewed you out if you hadn't demanded proper identification."

"Thank you, sir."

"Captain, I'm going to recommend you for a temporary appointment as chief pilot of the Wing at Rhein/Main. It's a big job. Cut the buck and I'm sure it's yours permanently. You've got a lot to be briefed on to get the picture of what we're up against here, so I'll turn you over to Colonel Beck again."

"General . . . I . . . uh . . ."

"Well?"

"Sir, I appreciate the General's confidence . . . even on a temporary basis. However, sir, I'm afraid I might let you down. I'm just not much on the administrative end of things."

"You can speak better English than that."

"If the General gives me leave to speak."

"The General does."

"Sir, I made myself live when I should have been dead so I could fly again," he said with a southern charm, sincerity, and appeal that could melt the hardest heart. "I lay there in a bed for six months while they were pulling lead and aluminum out of me and pumping me full of blood. The only thing that made me pull through was the thought of flying, General . . . I'm just not cut out to play wet nurse to boy pilots or pin up numbers in a chart room."

Crusty knew the breed all right. The old crushed-hat gang, a direct descendant of the barnstormer. They would fly into brick walls and the eye of a hurricane, but you couldn't give them a command or make them make decisions.

But Hiram Stonebraker also knew men. He liked something in this boy and he wanted to believe he could get the best from him. Scott was the first in with the Skymasters and certainly the best pilot who had shown up so far.

"You'll do what I tell you to do. Now get down to Operations and learn your goddamned job."

Throughout the night weight and balance supervisors removed excess items from the craft in from Hawaii. The long-range navigation equipment, navigator's stool, wash water, forward fuselage tanks, bladders, partitions, troop benches were peeled out to make room for another ton of pay-load cargo to Berlin.

Matt Beck personally briefed the new arrivals and would take the number one craft today to Berlin as their time bloc approached. Ten planes would make the flight. The eleventh was to remain at Rhein/Main for a special detail, Captain Scott Davidson to fly it. Clinton Loveless briefed him on the plan.

"Bomb coal!" Scott cried. "Somebody's out of their goddamned mind."

"Captain, this is the general's idea. No matter what happens to this experiment, you just keep your mouth shut. You're too cute to have your head shrunk."

"But, Colonel . . . anybody in his right mind knows you can't bomb coal."

"If, just if, we can drop coal sacks in Berlin in an open field . . . just if, I say, it would save thousands of hours of landing, unloading, and turning around. We've got to try out all ideas."

Scott shook his head. "Your show, sir."

Scott made a short flight to the outskirts of Offenbach to where an open field was marked out for the experiment. He flew low over it and flapped his wings to tell the ground observers he had spotted the target area.

On the edge of the white circle stood Hiram Stonebraker, Clinton Loveless, Perry Sindlinger, and a half-dozen other eager members of the staff.

Scott circled the craft to come in downwind, dropped to three-hundred-foot altitude, reduced air speed, and as he hit the edge of the circle a signal was sent back to a crew who released duffel bags filled with coal. They zoomed earthward. He made two more passes flying slower and lower, enabling many more sacks of coal to be thrown out of the door.

The duffel bags burst into shreds as they hit the ground and the coal was splintered into fractions. An angry black column of dust arose, raining down a storm of coal, and the winds sprayed and spewed it for miles beyond the target area.

The observers on the ground were gagged and blanketed with dust and in a moment resembled characters in a high school play using burnt cork on their faces.

Clint saw Perry Sindlinger, whose eyes resembled two burned holes in a blanket. He started to laugh, tried to control himself, because somebody there didn't think it was very funny. They bit their lips to contain themselves as a pitch-black Hiram Stonebraker faced them.

"Doesn't work," Stonebraker said.

CHAPTER FOURTEEN

Marshal Alexei Popov had made an error. He decided to allow a Western journalist to tour the Soviet Zone of Germany to "prove" freedom of the press. Nelson Goodfellow Bradbury was chosen.

His articles became increasingly more terse and when faced with censorship he began smuggling out stories through those mysterious channels known only to the society of newspapermen.

The last article had deep repercussions:

POPOV'S FOLLY. A FARCE IN THREE ACTS by Nelson Goodfellow Bradbury

Until recently the Communists continued to go to elaborate lengths in East Germany to parade in public members of opposition parties to "prove" political freedom existed in the workers' paradise. Berthold Hollweg is their most famous relic.

This farce of show-casing a few inept democratic politicians is over. Also over is freedom of speech, assembly, justice, worship, and all those other petit bourgeois annoyances tolerated by the decadent capitalist society.

The consolidation of the Soviet Zone of Germany is complete. The last voice of freedom is still. Any hope for democracy is dead.

V. V. Azov, a mysterious puppet master, calls the plays from a shuttered mansion in Potsdam.

The life and times of Comrade Rudi Wöhlman show him to be perfect in the role of a ventriloquist's dummy. Wöhlman is about ready to call together a "people's" congress. At the end of the congress plans will be announced for a "People's Republic" with Leipzig as the provisional capital.

Later, when the West is hopefully squeezed out of Berlin, this city will be named capital of the newest police state.

A four-hundred-thousand-man para-military "People's Police," which is the nucleus of an East German Army, are in existence to persuade the people that this is the right thing. The existence of this organization is in violation of all agreements to cleanse militarism from German life.

A back-up force of twenty divisions of infantry and armor under the command of Marshal Popov ensures full acceptance of the new way of life.

Why is there such a panic to form a People's Republic while the Communists continue to talk out of the other side of their mouths for unification?

The call for unification is the most hideous libel in all of the postwar Soviet profanities. The fact is the Soviet Union lives in terror of a reunited Germany which they cannot control.

They cannot control Germany so long as the West remains. They cannot win Germany through free elections.

The West is beginning to hammer out its own plans for the political and economic merger of their zones and, therefore, the Soviet Union must make unification impossible by the creation of a puppet state.

The fat, sad-eyed reporter was denounced in traditional terms as a "reactionary tool of yellow journalism" and ejected from the Soviet Zone through the Brandenburg Gate and advised he could never, never return.

Sean was happy to learn that Big Nellie was back in Berlin, for life granted him few real friends. The Press Club in Dahlem was jammed with journalists now who had been caught up in the Berlin story. It was good, Sean thought. The press had been a faithful ally of General Hansen from the beginning, and at last the Airlift story was catching the public fancy.

Sean brought Big Nellie up to date on the events in Berlin. The Lift had set down two thousand tons the day before. This was less than half the required daily minimum, but more Skymasters were on the way. He spoke of the big building programs at Tempelhof and Gatow.

"As a matter of fact, I just left two of Stonebraker's men. They're scouting around in the French Sector for a site for a third airfield."

Sean said the Berliners were holding up unbelievably under intolerable conditions, but there was a growing fear among Falkenstein and the German leaders that the West might negotiate Berlin away without their having a voice in their own fate.

Big Nellie handed Sean a copy of the column he had just filed. "It's a masterpiece," he said.

Sean smiled. As usual, he had found a unique thesis.

SOPHISTICATED SIEGE by Nelson Goodfellow Bradbury

All of the classic definitions of the word "siege" are defied by the bizarre blockade of Berlin. It is a situation unique in history.

Man has laid siege to man from the mythological siege of ancient Troy to the Biblical sieges of Jerusalem and Jericho on through to the sieges of Carthage and Paris and in recent years we saw it in the blockades of the Spanish Civil War.

Until Berlin, all sieges have had the goal of military victory. Long and involved sieges were embarked upon to starve and demoralize the besieged and followed by an attack that spelled destruction or submission. The Siege of Berlin breaks all of the rules and in many ways does the complete opposite of historic conceptions. In Berlin the enemies live side by side, eat together in the same cafes, swim in the same lakes, attend opera together, and in some instances have social contact.

Here, the enemies go to extremes NOT TO GET INTO A FIGHT.

This is a battle of will power. The protagonists battle for the minds and souls of men.

The phenomenon runs through the performance of normal life. The railroads, canals, sewage plants, phone systems continue to function only by cooperation between the Russians and the West even though there is no official contact between them.

Even the Airlift is closely watched by Russians in a four-power Air Safety Center.

Two separate police forces cooperate on certain criminals. Populations shift daily by hundreds of thousands through public transportation facilities.

The city administration has the ridiculous and near impossible task of trying to serve two masters while being voted into office to serve a third. And while the Berlin Magistrat is forced to take orders from both sides you will find duly elected Communists in public office in the Western Sectors and duly elected borough mayors from the democratic parties in office in the Soviet Sector.

Two currencies wage a battle for recognition confounding every rule of economics. This fight for the money is a good measuring stick of the way the people think, for despite its impossible physical position the Western B marks continue to thrash the "wallpaper marks" of the Russians.

In this, strangest of all sieges, the West continues to hang on by the skin of its teeth while in Karlshorst and Potsdam Trojan horses are being built for the Berliners, and in Moscow, Trojan horses are being built for the West.

Sean handed the column back to Nellie. "Like you said, nothing short of brilliant."

"Sean," Big Nellie said abruptly, "you're wearing your heart on your sleeve. Tell me to mind my own business."

"Things used to be clear to me."

"None of us like to see our magnificent points of view moderated by shades of gray. It's like admitting defeat. You were once a mean, exacting, German-hating son of a bitch."

"Only a Russian clings to something as absolute truth . . . until the commissars replace it with another absolute truth."

"Don't play verbal gymnastics with me, Sean."

"Am I chasing windmills? Do I see changes in these people because I want to, or are they really happening?"

Big Nellie grunted. It was still that girl, and Sean was seeking justifications. "Talk to most of our people in Germany and they'll tell you what a sweet, kindly, sentimental folk the Germans are. They may have been slightly misled by Hitler, but we apologize for them. Most Americans in Germany will tell you that most Germans didn't know what the Nazis were doing." Sean grunted.

Bradbury shook his mop of hair. "My distinguished colleagues are quick to sing odes to the noble Berliner. The Germans haven't changed, Sean, they've just shifted a little with the prevailing winds. Wait till this blockade goes into a sixth month and all those unity rallies around Germany will vanish in smoke. Wait until a Berlin tax takes a liverwurst sandwich out of their lunch buckets and you'll see how fast they get tired of Berlin. I've already heard it . . . Berlin was really never our capital . . . Berlin is a problem of the Americans."

As Big Nellie attacked the wall of justification he was building Sean wondered how far he had committed himself to making peace with the Germans in order to have Ernestine. Was he groping for signs that did not exist?

"The German people," Big Nellie said, "are not going to make a democratic state out of the Western Zones because they long for democracy. They'll do it because we order them to do it. Their political convictions and their love of freedom begins and ends with a full lunch bucket. They do not possess the inner convictions to survive an assault on a democracy. They're out to make the best deal they can to save their asses and they'll turn to the first strong man again who keeps their lunch buckets full. Heard enough?"

"You might as well finish."

"No one was more shocked than the Russians when they learned how easy it was to control Germans. We say, make a democracy. On the other side of the gate they say, make a police state. Think they'll rebel? Hell no, they'd have to tramp on somebody's lawn to do that. Three years after Hitler and they're marching over there with torches and banners. Three years and they've got block wardens and kangaroo courts again. Neighbor rats on neighbor in the grand old German tradition. You use informers. You know it's no sin to them to spill their guts to save their necks."

Big Nellie heaved a deep sigh, touched Sean's hand. "I get a little wound up in this, but somehow I can't get used to my new peace-loving democratic German ally."

"I had it coming," Sean said.

"You're my pal, Sean. The things you feel are deep and intense. If you try to cover them, they'll come back and haunt you."

CHAPTER FIFTEEN

"Beaver! Get your ass in here!"

"Sorry, sir, he's at the Press Club with the daily handouts."

"I want him in here the minute he gets back."

"Yes, sir."

Hiram Stonebraker held before him a copy of the *Task Force Times*, a one-page daily paper edited by Woody Beaver with a headline read-ing: *Sidney Hops Into Hamburg.*

It appeared that Woody Beaver had got hold of a kangaroo and was having the animal escorted around Germany appealing to Germans to fill its pouch with presents for West Berlin and particularly toys for the children. Sidney was collecting more tons than the Airlift was flying and getting more space in the *Task Force Times* than the C-54's.

Woody Beaver had learned his job, all right. Too damned well, Stonebraker thought. The Press Club was a converted mansion once belonging to a cement king and sat in West Biebrich on the Rhine. Beaver wheeled and dealed, planting Stonebraker's views, and when they differed with Buff Morgan's resorted to devious methods.

In public he rarely left the general's side, and was quick to tap his shoulder when he felt the general was about to make a salty utterance, particularly about the occupation country club.

Beaver started the *Task Force Times* on twenty-four hours' notice because Stonebraker thought it would be good for morale. At first Buff Morgan did not take kindly to a separate entity and said, "*The Stars and Stripes* is good enough for the rest of us peasants."

When he finally did authorize it, he conveniently forgot to allot paper, but Beaver proved equal to the task by foraging and scrounging so that the first issues came out in a variety of shapes and colors.

One of Beaver's brain storms was to hold a contest to give the Airlift an even more romantic name. "Operation Vittles" won the day and was good for copy in the world press. The contest winner, by coincidence, was a WAF working in Headquarters whom Beaver just so happened to be dating at the time.

Stonebraker decided to humble his rambunctious press officer by pouring on flight duty. On his third flight to Berlin, Beaver happened to pick up a passenger, a fraulein working at the mobile field canteen at Tempelhof. Their return flight somehow went wrong and they ended up in Marseilles.

The girl stuck to her story that she stowed away, and Beaver insisted that his instruments got fouled up by a strange magnetic phenomenon. Stonebraker told him to concentrate on his public-information efforts.

"Beaver has just entered the building, sir."

Stonebraker emitted a low, ominous gurgle like a stewing volcano.

"Beaver! Where did you get this goddamned animal."

"You mean Sidney, sir? Well, I was up at Fühlsbuttel covering the arrival of the first Australian crews and this kangaroo was their mascot and . . . anyhow . . . I thought . . ."

"Beaver, I'm not running a zoo."

"Sir, yesterday we got a ton of toys in Lübeck and we've got a pledge of a ton of sausage from Bremen. Now you know these Germans have never been hot for each other. This is a very good sign."

"What the hell are you, a political philosopher? How the hell we going to get this junk to Berlin?"

"By the end of the year we might be able to spare a few planeloads for an Operation Santa Claus."

"Santa Claus!"

"Just look at all these things we've collected."

Stonebraker realized it was a great public relations idea and backed off ever so slowly.

"After all," Beaver said, "you commanded me to use my initiative and make advance planning."

"Well . . ."

"Sidney's brothers, Humphrey and Octavius, have just arrived. We can cover all theee zones if the General will just sign this authorization for some extra trucks."

Stonebraker scratched his name on the requisition, then proceeded to chew Beaver's tail out for a cartoon in the *Task Force Times* making jest of what the Airlift referred to as "temporary duty."

"Beaver, I see by a decent paper, *The Stars and Stripes*, that Bob Hope is giving a show in Paris. It is my opinion that Bob Hope would be good for the morale of our people."

"Excellent idea, sir. I'll write an invitation for your signature."

Hiram Stonebraker shook his head, no.

"You go to Paris and bring Bob Hope back with you, personally."

"But . . . but . . . but . . ."

"Beaver, I believe in you."

"Yes, sir," he croaked. He slunk toward the door.

"And Beaver," the general said, chuckling devilishly, "don't come back without him."

CHAPTER SIXTEEN

Clinton Loveless was deeply involved in the Airlift Control Center of Headquarters on Taunusstrasse in Wiesbaden. Here were direct lines to Frankfurt Air Traffic Control Center and Tempelhof Approach and Gatow and all the fields in the zones. Minute to minute records were kept twenty-four hours a day recording movement of all air traffic, the status of each squadron, weather maps, and forecasts. And mainly, the Howgozit board showing the tonnage set down in Berlin. In these days it had edged to three thousand tons a day.

Statistical Service turned the Control Center and the staff conference room into mazes of charts and graphs showing turn-around times, engine availability, utilization of craft, flying hours per crew, and all those facts needed to keep a precision control as accurate as the precision of flying in the corridor itself.

A dozen Skymasters from the 46th at Bergstrom had come; sixteen from the 22d Transport from Fairfield, California; nine came from Great Falls, Montana; they came from Westover; more were on the way from Hickam and Tokyo and Kelly in Texas; the Airlift was growing larger than its parent, MATS.

The Air Materiel Command secured spare parts from all over the world and manufacturing lines rolled again for yet more parts. At Erding outside Munich a German/American manual of parts was written and German technicians hired to fill the growing gap prepared to renew 40,000 spark plugs a month and break down and reconstruct any and all instruments in the Skymaster.

The unpronounceable base of Oberpfaffenhofen, known as Obie, was activated for the two-hundred-hour overhaul; engine build-up was begun at Rhein/Main; daily spare-parts trains ran from Obie and Erding to the new rail head of Zeppelheim, which fed into Rhein/Main and Y 80.

Ten thousand Americans were there or on the way and with other thousands of British, Germans, and displaced persons some 50,000 people would be involved in supplying Berlin.

A Sea Lift to support the Airlift, called Marine X, poured in ten million gallons of aviation fuel a month and brought in new engines built in Texas and wheat from Canada.

The Headquarters of the Weather Wing was established in a confiscated house once belonging to the Von Ribbentrops, which had been used as a Gestapo horror house. They built up the most extensive system of gathering weather data from stations around the world ever known to aviation.

At Rhein/Mud the Operations office had a sign which read: COAL AND FEED STORE, FREE DELIVERIES, H. BALL BREAKER, PROPRIETOR.

In the Pilot's room at Y 80 another sign read: CONGRATULATIONS, YOU MADE IT AGAIN.

As the Americans flew the southern corridor with ever-growing precision the British flew into the northern corridor out of their fields at Fassberg, Celle, Lübeck, Fühlsbuttel, and Wünstorf.

As August wore on it became apparent that closer liaison would have to be established with British Headquarters which was located in the medieval town of Lüneburg and exchanges of personnel began to take place.

British Operation Plain Fare put on a magnificent show. The British had but a hundred aircraft, many of which were Dakotas, their counterpart of the Gooney Bird. They were closer to Berlin than the American Zone so their craft could make three round trips a day, but they had only two crews for each craft.

The main British effort was flour, which accounted for half their cargo tonnage. The British solved the cumbersome problem of flying in Berlin's gas and oil, which was loaded in bulky barrels. They contracted civilian tanker planes. Shortly, the Tudors and Lancasters flew in all of Berlin's liquid fuel by flying tanks.

The British solved the most perplexing problem of flying salt, which had proved to be deadly corrosive. It was beaten by flying the salt in the belly of waterproof Sunderland seaplanes, which landed on Berlin's Havel Lake.

In preparing for the winter, when the lake would freeze, they were designing panniers that could be slung under the craft . . . as salt was carried in ancient caravans.

"Get on this thing and whip it, Clint," Hiram Stonebraker said.

Clint drew up cargo-loading charts on every Skymaster in the Lift, dozens of ideas for lightweight packaging, and a manual for proper loading.

"Clint, go over to Hanau and do something about this coal situation."

Clint told the people at Hanau responsible for coal procurement that he wanted them to buy a better grade and weigh each sack more accurately because they were overloading the planes.

Coal was being carried in surplus duffel bags that had to be wetted down to cut down seepage, which was wrecking cable systems and instruments. Wetting-down added to the weight of the cargo; he wanted to test out a five-ply paper sack. Although paper sacks would only last for three flights against the duffel bag's twenty, it would still be cheaper. It would mean a half-million new sacks a month.

At Hanau Clint looked over the new ideas for tie-down rods. The canvas webbing was wearing out too fast. He liked the looks of light metal webs and rods and wanted to test it immediately.

At Hanau, Clarence Drinkwater had established a school to teach the Germans the tricks in cutting up heavy machinery and they went to work cutting up the shipments of small generators brought in by Marine X to raise Berlin's capacity.

"Clint, Chip Hansen phoned to say they are down to a four-day supply of newsprint. He feels it is vital to the morale of the Western Sectors to keep the press going."

Clint flew to Sweden, where he and a paper manufacturer designed an undersized roll of newsprint weighing only five hundred pounds.

"Clint, get down to Obie and see what the bitching is all about on the maintenance docks."

The wooden docks were inadequate. Clint wanted light metal ones that could be assembled like temporary grandstands. He put in a priority message to Air Materiel Command to procure them and Sea Lift them at once through Marine X.

Hiram Stonebraker came to the end of a sizzling argument with Buff Morgan over the red-line phone about air time and space. Stonebraker insisted that the air had to be clear of USAFE and civil traffic at Rhein/Main and Y 80 during the Airlift bloc times.

It was causing a nightmare of scheduling, but Stonebraker would allow nothing to interfere with the Lift's priority. The argument ended with Buff Morgan threatening to take the matter up with Chip Hansen.

Hiram slammed the phone down and continued with a number of well-chosen words about the USAFE country club when a message from Air Materiel was handed him: NAVY TURNING OVER ONE HUNDRED C-54 ENGINES AT ONCE. FLYING FIFTEEN OVER VIA C-82. BALANCE WILL ARRIVE BY MARINE X BY END OF MONTH.

Holding the message in his hand, he walked to the Control Center and studied the engine availability board. The navy engines would come just in time.

Because of the high usage of craft, the type of cargo, the pressure of heavy loads, and numbers of takeoffs and landings, the breakdowns were mounting so that nearly 20 per cent of the craft were on the ground at a single time for spare parts and repairs.

On the squadron level there were inspections at twenty and fifty hours in addition to unscheduled repairs. At a hundred hours each craft was given a more detailed inspection. At a thousand hours the craft were sent back to America for complete overhauls.

A bottleneck had developed at the two-hundred-hour interim overhaul at the new base at Obie. This two-hundred-hour inspection meant the training of hundreds of Germans and the loss of thousands of flying hours. Stonebraker wanted to eliminate the Obie Base and the two-hundred-hour overhaul, but both USAFE and MATS were against him. He returned to his office to receive a call from Clint Loveless, who had just gotten in from his latest trip, this one to British Headquarters on the possibility of setting up a jointly run operation at their fields at Celle and Fassberg. The British had more fields than planes to fill them, was closer to Berlin, and more Skymasters were coming into the American Zone than their two fields could handle.

Clint went to the general's office and was startled at first sight. The general seemed to be chalky-colored. He showed Clint the message on the navy engines. Clint blew a sigh of relief.

The general called in his aide, told him to phone M.J. and say he would not be there for dinner, and told his aide to get something to eat for Colonel Loveless and himself.

"Clint. This hundred navy engines won't be enough. I'm meeting with USAFE tomorrow to try to cut out the two-hundred-hour inspections. I want you to support my position."

Clint pondered. The Skymasters were being asked to do a job for which they were never designed. All the manuals no longer applied.

The chief pilots had worked out methods to get the greatest efficiency with the least wear through absolute power settings and by cutting down ground-idling time.

Yet, the repeated stress of take-offs with heavy loads and high manifold pressure had resulted in piston erosion. The high usage of craft simply played hell on combustion chambers and there was excessive wear on seals, gaskets, ignition wiring.

Hydraulic systems, particularly the gear-retracting mechanism, were overworked and the coal and flour cargoes eroded cables, wires, contacts, plugs, instruments, radios.

There were breakdowns on the long, delicate nose wheel, never designed for the unusual poundings they were receiving in the many take-offs and landings; fuel leaks were a constant source of headache.

The two-hundred-hour overhaul meant they needed greater logistical support, would have to find and build up 30 per cent more spare parts, find facilities and train aircraft and engine mechanics far beyond the capacity of the base at Obie.

Clinton Loveless and Hiram Stonebraker knew that in the unromantic, poorly lit, drafty hangars, mechanics torn from families and living in muddy tin-hut camps were going to make or break the Airlift.

It was the one problem that could never be solved, only appeased, for the Lift demanded the greatest maintenance and logistics operation in aviation's history.

"What about it, Clint?"

"I'm sorry, General. I can't support your view. We have to continue the two-hundred-hour overhaul."

Stonebraker knew he was whipped. His own staff would not back him on this issue. The Obie Base could only work during summer and autumn and there was no base in Germany that had the facilities to do a two-hundred-hour overhaul in winter. It meant that a wartime British base would have to be reactivated and the C-54's would have to fly out of Germany.

The dinner came. General Stonebraker ate at his desk, Clint on the coffee table in front of the couch.

"You'll have to go to England, Clint. Some MATS people will be looking over bases. I have the old Burtonwood Base in mind. Let me know if we'll be able to get it into shape quick enough."

"When do I go, sir?"

"Well . . . you might as well take a day off tomorrow." He nibbled at his food and asked Clint how the cooperation with the British was shaping up. Clint said, no strain. The general knew the British would come through from the old CBI days. With joint American/British bases operating soon in Fassberg and Celle and running nothing but coal perhaps they could build up the precariously low reserves in Berlin.

Lieutenant Beaver knocked, entered. Stonebraker ran through his papers, studied the cartoon for the next day's *Task Force Times*. It depicted Airman Kimacyoyo (Kiss My Ass, Colonel, You're on Your Own) at a desk marked, DEPENDENTS HOUSING PROCUREMENT. An exploded cigar had blackened his face and the caption read: "I Told You it was a Thankless Job." Hiram snickered as he initialed an okay. The cartoon would burn up Buff Morgan.

He studied the incoming VIP list. Beaver persisted that one of the journalists was a "must see." There was a British Cabinet Minister to be escorted on an inspection of Y 80 and also a French general.

"Frigg the French. They're not doing a goddamned thing for the Airlift."

"They fly the flag in Berlin, sir, and we're intending to lay down an airport in their sector."

"Any more of your goddamned friends coming in here to interfere with this operation, Beaver?"

The next week Vice President Alben Barkley was due and Garry Moore was scheduled to put on a show at the requisitioned Opera House.

"Where the hell are the Howgozit figures?"

Beaver produced a slip of paper taken from the Control Center with figures listing by squadron the number of flights and total tonnage. It was a terrible day. They had only set down six hundred tons when the weather put the Lift out of business.

His face grew long. How do you whip the weather? He thanked Beaver quietly and dismissed him.

A phone call came on the red line from Chip Hansen in Berlin. Buff Morgan had taken the air-space beef to him. Stonebraker refused to back down; Hansen said he would try to smooth USAFE's ruffled feathers.

"Crusty, I just got the figures on the new airfield."

"How many barrels of asphalt?" Stonebraker asked quickly.

"Ten thousand."

Stonebraker grunted.

"And Crusty . . . the Magistrat appealed to Neal Hazzard today. The hospital inventories are dangerously low. We are going to have to get several thousand tons of emergency drugs and supplies in immediately." At last, Chip Hansen sent his regards to M.J.

Stonebraker set the phone down slowly. "We have to fly in ten thousand barrels of asphalt," he said to Clint.

Clint wanted to cry.

"What the hell, Clint. No matter how rough we have it, it's ten times rougher on those people in Berlin."

Stonebraker pulled himself out of his chair. He reeled back suddenly, falling against the wall, groaned from a terrible pain in his chest, sunk to his knees, then began to crawl back to his desk.

"General!"

"Clint . . . top . . . drawer . . ."

Clint found a box of nitroglycerin tablets. *Take One in Case of Attack.* He administered the pill, laid a cushion beneath his head, loosened his collar, and went back to the phone as the general writhed and gasped for breath.

"No . . . no . . . phone . . . lock . . . door . . ."

Clint wavered. The general's life hung in the balance, yet with pain-wracked effort it had the sound of an order. Clint set the receiver down, and locked both entrances.

The general groaned and broke into a cold sweat, and then it subsided. Clint wiped his face with a damp rag.

The general clutched his wrists. "You keep your mouth shut about this."

"It's not worth your life, General. We're not going to make it, anyhow."

"Goddamn you, Clint! Goddamn you! Don't let me ever hear you say that again."

CHAPTER SEVENTEEN

A flight surgeon, sworn to secrecy, left the general's suite after assuring M.J. and Clint that he was resting well.

Clint remained shaken and M.J. tried to comfort him. "His seizures come and go. It is something we have to live with and I made up my mind a long time ago we weren't going to live in fear."

"They had no right to call him back," Clint said.

"At first, I thought that. But it would have killed him quicker if they had left him behind."

"This mission burns out airplanes and breaks down men. Neither we nor the machines are meant to stand up under this kind of pounding."

"Then, Clint, the only way the general will survive is if he continues to believe it can be done."

Clint returned to his room at the Rose Hotel and was awake far into the night. Hiram Stonebraker, those G-5 people in Berlin, the flyers at Y 80, and the mechanics at Rhein/Mud made up for a lot of those whorehouses on Madison Avenue. He was glad now that he had come.

The next day was Sunday; he called M.J. to inquire.

"The general has gone to his office," she said.

"I'll be damned."

What a day! Clint looked around the street outside the Rose Hotel. His first day off and the sun was shining.

Stonebraker kept his staff housed in a cluster of requisitioned hotels diagonally across the Koch Brunnen Square from Headquarters. The plush Schwarzer Bock, Rose, and Palast held the top-ranking people. Lesser hotels scattered all over the city were requisitioned for junior officers and enlisted personnel.

Clint walked to the main exchange for toilet gear and cigarettes. Wiesbaden had been spared except for a single stray stick of bombs. In the heart of the city all the grandiose civic and commercial buildings had been requisitioned by the Air Force for USAFE and all those other offices and wings needed to run the tremendous air establishment. Beer halls had been converted into mess halls and the late-comer, the First Airlift Task Force, took a block on Taunusstrasse with shops and apartments and converted it into a makeshift command post.

Clint returned to the Rose, wondered what the hell to do. He went to the Bier Stube at the Palast, a congregation point for Airlift people. The Lift was back in full operation; no one was around this early. Might as well see a little of Wiesbaden, he thought, and strolled to the Wilhelmstrasse along a line of once elegant shops and still lovely sidewalk cafes.

Out of the immediate bailiwick of Headquarters Clint could see that the city was a crown jewel, with tradition and grandeur. It had a history as a spa dating back to Roman times, and was heavily patronized by the aristocracy and Rhineland industrialists.

He crossed the Wilhelmstrasse to the flower-studded colonnade, which began with a statue of Bismarck. On one side was the Opera House and on the other a park and fountains. As airmen and their girls passed him, he began to feel lonely.

Clint hummed, "Sunday in the Park." Christ, he hated Sunday in the park in New York; it was like a ghetto boxed in by sheer walls of high buildings.

He was drawn toward the end of the colonnade by the sound of the Air Force band playing a Sunday concert before the Kurhaus.

AQUIS MATTIACIS read the carved lettering above six columns supporting the domed roof of the Kurhaus. The original Roman name of the city and the site of the springs with curative powers held a building rumored to have been built by twenty-six millionaires each having put up huge sums.

The Kurhaus had been requisitioned as the Eagle Club to serve American families. Ping-pong tables stood on marble floors and a soda fountain was installed in one end of a dining room. The German books were gone from the oriental-carpeted library and replaced by English tomes.

Behind the Kurhaus stretched a magnificent park of lakes and little bridges and riding trails and tennis courts, once patronized by arrogant monocled barons, slash-cheeked steel kings, and their hourglass-figured ladies.

He could hear the band playing "William Tell Overture." Why the hell did all bands play "William Tell Overture"? Maybe it wasn't a good idea having a day off.

Clint caught a taxi and drove up the hills to the Neroberg Officers' Club. The great hotel was in a lush setting, a forest on a foothill of the Taunus Mountains looking down on Wiesbaden and the Rhine. Clint sat at the bar, listened to Egon at the piano.

There were mostly USAFE people around and even though they didn't give a damn what was happening at Erding and Rhein/Main and Obie they could not escape the Airlift. Along with the gossip and complaints of how tough it was to live off the German economy, there was tension. There was a lot of talk about wanting to get dependents out of Germany before the Berlin thing blew up.

Clint looked around in growing desperation for a face from Headquarters. He bought Egon a round; the German played, "This Love of Mine," which he and Judy thought of as "their" song.

He bummed a bathing suit, took a drive down to the Opelbad, a luxurious pool set in the woods and vineyards over the city. He studied the women at pool side with a practiced eye, but none of them was as voluptuous as Judy. . . . Screw it, Clint thought.

"Where to, sir?" the taxi driver asked.

"Airlift Headquarters."

Clint sighed with relief as he entered Taunusstrasse 11. He went first to the Control Center and chatted with the duty control officer, who gave him a capsule briefing, then went upstairs to Operations and made his own hasty calculation that they would set down three thousand tons.

He went to his office, put the hot plate on for coffee, took off his blouse, and began to read over the preliminary agreement drawn up with the British for the joint operation of bases at Celle and Fassberg. He dialed General Stonebraker's office.

The general's secretary answered.

"This is Colonel Loveless. General in for me?"

"Hello."

"Clint Loveless, sir."

"Yes, Clint."

"How's your . . . indigestion, sir."

"Fine."

"I'm working over the agreement with the British. I'll try to have it on your desk tomorrow afternoon before I shove off for Burtonwood."

"I thought I gave you the day off."

"You did, sir. I don't know what to do with a day off."

"Well, long as you're here, have the agreement on my desk this afternoon."

Clint clenched his teeth for a long second. "Yes, sir. By the way, General, did you see the memo on how the British are getting the sparrows off the Gatow airfield?"

"No."

"Seems like one of their airmen used to train falcons for hunting. They're sending some over from England. Say they'll have those sparrows out of there in an hour."

"Why the hell didn't we think of that!"

"Guess we're not too much on falconry."

"By the way, Clint, M.J. is having cocktails and dinner for some of the staff and wives who are particularly angry at me. Why don't you join us at the dining room at seven."

"Sounds like a winner, sir."

Clint dug into the agreement, now happy he had returned to work. His phone rang.

"Colonel Loveless."

"Suh, this is Sergeant Bufford," a Texan drawled. "I'm here at Rhein/Main at the Lost Wives' Club. We got us a Mrs. Clinton Loveless who came in by commercial aircraft. We reckon she belongs to you, suh."

Clint blinked with disbelief. "Has she got two pale kids with her?"

"Ma'am, you got two pale kids?"

Judy took the phone. "Clinton. Will you *please* come over and get us."

"I'll be damned."

The general grumbled that the agreement would be late reaching his desk, but nevertheless gave Clint his own staff car and had his aide contact the hotel to arrange a suite.

Judy didn't know for sure if she had done the right thing by coming to Germany without telling him, but when they embraced and he sniffled while he hugged the children, she knew it was all right.

Tony and Lynn were deposited in a bathtub the size of a small swimming pool while the travel-weary wife collapsed with a martini.

Clint got the children fed. They were terribly impressed by the waiters in formal suits who scraped and bowed and carried on with a great deal of pomp. He unpacked and got them off to sleep.

Judy revived herself and came back to the parlor looking, feeling, smelling all woman and ready for love, but Clint was pensive.

"You aren't happy I came."

"We have a lot of rivers to cross." There hadn't been an exchange of letters for six weeks, except the one Clint had gotten from Milt Schuster. Judy had been to see him about a divorce.

"I was hurt and angry when I went to see Milt. And when the anger passed I was just plain lonely. Clint, doesn't the fact that I came here say that things will be your way. I guess I just don't like an empty bed."

"You'd have no trouble filling it with someone who shares your ideas about getting up in the world."

"I can't, Clint . . ." He stood and turned away from her. "I'll make it up to you, honey," she said. "We'll get a little house here . . ."

"Dammit, Judy. You don't just walk down the street and get a little house."

"What are you trying to say?"

"In the past six weeks I've been more alive than at any time in my life. We have an airman at a base outside Munich who figured out how to renew spark plugs for twenty-one cents a copy. New, they cost sixty

cents. We use fifty thousand of them a month. A young officer in Headquarters across the street has worked out a load calculator that helps
us carry up to five hundred more pounds of cargo on every flight. We
have displaced persons who can unload ten tons of coal in twenty minutes. We've done all kinds of miracles here . . . but we're whipped. I
know my girl Judy. She doesn't like a loser."

"Clint, I love you. I've just started to learn why and how much.
There's a part in this for me too."

He nodded and began to pour his heart out and Judy knew what
she had to do. She could take him away from this awesome thing for
little snatches at a time, brace him up, send him back to battle.

"That nasty old man is the greatest person I have ever known . . .
and he's going to die. He's got a time bomb in his chest."

After a while Clint was happy that she had come. He stretched out
on the bed. It was kind of like the early days when they scratched to
make ends meet; she was so wonderful then.

"Let's make a baby," Judy purred.

Clint agreed.

The phone rang.

"Clint, get over to Headquarters right away."

Clint didn't bother to ask what particular problem was annoying the
general.

"And we'll be flying out to Berlin tomorrow in the second time bloc
at Rhein/Main."

"What about my trip to England, sir?"

"It will have to hold. They got the ground-controlled approach
equipment in operation at Tempelhof. The weather is closing in again.
We've got to look it over and break that bottleneck."

"Be right over, General." He set down the phone and looked at his
astonished wife. "That's the name of the game," he said.

CHAPTER EIGHTEEN

It rained a deluge. Rhein/Mud was a lake.

Miserable teams of displaced persons and drenched airmen prepared
the line of Skymasters for flight. Hiram Stonebraker's car, bearing a

limp wet flag with two stars, stopped before Operations, 7497th Airlift Wing, as bloc time approached.

On sight of the general, the sign regarding Ball Breaker's Feed and
Coal Bin was stashed away for display at a more appropriate time.

Stonebraker, shaking the water off him, entered the chief pilot's
office.

"You going to run us up to Berlin, Captain?"

"Yes, sir," Scott Davidson answered. "We'll be number fifteen in the
bloc."

"When you reach Tempelhof Airways, tell them I want to try out
a ground-controlled approach."

Scott studied the wicked downpour outside. "Couldn't of picked a
better day for it, General."

"See you at the briefing. By the way, Scott, getting enough flying
time?"

"Plenty . . . sir."

As Stonebraker stepped back into the hall two pilots were reading
the *Task Force Times* and laughing. The cartoon depicted the weatherman having hung himself and two pilots on seeing the body commented, "Oh-oh, the weather's bad again."

Thirty crews drawn from a cross section of squadrons filed into the
briefing room. The weatherman stood before his map.

"The European Continent is under the influence of a deep low off
the British Isles causing a prognosis of bad flying weather for the next
forty-eight hours."

A grumble around the room.

"Ceilings will vary from zero to five hundred feet, visibility from
zero to one and a half miles."

"Lovely," Nick Papas mumbled.

"A tight pressure gradient causing strong winds aloft from the northwest, three hundred fifteen degrees. Winds will be forty to forty-five
knots."

It would be a long day.

Scott Davidson stood before the men and briefed them on new
VHF radio installations and beacons in the center corridor, then gave
a lecture about being fed up with the numerous little accidents on the
ground which were causing great time waste. He spoke of the tricks
of taxiing heavy loads, executing turns, and braking carefully to handle
the delicate nose wheel of the C-54.

As Hiram Stonebraker heard him speak he felt smug about his hunch on Davidson. Scott had been able to charm commanders' wives, con and duck responsibility in the past, but was quick to recognize that with Stonebraker his luck had run out, temporarily. Then, keeping the big birds in the corridor and getting tons into Berlin became like wartime all over. The mudhole of a base, the urgency of the Airlift, and the endless challenges were turning him into a fine chief pilot. Scott ended the briefing by repeating his own dislike of cigar smoking in the cabin . . . for Nick's benefit.

Stonebraker and Clint Loveless waited in the staff car near the craft as the rain pelted down on the team of a dozen Polish displaced persons and the American sergeant in charge of the loading. They became drenched beneath their ponchos as they filled the ship with sacks of coal, barrels of asphalt, and married the load to distribute it evenly with a number of lightly packaged cartons marked DANISH CHEESE.

Stan Kitchek and Flight Engineer Nick Papas walked around in ankle-deep water in the pre-takeoff inspection while Scott signed his clearance forms at Operations and picked up a flight kit.

The steps were rolled up and they all boarded. Clint sat in a jump seat installed in the rear of the flight deck. The general stood behind the copilot. Up and down the hardstands trucks drove off, stairs rolled away, wheel chocks were pulled, engines coughed to life, and the line of birds started taxiing carefully on the wet taxiways.

As bloc time approached Scott watched as the tower released the first plane. As its engines revved to takeoff power, sheets of water gushed off the wings. It sloshed down the runway leaving a high spray and went nearly to the end before becoming airborne. It disappeared immediately into the weather.

Stan intoned the check list.

"Nose wheel."

"Centered."

"Parking brake."

"Set."

At a three-minute interval the second bird disappeared into the gray overcast.

"RPM."

"Eight hundred."

"Fuel pressure."

"Seventeen."

"Oil pressure."

"Seventy."

Nick told Clint Loveless to buckle in because it was going to be rough. Clint hated it. Nick plugged into a jack and gave the general a pair of ear phones.

"Main tanks."

"On."

"Booster pumps."

"High."

"Cowl flaps."

"Trail."

"Generators."

"On."

Nick pushed against the windows to make certain they were locked. They were, but they were leaking.

By the time Scott was nearing the end of the runway he could see that rain had slowed the interval of takeoff.

Stan called the tower.

"This is Big Easy Fifteen calling Rhein/Main Tower for taxi and takeoff instructions."

"Big Easy Fifteen, this is Rhein/Main Tower. Bloc time is changed to zero seven three seven. Take off on runway two six. New altimeter setting is three zero, zero, zero. The time is zero seven three six, zulu."

"Roger."

"Big Easy Fifteen, clear to line up and hold."

Scott coaxed the bird into position at the end of the runway.

"Big Easy Fifteen, this is Rhein/Main Tower. You are cleared for takeoff."

As he pushed the throttle forward the multithousand-horsepower in the Pratt Whitney Engines leaped to life. He felt the strain of the great engines plowing through the water and he knew he would need most of the runway.

Stan Kitchek called out the speed. At eighty Scott eased the yoke back, tilting the nose wheel off the ground.

"Ninety, ninety-five."

Scott pulled the yoke and the bird lifted cleanly into the sky and was in an instant submerged in the weather and flying on instruments. He flew to nine hundred feet, banked south toward the Darmstadt Beacon, which his copilot had tuned in, crossed it, began his climb.

The ship bucked violently. Clint Loveless broke into a sweat. Stan
asked for and received clearance to go up to six thousand feet. Scott
fought the yoke as the turbulence threw the bird around, trying to gain
altitude for the forty-five-mile run to the Fulda Range.

Over the Fulda Range on the edge of the Southern corridor the
planes in the bloc checked their time with each other and adjusted
their speed to set up the precision chain into Berlin.

He turned to a heading of 057 degrees and subtracted 10 degrees
to crab into the wind, which was hitting from the northwest at forty
knots and pushing him to the right of course.

Clinton Loveless wanted to die. He tried to think of other things to
take his mind off his misery . . . about getting back to Wiesbaden and
making love to Judy. Even that didn't help.

Nick Papas sipped coffee from a thermos, offered some to the general.
He thought that two flights to Berlin today would be rougher than
hell. There was a big card game on tonight in Frankfurt . . . with luck
he would make it.

Scott and Stan were too busy keeping the bird on course to think
about anything.

Hiram Stonebraker felt it was a perfect day to try out the new ground-
controlled approach system up at Tempelhof. After they landed, he
planned to watch the GCA system land the next bloc from Wiesbaden,
and then spend the day in Berlin with Clint on a number of problems.

Hiram Stonebraker had few flyers' superstitions. One of them was
that on each of his twenty flights to Berlin, he flew with Scott Davidson.

They reached the midway point in the 211-mile run in the corridor.
While radio contact would be at a minimum, the general tapped Stan
on the shoulder, took the copilot seat, and switched on the intercom.

"Good day to try out the GCA."

"Yes, sir . . . a lulu." Scott nodded over his own shoulder. "Looks
like Colonel Loveless'd rather be somewhere else."

Clint's chalky lips seemed to mumble prayer between the pitches
and rolls.

"He's a good engineer. He should know how safe these birds are."
Stonebraker produced a long cigar. "Mind if I smoke, Captain?"

Scott hated cigar smoke in the cabin. Nick, who always chewed an
unlit cigar, shoved a light to the general's, then lit his own cigar with
a sigh of comfort. Scott grimaced.

The general saw the sweat glisten from Scott's forehead from battling the yoke. He could almost feel the ache in the flyer's hands and shoulders. The boy was doing a beautiful job of flying.

"How about that GCA landing, Scott. Can you handle it?" the general prodded.

"You can bet on it, General."

Scott crabbed into the wind again. "In weather like this, General, I'd like to see us carry a heavier load of gas."

Stonebraker pondered. The C-54's held large wing tanks. Clint and the production people had worked it so that in the short hauls of the Lift they would carry only 20 per cent capacity. This would make weight for greater cargo loads. At six pounds a gallon, this meant many hundreds more pounds of cargo.

"What's your reckoning, Scott?"

"In this kind of turbulence, the fuel splashes around violently. It's causing the tanks to split."

Gas leaks were a nemesis and they were having trouble sealing the tanks. He made a note to look into Scott's suggestion.

Scott flicked on Tempelhof. "This is Big Easy Fifteen calling Tempelhof. I want a center-line check, over."

"This is Tempelhof calling Big Easy Fifteen. You are one half mile right of center line."

Pretty slick, Stonebraker thought, pretty slick flying.

In Berlin the radarscopes, which could look through clouds and obstructions, were being blanked out by the rain pattern and were losing airplanes.

Inside the radar shack, the NCO made a frantic call for the officer in charge.

"Sir, we've picked up two planes from Gatow."

"What altitude?"

"Six thousand feet. They're drifting into the Rhein/Main stream."

The officer took the microphone. "Tempelhof to all Big Easy craft. Raise your altitude one thousand feet." Hiram Stonebraker detected the anxiety in the transmission.

In Tempelhof a call to Gatow confirmed that a bloc of British Yorks had stacked for landings and two of the craft had been blown out of their holding pattern toward Tempelhof.

The ground-controlled approach system was given an auspicious inauguration as the first three craft were "talked down" through the blinding storm.

Ground-controlled approach talked to Big Easy Four and started to lower him over Berlin in a large square pattern. Scott knew a relatively inexperienced pilot was at the yoke of Four.

When he missed his approach and was started around again it caused a chain reaction. As the Rhein/Main bloc hit the Planter Beacon they had to hastily climb into holding patterns.

Scott took his ship up to twelve thousand feet over the beacon and the crew broke out oxygen masks. The planes in back of him were forced to climb up to twenty thousand. It was like taking a long train of railroad cars and suddenly stacking them skyward, end to end. Scott looked out of the corner of his eye as the general's anger grew.

As the planes stacked higher the chatter over the radio became greater, breaking down the rigid discipline needed. In the radar shack, a new emergency arose as Big Easy Twenty-nine drifted clear out of the corridor.

The bloc was now like a tall column of cyclone-blown planes moving in a vicious circle. Across town the British were having the same trouble over Gatow.

Ground-controlled approach tried to nurse Big Easy Four down a second time but the inexperienced pilot missed his second approach by coming down the runway too fast.

The planes pushed up higher. A bloc would be following from Wiesbaden soon and breathing down their necks to make the situation impossible. Another plane from Gatow drifted toward Tempelhof. Communications collapsed.

Hiram Stonebraker knew that they would not be able to prevent a mid-air collision or a crash much longer.

"That's enough of this crap for one day," he mumbled. He picked up the microphone. "Clear the air! This is General Stonebraker in Big Easy Fifteen! This is a direct order! All craft will be diverted to their home bases immediately! Suggest the same procedure to Gatow."

A shattering silence followed. Their hearts sank as Tempelhof dispatched them one by one back to the zone.

Igor Karlovy had arrived early at the Berlin Air Safety Center so he could follow the progress of the day when he learned of the bad weather. He monitored the American and British confusion, and heard them sent home in defeat. He smiled inwardly as his prediction came to pass.

CHAPTER NINETEEN

Clint was so worried that the general would have a seizure on the return trip that he forgot how rough the flight was. But the general was amazingly calm. The worst had happened. While the young hands floundered, his years of experience averted a crash. On the return to Rhein/Main he sat at Nick's seat with a pad and pencil searching for an illusive bit of magic.

Clint Loveless was down as he had never been down. He hardly heard Judy's cry for joy when he returned to the hotel. As luck, or someone else's misfortune had it, an Army colonel from Camp Perry had broken with his wife and their house became available. Judy had seen it. It was a lovely six-room place on Gustav Freytag Strasse in a beautiful area where most of the American families lived in requisitioned houses.

What she did not know was that Hiram Stonebraker had threatened the housing procurement officer's life if he failed to find a place for the Loveless family.

"What the hell's the difference," Clint said sourly, "we'll probably be going back to the States soon. The Lift was finished today."

"Oh, Clint . . . I'm so sorry. The general?"

"He still refuses to believe it."

A mantle of gloom fell on Airlift Headquarters as the Tonnage Board in the Control Center read ZERO for the second straight day as the weather closed Berlin down.

Hiram Stonebraker stayed in his suite and studied. The Lift in basic form was two one-way streets into Berlin, the North and South corridors. A single one-way street, the Central corridor, was used to leave Berlin.

Similar makes of aircraft flew in bloc times at the same speed and staggered altitudes of five hundred feet. Precision flying in the narrow air lanes through absolute power settings had become a science. It all narrowed down to a single bottleneck—the air over Berlin.

The ground-controlled approach system had put down the first three planes of the bloc cleanly. When Big Easy Four made two missed approaches it caused the rest of the bloc behind him to stack . . . and then the breakdown in communications, radar control, holding patterns. The key lay somewhere in the behavior of Big Easy Four. What was it? What was it? What was it?

M.J. broke up Hiram's two-day meditation. There was to be a cocktail party and dinner to honor the arrival of his British counterpart, Air Commodore Rodman, for the formal signing of the joint Bases Agreement at Celle and Fassberg. He sent his chief of staff to meet the Commodore and his party at Y 80 and took him to the Schwarzer Bock Hotel.

Stonebraker stopped by at Rodman's suite later and apologized for not meeting him earlier.

Rodman understood. "Bloody nuisance, this weather," he said in the understatement of the year.

On the main floor of the Schwarzer Bock was a room rebuilt intact from a fifteenth-century castle. The general's cocktail parties were held here, and on such occasions he baffled his staff by making a lie of the terrible stories about him. He was the epitome of charm to the ladies and his British guests.

Over cocktails:

Judy Loveless gushed with joy over the new house. M.J. would be happy to go hunting for household wares.

Jo Ann Sindlinger, wife of the chief of staff, a tall, gravel-throated, happy Texan, gave Judy the word on where she might obtain a German maid. "They work for little more than room and board, you know."

Clint and Group Commander Dudley speculated about the Burtonwood Base. Clint didn't think that the base would be able to handle more than five craft a day on the two-hundred-hour overhaul.

Chief of Staff Sindlinger and Group Captain Cady were pleased with the way American/British cooperation was shaping up.

Sid Swing, the logistics chief, talked to Lieutenant Colonel Mendoza, the maintenance chief, and Ben Scudder, the chief communicator, about changing the VHF crystals at Erding and they told Squadron Leader Nevins they wanted to study the British Eureka/Rebecca radar systems more closely.

Sid's wife, Mary, was flirting with a British officer, as usual.

Ann Mendoza and Sue Scudder complained about the overcrowd
ing at the high school.

Lou Edmonds told Chief Pilot Matt Beck the weather might clear.

Sarah Beck told Betty Edmonds there was a crystal factory at Neu-
Isenburg that cut glass to your own pattern, was dirt cheap, and they
made a date to drive over.

Air Commodore Rodman said he had landed a twenty-two pound
salmon in Scotland on twelve-pound line. Hiram reckoned that the
best battle, pound for pound, was with the Chinook salmon and invited the Commodore to come to Malibu some day when the albacore
were running.

Dinner was served. As the first course arrived, Hiram Stonebraker
stood up suddenly. "Commodore. Would you ask your people to adjourn
immediately to the next room?"

The Englishman looked baffled.

"Ladies, will you excuse us?" Hiram said. "Gentlemen, please."

Those who knew Hiram Stonebraker were not surprised at the sudden conference call. He shut the door, then had a tablecloth pinned
on the wall. "Gentlemen. I have just solved the way to end the stacks
over Berlin."

They were all stunned.

He drew a diagram of the flow of the air bridge: planes following
each other at three-minute intervals to the Planter Beacon on the first
approach leg at Tempelhof.

"Here is the new difference. There will be no more stacking in case
of weather. If a plane misses his approach or for any reason cannot
land he is to return to his home base in the Center corridor and come
back in the next bloc."

If Big Easy Four had been sent back after his first attempt during
the fiasco, there would have been no stack over Berlin!

It was so utterly simple, but so utterly perfect!

"We will not only fly to Berlin in three-minute intervals, we will land
in three-minute intervals. The rhythm will not be broken by a missed
approach. The craft will return to base and the beat . . . beat . . . beat
will continue behind him."

For a moment no one moved, scarcely breathed.

"He's got it," sputtered Air Commodore Rodman.

"Why in the hell didn't we think of this earlier?" Stonebraker admonished himself. "Well . . . let's return to the ladies."

Born from the fiasco of Blue Monday and Black Tuesday, Hiram
Stonebraker had found the magic key to convert disaster into victory.
TO ALL AIRLIFT STATIONS: IN CASE OF MISSED APPROACH, AIRCRAFT IS
TO BE DIVERTED TO HOME BASE THROUGH CENTER CORRIDOR AND RE-
TURNED ON NEXT BLOC. UNDER NO CIRCUMSTANCES WILL AIRCRAFT
BE ALLOWED TO STACK. STONEBRAKER.

For the first time in the history of aviation the ancient ritual of stacking and holding patterns was eliminated and there was the feeling for
the first time that the Airlift could succeed.

In a matter of days the tonnage rose from three thousand to thirty-
five hundred tons . . . to four thousand tons . . . and then the daily
goal of forty-five hundred tons was reached. It was reached on a
stormy day during which ground-controlled approach talked down 80
per cent of the flights.

The joint British and American bases at Fassberg and Celle went into
operation with the arrival of more Skymasters. The daily tonnage went
over five thousand! The inevitable merger of forces came into being.
As in war, the old Allies combined in peace with Hiram Stonebraker
commander and Air Commodore Rodman vice commander of COM-
BINED AIRLIFT TASK FORCE.

The air bridge roared on day and night, and now the beat . . . beat
. . . beat . . . was that of a giant metronome, and with each beat another ten tons was transfused into the city of Berlin.

The engineers and the Berliners labored in a fury to complete the
third airfield at Tegel. Day . . . night . . . day . . . night . . . beat
. . . beat . . . beat . . . ten tons . . . ten tons . . . ten tons.

Although the miracle had come within grasp for the first time, the
greatest single challenge still lay ahead, for soon they would face that
long time ally of the Russians . . . General winter.

CHAPTER TWENTY

"How the devil did you get here?" Sean asked.

"Lil Blessing drove me over," Ernestine said. "Well . . . do you ask
me in?"

Sean held the door of his flat open, awkwardly.

"So this is your sanctum." It was a lovely flat, of course. The occupation forces took the best. "Well, aren't you glad to see me?"

"I wasn't prepared for an invasion."

"Look," she said, reaching into a shopping bag like those carried by all Berlin women. She produced two steaks.

"Where the hell did you get those?"

"Black market."

"You, in particular, with your uncle's name should never go to the black market," he lectured.

"Oh, stop it, Sean. Lil Blessing gave them to me. She said I could find my way to your heart with these, but you don't have one."

"Ernestine Falkenstein, look at me. I said, look at me. Are you tipsy?"

"Poo-poo-poo."

"You've been drinking."

"Poo-poo-poo. Just enough to have the courage to storm into your fortress."

Sean knew he must relent or he would have a bawling female on his hands. "Okay, there's the kitchen. Get busy. I'm starved."

Ernestine heaved a sigh of dismay. "Oh dear, I thought you would say that. Oh Sean, I studied so hard to be a lawyer I just never learned to cook. I'll just ruin the steaks and you'll never see me again."

"Well now, didn't you and your great friend Lil Blessing prepare for such a contingency?"

"You might just offer me a drink, you know."

He found the mildest liquor in the cabinet, sherry. She sipped, breathed contentedly, set the glass down. "I made reservations for us at Humperdink's. It is a fine restaurant, even though it happens to be in the Russian Sector. Uncle and I eat there often. Franz said he would personally attend to the steaks."

"You've got yourself a date. Stay away from the booze and I'll make myself dashing."

As he left the room, Ernestine walked to his desk and looked at the pictures of his brothers and his father.

Humperdink's, about the only building on Gernerstrasse not flattened, was a large house converted into one big room broken into paneled booths. The walls and crannies held boar and stag heads, beer mugs from the Middle Ages, Dresden figurines, and tapestries.

Lothar, an elderly blind man, played the zither at the entrance of the candlelit room. Actually his name was not Lothar, nor was he blind. As a former SS officer, the disguise proved excellent to keep him out of the hands of the justice seekers.

"Herr Oberst," Franz said bowing profusely again and again. "An honor, sir."

He took the steaks, swore to do them justice, escorted the two to a choice booth already enhanced with the presence of a bottle of chilled champagne. The room was warm and sentimental. Ernestine sipped, then sang to the zither melody. Sean, she thought to herself, have you grown tired of me before you even let yourself know me? Oh, you lion among men. It was growing painful now and she knew she could not show him. She longed to say, "*Ich liebe dich.*"

"What are you thinking about?" he asked.

"Nothing in particular."

Franz ushered three German couples to a large table in the center of the floor. She recognized her brother Gerd among them.

"Oh dear," she said, "I wanted tonight to be perfect. My brother has just come in and can be quite unpleasant."

Sean smiled. "I will be the epitome of restraint and charm," he promised.

Gerd nodded to Ernestine and she to him. He excused himself from his table and made his way to their booth. Sean arose.

"Hello, Erna."

"Gerd. Colonel O'Sullivan, my brother Gerd."

Sean shook his hand and asked him to have a seat.

"Only for a moment," Gerd protested. "My partners and our friends are having a small celebration."

Gerd's inference was plain to Ernestine. He was saying, see, Germans also can enjoy Humperdink's and there are still decent German girls left who prefer the company of German men.

On the other hand, Gerd could not say he was unhappy that his sister was in the company of a known Ami officer. He felt strongly that Germany's future lay in an alliance with the Amis and what better way to cement an alliance?

Erna and Uncle Ulrich made him look good. In fact, he had ditched his old Nazi friends and joined the Democratic Party. It was good business.

"Mother and Father?" Erna asked.

"Both well. Father devotes full time to managing our Wilmersdorf Branch. And our sainted sister?"

"Hilde has made a full recovery, thank you."

"She is in Wiesbaden, is she not?"

"Yes."

Sean felt the stilted air between them, was sorry for Ernestine's discomfort, and glad when Gerd turned the conversation to him.

"You have heard the news, Herr Oberst. Your people and the British landed nearly five thousand tons again today . . . and in such weather. I never cease to marvel at it."

"I've had the pleasure of dealing with the Airlift people. They are an extraordinary bunch."

"I should say so. If you land much more coal, you'll drive me out of business."

Gerd was trying to be pleasant. It was a bad joke. He was reaping a fortune from the blockade by the manufacture and sale of an ersatz coal called Blockade Briquets composed of compressed sawdust, dried grass, and low-grade peat. It smoked and it stank, but it did burn after a fashion and was desperately sought to augment the home supply.

Gerd accepted a glass of champagne from Sean. Decent chap, he thought. Held it up to toast. "Prosit. May we never be enemies again."

Sean did not answer.

"So here we are," Gerd said, "former enemies sitting as friends in the Russian Sector."

"In America we say that politics makes strange bedfellows."

Gerd smarted from the insult. "Very strange bedfellows," he said, looking directly at Erna.

Sean caught her pleading look and remembered his promise of restraint.

"Yesterday," Gerd continued pensively, "your airplanes brought bombs. Today the crowds stand and watch Tempelhof with a holy vigil." He deliberately offered Sean a very expensive cigar, lit his own. "I used to be an antiaircraft gunner. It is still strange for me to look up into the sky without trying to shoot you down."

Sean flung the champagne from his glass into Gerd's face.

"What the devil!"

"Gerd! His brother was a pilot."

Gerd stiffened, waved his friends back. A small smile formed at the corners of his mouth. "Forgive me, Herr Oberst."

The zither player picked up a melody quickly.

"Let's get out of here," Sean said.

"Sean," she said outside, "he did not know."

But he did not hear. There was not another word exchanged until he stopped the car before her uncle's flat.

"Good night. Please see yourself in."

"I cannot let you go away like this."

His fists clenched and his face contorted with rage and confusion. And he could hold it no longer. He buried his hands in his face . . . lost . . . alone. She tried to touch him but he became rigid.

"Oh God," she cried, "I cannot stand it any longer. Please take me to your room . . . please, Sean . . . please."

I will drink the bitterness from you . . . I will give you love for every hour you have known hate . . . I will overcome all of that in us that you despise . . . my love is strong enough to do this . . . yes, my love is strong enough.

German woman! I am making love to a German woman! Me! Me and that Nazi! In the dark blurs and whirls he could hear the roar of engines over the rooftop . . . the static of the radio, its station off the air. . . . In an instant of realization he was being devoured with a desire to snap her neck . . . and it was like no love he had ever known. The fury to love and to kill at the same instant transcended all things.

And then he lay in disgust at his weakness in a strength-ebbed silent oratory of self-condemnation.

Ernestine was tight beside him.

It is done, she thought. You are my man now, Sean. . . . You are my man.

Ernestine sat in the deep window frame as the daylight came. There was little to be seen outside; the fog swirled angrily close to the ground.

Overhead there was the unabated thunder of the engines on the first leg of the approach to Tempelhof. Ernestine walked back to the bed and brushed his hair with her fingers. There was sadness in his eyes.

"I did not know I could ever listen to the sound of engines again without terror. Now, they are like a lullaby, like the sound of waves coming in to the shore."

She lay beside him and he folded his arms about her without words.

There were a few remarks while they dressed, as he made an effort to spare her pain.

"Hello, Uncle Ulrich . . . I am sorry I did not phone . . . I was with a girl friend and it became late. . . . Yes . . . I am going straight to work."

Sean kept thinking that it would be best if they got out before his housekeeper arrived. She was the niece of Ulrich Falkenstein and had to be spared an indignity, but he could say nothing.

They drove away, silently.

"If you will leave me off at the Tempelhof Station, I can take a train to work."

He agreed, it would not look right to pull up in front of her building.

The usual morning crowd of Berliners was clustered near the station watching the planes take off and land, take off and land, take off and land.

This morning the birds groped through a heavy fog under ground-controlled approach. The Berliners gasped with each new landing as they caught sight of the craft at the last instant, bursting through the white shroud.

He stopped the car. There was an awkward moment of not knowing how to say good-by. Ernestine knew enough to go with dignity. She swung the car door open.

Sean grabbed her wrist. "I don't know what to say."

"Will it make you happier to know that I knew you wanted to murder me last night. If that is what you would have chosen to do, I would not have uttered a protest. If I cannot bring you life, I am yours to kill."

"I've got to see you again," he said, not believing his own words. "To-night."

"*Aufwiedersehen.*" She ran quickly out of the car and he watched her disappear up the steps of the elevated. The crowd on the platform screamed at the same instant. A Skymaster dropped almost on top of them!

The ground quaked as the plane smashed into the side of a building several blocks away, and after an ear-splitting blast, glass, brick, and pieces of the craft spewed . . . a belch of flame. There was a terrible second of silence . . . then the explosion!

Sean was swept into the midst of a mass of running humanity. The plane and the building were demolished. All that was left was a section of the tail, the American Star, and MATS, ALASKA.

There was a sorrowful wail of the horns of ambulances and police cars over the screams of horror. Sean O'Sullivan was transfixed by the leaping flames of the pyre.

"Tim! Tim! Tim!"

"Herr Oberst!" a German policeman begged, "Herr Oberst, do not go closer! They are all dead!"

"My brother is in that plane! Let go of me you goddamned fool!"

"Herr Oberst! Someone . . . please help me with him . . . he will be killed."

Sean was dragged away from the scene and held until he calmed. He was brought back to reality by the voice of the Lorelei . . . the voice of Ernestine!

"Sean! Come to your senses!"

He looked up at her. She was framed by the flames and the wreckage. His eyes were black with a hatred she had never seen.

CHAPTER TWENTY-ONE

"General Hansen," Ulrich Falkenstein said, "I must tell you how deeply my own grief runs."

"It was bound to happen," Hansen replied.

The two had always had misgivings. At this moment the German feared the city's freedom was being talked away in a four-power conference in Moscow. Hansen retained his universal doubts about the Germans. Yet, the death of the three American flyers had a shocking and sobering reaction. The Berliners thought that perhaps the alliance with the Americans was not so weak after all. And for the Americans it was a time of awakening to an understanding of the depth of their commitment.

Hansen's aide said that the official party was formed in the outer office. Soon a line of cars bore the mourners to the place of the wreckage.

The scene was that of a stilled battlefield. The debris had been taken away, the blood washed from sight, the agony of the inferno stilled, and what remained was a new shrine . . . a tail section of a Skymaster welded into a mangled wall, a torch marking the spot of impact.

Long orderly lines of thousands of Berliners passed by slowly and other hundreds knelt in the streets and prayed. Thousands of flowers were brought and a great sense of tragedy swept the city.

Sean O'Sullivan remembered another line of Germans a few years back whom he had ordered to tour a concentration camp. They, too, wept openly, but for reasons strangely removed.

Hanna Kirchner, weary from the burden of office under feuding masters, lay a wreath in the name of the city and said what was expected. "We will never forget this. It will give us the courage to survive."

As the photographers recorded the scene, the sound of the engines over them continued in three-minute intervals.

Andrew Jackson Hansen returned to his car, feeling that he had passed a Rubicon. A strange kinship had been born and for the first time he realized that the people of Berlin would hold.

Sean returned from the ceremonies pale. He closed the door of his flat behind him and unbuttoned his blouse slowly, then saw Ernestine standing before the fireplace.

"Your maid let me in," she said.

Sean nodded, hung up his blouse. The iron man who had played at God was still puzzled by his own mortal weakness.

"Do you know what happens to a man who worships hate as you do?" she asked.

"I love you, Ernestine," Sean whispered, "and I hate myself for loving you."

"Our only chance, Sean, is finding a great love that can overcome all else."

"We're just people, not gods," he said. "We're asking too much."

"Look at me, Sean. I am a German woman. Nothing can change that. You are my man. Nothing can change that, either. Whatever will happen now will happen. I can never leave you."

He held her and was overcome with a longing for peace, for the voices to be stilled. And for a moment, he was happy.

CHAPTER TWENTY-TWO

My Dearest Sister Ernestine:

So, you are in love! Knowing you, it must be serious. I wish I were there to hold your hands and dry your eyes when things go badly.

For me, the news is so sad. Colonel Smith has gotten his orders to transfer to Japan. The Americans seem to be sent everywhere in the world. I have grown to love their children as my own and I don't know how I'll be able to get along without them. Oh, Erna if I could only have my own children without the trouble of a man.

I cannot go back to the Brueckner home. They are barely making ends meet so I will try to find another American family to work in. Colonel and Mrs. Smith promise a high recommendation.

Wiesbaden is consumed with the Air Bridge and you know how flyers behave away from their airplanes. I rarely leave the house except once a week to see the cinema or to visit the Brueckners. The Americans have brought many new films over. Actually, they are old ones, but we could not see them during the Nazi days.

I close now. Be careful with your heart, Erna.

Your loving sister,

Hilde

The first months after her escape from Berlin, Hildegaard Falkenstein lived in an ennui. The Brueckners, an elderly couple who were dear friends of Uncle Ulrich, took her in with open arms; they had lost two sons in the war and their house was empty.

For a time they existed well. This was fortunate, for Hildegaard needed much care until she mended and was able to walk again in the sun. When she came to her senses she behaved like ages of harlots before her. Redemption became a fanatical cause. Her brush with near doom left a lasting mark.

Hildegaard became like a daughter to the Brueckners, changing her past ways to an unselfish giving of which she had never before been capable.

After a while the Amis requisitioned the Brueckner house, forcing her and the old couple to move up into the hills into cramped quarters with the rest of the Germans. Then Herr Brueckner became ill. Hildegaard realized that both Ernestine and her Uncle Ulrich had been contributing to her support beyond their means. For the first time she wanted to find work, but there was little she was trained to do.

She found a job as a shopgirl, but it was meager compensation. Later she became a waitress in a cafe on the Wilhelmstrasse where the Ami airmen were generous with their tips. Hilde was still beautiful and flyers were still flyers and they wanted to have the one they could not get.

When Herr Brueckner's need for medical attention grew greater, she swallowed her pride and applied for work as a domestic for an American family. At first she feared her past in Berlin might have followed her to Wiesbaden, but that proved unfounded.

She had on her side the fact that she spoke creditable English, made a lovely appearance, and carried the respected name of Falkenstein. She made application, answered the Fragebogen, took the necessary medical examination, and passed all clearances.

Colonel Carter Smith and his wife hired her as a housekeeper and governess for their three small children. At last there was a chance to eat decently and earn a few extra packs of cigarettes a week. With tobacco a medium of exchange, she could buy Herr Brueckner the services of a good doctor and bring them precious ounces of meat and butter.

In the home of Colonel Carter Smith, Hildegaard had her first true love affair. She fell in love with the children, and they with her.

Tony and Lynn Loveless jumped on Daddy as he turned into the gate and showered him with a batch of new German words. He played in the yard with them until the weariness of the day overcame him.

"Martini. I'm bushed," he said, bussing his wife.

"Here, lover," Judy said, pouring it from the tall mixer. She stood behind his chair, rubbed the back of his neck. He groaned.

"We knocked them over today," Clint said. "Six hundred ground-controlled approach landings in Berlin. Crusty was so pleased he forgot to chew us out at the staff meeting."

"How many tons?"

"Over five thousand."

"That's wonderful."

Clint sipped, purred his deep content as her fingers massaged magic spots.

"Clint, I found a German maid, pending your approval."

"Speak English?"

"Fluently."

"Where'd you dig her up?"

"She belonged to a Colonel Carter Smith, Army people. They are being shipped out to Japan. She has an A-1 recommendation. Mrs. Smith says the children are beside themselves with grief to be separated from her. She taught them German. Anyhow, she has a famous name to boot. I hear her uncle is practically the political leader of Berlin."

Clint smiled inwardly. That would be like Judy. She still had a little of New York in her. She'd have a name to drop.

"Honey, that's your department," he said.

"Well, you *must* interview her. Everyone says it is important to establish that the man is the head of the house to a German."

"Okay, okay, let's see it."

"Fraulein Falkenstein, would you come in, please?"

Clint knocked over his martini. He cleared his throat authoritatively and asked a few questions . . . to make it official.

"Jesus H. Christ!" Clint commented when she left the room.

"Lover," Judy said, "be an angel and don't try it or Momma will slit your throat."

"Jesus H. Christ," he repeated.

Ernestine opened the envelope, which, in addition to regular postage, had affixed a special "Berlin Tax" stamp issued to support the city.

My Dearest Sister Ernestine:

I must be the lucky cat who always lands on her feet. I adore my new home with the Loveless family. It has taken much of the pain away by the departure of the Smiths. My room is quite decent and comfortable. The boy is Tony, nine years old and the girl, Lynn, who is ten. They are very affectionate and well behaved, for American children.

At the end of my first week, Mrs. Loveless gave me a carton of cigarettes upon learning my responsibility to the Brueckners and she promises a bonus of a carton a week. Erna! Do you know what that means? They passed off the kindness by saying they were both trying to cut down on smoking. They are a typical American family with extreme generosity. She is the true master of the family as was Mrs. Smith, but is clever enough not to let him know it.

The Americans are strange people, but they fool you. Just when I am beginning to think Colonel Loveless is shallow-minded, he shows his genius in other ways.

I remember how Father used to treat our maids and I suppose that was what bothered me the most when I began working. Yet, I am never treated as a maid. Not the way we treated them.

I am glad to hear that Colonel O'Sullivan has found a room away from his own quarters. It will save you embarrassment. How does Uncle Ulrich look upon all of this?

I must run. Each night I read to my babies in German and I look forward to it so much. I hear them calling "Hilde" so I rush this letter to you with love.

Hilde

In downtown Wiesbaden, Die Valkyrie Club, a traditional old beer hall, had been converted into a garish, stadium-sized nightclub—Winkelmann, proprietor.

Sturdy old cement pillars were painted off-pink; sequined drums and trumpets revolved from the ceiling; purple drapes encased the band stand and special up-chuck bowls had been bought from a Luftwaffe barracks and installed in the men's room.

Winkelmann was a decent sort of chap. No airman was cheated or mistreated within his walls. The prostitutes working out of the place had to guarantee fair play, correct prices, and no clipping or rolling.

The semiprofessionals and just plain nice kids who wanted a place to have a glass of beer and dance lent an air of respectability.

Drunks were always sent home at Winkelmann's expense by taxi, after checking in their wallets for safekeeping.

The American authorities realized that in any military town Die Valkyrie Clubs had to exist. Actually, Winkelmann was doing them a good turn by running a trouble-free operation. All of this gave Winkelmann a great deal of pride. He took particularly good care of choice friends with his personal inner-circle stock.

Before the war he had been a poor boy who had spent his life in servitude of the arrogant Wiesbaden aristocracy, and he hated them. His coming into a position of importance paled the old Wiesbaden gentry. When Wiesbaden was Wiesbaden, bawdy houses like Die Valkyrie could never have existed! Winkelmann was a good soldier, but never a Nazi. He felt that the sponsors of the city, particularly the Rhineland industrialists, were Nazi to the core.

Nick Papas, a personal favorite, entered the tarnished portals and was led to Herr Winkelmann's personal bar built around an oversized

mock coffin with a plaster cast of a nude adorning the lid. Matches were
struck on either breast.

"Hello, Nick. Was gibt's?"

"Need a favor."

"Of course."

"You know Stan Kitchek?"

"Your copilot?"

"Yeah. The Looey needs a broad."

"Send him in."

"Stan's a funny kid. He's shy. Besides, he would never go for a broad
on an out-and-out business deal. Something to do with his childhood
training."

"So, we'll get him a girl who will go for car fare and cigarettes."

"No . . . I told you Stan's funny. He's got to feel, you know . . . in
love. He likes the big story, the hand-holding, the fond farewell."

Winkelmann shook his head. "I never understand people like that.
Well, it takes all kinds."

"So, you know a broad with puppy-dog eyes and a sad story who
speaks English?"

Winkelmann thought, lit up with an idea. "There's a German restaurant two blocks down and left on the alley called Mutter Rubach's.
There's a waitress there named Monika. I'll give her a call and you
take it from there."

"What's the tab?"

"For you, nothing. How about you and Captain Scott? I got three
new additions to my personal stock. They just escaped in from the Russian Zone, eighteen and nineteen years old. Maybe you boys will come
up to my place later and we can take some pictures and have a group
therapy session."

"Sorry . . . dammit . . . we got to fly the second time bloc tomorrow.
After we get Stan started, maybe we'll strafe the strasse for a quick one."

The sudden appearance of three Amis in Mutter Rubach's, a German sanctuary, caused the entire tone of the room to soften to a hush of
suspicious whispers.

Monika was there and waiting. They played the game out. She
served them. Stan thought she was very pretty. Scott said to her, my
pal would like to know you better and Monika said if Stan waited in a
bar down the street she would join him for a drink after she went off

duty, and Stan went away happy, leaving Nick and Scott with big mugs of beer.

By now, assured that the Ami intruders were merely flyers and not counter-intelligence looking for Nazis, the place returned to normal.

A combo of accordion, piano, and drums played a medley of Viennese waltzes with the roving musician hovering over the Ami table and patronizing them. Nick winked to Scott as the accordion player finished and hoped for a tip.

"Speak English?"

The accordion player said he did, a little.

"Have a cigarette. Here, take a few for your drummer and piano player."

"Oh, thank you, sir."

"Keep the pack."

Deep bows. He held the pack for the other two to see. They stood and bowed.

"What would you like us to play, sir?"

"A nice German song."

"A polka, perhaps."

"Naw . . . I'd like to hear a good old German marching song . . . like my grandpoppa played in the band in Milwaukee."

"Sorry, sir! I don't know any."

Nick's magic pocket produced another pack of cigarettes. The accordion player's eyes bulged. He walked back to the platform, spoke rapidly to the other two to weigh the prize against the risk of playing forbidden music.

They decided to go it! The combo broke into the "Westerwald March!"

After the first three notes many of the Germans scurried from their tables, paid their checks, and hustled out of Mutter Rubach's.

Others sat mesmerized. Nick and Scott waved friendly to them to show how much they were enjoying it and put another pack of cigarettes on the piano and the medley was now in full swing with the "Schwabenwinkel."

Backs became ramrod; there were smiles of nostalgia on old, moustached lips; surges of pride . . . beer mugs tapped the table tops in rhythm, and a few tears flowed. The musicians became carried away by their own candor and swept into a marching medley.

As the music crackled off the walls of Mutter Rubach's and turned into a second and third chorus, voices began singing and tables were being thumped in a frenzied joy.

Scott wanted to blow a whistle when he got outside to watch them tear the place apart escaping, but Nick talked him out of it. Nick had a '41 De Soto which he had inherited at the end of a large card game. "A little strasse strafing to round out the evening, *mein kapitan!*"

"*Jawohl.*"

"I'll flip you for first run."

Scott lost the flip of the coin so he took the wheel for Nick to operate. "Where to?"

"Platter Strasse."

It was a good arterial because it ran from the downtown area toward the Neroberg Hills, where most of the Germans lived. There would be a number of girls looking for rides home, generally.

They trailed a lone girl making her way along the street. "Make a pass," Nick said. The front looked okay. The girl smiled at his greeting. "Full flaps, landing gear down, cut engines. This will make nine straight kills, mein kapitan. In no time I will be a double ace."

He left the car, gently blocked the girl's route, and told her in fractured German that she had lovely legs which should be encased in nylons . . . which he just happened to have . . . and would she like a ride home?

They parted an hour later, the best of friends, without knowing each other's name, the girl several gifts richer.

Nick took the wheel.

"What the hell were you doing up there? Making a lifetime career?"

Nick grunted a happy grunt.

Scott was bored. "I'd shack regular if I could get a place away from that cruddy BOQ and if that Crusty bastard gave me ten minutes free time. This strasse strafing is like shooting fish in a barrel."

"I miss now and then," Nick said, "but that's because I'm ugly. Tell you what, Captain, let's make it sporting. I'll bet you a ten spot I can pick out a Schatzie you can't connect with."

"You're kidding."

"*Ja oder nein?*"

"It's your ten bucks, Nick . . . only, no animals."

"Legit broad . . . all the way . . . for ten?"

"You've got a bet."

Scott checked his watch. The German movie house would be empty-ing. He told Nick to drive him along Rhein Strasse in the general di-rection of the Kurhaus, where many maids working in American homes would be passing. They checked out a half-dozen girls, passed them up . . . then both of them saw her at the same time!

Click, click, click went the heels of Hildegaard Falkenstein.

"I may not even take your ten dollars," Scott said.

"Some guys are just born lucky . . ."

Nick blocked the intersection. The girl walked boldly around the front of the car looking straight ahead. Nick began to feel he might have a winner.

"Fraulein," Scott called, "could you please help us. We're lost."

She answered in rapid German, which they could not understand, and continued across the street.

"Ten bucks."

"Not yet." Scott got out of the car, blocked her way, gathering all of his boyish innocent charm, holding his hands apart helplessly and agonizing the conversation along in German. He mumbled a few choice words about the girl's beauty under his breath.

Hilde tried to step around him, but he wouldn't let her pass. Behind him, he could hear Nick Papas roar.

Words like "nylons" "chocolate" "perfume" were making no impres-sion.

Hilde grew short. "If you do not stand aside," she said in perfect English, "I will call for the police."

"Well . . . I'll be damned."

"Please let me pass. I do not play with little boys."

"Little boys! Oh honey, if you knew what you were missing, you'd cut your throat."

"Let me by or you'll cut your own throat."

She stepped forward, daring him to lay a hand on her. Scott backed off. She continued down the street and turned the corner at Gustav Freytag Strasse and walked into the Loveless house.

Nick Papas laughed until the tears streamed down his grizzly cheeks. "All right, you Greek bastard, you want to sweeten that bet?"

"Jawohl!"

"Fifty says I have her in the sack in a week."

"A bet," and he began laughing all over again.

Scott slowed the car before the house of Lieutenant Colonel Clinton Loveless and made a note of the address.

The flight of Big Easy Four contained a crew beset with mixed emotions:

Stan Kitchek was star-gazed by a large romance. He ran on and on about Monika. Sweet girl supporting her child and old mother. But she had never really been in love. It was happening, just like that.

Scott was almost mad enough to tell Stan that Monika was a tank job . . . but not quite.

Nick was a mosaic of assorted grins glorying in Scott's discomfort.

As they talked to Tempelhof Airways, Stan got out of his seat for a moment and took a big carton from under the flight engineer's table and handed it to Nick.

"What the hell's that?" Scott asked.

"Well, every clear day I see little kids standing on the rubble piles at the end of the cemetery watching us land. Lot of times they're at the airport, too. But did you ever notice that none of them ever came close to us, talked to us?"

"That's the way krauts are," Scott answered.

"Kids shouldn't be that way," Stan said, "anyhow, I thought I'd try something."

"What's in there?" Nick asked.

Stan opened the carton. The other two looked in curiously. Nick's big paw fished out a tiny handkerchief parachute. Attached to the strings was a bar of candy. The carton held over a hundred parachutes and candy bars. "I rigged them up in my spare time," Stan said. "I want you to toss them out of the back door just before we land."

Nick was touched. Scott shrugged as though Stan were crazy.

The final right turn around the Tempelhof Beacon at five hundred feet began the steep glide that took them over the St. Thomas Cemetery between rows of half-bombed-out apartment houses. Stan looked out. Yes, the children were there on the rubble near the end of the runway. Full flaps . . . the big bird slowed. Nick was at the back door throwing out the toy parachutes. They billowed, floated to earth. The children scrambled for them as the craft touched down on the end of the runway.

Within seconds hysterical phone calls were made from Russian spies in the apartments at the end of the runway, and from the Air Safety

Center. Strange objects over St. Thomas Cemetery! Parachutes! What kind of new sabotage were the Americans up to!

Candy bars?

Candy bars!

Candy bars!

People's Radio decried it with passion. "The latest American trick is to bribe little children in a heartless effort to justify remaining in Berlin."

In the days that followed, children in the zone made thousands of toy parachutes for their "friends" in Berlin. Sidney the Kangaroo hopped all the way to New York to collect tens of thousands of candy bars. The ritual of the candy drop took place from many Skymasters every day.

Ulrich Falkenstein said, "It is good for little children to look up to the sky and see a rain of candy bars."

And thus, the legend of Stan Kitchek, "The *Chockolade* Flyer," came to be.

CHAPTER TWENTY-THREE

A battered alarm clock sounded. It was two in the morning. Sean reached over the bed for Ernestine. "Honey, don't get up," he said, half asleep.

"I will be back as quickly as I can."

She left the bed groggy and shivering and bundled herself in a heavy robe.

Reinickendorf Borough was receiving its two-hour morning allotment of electricity. Like the rest of the women in the building she yawned around in the middle of the night.

She heated several pans of water. They would be lukewarm by morning, but they could be partly reheated by a "blockade blitz pill" so Sean would not have to shave and wash in icy water. She put up hot thermoses of coffee and breakfast broth, ironed a few pieces of clothing, did a light wash, and cleaned, and did all of the chores that required light and electricity.

Propriety had to be served. This meant finding a room away from

his own quarters for himself and Ernestine. It was a room in Reinickendorf in the French Sector close to where the new airfield was being
built, a third floor walk-up with some bomb damage, but it did have its
own tiny bath and kitchen alcove.

Except for a telephone that could reach him from Headquarters they
lived like Berliners. Reading, eating, bathing by candlelight or by the
flicker of a kerosene lamp.

"Above all, stand tall," Berliners were told every night at another rally.

It was hard to stand tall after hours-long waits for rations, scrounging for rare and precious articles such as soap, patching unpatchable
clothing, stuffing paper in shoe soles, walking five miles to and from
work in darkness. Life was further reduced to semiprimitive existence.

Hospitals scheduled operations and X-rays at rare hours; schools struggled on without heat, light, textbooks. Radios were heard by pooling
to save precious batteries; most of the news was broadcast on mobile
trucks.

Dentists' wives supplied power for drills by generating electricity by
pumping bicycle wheels; concerts and lectures and rallies were held by
candlelight; cinemas played in the middle of the night to audiences
who often walked across half the city to get to them.

There was no glass to replace a broken window, no parts to repair a
watch, no automobiles for civilians, no malt for beer; no typewriter
ribbons for offices, no paint, no cosmetics, no hardware, no machine
parts.

Rubble fields were bulldozed or cleared by hand and blockade gardens attempted to induce a few vegetables from the earth with seeds
donated from Munich and Hanover and Heidelberg.

Blockade runners crossed from the Russian Zone at great risk and
their black market prices were high. The Americans "officially" frowned
on it, but quietly saw to it that the blockade runners got enough gasoline to keep in business, for even at smugglers' prices any food augment
was precious.

Yet, out of this darkness a legacy came into being. Berliners were
hanging together, shrugging at hardship, laughing at their own plight:

"Better dried potatoes than Kumm Frau."

"Thank goodness the Americans aren't blockading and the Russians
trying to Airlift us."

The life of powdered eggs, scavenging for twigs, the long lines, the
candlelight, the Russian abuses, the checkpoints went on, but the peo-

ple became tougher with an infectious feeling of martyrdom cementing them together.

The only moment a Berliner's heart leaped with fear was when the beat of the engines stopped above them. Berlin lived on one lung and its faint heartbeat was the sound of the engines of the birds.

In this battle of will power, they held their share of the fortress wall.

A short way from where Sean and Ernestine had their room, the third airfield raced to completion.

The engineers of the 350th Support Squadron in Berlin picked an area adjoining French Headquarters, near the Tegel Forest—a flat field an equal distance from Tempelhof and Gatow. They scoured Berlin for heavy construction equipment, but were able to come up with little more than steam rollers dated from the turn of the century.

At the Hanau Base in the American Zone the heavy equipment was assembled, cut up by torches, transported in the C-74 and C-82 transports, and put on special flying duty on the Lift. Ten thousand barrels of asphalt were brought to Berlin along with pierced steel planking.

The Airlifting of the thousands of tons of machinery and supplies for the new runway was the minor part of the story.

There was no steel or rock for foundation of a runway that had to measure from two to ten feet in thickness. Western Berlin was searched for unused rail lines which were pulled up and carted to Tegel. Rubble and paving stones were hauled in.

A volunteer labor force was assembled from the people. The pay was poor, but there would be a hot meal served on each shift to keep them going. Twenty thousand Berliners answered the call!

Nearly half this force were women and they reported to work wearing dresses, business suits, dilapidated army uniforms, wooden shoes, tennis shoes, barefooted, wearing bathing suits in the heat, rags in the rain.

Every facet of the social and professional life was represented in this labor army that in the aspects of its massiveness resembled the construction of an Egyptian pyramid. But, unlike Egyptian slaves, these people worked themselves into exhaustion with a tenacity beyond measure, for there is no way to measure human determination.

A small force of fifteen American officers and less than a hundred enlisted men governed them as they cleaned, salvaged, crushed, carted, shoveled, and spread by hand a million feet of rock and brick.

The airport which they said could not be built in a year under the circumstances was nearing completion in a mere ninety days!

Ernestine returned to bed as the lights of Reinickendorf went out and the neighboring borough of Wedding was given their two-hour quota. Sean had fallen back to sleep. She hoped there would be no early call from his Headquarters today.

CHAPTER TWENTY-FOUR

Nelson Goodfellow Bradbury inherited the deal at a table of colleagues at the Dahlem Press Club.

"Low ball," he announced.

"They landed another five thousand tons by GCA today," Clarke of AP said.

"I'll open," said Whittsett from Hearst.

"The next Russian move has got to be a corker," Clarke mumbled.

"My next move is to call you."

"Call."

"Beats me."

"Call."

"What do you think, Nellie? Where do they hit next?" Bishop of CBS pondered.

"They've got a number of possibilities. Clamp down on smuggling, try a physical take-over of the City Hall and Magistrat . . . number of possibilities."

A waiter behind him bent forward to speak. "Telephone, sir."

He passed the deal to Clarke and lumbered to the phone booth.

"Hello, Nelson Bradbury speaking."

"You know who is here speaking?"

Nellie recognized the gauzed mouthpiece "disguise" of a Russian press officer named Sobotnik.

"Yes."

"It would be in your interest to leave the club now and walk west on Argentinische Allee for further contact."

Click.

Nellie shook his mop. The great Russian mania for secrecy and mystery had to be served. He cashed out of the game and left the club. The streets looked like London during the blackout days.

He walked a great enough distance to establish that he was alone and unfollowed. Sure enough, a black staff car from the Russian Embassy trolled past slowly from the other side of the street. Nellie stopped at the corner, yawned, waited for the car to make a second pass.

Two men emerged, unmistakably NKVD. They could be distinguished even in the poor light . . . they played their parts like bad actors: large brim hats, ill-fitting double-breasted suits, bony faces, sinister manner.

He got into the car on orders and held up his handkerchief to offer it as a blindfold. The NKVD men did not think it was funny. They drew the curtains and whisked down the Potsdamer Chaussee and over to the suburb of castles and mansions. He was driven to the fortress of Marshal Alexei Popov, led to a library, and closed in.

He speculated on the nature of his midnight summons. The Soviet strategy was clear. They wanted to keep the West talking and force concessions because of the pressure of the blockade. Yet, they were in no hurry, because all the top Soviet planners predicted a collapse of the Airlift in the winter.

In Moscow and at the United Nations their statesmen talked in circles. Just as the West indicated breaking off negotiations, the Soviets yielded just enough to keep the talks on. They agreed to a plan for new four-power currency for Berlin. On the surface it appeared to be a Russian softening. However, Marshal Popov received instructions to prevent actual execution of the agreement.

Despite the blackmail card of the blockade, Nellie felt a number of things were giving the Russians short hours of sleep. The Berliners were proving to be pressureproof. The Americans and British came back from the disaster of Blue Monday with the ground-controlled approach landings and now some sort of engineering miracle was taking place at Tegel. The Russians wanted no part of the coming December elections in Berlin.

Finally, a rising anger of world opinion was stronger than expected. Rallies for Berlin were erupting everywhere and the German people were showing a unity that was frightening to the Russian mind.

The silver fox of the Soviets, Marshal Alexei Popov, came to the library in an amiable mood.

"So good of you to come."

"Are you going to behead me, Marshal?"

Popov slapped Bradbury on the shoulder. "I have liked always your candor. Sit, please."

Nellie loaded his glass with vodka and whacked away at the tray of caviar, paper-thin slices of Polish ham, smoked sturgeon, and other delectables long missing on the other side of the Brandenburg Gate.

"I want to clarify misconceptions of the Soviet position. Your press should expose your people to the truth of the situation."

In all of his travels Big Nellie always wondered if they believed their own words. "Let us say, sir, that we expose our people to your side of the question . . . almost as you expose the Russian people to our side."

Popov laughed heartily. He knew he could not bully the journalist and wished no further repartee with him.

Popov reviewed the situation, said the West was in Berlin illegally, and had turned the city into a base for spies. In the zones of occupation Nazis were being used to rebuild the German military for a war of revenge against the Soviet Union.

Nellie doodled some notes, hearing nothing new, and knowing this was not why he was called to Potsdam.

Popov continued to say that the friendly and peace-loving Soviet people had tried to make a settlement, but talks had failed because of Western treaty-breaking.

"Mainly, it is a lie that the Soviet Union is using the threat of starvation in Berlin. There is no blockade of Berlin!"

The body blow had been delivered!

"The Airlift aggression is unnecessary. The Soviet Union guarantees food for every Berliner and to return to work all of those workers unemployed by the American and British aggression."

Nelson Goodfellow Bradbury went away from Potsdam a worried man. No one in the American and British headquarters, and not the most optimistic Berliner, believed the Airlift could keep the city going during the winter.

The Russian guarantee of food and jobs might prove irresistible to the Berlin housewife with a couple of children and the man thrown out of work and was meant to crush the West, for the price of Russian food and jobs was acceptance of the Russian currency.

He was deposited a few blocks from the Press Club, and immediately called Sean, who was in the room at Reinickendorf. "You better get me to see General Hansen," he said excitedly.

In the middle of the morning the Western governors, the Berlin commandants, and the German political leaders floundered without course. Popov and the Russians had trapped them. There was no choice but to wait and see.

General Trepovitch was selected to read the proclamation on People's Radio the next day.

"There is no blockade of Berlin! The Soviet Union can no longer stand by idly and watch the Airlift aggression bring further suffering to the workers of Berlin. Your Soviet brothers hold out their open arms.

"Beginning Monday the people in the so-called American borough of Neukölln may cross to their brothers at the borough town hall of Treptow in the Soviet Sector and turn in your illegal ration cards and B marks. You will be issued a new ration book guaranteed by the Soviet Union giving you five hundred more calories of food a day. Your illegal B marks will be exchanged for regular marks at the rate of one to one."

An awesome moment of decision had come! Every man and woman had to search deeply and alone to find his own answer. Face starvation in the winter; if you survive the winter . . . what then? Continue to live in fear of another Russian onslaught of another kind? Perhaps direct invasion . . . like the last one.

Would it not be better then to simply submit to survive and accept the Russian offer as the only way out of an impossible trap. The revenge would be horrible if the Russians were rejected.

The procedure was simple. On given days, citizens of a Western borough were to go to a neighboring Russian borough and exchange ration books and currency. There were over two million people in the Western Sector. The Soviets figured if only half of them crossed over initially the shaky city administration would collapse and the West would be hopelessly deluged by Russian marks.

In the Russian boroughs of Treptow, Freidrichshain, Pankow, Mitte, and Prenzlauer Berg they staffed for the onslaught!

The week of great decision came and went with no change in the life of Berlin. Two per cent of the people in Western Sectors changed to Russian rations.

CHAPTER TWENTY-FIVE

Clint Loveless studied the list for repair or replacement of equipment. The top priority read: starters, landing lights, harnesses, inverters, indicator master gyro fluxgate compasses, ammeters, indicator gyro horizons, and on down to windshield wipers, transmitter oil pressure, propellors.

The general had had him at Erding to break the spare-parts repair bottleneck.

There was a knock on his door.

"Come in."

Scott Davidson entered. "Hello, Scott."

"I had to come to Headquarters on some other business and wondered if I could see you for a few minutes."

"Sure."

He pushed his paperwork aside and rubbed his eyes. Scott studied his office curiously. It was a wonderland of charts and maps.

MAJOR PROBLEM AREAS
PRIORITY PROJECTS
CAUSES OF PILOT FATIGUE

Scott had always seen the colonel as a guy on the general's coattails, always looking green when he left the plane in Berlin. This first sight of his office gave him a sudden new respect.

"Sir," Scott said, "I've just finished this report and wanted you to have a look at it."

Clint took the folio. The cover read: THUNDERSTORM FLYING by Captain Scott Davidson, Chief Pilot, Airlift Wing, Provisional.

Clint made a sour face. "This is out of my line. All I know about it is that I hate it."

"That's just the point, Colonel. Before I submit it to the chief pilot here, I'd kind of like a layman's opinion."

Clint shrugged, put the folio on a stack of papers, and said he'd read it.

"Colonel, long as I happen to be here, I just happened to remember something else. You are in a hell of a position to do me a favor."

"So?"

"Shall I get to the point?"

"By all means," Clint said, handing him back the report on thunderstorm flying.

Scott smiled. "Sir . . . I'd like an introduction to your housekeeper."

"No."

"But . . ."

"I don't want any of you crushed-hat bastards knocking her up. She's too good a maid."

"Colonel, I don't have that in mind at all."

"Then you must be queer."

"The truth is that I met her once and well . . . I was pretty damned crude. I'd like to make amends."

Clinton Loveless had grave doubts about the sincerity of Scott Davidson. But what the hell . . . trying to keep men away from Hilde was as ridiculous as . . . trying to keep men away from Hilde. Furthermore, Clint flew with Scott and placed his life in the man's hands too often to be uppity.

"Colonel, could I just happen to drop around your house, like for dinner . . . or something?"

"Like maybe you've thought this over?"

"Well, sir, as a matter of fact, with me flying two runs a day to Berlin and all my paperwork, I've got limited time off."

"Like when do you have in mind?"

"Like tonight . . . Colonel?"

Clint was amused by Scott's gall. "Cocktails are at six-thirty. I assume you've already cased my house and know how to find it."

"Goddamn, Colonel, you're a good troop."

Judy thought Scott Davidson was adorable and just loved being part of the scheme. When Hilde served drinks in the living room she was introduced to the captain and matter-of-factly said she had met him. If she was uncomfortable about his sudden appearance, she did not show it.

"Won't you join us for dinner, Captain?"

"Oh no, that would be putting you to too much trouble."

"Nonsense."

"Well . . ."

"We insist, don't we Clint."

"We insist."

"Hilde, set a place for Captain Davidson." She nodded, went to the kitchen for her own dinner and to feed the children.

Scott waited until a reasonable time had passed in order to give proper attention to the hostess, then found a pretense to get into the kitchen.

Hilde was at the kitchen table joking with Tony and Lynn. Scott poured himself a glass of water, edged his way into the group, and quickly endeared himself to the children in the continuation of his out-flanking her by having the family go crazy about him.

Tony and Lynn were sent off to put on their pajamas and study. Hilde flitted about the kitchen putting the final touches on the dinner as Judy and Clint discreetly remained in the living room with the mar-tini mixer.

"Sure is a pleasant coincidence," Scott said.

"I think not," she answered.

"Look, I wanted to find you to tell you I'm sorry about the other night. We were tired and I just had too much to drink."

"I don't think you're sorry."

"I went to a lot of trouble to find you so I could show just how sorry I am."

"What you are sorry about is that your ridiculous pride has been damaged. This trouble you are going to now is an attempt to redeem it."

Hilde was neither amused, charmed, or swept up by him. The re-sistance was failing to melt on schedule for Scott Davidson.

"Can't I have a clean slate?" he persisted.

Hilde set the bread knife down, wiped her hands on her apron. "This town is filled with easy girls who should be able to fill your appetite. You're only going to damage your pride further if you attempt to see me."

"You're being too rough. I'm a lot of fun, Hilde."

"Strange, Captain. I find you dull, spoiled, and immature."

Nick Papas snapped his fingers together eagerly. It was the first bet he had ever collected from Scott. "Poop, Captain, poop."

Scott peeled off five bills of ten-dollar military script.

"Fifty bucks." Nick kissed the money with mock ecstasy. "Most beau-tiful bet I ever collected. Five O!"

"What's up?" Stan Kitchek asked in amazement.

"I asked the captain to donate to buy candy bars for you to parachute to the kids in Berlin. Look what he did. He gave me fifty bucks."

"Gee, Scott," Stan Kitchek said with a catch in his throat, "that's awful nice."

CHAPTER TWENTY-SIX

The Berliners' rejection of Russian rations forced Marshal Popov to advance the timetable for the take-over of the city. They clamped down on the blockade runners, sending a half dozen of them to the firing squad. Harassment of Berliners at the checkpoints against the B marks reached a new high. And then an assault on the city government just short of all-out war!

Action Squads trained with military precision assembled in Marx/ Engels Platz under the control of Russian officers in civilian disguise. They poured in, over five thousand strong, many in American lend-lease trucks.

They converged on the City Hall and the Magistrat buildings armed with clubs, knives, stones, carrying banners and slogans.

This was the tactic that crumbled freedom in Czechoslovakia. This was the replay of the Prague riots. The Action Squads broke into the buildings, smashed up offices, and left the main chambers in a shambles. American, British, and French liaison officers were beaten up and the phone lines to the Western Sectors were cut.

The riot grew! Neither the Russian Sector police or the Red Army were anywhere to be seen, allowing the Action Squads free hand. At the end of the day Oberburgermeister Hanna Kirchner was able to see General Trepovitch to demand protection.

The Russian shrugged. "I cannot keep the workers from staging a democratic demonstration. They hate the imperialist Airlift aggression. It is the free right of the workers to protest."

The angry little lady came to her feet. "I never believed," she spat, "there could ever again be anything as loathsome as the Nazis. The Soviet Union has won that honor."

Trepovitch sprung to his feet.

"Go on, hit me," she dared.

He dared not. She spat on his desk and walked out.

The next day the "riots" continued.

Hanna Kirchner defiantly drove to her office, but the doors were now blocked by Red Army guards and she was not allowed to enter.

People's Radio announced more Red Army guards were coming, explaining that the anger of the workers compelled the Soviet Union to protect the citizens of Berlin from their corrupt officials.

Andrew Jackson Hansen returned to his old posture as Eric the Red. He spewed a stream of oaths in frustration against the outrage. When Neal Hazzard and Sean were able to calm him down they entered a conference with the British and French to reach a mutual decision.

The third day of riots at the City Hall and Magistrat was allowed to continue. The Western commanders then contacted Hanna Kirchner and told her that the Berlin Assembly and Magistrat could continue operation in the Western Sectors of the city.

On the fourth day of riots, Oberburgermeister Hanna Kirchner called for the Assembly to come into session in the British Sector at the Student's Haus on Seeinplatz.

People's Radio retorted that night, "The workers of Berlin have been abandoned by flunkies carrying out the dirty work of the imperialists."

Armed now with the "fact" that the Democrats, Christians, and Conservatives had "abandoned" their offices, the Soviets swept all non-Communists from borough offices in their sector, including three mayors. The Russians padlocked vital files at the Magistrat.

A massive shift of population and offices followed as members of the free parties fled to the new sanctuary of the West. Each day a new department of the government splintered off and opened new offices there. The climax was an assembly of sixteen hundred Communists at the Admiral Palast.

"The people of Berlin have been left to the mercy of the revenge seekers," Rudi Wöhlman cried to his audience. "Look at the Magistrat and Assembly. They have been abandoned! This is the time to elect representation for the workers!"

This rump meeting of Communists by hand proclamation declared Heinz Eck as Oberburgermeister of "Free" Berlin. A new Magistrat now to be known as the Berlin Soviet was proclaimed without debate, protest, or formal vote.

In the beginning of September 1949, the Soviet Union had evaded an open election and split the city into two parts.

"My God!" Nelson Goodfellow Bradbury said, "my God!"

From his vantage point high in the shell of the gutted Reichstag he looked down on the Platz der Republik. The people had gathered to protest Russian atrocity.

A mass of humanity jammed the square; they were packed solid in the destroyed Tiergarten. The great Charlottenburger Chaussee was a solid bulk of people backed all the way to the Victory Column restored by the British. Berliners spilled over the area against the Brandenburg Gate where it touched the Russian Sector. There had never been a gathering like this. A half-million Berliners rose in anger.

Usually an orderly people, they became enraged when the Russians saw fit to change the guard at a monument which sat just inside the British Sector. The Berliners called it "Tomb of the Unknown Raper." A student climbed the flag pole on the Brandenburg Gate and ripped the hammer and sickle from its mast. Only courageous action of the British guards prevented a full-scale uprising.

It rained and they were drenched, but it did not seem to matter. One by one the leaders came to the rostrum and defied the Soviet Union.

The great figure of Ulrich Falkenstein, hatless and refusing the protection of an umbrella, faced this unprecedented sea of human wrath. He had kept his sacred word to General Hansen. The people had held.

"Berliners!" his voice echoed through them in the midst of their ruin. "I have said that you were never Nazis. And I say now: Berliners will never be Communists!"

CHAPTER TWENTY-SEVEN

Scott Davidson had fallen upon hard times. First he ran into a new boss like Hiram Stonebraker. Now a rebuff by a German maid! . . . . No broad had ever called him dull!

Scott had accumulated four days' leave. He and Nick went on an historic binge from Rüdesheim to Wiesbaden to Frankfurt to Mainz, which ended with Nick's car sinking slowly in the Rhine River. And he had plenty of Schatzies . . . six girls in four days.

But, as Hildegaard had suggested, they were rather easy. This annoyed Scott. He was going to show her! Actually, all he showed was a throbbing headache and a queasy stomach. It was a strange, unique, humiliating experience to be so bluntly rejected. Scott proved her contention that he was spoiled and immature. He was left with no choice but to strike his banners in defeat and forget her, but he couldn't.

He was edgy for a week after his binge. Scott seemed disinterested even when Nick told him he had gotten a two-room flat in Frankfurt. Nick and Stan became worried. He had never acted like this before.

The Ring Church on Friedrichstrasse emptied of old aristocrats in threadbare finery who stopped for a word with the black-robed minister. Hilde came from its confines with Tony and Lynn Loveless. They all thought it would be good for their German lessons to hear the sermon in the language.

She stepped into the sudden light, shading her eyes, a cameo in lace and white gloves. The Loveless children, scrubbed and polished, circled around her, running off their relief to be free from the confinement.

"Lovely sermon."

Hilde turned and faced Scott Davidson.

"Hi kids," Scott said, "how about a milk shake at the Eagle Club. I always like a milk shake after church."

"I am afraid not. It will spoil their dinner."

"Aw, Hilde," Tony complained.

"I said, no."

"Well, we got to listen to our Aunt Hilde," Scott said. "Mind if I walk you home?"

"Otherwise you plan to make a scene here in front of the church," she hissed in a low voice.

"Hey, you kids run on ahead. I'll see if I can't get Aunt Hilde to change her mind."

Tony gave a sour "ugh, girls" look and trotted off with his sister.

Hilde looked beautiful; he offered her his arm but she ignored it.

"Wouldn't like to see a dull, immature, spoiled flyer from time to time, would you?"

"Captain Davidson, the kind of friendship I am interested in goes against your manly nature."

"I thought about that and I'd like to see you anyhow. Maybe I'm maturing?" He was eating crow now and there was no use rubbing it in.

"I accept your apology because I believe you mean it now. However, I do not wish to see you."

Hilde did not believe in platonic relationships between men and women. It might begin that way with the best of intentions, sooner or later it would drift toward sex. With a man like the flyer, sooner. In Berlin, in the old days, she had been too self-centered to be excited by the beginning of a romance. Later, a deep hatred of men was born.

Some of it had mellowed in the home of Colonel Smith and of the Loveless family. Now wisdom told her that there were good men and there was good love in the world, but she always excluded herself from the possibility.

They gathered the children, crossed the street, continued quietly.

"Don't get angry," Scott said after a time, "but I learned that you never go out on dates."

"Life is much more simple that way," she answered.

"I promise I won't complicate things."

It had been a lonely year for Hilde. Scott was charming and he could be controlled now that she had his absolute respect. She knew she was trying to fool herself because in three or four dates he would return to being what he really was. Yet, she did not want to send him off again. They came to the head of the colonnade.

"Why don't we have that milk shake," she said. "I can always feed them an hour later."

He started to offer her his arm again, but held it back. He had entered a strange new world of the fear of rejection.

Hilde took his arm and they walked down the colonnade.

CHAPTER TWENTY-EIGHT

Tegel Airfield neared completion a mere three months from the day the first shovel was set into the earth.

One obstacle remained in this strange blockade—the transmitter of People's Radio sat near the end of the runway.

Although the French role had been minor, it was dramatic. Colonel Jacques Belfort personally supervised the dynamiting of the Russian tower. The Russians branded them "cultural barbarians," but to no avail.

The first Skymasters from the zone set down in Tegel in autumn of 1948, pushing the daily tonnage to six thousand.

The Soviet concept of the blockade, a logical and routine political maneuver, had failed to achieve its initial aims. The whole matter was getting out of hand. While the Russians continued to be certain of ultimate victory, much of their confidence was undermined by the small miracles performed by the West.

The Kremlin sent out a contagious new line of thinking to probe for a way out of the blockade mess without a loss of face.

V. V. Azov was a prisoner in his Potsdam mansion. It was in the wind that he would be liquidated. Indeed, an undercurrent of anxiety ran beneath the entire Soviet command. Even Marshal Alexei Popov, the greatest Soviet war hero, might be falling out of favor.

Igor Karlovy placed his own good fortune on the fact that he was the foremost aviation traffic expert in the command. However, this technical skill could not sustain him in Berlin forever.

"How can you remain so certain," V. V. Azov demanded of Igor, "that the operation of the new runway at Tegel will not allow the Airlift aggression to continue indefinitely?"

The commissar's face was ashen and he had developed a bad twitch. At times, Igor thought, he seemed to be on drugs.

"If they had ten runways in Berlin, the Lift would still collapse in winter. There is an entirely new set of problems never solved in aviation."

"It seems the Americans have ways of solving quite a number of unsolvable problems."

"I assure you, Comrade Commissar, they are barely holding even now. Coal reserves have fallen to less than a two-week supply. A single streak of bad weather in December and they have no choice but to quit."

"Igor," Lotte pouted, "you sit for hours and stare and say nothing."
"Huh . . . what . . . what did you say?"

"You are bored with me."

"No, no my pet."

"You used to sing to me all the time, even when you were not happy."

"Do you want a man or a nightingale! Dammit, woman! I have problems on my mind!"

Lotte cried. In the last week or two all he had to do was look at her crossly and she would cry. She wept over nothing. He walked into his study and slammed the door behind him.

His frequent black moods were not caused by the growing desperation of the Russian command. Igor was an engineer and he would not be bullied against his judgment. What was getting him down like a growing poison was the hatred and rejection of the Berliners. The defiance of a half-million workers, their scathing humor, their willingness to sacrifice anything to avoid the Soviet way of life.

And the damned Americans and their damned chocolate flyers . . . the kangaroo and the candy bars. . . .

Sean looked at his watch; Ernestine would be at the room in a few moments. He emptied the bag of groceries. There was a knock on the door. Strange, he thought, Ernestine has a key. He opened the door and faced Igor Karlovy.

"Come in," Sean said.

Igor looked about the shabby room. It reminded him of rooms in Moscow. "Forgive me for showing up in this manner, but you know how things are done in Berlin. It has been a long time, O'Sullivan."

They shook hands.

"So, we are all just men," Igor said, "and all in the same boat."

"Can I expect to be reading about my frailty in your papers tomorrow?"

"Of course not," Igor said, "there are certain things we Russians honor. Besides, everyone from Popov on down is too vulnerable."

Sean scrounged the cupboard, found a half bottle of vodka, and offered Igor a cigarette.

"The record of our past friendship appears to have gained value in our command," Igor said. "I have been told to bring you a message."

"Go on."

"We are ready to implement a four-power currency control immediately and guarantee your access routes to Berlin."

Sean knew that the Russians were capable of reversing themselves overnight on any given issue and offer an unexpected treaty without apparent reason. "I'll see that General Hansen gets the message."

"With your personal recommendation, I hope."

"As a matter of fact, no," Sean answered.

"Between friends," Igor said, "this whole quarrel is becoming costly for both sides. The prospect of having to impose a blockade during the winter is not pleasant. On the other hand, there is no way your Airlift can run through the winter. We have both proved our points. I believe we should both save face as gracefully as possible."

Sean laughed. "Come on, Colonel Karlovy. What's a few thousand Germans starving to death? You're bringing this offer because you don't want to go into the winter and find out we can pull the city through."

The Russian stiffened. "When can I have your answer?"

"You know the address here."

The door burst open and Ernestine saw the Russian first and became masked in fright.

"An old friend," Sean said, stepping into the candlelight.

Igor tipped his fingers to his cap and thought it time for him to go. "Good-by, Colonel . . . aufwiedersehen, fraulein."

Igor locked himself in his office, shocked by O'Sullivan's abruptness. Had O'Sullivan spotted a Soviet weakness that quickly? Had he in truth been sent to transmit Russian fears?

He reached up on a shelf, took his mandolin down. It was covered with dust. He blew the film away, tuned the sour strings, then remembered that Lotte had not greeted him. He found her asleep on the living-room couch.

She fluttered her eyes open. "I lay down for a moment. I must have dozed," she said.

She was quite pale. What the devil was getting into her? She had always been a picture of health and energy. Now all this weeping and dragging about.

In the topsy-turvy world of working by night and running days together one was apt to overlook small things. Igor thought . . . how long has it been? How long?

"You little fool!"

She did not answer.

"You are pregnant."

"Yes," she said.

He was seized with panic! Where to run! What to do!

She took his hand and made him sit. "I have always loved you, Igor. I am not afraid."

He knelt beside her and lay his head in her lap. "You little fool . . ."

"I must have something when you are gone."

CHAPTER TWENTY-NINE

Scott shoved a bouquet of roses into Judy Loveless' hand. "You are a sexy babe . . . it's you I really crave."

"I also think you're great . . . but damn, you're ten years late. Come in, Scott, Hilde will be down in a minute."

Lynn and Tony picked Scott's pockets for the ransom that usually turned up. Tony found a wooden Hussar carved in the Black Forest, and Lynn a charm in the shape of a heart to go on a bracelet they were building.

He began to tell the children about a hair-raising landing with three Jap Zeros on his tail, which he never made, and they didn't think he made, but it was exciting the way he told it.

Hilde entered dressed the way Judy had advised for a football game. She looked like a co-ed from William and Mary.

"We better get in gear or we'll miss the kick-off."

"I won't be too late, Mrs. Loveless."

"No rush."

"Wiederschen, children."

A chorus of soldiers' whistles greeted Hilde as Scott led her to their seats. She settled between him and Nick Papas. Scott explained that the enemy was the team in the blue shirts, the Army from Heidelberg, and the whites were the Air Force, Wiesbaden. Nick Papas had three bills riding on the outcome.

At the first crunching blocks, Hilde's eyes bulged. "Mein Gott! They're killing each other!"

"The idea, honey," a perplexed Nick Papas explained for the third time, "is the man who is running . . . well, his team has four turns to advance the ball ten yards . . . or meters. Then, they are entitled to another four chances . . . see?"

She jabbed Scott in the ribs. "Why didn't you explain it that way?"

"For Christ's sake, watch the game."

"Nick?"

"Yeah?"

"If he must only make ten meters, why did he just run twenty-five meters?"

"Because . . . because his true objective is to get it all the way down the field and score a goal."

"Ja, ja, now I see."

"Good."

"Nick?"

"Yeah?"

"Why does he kick the ball?"

"For Christ's sake, watch the game."

"Mein Gott!" Hilde hid her face in Scott's shoulder as the Air Force safety man took the punt and the Army gang tackled him viciously.

"Come on, Hilde," Scott said. "He isn't hurt and he isn't mad. Look, he's running back to play . . . he likes the game."

"I will watch and I will be very still."

The stands came to their feet. The soldiers were in a state of hysteria over an interception.

"Who has the ball, Nick? I did not see?"

The Army officers were guests at the Scala Officers' Club and celebrated their victory rousingly. Hilde changed to high heels as Judy had instructed her to do.

Scott was barely able to have a dance without being cut in on. Anyhow, it was kind of nice to study her from a distance. She danced near their table with a pink-cheeked, fuzz-faced Army second lieutenant, and winked to Scott. He appraised her backside, her legs, her bust. It all checked out . . . gorgeous. He didn't know how long he would be able to keep his promise.

A wild, barefoot congo line circled the club, a converted theater, moving from the little bar and dance floor to the main bar, where the band on the stage joined as they picked up dancers. They congoed up the stairs to the balcony where couples were necking and back down again and Hilde laughed until her sides hurt. She continued to bubble all the way home.

"It has been a wonderful day . . . the most wonderful day since . . ." Since the last time she saw Scott. Scott was wonderful days.

But she understood by his silence what was happening and was bound to happen. He pulled up to the curb.

"Let's sit and talk a moment," he said.

"Okay. I don't know how to thank you for the day."

"That's a bad question to ask me. How long you figure we're supposed to go on like this?"

"That's up to you."

"Hilde, we've got to bend a little. I'm a nice guy."

She shook her head. "That is just the trouble. You aren't a nice guy. You are a rat, just like I am. We are two of a kind. I do not dislike you because you are a rat . . . but I know you."

"All right, so we're both rats. Then what's the harm?"

"Good night, Scott."

Hilde tried to compose a letter to Erna, but found herself contradicting her own ideas.

When it came to a definition of love she did not know it. Scott was a wanderer who would never change his ways. Yet, she had never cared for a man as she did for him. She even desired him, but to give him sex would be the beginning of the end.

From the time she began to work for her first American family, Colonel and Mrs. Smith, a new experience began. The colonel was a great bear of a man who spoke softly and with warmth. He called her "Miss Hilde." He was a gentle person, perhaps like Uncle Ulrich would be if she knew him better. The colonel's children loved to cuddle on his lap for their story.

But there was strength in Colonel Smith too. One could tell that by the respect his officers showed, although they seemed at ease around him.

She and Mrs. Smith shopped together and she was allowed to join certain family outings, and after a while they even gossiped together. It was strange, this nice way the Americans treated each other. It was how an officer like Scott and a man from the ranks like Nick could share a brotherly love.

Hilde remembered her shock the first time she saw Colonel Loveless chase his wife through the garden calling, "Me Tarzan, you Jane."

And she remembered standing in the hallway in the morning listening at their bedroom door when Tony and Lynn jumped into bed with them and they all wrestled.

At first Hilde resented Ami laughter. Sure, the Amis could laugh . . . they were not hungry. Their cities were not in ruins, but they laughed as much about themselves and their own failings as anything else.

In the rigid adherence to reverence for her father Hilde remembered little laughter and little warmth for anyone but Ernestine. She had never known a German man who did not take himself seriously. Perhaps, she wrote to Ernestine, the Americans deserve laughter.

Judy knocked on Hilde's door the next morning as she sat before the mirror brushing her long, thick brown hair. Mrs. Loveless muttered something envious.

"Hilde, Colonel Loveless has managed to get three days off starting Saturday. We would like to get away, just anywhere. He hasn't seen a thing of Germany except air bases."

"I hope he isn't called back to his office like the last time you tried to get away."

"Never can tell."

"Everything here will be fine."

"By the way, it will be all right to entertain Captain Davidson here while we're gone."

"I don't know if we will be seeing each other again."

"Little fight?"

Hilde shook her head.

"Oh, I'm sorry, Hilde."

She set the brush down and felt a need to speak to Mrs. Loveless. "In German we have a word. He is filled with *Wanderlust* . . . he is a rover."

Judy lit a cigarette and sat on the edge of the bed. "A lot of people who care for each other see that life rewards in different ways. We say in America, half a loaf is better than none. Hilde, may I speak to you frankly?"

"Yes, ma'am."

"When I interviewed Mrs. Smith about hiring you, she was quite

frank with me. As you know by their letters and gifts, they care for you
very much. So do I. So, I talk as a friend. Mrs. Smith told me, one thing
you will notice about Hildegaard . . . she never laughs. And she said
. . . I don't think Hildegaard has ever laughed from the day she was
born. I don't think she knows how."

Hilde was surprised by the truth of the discovery.

"Scott Davidson makes you laugh. You are a happy woman when
he enters the room. In the end, this might have to be worth a few tears."

Shortly after Scott arrived in Germany he accepted a Permanent
Change of Station status. The definition of Temporary Duty on the
Airlift was vague and taking Permanent Station in Germany meant a
lot of privileges. Anyhow, Scott didn't really give a damn where he was
stationed.

Hiram Stonebraker brought the first changes of his ways. As a chief
pilot of an Air Wing he found himself constantly fretting about housing for his crews, their fatigue, the ground-controlled approach landings in the steep glide paths over crowded cities, a beacon which gave
off a weak signal, and a number of other things he didn't give a damn
about before. And then came Hildegaard Falkenstein.

Stan Kitchek was glad about Hilde. He was a purist. He had a nice
girl back in Seattle and would have her till hell froze over. He was
riddled with guilt when he needed another woman.

Nick didn't get to do so much bumming around with Scott after
Hilde came into the picture, but he was crazy about her. Scott had a
judgment day coming all his life and Hilde was the first girl Nick knew
with the stuff to pull it off. She showed it by not giving in.

The Air Force and Army had set up low-cost holidays in requisitioned German resorts in Bavaria. Scott's leave was overdue. He had
flown nearly a hundred flights to Berlin, but his own growing sense of
duty kept him at his desk.

Stan and Nick Papas shoved off for Bavaria hunting a couple of new
Schatzies. Scott stayed on to fly the general and Colonel Loveless to
Burtonwood in England, recommissioned as the 59th Air Depot. Clint
headed a team of production control people to try to break the bottleneck of the 200-hour overhaul.

The Skymasters went to a hangar known as Station Number One

where the process began with a stripping of radios and instruments and continued from hangar to hangar where they were steam-cleaned to remove the coal dust, then parts and instruments and engines were broken down, rebuilt, tested, reinstalled, checked out.

Only five Skymasters a day could be completed on the line. Others were backing up in Germany awaiting overhaul.

Douglas and Lockheed Aircraft sent engineers over to consult with Clint on proper methods to stop tank leaks, a continuing menace. A special team from Erding Base was given a course on a sealing method known as TC 48 so they could teach it to all maintenance crews in Germany.

After the general and Clint Loveless finished their inspection Scott remained to confer on pilots' complaints about hydraulic-system seepage, tire wear, faulty wiring, fire hazards, foreign matter in oil screens, and those other things a chief pilot worried about.

Five days after he arrived in Burtonwood, Scott picked up a renovated Skymaster at Station Number Five and flew it back to Rhein/Main.

Scott stood before the door of the Loveless house not having the slightest idea why he should return. Hilde opened the door, and felt a sense of relief on seeing him for the first time in two weeks, but stifled her joy.

"Bad penny," he said.

"Come in."

"Anybody in?"

"Colonel and Mrs. Loveless are out and the children are asleep. If I had known you were coming I would have kept them up."

"I'm hungry," Scott said.

He sat at the kitchen table. She served him cold chicken and noodles and dark bread.

I am so glad you're back, she thought.

I must be crazy, he thought.

CHAPTER THIRTY

"Clint!" Hiram Stonebraker barked, "what have you done for Fassberg today?"

"For Fassberg, sir?"

"Goddammit, we've got to think about Fassberg! I'm away for a week on an inspection and Fassberg has fallen three hundred tons a day behind Celle. When you return for the staff meeting, you damned well better tell me what you intend to do for Fassberg!"

"Yes, sir."

Stonebraker had gone to the States with his Logistics people to inspect a materiel depot built at Middletown, Pennsylvania, to support the Airlift. While he was gone, Lieutenant Woodrow Beaver struck!

Beaver had quietly written to Al Capp, creator of *Lil' Abner* and father of the Shmoo, an American leprechaun put on earth to cure man's ills. Beaver reckoned the Shmoo could be helpful to the Airlift.

The lovable pear-shaped little fantasy could be converted into beef, ham, or cheese if one was hungry. You could build a house out of a Shmoo or make them into dresses and shoes. Shmoos could be converted into any denomination of currency. There was nothing Shmoos couldn't do.

Al Capp agreed to help. Beaver had some inflatable Shmoos made and all was in readiness for the moment Hiram Stonebraker left Germany on the Middletown inspection. Beaver had Armed Forces Radio dramatically announce that Shmoos were coming to Berlin!

Ten every day would be parachuted and those lucky Berliners who found them could convert them at the Red Cross for CARE packages.

At the end of the week, the Shmoos had won the heart of the Berliners.

"Beaver! Get in here!"

Stonebraker shoved a *Task Force Times* under his nose. "Well?"

Beaver studied the paper earnestly. "You mean the photo contest to name the Airlift Queen, sir?"

"I mean the goddamned Shmoos!"

Beaver handed the general cables from AP, UP, INS. The Shmoo had stormed the front pages. NBC was sending a top team to document the life of a Shmoo from birth, through a dramatic corridor flight, and on to the German family who found him in Berlin. Three Soviet papers carried front-page editorials denouncing the Shmoos.

"Get the hell out of here," Stonebraker said.

"Yes, sir."

"Beaver!"

"Sir?"

"What did you do for Fassberg today?"

"I sent them a Shmoo this morning."

When Beaver was out of sound-wave blast, a WAF secretary brought in a little plastic Shmoo and set it on the general's desk. The note tied around its neck read: "My name is Buff (Morgan) Shmoo and I have been presented to the boss by his devoted staff. I am guaranteed to triple housing procurement, break the bottleneck at Burtonwood, prevent fog at Tempelhof, predict the weather with unerring accuracy. I am a nice Shmoo and I desire only to serve humanity."

"Where in the hell has the Navy been?"

"Taking care of the Air Force wives!"

Two Navy squadrons of Skymasters arrived, flush with spare parts, wealthy with mechanics, and stuffy with a pride that told them they could put more tons down in Berlin than any squadrons in the Air Force. Now a fleet of two hundred Skymasters forged the Air Bridge with a hundred more of the British.

A huge new transport, the C-74, arrived in Germany with twenty tons of spare engines! An engine Lift began directly from the States.

Globemasters and other new transports came to be used in flying special loads of heavy and bulky machinery. They brought in a dozen new generators for the Western Sector power plant.

Multimillion candlepower, high-intensity lights were installed extending from the center line of the Tempelhof runway through the St. Thomas Cemetery. EVEN THE DEAD CANNOT SLEEP IN PEACE FROM THE AMERICAN AGGRESSION, cried People's Radio.

Superb new beacons and ranges lined the corridors; radar control became absolute; ground-controlled approaches in Berlin gave a promise that this was the miracle to beat . . . General winter.

An army of transportation on the ground kept the rhythm of movement from mines and ports and depots and railheads and marshaling yards to the ready lines at the air bases in uninterrupted tempo.

New tie-down straps, new weight charts, new communication systems . . . loading crews could empty a ten-ton trailer into a Skymaster in twenty minutes. In Berlin, unloading crews could unload ten tons in fourteen minutes.

A direct coal line ran from the Ruhr mines to the sacking plants at Hanau to the air bases at Celle and Fassberg. Mobile weather and operations trucks now briefed the pilots at planeside to cut down turn-around time.

Mobile canteens fed them at planeside; mobile maintenance trucks cured minor ills; turn-around time in Berlin was whittled to a mere thirty-two minutes from touch down through unloading to takeoff.

The immense weather-gathering data centers funneled in data and weather forecasts were changed every half hour. At Gatow in Berlin a method of using the canals to carry the coal by barge to the power plant cut out trucks and saved thousands of gallons of gasoline.

At Great Falls in Montana, MATS laid out an exact duplicate of the Berlin corridors where new crews were trained. Skymasters were loaded exactly as they would be at Fassberg, Rhein/Main, Y 80, Celle. They flew the Montana countryside along beacons and ranges duplicating those in Germany. They landed by GCA around beacons and at glide angles that matched Tempelhof, Gatow, and Tegel in every detail.

On Air Force Day in 1948 the Combined Airlift Task Force set down 6800 tons of coal in Berlin. The next day a special Lift of shoes, blankets, and warm clothing was flown in. Fifteen thousand children were flown out by the British to foster homes in the zones.

There were tears and smiles at Tempelhof. The people of Berlin showered the flyers with gifts that ranged from family heirlooms to trinkets made by school children.

As the first tests of winter were upon them, the American President announced that sixty more Skymasters were coming to Germany! The might of the American nation and the audacious British fortitude had been molded into the most magnificent use of the military in a time of peace.

It rolled now with unstoppable momentum from the engine build-up plants in Texas and California;

from the Materiel Centers around America;

by the Sealift, Marine X;

by the engine Lift;

by the assembly lines of the factories;

by the energy and ingenuity at Erding and Burtonwood and Hanau;
by the raw courage and the skill of the flyers;
by the sleepless hours and labor in bad light and cold of the mechanics and laborers.

As the Gooney Birds were retired one by one from the Lift the beat
. . . beat . . . beat . . . of the giant metronome that Hiram Stonebraker envisioned had been created with the hands of selfless dedication.

CHAPTER THIRTY-ONE—*December 2, 1948*

Berliners awakened by candlelight in icy hovels. The first snows of winter floated down on long shivering lines of voters waiting at the polls. With the Soviet Union boycotting the election, the Democratic Party won a majority in the Western Sector. The first act of the new Assembly was to vote Ulrich Falkenstein as Oberburgermeister of West Berlin.

The United States, Britain, and France then resumed a three-power Kommandatura for the Western boroughs. Among their first duties was to ascertain, with the new Magistrat, how much coal could be rationed to the people. Stocks were at a perilous new low and winter was going to make greater demands.

It was then announced to the Berliners that they would be rationed twenty-five pounds of coal per family for the winter. Ulrich Falkenstein appealed to the Kommandatura to allow them once again to put the forests to the ax to augment this sparse allotment and it was agreed.

Hanna Kirchner, now speaking for the Berlin housewives, told her old comrade that the beloved trees should be spared and taken only as a final desperation.

"Hanna," he said, "trees can grow again in the same place. But if we leave Berlin, we shall never grow here again."

The last of the birches and pines and lindens of once proud forests were felled and People's Radio mocked, "The last act of Western vandalism is to destroy Berlin's watershed and beauty." Meanwhile, at the town of Helmstedt in the British Zone, long lines of coal trains waited in hope for an act of Soviet humanity to allow them to clear and go to Berlin. The trains grew white with snow and rusted in silence.

The defiance in Berlin continued to grow.

Brigadier General Neal Hazzard announced that Americans would help establish a new university in their sector. As thousands of students and faculty broke out of their academic prison in the Soviet Sector, the Free University of Berlin was born and took its first tottering steps in classes held in a hundred damaged, patched-up buildings around the borough of Steglitz.

From the moment of the first Airlift death, Neal Hazzard forbade social contact with the Russians. The breach between the two cities widened on other lines as the Berlin Symphony was forbidden to play on the other side of the Gate and all cultural contact melted.

The Russian prodding never ceased. A threat to cut the American phone lines to the zone was countered by an American promise to cut Soviet phone lines.

Soldiers on both sides became touchy and a sudden battle nearly erupted when Marshal Popov was hauled down for speeding through the American Sector and overzealous Russian guards became threatening.

The Soviet Union seemed obsessed with the building of a War Memorial Cemetery to their dead in the Battle of Berlin in Treptower Park. It was not understood how this could endear them to the Berliners, even of Wöhlman's ilk. A grotesque ode to death was being imposed upon a fallen enemy. First, the pink marble from Hitler's demolished Chancellory was taken to the place and great plaques and monuments bearing Stalin's words, histories of battles, great metal wreaths and statues depicting the agony of Russian heroism were ordered.

In this odd battle of wills, many of the bronze castings were ordered from West Germany. Neal Hazzard played upon the Soviet mania for the project by holding up delivery of the castings until everything was paid for in Western currency.

Counter-Intelligence reported that many of the Soviet Command were leaving. One by one, members of the Russian staff failed to show up at normal public functions. A new crop of officers appeared on the scene. And then it was confirmed that V. V. Azov had disappeared!

A week after Azov vanished, the opera box belonging to General Nikolai Trepovitch was empty at a performance of *Aïda*. Three days

later a small five-line box on the last page of the Red Army publication
announced that Marshal Popov would assume General Trepovitch's
duties in addition to his own.

As the West continued to meet the challenge of winter head on and
the temper of the Berliners turned to pure iron, Popov ordered more
Yak fighter planes into the corridor. They buzzed dangerously close
to the Skymasters and British Yorks. Antiaircraft fire was apt to com-
mence in the corridors close to the stream of planes without prior warning. Target sleeves were towed into the paths of incoming blocs. . . .
But the Sky Bridge did not waver.

The French followed the softest line, insisting to the last that the
Soviet Union could be negotiated with . . . and then their patience
collapsed.

The three military governors of the West called together a press conference to make a dramatic announcement. The honor was given to
General Yves de Lys, who stood before the microphone looking into a
room crammed with journalists from both sides of the Gate.

"As of 0600 this morning, all trade from the Western Zones of Germany to the Soviet Zone is suspended. All transit by waterway, highway, and rail through the Western Sectors of Berlin is ceased."

The West had launched the counterblockade!

CHAPTER THIRTY-TWO

Periodically, M.J. made Hiram throw a party for staff and wives as a
peacemaking gesture. Clint and Judy trotted off to it.

It was snowing when Scott arrived. He went upstairs to see the children. Lynn was down with a sore throat. His magic pocket turned up
a charm of a little Berlin bear. For Tony there was a figurine of a top-
hatted, ladder-carrying chimney sweep. They were made up by the
Berlin Chimney Sweep Association and given as presents to several
hundred Airlift crew members. A welcome fire crackled when he came
down to the living room.

"How were your flights today?"

"Germany has a monopoly on weather," he said. He never complained, so it must have been rough.

"I didn't get a chance to phone your sister," he said, "but I did find an old pal at Tempelhof who said he'd deliver a package."

"That is wonderful. I will give you a box tonight before you leave."

Hilde had made up a parcel for Ernestine of shoes, a warm sweater, underclothing, cosmetics, some tinned food.

"I hope you meet Erna someday," Hilde said. "She is a wonderful girl. It is a shame we only got to know each other so late and under much hardship. I look forward so much to good times with her one day."

Scott sat on the big hassock and stared into the fire. "I'm getting grounded for a few weeks," he said.

"Is anything wrong?"

"No. The flight surgeon says I've flown too many hours, even by Stonebraker's standards."

"Scott, I have never said it, but I want you to know how wonderful this thing is that you do for Berlin. With Erna there, it means even more to me."

He shrugged. "We didn't vote on coming to Germany. We're told where to fly."

"And to drop candy bars to children? And to give up a good life like Colonel Loveless and your general?"

"It has been an interesting challenge," Scott said in what was a semi-official tone of voice.

"Anyhow," she said, "I am glad you won't be flying for a time. You need a rest."

"I'll be taking a leave, Hilde. I want to go away someplace for a week where they don't know about airplanes. Will you go with me?"

She did not go through with her reflexive reaction to say no because that could mean sending him away for good . . . nor could she tell him she really wanted to go. "It would be a mistake, Scott."

"No strings," he said. "Don't answer tonight. I'll call you between flights to Berlin tomorrow. My leave starts day after tomorrow."

As Scott drove to Rhein/Main he knew it would be a long day. A light, freezing rain had iced the road.

Bloc time neared. The crews reported to Operations. Scott's ship would be Number One with a mixed cargo of flour and coal married to malt.

Navigation kits with maps and routes from Italy to England were issued. They were briefed on altitudes, the hack watches synchronized. En route frequencies were gone over.

Plane Number Eight would carry a weather observer;

Plane Number Nine, a check pilot;

Plane Number Ten, an intelligence photographic unit;

Plane Number Twelve, a team from *Time* and *Life*;

Plane Number Fourteen, three VIP's from the State Department.

The weatherman said, "After climbing through moderate to heavy icing you will break through on top at five thousand feet. It will be visual all the way on top. Winds are light, averaging fifteen knots from 320 degrees. A low-pressure cell is slowly developing in the North Sea area which might cause a significant weather in the next forty-eight hours."

An Intelligence briefing stated that Russian Yak fighter-plane activity had increased between Eilsleben and Bernsburg.

Outside, the ten-ton trailers loaded the Skymasters. Loading sergeants supervised the teams of twelve Polish laborers who deftly filled, married, and tied down the cargo.

Jet engines mounted on trucks blasted hot air onto the wings of the Skymasters to de-ice them. After many systems were tried and given up, this proved the best. It was developed by a group of enlisted men at Rhein/Main.

Scott and Stan reached Big Easy One as the jet engines were being driven off. Nick handed Scott his visual-inspection sheet.

A second inspection was made with the pilot and copilot walking around their bird checking wing-tip skin for cuts, loose rivets, checking the de-icer boots, the prop blades for pits and looseness, looking for frayed cables and loose cowlings, for foreign matter in the air scoops, for leaks, for tire conditions, for faulty shuttle valves. The inspection continued in the efficient silence of a pair of surgeons in a medical amphitheater.

Inside the craft, Nick checked the cargo compartments for fire extinguishers, checked the cargo tie-downs, the hydraulic fluid gauges for levels. In the cockpit, Stan went down his list: cabin heater, circuit breakers, reserve fluids.

The three pairs of trained eyes were unable to determine a flaw. Nick brought three boxes into the cabin. One was for delivery to Hilde's sister in Berlin. A second box contained toy parachutes and candy bars. The third box held a number of small toys collected from school children to be distributed in Berlin for a planned Operation Santa Claus at Christmas.

Stan droned down the check list as the trailers drove off.

"Auto pilot servos."

"Off."

"Wing flaps."

"Up."

"Cross Feeds."

"Off."

The dialogue continued until stationtime. The tower called Scott's ship, Big Easy One. He taxied to the end of the runway, lined up, and held.

At precisely 0700, zulu, Frankfurt Air Traffic Center atop the I. G. Farben Building turned the bloc to Rhein/Main. The tower cleared the bloc for takeoff and at three-minute intervals they were airborne.

Scott held his takeoff heading executing a turn at the Darmstadt Beacon climbing at exactly 350 feet per minute at 125 miles per hour. He went over the Darmstadt Beacon at 900 feet on the button, continued to climb toward the assigned altitude, watching for icing.

On a heading of 085 degrees, Stan tuned in for the Aschaffenberg Beacon. In moments its signal, a faint dit-da-da-da-dit was heard . . . became louder. Over the beacon the needle swung wildly, telling them they had reached the null.

Scott turned now to a heading of 033 degrees. Stan tuned in the Fulda Range that would lead them to the Southern corridor. Over Fulda, the bloc set up their precision chain. Each ship radioed his time as he passed over the range and they adjusted their spacing to the three-minute interval and an air speed of 170 mph.

The line of birds droned toward Berlin in flawless precision.

At that same moment, there was activity all over the zones and in the corridors.

A bloc of coal cargo planes from the Fassberg Base moved toward Berlin in the Northern corridor.

At the British base at Wunsdorf, a bloc of Tudor tankers drank in petroleum from underground storage tanks, scheduled to take to the air in forty-six minutes.

At Y 80, crews of the 333d Troop Carrier Squadron of Wiesbaden's 7150th Composite Wing were in the Operations briefing room.

In the Center corridor aircraft of the 40th Troop Carrier Squadron headed back to the joint base at Celle.

In Berlin, ships of Navy VR 6 were being unloaded at Tempelhof.

Nick checked the cargo, came forward. "Every time I look at all this coal, all I can think of is I'm sure glad we don't have to carry the ashes out of Berlin."

Scott didn't hear him. He was trying to face up to a rejection by Hilde. He flirted with the idea of telling her he loved her, even throw out a hint of marriage . . . but he knew she would see right through the scheme.

"We're picking up ice," Stan said.

This, Scott heard. "Wet the props down."

Stan adjusted the rheostat that sent a stream of isopropyl alcohol along each propeller blade. When an inch of ice formed on the leading edge of the wings Scott ordered the de-icer boots turned on. Chunks of ice flaked off into the air stream as the boots inflated and deflated.

The engines groaned under the new load until the plane burst on top into the sun at 5200 feet.

Their eyes burned with the sudden light. They fished about for their sunglasses. Below them lay a solid carpet of clouds.

Stan called Tempelhof. The weather was clear to Berlin. As they continued down the corridor the clouds below them scattered and they could see the ground. Today it held a mantle of new snow.

The magnificent cycle continued all around them:

at Rhein/Main the crews were at planeside making their checks;

at Fuhlsbuttel flour was loaded into British Dakotas and on the taxiways;

at Lübeck, newsprint in the new five-hundred-pound rolls was loaded on trailers to be carried out to the craft;

at Schleswigland, garrison supplies for the French and British had been cleared to take off.

Scott's bloc from Rhein/Main was now under control of Tempelhof Radars. Stan and Nick began the prelanding preparations.

Berlin burst below them, never failing to stun the eye. Chains of lakes and canals interwoven with the stubbed forests. And then mile after mile of gutted-out shells.

Tempelhof Airways slowed the bloc to 140 mph, brought them to 2000 feet. As Scott turned over the Tempelhof Range Beacon, the other bloc, which had flown in down the Northern corridor from Fassberg, had landed at Tegel and were already unloaded and in taxi position to take off.

Scott turned left over the Tempelhof Range. At Wedding Beacon over the French Sector he made his downwind leg to 1500 feet.

"Tempelhof to Big Easy One, use caution. Cross winds fifteen knots gusting to twenty-five knots, west to east. Braking action poor."

Nick grunted. There was always a kicker to landing in Germany.

"Blowers."

"Low."

"Auto pilot."

"Off."

Flaps were set to 10 degrees.

"Booster pumps."

"High."

"Landing gear."

The wheels groaned out of their prison, thumped down, locked.

"Flaps."

Scott set them full down. The bird lowered, chopped at the sudden bursts of wind shooting up from the ruins. The blitz of high-intensity lights in the St. Thomas graveyard led them to the runway. Scott's angle of descent dropped the ship below the level of the four- and five-story apartment houses on both sides of the cemetery.

A Russian spy in an apartment checked off his Skymaster as number 104 to land since midnight. This figure would be checked out against figures received at the Air Safety Center.

A hundred little parachutes billowed from the back door. Cold, numb children ran from rubble piles as the candy bars floated into the cemetery.

The Skymaster was put down deftly two feet after the beginning of the runway in the dead center, giving the full length to nurse it down the slippery steel planking. A FOLLOW ME jeep picked Scott up, led him to the west aprons.

Six seconds after Scott cut engines, a ten-ton trailer was backed to the door of his craft. The first German laborer, bone-thin and ragged, went to the pilot's cabin. Scott gave him a pack of cigarettes and told him to split it among the crew. Most of the pilots did the same.

Tie-down webs were freed. A human chain emptied the ten tons of cargo in sixteen minutes. Nick lost the toss and waited for the mobile canteen to buy coffee and sandwiches.

He watched the swarm of activity, never failing to marvel at the place. Once Tempelhof had been a parade ground for Prussian pomp. In the early days of aviation it had been made into an airfield with stands for barnstorming shows.

Hitler built an enormous edifice to house Goering's Air Ministry. Great steel canopies were high enough to shelter a plane while being loaded and unloaded along the crescent-shaped building.

The building itself, one of the largest in the world, ran from seven floors below the ground to seven above it. The Russians had flooded these subterranean basements, where fighter-plane assembly plants were safe from Allied bombers. Yet, with all of this massiveness, there was the irony that room was planned for but one undersized runway.

Stan found the Red Cross girl and gave her the package for the Operation Santa Claus collection while Scott ran down a buddy who promised to deliver Hilde's package to Ernestine Falkenstein.

A mobile Operations and Weather truck gave them planeside briefings on the return flight. Good luck . . . so far, the low in the North Sea had not developed into a front.

The VIP's were impressed; *Time* and *Life* were impressed.

Women laborers swept the coal dust off the apron and sacked it. Some days they swept up three or four tons.

A short ceremony had been staged for the journalists with their crew being presented with gifts from the Metal Workers' Union.

A number of the planes were partly loaded with light bulbs in crates bearing the crest of the Berlin Bear and the defiant inscription: MANUFACTURED IN BLOCKADED BERLIN.

In thirty-two minutes after touching down at Tempelhof they were going through takeoff procedures again. New blocs were en route, on the way back, or being formed up. The immense Traffic Control Center atop the I. G. Farben Building in Frankfurt mapped this endless parade.

Scott's heart was in his mouth as he cleared Berlin. In an hour and twenty minutes he would call Hilde and she would give him an answer.

CHAPTER THIRTY-THREE

"Hilde, you've been crying," Judy Loveless said, coming into the kitchen.

"I used to cry a lot. I haven't in a long time."

Judy closed the door behind her. "Scott? Your family?"

"Scott. Could I have your advice?"

"I don't think I should interfere, Hilde."

"Please."

"Okay."

Hilde dried her eyes and poured Mrs. Loveless a cup of coffee from the always ready pot, then she sat opposite.

"Scott is going on leave. He has asked me to go with him. Till now there has been nothing between us, I assure you. But he is how he is and he will not change. Somehow . . . I can't find the words to send him away."

"What do you want from him? A playmate? A dancing partner? Do you think it's fair to keep him hanging around?"

"Then what you say is, I must submit."

"What I say is you are so much on the defensive you're not giving yourself a chance to discover your own feelings."

"I don't love him."

"Hilde . . . look at me. Have you ever been in love?"

"No."

"I don't believe Scott Davidson has either. Eventually you must expose yourself to the risk of finding love."

"If I could believe I could have something like you and Colonel Loveless have . . ."

"We didn't pick it off of a tree, Hilde, or find it parked at our front door one day. Being in love is troublesome and it brings pain . . . and it also means being able to give of yourself."

Hilde bowed her head and swallowed hard.

"You're a big girl, Hilde. If you want love, you're going to build it on tears, room by room."

A contribution to the perfection of the Airlift was for the craft to radio ahead to its home base and give in code information on whether his ship needed maintenance or carried cargo.

Those planes needing minor repairs or carrying cargo from Berlin reported it ahead; the information was relayed to the various centers to have everything in readiness as the plane touched down.

Scott's plane was Number One. It would go to Hardstand Number One. A loading master had the chart of the plane and had a trailer loaded with cargo, Trailer Number One.

When each plane cut engines in the matching hardstand number the matching trailer pulled up to continue the cycle flawlessly. The mobile planeside briefings brought in the latest weather data and flight-plan changes.

Number Seventeen reported an oil leak, was pulled out of the bloc, and a new craft took the number.

The control centers charted each bit of loading and maintenance information, engine hours, cargoes, air-traffic bloc times, and fed the data back to the control center at Headquarters in Wiesbaden.

Turn-around time for the bloc was to be forty-nine minutes. Scott grabbed a ride to his office with the Production Control jeep.

He asked the operator for the Loveless number.

"Colonel Loveless residence."

"Hi . . . it's me."

"Hi, me."

Scott heaved a sigh. *"Ja oder nein?"*

"Ja."

"You . . . you mean it?"

"Yes."

"Listen, I got to run. I'll call you soon as I get back from Berlin. We take off in the morning."

"I'll wait to hear from you."

Scott returned to Big Easy One beaming. He clapped his hands together to beat off the cold. Nick handed him the trip sheet. He pinched Nick's cheek. "You're a nice Greek boy, Nick Papas, a nice, nice boy."

"What's it? What's it?"

"Tell Lieutenant Kitchek he's a nice Polish boy and to check out this nice bird."

"The way you're flying you might reach Berlin ahead of the bloc."

Nick grumbled off. He knew what had happened. Scott was going on leave tomorrow. Ten will get you fifty, Hilde was going with him. It was going to be like Cindy all over again. He wanted Hilde to have held out. The bastard always won.

"Before you get too happy," Stan said, "that low in the North Sea has deepened. Berlin is full of weather. It's a cinch we'll have to land by GCA."

"Good," Scott beamed, "I need the practice."

Stan looked to Nick as if to say . . . is he crazy?

"Fly this bird," Scott said when they passed Fulda.

He needed to think. He stretched in a makeshift bunk. The long-eluded victory was almost his. Scott chastised himself for not confronting her with this decision earlier. What the hell, the longer the wait, the sweeter the victory!

He decided to play it smooth and wait until she gave all the signs. He had never wanted a woman as much as he wanted Hilde. And dammit, she never meant to let him go all the while!

Thirty-five minutes past Fulda, Nick shook him from his reverie. He returned to his seat.

"How's the weather?"

"Ceiling in Berlin is five hundred feet, visibility a half mile."

Scott grunted. It was getting close to minimums. The altimeter showed the plane losing altitude. Scott glanced out of the left window and saw the thin white line forming over the black boots, a sight that always quickened the pulse of a pilot.

"Watch the ice, Stan," he said, easing the yoke back to bring the plane to proper altitude.

While wetting down the props and concentrating on the instruments, they had no way of knowing a fuel line in the engine was breaking from metal fatigue and would drip raw gas onto the hot cylinders.

"Tempelhof Airways, this is Big Easy One forty minutes east of Fulda at six thousand feet. Center-line check."

"Big Easy One, this is Tempelhof Airways. We have you under radar control. You are on center line. Report at each thousand-foot level. You are cleared to descend to four thousand."

"Roger."

The fuel line ripped open.

"Big Easy One this is Tempelhof. Ceiling three hundred feet, visibility one half mile. Winds fifteen knots from the northwest, braking action poor. Turn over to Jigsaw at forty-five."

Jigsaw! The code name for ground-controlled approach. A chain reaction of tension was set off down the entire bloc. They were all flying blind. Teams of specialists in the electronic shacks on the side of the runways would soon guide their flight by ethereal voices.

As turbulence shook Big Easy One the hot exhaust ignited the trailing fuel.

"Christ!"

A streak of fire poured from the number-three engine down the side of the plane the instant the fire-warning light came alive.

"Oh shit," Nick said.

Scott reached over Stan, pulled the fire wall shut-off valve, and looked at his watch to let thirty agonizing seconds pass.

"This is Big Easy One. Emergency. Engine on fire."

Scott pulled the CO_2 extinguisher handle discharging white foam to battle the flaming engine, set down the landing gears to ventilate the wheel housing. The fire smothered to stillness.

Scott's trained hand closed the cowl flaps and retarded the throttle on the smoking engine. He nodded to Stan, who pushed the feathering button and snapped off the booster pump. The giant prop slowly turned right-angled to the air flow and came to a halt.

"Tank."

"Off."

Scott flipped the ignition switch. Stan looked out of the window. "I think we've got it."

Scott looked over his shoulder at Nick. The unlit cigar had been chewed in half. He flipped a book of matches back. "Go on, light it."

"All heart, you're all heart."

"This is Big Easy One calling Tempelhof Airways. Fire under control, number-three engine feathered."

The bloc behind Scott held rigid discipline. A struggle was now on to bring in the wounded bird.

"This is Tempelhof calling Big Easy One. Contact Jigsaw on Charlie Channel."

Stan switched to the emergency channel and established contact with GCA.

"This is Jigsaw. What are your intentions?"

With the immediate emergency under control Scott wanted to try for Gatow or Tegel, where the landing would be easier than the steep glide over the cemetery.

"This is Big Easy One calling Jigsaw. Can you give me permission to land at Gatow or Tegel?"

"Stand by."

Gatow had an emergency. A plane had blown a tire and the runway was out of use. Tegel had fallen below minimums and was shut down.

"Big Easy One this is Jigsaw. Cannot comply with your request. Both fields out of operation. Can you turn around and go back to the zone, over?"

Stan and Nick kept quiet. The few seconds to decision did not allow the luxury of discussion or prolonged procrastination. Scott did not know for certain what had caused the fire and therefore not certain it would not erupt again. There was nothing left to fight it with. He had ten tons of cargo on three engines and an icing condition.

"Let's get this mother down," he said to his crew over the intercom. They nodded in agreement.

"This is Big Easy One calling Jigsaw. We want to make an immediate landing at Tempelhof."

Stan and Nick were already going through the emergency procedures, leaving Scott free to concentrate on the instruments. Nick looked outside. Nothing could be seen.

They listened as Tempelhof Radar diverted the rest of the bloc into the Center corridor and back to Rhein/Main.

"This is Jigsaw calling Big Easy One. We have you positive. What is your altitude?"

"This is Big Easy One. We are at fifteen hundred."

"Maintain that altitude until further advised."

Nick and Stan worked down the prelanding check list.

"This is Jigsaw," an airman named Ed Becker said, wondering why he had come to Germany, why he was sitting before this luminous green scope being thrust into the role of the Lord. "Turn left Heading 337."

"Left Heading 337," Stan repeated after Scott's execution.

Fire wagons, ambulances, crash trucks tensed in readiness as the fog began to fall close to the ground.

"This is Jigsaw," Ed Becker said. "You will land on left runway two seven. Wind fifteen knots northwest, cross winds from right, altimeter three zero zero three."

"Roger. Altimeter three zero point zero three."

The NCO behind Ed Becker handed him further weather. "Big Easy One this is Jigsaw. Ceiling one hundred feet, visibility one eighth of a mile."

"Oui vay," Nick whispered.

Stan pretended he didn't hear the transmission, kept working around Scott on the control panel.

"Ask them if they have the high-intensity lights to maximum?"

"This is Jigsaw calling Big Easy One. Lights are on full. You are over Wedding Beacon. Turn right to a heading of ninety degrees, maintain fifteen hundred feet."

"This is Big Easy One. Right ninety degrees, altitude fifteen hundred."

Fog-entombed Tempelhof grew deathly silent. The theodolite measuring the ceiling tried vainly to pierce the thickening fog. Airman Ed Becker studied the blip on the radar screen with a growing ache in his chest and back. The blip was approaching the base leg.

"This is Jigsaw. Turn right to a heading of 180 degrees, maintain fifteen hundred feet, perform prelanding cockpit check."

Stan repeated the instructions.

The clock in the dark room ticked, ticked, ticked. Strange glows cast from the screens put an eerie color on their drawn faces. The blip inched along the scope.

"This is Jigsaw. You are approaching final leg." Ed Becker calculated a correction for wind drift. "This is Jigsaw. Turn right to a heading of 276."

Ed Becker's job was done.

"This is Jigsaw. Stand by for final controller."

Master Sergeant Manuel Lopez of San Antonio had Big Easy One in the precision scope.

"This is Jigsaw calling Big Easy One," said a mixture of Texas drawl and Spanish. "How do you read me?"

"Loud and clear."

"This is Jigsaw. I read you five square. You need not acknowledge further instructions."

Everyone in the shack gathered behind Sergeant Lopez's chair. His job was to keep the plane on proper azimuth, an imaginary line in the sky that ran to the beginning of the runway to keep the craft at proper glide.

"You are a little right of center line. Correct five degrees left to 270."

The blip on the precision scope was now in dead center, heading at the runway.

"Big Easy One, you are on center line six miles from touchdown and approaching glide path."

The million-candle-power krypton lights could not force the fog to yield.

"Big Easy One, ten-second gear warning."

Nick pushed the gear handle. The nacelle doors reopened and the plane shuddered as the gears extended.

"You are in the glide path. Begin descent at 550 feet per minute." Lopez watched the glide scope as it settled high. "You are above glide path one hundred feet, increase your rate of descent."

The flaps were set. Stan and Nick had completed the final check and reported to Scott. Nothing left now but that voice and Scott's nerves. Scott focused himself on the instruments, thought of, but gave up, the idea of a stick of gum. The other two looked outside into nothing. Stan flicked on the wipers. No light at all.

"This is Jigsaw. You are cleared to land. You are four miles from touchdown . . . you are drifting slightly below the glide path . . . adjust rate of descent up twenty-five feet . . , turn right to 272 degrees.

Beat . . . beat . . . beat . . . beat. . . .

"Big Easy One this is Jigsaw. You are one mile from the end of the runway approaching GCA minimums and coming up on the cemetery. You are on center line, excellent rate of descent . . . you are a quarter of a mile from touchdown . . , you are on the glide path . . . on center line . . . you are fifty feet above glide path over the runway. Take over and land."

Lopez closed his eyes and prayed.

"I see the lights!" Stan cried.

Scott saw the runway lights rush by! His speed was high due to excess turbulence and altitude at the end of the runway. He had all the power off. Big Easy One cannonaded far down the runway.

Scott shoved the nose wheel down and as it bounced hard on the runway he started gingerly hitting the brakes as the plane careened, slipped closer to the end.

They hit the overrun. Scott plied the brakes as hard as he dared. Big Easy One halted two feet from the railroad track siding.

They sat for several seconds. Stan took off his earphones and got out of his seat. "Wise guy," he said.

"Smart ass," Nick said.

The fog was so thick that the FOLLOW ME jeep which drove them to Operations became lost en route and ended up in the old Luftwaffe pistol range two miles on the other side of the second runway.

"Sorry, Captain Davidson, no takeoffs after dark with three engines, no three engine takeoffs from Tempelhof. No way to fix a fuel leak at Tempelhof."

"I know that, goddammit. I helped write the manual. I want the first ride back to Rhein/Main or Y 80."

"Sorry, Captain Davidson, operations are closed down."

"What the hell am I supposed to do?"

"Go to sleep, I think, sir. We've arranged quarters for you and your copilot at the Columbia Club and your engineer at Transit Airmen's Quarters. We trust you will be comfortable."

"Dammit, I'm supposed to start my leave tomorrow."

"It is ceiling zero. And please bear in mind that Berlin is blockaded by land and sea. I suggest that you do not try those routes."

"All right, wise ass, I want to phone Wiesbaden."

"Sorry, Captain, you need a priority to get a phone line out of Berlin."

As he left in utter defeat he turned at the door at the harassed young officer. "I don't like you," Scott said.

CHAPTER THIRTY-FOUR

Hildegaard Falkenstein had a lightness of heart and a happiness she had never known before Scott picked her up.

Things are on the way, he thought, as they drove into the country-side.

She had not been into the villages and forests for longer than she cared to remember. She had never traveled with this feeling of wonderment. How lovely it was. How lovely Scott Davidson was. Hilde's eyes glowed with the discoveries that came from her daring to open locked doors.

At the end of the first day's drive they decided to stop for the night at Rombaden, about halfway to the Bavarian Alps.

Over the Landau River from the city, the Four Seasons Hotel had rooms available to American officers. Hilde remembered being in Rombaden once with her father in the early days of Hitler. It was a big Nazi city then.

The Four Seasons was a bit seedy from the lack of upkeep and new replacements and the uniforms were threadbare, but there was still a touch of the old elegance.

Scott was warm. Scott was understanding. He brushed away all awkwardness by taking separate rooms on different floors.

Dinner was only adequate, but the aristocratic service made her feel like a queen.

They drove across the bridge to Rombaden and for the next hours engaged in pub-crawling along the wild and reputed Princess Allee filled with the bawdy, the singing, the risqué.

They were happy crossing back over the Landau to the hotel. Off the lobby a great fire roared in the seventeenth-century fireplace and they sipped cognac, which Scott knew the bar could find if they really wanted to.

It was cozy and dreamy. Hilde cuddled close to Scott and lay her head on his shoulder.

For Scott Davidson, the long-awaited, long-denied sign was being given. World flyer and past master of the moment of woman's surrender; triumph was close at hand. He allowed Hilde to loll in her joy, let her approach the delicate moment. He must do nothing to deter her own train of thought. He became deliberately passive.

Hilde's inner conflict began the moment she decided to go away with Scott. She began to realize that she deliberately invited temptation in the hopes of having him. She remembered so many things now. The voices, the sounds, the smells. Scott was American. He was a big man and he smelled good. He was clean, like they were.

"Honey, we'd better turn in," he whispered. "We have a long drive tomorrow. I'll see you to your door," he said in pure Virginian.

He turned her lock.

"Good night, Scott. It has been a most beautiful day."

"Good night, honey," he said boyishly.

Hilde took his hand and brought him into her room. Scott, like a little child, allowed himself to be led. Hildegaard's embrace had none of the calculation or sophistication of a trained lover. She was crazy with desire.

Scott knew her eruption had to come from the liberation of long-imprisoned emotions. Careful, he said to himself, careful, Scott. He handled her with deliberate slowness . . . and then they were at the bedside.

Even in this mad moment Hilde longed to cry out, "I love you, Scott," but she could not do it. She writhed with passion, fearing that her declaration would be a sign of weakness.

She almost cried in desperation, begging him to assure her that he loved her. But Scott gave no word. They lay, side by side, like a pair of animals unable to declare love.

As suddenly as Hilde's passion rose, it collapsed. She rebelled at his touch. They lay stiffly, awkwardly, dumbfounded, silent.

Hilde spoke first . . . a harsh whisper to ask him to leave. Scott did not like men who either pleaded with women or tried to manhandle them. Even at the brink, a man has to keep his pride. He had guessed wrong before . . . he guessed wrong again.

Scott left her without a scene, got into his car, returned to Princess Allee, and drank himself into a stupor. Near dawn the German owner called for the American Constabulary, which established that the captain belonged at the Four Seasons and returned him to the hotel.

Scott's fingers felt the big, soft down pillow. It took a long time for him to fight his eyes open. The room was in shadow light from an opening in the drapes. He sat up, ever so slowly, held still until the thumping in his head beat more quietly, and smacked his lips to get rid of the foul taste.

The fire in the fireplace was nearly out. Scott moaned and shivered to the window, pulled the drapes open. The Landau River flowed below him. "Christ, where am I?" The Four Seasons Hotel . . . Rombaden . . . Hilde! Ugh! The marble floor of the bathroom chilled his feet. He dunked his head in the water basin, examined himself in the mirror. Hilde!

Hilde was packed and waited in the lobby for a taxi to take her to the train station in the city across the river. Scott Davidson approached with that damned boyish innocence with no trace of anger.

"I guess we should sit and talk," he said.

"I don't want a scene."

"Only women make scenes," he said. "Besides, I'm a sick man. Hilde, sit down. The one thing you should know is that, come hell or high water, I'm a gentleman."

She walked to the fireplace and edged onto a couch. "You are a clever man, Captain. I would suppose that your memoirs should rank with the greatest."

"Hilde, I don't get it. You know what I am and you went away with me . . ."

"Stop it," she demanded. "It is true that I love you and I need you. And I do thank you for arousing feelings in me I did not know I possessed. Scott, you are a fighter pilot by instinct. Your life is only for the moment of the kill."

"Then take me for what I am."

"For you, Scott, the kill is the beginning of the end. For me, love is going to be the beginning of the beginning."

The hall porter came and told Hilde a taxi was waiting. Scott said she would be ready in a few moments.

"If it will give you any consolation," she said, "this trip was my fault. It was unforgivable of me to put a little boy in a candy store and tell him not to touch."

Scott felt a need for a few light, face-saving remarks. "See you around."

"You are never to call on me again," she said firmly.

Scott saluted, grinned. "If you knew what you were missing, you'd cut your throat."

"My dear Scott . . . so would you."

Hilde left. Scott watched her disappear. As the cab drove off he seemed to remember faintly the tear-filled voice of his wife telling him that someday he would crash and it would be monumental; for when Scott Davidson got dumped a hundred people whose hearts he had broken would be standing on the side lines and cheering.

Nick Papas prepared the dining-room table for a payday card game. The captain came in.

"What the hell you doing back?"

"Phased out."

"Finished?"

"Kaput. That's baseball."

"You still care for her?"

"Hell no."

"It's just as well," Nick said. "Pour yourself a belt and sit down because I've got some poop for you. Remember Chuck Ames?"

"Airways, Philippines."

"That's right. Saw him last night in Frankfurt. He's just been transferred here from Berlin. Anyhow, he's been in Berlin from the first day of occupation."

"So?"

"He was here a couple weeks ago looking for housing and all that crap. He was at the Scala Club and he saw you there with Hilde."

"I didn't see him."

"He took off. Tell you why. He had met Hilde in Berlin over a year ago. Only then, her name was Hilde Diehl, and she worked in a joint called Paris Cabaret. Scott, them damned women fool you every time . . . she was a hooker."

CHAPTER THIRTY-FIVE

A maid led Gerd to his Uncle Ulrich's study. He was surprised by the austerity in which the Oberburgermeister of Berlin lived, although it was in keeping with his political image with the people.

The idealists such as his uncle were necessary for that transition period Germany was going through to keep the occupation authorities content. Soon enough, Gerd thought, the German people would look to the new generation of businessmen such as himself who were rebuilding Germany from its ashes. The Ulrich Falkensteins would pass on and no one would replace them.

Ernestine entered. "Hello, Gerd, won't you sit down?"

He made himself comfortable, lit an Ami cigarette. "Tomorrow is Christmas Eve," he said tersely. "It would please us if you paid us a visit."

"I see."

"It is Father's idea and I agree. We should try to become a family again."

"I am sorry," she said. "I will never go to your home so long as Hilde is not welcome."

"Erna, we must begin again somewhere. You will find a number of changes in Father's attitude."

Ernestine had met her mother secretly from time to time and learned that her father was in poor health. In their visits her mother had spent most of the time echoing Father's views about the cruelty of fate. Yet, this was a good moment. Ernestine had always desired a reunion and the first move had come from her father.

"Our parents," Gerd said, "must accustom themselves to a new generation which rebels at the kind of obedience we were forced to give. Having Frau Kirchner as Oberburgermeister of Berlin came as a prelude of drastic changes in the German society."

Ernestine had spoken about Frau Kirchner and the new generation of Germans with her uncle many times. Gerd, like most Germans, dropped the hostility of the defeat as well as their Nazi friends when it was no longer profitable. His attitude, arrogance, and ambitions had not changed. The only change was the way of doing business. Gerd was clever, she thought, and his kind will be able to convince people, particularly the Americans, about the "new" Germany.

"You will come?" he asked again.

"It is a matter I must discuss with Uncle Ulrich."

"By all means. I hope you decide favorably. I trust Uncle Ulrich will honor us with a visit," he added carefully, "and I should like you to meet my fiancée."

She spoke to her uncle about Gerd's visit later in his study where they had wiled away many hours just talking together.

"It is not like Father to either forgive or forget anyone whom he feels has wronged him," Ernestine said.

Ulrich nodded.

"From the time you were sent to the concentration camp until you returned to Berlin your name was forbidden as was Uncle Wolfgang's."

"Time," Ulrich said, "time softens us all up. It bleeds the will power that is needed to sustain a long feud."

"But do you really believe this comes from his heart?"

"I think," Ulrich said, "the ring is closing."

"Don't be a mystic, Uncle."

"But mystics we must be. Men such as Bruno are common in our people. They are certain their life is guided by a mysterious fate and not by themselves. Unavoidable 'fate' is a built-in excuse for failure. One, like your father, who sees himself as a victim of fate is apt to be superstitious, unclear of mind. Bruno cannot admit to himself his life was a lie. He has wrapped himself in 'fate' to avoid both guilt and shame of the Nazi era. But . . . every man and woman who lived in Nazi Germany in our generations must, in the end, seek an acquittal from God."

"Once I had a letter from that boy in the SS," Erna said. "It was his last, from Stalingrad. He wrote me that now that he was facing his Maker he was frightened because of the things he had done."

"Yes. And it is the same with Bruno. It will be the same with sixty million Germans. They will come to that place far up the road where they can no longer avoid the questions."

"But what does Father seek from us?"

"An avenue of redemption, a proof of his innocence. Some Germans will stand at the Lord's throne and say, see here, God, I had a Jewish friend. I did not like what happened to him. Bruno Falkenstein builds a case. He will say, God, my brother was in a concentration camp and he has returned to our family. My daughter has left my roof, but I am so great and generous I have forgiven her. Am I not worthy?"

"What should we do, Uncle?"

"He is your father . . . my brother . . . our burden, our cross."

Bruno advanced toward his daughter, took her hand, patted it. "It was good of you to come, Erna," he said, his voice choking with emotion.

"*Froeliche Weinachten, Vater,*" she whispered.

Herta ran from the room in order not to show tears.

"Sit, sit," her father said.

His old pinstripe suit was worn out, but there was still a trace of grandness in it. It hung on him poorly. Even by candlelight she was struck by how he had aged. It was this that gave her a sudden knowledge that a parent was slipping away.

They lived in the same rooms, but the rooms were warm while the others in the building were freezing. The candlesticks were silver.

The windows were not covered with tin and boards, but by heavy drapes. The little alcove shared by Erna and Hilde was a tiny luxury of leather couch and desk for Gerd.

As they spoke of small things she realized that his age, his illness, had caused a loss of anger.

"I have learned that you are not well these days, Father."

"The wear and tear of life. Fate has dealt us cruel blows."

"Gerd told me it is not necessary for you to work any longer. How do your days pass?"

"I am growing old. I make my peace with God." He rubbed the back of his hand nervously . . . faltered. "How is Hilde's health?"

"She is happy. She lives in Wiesbaden and works for an American family."

"The Amis are not too bad. They have paid back much for how they ruined Berlin with their bombs."

Gerd arrived with his fiancée, Renate Hessler. The girl was only nineteen years of age; Herta assured Erna she was from a "good" German family.

Renate was waxen-faced and moved with the forced gestures of a mannequin. Gerd had her lavishly decorated in a way that belied the hardships outside. Her speech was superficial. She could talk about almost nothing other than clothes.

Ernestine saw her as a decorative ornament for Gerd to parade in public. Renate would be trained in the German manner to serve her man. The luxuries Gerd would be able to bring her was ransom enough to assure him he would be allowed innumerable mistresses.

After an exchange of drivel, Erna was tempted to ask Gerd if Renate was a member of the new Germany or the old.

"Ulrich will come?" her father asked for a third time.

"Yes, but Christmas is a bad time for the Oberburgermeister of Berlin. He has many orphanages and hospitals to call upon."

"Yes, yes, I understand."

The electricity in Steglitz Borough was turned on an hour early as a Christmas gift from the Americans. Herta scampered to the stove to prepare the meal.

At long last the car of the Oberburgermeister stopped before the building. A number of passing people stopped, surrounded him. They stood in the snow to shake the hand of Ulrich Falkenstein . . . their new "father."

Erna watched all this from the window above and looked at Gerd and her mother and Renate, and wondered if anything had really changed at all.

As Ulrich disappeared into the building, Erna watched the excitement rise in her father. He stood, adjusted his dress, a shadow of the old pomp, shoulders back, erect.

Gerd welcomed his uncle at the door with a proper bow, then the brothers stood face to face. Ulrich opened his arms and Bruno came to him and they embraced.

"Froeliche Weinachten, Bruno."

For the first time in her memory, Erna saw her father cry.

CHAPTER THIRTY-SIX

Hildegaard thought that it was cruel of the Americans to order Colonel Loveless away on Christmas Eve. Clint came home in the afternoon and informed the family that he had to go to the Erding Base. There was a foul-up on the small-parts assembly lines.

Hilde rushed the dinner of goose. It was eaten half heartedly, the opening of gifts around the tree became confused and miserable. Clint pulled out when the staff car came.

On Christmas Day he phoned from Erding. Judy cried and Lynn cried because Daddy was alone. The children and Hilde all insisted Mommy go down to Erding and stay with him. Clint was miserable but protested the idea . . . weakly.

When everyone reassured her they wanted her to make the trip, she packed her bags in minutes. Clint meanwhile drove to Munich to find a hotel room.

When Hilde and the children saw Judy off at the railroad station it became a good Christmas for everyone.

Erna's letter came the next day. When the children had been put to sleep, she stoked the fire and read it over for a third time.

Erna was a saint. Hilde knew she would never have gone back to her father, first. Hilde did not hate him so strongly as she once believed. These days hate was tempered by pity and the wisdom of maturity.

Time healed so many things. Perhaps it could heal this too. Perhaps she would see her family again.

She wrote to Erna that the silly business with the flyer was over. Having lost her heart for the first time, it was proving difficult. She reaffirmed her contention that love was a bother and could bring nothing but pain.

Hilde wrote of thoughts of coming back to Berlin. She wanted to study so that in time she could carry her own weight. But mostly, she wanted to be with Erna and to help take care of Uncle Ulrich.

A phone call came from Munich. Colonel Loveless had gotten a room at the Bayerischer Hof. Hilde heard Mrs. Loveless giggle on the phone and whisper, "Clint, stop it." They were having a grand time. Mrs. Loveless said the colonel would have to stay at Erding till after New Year's.

Hilde assured her everything at home would be under control and insisted she stay with him. Colonel Loveless took the phone, "Hilde, I love you," he said. When the call was done, she returned to her letter to Erna.

The doorbell rang. Scott Davidson stood out in the cold. Except for rare moments, Hilde had learned complete control of herself; she walked away, leaving the door open. He trailed in slowly, holding his hat in his hand.

"Hi."

Hilde turned her back to him, braced herself.

"Know something. I've never been lonely at Christmas before. I'm lonely as hell."

"The children have missed you."

"How about you?"

"I cannot say I have been happy."

"Me, too, I'm not happy."

"Scott, I asked you not to see me. If you persist I will move away from here. It will make life very difficult for me."

"I've got a better idea. Why don't we get married." He came up behind her slowly. "I love you, Hilde."

She looked through misty eyes at the fire. Scott sat on the big hassock. "We act like a couple of people facing a firing squad."

"Once I believed that marrying an American would answer all my problems. I wanted a world that did not exist. And then . . . I had too much of another kind of world. Somewhere in between there will be a life for me . . . back in Berlin. As for us, Scott . . . it won't work."

"Hilde. I'm me. I won't ever change in a lot of ways and I couldn't promise that. But I know that you are the only one I've ever really wanted in my life and I know damned well that I'm going to do whatever is necessary to make it work."

A smile came from her heart. She believed him.

"We'll both have to learn how to give," he said. "I know you'll take care of me, Hilde . . . I never felt anyone ever could before. I want more than anything to take care of you."

"Scott, there is so much more to it."

"No, there isn't, except we've been damned fools."

"You don't understand. After the war survival had many prices. Berlin was a nightmare. I was very vain and foolish . . ."

"I don't give a damn what happened in Berlin."

She found the strength to face him, somehow. The shadow of the fire played on her face. "I did not go to sleep with you because the only thing that I could have from you was your respect . . . Scott, I was a prostitute."

"I know all about Hilde Diehl and the Paris Cabaret."

Hilde hid her face and cried softly. "Oh God . . . why did you come back?"

She felt his closeness and the love in him and she let herself be held and soothed. "I came back because I'd be some kind of a damned fool to let you go."

"Is there really a chance for us?"

"We know the worst in ourselves and each other and we've faced it openly. I guess a couple of people like us have the best chance in the world."

CHAPTER THIRTY-SEVEN

The New Year's office party was in full swing. Sean ducked it to get back to his own office to finish work on a pressing document.

There was the first rumblings of a shift in population from the

Soviet Zone. Because there was an avenue of escape Sean felt that there could be floodlike crossings of refugees in the future. They had to establish ways to weed out spies among the refugees, establish secret places to protect important defectors, arrange housing for ordinary refugees, ways to move them from Berlin into the zone quickly. Most of all, Sean underlined, *The Gate Must Be Kept Open.*

This is the only offensive position we hold against the Communists. We can physically bleed their economy by encouraging more people to defect. . . .

He was interrupted by the phone.

"Colonel O'Sullivan."

"Hi, this is Lil."

"Hi."

"I've been trying to reach Bless for half an hour."

"Last time I saw him he was feeling no pain and chasing a couple of WAC's around General Hansen's desk."

"That fat cop! He knows we've got a party tonight and he knows I've got to get to the commissary and he knows he's got the car."

Sean glanced at his watch. "I've got about a half-hour's work. I'll run you to the commissary because I think he's going to need a nap."

"You're a love."

"Ernestine said she'd be over by nine to help you get everything ready."

Sean put in a call to have "patrols" scour the halls for Blessing and send him to his office. He continued to work on his report.

"Just before the battle . . . mother . . .
I am thinking most of you!"

Sean sized up the alcohol content of his friend. Bless was about fifty-fifty, still in operating condition. He plopped into a chair, scratched his belly, and set his feet on Sean's desk. "You sent for me, sir?"

"Lil's got the storm flag up."

"Ohhhh, Jesus. I was supposed to take her to the commissary. Ohhhhh, Jesus. I bet she chews out my tail."

"If you'll crap out for fifteen minutes I'll run you home and take her to the store. You've got to get a nap if you're going to be jolly at the party later."

"Sean, you're a pal. You got it made. Don't get married."

"Matter of fact, that's kind of what I have in mind. New Year's is a good time to begin with a clean slate."

Bless became sober, quick. His feet dropped off Sean's desk with a thud and he broke into a sweat. "You better come to my office," he said grimly.

Sean was puzzled by the sudden change. He followed Bless across the hall; the door was locked behind them. Bless unlocked his desk and Sean was handed a familiar-looking folder. Blessing had his hands on his face. "I swear to God, I don't know what to do."

Without opening the folder, Sean sensed what had happened. "How long have you had this?"

"About two weeks ago CIC had him listed along with about twenty others for a routine check. It was only last week we found those hidden files from the Labor Ministry. No one has seen this but me . . . and you."

Sean opened the cover . . . BRUNO FALKENSTEIN.

His trained eye searched the pages of the Nazi documents. There had been three Falkenstein brothers all raised in the tradition of the pre-war Democratic Party labor movement.

Ulrich became a major figure in the unions and political life in Berlin. His brothers, lesser figures.

When Hitler came, Ulrich and Wolfgang were among the few who held to their beliefs in the face of disaster. Ulrich went to Schwabenwald Concentration Camp; Wolfgang was murdered by slow strangulation at Plötzensee for his part in the plot against Hitler.

Bruno was the mediocre of the three. Nazi doctrine appealed to mediocre men. The Nazis made mediocre men big, gave them positions beyond their ability in a normal society in exchange for unquestioning obedience. Bruno became a Nazi. Today he echoed the German chorus that he was forced into it to protect his livelihood, and because he had no choice.

Because of his background he was put into the Labor Ministry. Public knowledge of his activities was deliberately kept vague by him. Even his own family knew little except that he was considered a fairly important official; both his income and privileged way of life proved that out.

The documents Sean read were sealed in Bruno Falkenstein's own hand! He had planned and executed operations for the securing and shipment of tens of thousands of slave laborers from Poland for the

Krupp and I. G. Farben industries. Bruno Falkenstein, by his own signature, was a Nazi criminal.

Sean set the folder on Blessing's desk, glassy-eyed with confusion.

"I've been a cop for a long time, Sean," Bless said. "There were times I had a prisoner who I knew should be free. Listen to me, Sean . . . there is a time when a cop has to be judge and jury."

"He deserves what's coming to him . . ."

"Sure he does, but you don't and neither does Ernestine. Neither does his brother. Maybe they'll throw the book at him just to prove he isn't being protected by Ulrich Falkenstein. And don't forget, he may be a bastard, but it's her old man. Sean . . . there's thousands of these bastards getting away. This one won't matter."

Sean O'Sullivan sat in the darkness like an agonized Hamlet. Over their little room in Reinickendorf, British Hastings burst through the clouds into the snowfall, landing at Tegel.

What terrible forces were there that was making their love hopeless? They had struggled to overcome . . . they had nearly succeeded. Once he had judged a man harshly for the same thing. He had re-created the sin of Dante Arosa the moment he hid the files on Bruno Falkenstein. He who had never been able to understand Dante Arosa's human weakness.

Ernestine longed for a relationship that would bring Hilde back to the family. If Bruno Falkenstein were sent to prison the raging scandal and her own sense of guilt would make a life together impossible.

If he continued to keep the secret, he would have to ask her to begin life with a lie hanging over their heads that would grow instead of diminish. Sean's own sense of right and wrong told him that God could not permit such a lie to remain hidden and untested.

She came to their room, brushing the snow from her. At that moment he loved her more than right or wrong . . . more than his sense of duty. He wanted now only to survive for a month, a week, a day . . . and he was filled with fear.

CHAPTER THIRTY-EIGHT

"Comrade Colonel," Marshal Alexei Popov said to Igor, "one would gather that the Americans and British did not study your estimates of their collapse."

When a political commissar harassed you that was one matter. When a marshal of the Red Army questioned your competence, it was another.

"If you will recall the conference of our decision," Igor began his defense, "I explained at that time a great deal of the success or failure of the Airlift would depend on American determination. I was ordered to stick to mathematics."

"And what about your assurances the Airlift would collapse this winter?"

"If our intelligence had supplied me with proper information about the high development of ground-controlled approach systems, I would have made a different estimate."

It was, in fact, everyone's blunder, but no one's blunder. Popov realized that the faithful ally, General winter, had been beaten. The colonel was a good officer. Karlovy's estimation of the situation had been echoed throughout the entire Soviet command.

"Make contact again with the American," Popov said. "Inform him that I want to begin personal discussions with General Hansen."

Igor felt the same amazement as everyone at Headquarters. With only half the days of the winter considered safe for flying, the Airlift was setting down five thousand tons every twenty-four hours. From time to time, the operation was closed for an hour or a day. At times, the Western Sector's coal stocks dipped below a week's reserve and food became so scarce that part of the city was a hairline away from starvation, total darkness, freezing.

But the momentum of the Airlift was so powerful it was able to recover instantly. Beat . . . beat . . . beat . . . the giant metronome ticked on through driving winds and sleet-covered runways . . . beat . . . beat . . . beat . . . Tempelhof . . . Tegel . . . Gatow.

The electronic miracle wrought by GCA became so finely honed that the planes could be brought down in their interval virtually blind. GCA was the final link in solving the riddle. Beat . . . beat . . . beat

. . . Tempelhof . . . Tegel . . . Gatow . . . ten tons . . . ten tons . . . ten tons.

Soon it would be spring and the Airlift would soar to greater heights. The scent of colossal victory for the West was in the air.

"Look up to the sky, Berliners," Ulrich Falkenstein's voice came over the loudspeaker trucks, "look up to the sky for that is where freedom comes . . ."

Under his leadership they had made a city of their own with its own police, university, currency. Berliners knew their own strength and the strength of their allies. They took the offensive.

The Western counterblockade shut off raw materials from flowing into the Russian-raped Zone and it staggered the economy. Blockade runners risked bullets to crash into the Western Sectors. People stood up against the bully police of Adolph Schatz.

And then, in the scheme of things, Adolph Schatz was found to be no longer useful to the regime and he disappeared without mourners.

Beat . . . beat . . . beat . . . Tempelhof . . . Tegel . . . Gatow. "This is Jigsaw calling Big Easy Twenty-two. You are one mile from touchdown. You are on center line. You are on the glide path . . ."

"This is Jigsaw . . ."

"Big Easy Fourteen calling Jigsaw . . ."

"Tempelhof Airways calling Big Easy Thirty . . ."

"This is Jigsaw . . ."

"Gatow Airways calling Big Easy Six . . ."

"This is Jigsaw . . ."

The Soviet Union launched a last-ditch propaganda campaign attacking the legality of the air corridors claiming they were no longer valid. The precisely drawn and clearly stated documents made up three and a half years earlier by Hiram Stonebraker proved unassailable.

To back Soviet claims, Popov flooded the corridors with more fighter planes without advising the Air Safety Center. Ground firing erupted all through the Soviet Zone along the corridors. Searchlights were shined into the eyes of American and British flyers.

Beat . . . beat . . . beat . . . Tempelhof . . . Tegel . . . Gatow. "This is Jigsaw calling Big Easy . . ."

"I hope my arrival at this time of night is not awkward," Igor said.

"Of course not," Sean said.

"No, no, fraulein, please stay," he said to Ernestine. "This time I brought the vodka," he continued trying to be friendly. "I saw you were running low. May I?"

He took off his cap, sat at the table in the center of the room, and filled three glasses. Sean offered him a cigarette.

"Lucky Strikes. I confess I am going to miss these."

"Expecting to travel?"

Igor shrugged. "I have been guilty of gross underestimations." He spread his arms out like an airplane, pointed toward the window, where the engines' drone renewed itself each 120 seconds. "If I hadn't seen it myself, I would not have believed it possible."

Igor hoped that he would be allowed to work and teach the things he had learned about air safety and GCA at the Air University. He believed great efforts should be launched to imitate the American transport system although he realized no study of the Airlift would be allowed to be taught for that would be an admission of American superiority.

He touched glasses with Sean, drew hard on the cigarette. "My errand this time is to ask you if General Hansen is amenable to discussions with Marshal Popov?"

"The marshal knows our phone number," Sean answered.

So blunt and logical, Igor thought. Igor walked to the window, watched the procession of planes for several moments. "For some reason I do not like to leave like this. Nothing seems to be answered. I think I am most sorry about the fact you and I haven't become better friends."

"The doors were always open until our flyers started getting killed."

"When does all of this stop?"

"A long time ago we made a pact not to talk politics. It's too late in the day to get involved in Marxist dialogue."

"A parting thought perhaps. That would not be treaty-breaking."

"What good would it do, Colonel Karlovy? Where you are going you cannot pursue your curiosity."

"That does not keep me from being curious."

"It will end when the Russian people stop accepting their own degradation as a condition of life and when the Russian people refuse to allow themselves to be used to degrade other human beings."

Igor was white-lipped. "I'm sure I don't understand you."

"I'm sure you do," Sean said.

The Russian smiled, gulped down his vodka in the grand style, nodded to Ernestine, shook Sean's hand, coldly, and started for the door, then turned. "I should like your assistance on a personal matter," he sputtered.

Igor loathed himself for each step of his return. He sat, filled his glass again, stared glumly at the floor. "The girl, Lotte, is with child . . . she has a damned fool notion that doctors in the American Zone are better. In this instance, the mother bears the entire burden and I honor her decision," he lied. "Will you help her cross over?"

"Yes."

"Good, she will be pleased. What do you want her to do?"

"Is she able to move around freely?" Sean asked bluntly.

Igor was now faced with the first of his confessions. "No . . . the two of us do not go out together . . . because of the lack of transportation," he further lied.

"When you are at Headquarters, is she free to move?"

Igor did not want to answer, but knew he must.

"My chauffeur is from the . . . political side of things . . . she is always in his sight."

"Does she ever cross through the Gate?"

"From time to time she is driven to the free market in the Tiergarten."

"Good enough," Sean said. The quicker the execution was made, the better the chance for success. "Tomorrow," he said.

Igor's pain registered visibly.

"Tomorrow," Sean repeated, "between noon and two o'clock she is to come to Tiergarten. She is to carry absolutely nothing out. She will wear a red bandanna and look for a vendor named Braunschweiger. She will identify herself to him as Helen and ask to purchase a Swiss watch."

"The driver?"

"He will be accosted and delayed by some British security people the moment she makes contact. They will demand to see his papers and otherwise stall him. We will create a confusion and during it she will be taken out and hidden. I can't tell you how, but we'll get her back to the zone."

Igor nodded that he understood. The final degradation was on him now. He took a letter from his tunic and handed it to Sean. It was instructions to a West Sector bank where he had a blind, numbered account in B marks. "This will take care of her and the child for a number of years."

Ernestine realized that this was no spur of the moment plan, but a long thought out and dangerous move. "How can you let her go knowing you will never see your own child!"

Igor smiled pathetically. "I can assure you, fraulein, it is not easy."

Sean put his hand on Igor's shoulder. "We can get you over too."

Igor shook his head. "We don't learn, either of us. The greatest single mistake made by the Soviet command was not to understand how much an American loves his country. You see, Colonel O'Sullivan . . . a Russian loves his just as much."

"But in Berlin you are wrong," Sean said.

"That is the final love," Igor said. "To know the faults and the wrongs of that which you love . . . and go on loving just the same."

CHAPTER THIRTY-NINE

Scott Davidson was given a new toy to play with.

The first Boeing C-97, a mammoth multipurpose transport called the Stratofreighter, arrived at Rhein/Main. Twin-decked, its four powerful Pratt Whitney engines could cruise at half again the speed of the Douglas Skymaster and bring in a twenty-five-ton pay load.

The tail had a pair of clam-shell doors and a self-contained power hoist running the length of the plane that could load on and set in large pieces of machinery, trucks, cannons, then roll them forward on ball-bearing strips on the floor.

It was a magnificent ship destined to serve MATS as an interim plane until even larger and faster transports could be developed; America knew now that she must never again be without Airlift capacity.

The roomy forward-control cabin seemed like a summer palace after the confines of the Gooney Birds and Skymasters. Scott tested the ship with the Boeing people, certain that his new love of this big old bird was a sign of advancing age.

It was a long way removed from the first milk run to Berlin with the Gooney Birds setting down eighty tons a day . . . the Skymasters brought in six and seven thousand tons. Yet, it was less than a year that it all had started!

On flight number two hundred to Berlin, Hiram Stonebraker handed him a set of gold oak leaves. "Major," he said, "we're kicking your ass upstairs. We want you over at Headquarters as vice operations chief."

Scott would be the number two pilot in the entire Airlift. His first job would be to write a manual on the characteristics and use of the Stratofreighter in Operation Vittles.

As winter ended, old hands took new duties. New crews came with new ships. The long-standing joke of the Airlift, the illusive definition of "temporary duty" was finally explained. With the new crews coming from Great Falls, rotation from Germany was commenced.

Stan Kitchek was lost after Scott's transfer to Headquarters. He was promoted to captain, accepted "permanent change of station," made a first pilot, and transferred to the base at Celle which had been turned into the model of the Airlift, the epitome of precision of air-cargo transportation.

Master Sergeant Nick Papas was advised that he had a month's leave accumulated, which was now payable. He phoned Scott.

"Want to say good-by to an old Greek?"

They met in the bar of the NCO Rocker Club in Wiesbaden a little later. Nick was packed and ready to take off.

"So, what are you going to do now?"

"Check the bank balances in Chicago. Then, who knows? I got twenty years service come September. Maybe I'm getting a little old for this crap. I may just do it up in real Greek style, have the relatives send a girl over from the old country."

"Hey, how about that."

"I never said anything about you and Hilde. I've seen a lot of fighter pilots in my twenty years. Lot of them don't grow up. I never figured you'd get your wings clipped."

Scott cracked an egg, emptied it into the mug of dark beer, swirled it around. "Know what, Nick. I looked real close in the mirror today. I've got four gray hairs. When I think about it . . . I guess I'm the luckiest bastard who ever lived. It's easy to come out of the clouds when you've found something better on the ground."

"Sorry I won't be standing up for you. When do you figure to get married?"

"Lot of red tape. We're looking for a final clearance any day."

Nick looked at his watch, gulped his beer down. "It's that time."

Scott drove him to Y 80 where he had passage on MATS on a States-bound Skymaster.

In the end there were no words to cover six years of intimate comradery.

"See you around, Major."

"So long, Nick."

He waited until Nick's plane was out of sight, and with him a part of his own life had flown away.

German girls by the thousands were trying to marry American servicemen. Many wanted it only as an avenue of escape from the nightmare of their war-ravaged world.

American boys who had never been exposed to the open and free relationship of a European woman wanted one of their very own.

It became necessary for the American authorities to institute barriers and rigid screenings to prevent a flood of bad matches.

Scott went to Colonel and Mrs. Loveless and candidly discussed Hilde's past. Clint acted as her sponsor, engineered the papers with his own brand of deftness. His influence with General Stonebraker, the general's personal like of Scott, plus the Falkenstein name would all help to smooth the way. Even so, there was a long winter of red tape.

Clint went to see the final authority, the chief chaplain of USAFE, and judged him to be a true man of the cloth and decided to lay it on the line.

The chaplain found it refreshing. Finding a confessed prostitute was as rare as finding a confessed Nazi. After giving Mary Magdalene as the obvious parable, he interviewed Hilde and assured her she could set a date with Major Davidson.

Clint and Judy often said they had never seen two people more in love, more grateful for the existence of the other, more willing to give of themselves, more awed by their late discovery.

Colonel Matt Beck and his vice chief, Major Scott Davidson, sat before Hiram Stonebraker. The general chewed their asses out.

Incidents of Russian buzzings and close flying were mounting. A Skymaster had been bullied out of the corridor, was pounced upon by Yak fighter planes which forced it to land on a Soviet airfield. Matt Beck wanted fighter plane escorts.

The general said he didn't have grounds for the request. Both Intelligence and his own estimates were that the Russians were putting on a last-ditch show trying to force more landings for face-saving value.

"What have we got? Gutless wonders? Now I don't want any more of our people scared out of the corridors!"

When Scott and Colonel Beck were alone, they summarized the situation in a short sentence. "Too many replacement crews."

Most of the original Airlift crews had been on bombers during the war and were disciplined to hold formation in the face of flak and enemy fighters. While the Russians annoyed the old-timers, they never made them deviate from course.

The two worked on a revision of pilot rosters to keep the maximum number of old hands in every time bloc and squadron.

Next day, Scott came into Colonel Beck's office, annoyed. Y 80 had a time bloc scheduled for the 12th and 333rd Troop Carriers that showed it to be 75 per cent new crews who had never faced a buzzing. Moreover, nine of the crews were making their first run to Berlin. Russian activity was reaching a new peak.

"I think I'd better go down to Y 80," Scott said, "and take this bloc in and out of Berlin a couple of times."

The colonel agreed.

Major Scott Davidson briefed them. They looked to him with a sense of relief and with an admiration given an old flyer of his caliber.

"It's a game of trying to make you flinch," Scott said. "They're like yappy puppies. Don't let them know you know they're alive. Let's hack time now."

Bloc time was twenty minutes away. Scott phoned Hilde.

"Going to take a couple of runs to Berlin, today," he said, "we've got to get these people steadied down."

Hilde masked her disappointment as always. She hated him to fly, and was in knots until he returned. She knew, though, that she could never say anything about it . . . now or ever.

"I'll go to the hotel and wait for you," she said.

"I may be late."

"I'll wait . . . Scott . . . I go to my room and I look at the ring twenty times a day. Would it be bad luck if I wore it around my neck on a chain. That way I could tuck it into my bosom so no one can see I'm wearing it."

"Great idea. I can fish it out later."

"Scott!"

"Then . . . you can stick it through my nose."

"I'm serious. I want so much to have it close."

"Sure. Maybe you'd better get some use out of it before it turns green. I'll try to phone your sister if I have time."

"*Aufwiedersehen* . . . I love you . . ."

"Me too . . ."

He detected a tremor in her voice. Just sentimental . . .

Scott lined them up over Fulda. They moved into the Southern corridor. Below the ground was lush and green with the coming of spring.

The interval was established for the 110-mile run to Berlin. For twenty minutes it was clear and smooth. Soon they would be under the control of Tempelhof radars.

His copilot, a likable young redhead a few months out of flying school, was on the yoke while Scott stretched. He looked over his shoulder to the flight engineer, another youngster . . . and he missed Nick's cigar smoke.

"Big Easy Fourteen calling all craft. Three Yaks at one o'clock."

Scott took the yoke quickly. His copilot spotted them coming straight down the line. A hundred feet above them the Russians leveled off, ducked back into the clouds.

"They're just clowning today," Scott said on the intercom. "This is Big Easy One to all craft. Keep your interval. This is Big Easy One calling Tempelhof Airways. Are we under your radar control, over?"

"This is Tempelhof Airways. You are coming into Radar Control. Caution. There are twelve unidentified blips around your bloc."

Scott frowned . . . twelve . . .

Omar Kum Dag was a rarity in the Red Air Force. He was one of the few flyers from Ashkabad in the distant Turkman Republic. His comrades considered him reckless. Kum Dag could be counted upon to take abnormal risks. His squadron leader was worried that he had a compulsion to either kill himself or prove himself because of his yellow skin and the constant teasing of the others.

They were not pleased when Kum Dag was assigned to the mission.

After all, they were ordered only to have some harmless fun with the American birds.

"Look at that stupid son of a bitch doing a victory roll," Scott snarled as Omar Kum Dag's Yak zoomed and spiraled right in front of him.

The copilot was pale and unnerved. Scott gritted his teeth as the Russian dived perilously close again, now wishing for the first time he had the guns and speed to go after him. Fun was fun, but only a crazy man buzzed a defenseless craft like that.

The Russian captain leading the squadron admonished Kum Dag angrily as the Yak streaked up to the clouds and circled for another pass. He was ordered to quit, but Omar Kum Dag did not hear.

He was detached by the roar, the surge, the mania to come even closer so no one would ever again doubt his courage.

"This is Tempelhof calling Big Easy One. There's a blip on your tail . . ."

Hilde's hair fell into her eyes as she flitted about the kitchen in that sort of furor she always generated while making a meal. She talked to herself, admonished herself for the lack of seasoning in the soup.

She stopped for a moment, wiped her hands, felt through her blouse, and touched the ring that lay between her breasts. It made her happy and she began to sing . . . tonight she would love him and love him and love him.

Colonel Loveless closed the kitchen door behind him.

"What on earth are you doing home, Colonel? It is only three o'clock."

The colonel looked deathly sick and he began to tremble as an unintelligible sound came out of his throat. Hilde dropped the plates from her hand.

"No!" she screamed.

"Oh God . . ." Clint moaned. "Oh God . . ."

"Scott! Scott!"

He gripped the writhing girl and held her until a blackness overcame her.

CHAPTER FORTY

Springtime!

Ulrich Falkenstein had shepherded his people through the winter. He felt it proper now to respond to invitations and receive ovations for his people in Paris and London, New York and Washington.

In exactly four years after the last Russian cannon fired down the Unter Den Linden, the greatest paradox of the century had happened. Berlin had completely reversed its meaning in the eyes of the world. In the resurrection of 1949, a stunning series of events occurred that halted the Communist scourge on the European continent.

Western Europe, now infused with the blood of the Marshall Plan, staggered from its ruins and the despair was replaced by a dynamic new birth. The sound of building was heard again.

As the West took this new lease on life they declared that they would defend themselves from further Soviet outrage in unity. In this springtime of 1949, NATO, the common defense, was born as a son of the Truman Doctrine.

In the resurrection of 1949 a new German state of the three Western Zones was in the making. A constitution was drawn with mankind's hope that a new kind of Germany would emerge.

The Soviet Union had failed. They had failed to stop the formation of a Western-oriented Germany; they had failed to drive the West from Berlin. The Airlift poured six and seven thousand tons of goods into Berlin every day. The pressure was off the West for negotiations for a settlement.

More generators were flown in and as the coal stocks grew the electrical capacity was raised. Raw materials were flown in and the acute job shortage began to ease.

The Airlift was now putting down tonnage equal to what the rails and highways had delivered before the blockade.

Consumer goods began to appear in dribbles: clothing, soap, bedding, books, radios, shoes, pots, pans. The B marks were replaced by the same Western currency used in the zones.

Those devils who used the threat of starvation were now finding themselves on the receiving end. The Western counterblockade staggered Soviet Berlin and Soviet Germany, creating havoc and turning the tables. Time, that ally which the Soviet Union used as a merciless tactic, now turned into a tactical enemy . . . now it was they who wanted to make a peace.

Hiram Stonebraker ordered the Combined Airlift Task Force to create an all-out operational assault on every tonnage record with an elaborate plan. With weather promising, midnight of the day of April 16 was chosen as the start of the twenty-four-hour period. Woody Beaver seized upon the occasion to name it "The Easter Parade."

At midnight the first blocs moved for Berlin from Y 80 and Fassberg with all other bases in ready.

M.J. and Hiram breakfasted at his usual hour of 0600. As he ate, he called the Control Center. His chief of staff was already there and reported everything had moved through the night on schedule.

Stonebraker quelled his anxiety. It would be a long day, the plan was daring, and he wasn't sending in a single goddamned ounce of cheese.

"You know, M.J.," he said in a rare show of nostalgia, "I signed the order yesterday taking the last Gooney Bird out of the Lift. I've been thinking about it. It's a fine old ship. Maybe nowhere near as sophisticated as these new birds, but it knows all the tricks of the sky. When our backs were to the wall and it was needed . . . it came through. They tell me the Gooney Birds will all be retired, but I'll bet you that ten years from now in any air base in the world . . . you'll find a Gooney Bird."

His wife patted his hand. She handed him a small package. "This came after you turned in," she said. It appeared to be another of those gifts from the people of Berlin. A note was attached. He mused. "This is from Chip Hansen."

Dear Crusty,
We have convinced this former Berlin manufacturer of small parts for armaments to reorient his production to something more useful. The factory began yesterday in a small way. They wanted you to have Model #1, Serial #1.

Faithfully,
Chip

Stonebraker's leathery face beamed as he took out a stainless-steel spinning reel. "Look at this, M.J. It's even left-handed." He opened the bale, turned the handle, played with the drag adjustment.

"Maybe Chip Hansen is trying to say that we're just a couple of old Gooney Birds too. Why don't you start looking through the fishing magazines and catalogues you've been sending for and hiding. I put some of them in your briefcase."

He grunted, decided to carry the reel to his office, disguised.

At Taunusstrasse 11 the general went directly to the Control Center. Almost everyone was there and the suspense was rising.

The Easter Parade was now in daylight, having flown out the night. Weather was holding, no Russian harassment, no breakdowns.

Through the night they had been landing in Berlin in one-minute intervals. With seventeen hours left to go they had already set down four thousand tons.

Clinton Loveless was in his office, doodling on his desk. It was ironic, he thought, that the two letters should arrive on the same day. One was from J. Kenneth Whitcomb III on gold-embossed Whitcomb Associates stationery.

Clint:
I'll get right to the play. The deal we discussed before you took leave to go on your great patriotic mission is still open.
We need you, baby. Let me say that we've checked out what you've been doing and we're proud you're on our team. We Americans can score a touchdown in any league.
Clint, I've picked up the ball on a big one. We are developing the first no-deposit, no-return bottle in America. It will revolutionize the industry . . .

The second letter came on rather austere stationery from a mining company in Utah. It was from the president, who was the son of the founder. He wrote that his father had hand-dug the first claim at the turn of the century.

It was a good company with good products and a good reputation. It employed three hundred people. The letter stated they were not able to adjust to modern methods. He had heard that Clinton Loveless once helped out small companies in trouble and allowed them to survive without being gobbled up.

"Will you help us?" the letter asked.

Judy read both letters. She took the one from Pudge Whitcomb, tore it into a hundred parts, put it in the fireplace with a final comment. "That jerk."

Stonebraker poked his head into Clint's office.

"Morning, sir."

"Why aren't you in the Control Center with the rest of the peasants!"

"Sit down, General, take a look at this," he answered dreamily.

He spread out a set of drawings. Clint was playing with the idea of preloading cargo on pallets in the rounded shape of the airplane's fuselage. The pallets would be lifted to the plane by conveyer belts, rolled down the floor of the craft on ball bearings. There wouldn't be an inch of waste space.

Stonebraker realized Clint had an idea of great brilliance for that time when the jet transport was developed with its great capacity.

"Bring this crap into my office when we finish today. Looks interesting."

Finishing up "today," meant midnight. No one was about to leave Taunusstrasse until the final figure of the Easter Parade was known.

The day wore on. No breakdowns in the rhythm of the Lift. The tonnage reached and passed five thousand . . . six . . . seven . . . eight.

Ten o'clock that night Hiram Stonebraker was concentrating on a Penn Fishing Tackle Catalogue. He shoved it into his desk drawer as Woody Beaver came in and began stuttering.

"Speak up, Beaver!"

"Ten thousand tons, General. We're landing them every sixty-three seconds!"

"Well, don't get your bowels in an uproar. We still have two hours left."

Phone calls came from British Headquarters in Luneberg. Air Vice Commodore Rodman was beside himself. A phone call came from Ulrich Falkenstein; a phone call came from Chip Hansen. Finally, a phone call came from the White House.

Everyone at Taunusstrasse was jammed into the Control Center as the direct lines from Gatow, Tegel, and Tempelhof kept edging the tonnage up.

Hiram Stonebraker remained in his office reading an article about the high hopes of a record albacore run off Catalina.

The clock moved up to 2400. Beaver got to the general's office first. "Twelve thousand, nine hundred tons!"

Stonebraker grumbled contentedly. "Advise General Buff Morgan, our erstwhile USAFE commander of his great feat, and call the boys in for a celebration."

The general arose, walked a few steps, winced, gasped . . . and stumbled.

"Beaver . . ." he called shakily, "pill from the top drawer . . . water . . ."

Beaver responded quickly. The general allowed himself to be helped to his couch. "Get outside . . . keep everyone out . . . don't say . . . anything . . ."

Clint was next to reach the general's office before Beaver could act. "General doesn't want to . . ."

"Outside, Beaver . . . don't let anyone in . . . move dammit, I've seen this before."

He half shoved Beaver through the door, locked it, went to the phone.

"Get away from that phone."

"Not this time, General."

"You're lucky," the flight surgeon said. "That bomb was about ready to explode. It's a good thing Loveless called."

"I'll bust his ass."

"No you won't. You'll thank him for having the sense to do what you should have done. He saved your life, General."

"Well . . . send the bastard in."

"We've all had a big day. Tomorrow will be soon enough."

"I said I want him in here."

The flight surgeon weighed the alternatives. The aggravation of refusal could cause him more damage than a short visit by his vice chief.

Clint pulled up a chair next to the bed. "We really clobbered them today, General."

"You know what makes me so smart, Clint? I'm smart enough to have people like you working for me."

"You must really be sick, General."

"Clint, it isn't even a year since we had lunch together in New York.

This country of ours can do anything. You know why? Because enough men like you have a sense of values that tells them to help a little mining company in Utah. That pretty little wife of yours told me about it and she said . . . how proud she was to be the wife of an American."

"For Christ sake . . . knock it off."

"Twelve thousand, nine hundred tons . . . I wish that Scott and some of the other boys could have lived . . . so, they'll phase out the operation, they'll phase us out . . . like old Gooney Birds . . . and Buff Morgan will run around picking up medals in our behalf. When you're in Utah . . . get yourself down to Malibu so we can do a little fishing."

Clint caught the flight surgeon's eye. So did the general.

"I'm supposed to thank you for saving my life," he said wearily. "Thanks."

CHAPTER FORTY-ONE

"Berliners! The Blockade is over!"

At midnight of June 11, nearly one year after the Soviet blockade, the first convoy of trucks rolled onto the autobahn through the Soviet Zone and beyond the checkpoint at Helmstedt.

Denied a celebration for many years, the Western Sectors erupted into the wildest night the city had ever known. Great delirious crowds surged before the American and British headquarters. Before the Borough town halls they chanted by torchlight for their leaders.

Soldiers from the West were mobbed on the streets and kissed and loved by the women and embraced by crying, usually unemotional German men.

In the middle of the night the first trucks of the convoy reached Berlin and were drenched in flowers.

Across the Brandenburg Gate in the Soviet boroughs of Köpenick, Treptow, Lichtenberg, Friedrichshain, Prenzlauer Berg, Weizensee, Pankow and Mitte the streets were empty. It was gloom and quiet, an ominous forecast of the life to come.

Igor Karlovy received a knock on his door. A squad of NKVD men told him to pack a single bag, immediately.

Sean sat alone in the room in Reinickendorf. Down below he could hear the singing, the cheering, see the torchlights.

The end of the blockade had come to him as a bittersweet victory. He could no longer hold his secret in him. Ernestine arrived rumpled and breathless and bursting with joy but she saddened the moment she saw Sean.

The black mood had come over him again. She had been patient. In the beginning it seemed that they were going to pull through. They were much in love and struggled together to overcome. For a time she believed they had passed the crisis.

And then something happened that Sean kept buried in him. He would cling to her in desperation . . . then drift away beyond her reach.

He had taken it badly when Blessing and his family returned to America to resume civilian life. His periods of detachment grew more often after that.

It became unbearable at times. She brought herself to the point of having it out. But the fear of losing him kept her quiet at the last instant and she was patient. While Berlin bathed in revelry, Sean drifted away once more.

Again that night he floated in the half world of nightmares. Ernestine lay awake seeing him fall down, down, down, beyond all help. His tortured dreams were punctured by the hilarity in the streets.

"Ja! Ja! Berlin *bleibt!*"

"*Wunderbar! Alles ist Wunderbar!*"

"Ja! Ja! Ja! Ja!" they chanted. "Ja! Ja! Ja! Ja!"

Sean saw himself stand in a rage above Dante Arosa. German woman! How could you do it with a German woman! He groveled at Dante's feet and the young officer kicked his ribs . . . German woman! Arosa taunted . . . I give you the choice to resign from the Army or join the SS!

Maurice Duquesne laughed hilariously. Naïve American. You must roll in the sweat of your enemy!

Ja! Ja! Ja! Ja!

Ernestine tried to touch him as he sweated and knotted with the pain of his dream.

Boom! Boom! Boom! Boom! beat a makeshift drum made of a dishpan.

Torches! Lines of snaking people in the streets . . . lines in the dirge to the Schwabenwald Concentration Camp. Look at the concentration camp, you people! I am O'Sullivan! I am the law! Look, dirty Germans, look!

Boom! Boom! Boom! Boom!

> Kathleen Mavourneen, the gray dawn is breaking . . .
> The sound of the hunter is heard from the hill . . .

Sorry Liam . . . sorry Tim . . . sorry Father . . . hear that other voice . . . that is Ernestine . . . I must go to her. Ernestine! Where are you! I told them I was coming to you! I told them about your father! No . . . I did not tell them.

> *"Deutschland, Deutschland, Ueber Alles,*
> *Ueber Alles in der welt!*
> *Deutschland, Deutschland Ueber Alles . . ."*

"Forbidden!" Sean cried, coming out of his dream. "That song is forbidden!"

The voices faded down the street . . . faded . . . faded.

> *"Deutsche Frauen, Deutsche Treue,*
> *Deutsche Wein und Deutsche sang!"*

He staggered to the window, saw the torchlights turn the corner. Ernestine was a shadow on the bed.

"We can't go on like this," she said.

He slumped in the chair, waited for his breath to slow, his heart to quit the pounding.

From the hallway in the landing below there was riotous laughter by a woman being embraced by an overzealous drunk.

"What happened last New Year's Eve, Sean?"

For a moment all that could be heard was the deep unevenness of his breathing. "Your father is a criminal Nazi. I have hidden the files."

"Oh, my God."

She appeared standing over him, knowing now the reason for his torment. And she knew the depth of his love. "I am as much to blame as you. I lived with him and closed my eyes and my ears."

"Erna . . . what are we going to do?"

She was numb as he had been numb for months. "Your life," she whispered, "and the work of my uncle are too good to throw away on a Nazi. You will go to General Hansen and tell him."

"No . . . I can't . . ."

"You will do what you must do."

"I won't give you up! We did not make this . . ."

"Germans," she mumbled almost incoherently, "redeem the sins of your fathers."

"Stop it!"

She laughed with bitter tears. "We make an exception of Colonel O'Sullivan's German Schatzie. Oh God . . . we were insane from the first minute."

"Hear me, Erna . . . we will overcome this."

"And you will spend a lifetime hearing me cry in my sleep with my father in prison and my mother withering to death. What of my sister, who grieves beyond grief for that flyer who died, or my uncle, who struggles to restore us to our dignity."

"To hell with them!"

"Oh my Sean, I love you so. I will not let you become an instrument of your own destruction. I will not let you disgrace your uniform . . ."

> *"Deutschland, Deutschland, Ueber Alles . . .*
> *Ueber Alles in der Welt . . ."*

"Ernestine! Ernestine!"

"I am a German woman."

"Ernestine!"

"Germans are a superstitious people. We are guided by fates we cannot control."

"Erna! I swear to you we'll find the strength."

"Liam! Tim! Those names you cry out in your dreams. Sean! Give me your brothers' blessings."

He sunk to his knees and buried his head in her belly.

"Oh God!" she cried in anguish, "we tried so hard!"

CHAPTER FORTY-TWO

Sean walked slowly toward General Hansen's desk. He lay the file of Bruno Falkenstein on it. The general glanced at it, set it aside.

"I'm glad you made the decision to bring this in," he said.

"Sir . . . I am guilty . . ."

"Sean. These papers took a long time being processed at your desk. That is all there is to it."

"Sir . . ."

"That is all there is to it, understand."

"Not after what I did to another man for the same thing."

"There are differences. You will refuse to recognize them now because of the punishment you are inflicting on yourself. I should like to know about Fraulein Falkenstein?"

"She sent me away."

Hansen realized that the girl's decision had come out of love for him to allow him to try to create some kind of normal life.

"I'm sorry, Sean."

"Our wounds run too deep. I cannot make peace with the Germans. Erna and I . . . tried to fool ourselves. No real peace can ever be made until we pass on and the new generation of Americans and Germans make it."

"I'm afraid you're right, Sean."

"General, please help me get out of Germany."

A PAUSE FOR REFLECTION by Nelson Goodfellow Bradbury

West Berlin is delirious with victory. The Western world has won its first and only victory of the cold war.

In a year's time, a quarter of a million flights into Berlin carried two and a half million tons of cargo flying over a half million miles.

It cost us a quarter of a billion dollars and seventy lives. This is cheap, as battles go. We gained immeasurable technical knowledge and this victory brought out the finest qualities of American courage and ingenuity.

We have renewed our bond with the British ally and we have found a new ally. In this first test, the Berliner was pure iron.

But those among us who believe this is a final victory are fools. The Soviet Union has had its momentum halted by the Truman Doctrine, the Marshall Plan, NATO, and the Airlift. The Kremlin is merely pausing to reflect.

The agreement ending the Berlin blockade, like all Soviet agreements, is useful to them for the moment. They have not changed an iota of the promise to devour the human race with communism.

The Soviet Union will catch its bearings and shop around for cheap victories. The West will be tested again and again.

In the end, the Soviet Union must always come back to Berlin, the scene of their defeat. As long as the West remains, the Soviet Union cannot consolidate her colonies behind closed doors and is faced with living with exposure of her way of life.

Already one sees the drab existence that lies in store for the Russian Zone of Germany, now contrasted by the surge in West Germany. The Kremlin cannot stand such public exposure and they must try to run us out of Berlin again and again. A battle is won. The war goes on.

The end of the Second World War saw the Russians, secluded for centuries, suddenly come out of their shell and pour beyond their borders.

I think it will take a long time for them to learn to live with the rest of the world and to learn that most of the human race has no desire to be made over in their image.

American determination must make new Russian victories come harder. Then will they look into their own house, cleanse their own ills and decide to join the family of man and let the world live in peace. Until the Soviet Union learns this, we are in for many hard years.

And what about the Germans?

The present generation would like to forget the Nazi era. Tough luck. They are bathed in the blood of thirty million dead. There is no way to cleanse themselves.

What of the German who swears he was not a Nazi?

Before we pass judgment on the Germans let me say that I have never found an American who has expressed personal guilt over the fact that we destroyed a people and their civilization in brutal indifference to gain the North American continent. And damned few feel guilt as Americans for the dropping of atomic weapons on undefended civilian cities.

Fewer still take personal responsibility for the fact that twenty million Americans live as second-class citizens in our country. While it is easy for us to see the faults in the Germans and the Russians, we most conveniently fail to see them in ourselves.

The Germans tell us that all men are inhuman. True. Nonetheless, when the final book on man's inhumanity to man is written, the blackest chapter will be awarded to the German people in the Nazi era.

How about the coming generation of Germans? Are they to be held responsible for the sins of their fathers? Can a German boy be any more innocent than the Polish boy who must live with the scars inflicted by the German?

All of us are the sum total of our past. The Nazi era is part of the sum total of the heritage of unborn German generations. Yes, they are responsible.

The road to redemption is to face up to the truth of the past. Only the successful experience of a democracy will ever bring these people around.

The German citizen who has historically permitted himself to be politically ignorant must stop turning his "fate" over to the "father" who fills his lunch bucket.

There must be more to German political stature than a loaf of bread and making the best deal to survive. Already we hear complaints about the taxation to save Berlin. Yet, we must be skilled and patient and hope that by living with Americans some of it will rub off on them.

If there is ever to be a redemption of the German people, it began in Berlin.

Berliners boast that they are different. So do the people of Hamburg, Munich, and San Francisco. Which Berliners are different? The ones in the Western Sectors or those in the Soviet Sector?

We see too many fearsome signs of Nazi-like revivals across the Brandenburg Gate. The only difference is the color of the flag and the hammer and sickle replacing the swastika. All the rest is the same. They are, in fact, a weak people who must lean upon someone else.

Some leaders in Berlin will tell you that Berlin has always been the heartstone of democratic German thought. It has a long tradition of labor and liberalism. This is true.

It is also true that it was the heartstone of Prussian militarism and the German General Staff that brought the world to such misery.

Other Berliners will tell you they were never Nazi. I saw the Hitler legions goose-step through the Brandenburg Gate past fanatical mobs of Berliners screaming "sieg heil."

Giving the Berliner all the benefits of the doubt that they were still partly Nazi and I ask, "How much is being a little bit Nazi?"

Berliners will say they saw tyranny before and were quick to spot it again. When they did, they stopped it. This is a hard point to take issue with. Even professional German haters who may claim that Berlin stood because of terror of the Russians cannot answer why they decided to do this while expecting the West to quit the city.

We conclude: The people of Berlin have achieved a victory for democracy. This victory neither exonerates them nor pays the bill for their participation in Hitler's Germany.

Berlin was the Nazi capital. Nothing can change that.

West Berlin has contributed more for the freedom of mankind than any people in the world since the end of the war. Nothing can change that fact, either.

When I asked a wise American general, "Will the German people change?" he answered me with the wisdom of all great men. He said, "Come back in twenty-five years and I'll give you an answer."

CHAPTER FORTY-THREE

"Ernestine."

"Yes, Uncle?"

"Can you take a little something to eat, child?"

"I am not hungry, Uncle."

"You have just sat here day after day with almost no food or sleep. You will be very ill."

"Please do not worry about me."

"I must go to make a public appearance with General Hansen. Won't you come with us?"

"I am tired, Uncle. I wish to stay."

"Erna . . . Hilde is coming back to Berlin today. She is flying home from Frankfurt. She will be with us tonight."

"Hilde?"

"Hilde, your sister, will be here tonight."

"How wonderful it will be to see her."

"I hear the doorbell. It must be General Hansen's aide."

"Uncle . . . why doesn't Sean call me?"

"You must forget him. He flies away today."

"Why didn't he call to say good-by?"

"Erna . . . he did call many times, but you would not talk to him."

"Oh, yes . . . yes . . . I remember now."

"The general's aide is here. I must go now. Shall I open the curtain and let in some light?"

"No, I am more comfortable this way."

"How is the girl?" General Hansen asked in the car.

"She is beyond sorrow. I will thank God when this day is over, knowing that her sister has returned. It will take a long time for her to get over this."

"Herr Falkenstein . . . please know, sir, that that boy is like a son to me. He tried beyond human limits. I swear that to you . . . he tried."

"My concern is not for him."

The two old warriors drove off to meet their cheering publics. Through the hell they had survived together, they had formed a deep mutual admiration. Ulrich Falkenstein gave the general a copy of a law passed by the Berlin Assembly granting an education without cost at the Free University to every son and daughter of an American who died on the Air Bridge.

The presence of the American Commandant General Neal Hazzard set off a wild ovation by the crowd assembled before Tempelhof. His car was swamped. Neal was weary from drinking and celebrating in what must have been every German bar in the Western Sectors. As he shoved through, babies were thrust into his face to be kissed and he was embraced. Women grabbed his hand and kissed it. It could be said that no occupation governor in the world's history was held in such esteem by those he had conquered.

He finally was able to get into the main building and found the office where Colonel O'Sullivan awaited departure. Sean, his mighty friend through battle after battle of nerves, was a shell of himself.

"Sean, are you going to be all right?"

"Why wouldn't she say good-by to me . . . why . . . why?"

Hiram Stonebraker's personal Gooney Bird had been sent to take O'Sullivan to Frankfurt. An aide said the plane was in readiness.

"Can you make it?" Neal asked.

Sean nodded.

Beyond the building in the square the festivities were reaching a new pitch. They could hear an Army band play "Stars and Stripes Forever." They could hear the wild shouts and ovations of the Berliners.

Neal Hazzard walked slowly, supporting Sean. They entered the Gooney Bird. Neal waved the crew away. "The colonel has a virus. Stay away from him and let him rest."

"Good-by, Sean," Neal said. "God bless you."

"So long, Neal," he whispered.

A deafening roar burst anew from the crowd which had jammed into every possible space in the plaza before Tempelhof.

Oberburgermeister Ulrich Falkenstein had arrived with General Andrew Jackson Hansen.

Neal Hazzard pushed his way through the adoring mob to join them near the speaker's stand, and when they saw him ascend the steps the hysteria of West Berlin burst anew. They ascended the steps together, waving to the multitudes.

"Falkenstein! Hansen! Hazzard!" a hundred thousand throats chanted. "Falkenstein! Hansen! Hazzard!"

For a terrifying second the three men stopped and looked at the sky as Tempelhof Tower cleared the Gooney Bird bearing Sean O'Sullivan.

The Gooney Bird passed above Ulrich Falkenstein's flat.

Ernestine watched it disappear and drew the curtain. She walked slowly into the kitchen, shut the door, pulled down the window, and drew the blind. She went to the stove, stood over it a second, her eyes transfixed on the gas jets. Her hand reached out and she turned them on. They hissed. Ernestine sat back in a chair as the smell reached her nostrils. She drank it in deliciously. And soon her eyelids grew heavy and she began to doze.

Judy Loveless held Hilde's hands on a wooden bench at the Frankfurt Airport on the civilian side of Rhein/Main. Clint stood in front of them, his hands in his pockets. Tony imitated his father. Lynn sat on Hilde's lap, sobbing.

"Hilde," Judy said, "the offer to come and stay with us is always open. You know we mean it."

Hilde smiled. "My father needs me. He has asked for me. It will be a terrible ordeal. And that foolish sister of mine went and lost her heart when I warned her not to."

"And you, Hilde? What about your heart? Will you get over Scott?"

"We are two foolish sisters."

"You must write to us."

"I promise, Mrs. Loveless. Colonel, I am so glad you are going home."

"Well," he said, "Utah isn't exactly home."

"You and Mrs. Loveless will always have a home . . . because there are the two of you."

At the moment that life passed from Ernestine, her uncle stood before his people.

"Berliners," he said, with a voice echoing over the mass, "we cannot express our gratitude by the mere naming of this place as the Airlift Plaza. We cannot tell what is in our hearts. The way we shall express our thanks to those American and British flyers who have given us freedom is to keep this city a fortress. I beg you now to all stand in silent reverence to those who have given their lives for Berlin."

The Gooney Bird touched down at Rhein/Main. Colonel O'Sullivan was met and driven to the civilian side of the field where a MATS flight would return him to the States.

At that moment the loudspeaker called for German Nationals to board a Pan-Am flight to Berlin.

The scene around Hilde was filled with tears and embraces. When, at last, she was told she could delay no longer, she ran out a few steps and blew a kiss to the Loveless family.

Past the gate she was on the field. In her haste she did not see the American Army colonel coming in her direction. They bumped together. The packages in Hilde's arms tumbled to the ground and they both knelt instinctively to pick them up.

"I beg your pardon, fraulein," Sean said.

"I am clumsy, it was my fault," Hilde answered.

"Please let me help you."

He fitted the packages into her arms. He put his fingers to his cap in a salute. "*Aufwiedersehen*, fraulein," he said.

"*Aufwiedersehen*," she answered.

The two of them went their separate ways.